Black Jack

Volume 1

Osamu Tezuka

VERTICAL.

Translation—Camellia Nieh
Production—Glen Isip
Hiroko Mizuno

Published by Vertical, Inc., New York.

Originally published in Japanese as *Burakku Jakku 1*
by Akita Shoten, Tokyo, 1987.
Burakku Jakku first serialized in *Shukan Shonen Champion*,
Akita Shoten, 1973–83.

ISBN: 978-1-934287-27-9

Manufactured in the United States of America

First Edition

Fifth Printing

Vertical, Inc.
451 Park Avenue South 7th Floor
New York, NY 10016
www.vertical-inc.com

CONTENTS

IS THERE A DOCTOR?

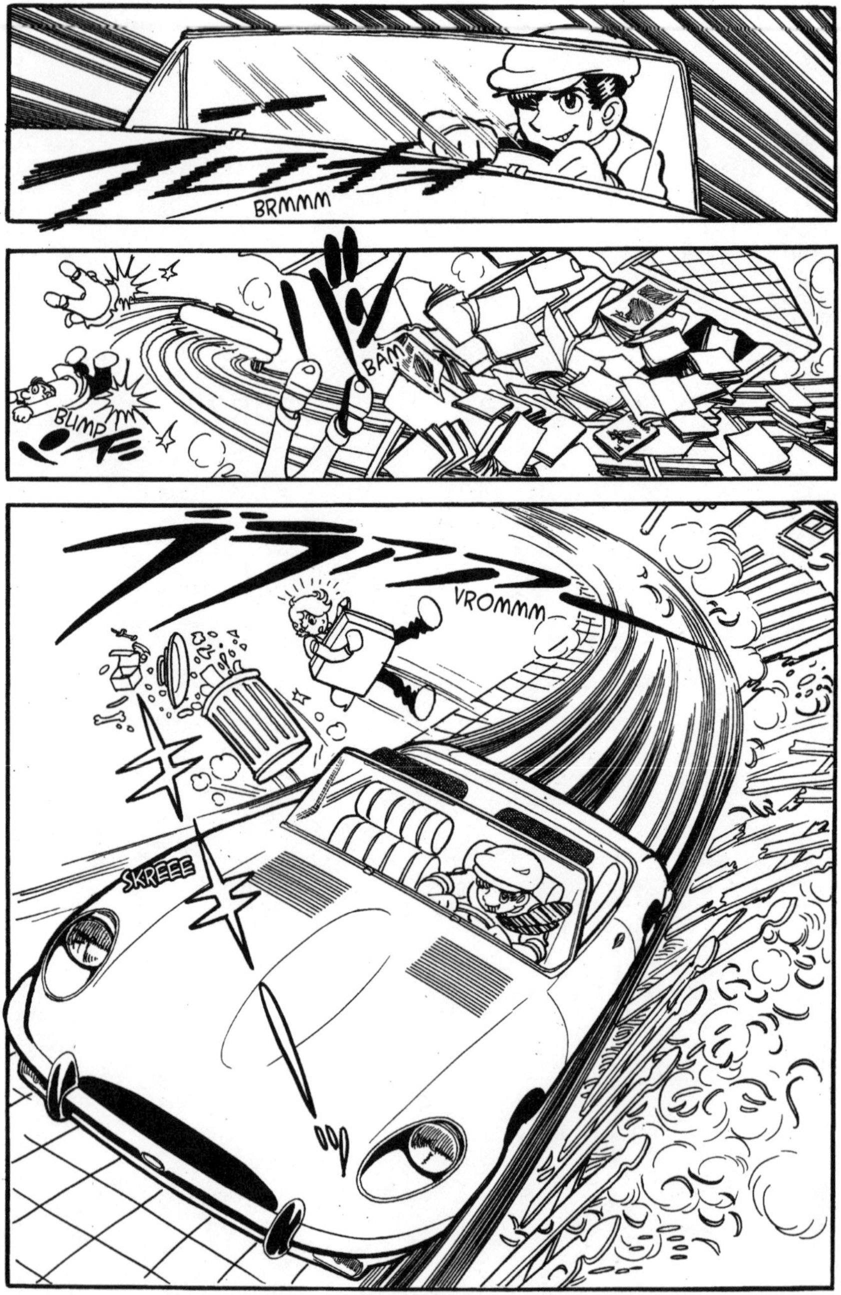
BRMMM
BAM
BLUMP
VROMMM
SKREEE

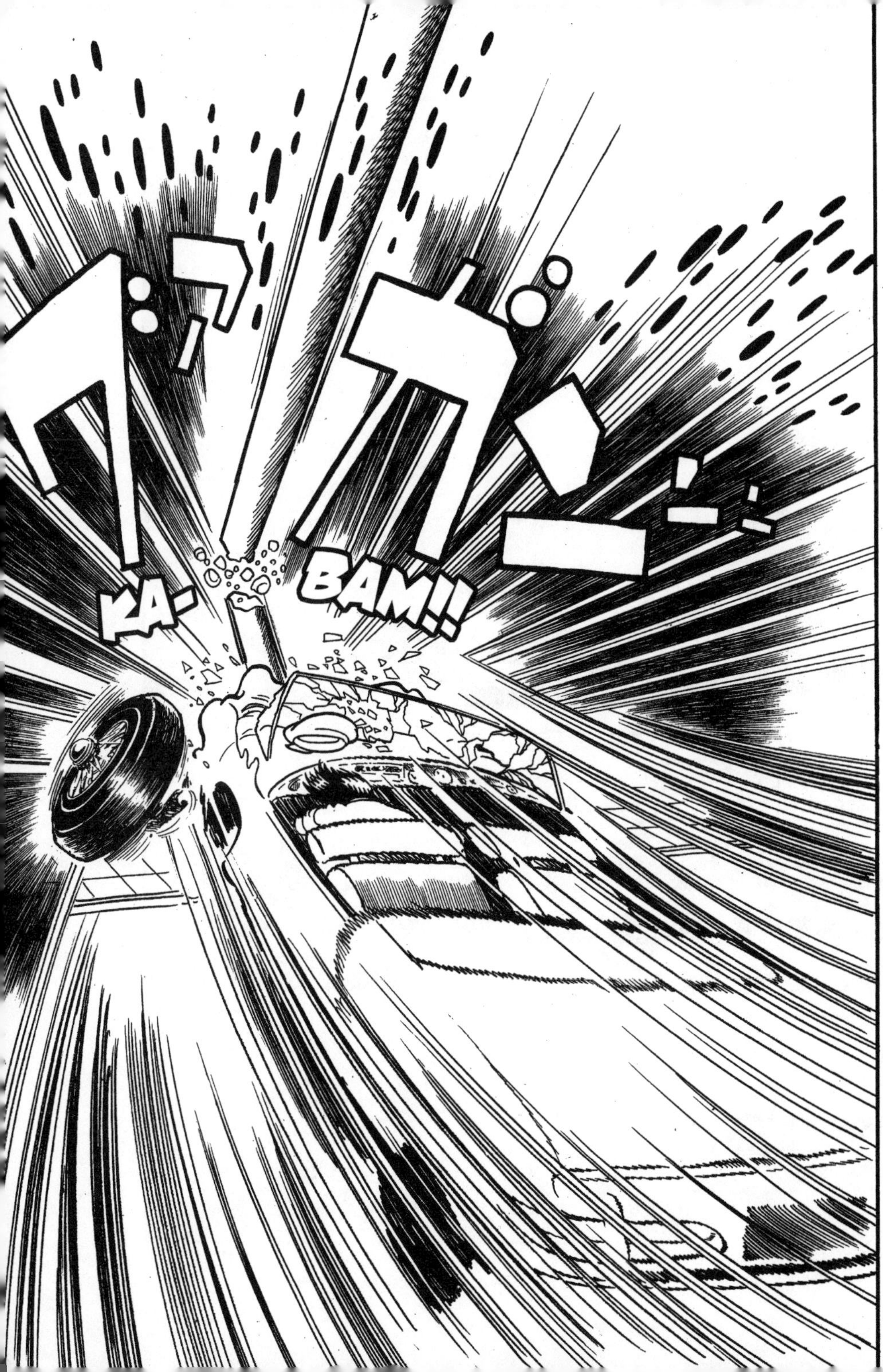
ガガーン
KA-
BAM!!

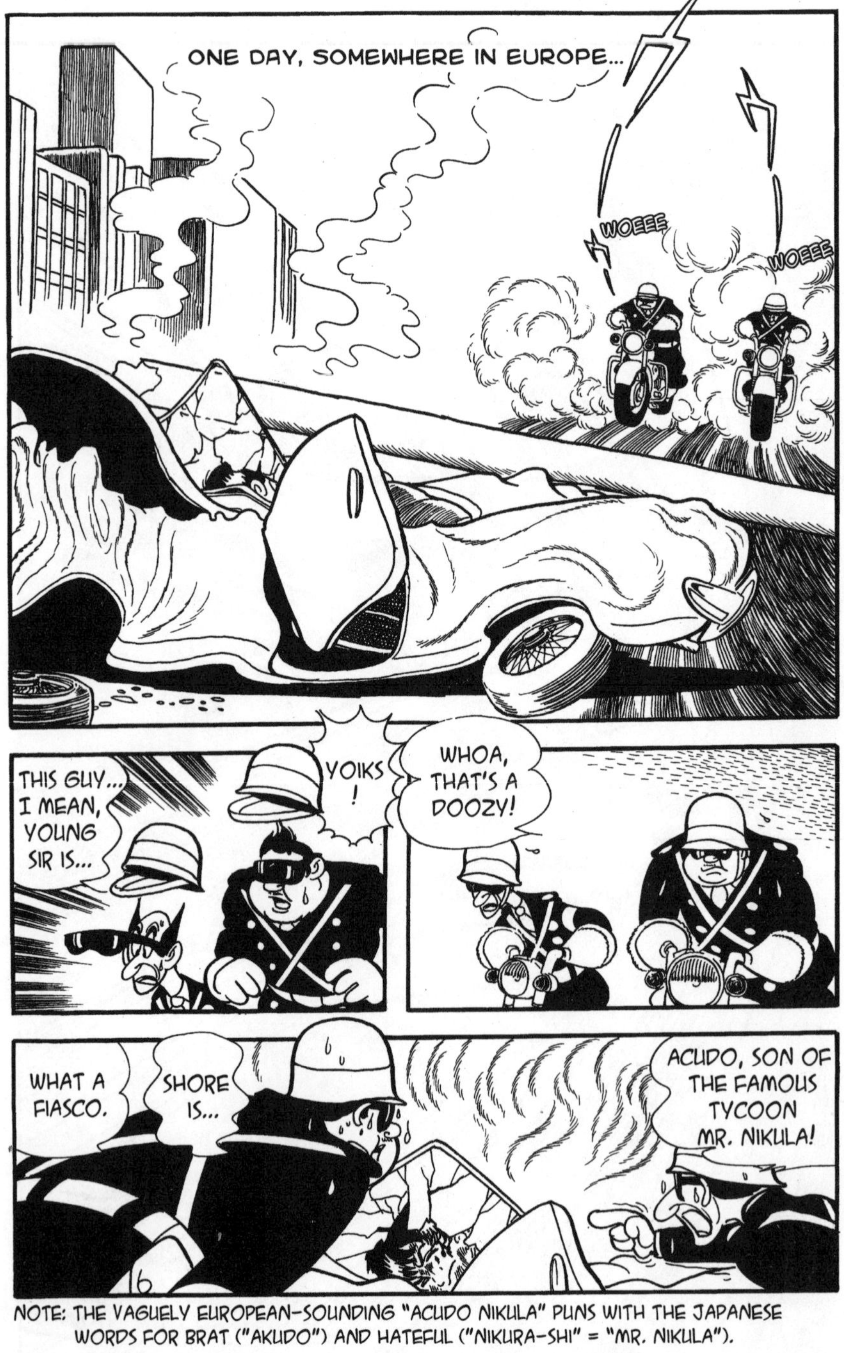
ONE DAY, SOMEWHERE IN EUROPE...
WOEEE
WOEEE
WHOA, THAT'S A DOOZY!
YOIKS!
THIS GUY... I MEAN, YOUNG SIR IS...
ACUDO, SON OF THE FAMOUS TYCOON MR. NIKULA!
SHORE IS...
WHAT A FIASCO.

NOTE: THE VAGUELY EUROPEAN-SOUNDING "ACUDO NIKULA" PUNS WITH THE JAPANESE WORDS FOR BRAT ("AKUDO") AND HATEFUL ("NIKURA-SHI" = "MR. NIKULA").

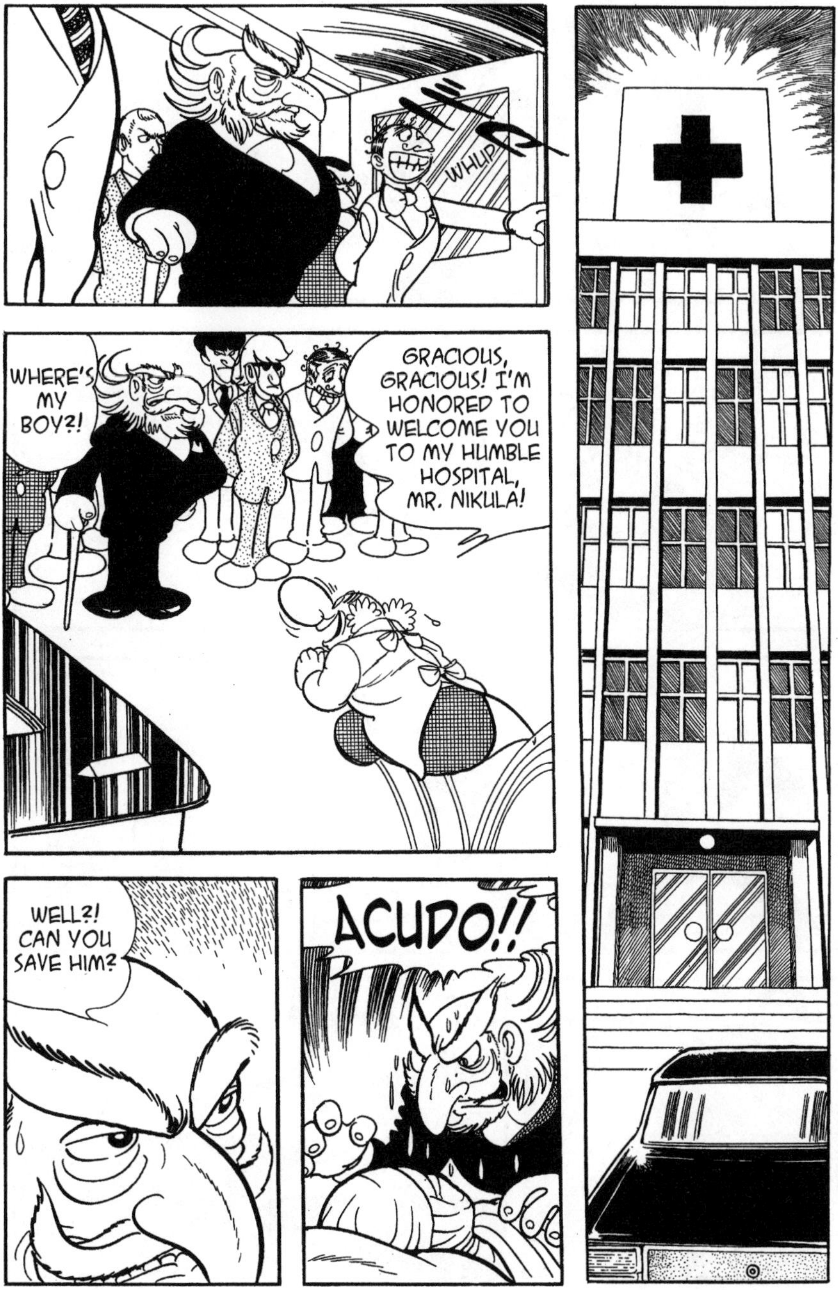
WHUP
GRACIOUS, GRACIOUS! I'M HONORED TO WELCOME YOU TO MY HUMBLE HOSPITAL, MR. NIKULA!
WHERE'S MY BOY?!
ACUDO!!
WELL?! CAN YOU SAVE HIM?

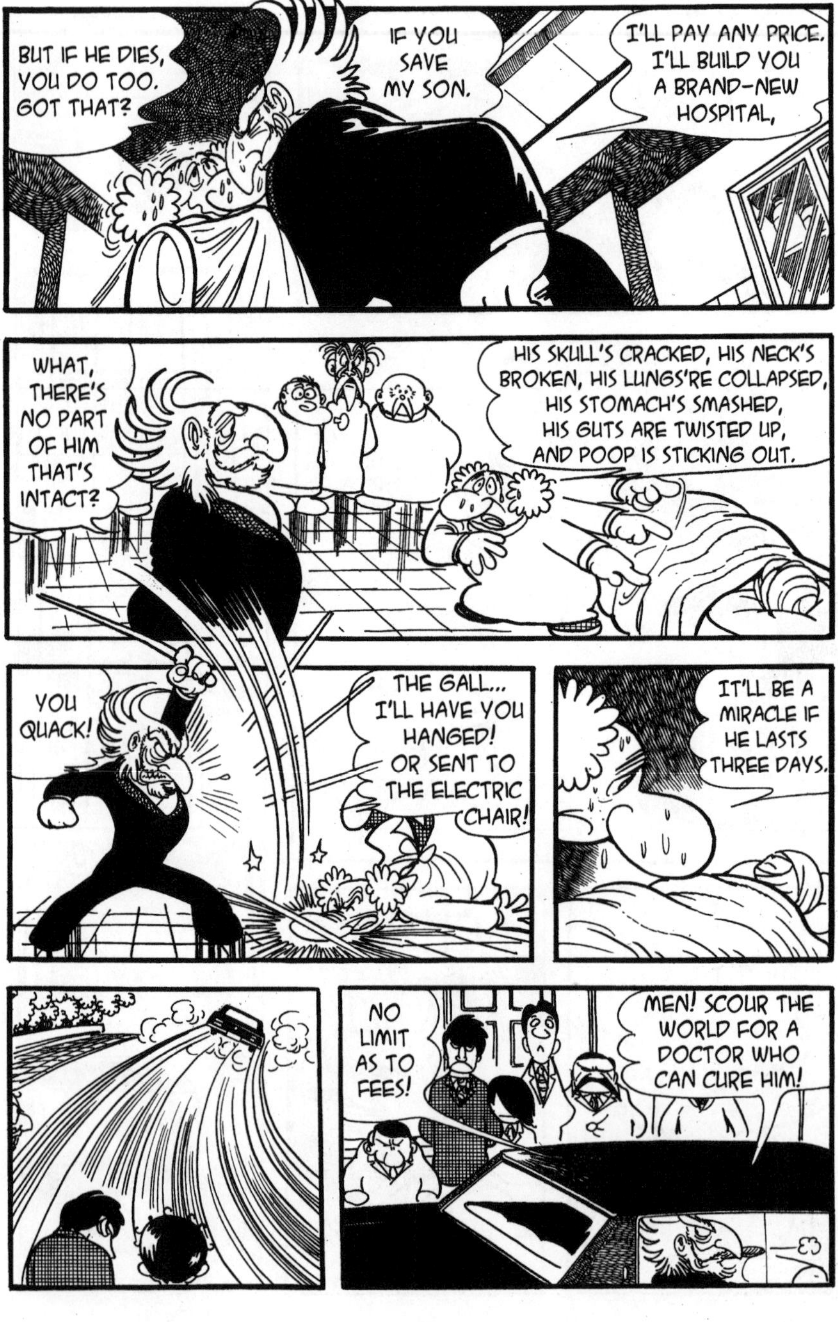
I'LL PAY ANY PRICE. I'LL BUILD YOU A BRAND-NEW HOSPITAL,
IF YOU SAVE MY SON.
BUT IF HE DIES, YOU DO TOO. GOT THAT?
HIS SKULL'S CRACKED, HIS NECK'S BROKEN, HIS LUNGS'RE COLLAPSED, HIS STOMACH'S SMASHED, HIS GUTS ARE TWISTED UP, AND POOP IS STICKING OUT.
WHAT, THERE'S NO PART OF HIM THAT'S INTACT?
IT'LL BE A MIRACLE IF HE LASTS THREE DAYS.
THE GALL... I'LL HAVE YOU HANGED! OR SENT TO THE ELECTRIC CHAIR!
YOU QUACK!
MEN! SCOUR THE WORLD FOR A DOCTOR WHO CAN CURE HIM!
NO LIMIT AS TO FEES!

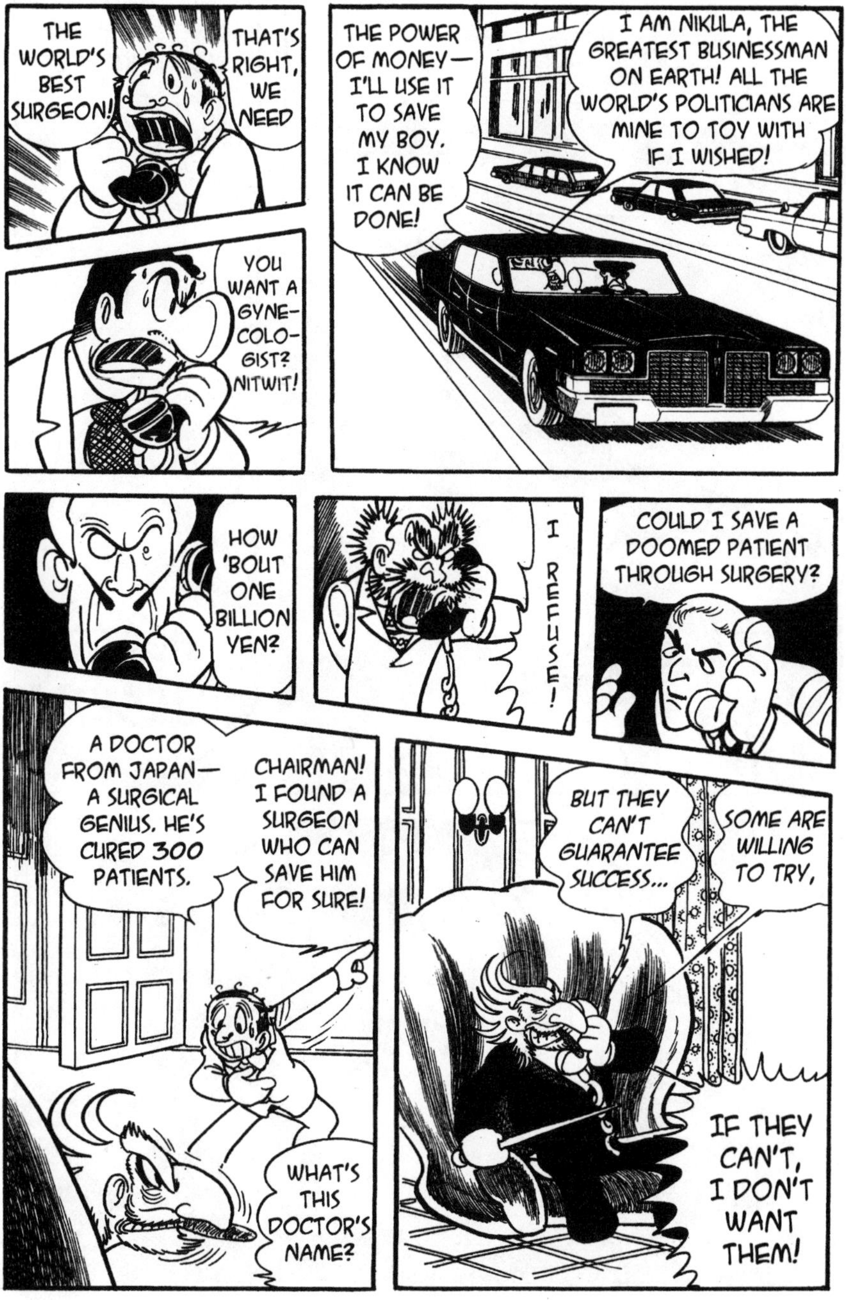
I AM NIKULA, THE GREATEST BUSINESSMAN ON EARTH! ALL THE WORLD'S POLITICIANS ARE MINE TO TOY WITH IF I WISHED!
THE POWER OF MONEY— I'LL USE IT TO SAVE MY BOY. I KNOW IT CAN BE DONE!
THAT'S RIGHT, WE NEED
THE WORLD'S BEST SURGEON!
YOU WANT A GYNE-COLO-GIST? NITWIT!
COULD I SAVE A DOOMED PATIENT THROUGH SURGERY?
I REFUSE!
HOW 'BOUT ONE BILLION YEN?
SOME ARE WILLING TO TRY,
BUT THEY CAN'T GUARANTEE SUCCESS...
IF THEY CAN'T, I DON'T WANT THEM!
CHAIRMAN! I FOUND A SURGEON WHO CAN SAVE HIM FOR SURE!
A DOCTOR FROM JAPAN— A SURGICAL GENIUS. HE'S CURED 300 PATIENTS.
WHAT'S THIS DOCTOR'S NAME?

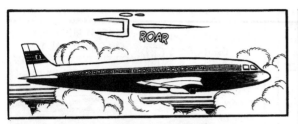

ROAR

I DON'T KNOW HIS REAL NAME, BUT THEY CALL HIM BLACK JACK.

JAL

JAL

BLACK JACK?

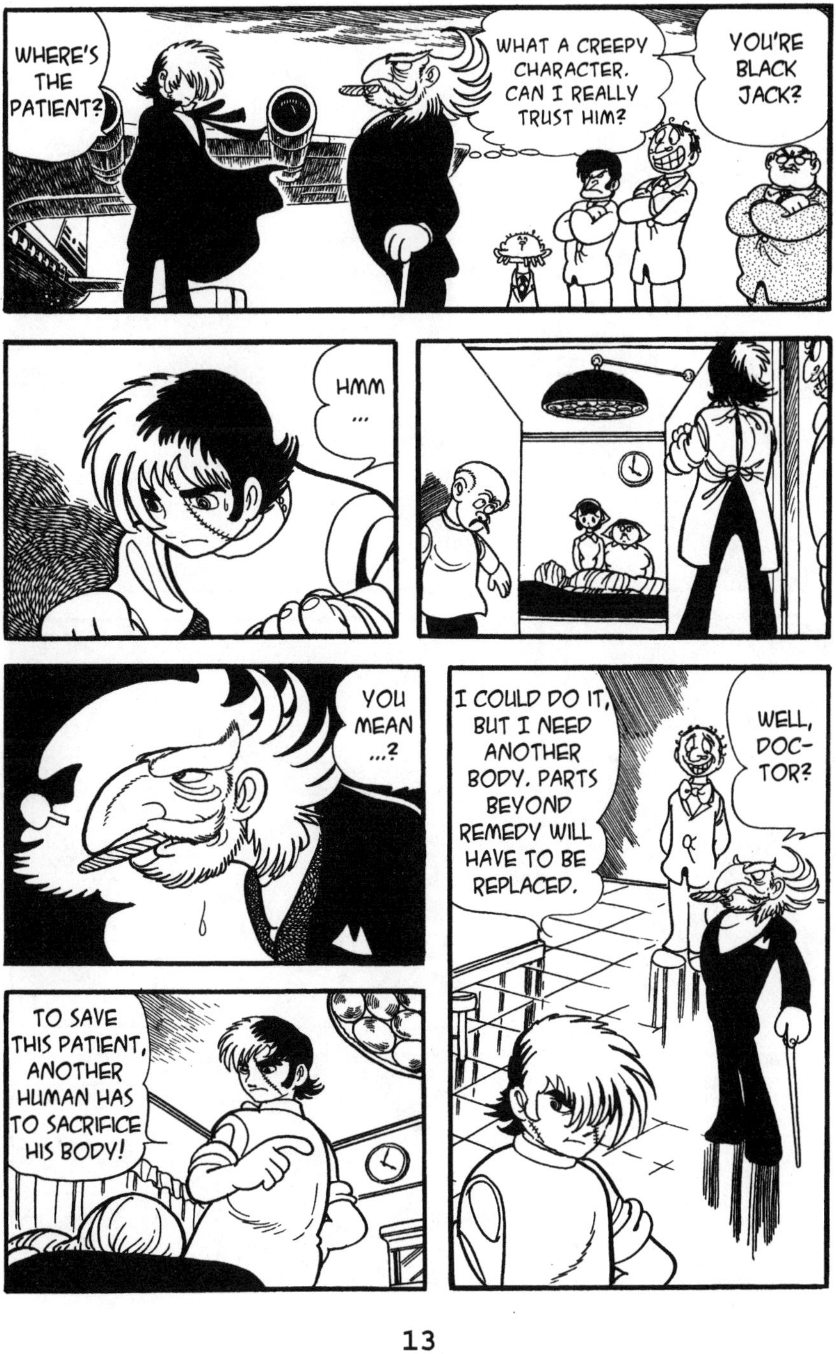
YOU'RE BLACK JACK?
WHAT A CREEPY CHARACTER. CAN I REALLY TRUST HIM?
WHERE'S THE PATIENT?
HMM ...
WELL, DOC-TOR?
I COULD DO IT, BUT I NEED ANOTHER BODY. PARTS BEYOND REMEDY WILL HAVE TO BE REPLACED.
YOU MEAN ...?
TO SAVE THIS PATIENT, ANOTHER HUMAN HAS TO SACRIFICE HIS BODY!

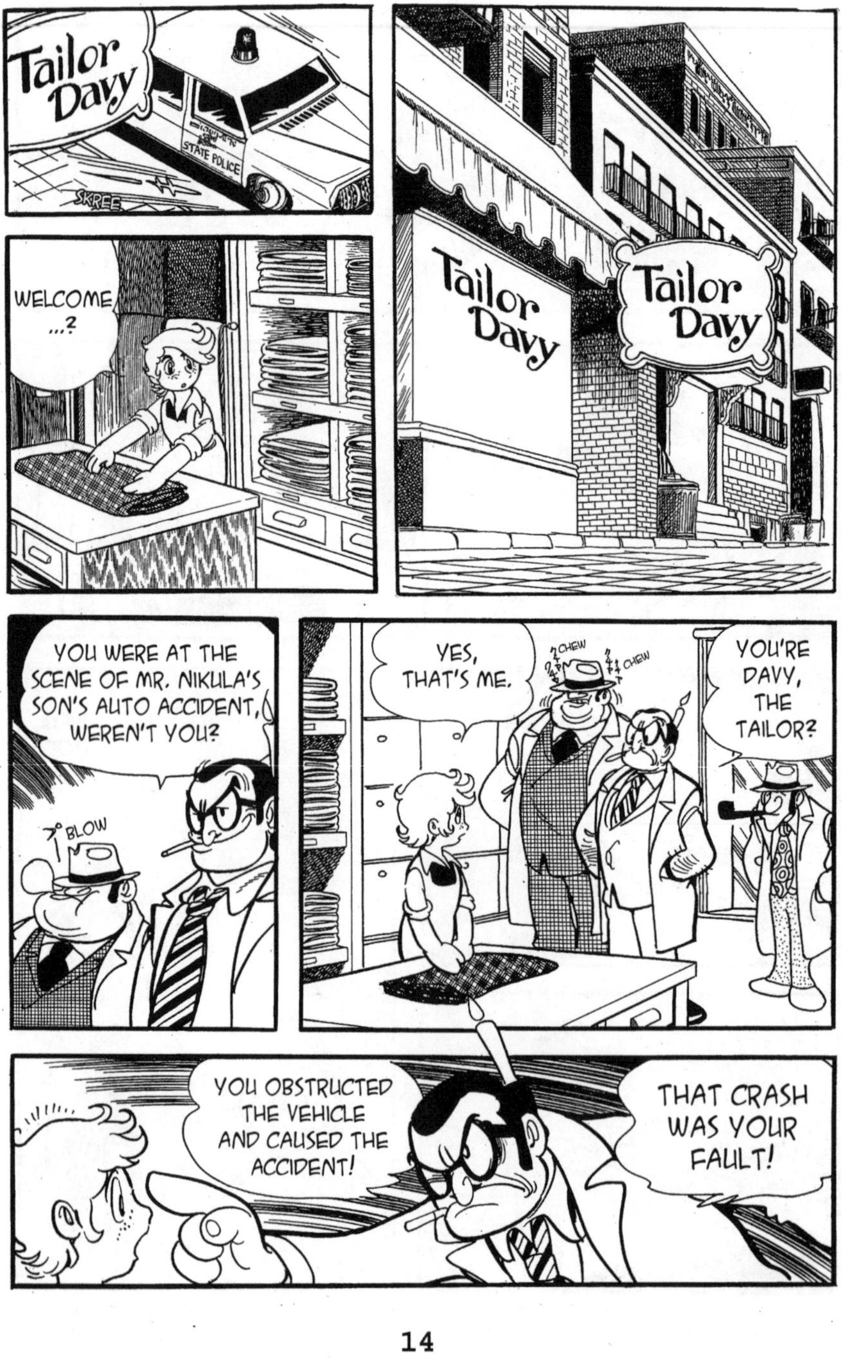
Tailor Davy
Tailor Davy
Tailor Davy
STATE POLICE
SKREE
WELCOME ...?
YOU'RE DAVY, THE TAILOR?
CHEW CHEW
YES, THAT'S ME.
YOU WERE AT THE SCENE OF MR. NIKULA'S SON'S AUTO ACCIDENT, WEREN'T YOU?
BLOW
THAT CRASH WAS YOUR FAULT!
YOU OBSTRUCTED THE VEHICLE AND CAUSED THE ACCIDENT!

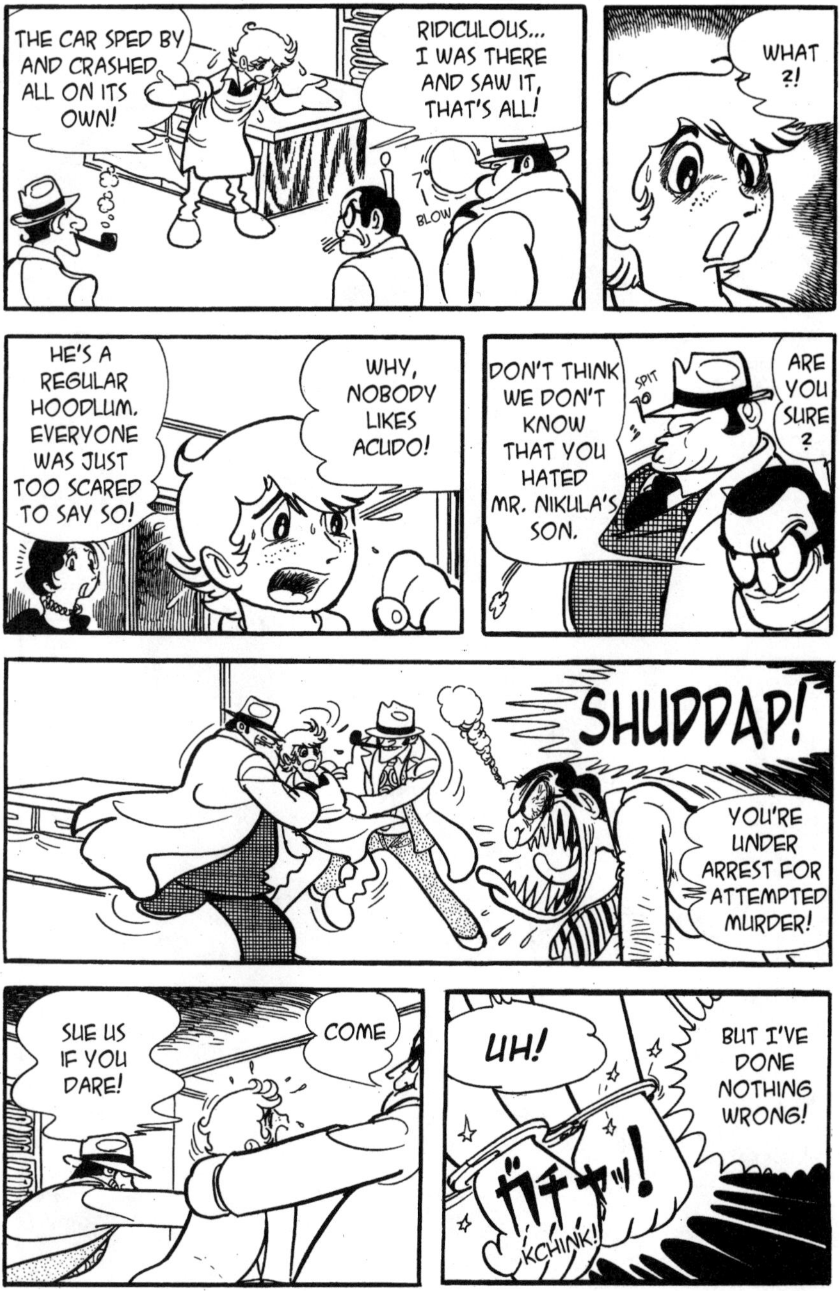
WHAT ?!
RIDICULOUS... I WAS THERE AND SAW IT, THAT'S ALL!
THE CAR SPED BY AND CRASHED ALL ON ITS OWN!
BLOW
ARE YOU SURE ?
DON'T THINK WE DON'T KNOW THAT YOU HATED MR. NIKULA'S SON.
SPIT
WHY, NOBODY LIKES ACUDO!
HE'S A REGULAR HOODLUM. EVERYONE WAS JUST TOO SCARED TO SAY SO!
SHUDDAP!
YOU'RE UNDER ARREST FOR ATTEMPTED MURDER!
BUT I'VE DONE NOTHING WRONG!
UH!
ガチャッ!
KCHINK!
COME
SUE US IF YOU DARE!

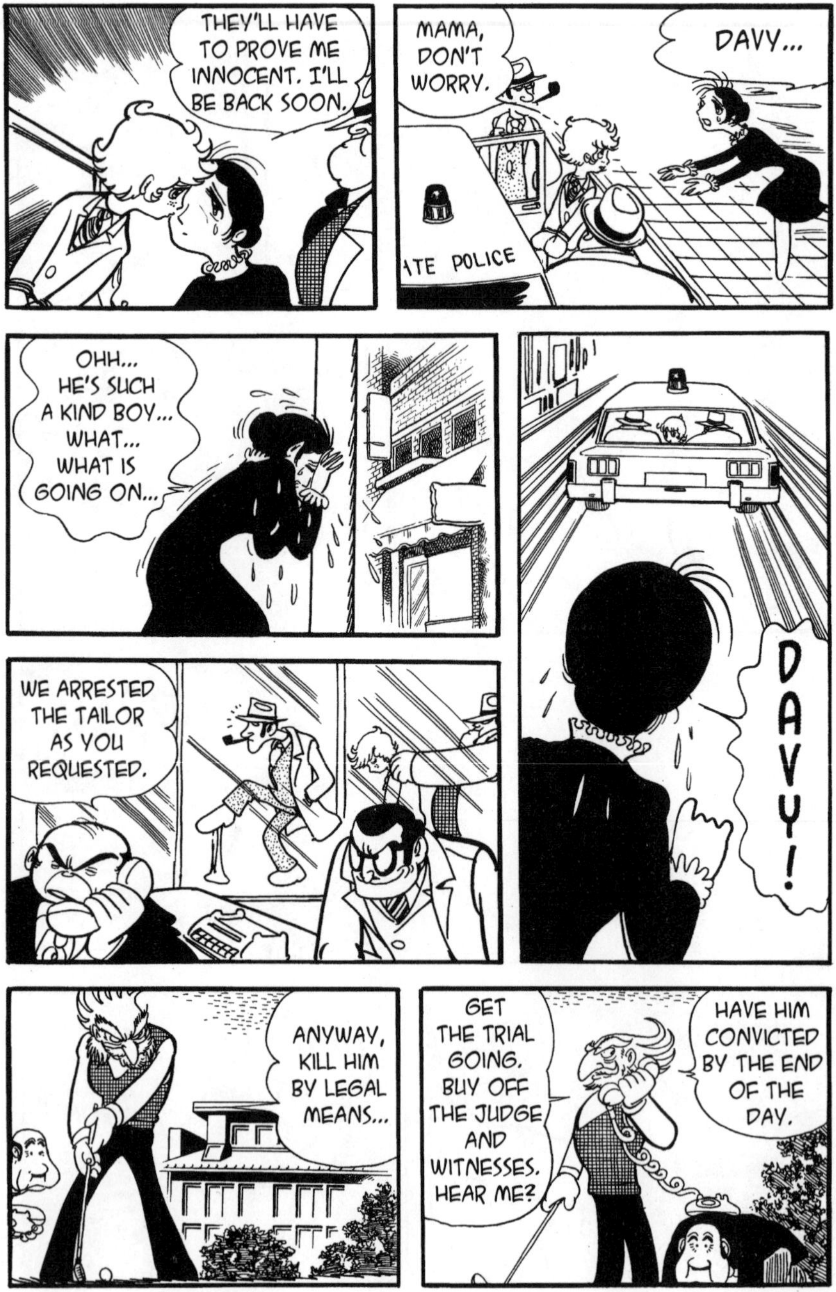
DAVY...
MAMA, DON'T WORRY.
ATE POLICE
THEY'LL HAVE TO PROVE ME INNOCENT. I'LL BE BACK SOON.
DAVY!
OHH... HE'S SUCH A KIND BOY... WHAT... WHAT IS GOING ON...
WE ARRESTED THE TAILOR AS YOU REQUESTED.
GET THE TRIAL GOING. BUY OFF THE JUDGE AND WITNESSES. HEAR ME?
HAVE HIM CONVICTED BY THE END OF THE DAY.
ANYWAY, KILL HIM BY LEGAL MEANS...

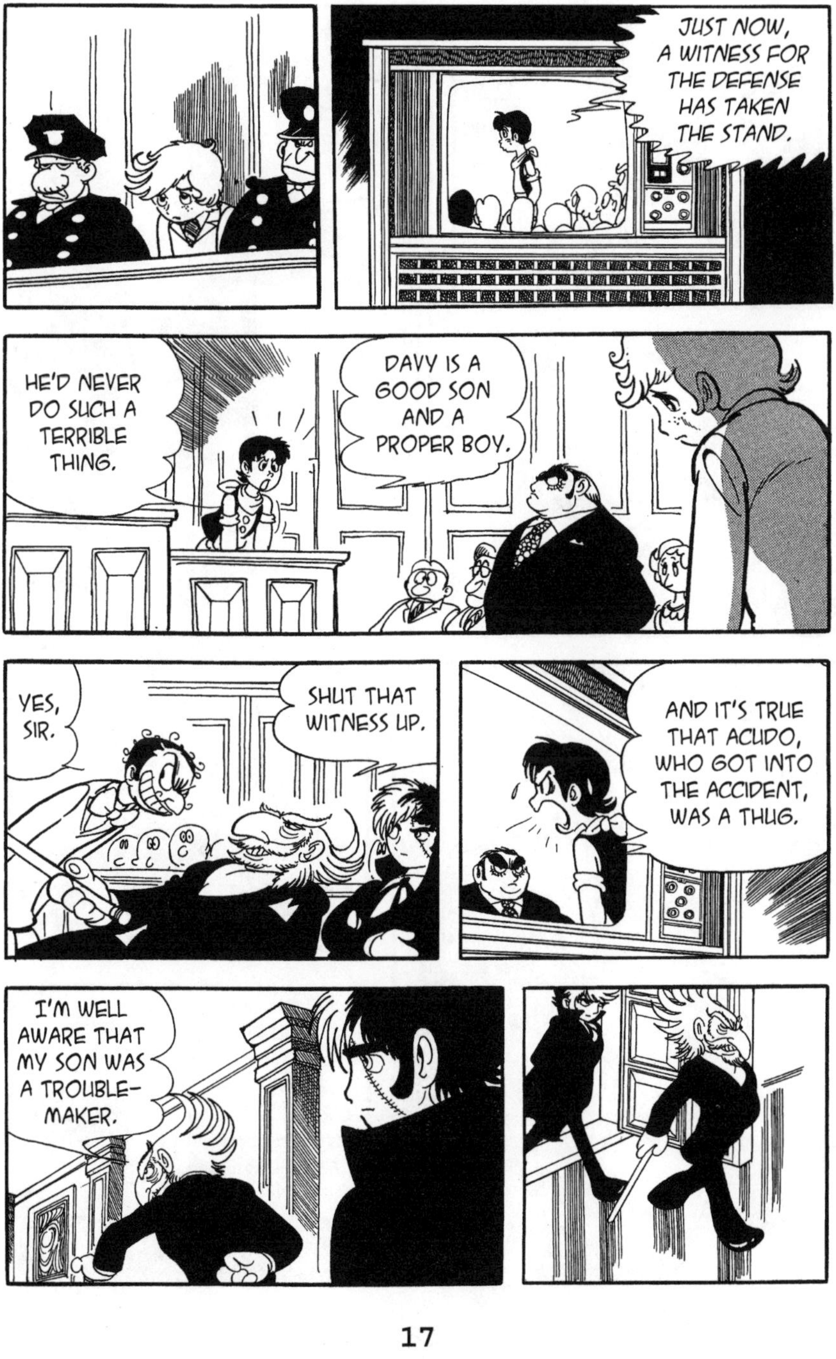
JUST NOW, A WITNESS FOR THE DEFENSE HAS TAKEN THE STAND.
DAVY IS A GOOD SON AND A PROPER BOY.
HE'D NEVER DO SUCH A TERRIBLE THING.
AND IT'S TRUE THAT ACUDO, WHO GOT INTO THE ACCIDENT, WAS A THUG.
SHUT THAT WITNESS UP.
YES, SIR.
I'M WELL AWARE THAT MY SON WAS A TROUBLE-MAKER.

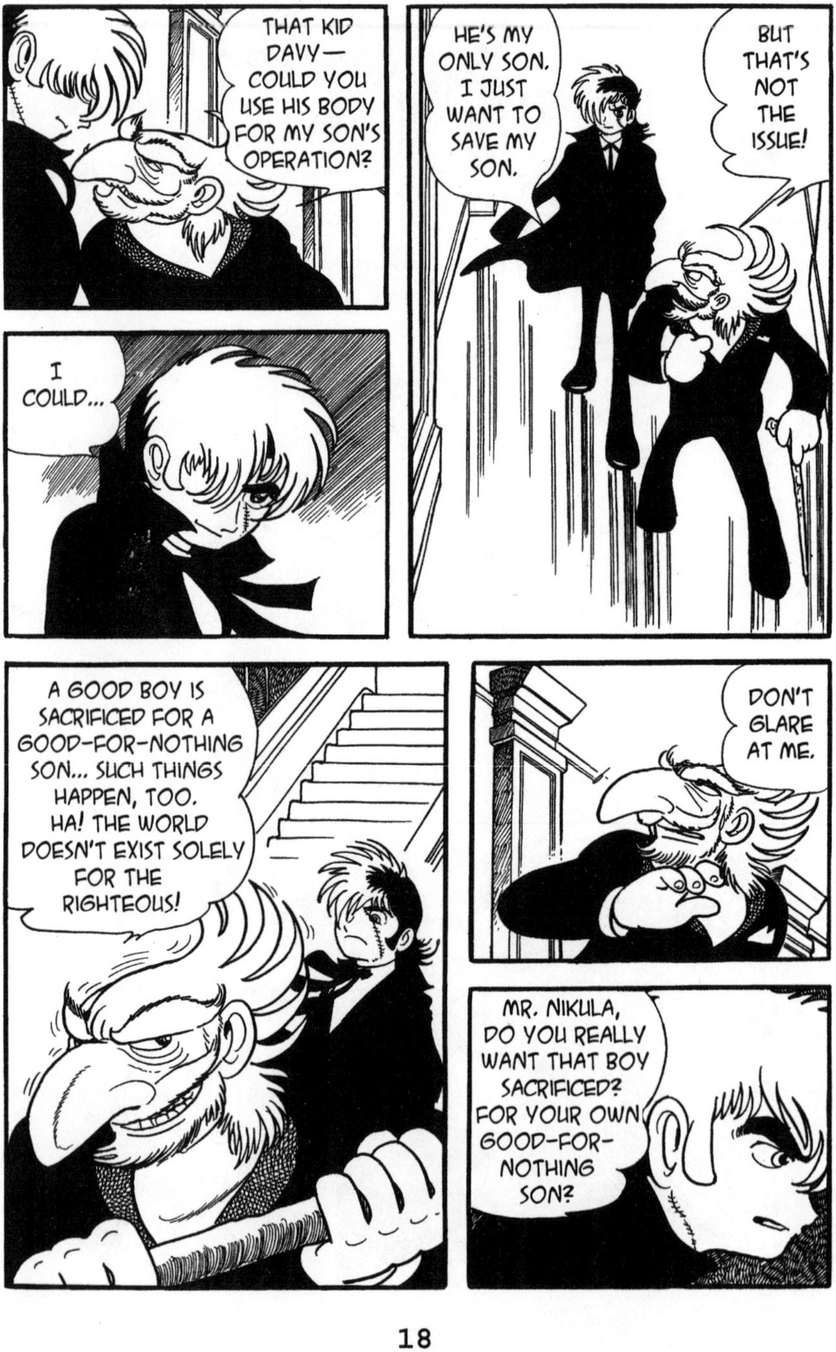
THAT KID DAVY— COULD YOU USE HIS BODY FOR MY SON'S OPERATION?
I COULD...
HE'S MY ONLY SON. I JUST WANT TO SAVE MY SON.
BUT THAT'S NOT THE ISSUE!
A GOOD BOY IS SACRIFICED FOR A GOOD-FOR-NOTHING SON... SUCH THINGS HAPPEN, TOO. HA! THE WORLD DOESN'T EXIST SOLELY FOR THE RIGHTEOUS!
DON'T GLARE AT ME.
MR. NIKULA, DO YOU REALLY WANT THAT BOY SACRIFICED? FOR YOUR OWN GOOD-FOR-NOTHING SON?

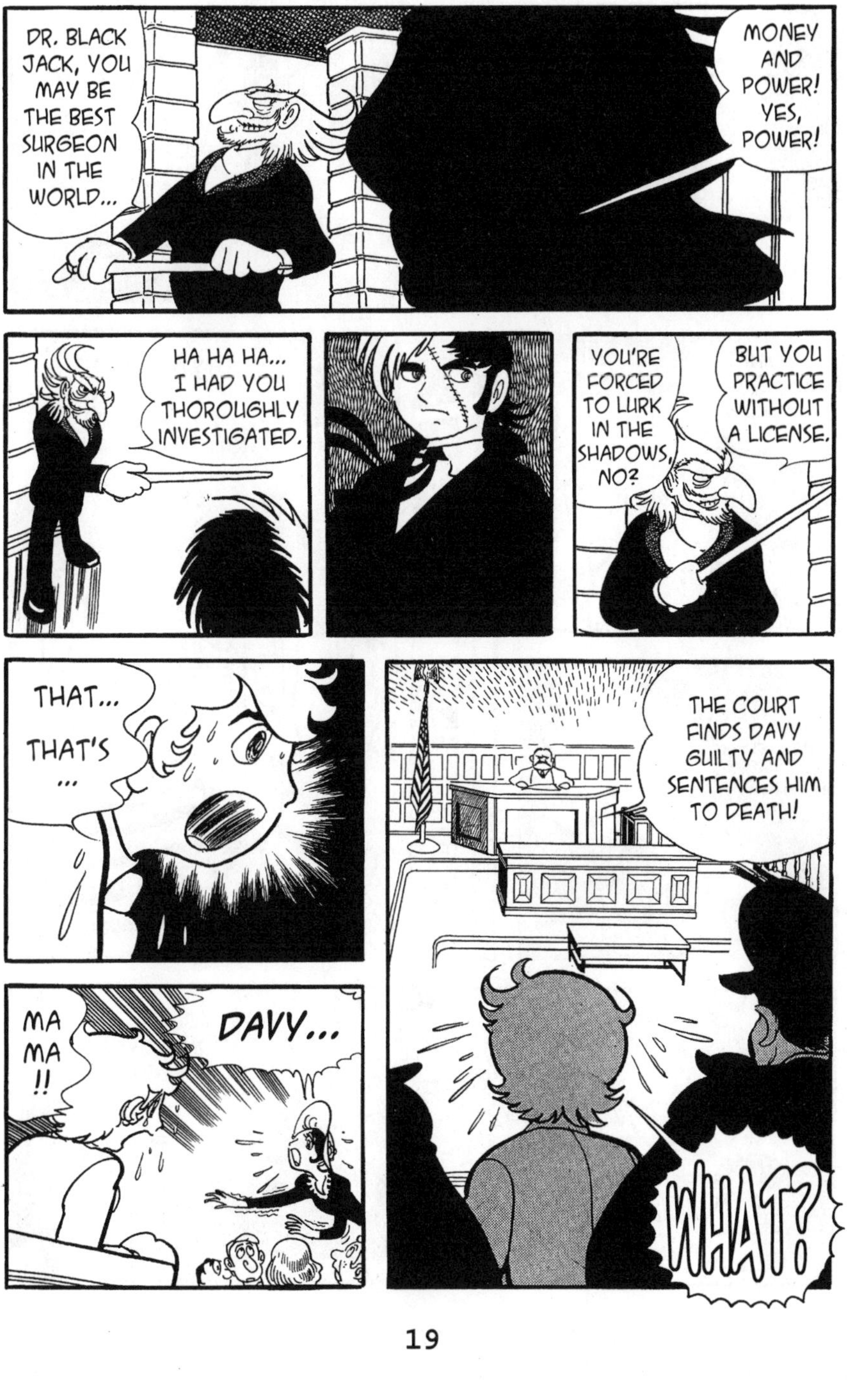
MONEY AND POWER! YES, POWER!
DR. BLACK JACK, YOU MAY BE THE BEST SURGEON IN THE WORLD...
BUT YOU PRACTICE WITHOUT A LICENSE.
YOU'RE FORCED TO LURK IN THE SHADOWS, NO?
HA HA HA... I HAD YOU THOROUGHLY INVESTIGATED.
THE COURT FINDS DAVY GUILTY AND SENTENCES HIM TO DEATH!
WHAT?
THAT... THAT'S ...
DAVY...
MA MA !!

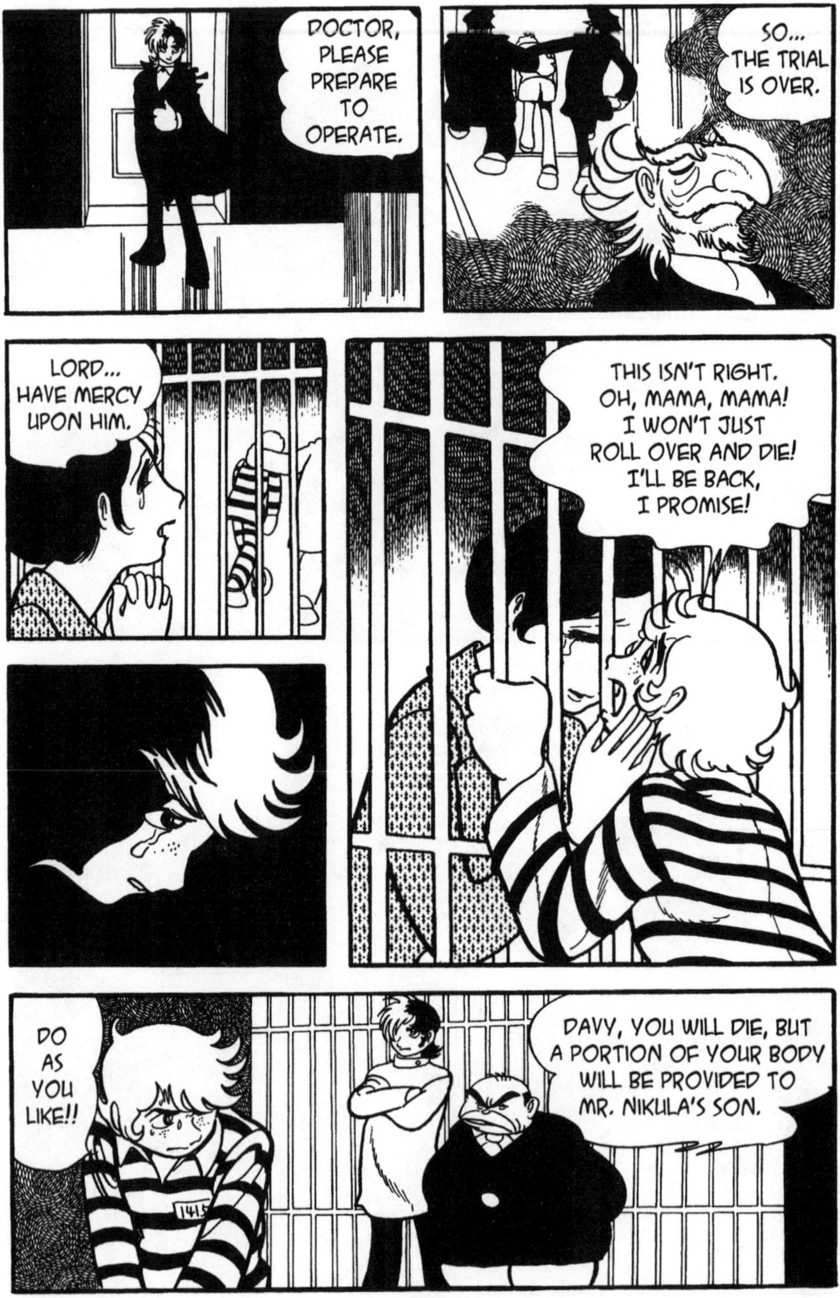
SO... THE TRIAL IS OVER.
DOCTOR, PLEASE PREPARE TO OPERATE.
THIS ISN'T RIGHT. OH, MAMA, MAMA! I WON'T JUST ROLL OVER AND DIE! I'LL BE BACK, I PROMISE!
LORD... HAVE MERCY UPON HIM.
DAVY, YOU WILL DIE, BUT A PORTION OF YOUR BODY WILL BE PROVIDED TO MR. NIKULA'S SON.
DO AS YOU LIKE!!
1415

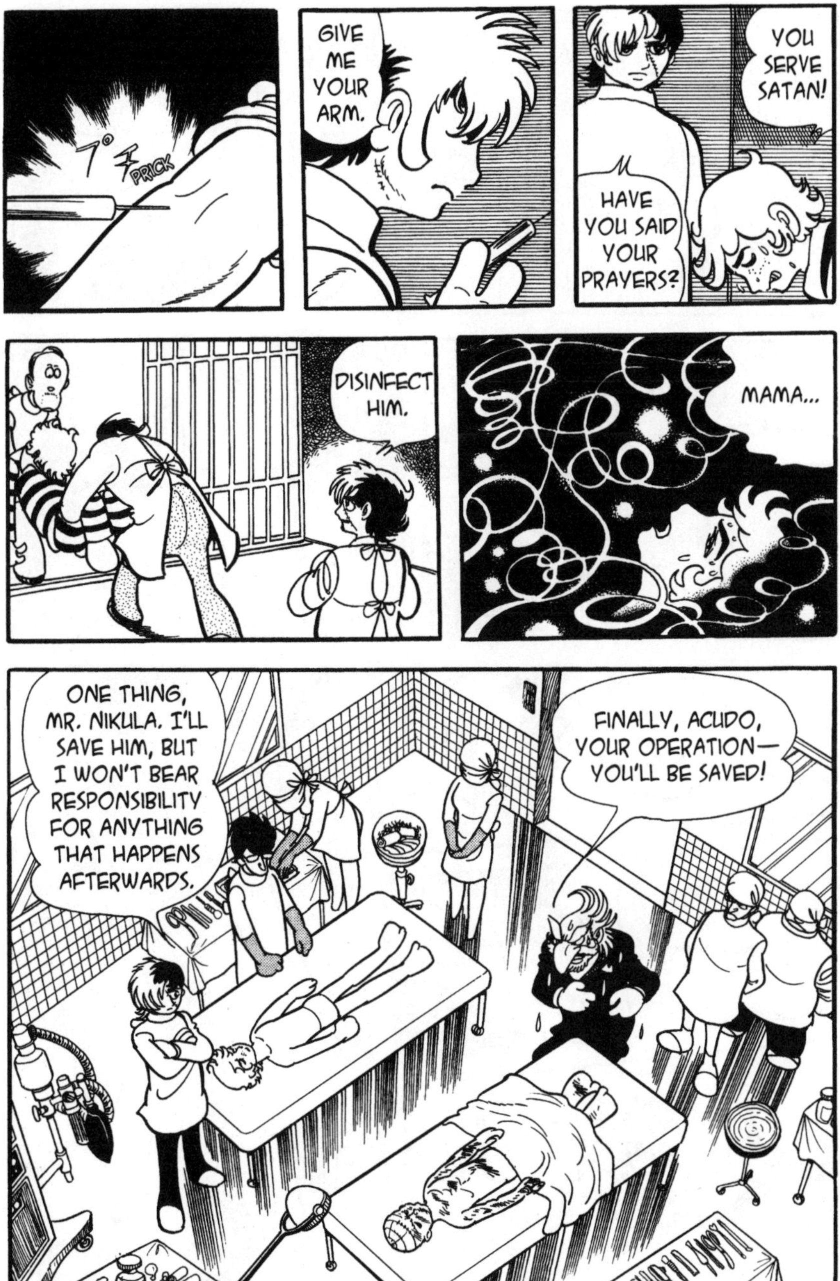
YOU SERVE SATAN!
HAVE YOU SAID YOUR PRAYERS?
GIVE ME YOUR ARM.
PRICK
MAMA...
DISINFECT HIM.
FINALLY, ACUDO, YOUR OPERATION— YOU'LL BE SAVED!
ONE THING, MR. NIKULA. I'LL SAVE HIM, BUT I WON'T BEAR RESPONSIBILITY FOR ANYTHING THAT HAPPENS AFTERWARDS.

THAT'S FINE! IF HE'S FULLY HEALED, I'LL HAVE NO COMPLAINTS.
ALL RIGHT THEN. WAIT OUTSIDE.
I'M DOING THIS ALONE!
SHOOP

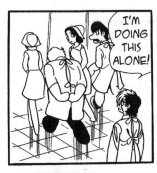

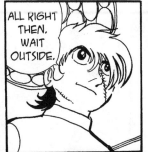

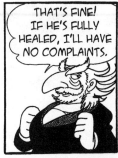

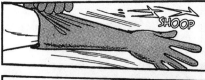

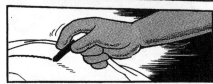

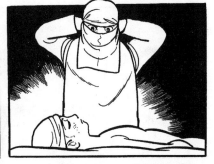

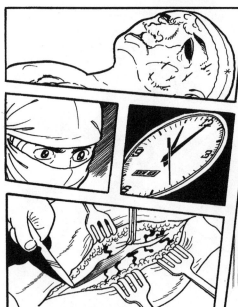

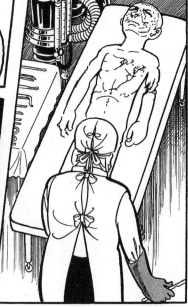

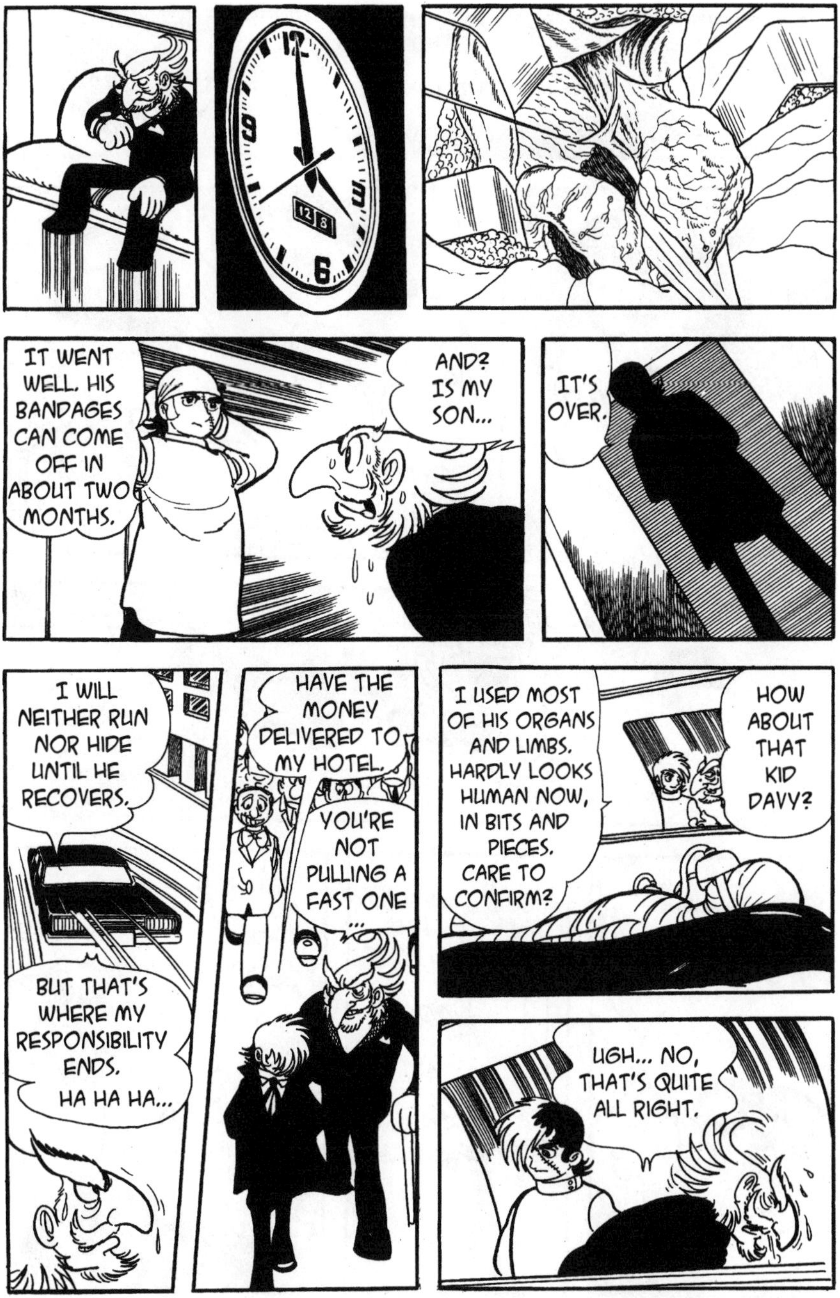
IT'S OVER.
AND? IS MY SON...
IT WENT WELL. HIS BANDAGES CAN COME OFF IN ABOUT TWO MONTHS.
HOW ABOUT THAT KID DAVY?
I USED MOST OF HIS ORGANS AND LIMBS. HARDLY LOOKS HUMAN NOW, IN BITS AND PIECES. CARE TO CONFIRM?
UGH... NO, THAT'S QUITE ALL RIGHT.
HAVE THE MONEY DELIVERED TO MY HOTEL.
YOU'RE NOT PULLING A FAST ONE ...
I WILL NEITHER RUN NOR HIDE UNTIL HE RECOVERS.
BUT THAT'S WHERE MY RESPONSIBILITY ENDS.
HA HA HA...

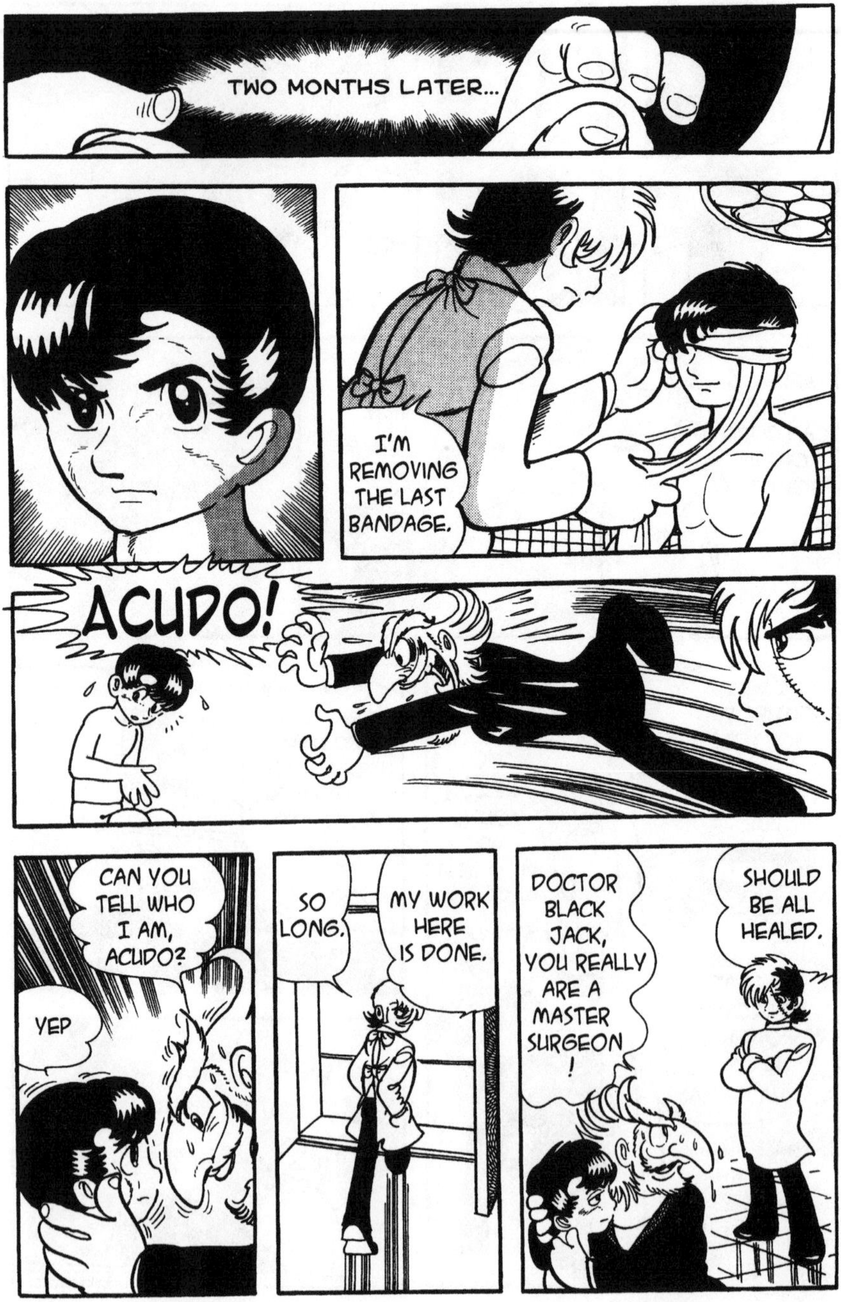
TWO MONTHS LATER...
I'M REMOVING THE LAST BANDAGE.
ACUDO!
SHOULD BE ALL HEALED.
DOCTOR BLACK JACK, YOU REALLY ARE A MASTER SURGEON !
MY WORK HERE IS DONE.
SO LONG.
CAN YOU TELL WHO I AM, ACUDO?
YEP

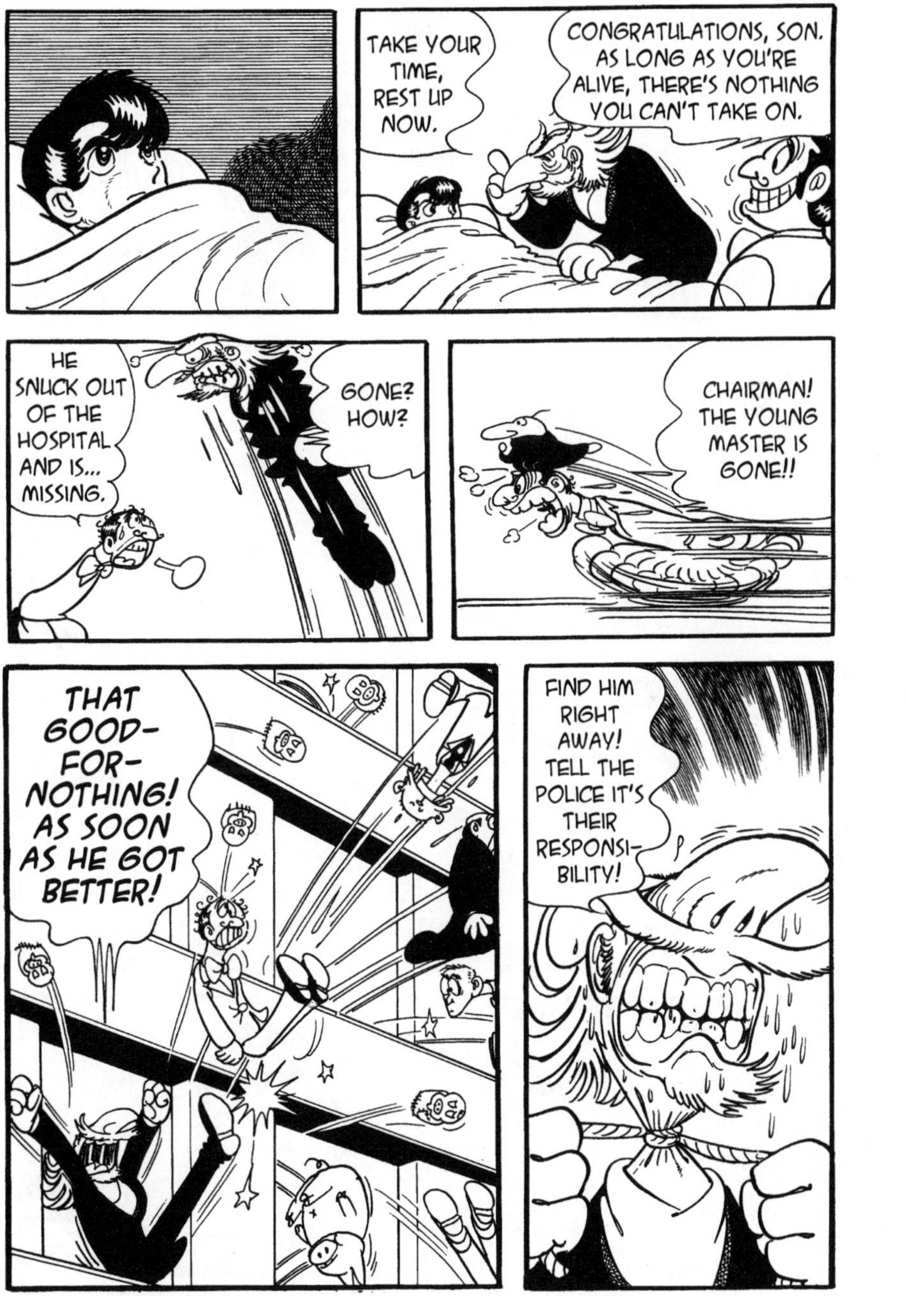
CONGRATULATIONS, SON. AS LONG AS YOU'RE ALIVE, THERE'S NOTHING YOU CAN'T TAKE ON.
TAKE YOUR TIME, REST UP NOW.
CHAIRMAN! THE YOUNG MASTER IS GONE!!
GONE? HOW?
HE SNUCK OUT OF THE HOSPITAL AND IS... MISSING.
FIND HIM RIGHT AWAY! TELL THE POLICE IT'S THEIR RESPONSIBILITY!
THAT GOOD-FOR-NOTHING! AS SOON AS HE GOT BETTER!

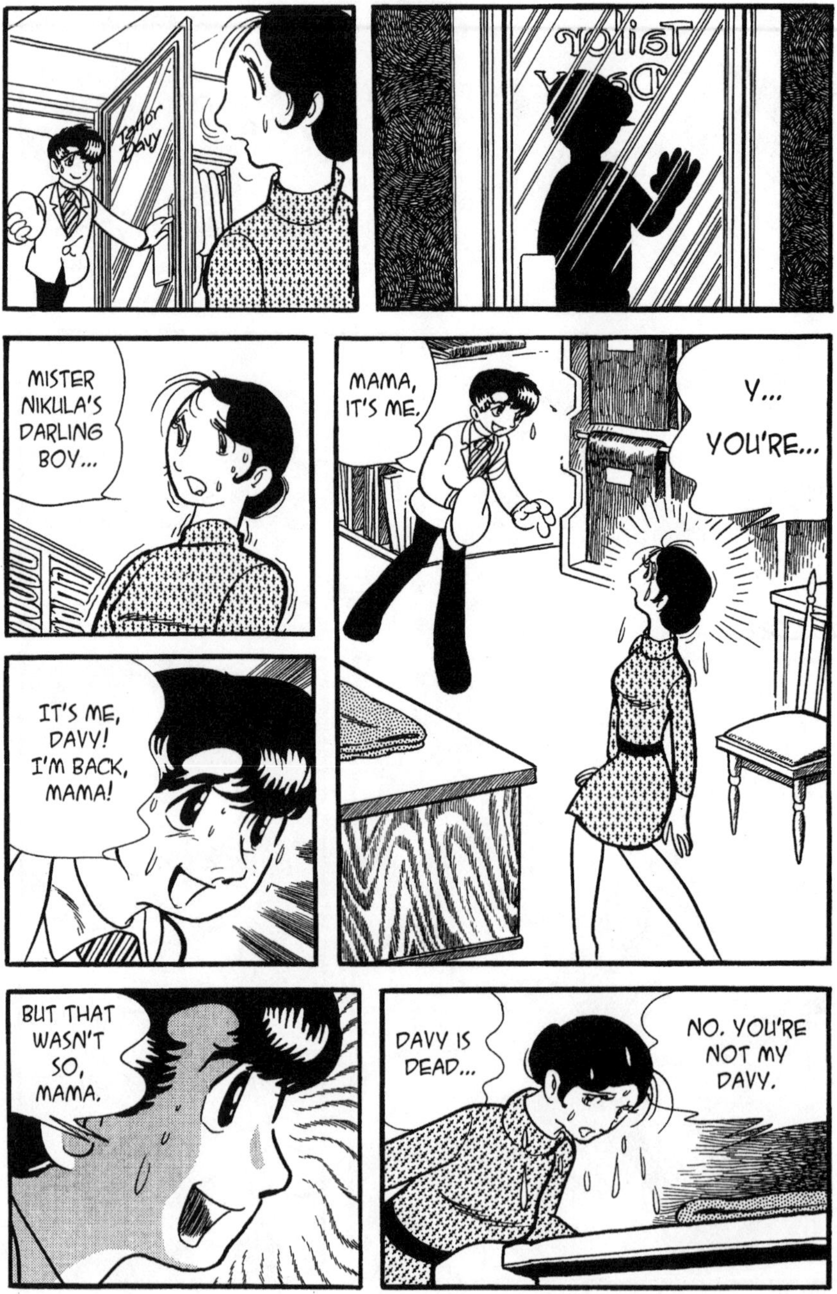
Tailor Davy
Y...
YOU'RE...
MAMA, IT'S ME.
MISTER NIKULA'S DARLING BOY...
IT'S ME, DAVY! I'M BACK, MAMA!
NO. YOU'RE NOT MY DAVY.
DAVY IS DEAD...
BUT THAT WASN'T SO, MAMA.

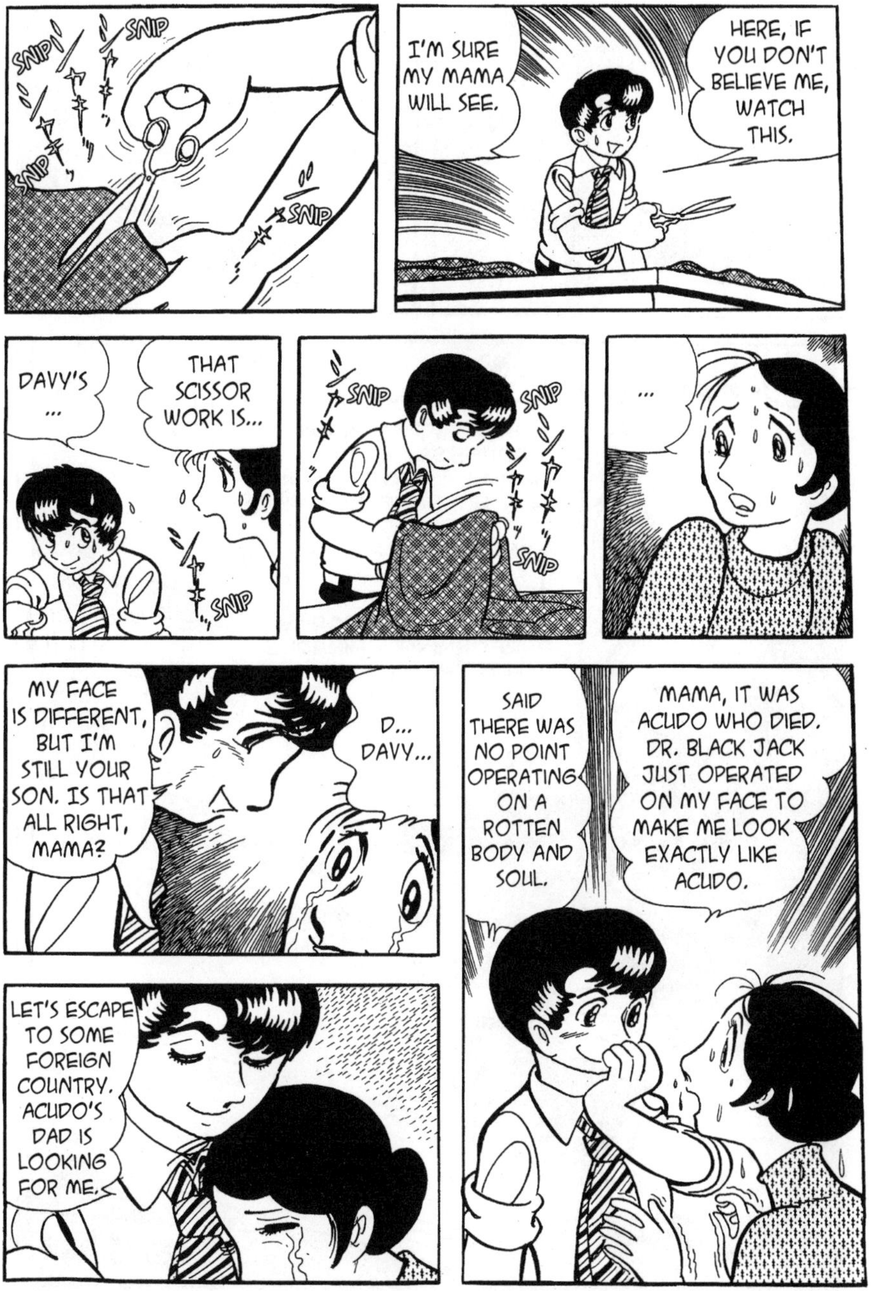
HERE, IF YOU DON'T BELIEVE ME, WATCH THIS.
I'M SURE MY MAMA WILL SEE.
SNIP
SNIP
SNIP
SNIP
...
SNIP
SNIP
SNIP
THAT SCISSOR WORK IS...
DAVY'S ...
SNIP
MAMA, IT WAS ACUDO WHO DIED. DR. BLACK JACK JUST OPERATED ON MY FACE TO MAKE ME LOOK EXACTLY LIKE ACUDO.
SAID THERE WAS NO POINT OPERATING ON A ROTTEN BODY AND SOUL.
D... DAVY...
MY FACE IS DIFFERENT, BUT I'M STILL YOUR SON. IS THAT ALL RIGHT, MAMA?
LET'S ESCAPE TO SOME FOREIGN COUNTRY. ACUDO'S DAD IS LOOKING FOR ME.

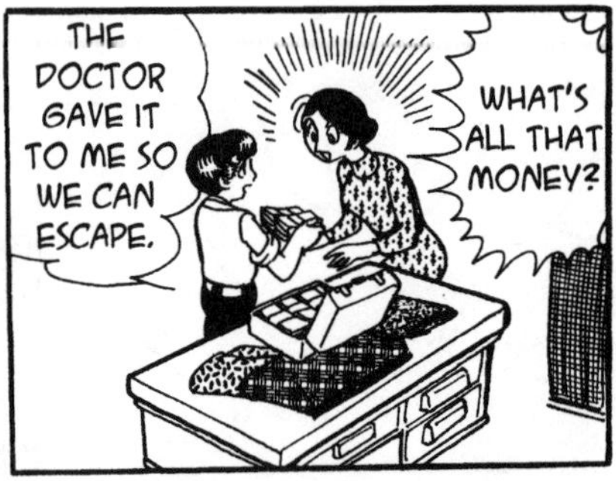
WHAT'S ALL THAT MONEY?
THE DOCTOR GAVE IT TO ME SO WE CAN ESCAPE.
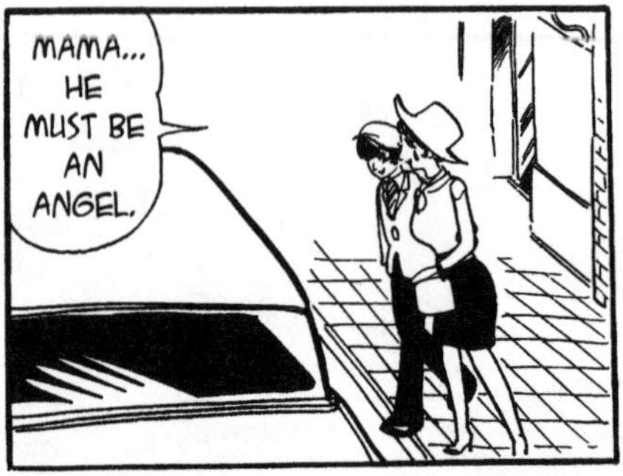
MAMA... HE MUST BE AN ANGEL.
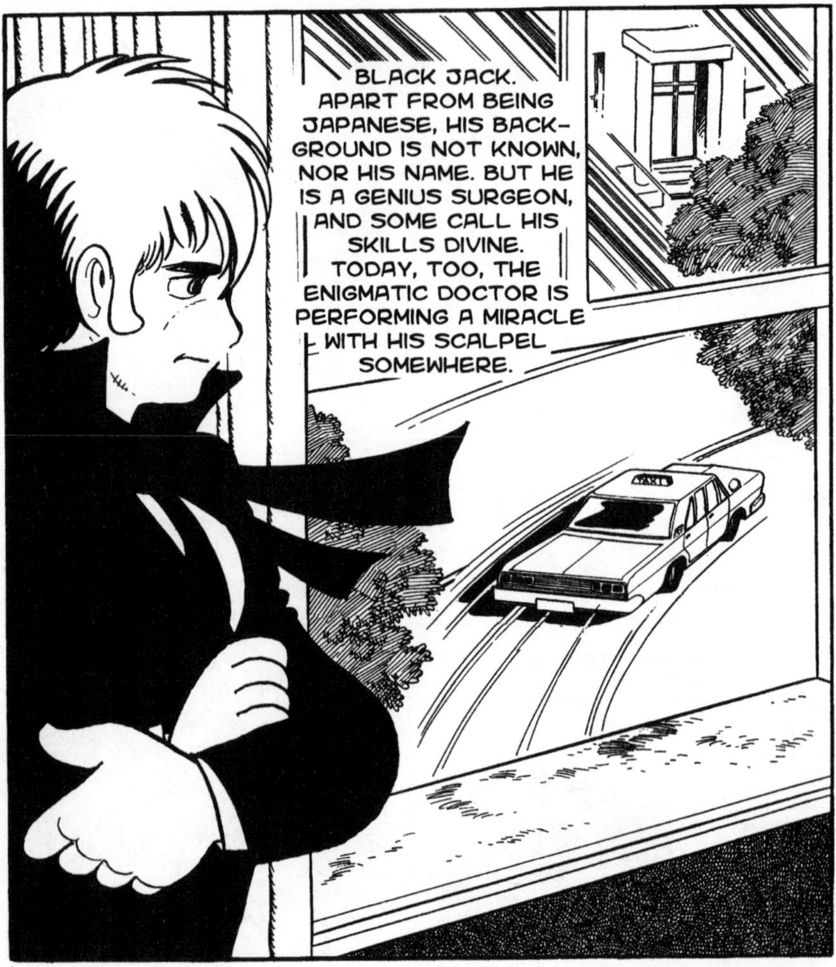
BLACK JACK. APART FROM BEING JAPANESE, HIS BACK-GROUND IS NOT KNOWN, NOR HIS NAME. BUT HE IS A GENIUS SURGEON, AND SOME CALL HIS SKILLS DIVINE. TODAY, TOO, THE ENIGMATIC DOCTOR IS PERFORMING A MIRACLE WITH HIS SCALPEL SOMEWHERE.
TAXI

THE FIRST STORM OF SPRING

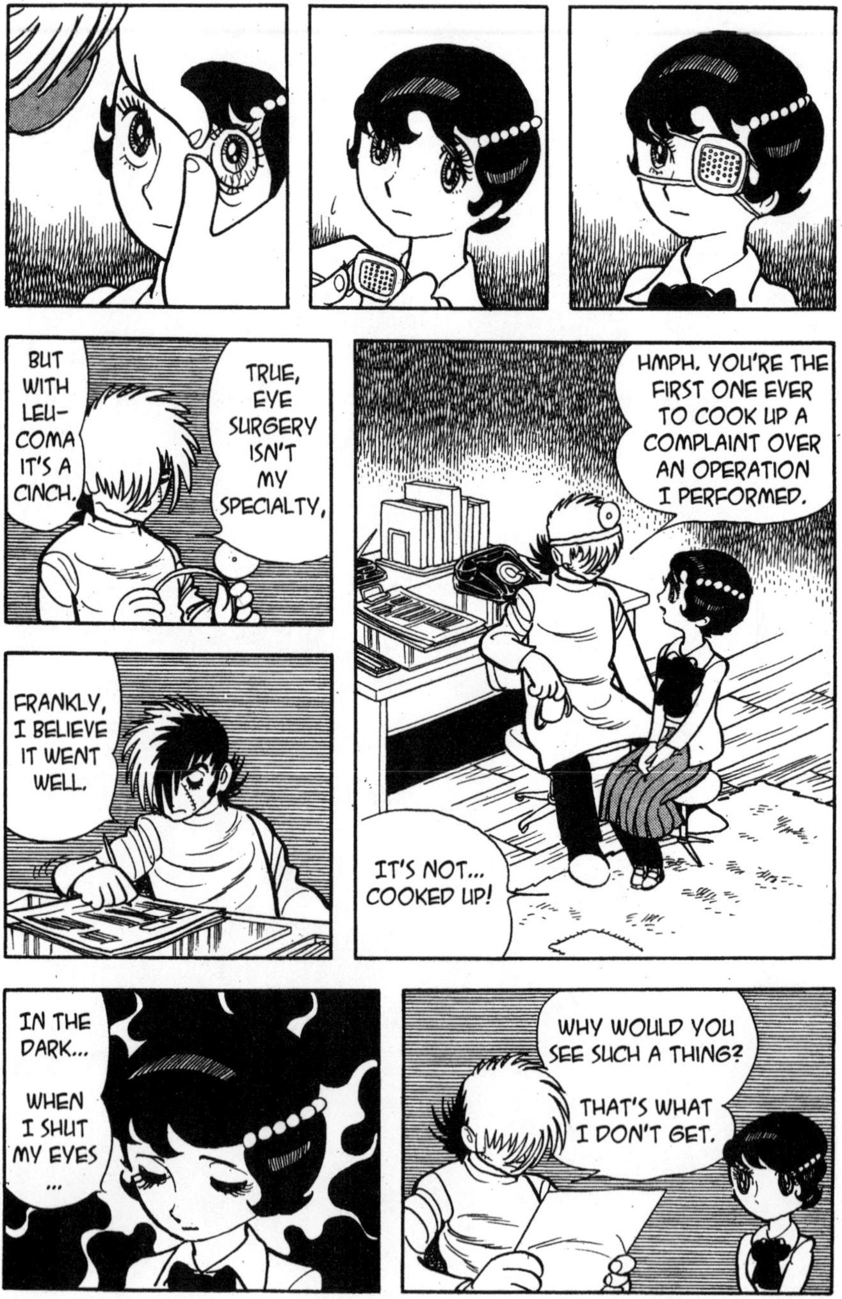
HMPH. YOU'RE THE FIRST ONE EVER TO COOK UP A COMPLAINT OVER AN OPERATION I PERFORMED.
IT'S NOT... COOKED UP!
TRUE, EYE SURGERY ISN'T MY SPECIALTY,
BUT WITH LEU-COMA IT'S A CINCH.
FRANKLY, I BELIEVE IT WENT WELL.
WHY WOULD YOU SEE SUCH A THING?
THAT'S WHAT I DON'T GET.
IN THE DARK...
WHEN I SHUT MY EYES ...

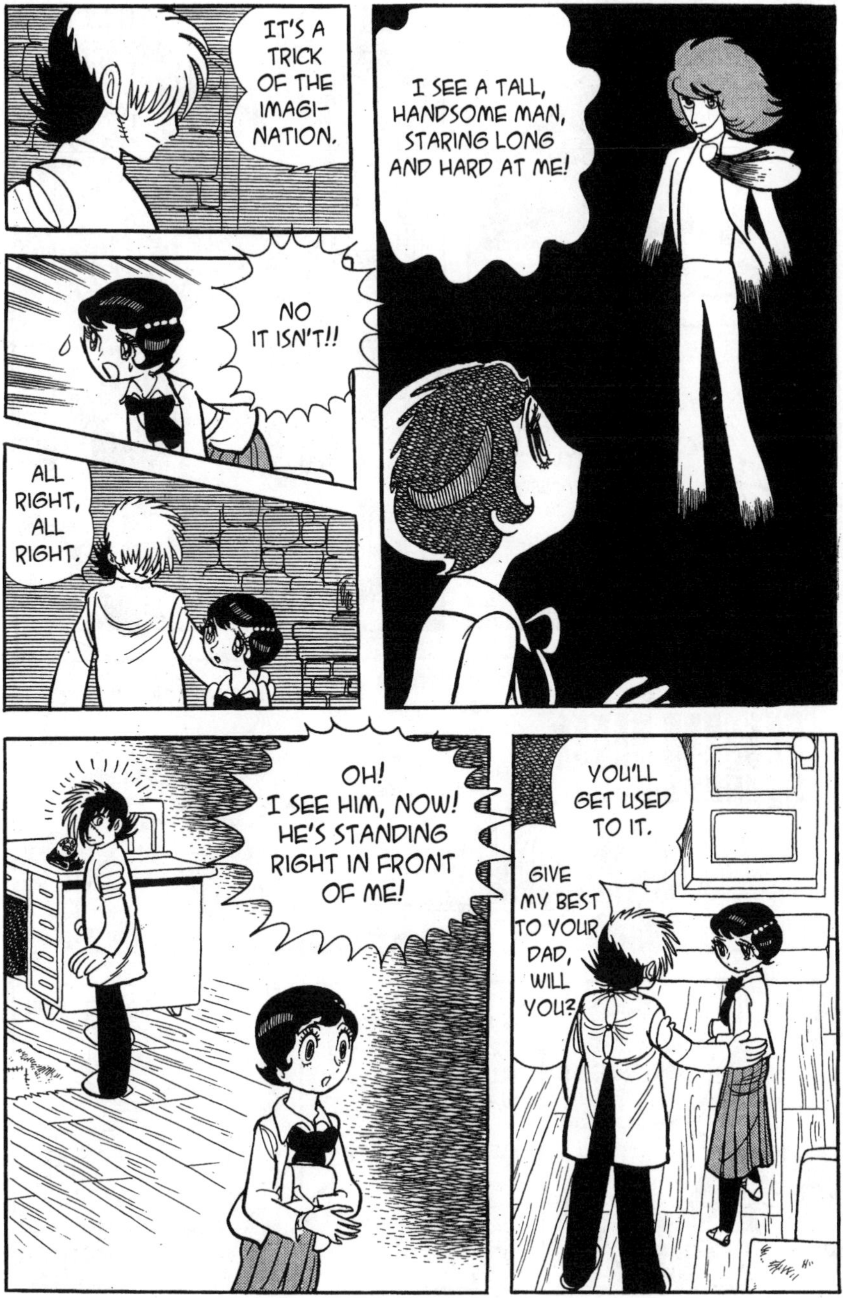

IT'S A TRICK OF THE IMAGI-NATION.
NO IT ISN'T!!
ALL RIGHT, ALL RIGHT.
I SEE A TALL, HANDSOME MAN, STARING LONG AND HARD AT ME!
OH! I SEE HIM, NOW! HE'S STANDING RIGHT IN FRONT OF ME!
YOU'LL GET USED TO IT.
GIVE MY BEST TO YOUR DAD, WILL YOU?

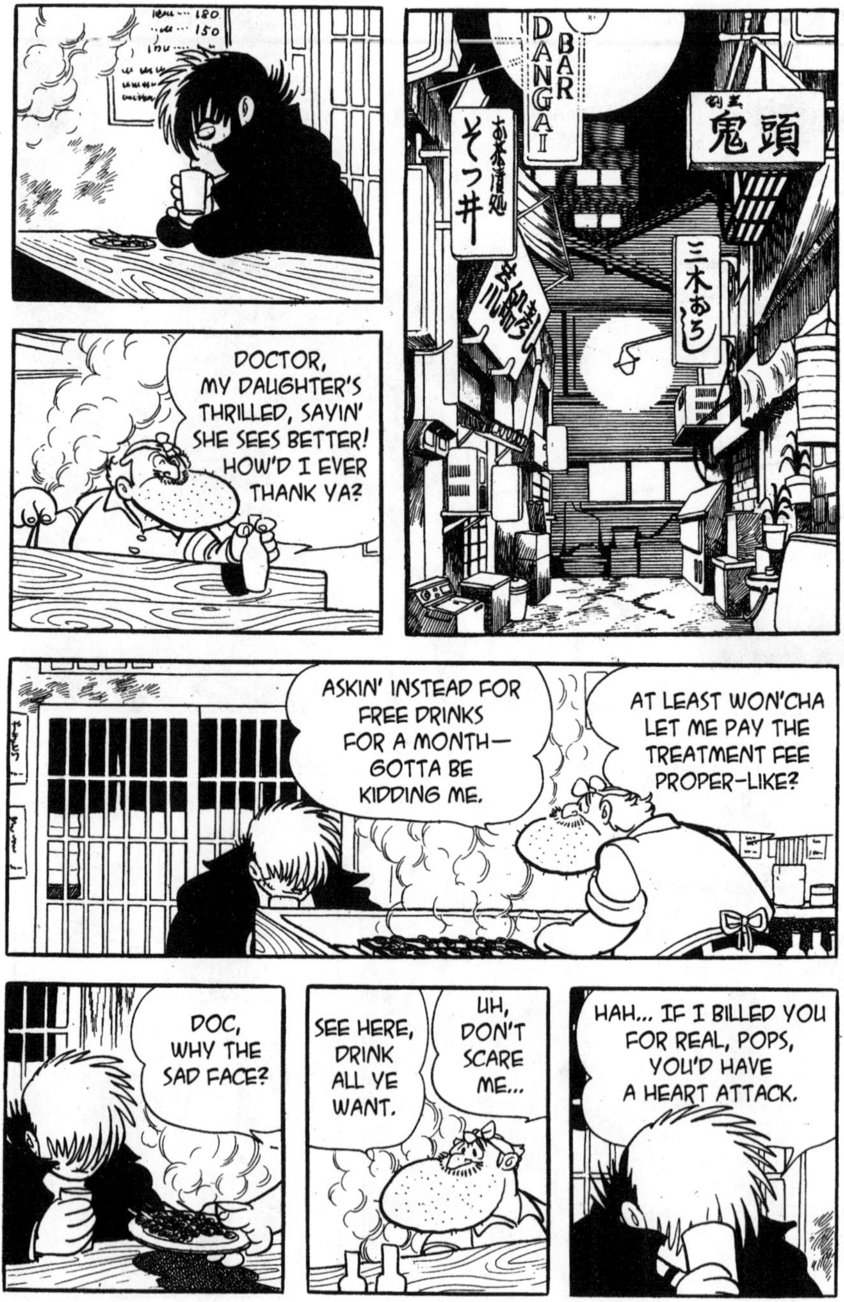
BAR
DANGAI
鬼頭
お茶漬処
そつ井
三木おろし
DOCTOR, MY DAUGHTER'S THRILLED, SAYIN' SHE SEES BETTER! HOW'D I EVER THANK YA?
AT LEAST WON'CHA LET ME PAY THE TREATMENT FEE PROPER-LIKE?
ASKIN' INSTEAD FOR FREE DRINKS FOR A MONTH— GOTTA BE KIDDING ME.
HAH... IF I BILLED YOU FOR REAL, POPS, YOU'D HAVE A HEART ATTACK.
UH, DON'T SCARE ME...
SEE HERE, DRINK ALL YE WANT.
DOC, WHY THE SAD FACE?

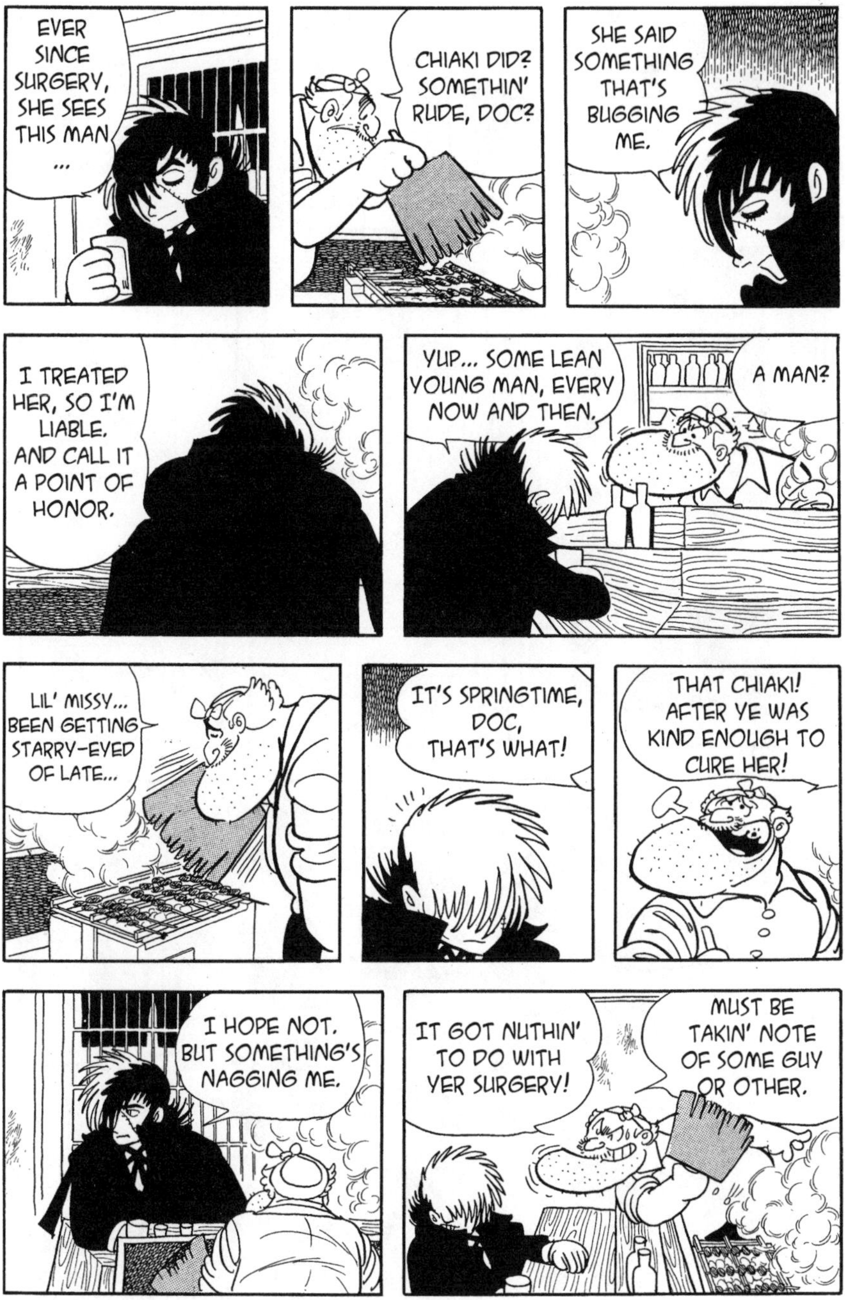
SHE SAID SOMETHING THAT'S BUGGING ME.
CHIAKI DID? SOMETHIN' RUDE, DOC?
EVER SINCE SURGERY, SHE SEES THIS MAN ...
A MAN?
YUP... SOME LEAN YOUNG MAN, EVERY NOW AND THEN.
I TREATED HER, SO I'M LIABLE. AND CALL IT A POINT OF HONOR.
THAT CHIAKI! AFTER YE WAS KIND ENOUGH TO CURE HER!
IT'S SPRINGTIME, DOC, THAT'S WHAT!
LIL' MISSY... BEEN GETTING STARRY-EYED OF LATE...
MUST BE TAKIN' NOTE OF SOME GUY OR OTHER.
IT GOT NUTHIN' TO DO WITH YER SURGERY!
I HOPE NOT. BUT SOMETHING'S NAGGING ME.

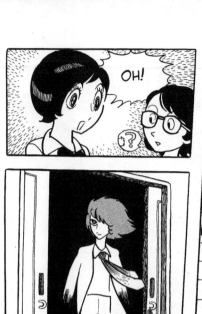

OH!
?
I SAW HIM, IN THAT DARK DOORWAY!
THERE SHE GOES AGAIN WITH HER PHANTOM GUY.
PITY... IT'S CUZ WE'RE AN ALL-GIRLS SCHOOL.
HE'S NOT A PHANTOM! HE WAS RIGHT HERE!
AT A PICKLES WAREHOUSE? THIS MORNING YOU SAW HIM IN THE GYM.
CHIAKI'S SURE GONE BOY CRAZY.

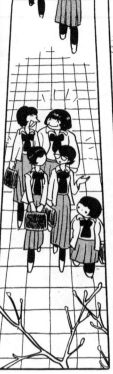

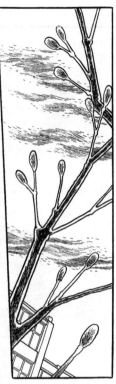

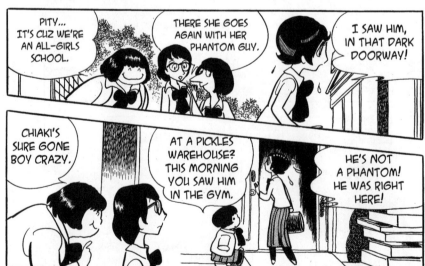

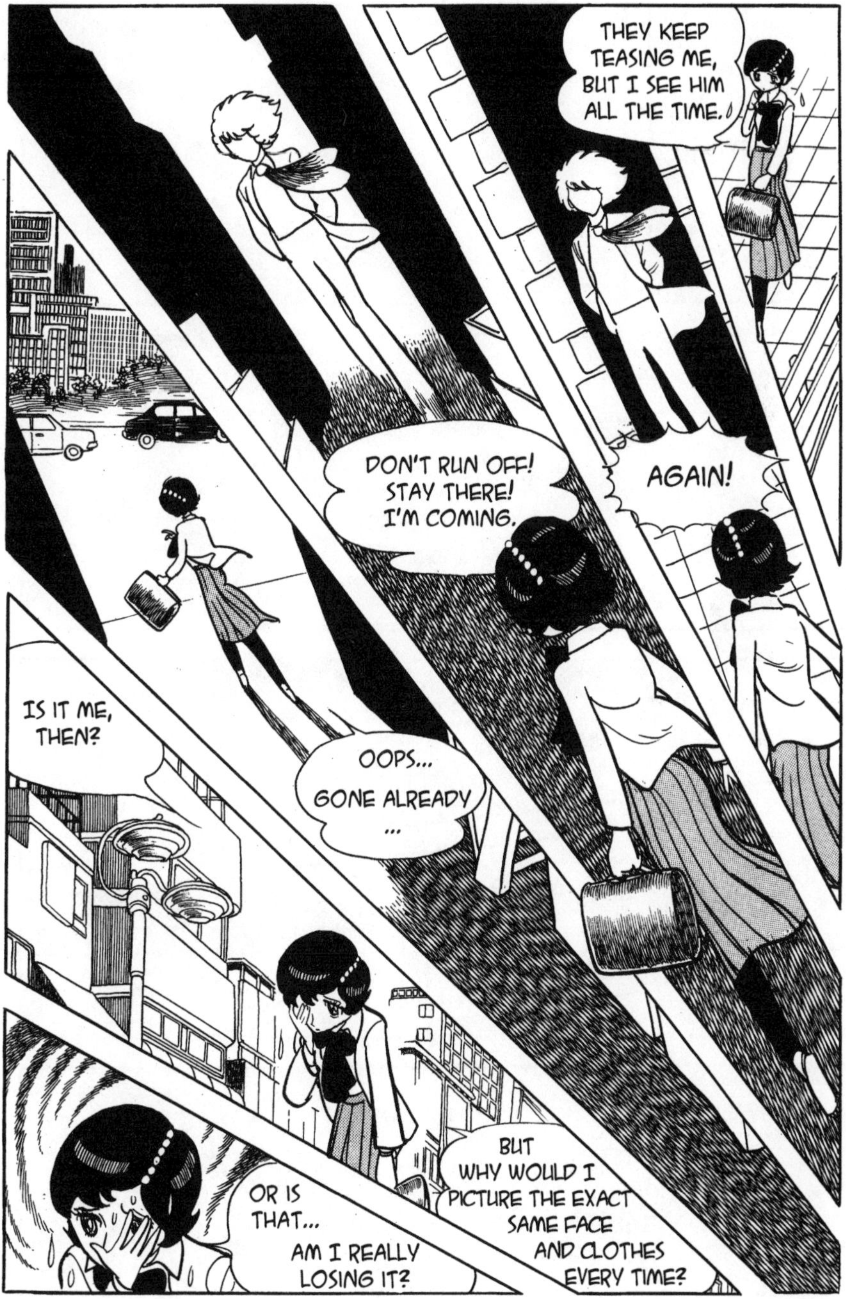
THEY KEEP TEASING ME, BUT I SEE HIM ALL THE TIME.
AGAIN!
DON'T RUN OFF! STAY THERE! I'M COMING.
OOPS... GONE ALREADY ...
IS IT ME, THEN?
BUT WHY WOULD I PICTURE THE EXACT SAME FACE AND CLOTHES EVERY TIME?
OR IS THAT... AM I REALLY LOSING IT?

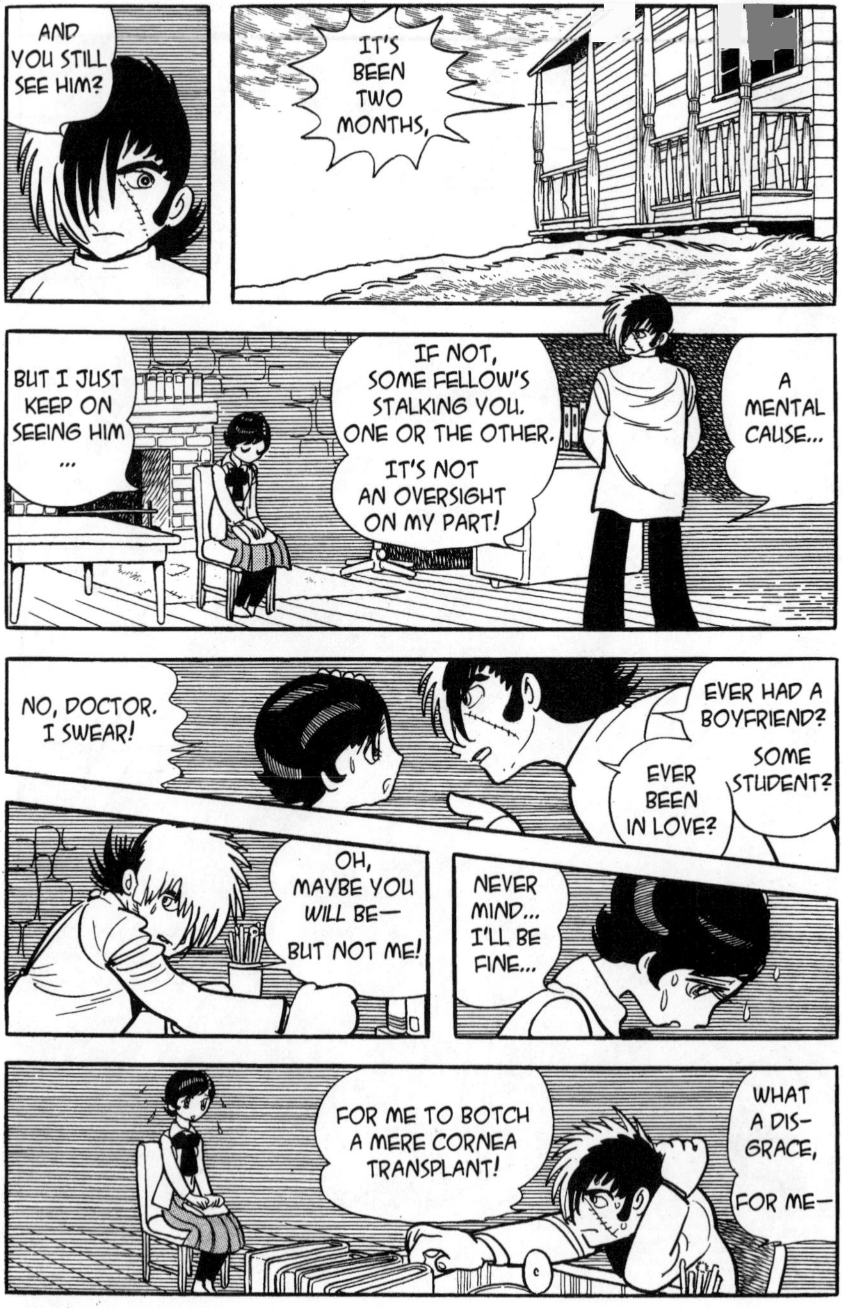
IT'S BEEN TWO MONTHS,
AND YOU STILL SEE HIM?
A MENTAL CAUSE...
IF NOT, SOME FELLOW'S STALKING YOU. ONE OR THE OTHER.
IT'S NOT AN OVERSIGHT ON MY PART!
BUT I JUST KEEP ON SEEING HIM ...
EVER HAD A BOYFRIEND?
SOME STUDENT?
EVER BEEN IN LOVE?
NO, DOCTOR. I SWEAR!
NEVER MIND... I'LL BE FINE...
OH, MAYBE YOU WILL BE— BUT NOT ME!
WHAT A DIS- GRACE,
FOR ME—
FOR ME TO BOTCH A MERE CORNEA TRANSPLANT!

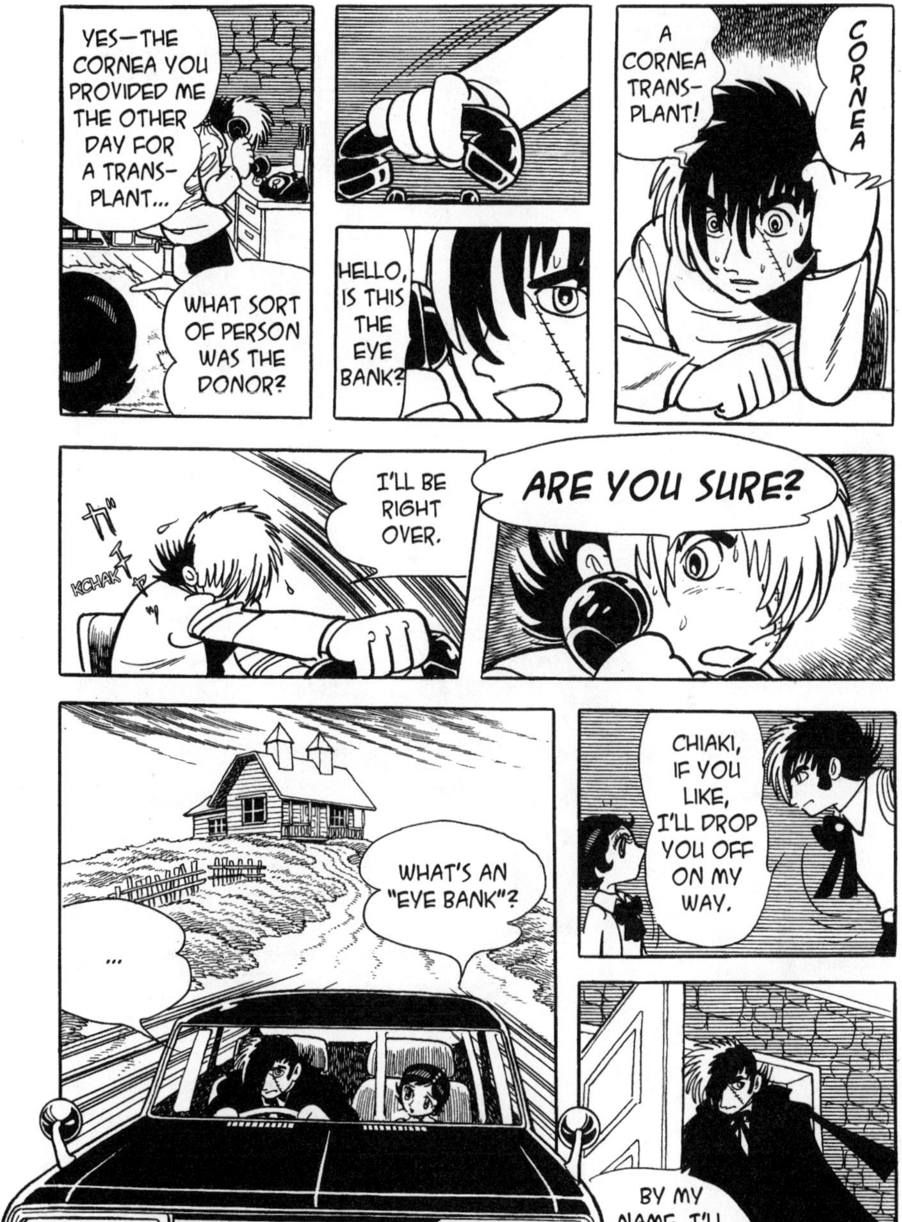
CORNEA
A CORNEA TRANS-PLANT!
HELLO, IS THIS THE EYE BANK?
YES—THE CORNEA YOU PROVIDED ME THE OTHER DAY FOR A TRANS-PLANT...
WHAT SORT OF PERSON WAS THE DONOR?
ARE YOU SURE?
I'LL BE RIGHT OVER.
KCHAK
CHIAKI, IF YOU LIKE, I'LL DROP YOU OFF ON MY WAY.
BY MY NAME, I'LL SORT THIS OUT.
WHAT'S AN "EYE BANK"?
...

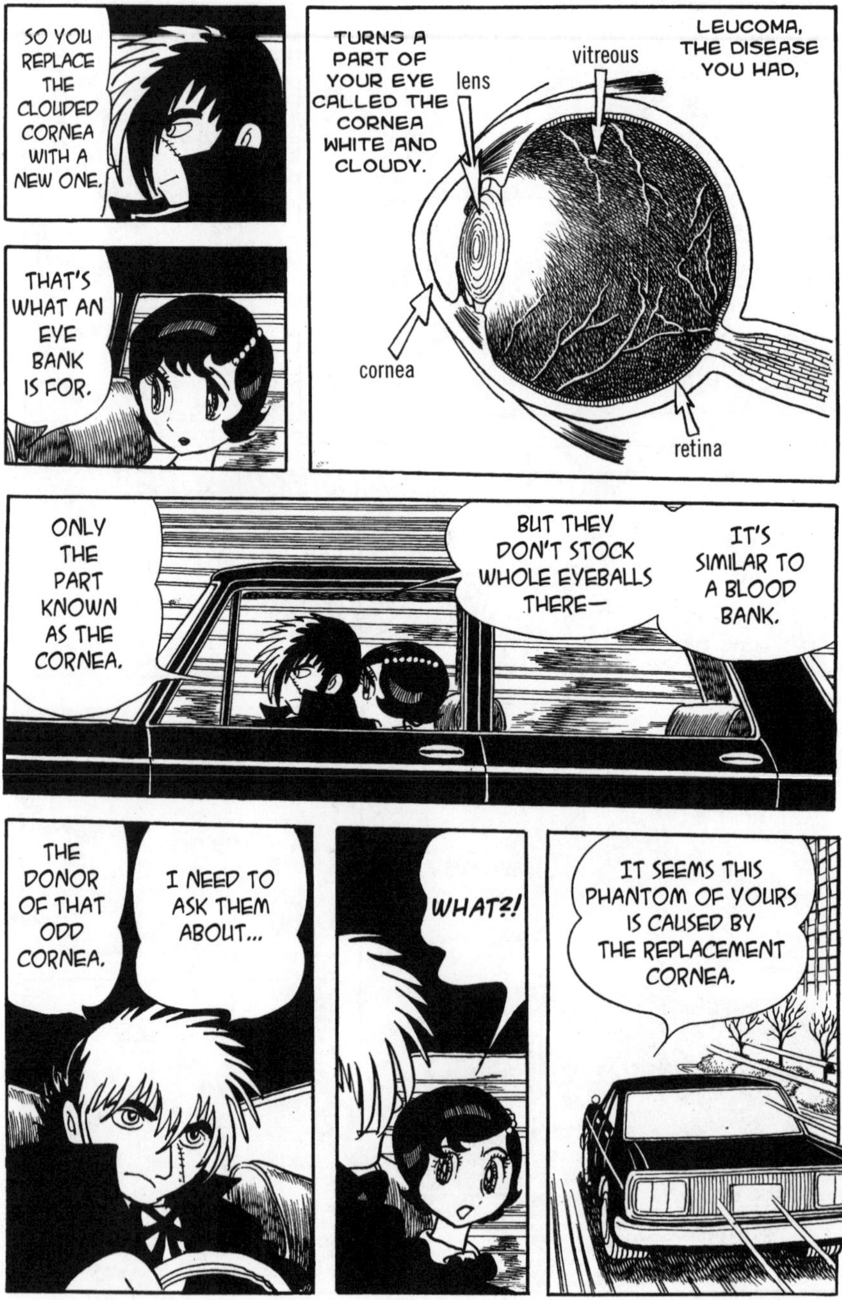
LEUCOMA, THE DISEASE YOU HAD,
TURNS A PART OF YOUR EYE CALLED THE CORNEA WHITE AND CLOUDY.
vitreous
lens
cornea
retina
SO YOU REPLACE THE CLOUDED CORNEA WITH A NEW ONE.
THAT'S WHAT AN EYE BANK IS FOR.
IT'S SIMILAR TO A BLOOD BANK.
BUT THEY DON'T STOCK WHOLE EYEBALLS THERE—
ONLY THE PART KNOWN AS THE CORNEA.
IT SEEMS THIS PHANTOM OF YOURS IS CAUSED BY THE REPLACEMENT CORNEA.
WHAT?!
I NEED TO ASK THEM ABOUT...
THE DONOR OF THAT ODD CORNEA.

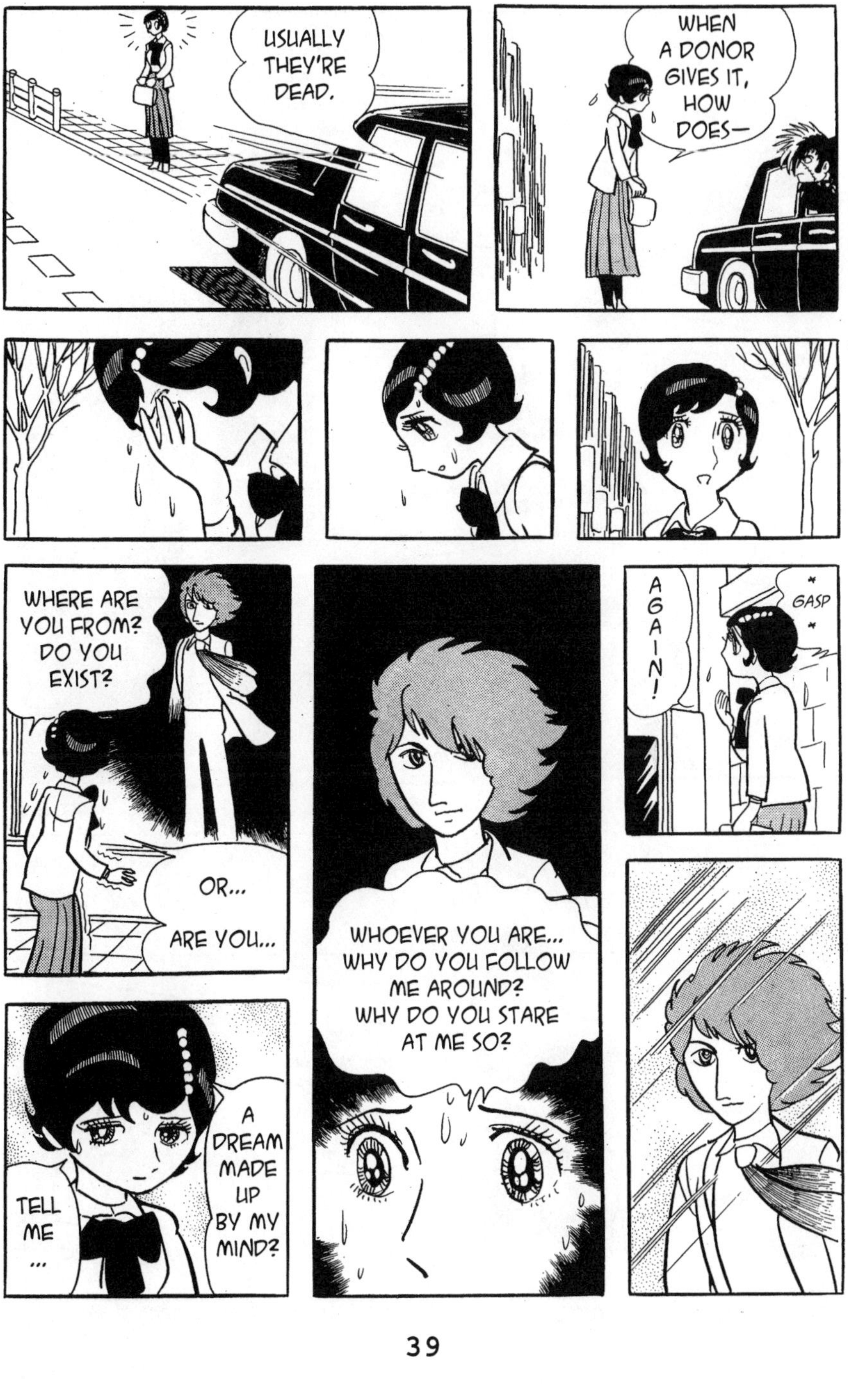
WHEN A DONOR GIVES IT, HOW DOES—
USUALLY THEY'RE DEAD.
AGAIN!
GASP
WHOEVER YOU ARE... WHY DO YOU FOLLOW ME AROUND? WHY DO YOU STARE AT ME SO?
WHERE ARE YOU FROM? DO YOU EXIST?
OR... ARE YOU...
A DREAM MADE UP BY MY MIND?
TELL ME ...

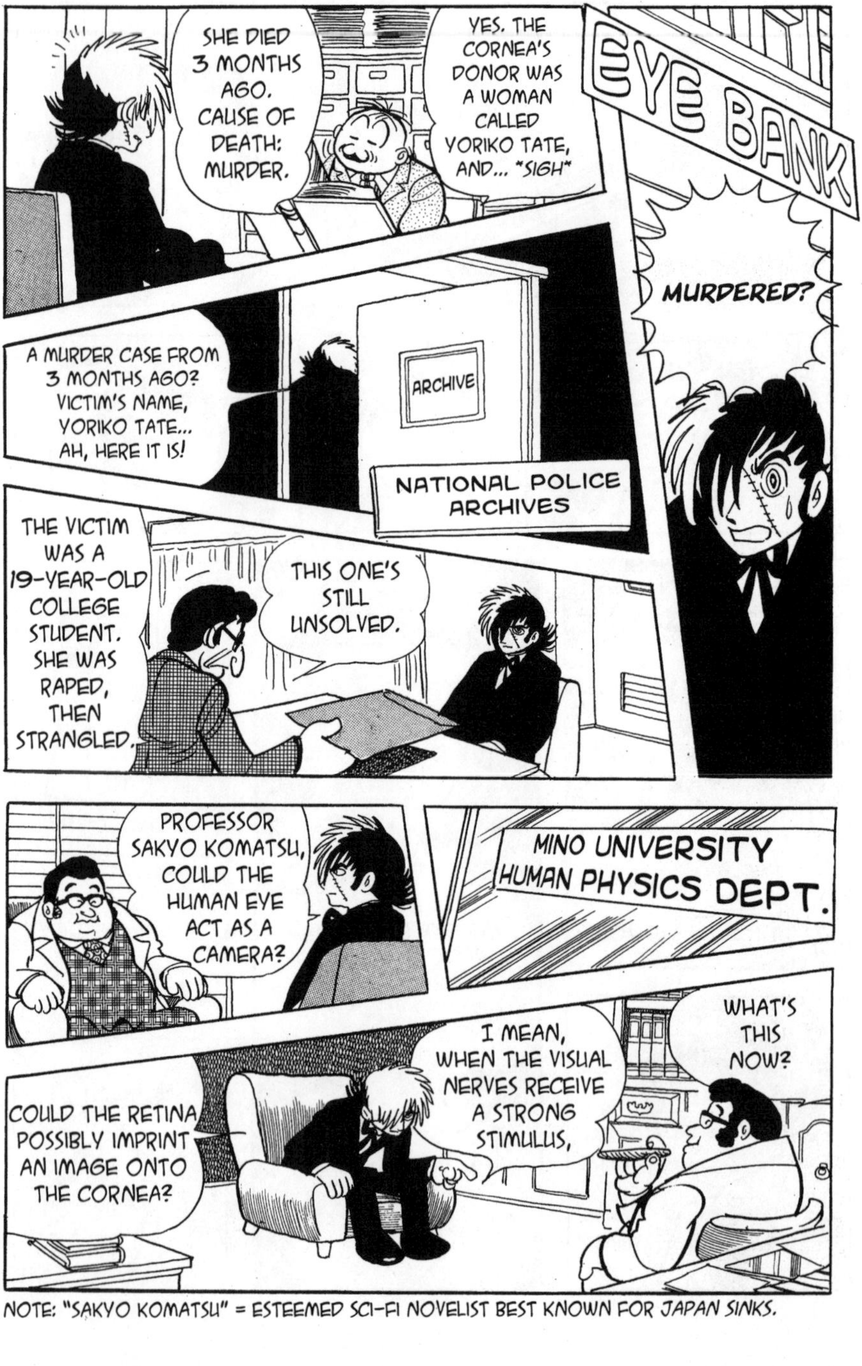
EYE BANK
YES. THE CORNEA'S DONOR WAS A WOMAN CALLED YORIKO TATE, AND... *SIGH*
SHE DIED 3 MONTHS AGO. CAUSE OF DEATH: MURDER.
MURDERED?
NATIONAL POLICE ARCHIVES
ARCHIVE
A MURDER CASE FROM 3 MONTHS AGO? VICTIM'S NAME, YORIKO TATE... AH, HERE IT IS!
THIS ONE'S STILL UNSOLVED.
THE VICTIM WAS A 19-YEAR-OLD COLLEGE STUDENT. SHE WAS RAPED, THEN STRANGLED.
MINO UNIVERSITY HUMAN PHYSICS DEPT.
PROFESSOR SAKYO KOMATSU, COULD THE HUMAN EYE ACT AS A CAMERA?
WHAT'S THIS NOW?
I MEAN, WHEN THE VISUAL NERVES RECEIVE A STRONG STIMULUS,
COULD THE RETINA POSSIBLY IMPRINT AN IMAGE ONTO THE CORNEA?

NOTE: "SAKYO KOMATSU" = ESTEEMED SCI-FI NOVELIST BEST KNOWN FOR JAPAN SINKS.

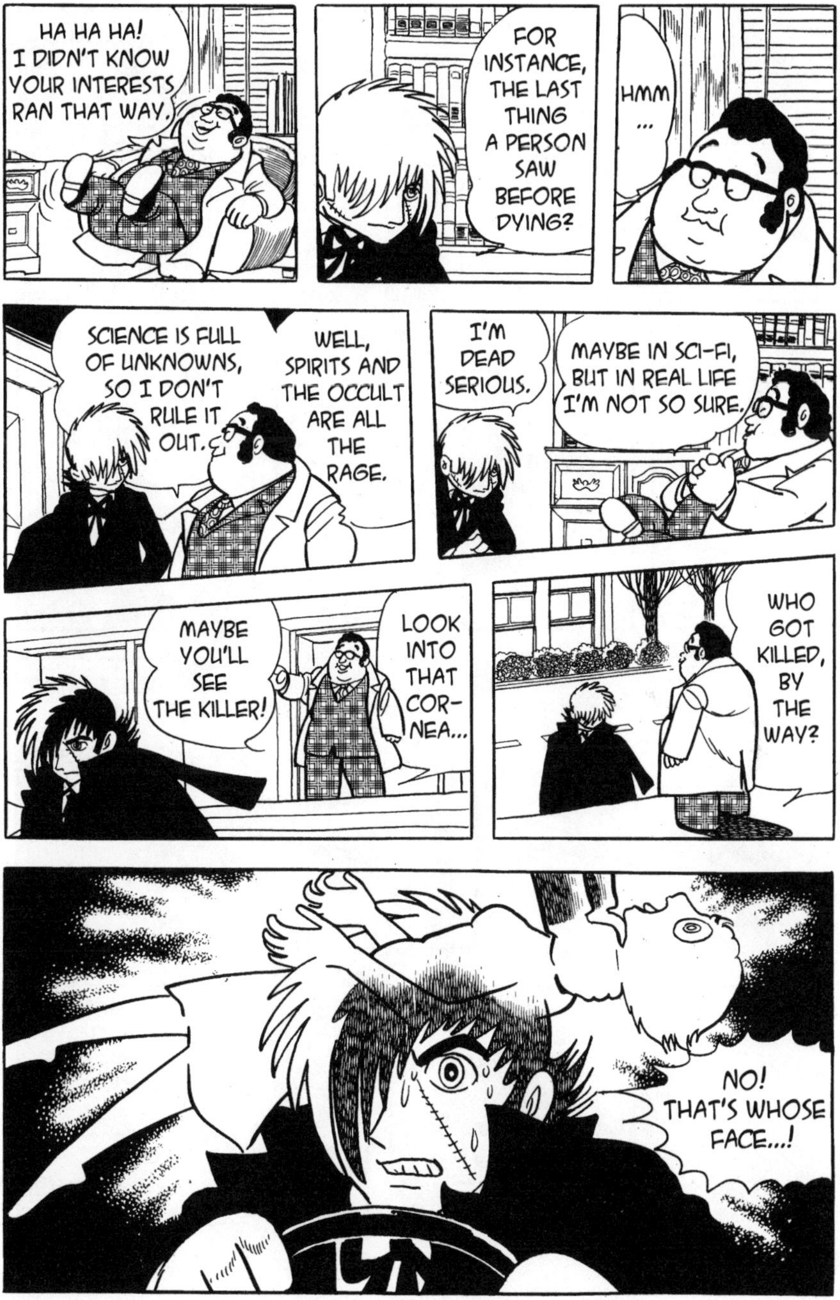
HMM ...
FOR INSTANCE, THE LAST THING A PERSON SAW BEFORE DYING?
HA HA HA! I DIDN'T KNOW YOUR INTERESTS RAN THAT WAY.
MAYBE IN SCI-FI, BUT IN REAL LIFE I'M NOT SO SURE.
I'M DEAD SERIOUS.
WELL, SPIRITS AND THE OCCULT ARE ALL THE RAGE.
SCIENCE IS FULL OF UNKNOWNS, SO I DON'T RULE IT OUT.
WHO GOT KILLED, BY THE WAY?
LOOK INTO THAT COR-NEA...
MAYBE YOU'LL SEE THE KILLER!
NO! THAT'S WHOSE FACE...!

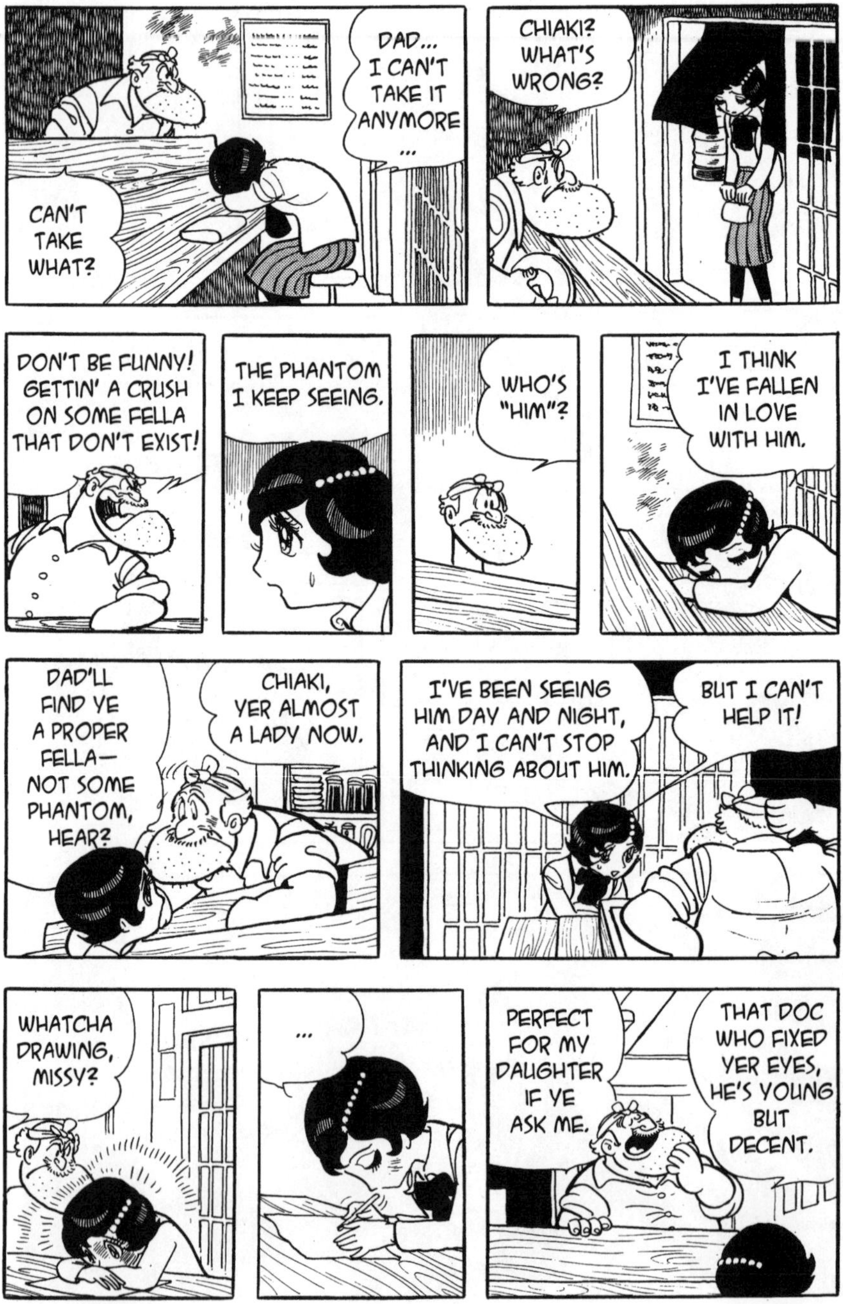
CHIAKI? WHAT'S WRONG?
DAD... I CAN'T TAKE IT ANYMORE ...
CAN'T TAKE WHAT?
I THINK I'VE FALLEN IN LOVE WITH HIM.
WHO'S "HIM"?
THE PHANTOM I KEEP SEEING.
DON'T BE FUNNY! GETTIN' A CRUSH ON SOME FELLA THAT DON'T EXIST!
BUT I CAN'T HELP IT!
I'VE BEEN SEEING HIM DAY AND NIGHT, AND I CAN'T STOP THINKING ABOUT HIM.
CHIAKI, YER ALMOST A LADY NOW.
DAD'LL FIND YE A PROPER FELLA— NOT SOME PHANTOM, HEAR?
THAT DOC WHO FIXED YER EYES, HE'S YOUNG BUT DECENT.
PERFECT FOR MY DAUGHTER IF YE ASK ME.
...
WHATCHA DRAWING, MISSY?

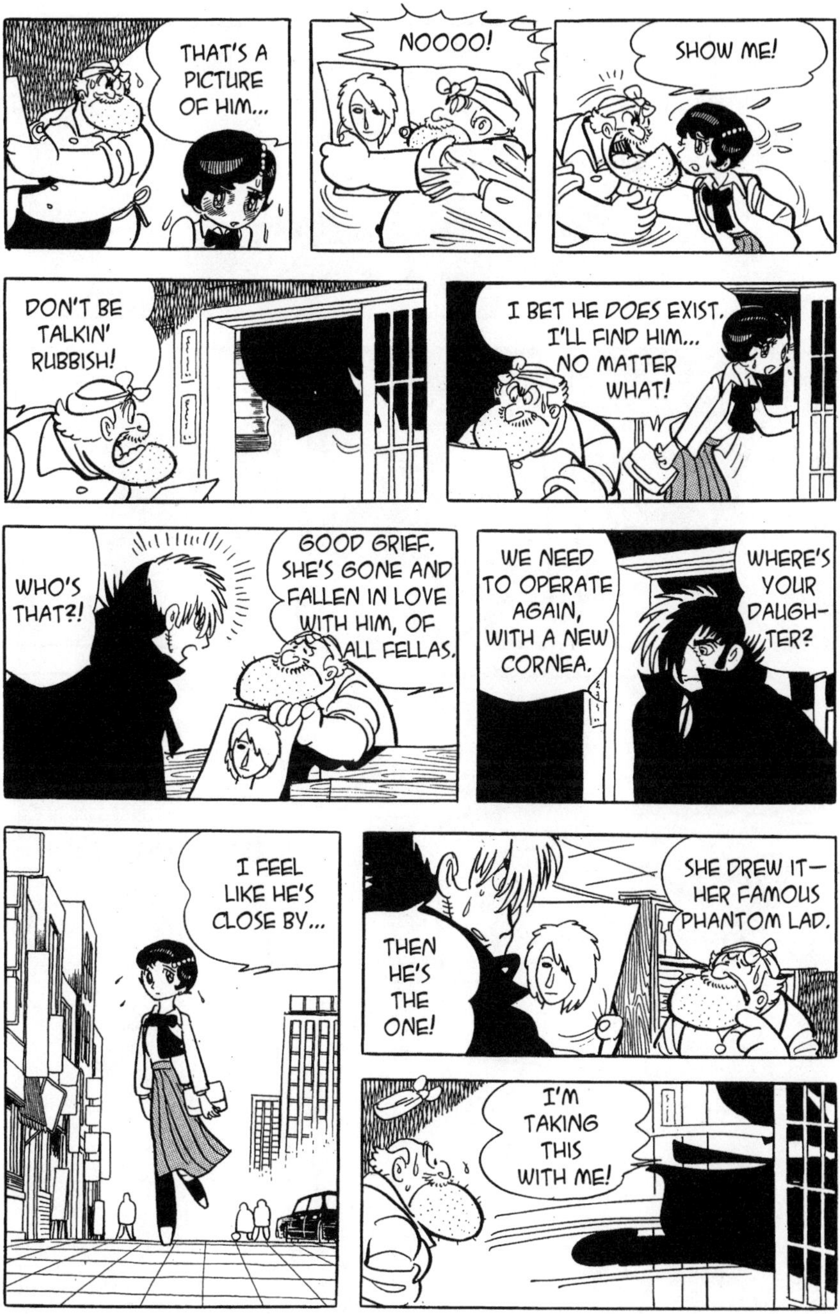
THAT'S A PICTURE OF HIM...
NOOOO!
SHOW ME!
DON'T BE TALKIN' RUBBISH!
I BET HE *DOES* EXIST. I'LL FIND HIM... NO MATTER WHAT!
GOOD GRIEF. SHE'S GONE AND FALLEN IN LOVE WITH HIM, OF ALL FELLAS.
WHO'S THAT?!
WE NEED TO OPERATE AGAIN, WITH A NEW CORNEA.
WHERE'S YOUR DAUGHTER?
I FEEL LIKE HE'S CLOSE BY...
SHE DREW IT— HER FAMOUS PHANTOM LAD.
THEN HE'S THE ONE!
I'M TAKING THIS WITH ME!

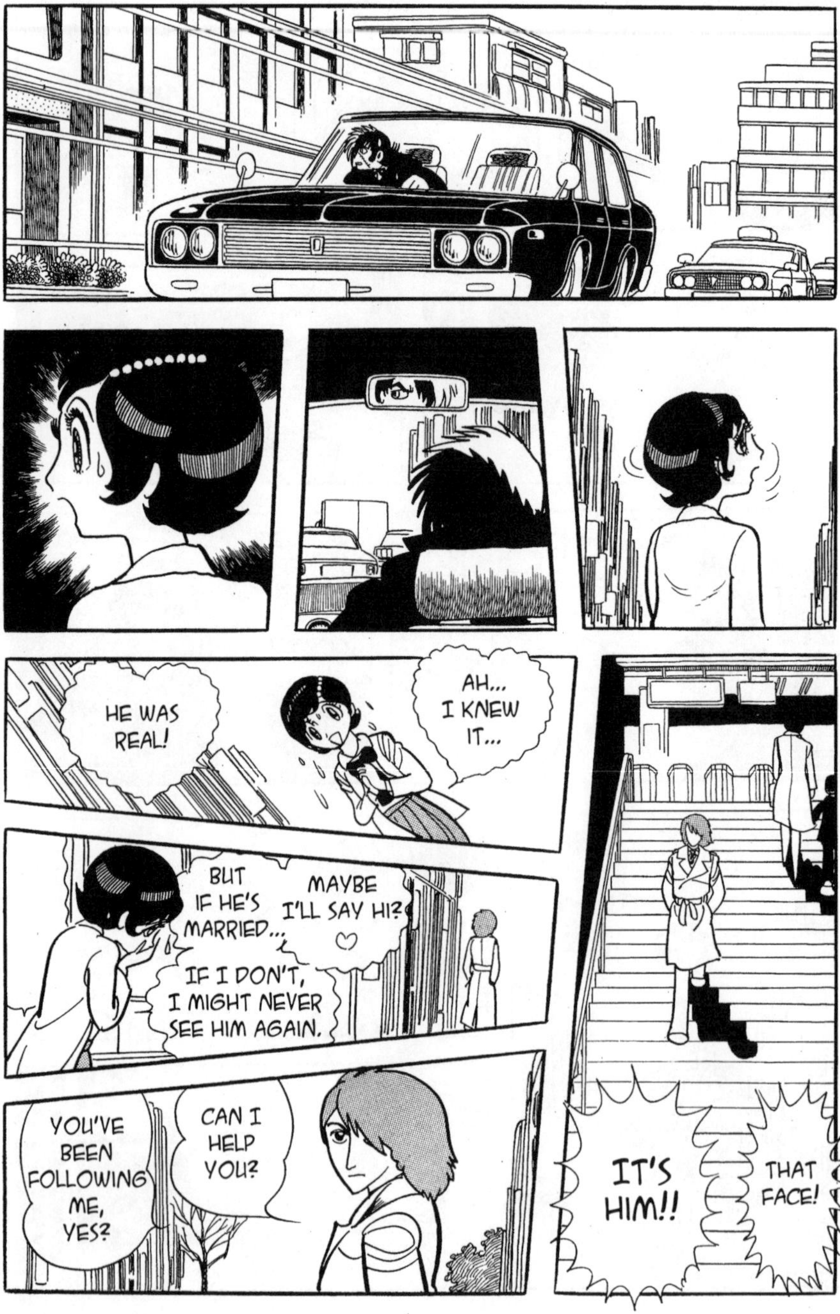
THAT FACE!
IT'S HIM!!
AH... I KNEW IT...
HE WAS REAL!
MAYBE I'LL SAY HI?
BUT IF HE'S MARRIED...
IF I DON'T, I MIGHT NEVER SEE HIM AGAIN.
CAN I HELP YOU?
YOU'VE BEEN FOLLOWING ME, YES?

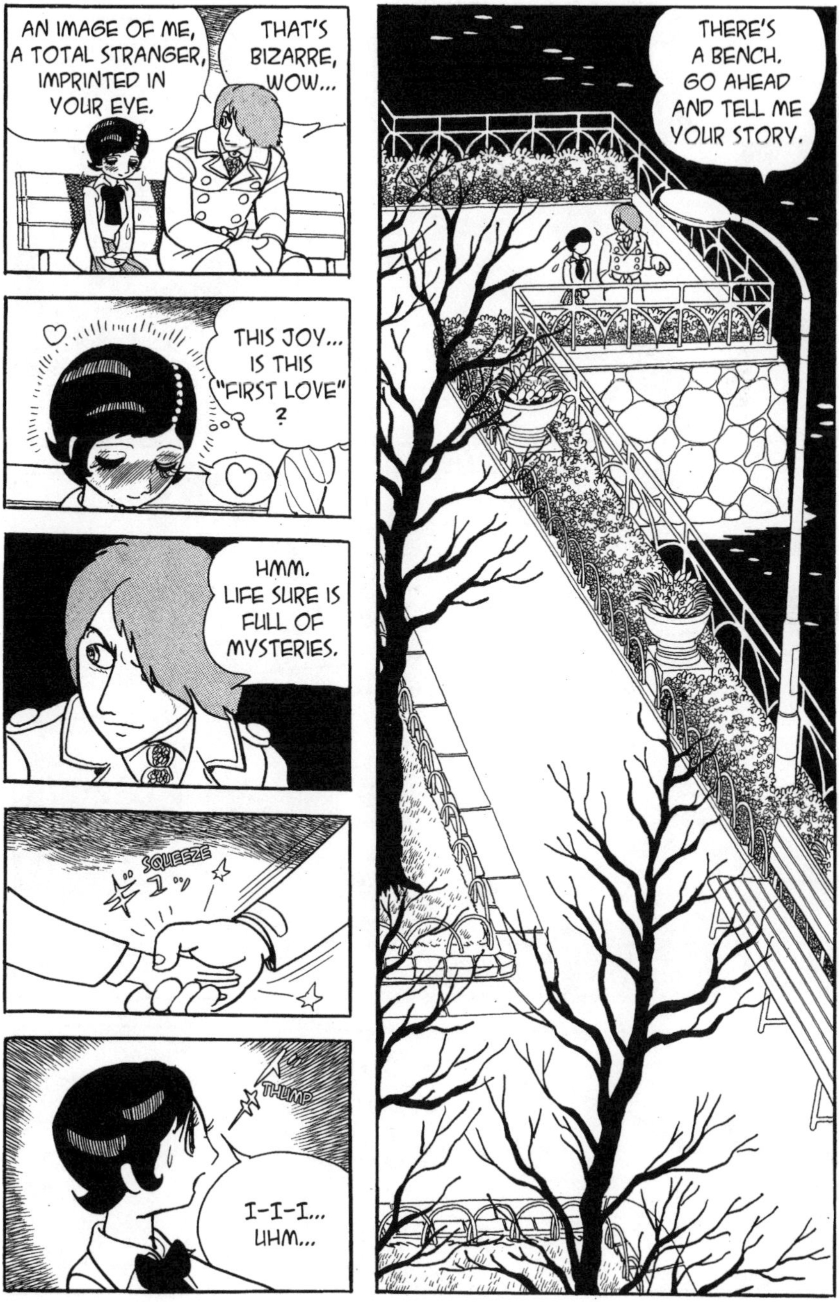
THERE'S A BENCH. GO AHEAD AND TELL ME YOUR STORY.
THAT'S BIZARRE, WOW...
AN IMAGE OF ME, A TOTAL STRANGER, IMPRINTED IN YOUR EYE.
THIS JOY... IS THIS "FIRST LOVE"?
HMM. LIFE SURE IS FULL OF MYSTERIES.
SQUEEZE
THUMP
I-I-I... UHM...

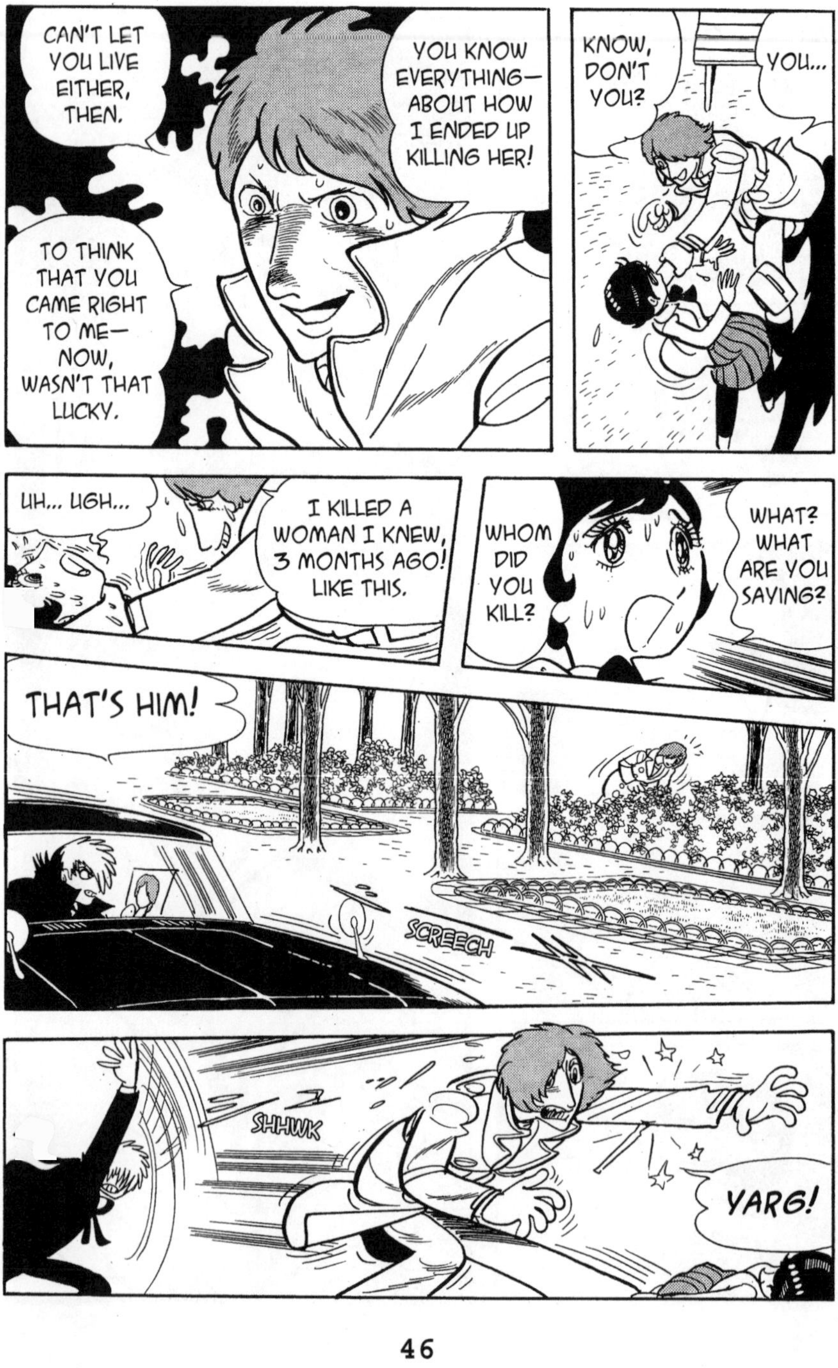
YOU...
KNOW, DON'T YOU?
YOU KNOW EVERYTHING— ABOUT HOW I ENDED UP KILLING HER!
CAN'T LET YOU LIVE EITHER, THEN.
TO THINK THAT YOU CAME RIGHT TO ME— NOW, WASN'T THAT LUCKY.
WHAT? WHAT ARE YOU SAYING?
WHOM DID YOU KILL?
I KILLED A WOMAN I KNEW, 3 MONTHS AGO! LIKE THIS.
UH... UGH...
THAT'S HIM!
SCREECH
YARG!
SHHWK

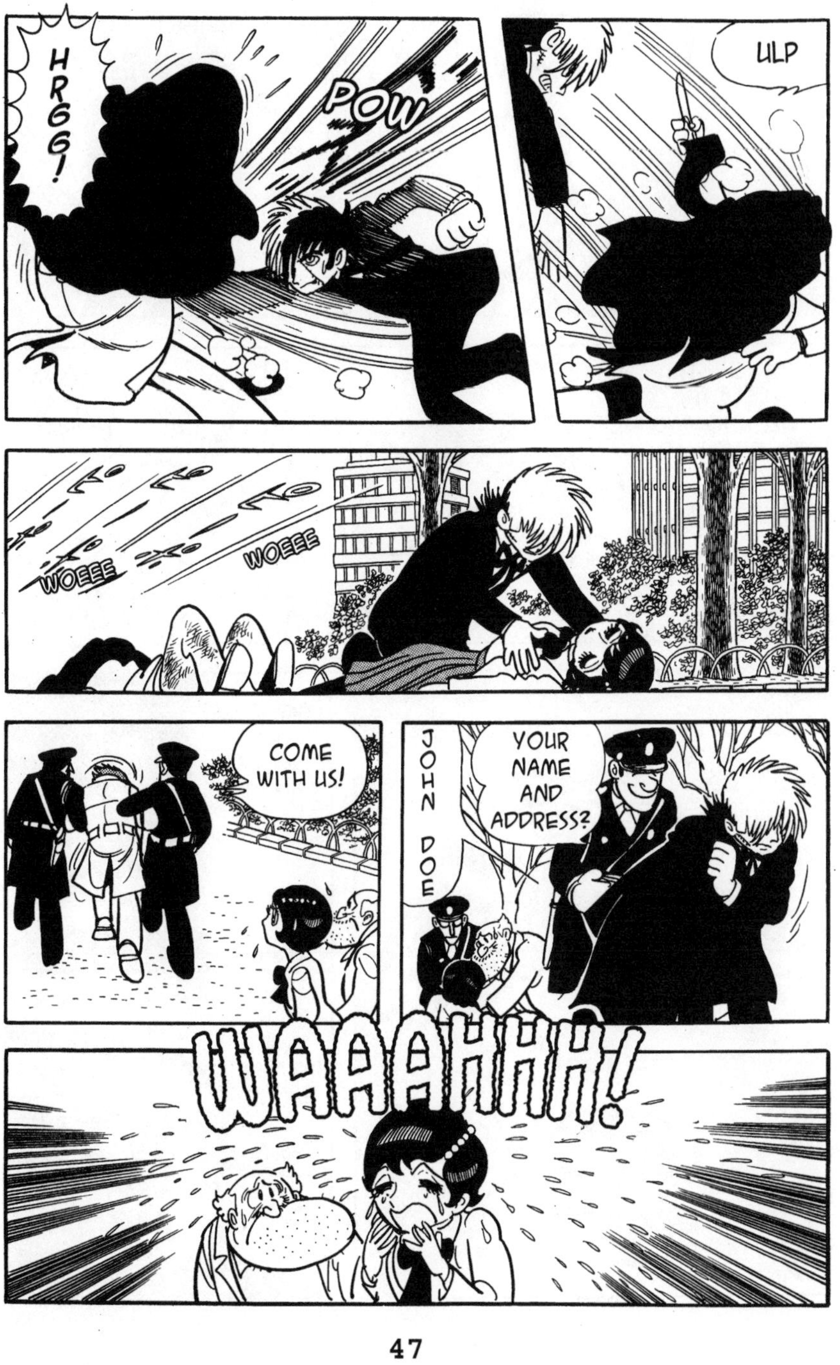
ULP
HRGG!
POW
WOEEE
WOEEE
YOUR NAME AND ADDRESS?
JOHN DOE
COME WITH US!
WAAAHHH!

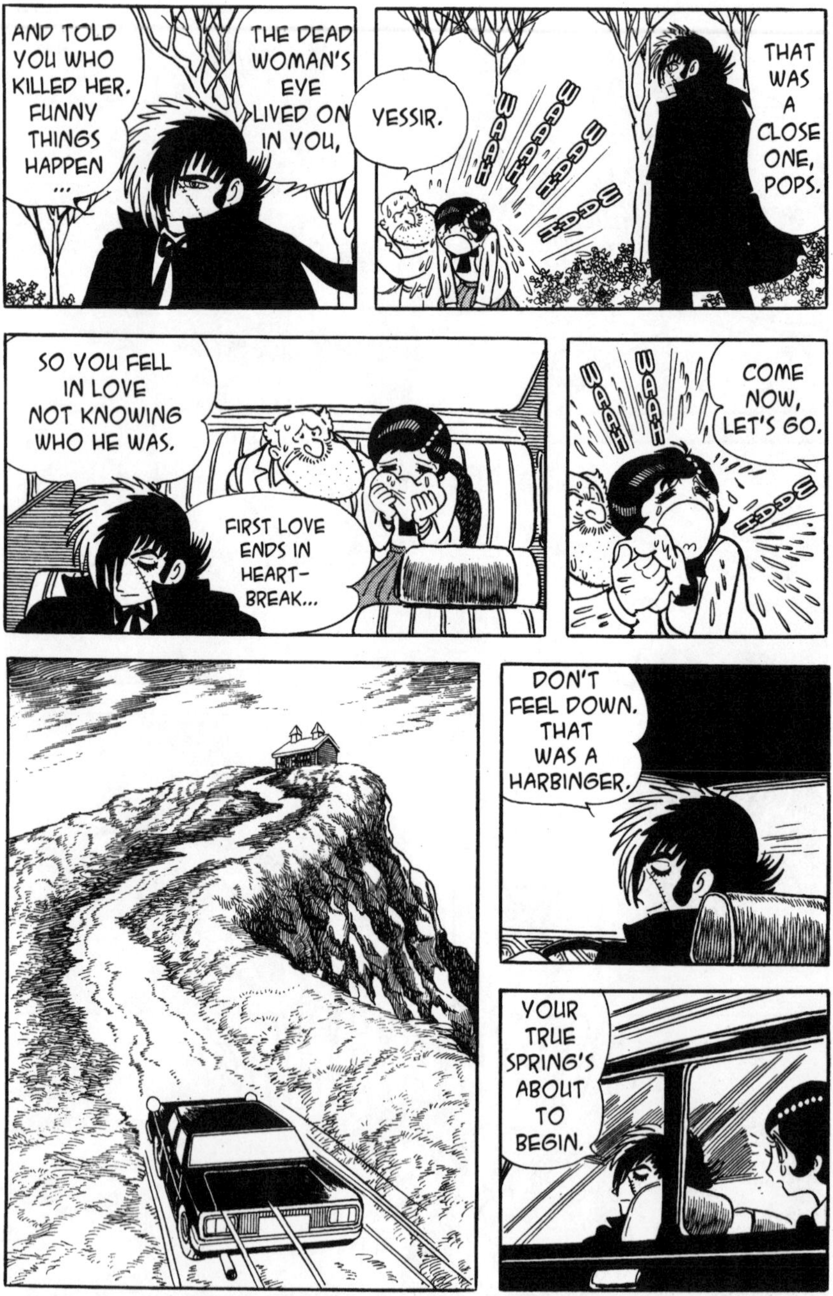
THAT WAS A CLOSE ONE, POPS.
YESSIR.
THE DEAD WOMAN'S EYE LIVED ON IN YOU,
AND TOLD YOU WHO KILLED HER. FUNNY THINGS HAPPEN ...
COME NOW, LET'S GO.
SO YOU FELL IN LOVE NOT KNOWING WHO HE WAS.
FIRST LOVE ENDS IN HEART-BREAK...
DON'T FEEL DOWN. THAT WAS A HARBINGER.
YOUR TRUE SPRING'S ABOUT TO BEGIN.

TERATOID CYSTOMA

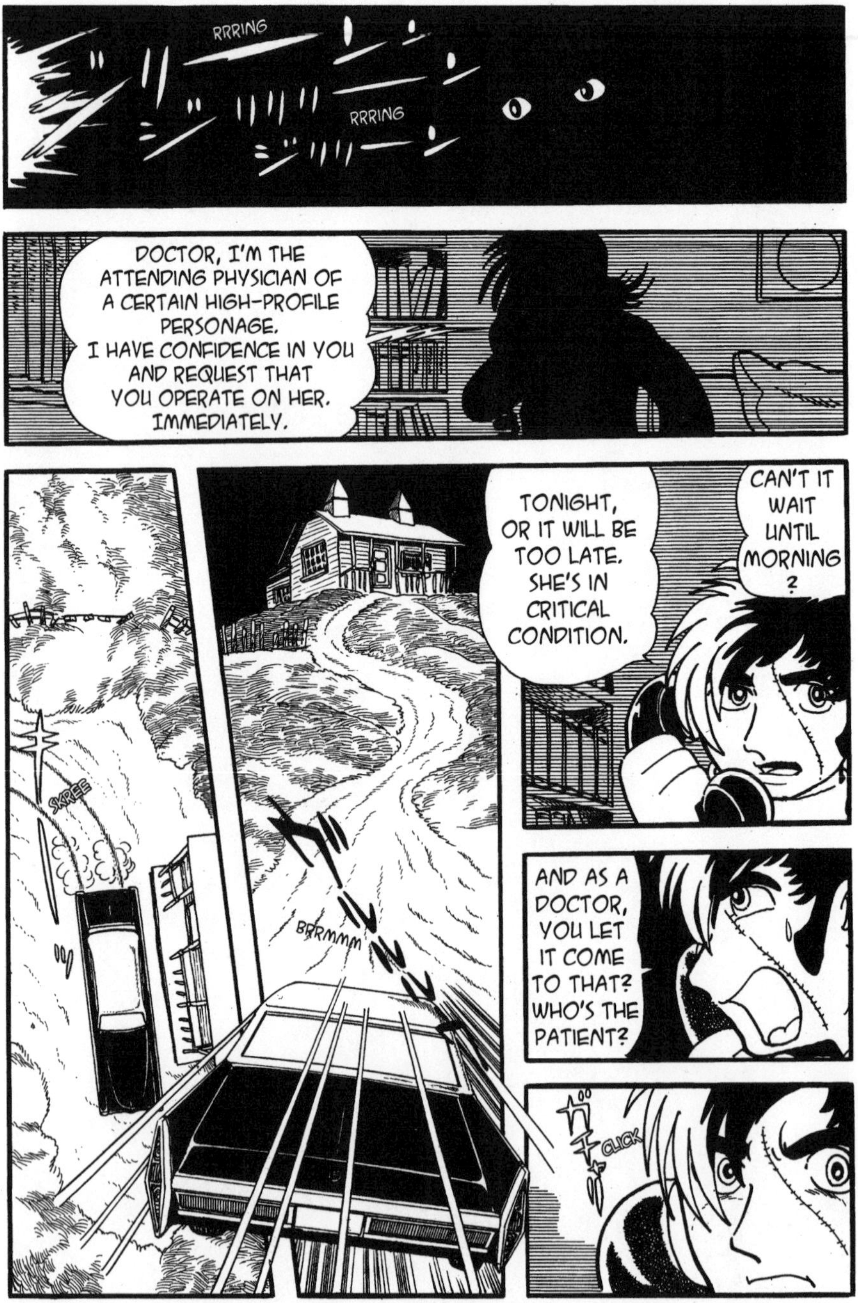
RRRING
RRRING
DOCTOR, I'M THE ATTENDING PHYSICIAN OF A CERTAIN HIGH-PROFILE PERSONAGE. I HAVE CONFIDENCE IN YOU AND REQUEST THAT YOU OPERATE ON HER. IMMEDIATELY.
CAN'T IT WAIT UNTIL MORNING?
TONIGHT, OR IT WILL BE TOO LATE. SHE'S IN CRITICAL CONDITION.
AND AS A DOCTOR, YOU LET IT COME TO THAT? WHO'S THE PATIENT?
CLICK
BRRMMM
SKREE

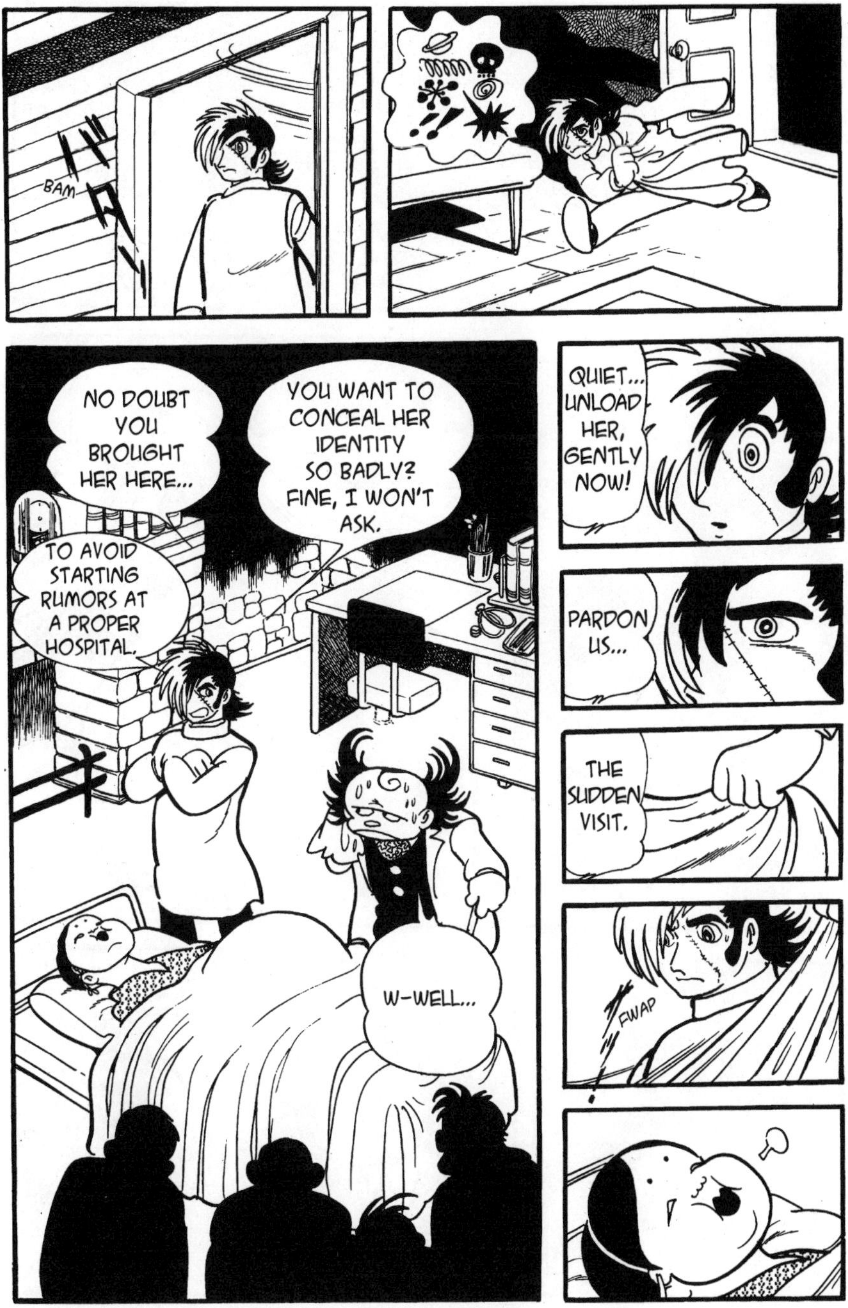
BAM
QUIET... UNLOAD HER, GENTLY NOW!
PARDON US...
THE SUDDEN VISIT.
FWAP
YOU WANT TO CONCEAL HER IDENTITY SO BADLY? FINE, I WON'T ASK.
NO DOUBT YOU BROUGHT HER HERE...
TO AVOID STARTING RUMORS AT A PROPER HOSPITAL.
W-WELL...

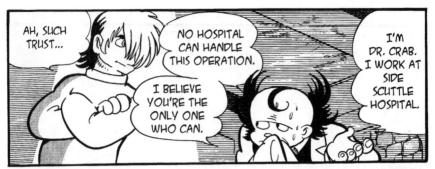

I'M DR. CRAB. I WORK AT SIDE SCUTTLE HOSPITAL.
NO HOSPITAL CAN HANDLE THIS OPERATION.
I BELIEVE YOU'RE THE ONLY ONE WHO CAN.
AH, SUCH TRUST...
A TUMOR ?
PHEW, IT'S HUGE.
IT'S A CYSTOMA.
AND YOU WANT ME TO REMOVE IT.
IT'S A TERATOID CYSTOMA.
AH HAH.
I SEE ...

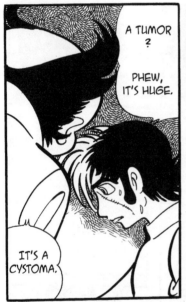

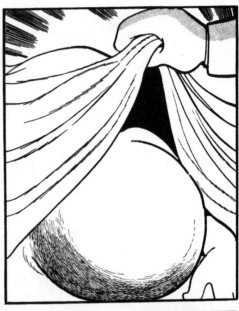

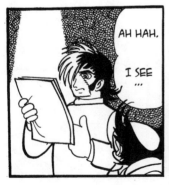

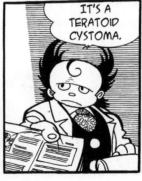

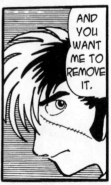

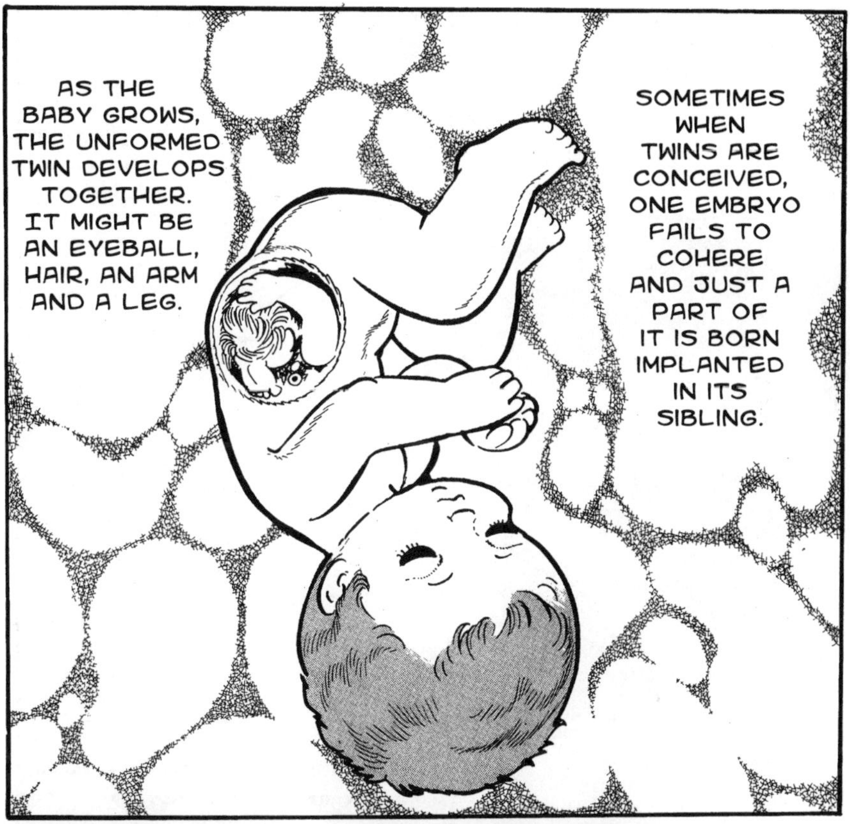
SOMETIMES WHEN TWINS ARE CONCEIVED, ONE EMBRYO FAILS TO COHERE AND JUST A PART OF IT IS BORN IMPLANTED IN ITS SIBLING.
AS THE BABY GROWS, THE UNFORMED TWIN DEVELOPS TOGETHER. IT MIGHT BE AN EYEBALL, HAIR, AN ARM AND A LEG.

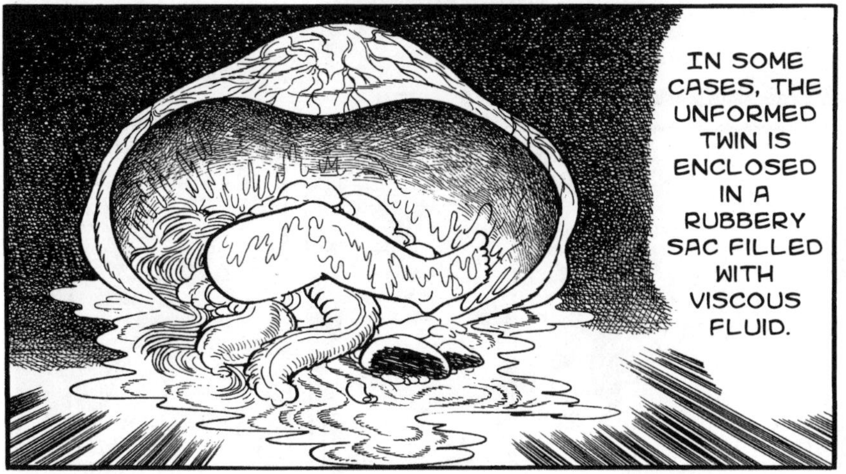
IN SOME CASES, THE UNFORMED TWIN IS ENCLOSED IN A RUBBERY SAC FILLED WITH VISCOUS FLUID.

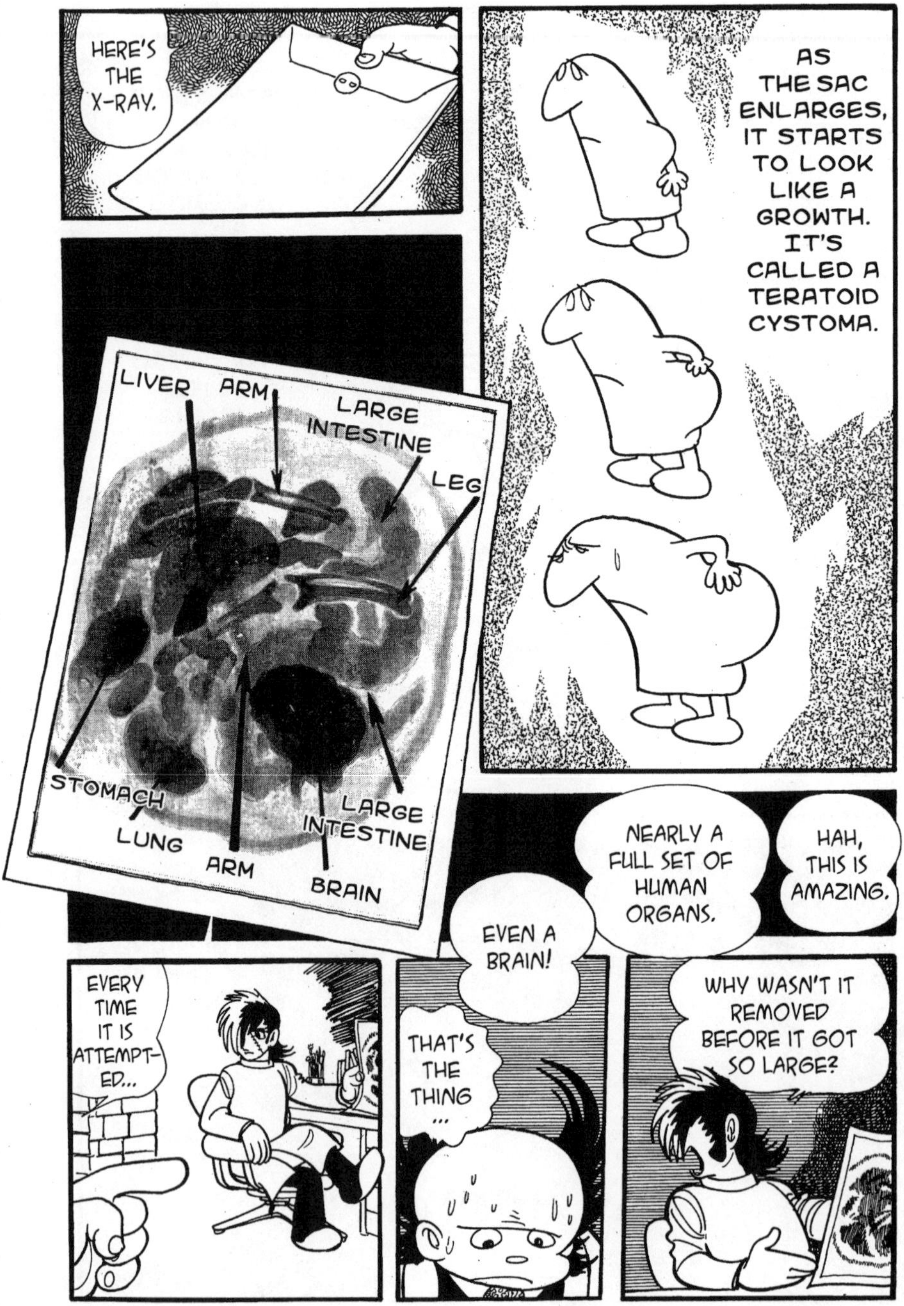
AS THE SAC ENLARGES, IT STARTS TO LOOK LIKE A GROWTH. IT'S CALLED A TERATOID CYSTOMA.
HERE'S THE X-RAY.
LIVER
ARM
LARGE INTESTINE
LEG
STOMACH
LUNG
ARM
BRAIN
LARGE INTESTINE
HAH, THIS IS AMAZING.
NEARLY A FULL SET OF HUMAN ORGANS.
EVEN A BRAIN!
WHY WASN'T IT REMOVED BEFORE IT GOT SO LARGE?
THAT'S THE THING ...
EVERY TIME IT IS ATTEMPT-ED...

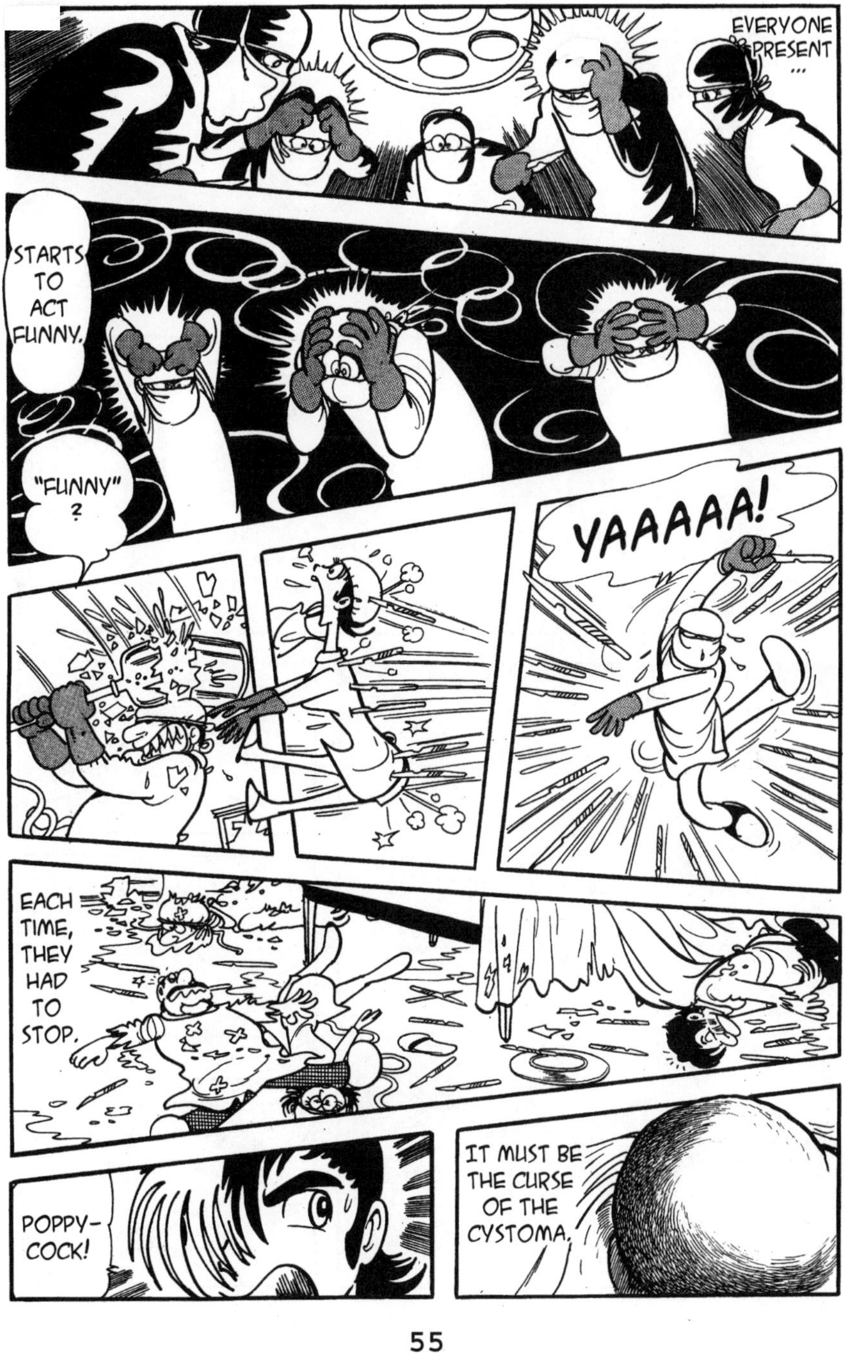
EVERYONE PRESENT ...
STARTS TO ACT FUNNY.
"FUNNY" ?
YAAAAA!
EACH TIME, THEY HAD TO STOP.
IT MUST BE THE CURSE OF THE CYSTOMA.
POPPY-COCK!

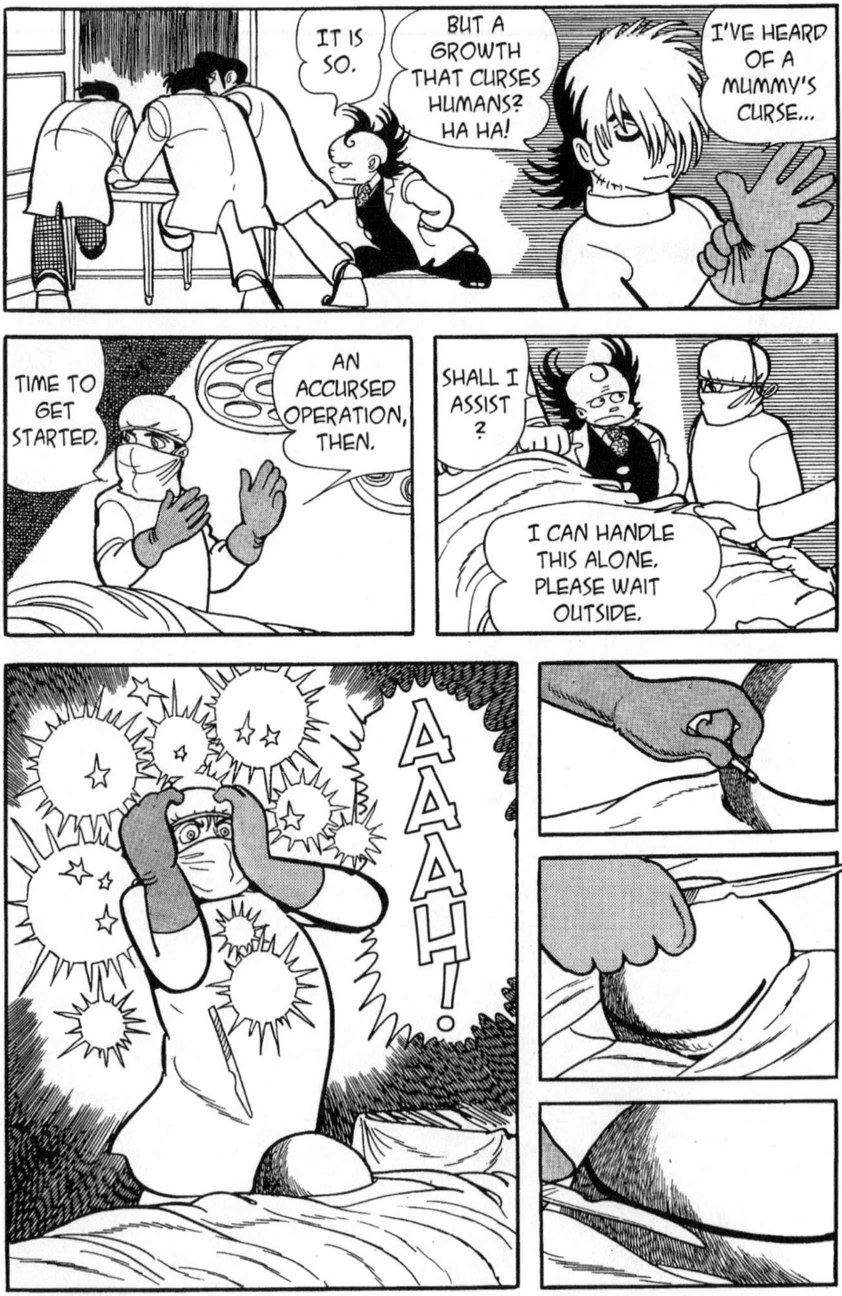
I'VE HEARD OF A MUMMY'S CURSE...
BUT A GROWTH THAT CURSES HUMANS? HA HA!
IT IS SO.
SHALL I ASSIST?
I CAN HANDLE THIS ALONE. PLEASE WAIT OUTSIDE.
AN ACCURSED OPERATION, THEN.
TIME TO GET STARTED.
AAAAH!

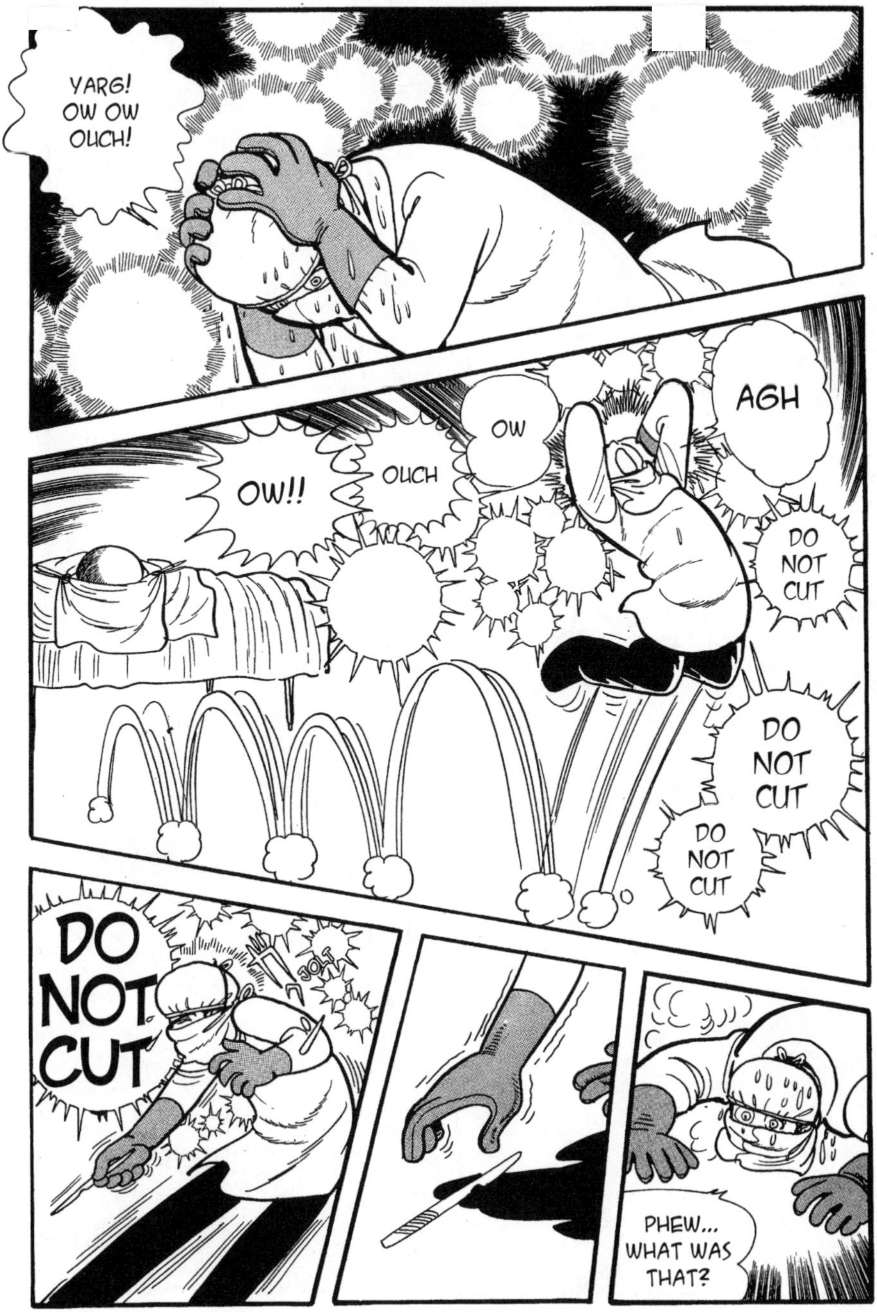
YARG! OW OW OUCH!
AGH
DO NOT CUT
DO NOT CUT
DO NOT CUT
OW
OUCH
OW!!
PHEW... WHAT WAS THAT?
DO NOT CUT
JOLT

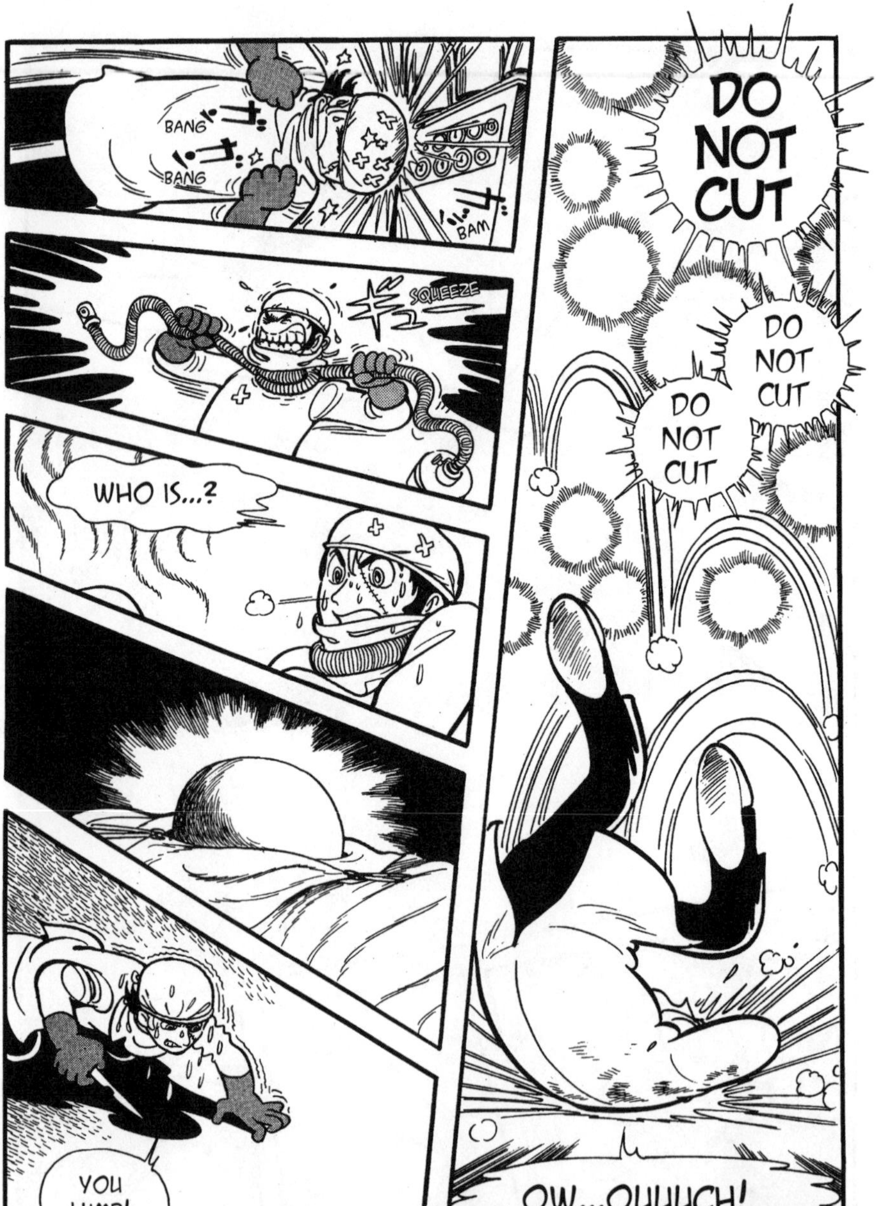
DO NOT CUT
DO NOT CUT
DO NOT CUT
OW...OUUUCH!
BANG
BANG
BAM
SQUEEZE
WHO IS...?
YOU LUMP! IS IT YOU?

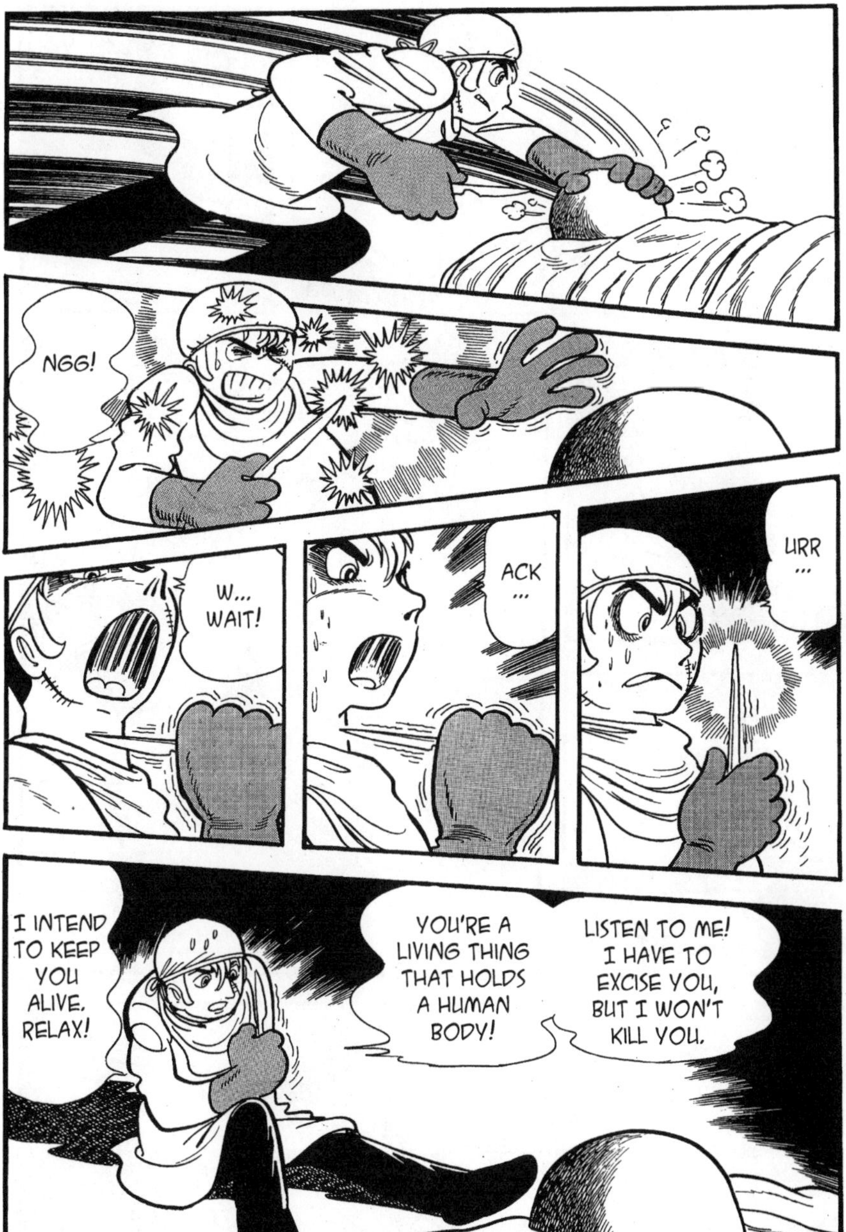
NGG!
URR ...
ACK ...
W... WAIT!
LISTEN TO ME! I HAVE TO EXCISE YOU, BUT I WON'T KILL YOU.
YOU'RE A LIVING THING THAT HOLDS A HUMAN BODY!
I INTEND TO KEEP YOU ALIVE. RELAX!

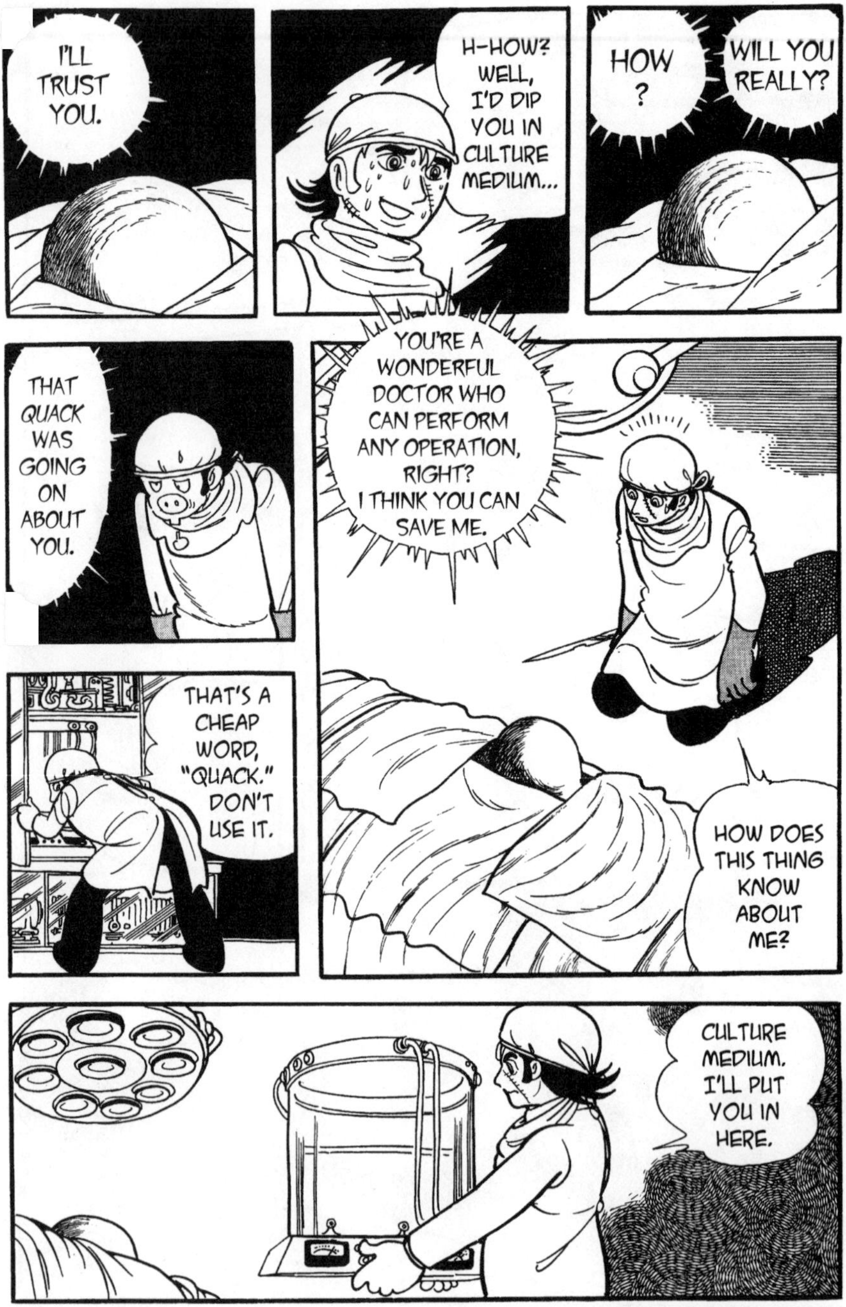
WILL YOU REALLY?
HOW ?
H-HOW? WELL, I'D DIP YOU IN CULTURE MEDIUM...
I'LL TRUST YOU.
YOU'RE A WONDERFUL DOCTOR WHO CAN PERFORM ANY OPERATION, RIGHT? I THINK YOU CAN SAVE ME.
HOW DOES THIS THING KNOW ABOUT ME?
THAT QUACK WAS GOING ON ABOUT YOU.
THAT'S A CHEAP WORD, "QUACK." DON'T USE IT.
CULTURE MEDIUM. I'LL PUT YOU IN HERE.

THIS WILL KEEP YOU ALIVE FOR THE TIME BEING.
ARE YOU READY ?
DON'T INTERFERE THIS TIME.
JOLT
I TOLD YOU TO STOP IT.
I'M GIVING YOU AN ANESTHETIC.
...
NAP FOR A WHILE.

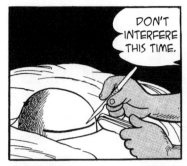

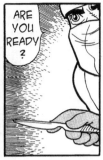

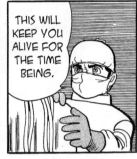

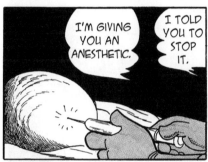

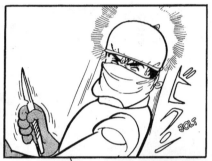

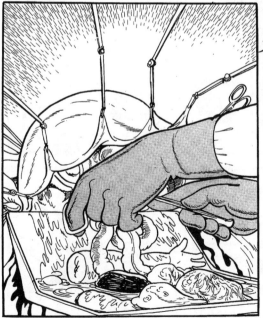

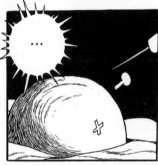

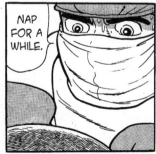

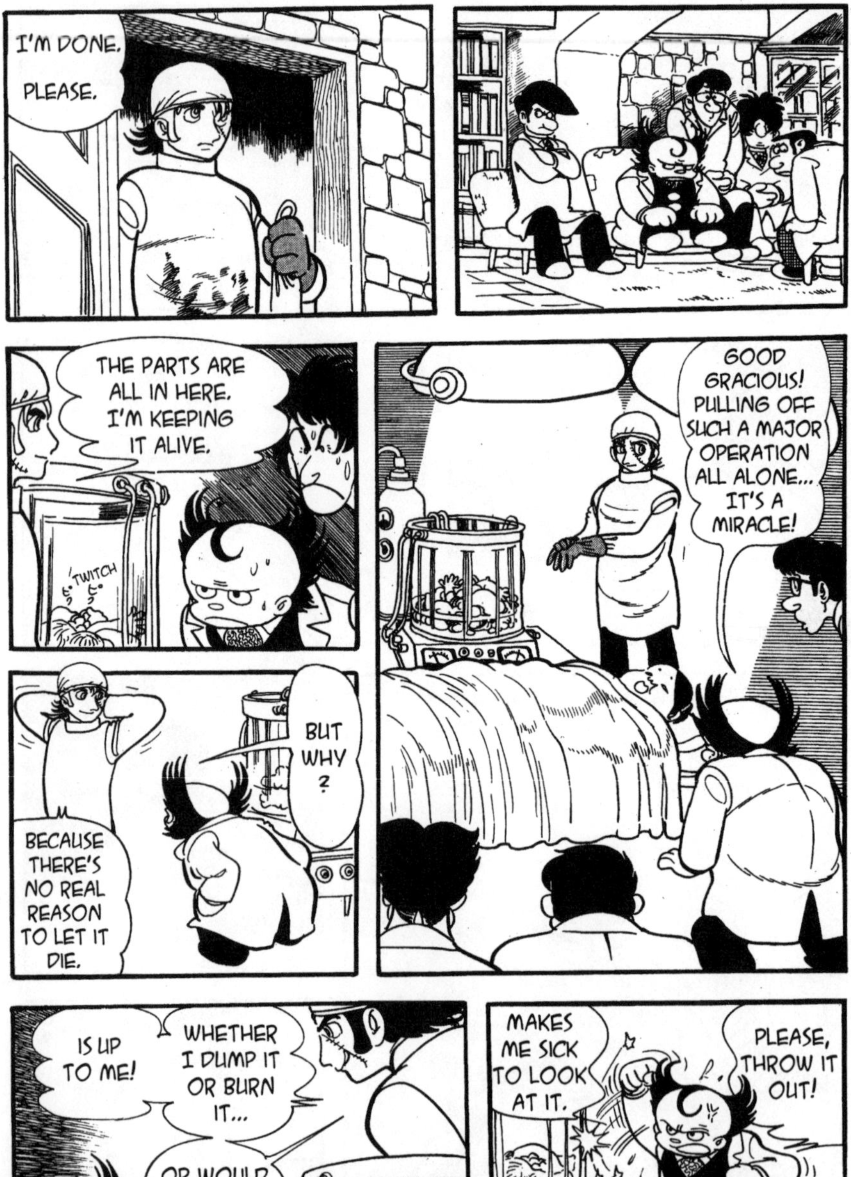
I'M DONE.
PLEASE.
THE PARTS ARE ALL IN HERE. I'M KEEPING IT ALIVE.
TWITCH
BUT WHY?
BECAUSE THERE'S NO REAL REASON TO LET IT DIE.
GOOD GRACIOUS! PULLING OFF SUCH A MAJOR OPERATION ALL ALONE... IT'S A MIRACLE!
WHETHER I DUMP IT OR BURN IT...
IS UP TO ME!
OR WOULD YOU BUY IT FOR A MILLION YEN?
PLEASE, THROW IT OUT!
MAKES ME SICK TO LOOK AT IT.
IT WILL PUT A CURSE ON YOU.

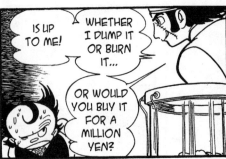

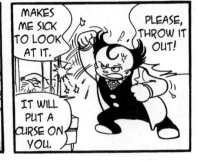

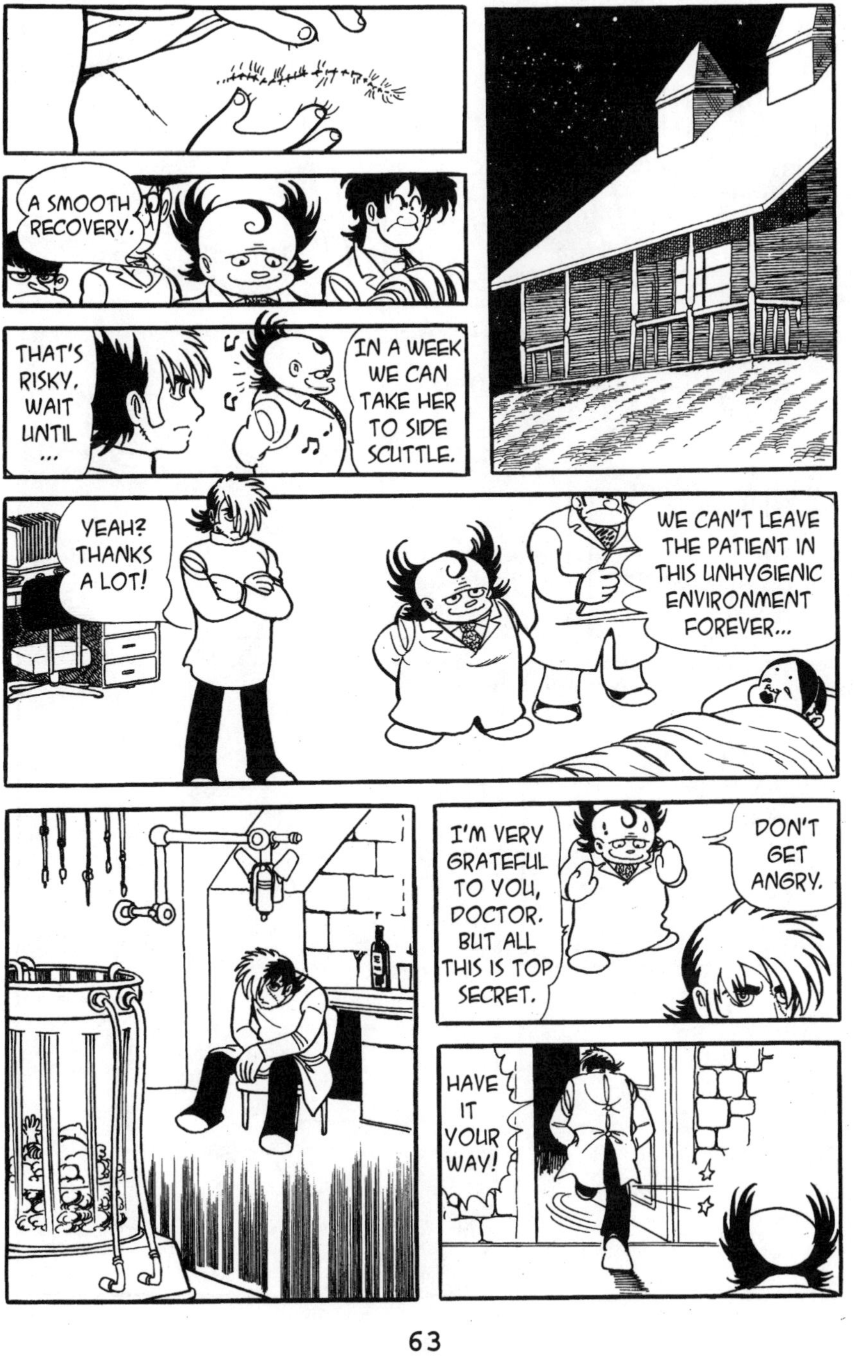
A SMOOTH RECOVERY.
IN A WEEK WE CAN TAKE HER TO SIDE SCUTTLE.
THAT'S RISKY. WAIT UNTIL ...
WE CAN'T LEAVE THE PATIENT IN THIS UNHYGIENIC ENVIRONMENT FOREVER...
YEAH? THANKS A LOT!
DON'T GET ANGRY.
I'M VERY GRATEFUL TO YOU, DOCTOR. BUT ALL THIS IS TOP SECRET.
HAVE IT YOUR WAY!

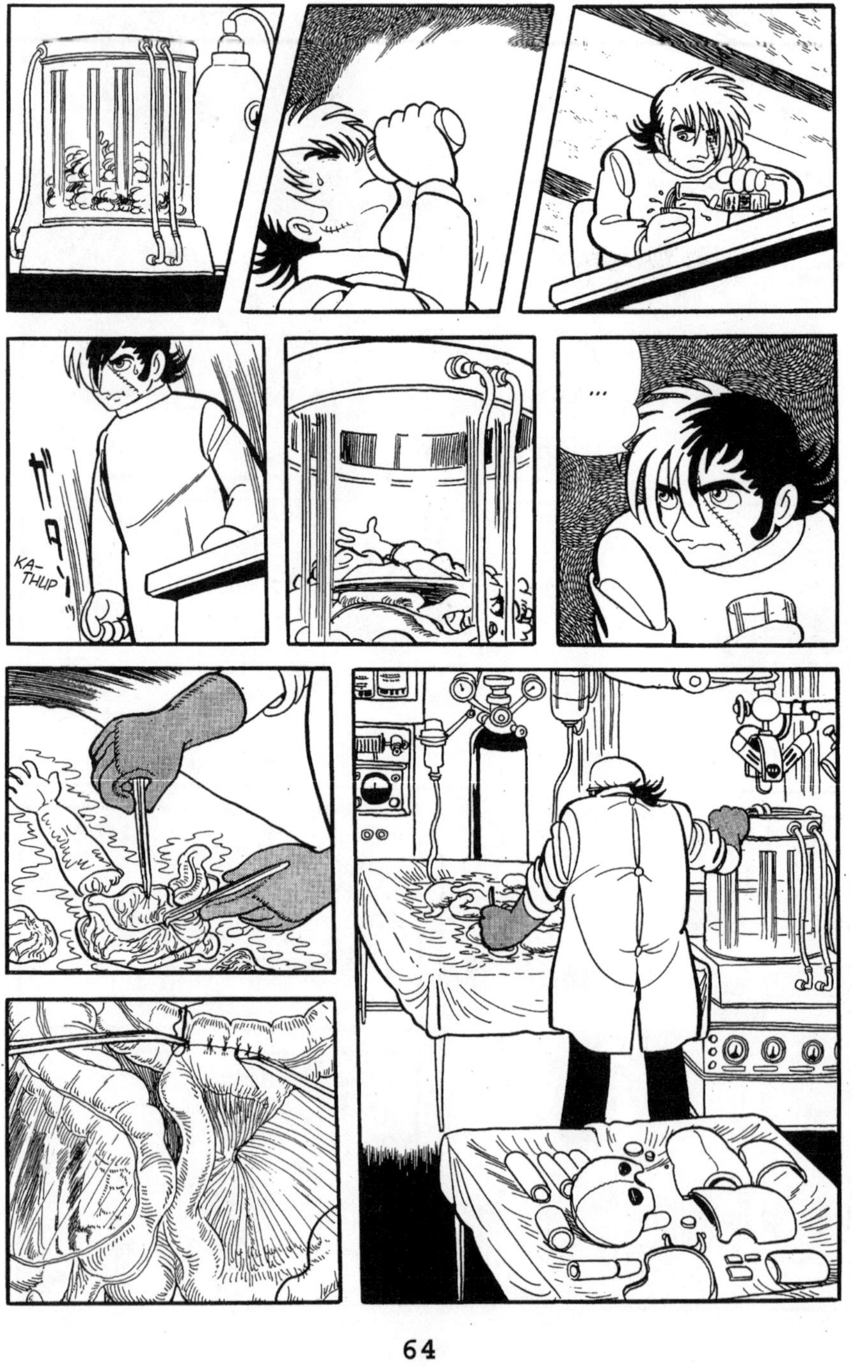
...
KA-THUP

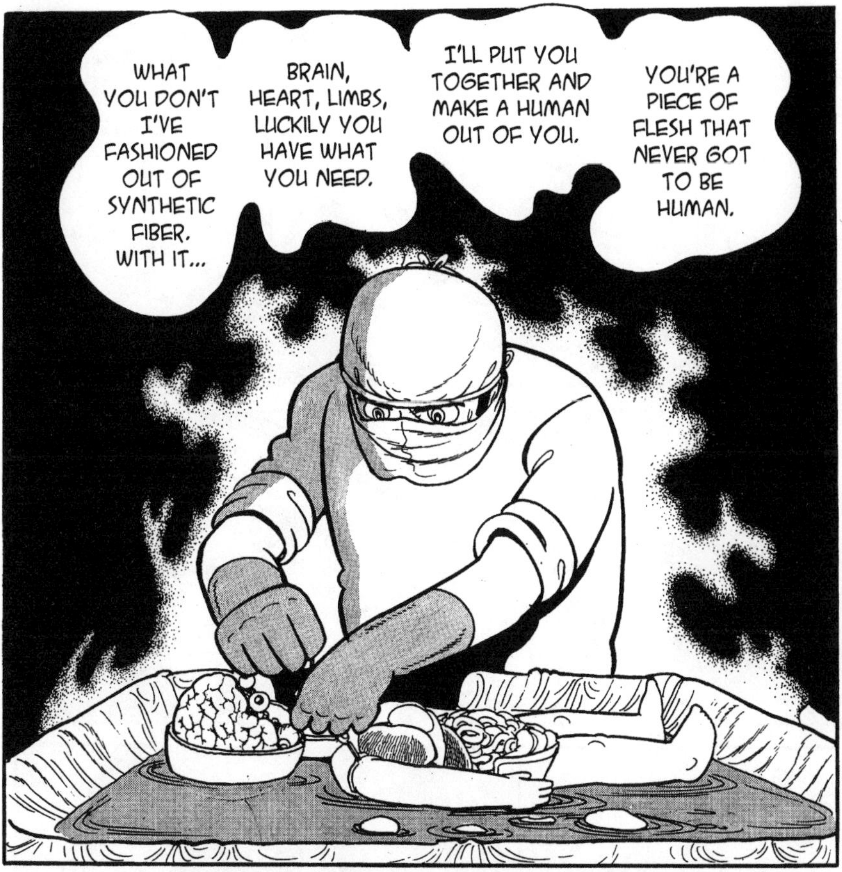
YOU'RE A PIECE OF FLESH THAT NEVER GOT TO BE HUMAN.
I'LL PUT YOU TOGETHER AND MAKE A HUMAN OUT OF YOU.
BRAIN, HEART, LIMBS, LUCKILY YOU HAVE WHAT YOU NEED.
WHAT YOU DON'T I'VE FASHIONED OUT OF SYNTHETIC FIBER. WITH IT...

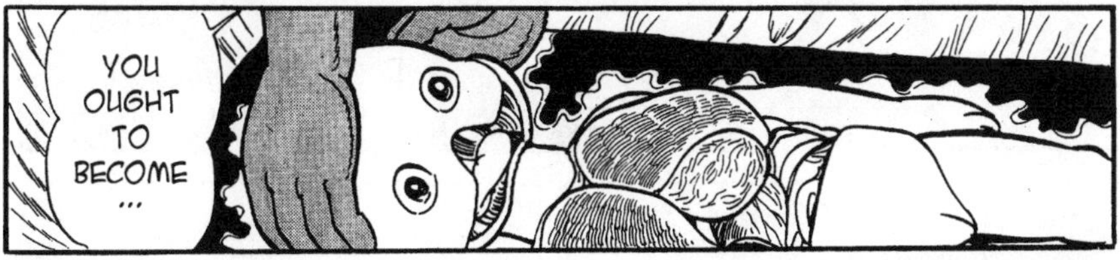
YOU OUGHT TO BECOME ...

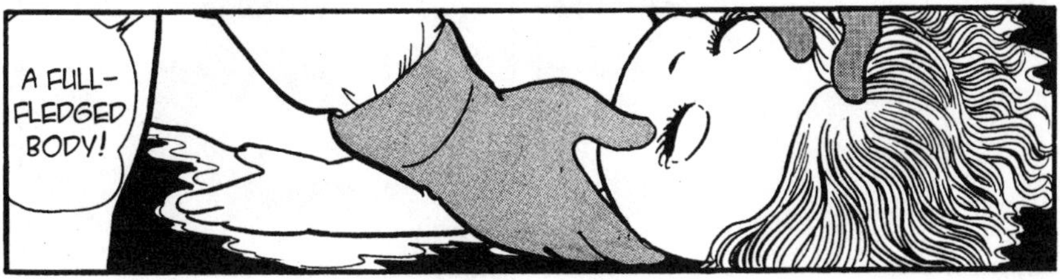
A FULL-FLEDGED BODY!

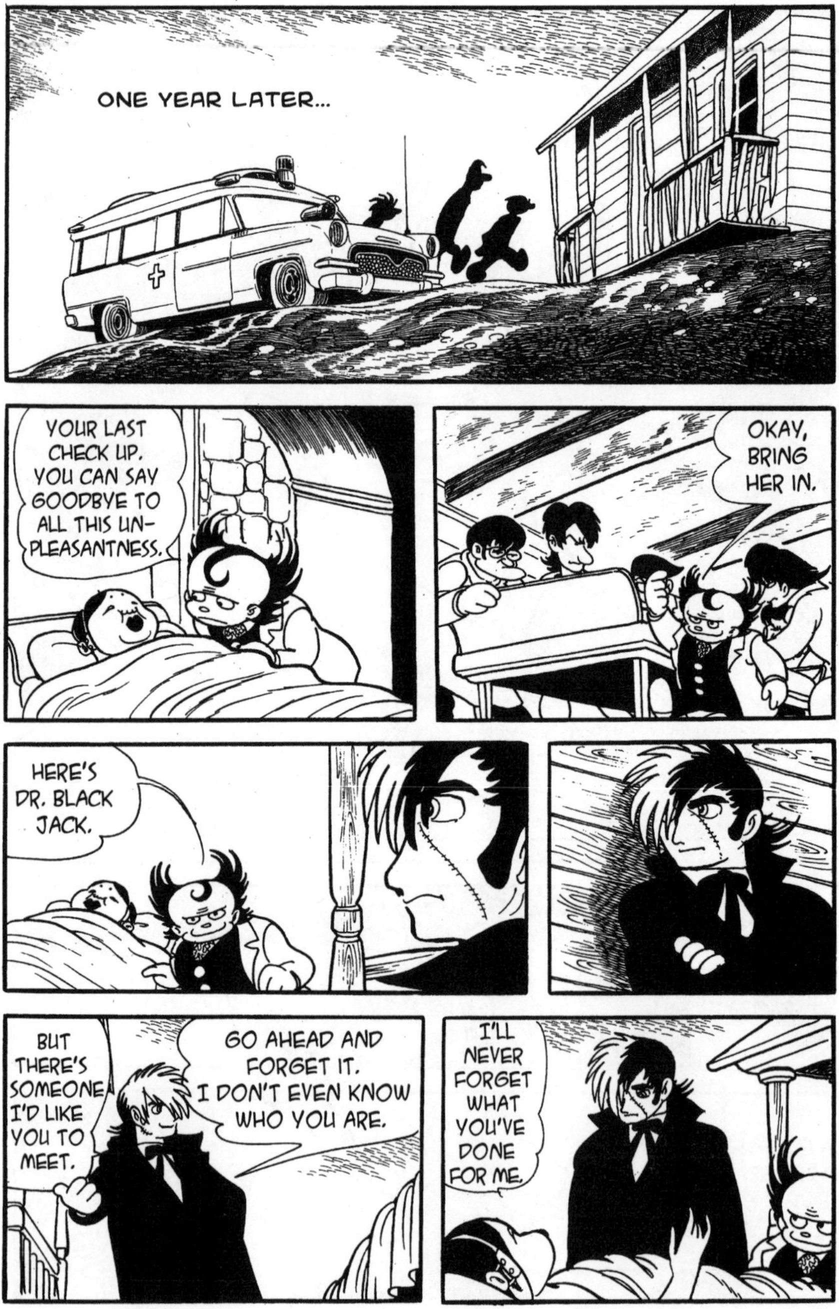
ONE YEAR LATER...
OKAY, BRING HER IN.
YOUR LAST CHECK UP. YOU CAN SAY GOODBYE TO ALL THIS UN-PLEASANTNESS.
HERE'S DR. BLACK JACK.
I'LL NEVER FORGET WHAT YOU'VE DONE FOR ME.
GO AHEAD AND FORGET IT. I DON'T EVEN KNOW WHO YOU ARE.
BUT THERE'S SOMEONE I'D LIKE YOU TO MEET.

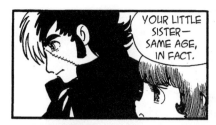

YOUR LITTLE SISTER— SAME AGE, IN FACT.
WHAT... I DON'T HAVE A SISTER.
YOU'VE NEVER MET...
BUT SHE GREW UP WITH YOU, YOUR LITTLE SISTER.
MUR DER ER
CADA VER
IDIOT
GOOD FOR NOTHING
OGRE
BEAST
VAMPIRE
STOP!

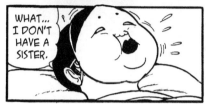

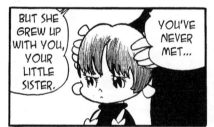

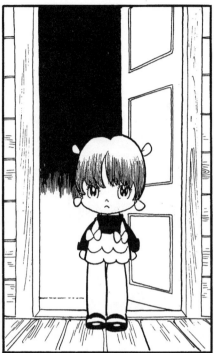

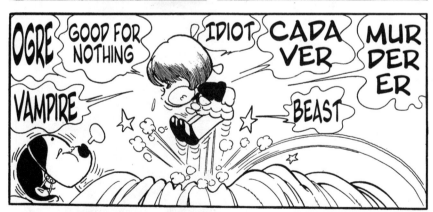

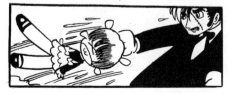

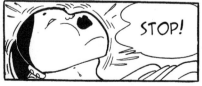

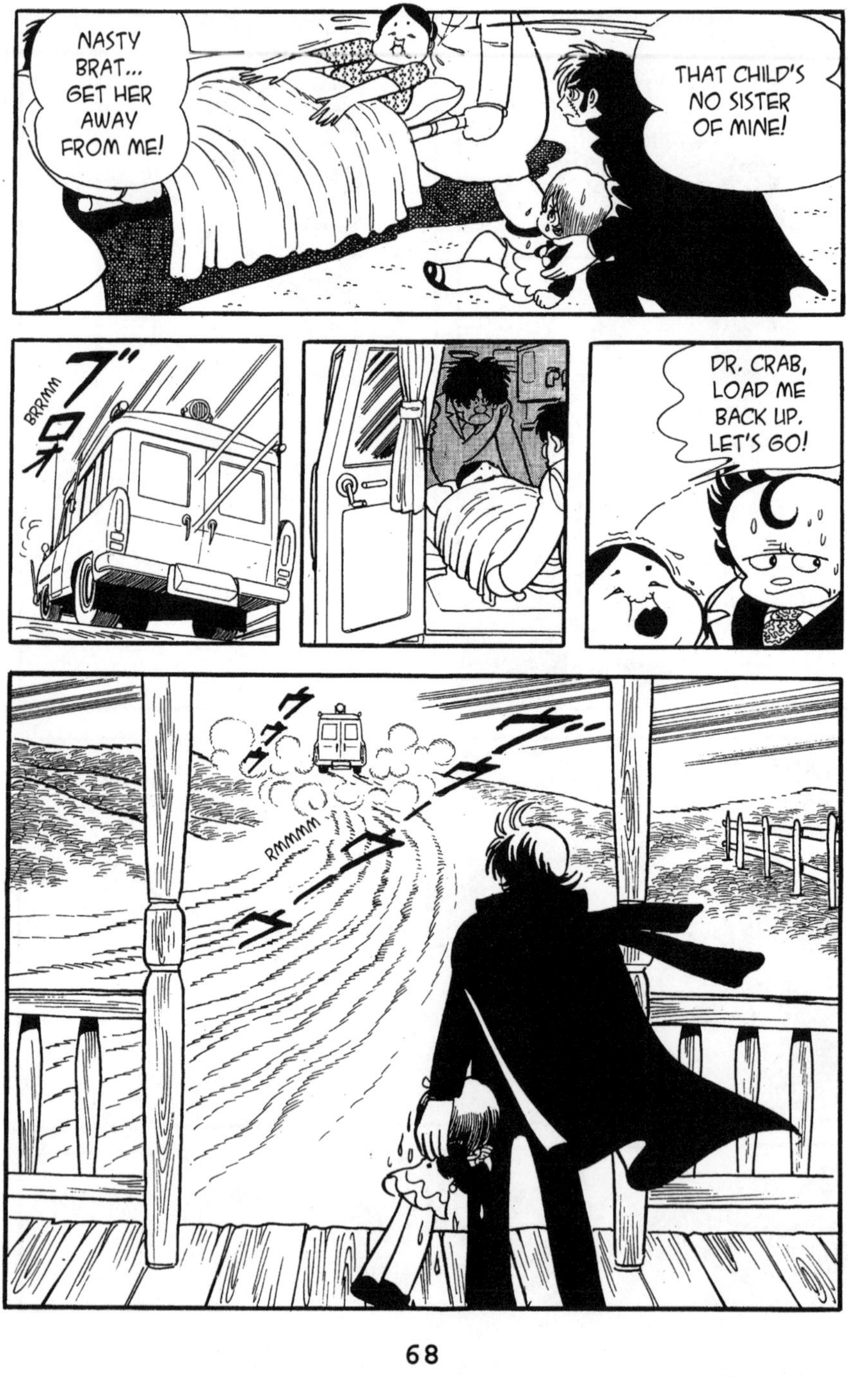
THAT CHILD'S NO SISTER OF MINE!
NASTY BRAT... GET HER AWAY FROM ME!
DR. CRAB, LOAD ME BACK UP. LET'S GO!
BRRMM
RMMMM

THE FACE SORE

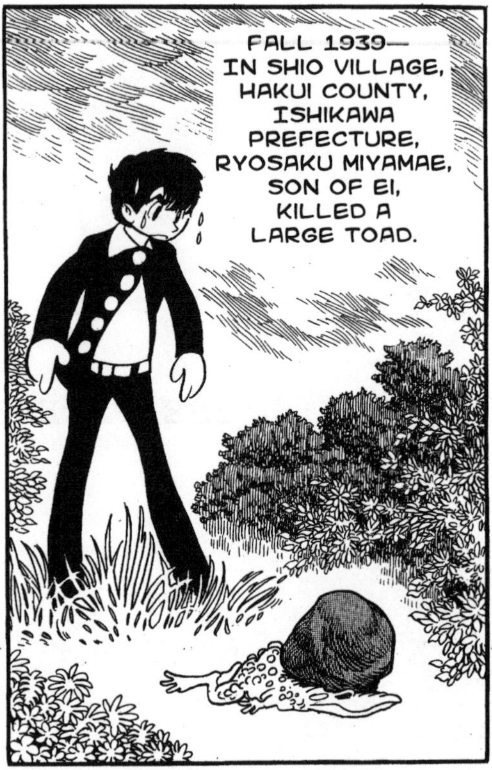
FALL 1939—
IN SHIO VILLAGE, HAKUI COUNTY, ISHIKAWA PREFECTURE, RYOSAKU MIYAMAE, SON OF EI, KILLED A LARGE TOAD.

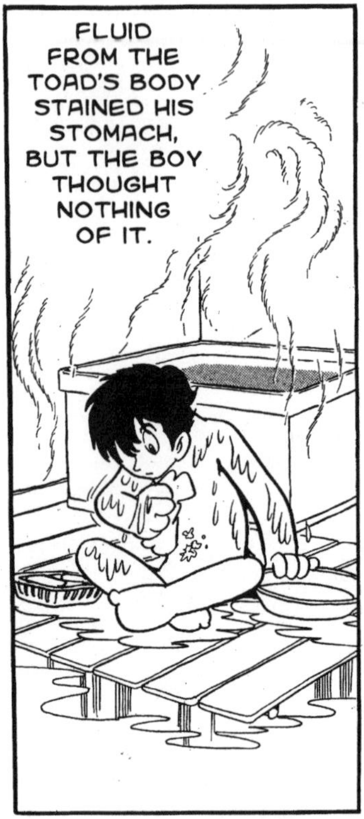
FLUID FROM THE TOAD'S BODY STAINED HIS STOMACH, BUT THE BOY THOUGHT NOTHING OF IT.

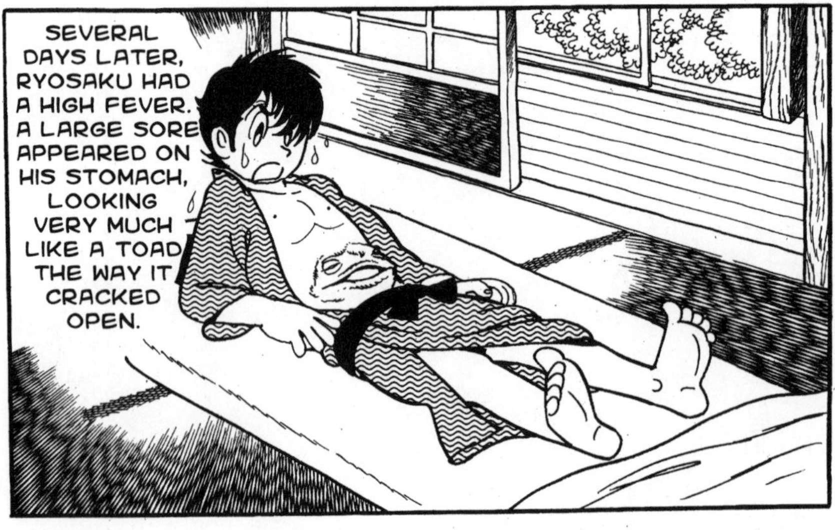
SEVERAL DAYS LATER, RYOSAKU HAD A HIGH FEVER. A LARGE SORE APPEARED ON HIS STOMACH, LOOKING VERY MUCH LIKE A TOAD THE WAY IT CRACKED OPEN.

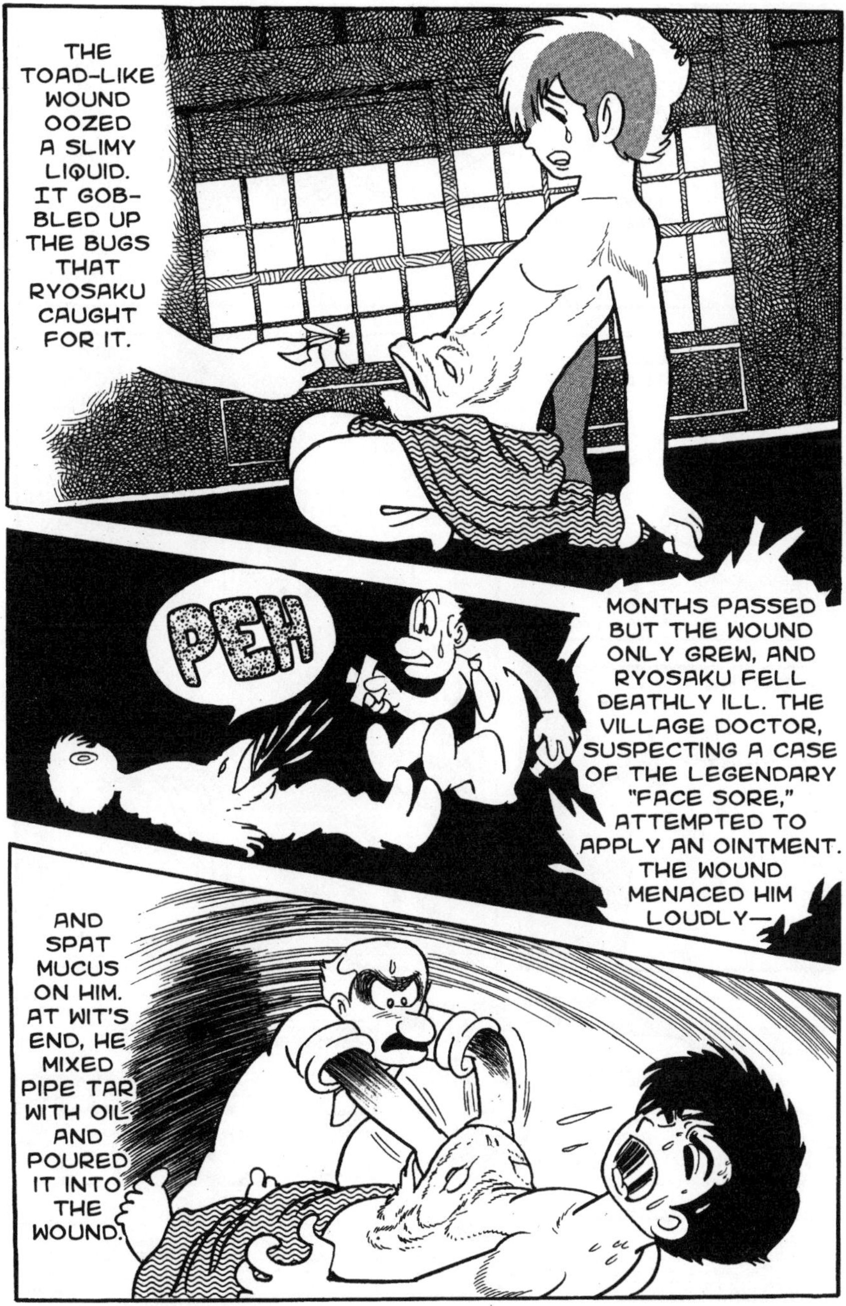
THE TOAD-LIKE WOUND OOZED A SLIMY LIQUID. IT GOBBLED UP THE BUGS THAT RYOSAKU CAUGHT FOR IT.
MONTHS PASSED BUT THE WOUND ONLY GREW, AND RYOSAKU FELL DEATHLY ILL. THE VILLAGE DOCTOR, SUSPECTING A CASE OF THE LEGENDARY "FACE SORE," ATTEMPTED TO APPLY AN OINTMENT. THE WOUND MENACED HIM LOUDLY—
PEH
AND SPAT MUCUS ON HIM. AT WIT'S END, HE MIXED PIPE TAR WITH OIL AND POURED IT INTO THE WOUND.

NOTE: "FACE SORE" = JINMENSO, A MONSTER FROM JAPANESE FOLKLORE

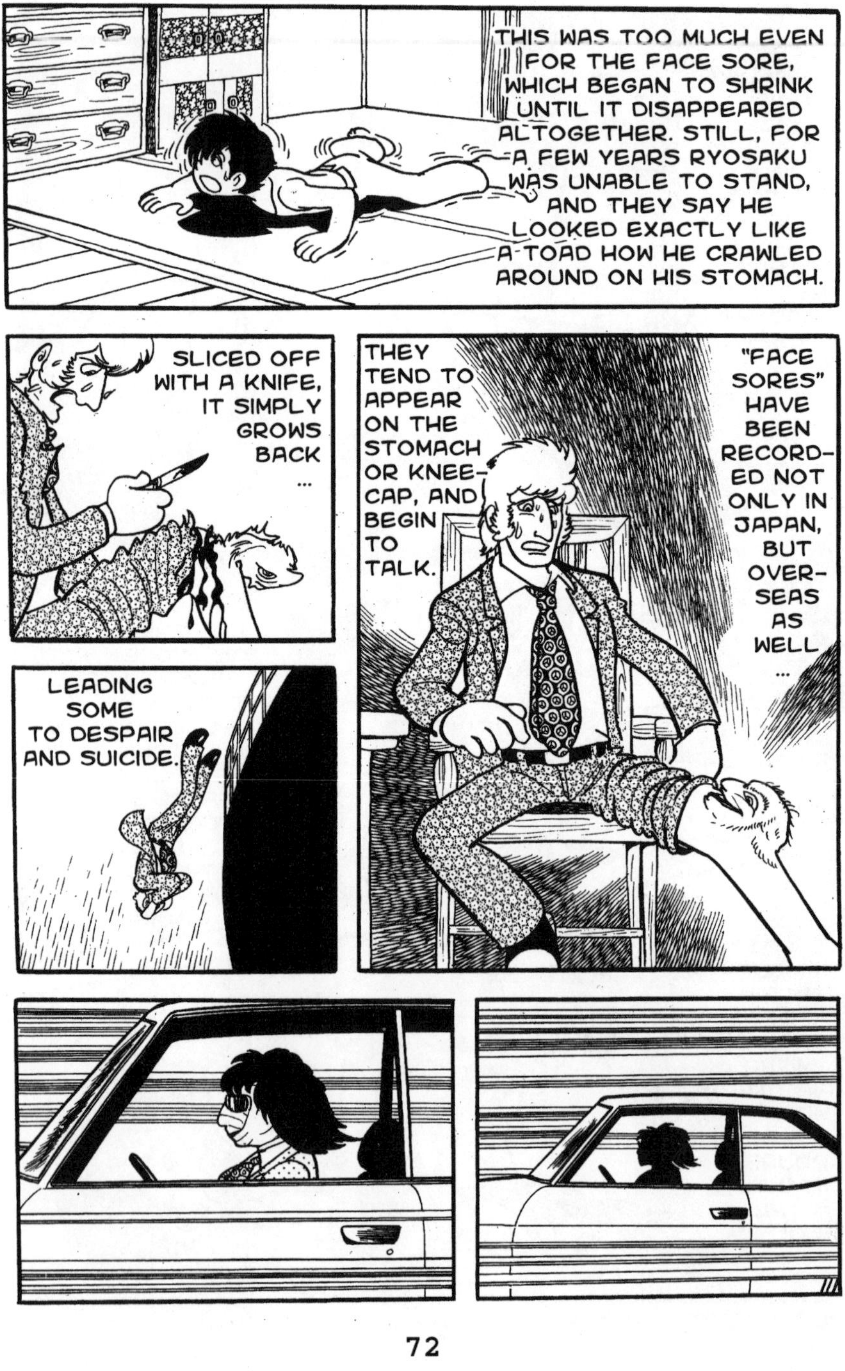
THIS WAS TOO MUCH EVEN FOR THE FACE SORE, WHICH BEGAN TO SHRINK UNTIL IT DISAPPEARED ALTOGETHER. STILL, FOR A FEW YEARS RYOSAKU WAS UNABLE TO STAND, AND THEY SAY HE LOOKED EXACTLY LIKE A TOAD HOW HE CRAWLED AROUND ON HIS STOMACH.
"FACE SORES" HAVE BEEN RECORDED NOT ONLY IN JAPAN, BUT OVERSEAS AS WELL ...
THEY TEND TO APPEAR ON THE STOMACH OR KNEE-CAP, AND BEGIN TO TALK.
SLICED OFF WITH A KNIFE, IT SIMPLY GROWS BACK ...
LEADING SOME TO DESPAIR AND SUICIDE.

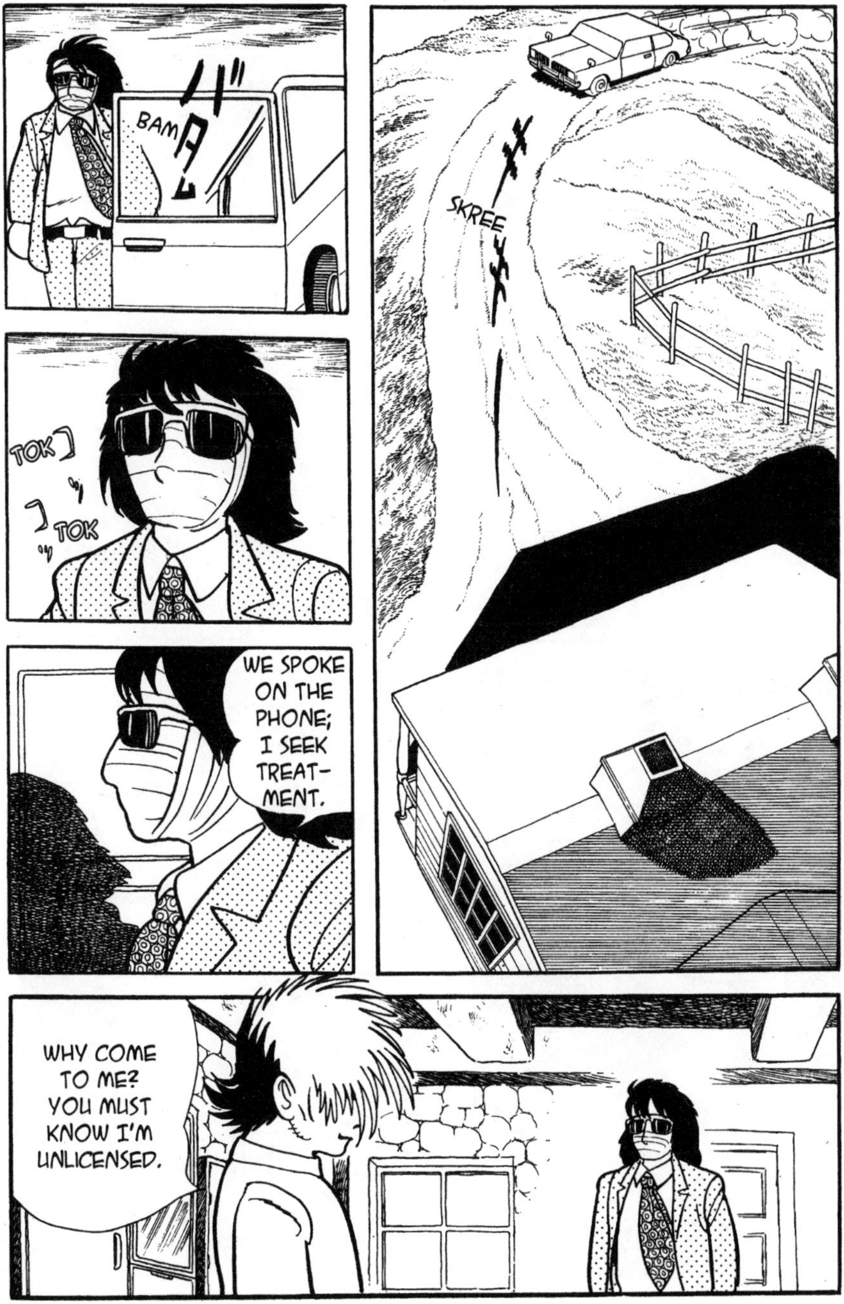

SKREE
BAM
TOK
TOK
WE SPOKE ON THE PHONE; I SEEK TREATMENT.
WHY COME TO ME? YOU MUST KNOW I'M UNLICENSED.

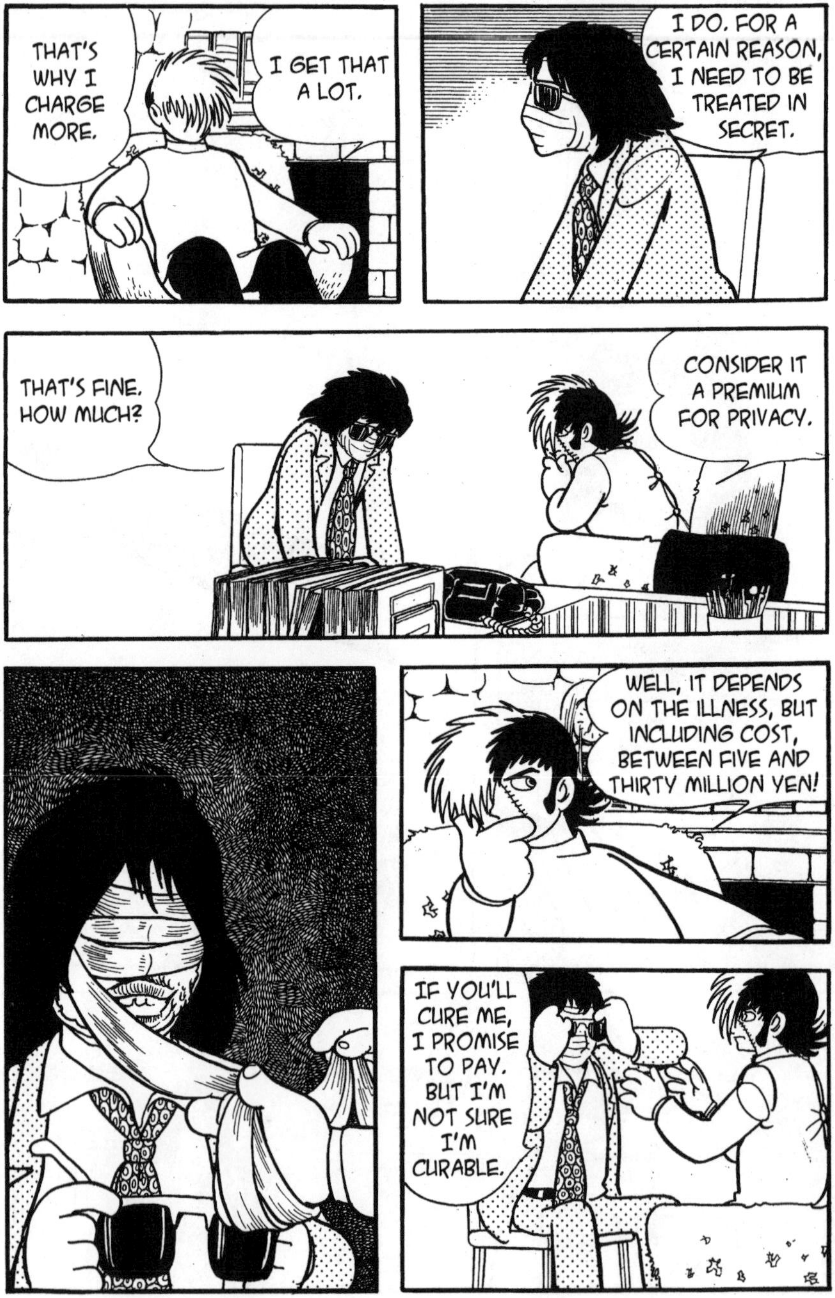
I DO. FOR A CERTAIN REASON, I NEED TO BE TREATED IN SECRET.
I GET THAT A LOT.
THAT'S WHY I CHARGE MORE.
CONSIDER IT A PREMIUM FOR PRIVACY.
THAT'S FINE. HOW MUCH?
WELL, IT DEPENDS ON THE ILLNESS, BUT INCLUDING COST, BETWEEN FIVE AND THIRTY MILLION YEN!
IF YOU'LL CURE ME, I PROMISE TO PAY. BUT I'M NOT SURE I'M CURABLE.

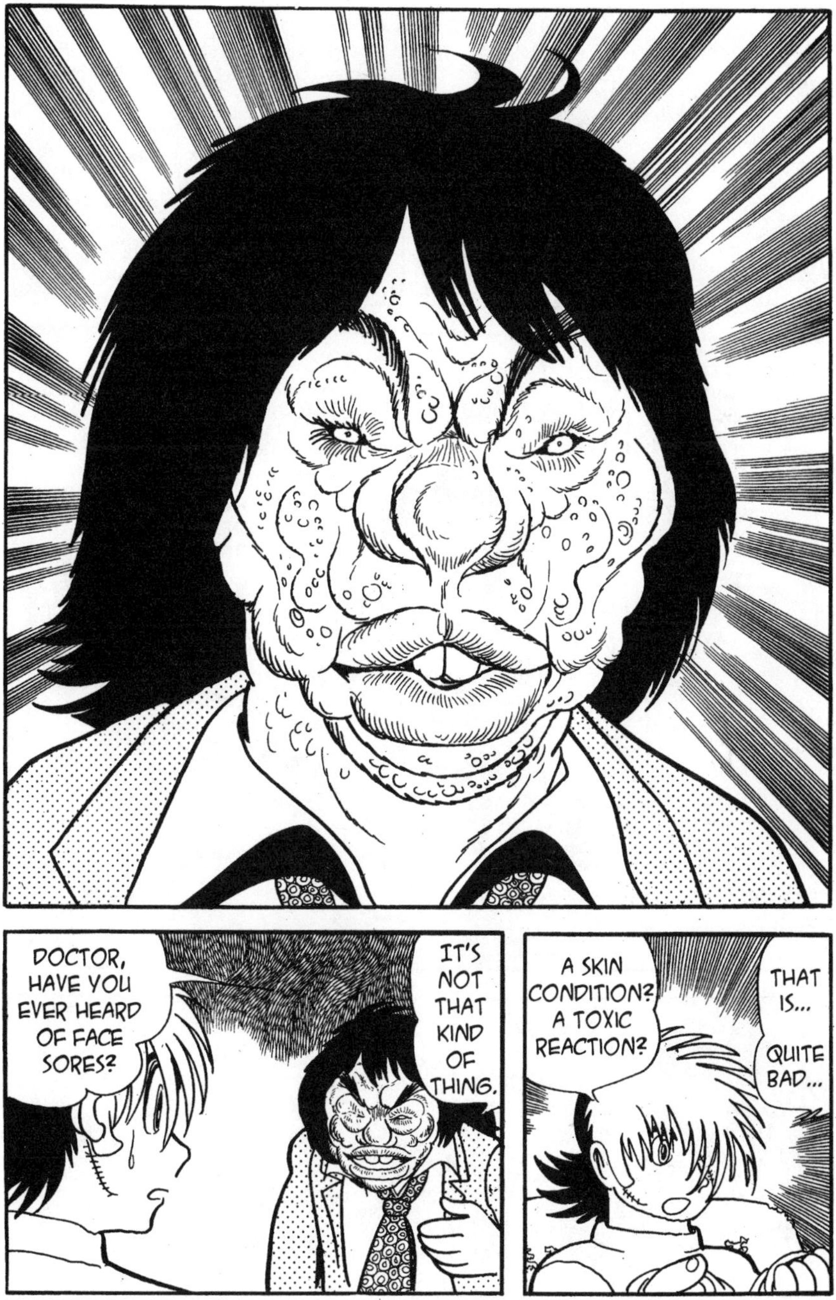
THAT IS...
QUITE BAD...
A SKIN CONDITION? A TOXIC REACTION?
IT'S NOT THAT KIND OF THING.
DOCTOR, HAVE YOU EVER HEARD OF FACE SORES?

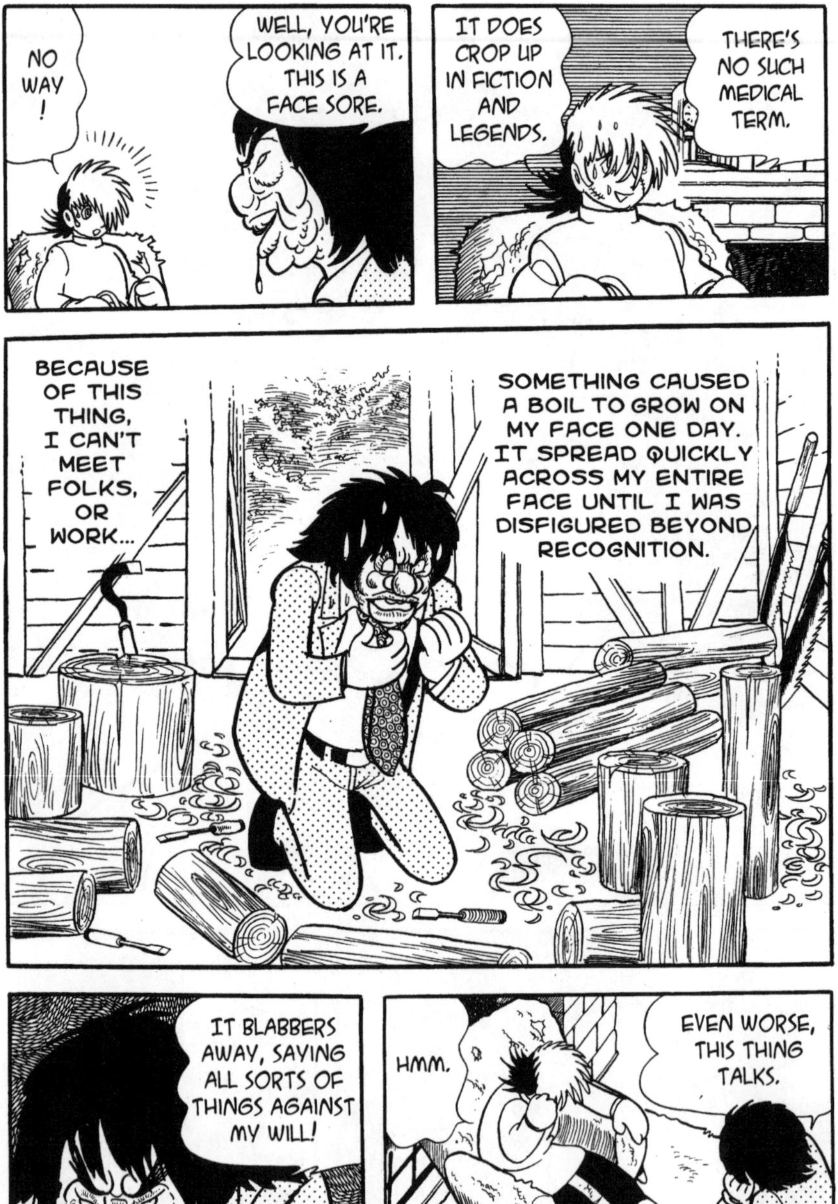

THERE'S NO SUCH MEDICAL TERM.
IT DOES CROP UP IN FICTION AND LEGENDS.
WELL, YOU'RE LOOKING AT IT. THIS IS A FACE SORE.
NO WAY!
SOMETHING CAUSED A BOIL TO GROW ON MY FACE ONE DAY. IT SPREAD QUICKLY ACROSS MY ENTIRE FACE UNTIL I WAS DISFIGURED BEYOND RECOGNITION.
BECAUSE OF THIS THING, I CAN'T MEET FOLKS, OR WORK...
EVEN WORSE, THIS THING TALKS.
HMM.
IT BLABBERS AWAY, SAYING ALL SORTS OF THINGS AGAINST MY WILL!

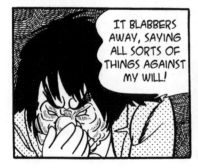

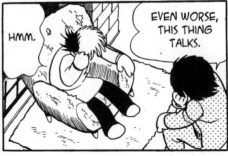

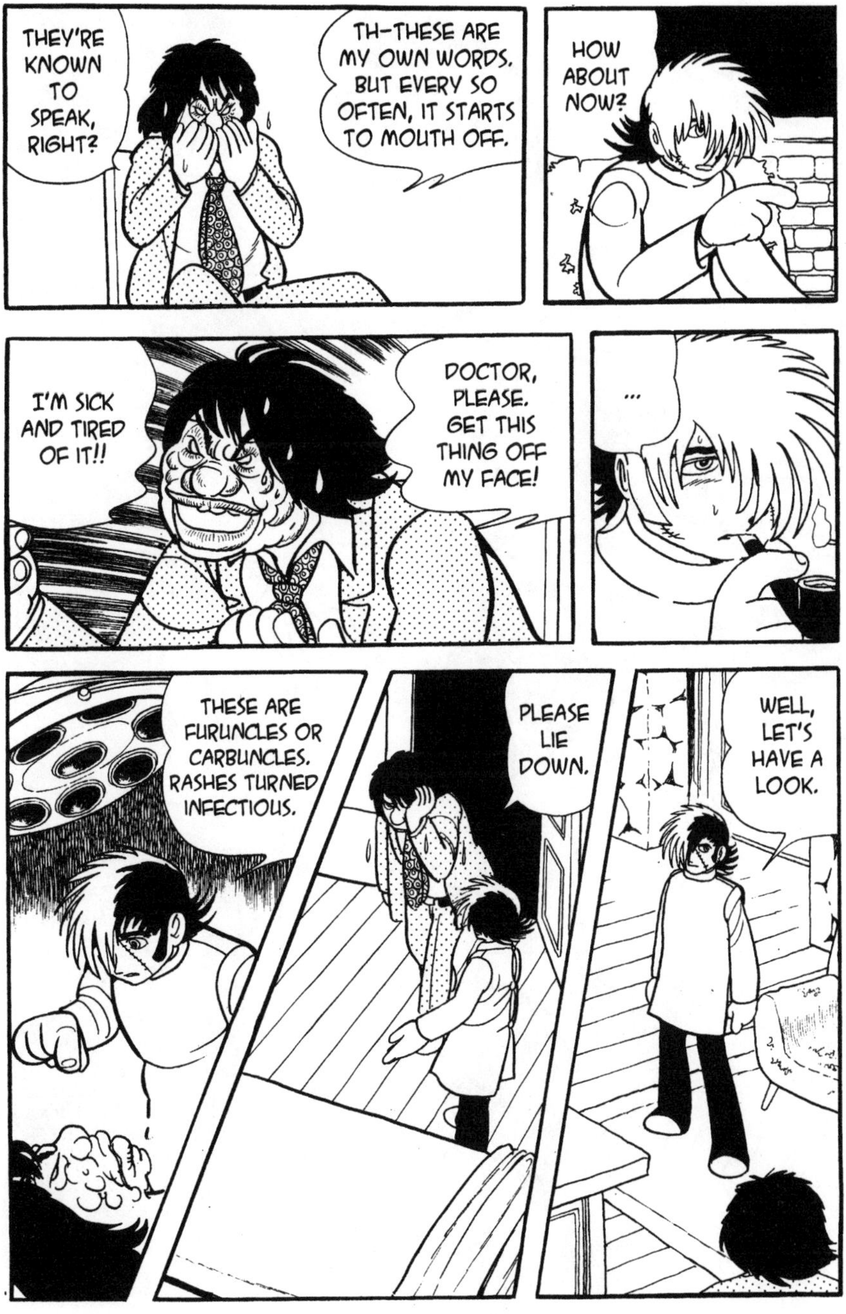
HOW ABOUT NOW?
TH-THESE ARE MY OWN WORDS. BUT EVERY SO OFTEN, IT STARTS TO MOUTH OFF.
THEY'RE KNOWN TO SPEAK, RIGHT?
...
DOCTOR, PLEASE. GET THIS THING OFF MY FACE!
I'M SICK AND TIRED OF IT!!
WELL, LET'S HAVE A LOOK.
PLEASE LIE DOWN.
THESE ARE FURUNCLES OR CARBUNCLES. RASHES TURNED INFECTIOUS.

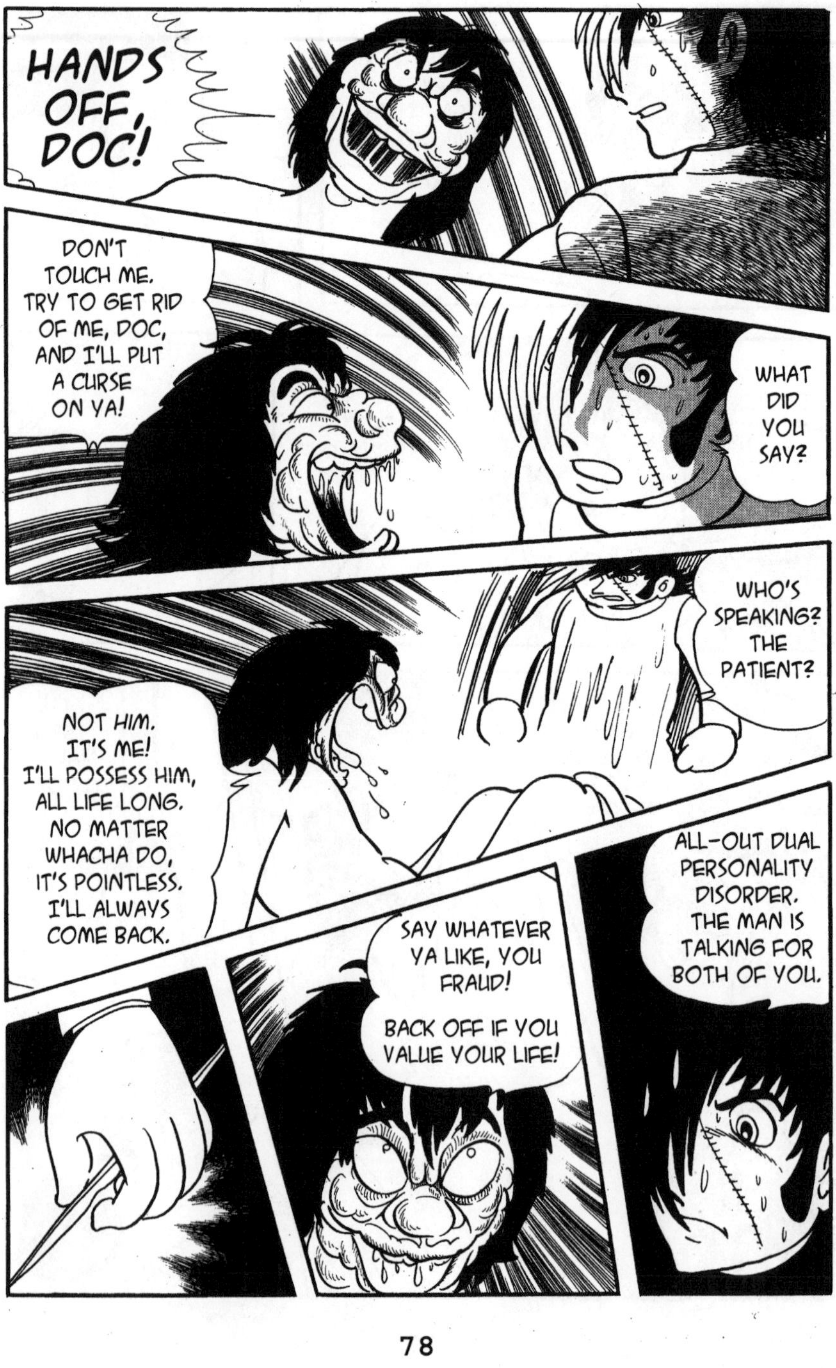
HANDS OFF, DOC!
WHAT DID YOU SAY?
DON'T TOUCH ME. TRY TO GET RID OF ME, DOC, AND I'LL PUT A CURSE ON YA!
WHO'S SPEAKING? THE PATIENT?
NOT HIM. IT'S ME! I'LL POSSESS HIM, ALL LIFE LONG. NO MATTER WHACHA DO, IT'S POINTLESS. I'LL ALWAYS COME BACK.
ALL-OUT DUAL PERSONALITY DISORDER. THE MAN IS TALKING FOR BOTH OF YOU.
SAY WHATEVER YA LIKE, YOU FRAUD!
BACK OFF IF YOU VALUE YOUR LIFE!

STOP!! YOU MORON! IMBECILE! CRETIN! YOU'RE REALLY GONNA OPERATE?
UGH ...
DOCTOR... CAN YOU REALLY CURE ME?
PIECE OF CAKE. IT'S NOT LIKE I HAVE TO REPLACE YOUR HEAD.
NYAH!! JUST YOU TRY IT! I'LL COVER YOU IN POISON AND GIVE YOU POCK-MARKS!
WILL YOU PLEASE SHUT HIM UP?
A LOCAL ANESTHETIC WOULD BE ENOUGH, BUT I'M PUTTING YOU BOTH TO SLEEP.
YAK
YAK
YAK

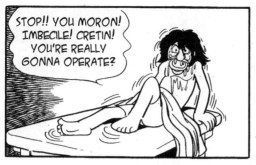

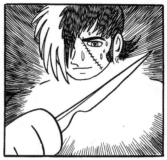

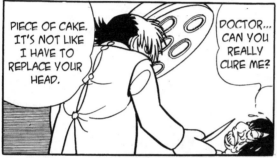

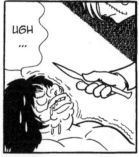

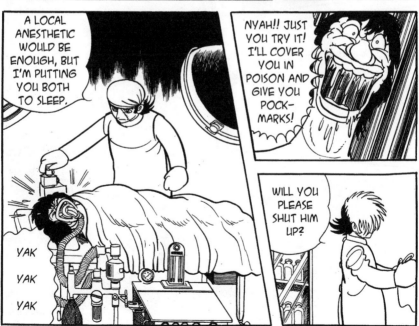

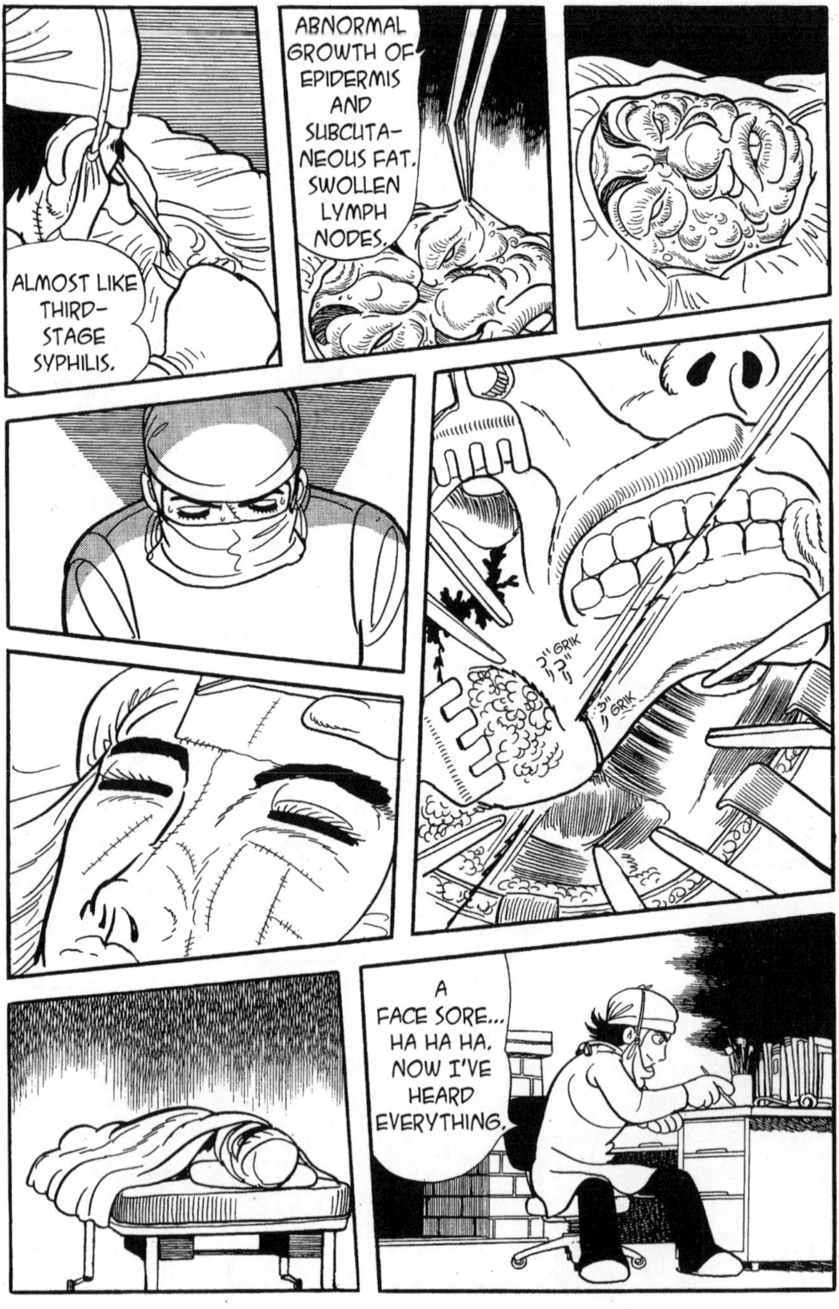
ABNORMAL GROWTH OF EPIDERMIS AND SUBCUTANEOUS FAT. SWOLLEN LYMPH NODES.
ALMOST LIKE THIRD-STAGE SYPHILIS.
GRIK
GRIK
A FACE SORE... HA HA HA. NOW I'VE HEARD EVERYTHING.

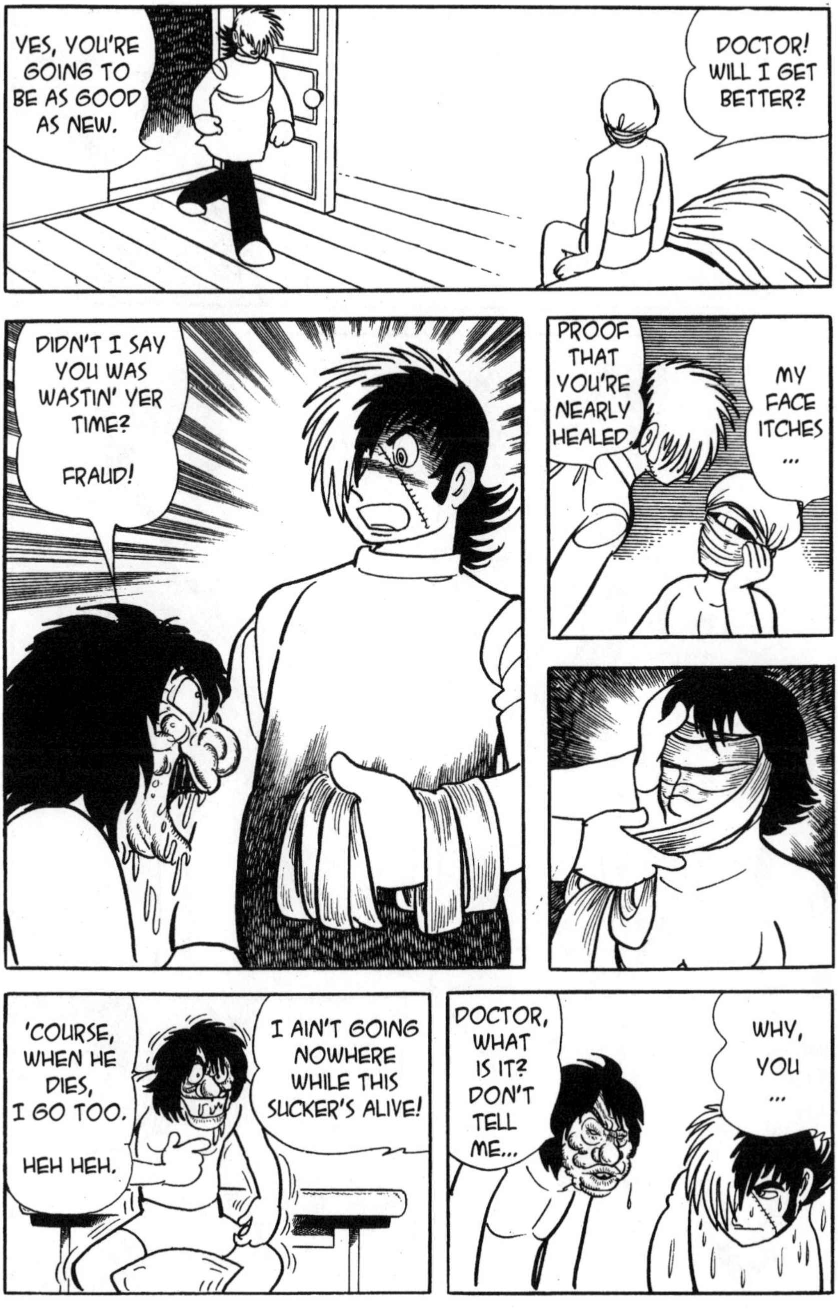
DOCTOR! WILL I GET BETTER?
YES, YOU'RE GOING TO BE AS GOOD AS NEW.
MY FACE ITCHES ...
PROOF THAT YOU'RE NEARLY HEALED.
DIDN'T I SAY YOU WAS WASTIN' YER TIME?
FRAUD!
WHY, YOU ...
DOCTOR, WHAT IS IT? DON'T TELL ME...
I AIN'T GOING NOWHERE WHILE THIS SUCKER'S ALIVE!
'COURSE, WHEN HE DIES, I GO TOO.
HEH HEH.

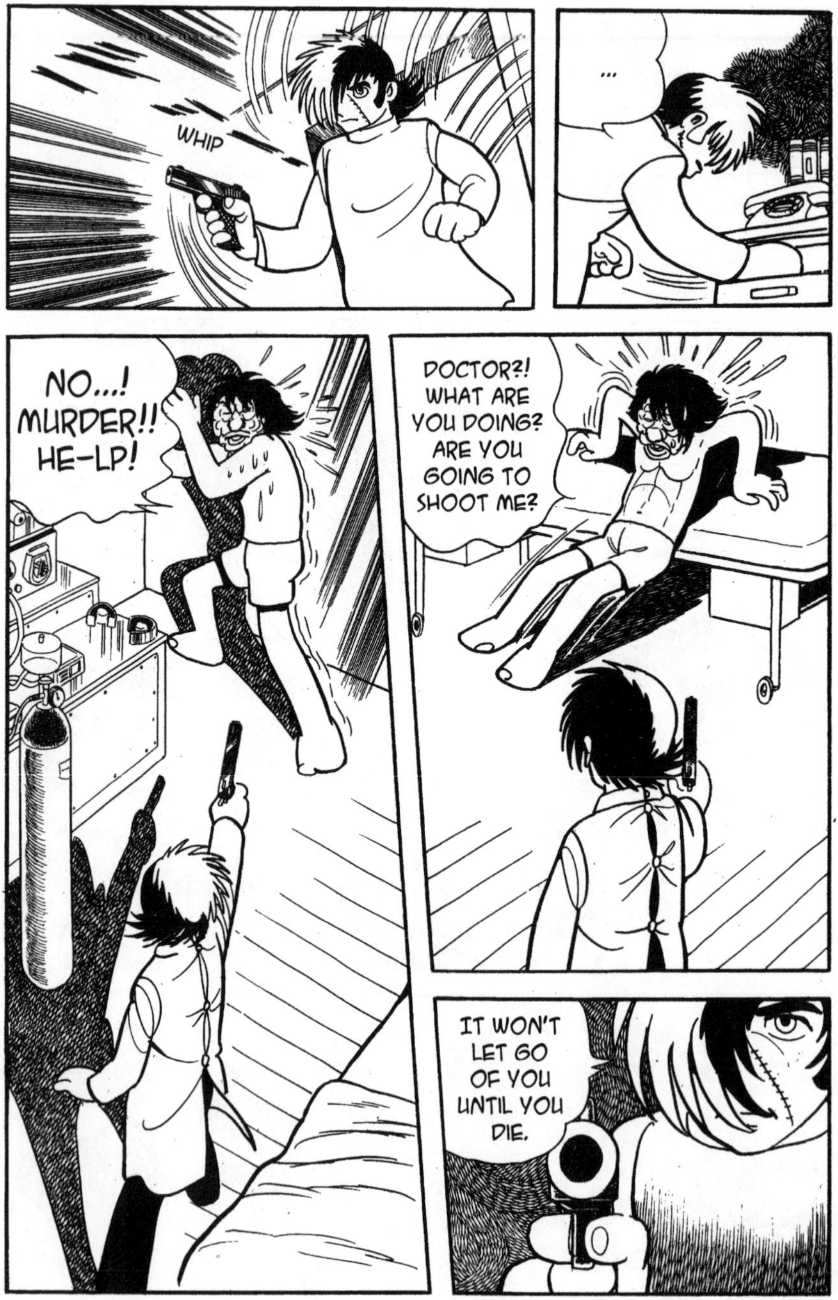
...
WHIP
DOCTOR?! WHAT ARE YOU DOING? ARE YOU GOING TO SHOOT ME?
IT WON'T LET GO OF YOU UNTIL YOU DIE.
NO...! MURDER!! HE-LP!

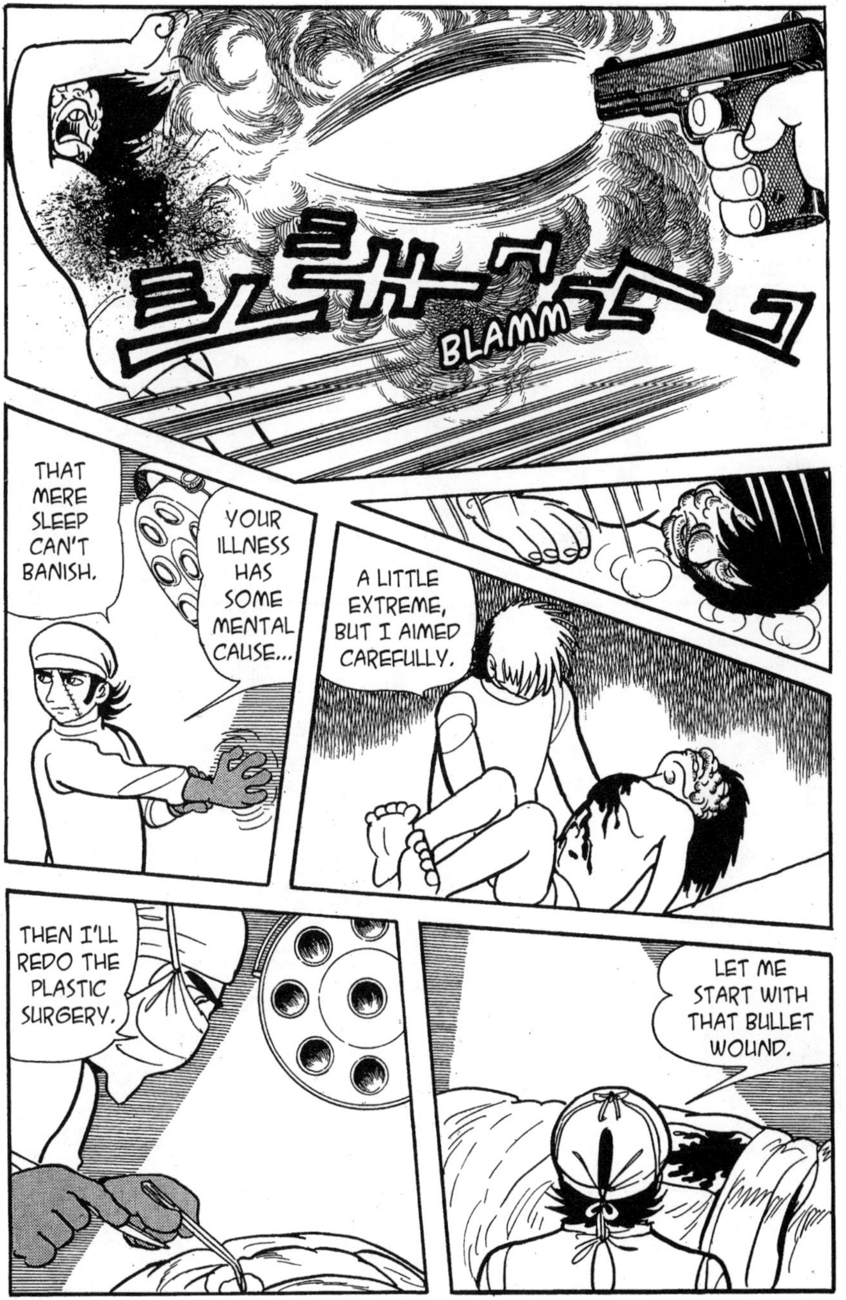
BLAMM
A LITTLE EXTREME, BUT I AIMED CAREFULLY.
YOUR ILLNESS HAS SOME MENTAL CAUSE...
THAT MERE SLEEP CAN'T BANISH.
LET ME START WITH THAT BULLET WOUND.
THEN I'LL REDO THE PLASTIC SURGERY.

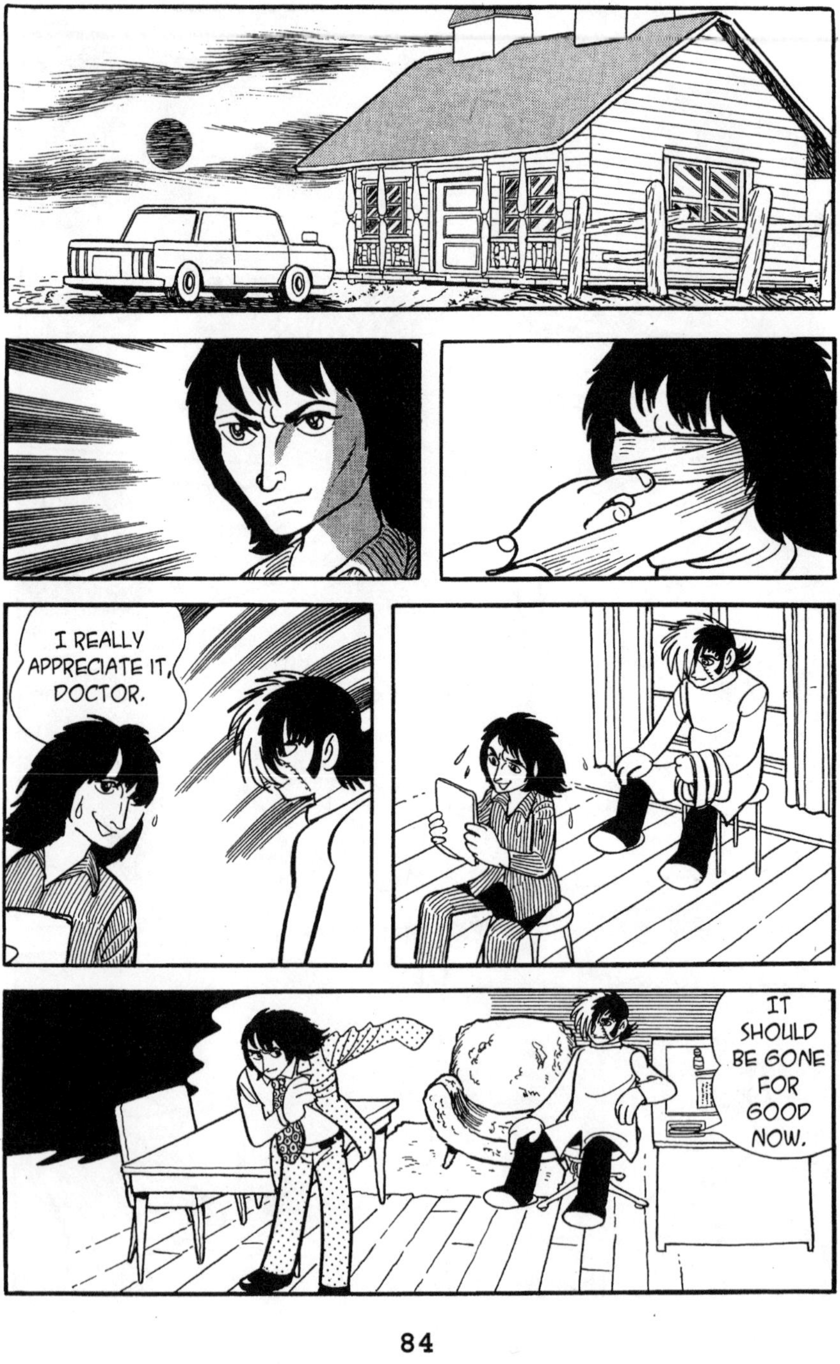
I REALLY APPRECIATE IT, DOCTOR.
IT SHOULD BE GONE FOR GOOD NOW.

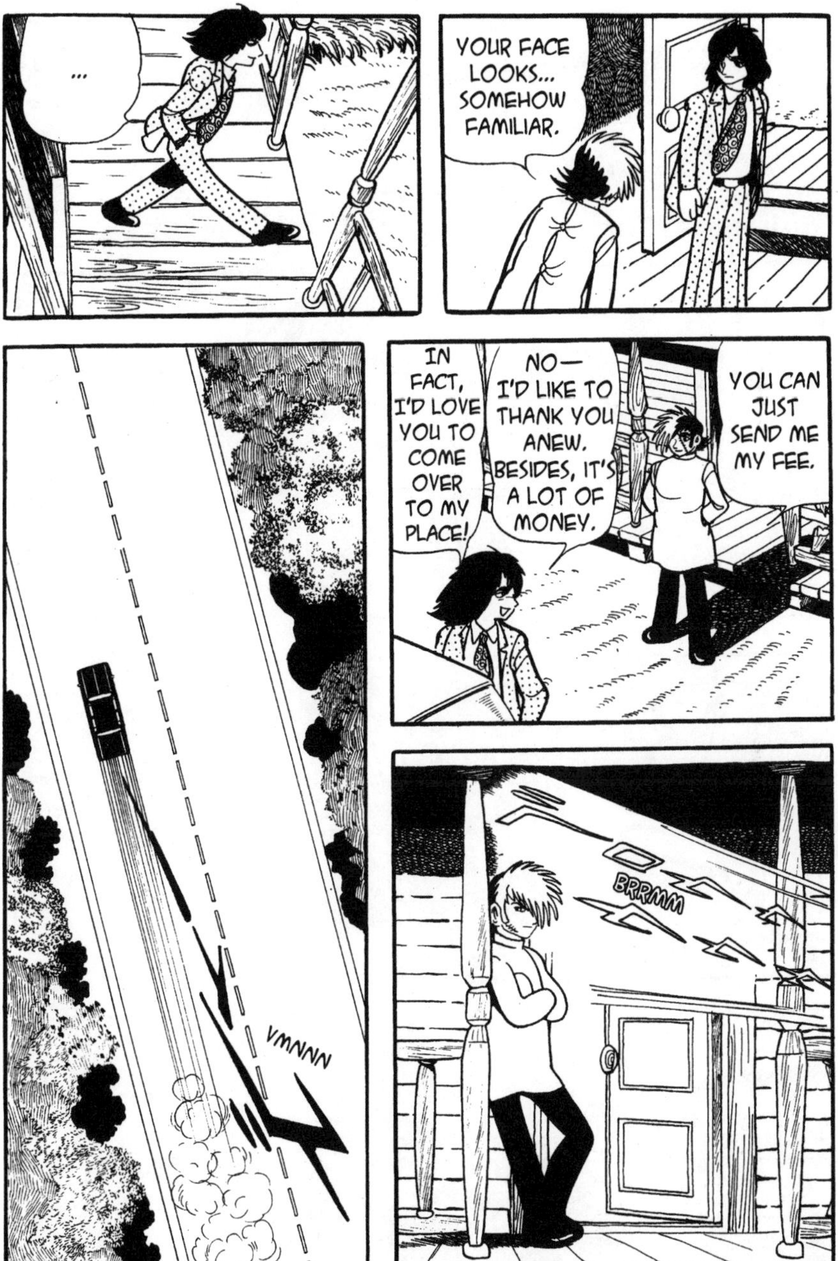
YOUR FACE LOOKS... SOMEHOW FAMILIAR.
...
YOU CAN JUST SEND ME MY FEE.
NO— I'D LIKE TO THANK YOU ANEW. BESIDES, IT'S A LOT OF MONEY.
IN FACT, I'D LOVE YOU TO COME OVER TO MY PLACE!
BRRMM
VMNNN

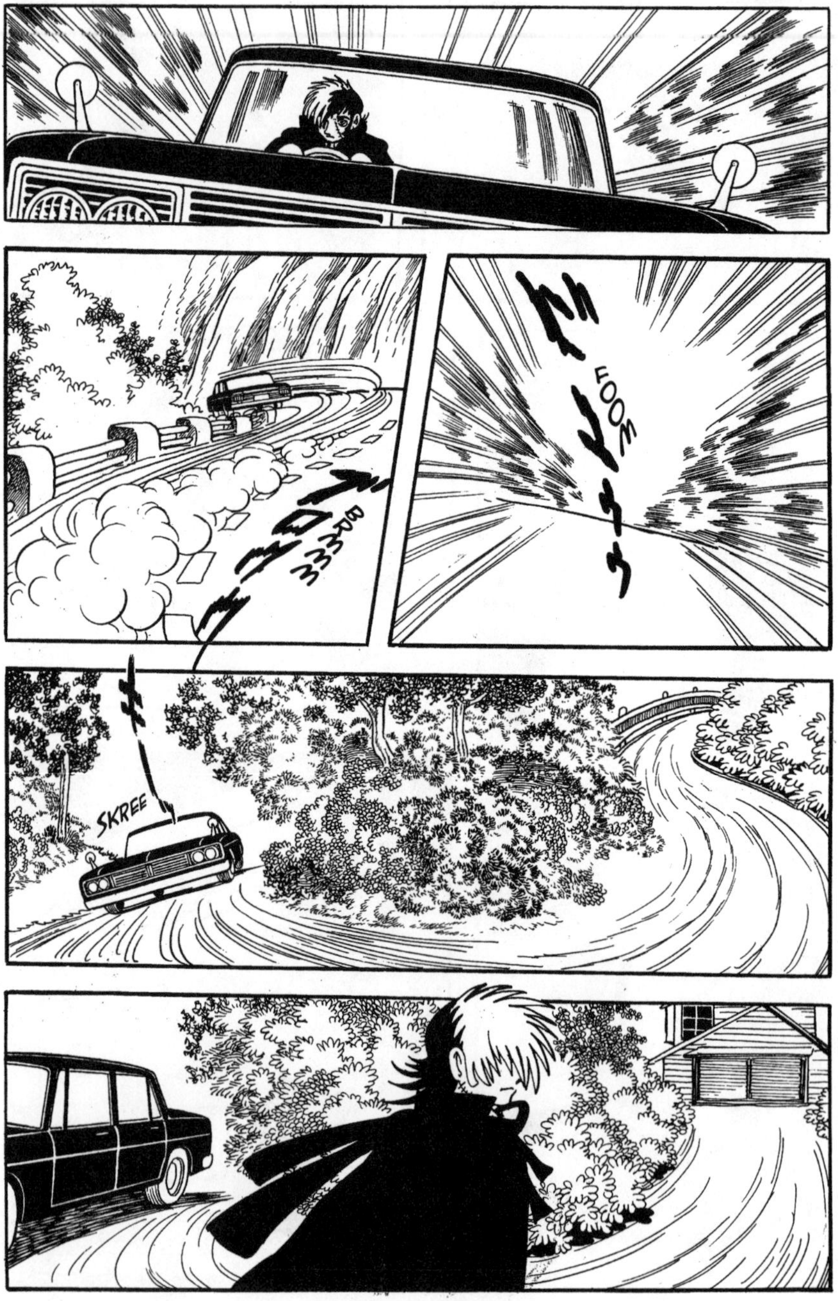
FOOM
BRMMM
SKREE

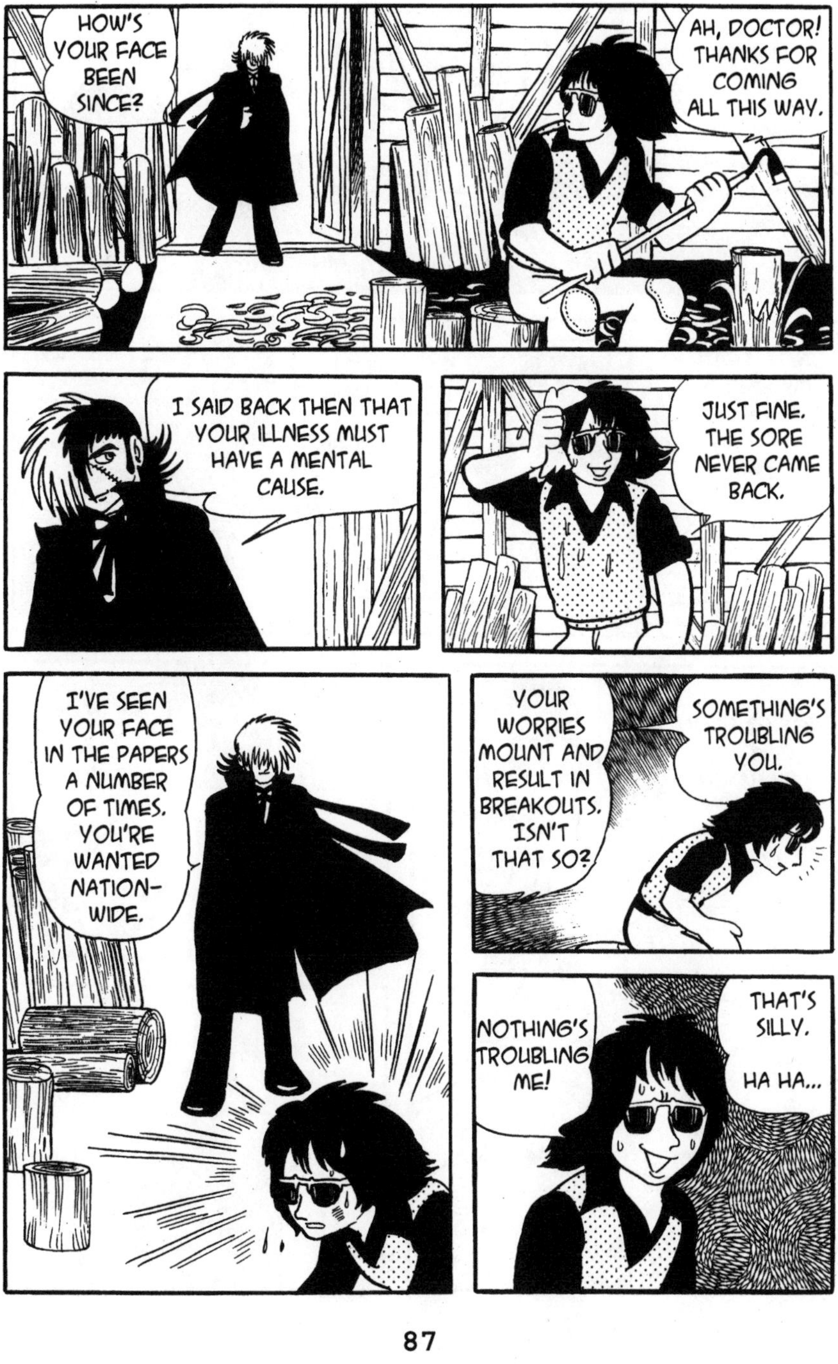

AH, DOCTOR! THANKS FOR COMING ALL THIS WAY.
HOW'S YOUR FACE BEEN SINCE?
JUST FINE. THE SORE NEVER CAME BACK.
I SAID BACK THEN THAT YOUR ILLNESS MUST HAVE A MENTAL CAUSE.
SOMETHING'S TROUBLING YOU.
YOUR WORRIES MOUNT AND RESULT IN BREAKOUTS. ISN'T THAT SO?
THAT'S SILLY.
HA HA...
NOTHING'S TROUBLING ME!
I'VE SEEN YOUR FACE IN THE PAPERS A NUMBER OF TIMES. YOU'RE WANTED NATION-WIDE.

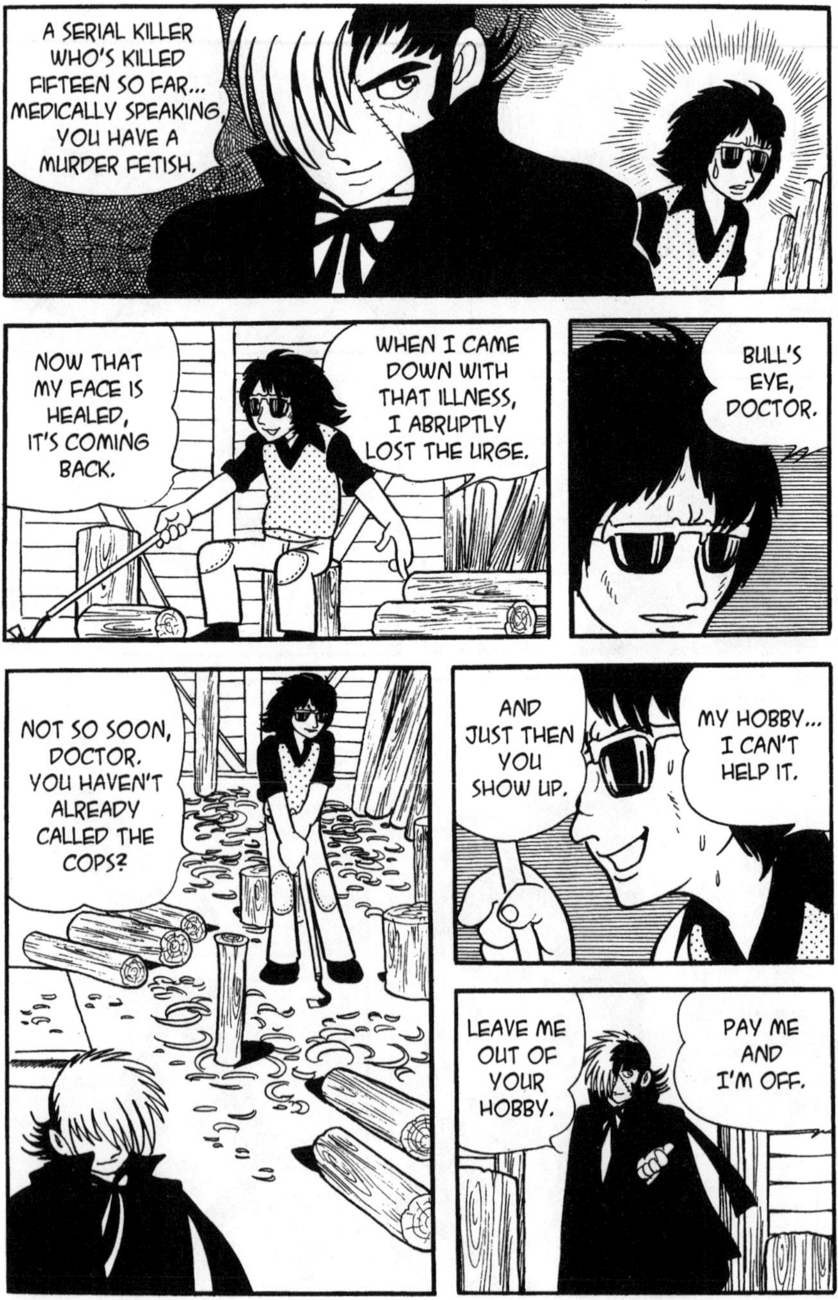
A SERIAL KILLER WHO'S KILLED FIFTEEN SO FAR... MEDICALLY SPEAKING, YOU HAVE A MURDER FETISH.
BULL'S EYE, DOCTOR.
WHEN I CAME DOWN WITH THAT ILLNESS, I ABRUPTLY LOST THE URGE.
NOW THAT MY FACE IS HEALED, IT'S COMING BACK.
MY HOBBY... I CAN'T HELP IT.
AND JUST THEN YOU SHOW UP.
PAY ME AND I'M OFF.
LEAVE ME OUT OF YOUR HOBBY.
NOT SO SOON, DOCTOR. YOU HAVEN'T ALREADY CALLED THE COPS?

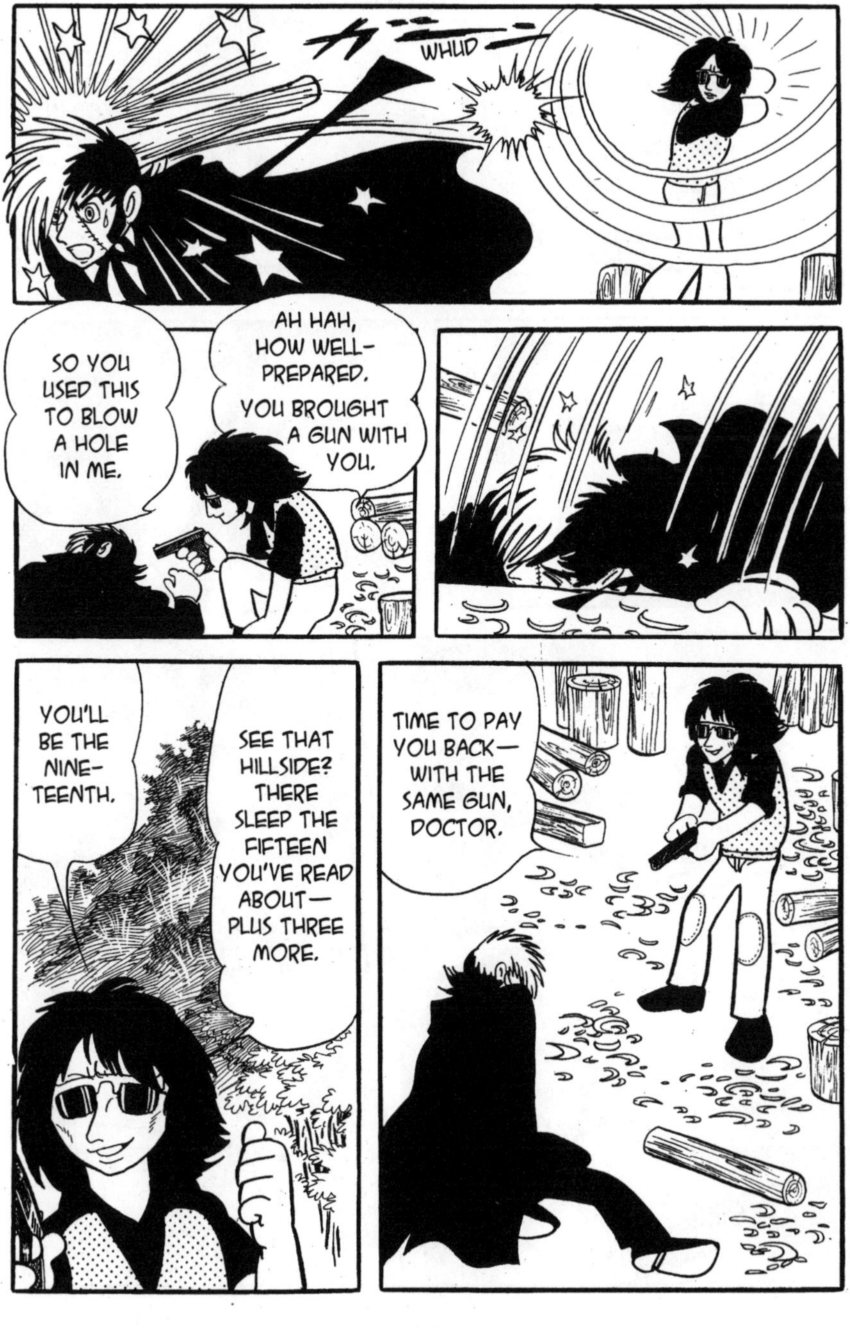
WHUD
AH HAH, HOW WELL-PREPARED. YOU BROUGHT A GUN WITH YOU.
SO YOU USED THIS TO BLOW A HOLE IN ME.
TIME TO PAY YOU BACK—WITH THE SAME GUN, DOCTOR.
SEE THAT HILLSIDE? THERE SLEEP THE FIFTEEN YOU'VE READ ABOUT—PLUS THREE MORE.
YOU'LL BE THE NINE-TEENTH.

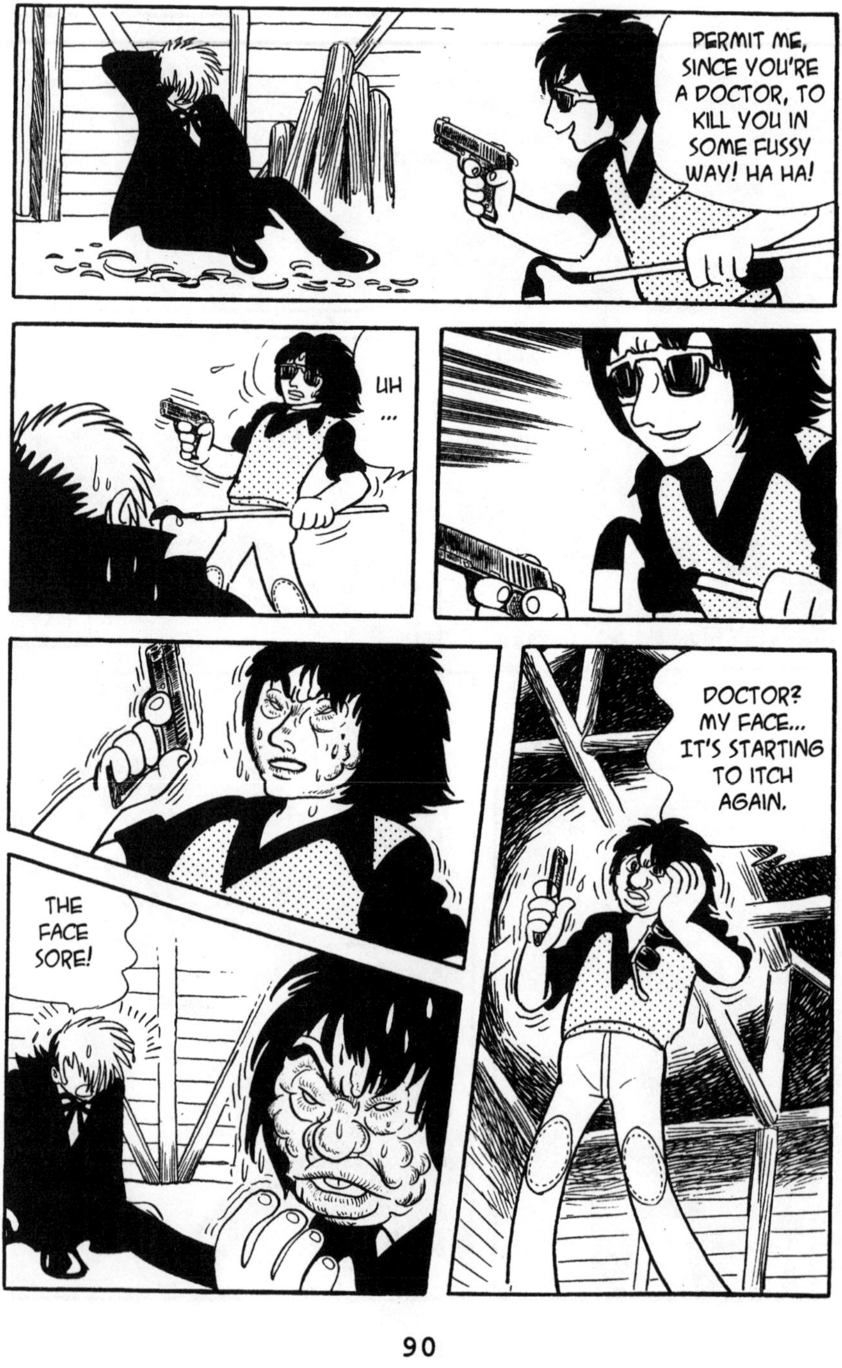
PERMIT ME, SINCE YOU'RE A DOCTOR, TO KILL YOU IN SOME FUSSY WAY! HA HA!
UH ...
DOCTOR? MY FACE... IT'S STARTING TO ITCH AGAIN.
THE FACE SORE!

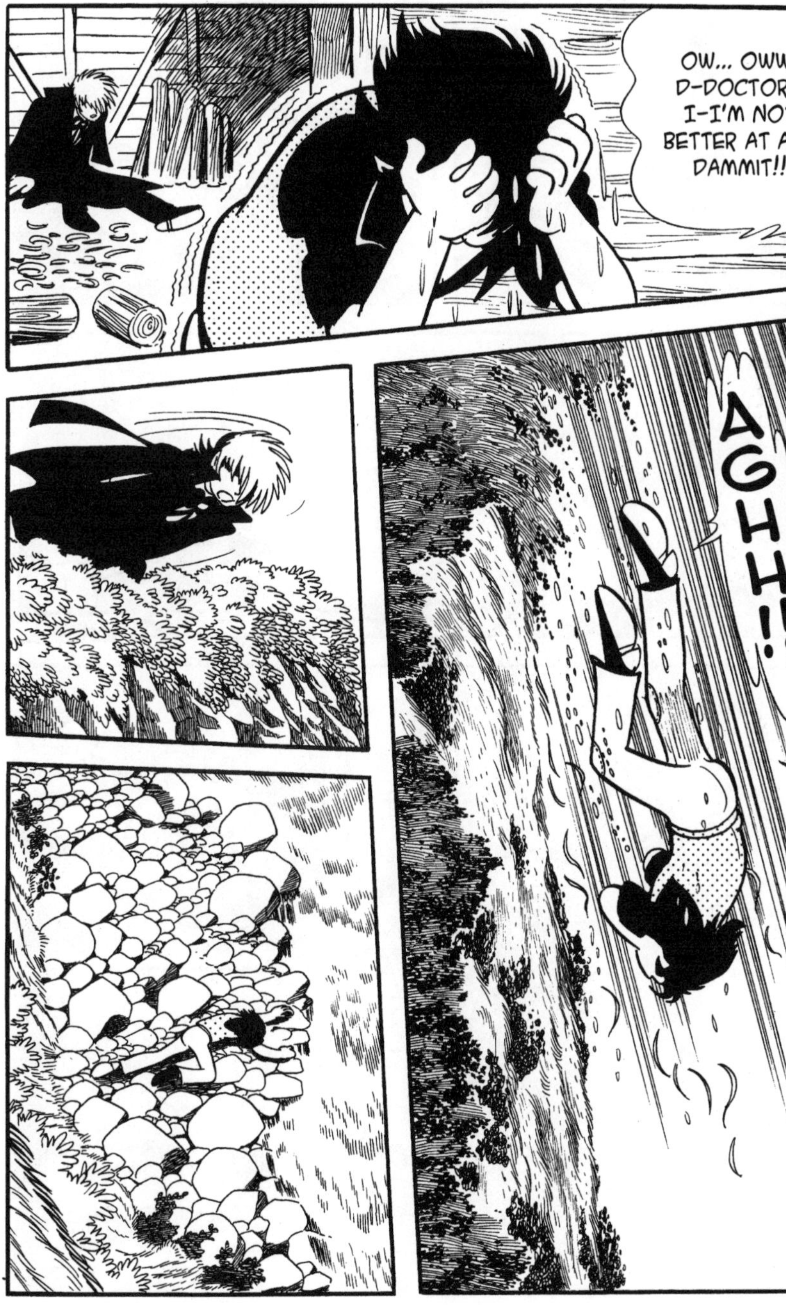
OW... OWW! D-DOCTOR!! I-I'M NOT BETTER AT ALL, DAMMIT!!
AGHH!!

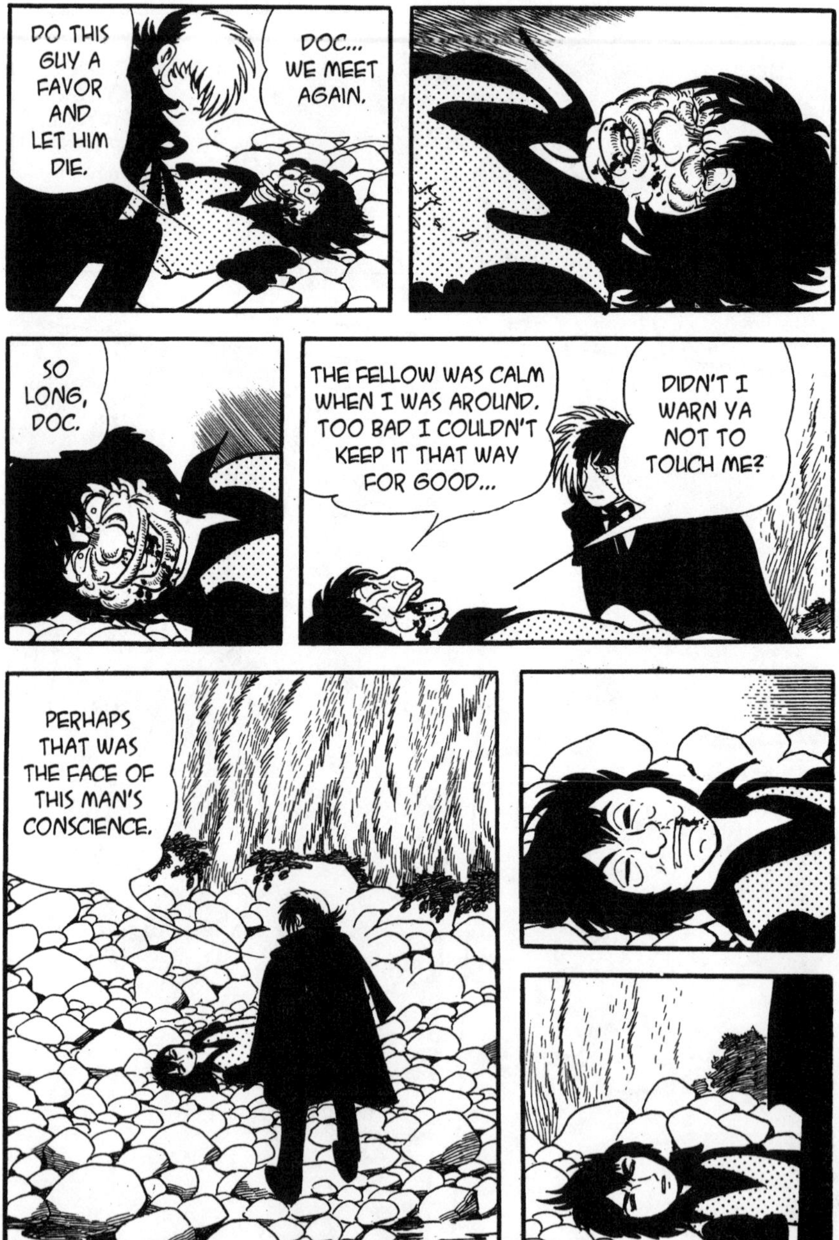
DOC... WE MEET AGAIN.
DO THIS GUY A FAVOR AND LET HIM DIE.
DIDN'T I WARN YA NOT TO TOUCH ME?
THE FELLOW WAS CALM WHEN I WAS AROUND. TOO BAD I COULDN'T KEEP IT THAT WAY FOR GOOD...
SO LONG, DOC.
PERHAPS THAT WAS THE FACE OF THIS MAN'S CONSCIENCE.

SOMETIMES LIKE PEARLS

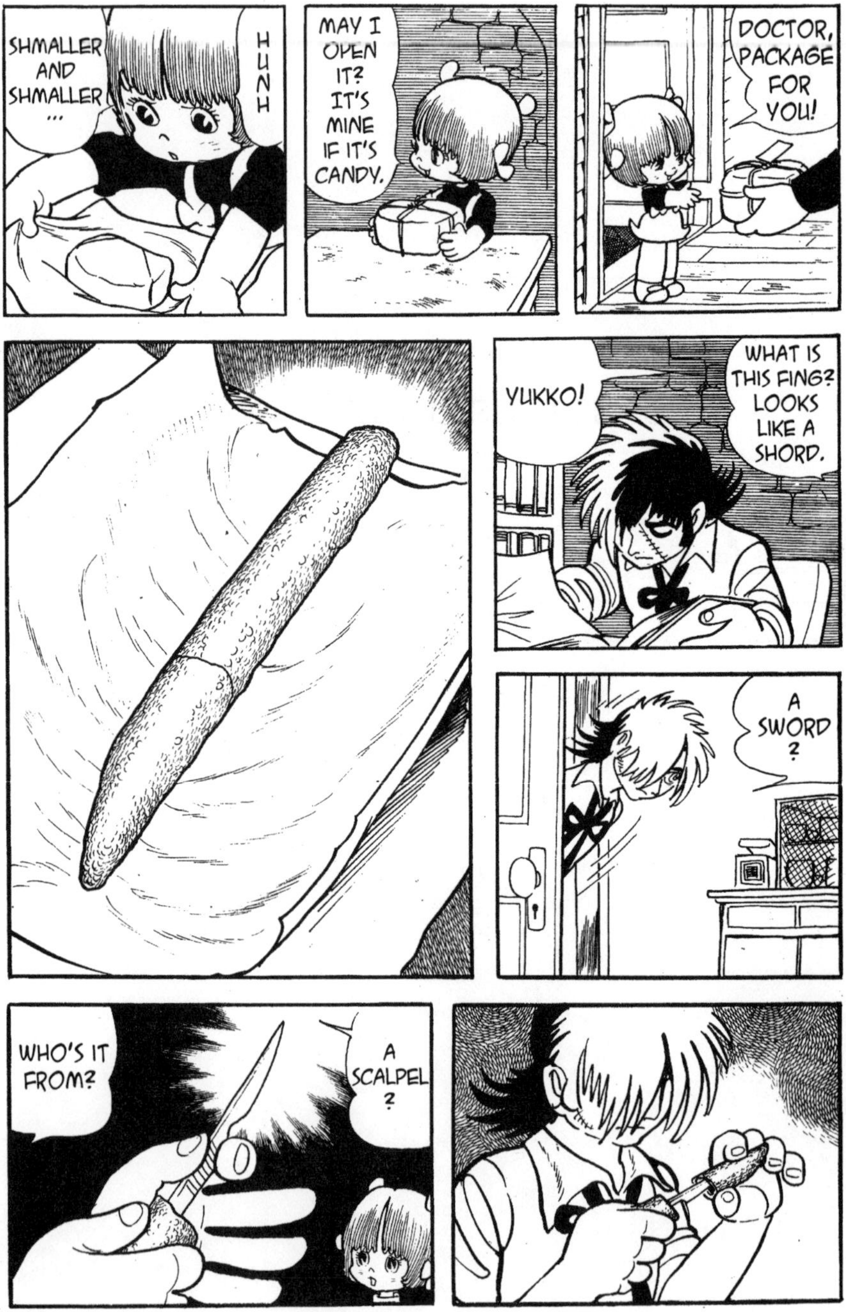
DOCTOR, PACKAGE FOR YOU!
MAY I OPEN IT? IT'S MINE IF IT'S CANDY.
HUNH
SHMALLER AND SHMALLER ...
WHAT IS THIS FING? LOOKS LIKE A SHORD.
YUKKO!
A SWORD?
A SCALPEL?
WHO'S IT FROM?

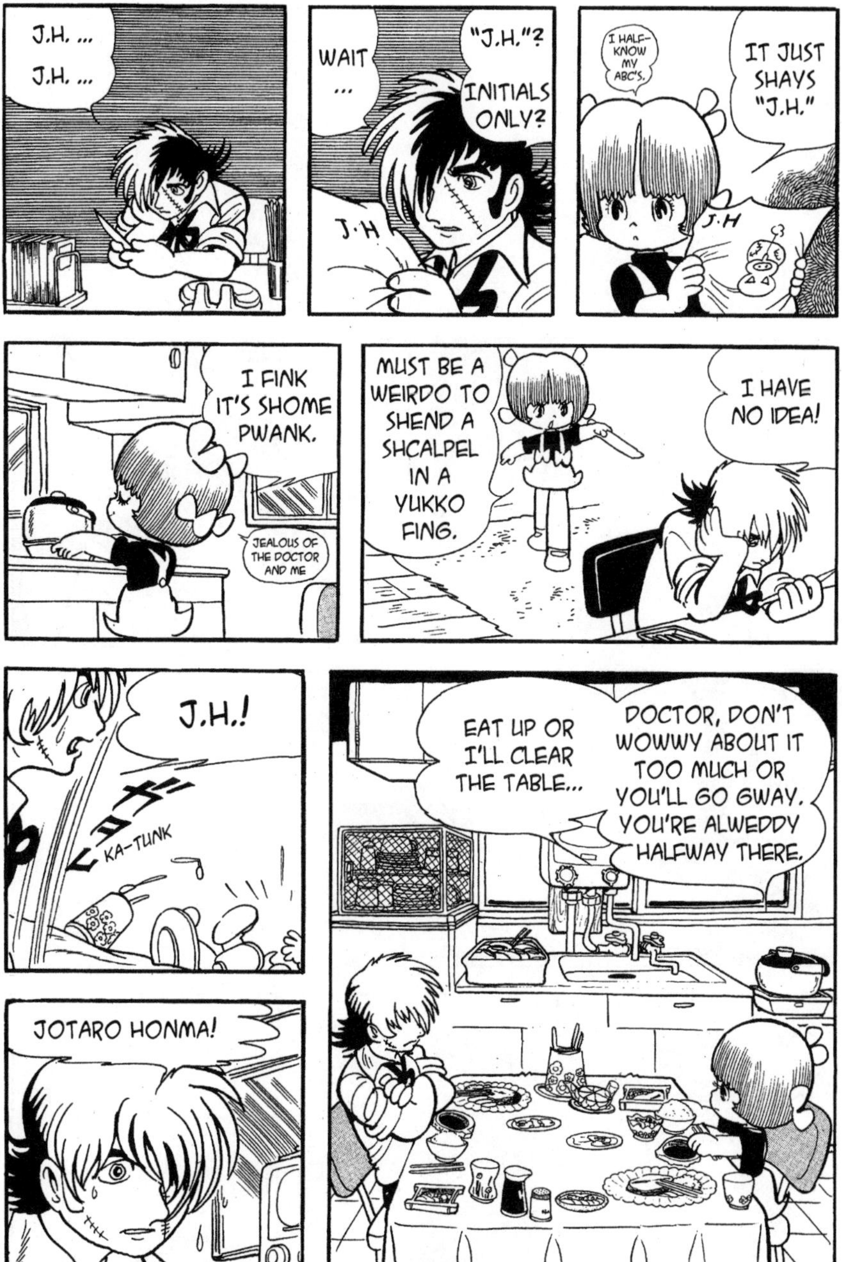
IT JUST SHAYS "J.H."
I HALF-KNOW MY ABC's.
J·H
"J.H."? INITIALS ONLY?
WAIT ...
J·H
J.H. ... J.H. ...
I HAVE NO IDEA!
MUST BE A WEIRDO TO SHEND A SHCALPEL IN A YUKKO FING.
I FINK IT'S SHOME PWANK.
JEALOUS OF THE DOCTOR AND ME
DOCTOR, DON'T WOWWY ABOUT IT TOO MUCH OR YOU'LL GO GWAY. YOU'RE ALWEDDY HALFWAY THERE.
EAT UP OR I'LL CLEAR THE TABLE...
J.H.!
KA-TUNK
JOTARO HONMA!

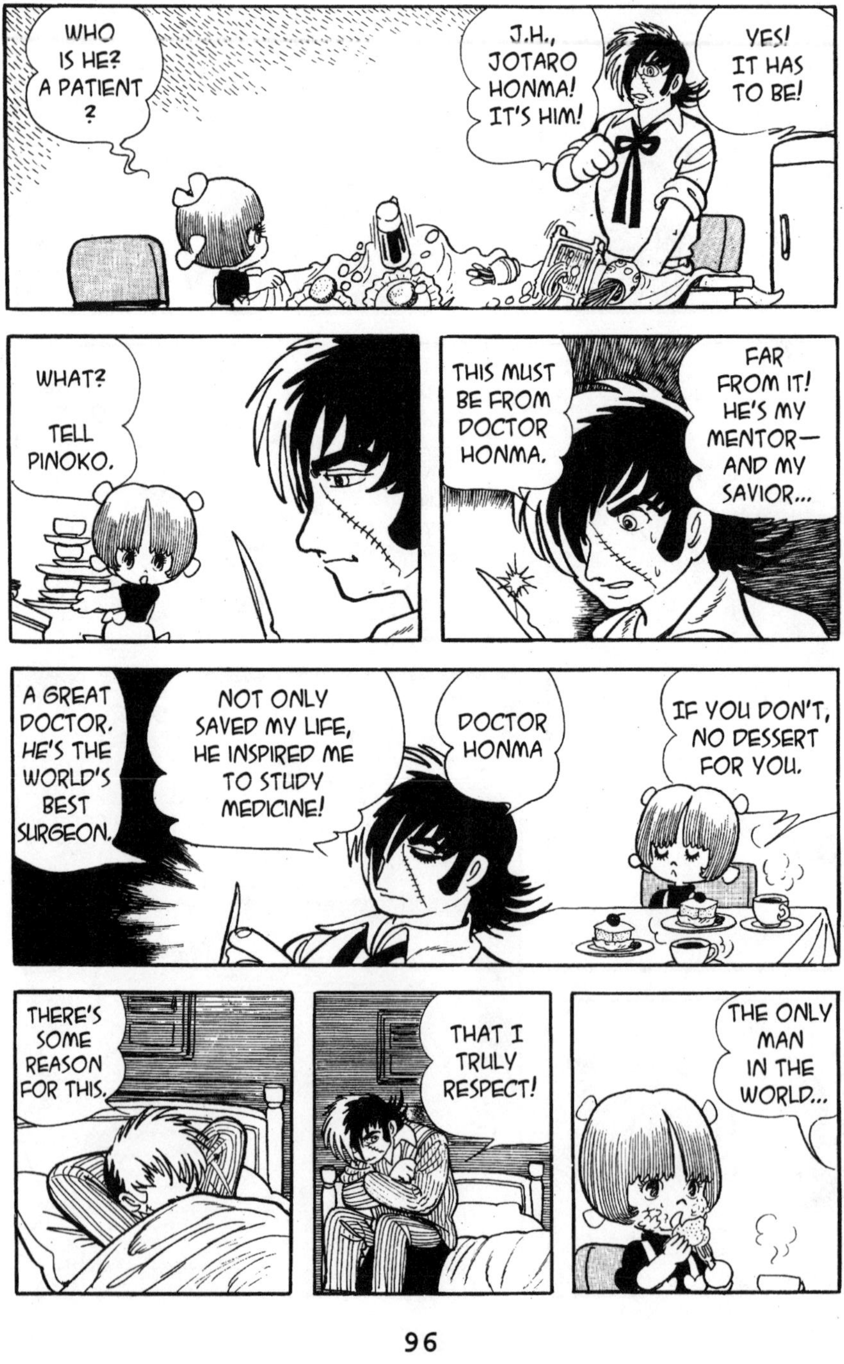
YES! IT HAS TO BE!
J.H., JOTARO HONMA! IT'S HIM!
WHO IS HE? A PATIENT ?
FAR FROM IT! HE'S MY MENTOR— AND MY SAVIOR...
THIS MUST BE FROM DOCTOR HONMA.
WHAT? TELL PINOKO.
IF YOU DON'T, NO DESSERT FOR YOU.
DOCTOR HONMA
NOT ONLY SAVED MY LIFE, HE INSPIRED ME TO STUDY MEDICINE!
A GREAT DOCTOR. HE'S THE WORLD'S BEST SURGEON.
THE ONLY MAN IN THE WORLD...
THAT I TRULY RESPECT!
THERE'S SOME REASON FOR THIS.

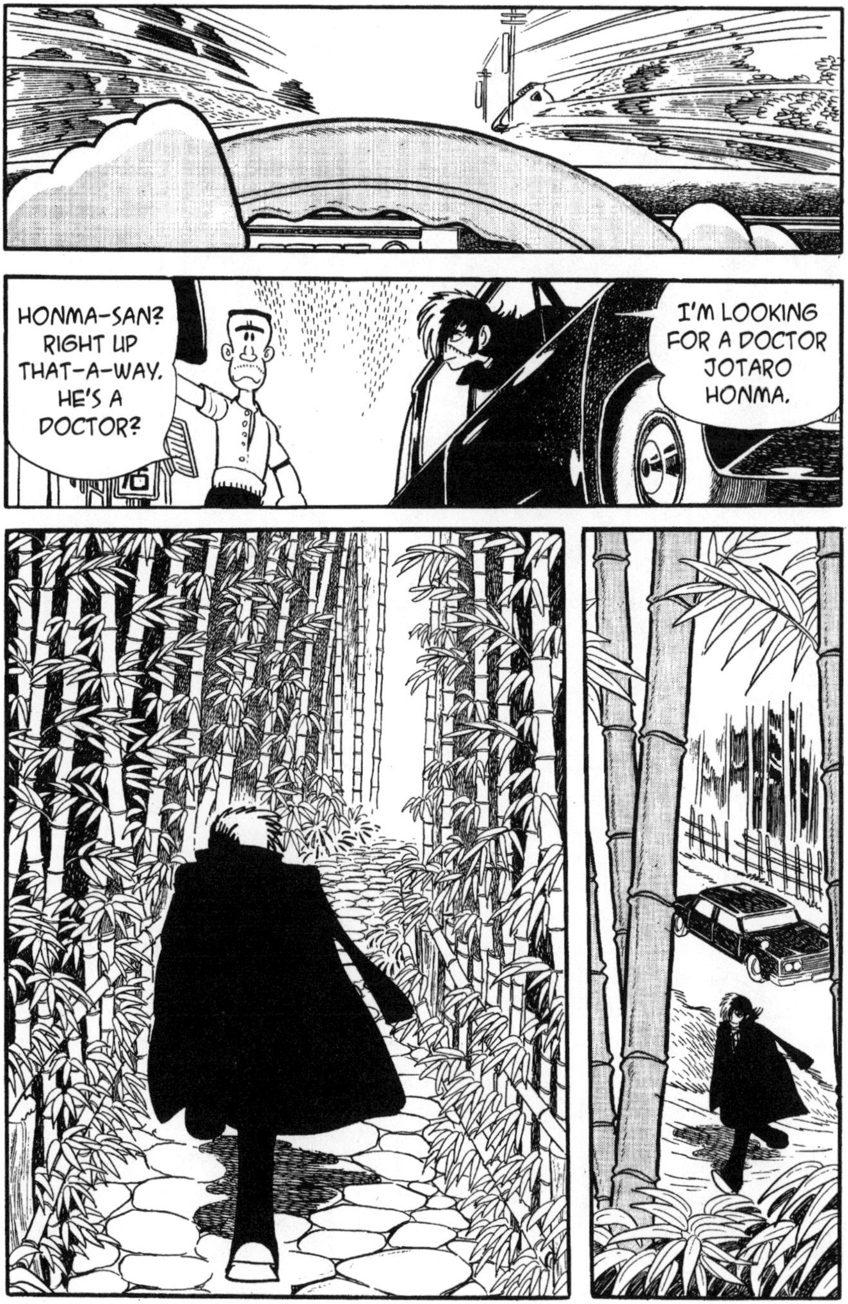
I'M LOOKING FOR A DOCTOR JOTARO HONMA.
HONMA-SAN? RIGHT UP THAT-A-WAY. HE'S A DOCTOR?

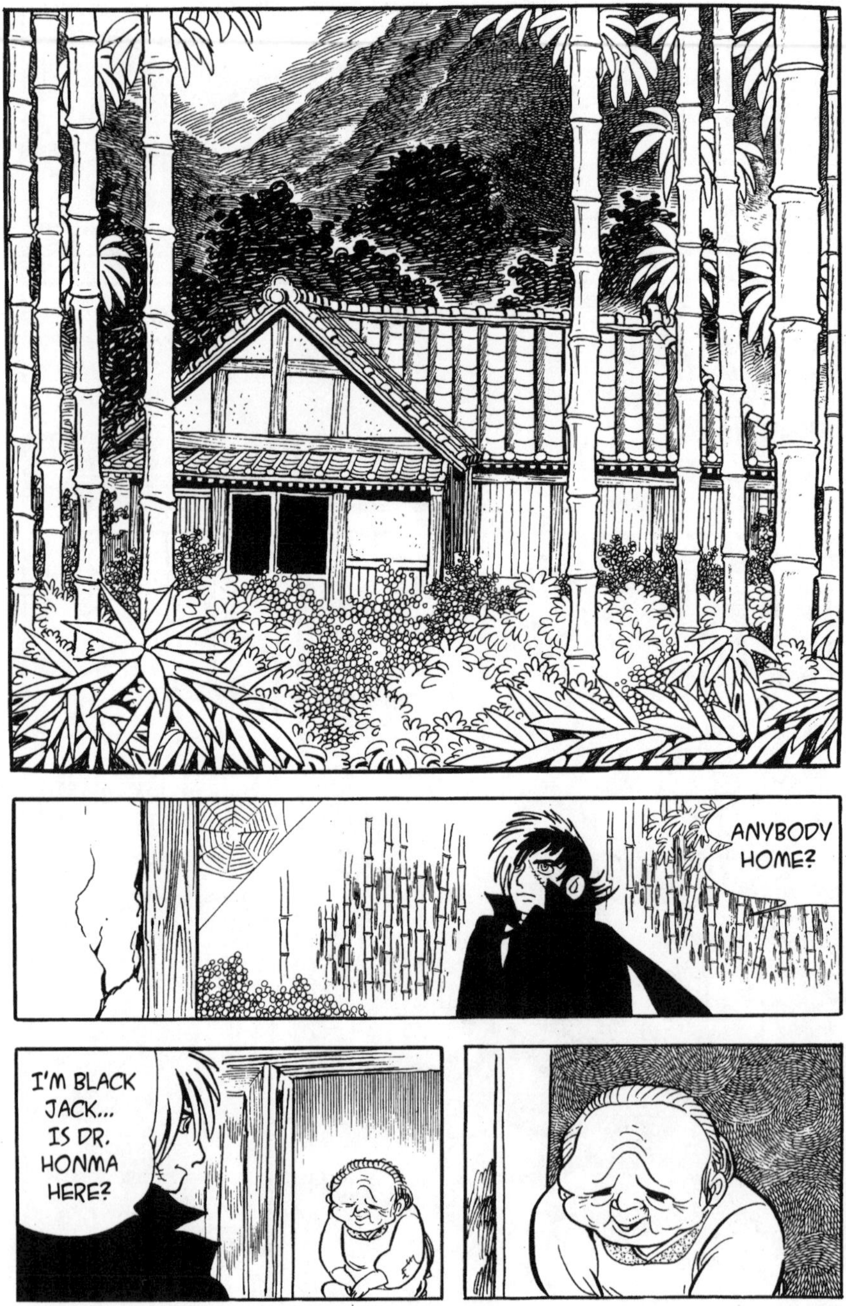
ANYBODY HOME?
I'M BLACK JACK... IS DR. HONMA HERE?

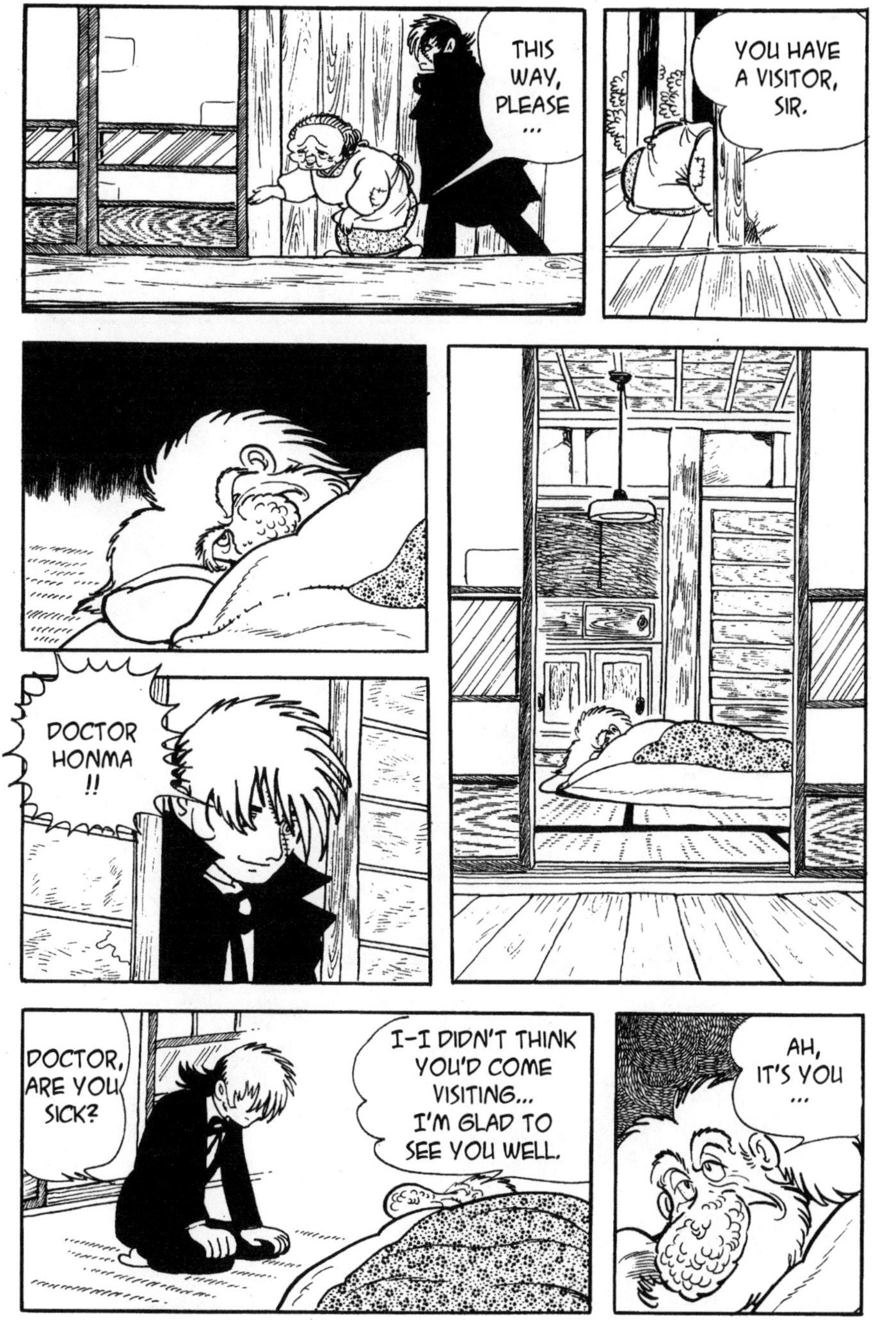
YOU HAVE A VISITOR, SIR.
THIS WAY, PLEASE ...
DOCTOR HONMA !!
AH, IT'S YOU ...
I-I DIDN'T THINK YOU'D COME VISITING... I'M GLAD TO SEE YOU WELL.
DOCTOR, ARE YOU SICK?

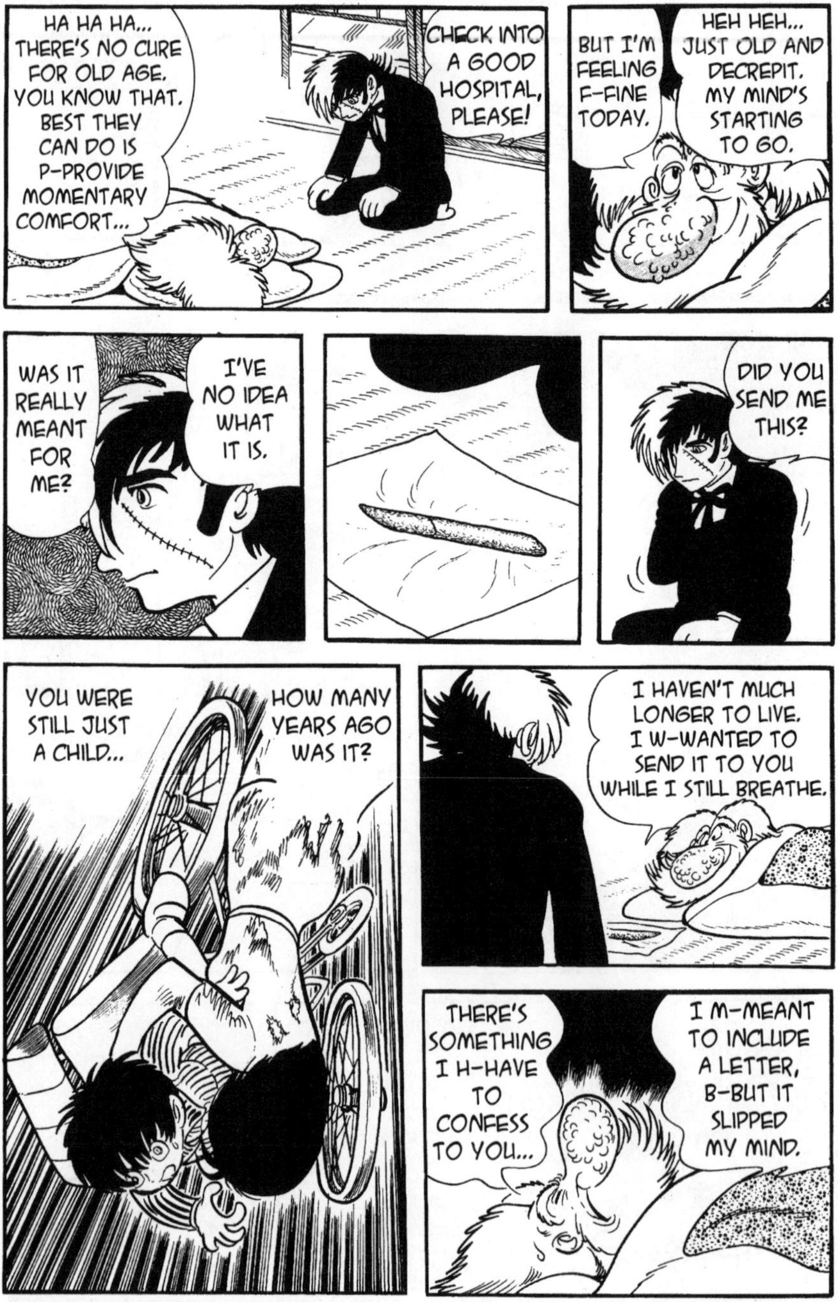
HEH HEH... JUST OLD AND DECREPIT. MY MIND'S STARTING TO GO.
BUT I'M FEELING F-FINE TODAY.
CHECK INTO A GOOD HOSPITAL, PLEASE!
HA HA HA... THERE'S NO CURE FOR OLD AGE. YOU KNOW THAT. BEST THEY CAN DO IS P-PROVIDE MOMENTARY COMFORT...
DID YOU SEND ME THIS?
I'VE NO IDEA WHAT IT IS.
WAS IT REALLY MEANT FOR ME?
I HAVEN'T MUCH LONGER TO LIVE. I W-WANTED TO SEND IT TO YOU WHILE I STILL BREATHE.
I M-MEANT TO INCLUDE A LETTER, B-BUT IT SLIPPED MY MIND.
THERE'S SOMETHING I H-HAVE TO CONFESS TO YOU...
HOW MANY YEARS AGO WAS IT?
YOU WERE STILL JUST A CHILD...

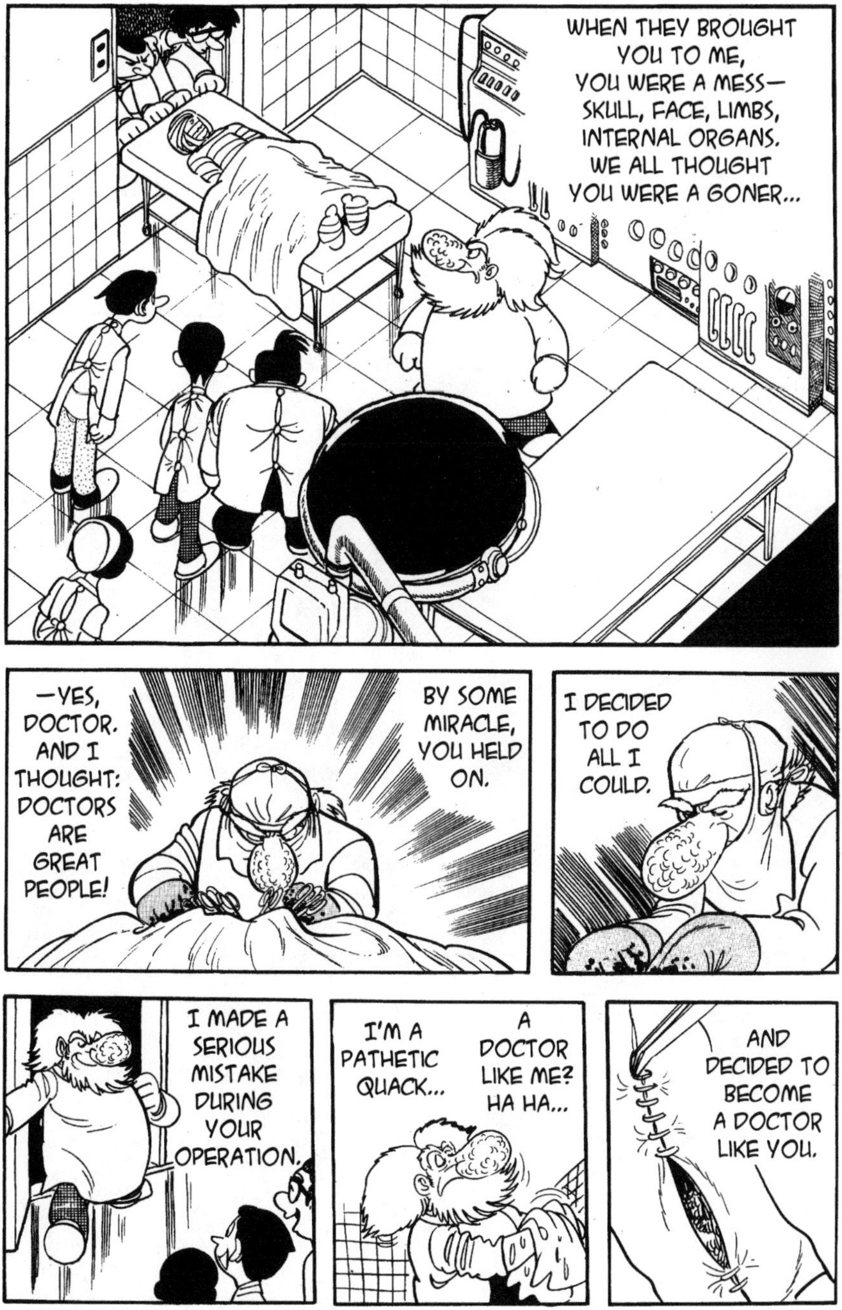
WHEN THEY BROUGHT YOU TO ME, YOU WERE A MESS— SKULL, FACE, LIMBS, INTERNAL ORGANS. WE ALL THOUGHT YOU WERE A GONER...
I DECIDED TO DO ALL I COULD.
BY SOME MIRACLE, YOU HELD ON.
—YES, DOCTOR. AND I THOUGHT: DOCTORS ARE GREAT PEOPLE!
AND DECIDED TO BECOME A DOCTOR LIKE YOU.
A DOCTOR LIKE ME? HA HA...
I'M A PATHETIC QUACK...
I MADE A SERIOUS MISTAKE DURING YOUR OPERATION.

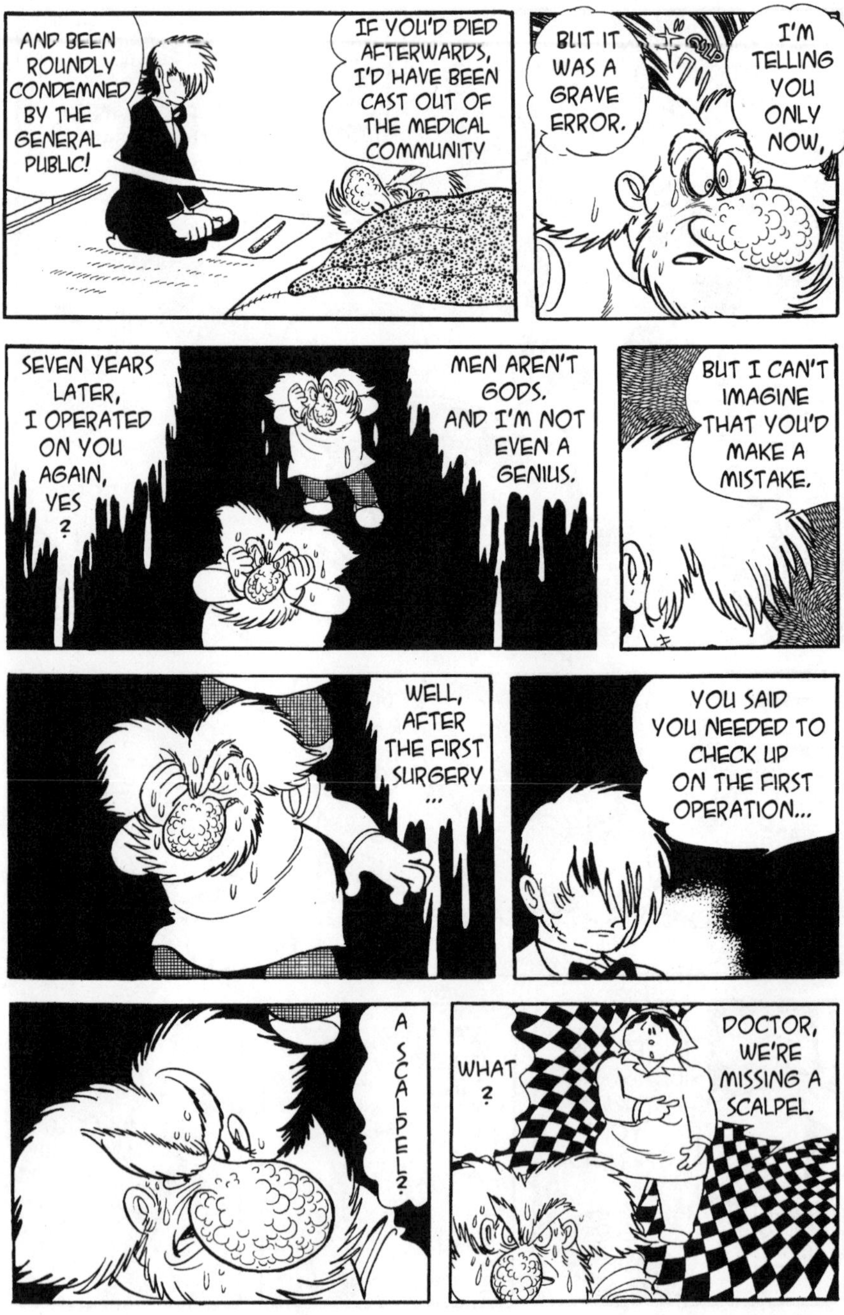
I'M TELLING YOU ONLY NOW,
BUT IT WAS A GRAVE ERROR.
IF YOU'D DIED AFTERWARDS, I'D HAVE BEEN CAST OUT OF THE MEDICAL COMMUNITY
AND BEEN ROUNDLY CONDEMNED BY THE GENERAL PUBLIC!
BUT I CAN'T IMAGINE THAT YOU'D MAKE A MISTAKE.
MEN AREN'T GODS. AND I'M NOT EVEN A GENIUS.
SEVEN YEARS LATER, I OPERATED ON YOU AGAIN, YES?
YOU SAID YOU NEEDED TO CHECK UP ON THE FIRST OPERATION...
WELL, AFTER THE FIRST SURGERY...
DOCTOR, WE'RE MISSING A SCALPEL.
WHAT?
A SCALPEL?

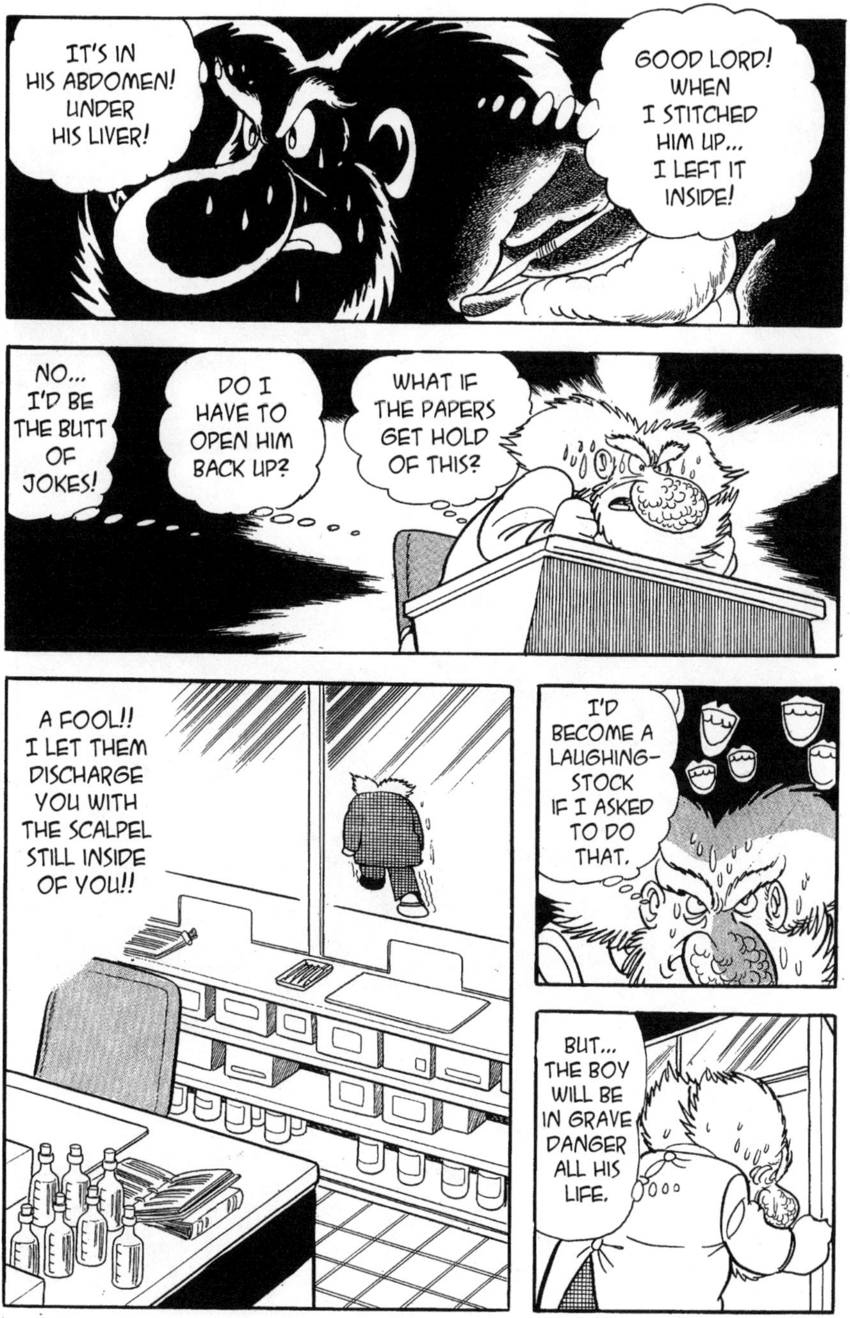
GOOD LORD! WHEN I STITCHED HIM UP... I LEFT IT INSIDE!
IT'S IN HIS ABDOMEN! UNDER HIS LIVER!
WHAT IF THE PAPERS GET HOLD OF THIS?
DO I HAVE TO OPEN HIM BACK UP?
NO... I'D BE THE BUTT OF JOKES!
I'D BECOME A LAUGHING-STOCK IF I ASKED TO DO THAT.
BUT... THE BOY WILL BE IN GRAVE DANGER ALL HIS LIFE.
A FOOL!! I LET THEM DISCHARGE YOU WITH THE SCALPEL STILL INSIDE OF YOU!!

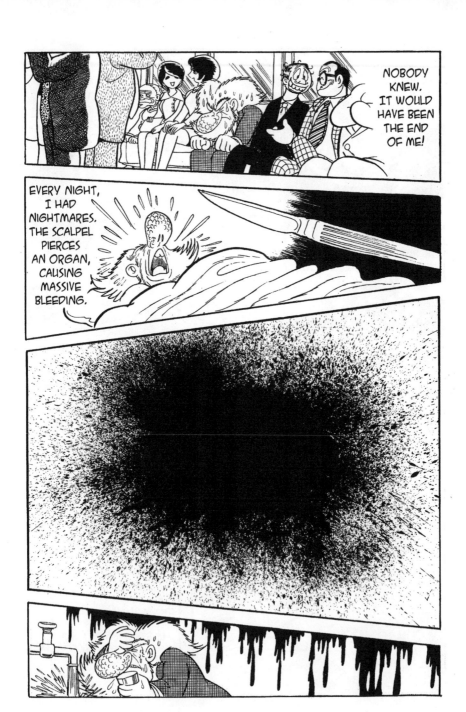

NOBODY KNEW. IT WOULD HAVE BEEN THE END OF ME!

EVERY NIGHT, I HAD NIGHTMARES. THE SCALPEL PIERCES AN ORGAN, CAUSING MASSIVE BLEEDING.

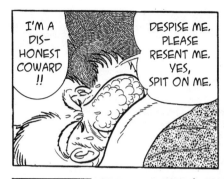

WHEN I FINALLY GOT THE CHANCE TO OPEN YOU UP AND REMOVE THE SCALPEL...
SEVEN WHOLE YEARS HAD PASSED!
DESPISE ME. PLEASE RESENT ME. YES, SPIT ON ME.
I'M A DIS-HONEST COWARD!!
WHY HADN'T THE SCALPEL'S SHARP BLADE PIERCED YOUR LIVER, YOUR STOMACH, OR YOUR INTESTINES FOR SEVEN LONG YEARS?
...I FELT AROUND UNDER YOUR LIVER, AND FELT SOMETHING.
WHAT I EXTRACTED WAS...
A STICK OF STONE!

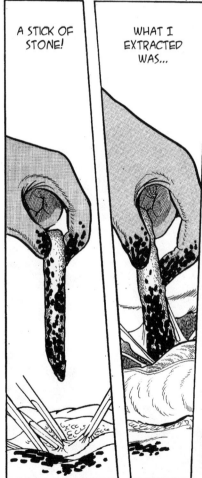

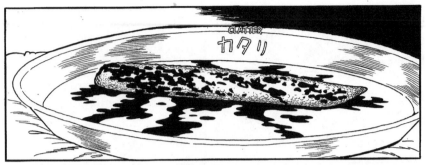

CLATTER
カタリ
SAW SAW
THERE WAS A SCALPEL IN IT!!
ASTONISHING. THE SCALPEL HAD BEEN CAREFULLY SHEATHED IN CALCIUM AND PRESERVED.

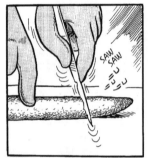

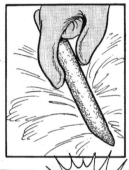

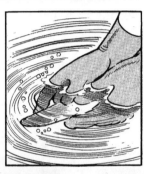

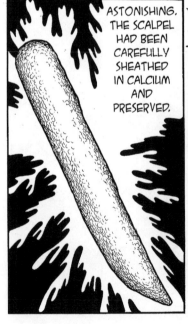

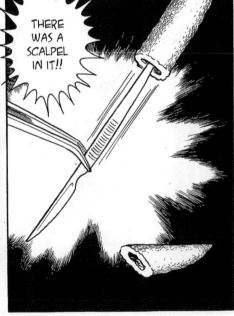

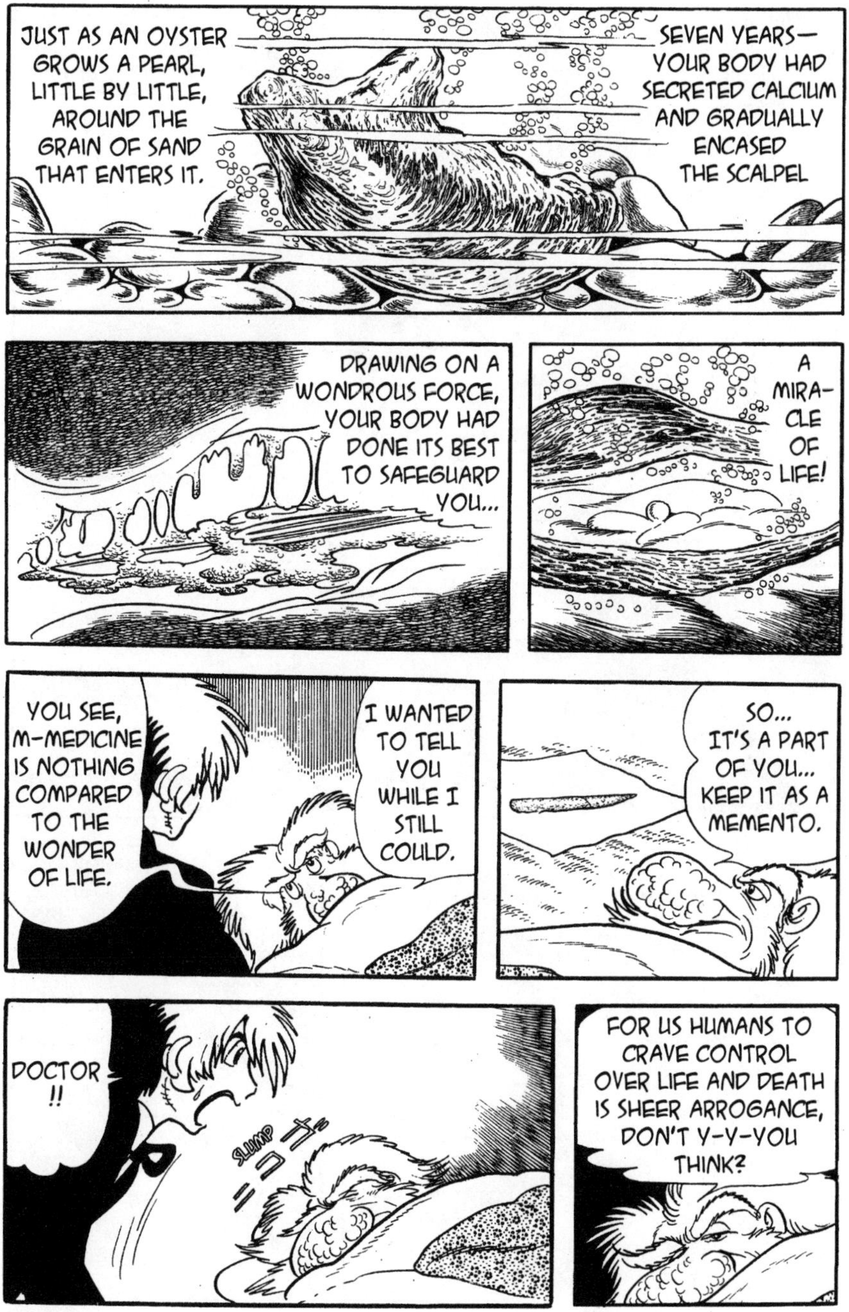
SEVEN YEARS— YOUR BODY HAD SECRETED CALCIUM AND GRADUALLY ENCASED THE SCALPEL
JUST AS AN OYSTER GROWS A PEARL, LITTLE BY LITTLE, AROUND THE GRAIN OF SAND THAT ENTERS IT.
A MIRA-CLE OF LIFE!
DRAWING ON A WONDROUS FORCE, YOUR BODY HAD DONE ITS BEST TO SAFEGUARD YOU...
SO... IT'S A PART OF YOU... KEEP IT AS A MEMENTO.
I WANTED TO TELL YOU WHILE I STILL COULD.
YOU SEE, M-MEDICINE IS NOTHING COMPARED TO THE WONDER OF LIFE.
FOR US HUMANS TO CRAVE CONTROL OVER LIFE AND DEATH IS SHEER ARROGANCE, DON'T Y-Y-YOU THINK?
DOCTOR !!
SLUMP

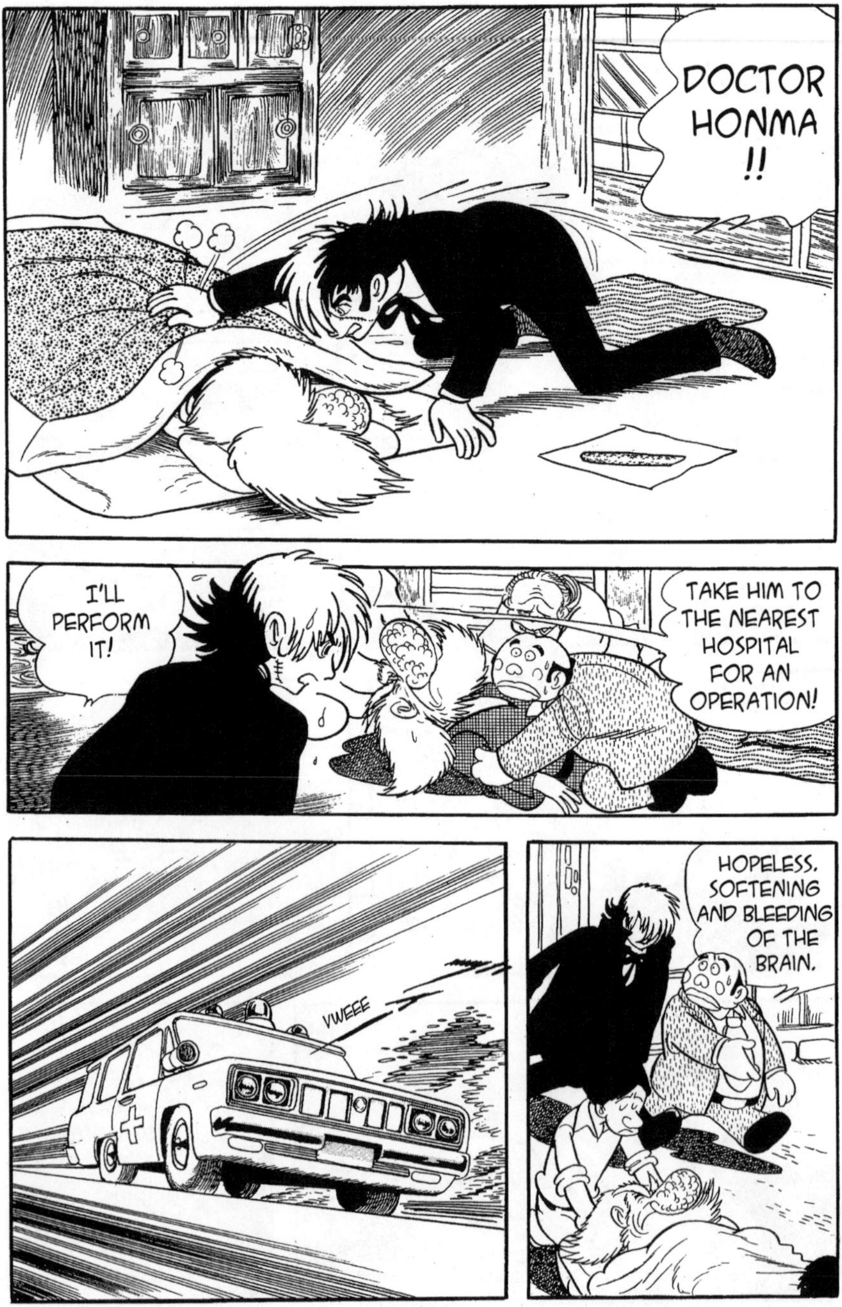
DOCTOR HONMA !!
TAKE HIM TO THE NEAREST HOSPITAL FOR AN OPERATION!
I'LL PERFORM IT!
HOPELESS. SOFTENING AND BLEEDING OF THE BRAIN.
VWEEE

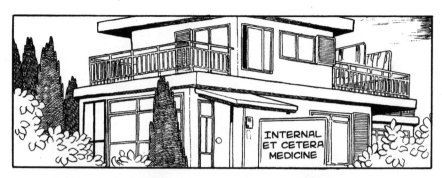

INTERNAL ET CETERA MEDICINE
THIS SURGERY IS FOR A CEREBRAL HEMOR-RHAGE.
HERE AT A COUNTRY CLINIC? WHEN IT'S HARD EVEN AT A BIG TOKYO HOSPITAL?
TREPA-NATION!
KSH KSH
OSCILLO-GRAPH!
NORMAL FOR NOW.

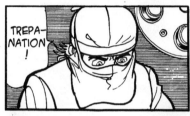

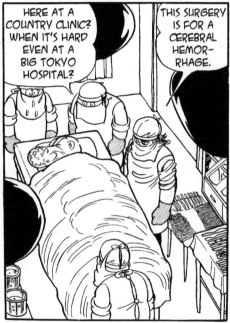

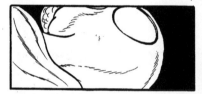

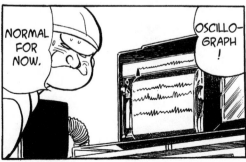

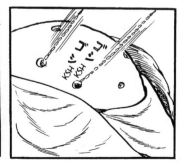

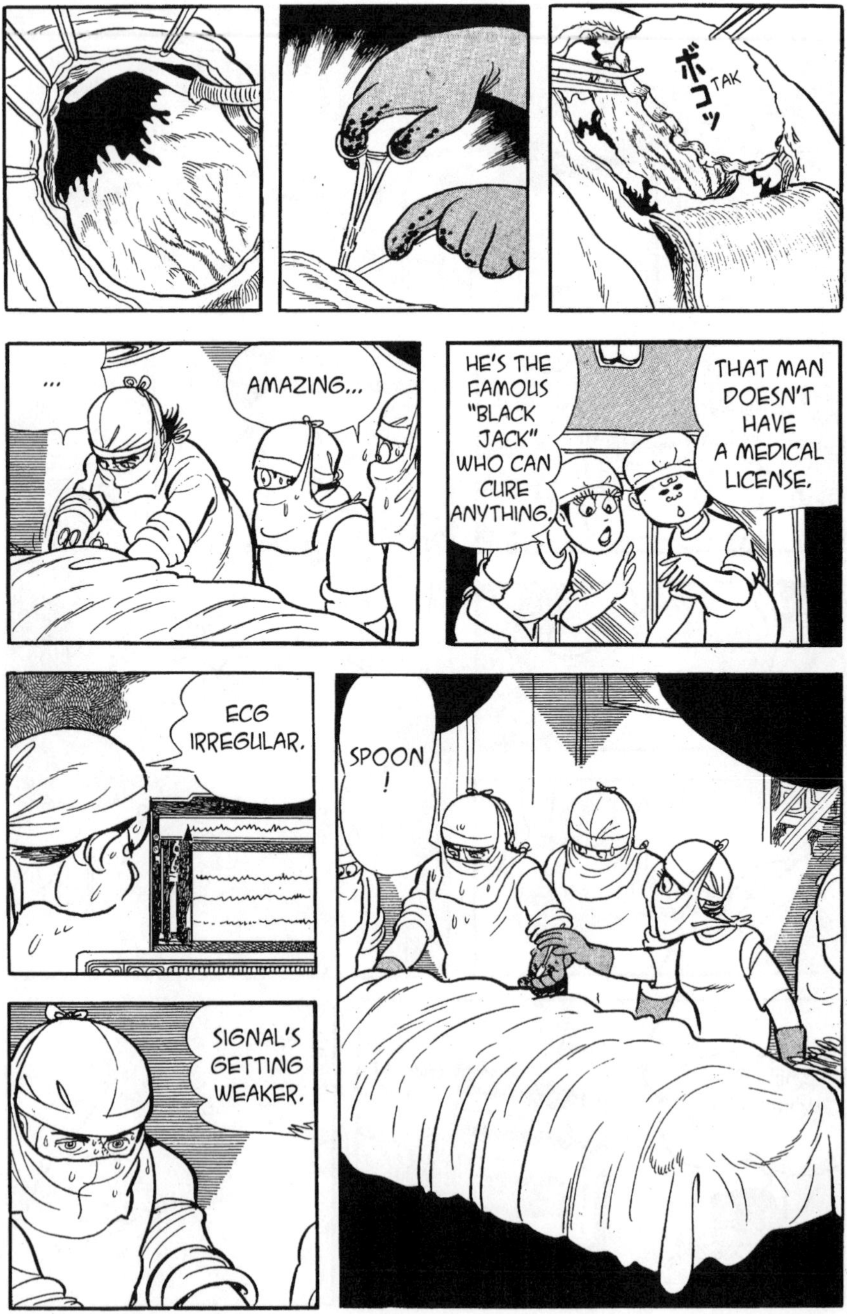
ボコッ
TAK
THAT MAN DOESN'T HAVE A MEDICAL LICENSE.
HE'S THE FAMOUS "BLACK JACK" WHO CAN CURE ANYTHING.
AMAZING...
...
SPOON!
ECG IRREGULAR.
SIGNAL'S GETTING WEAKER.

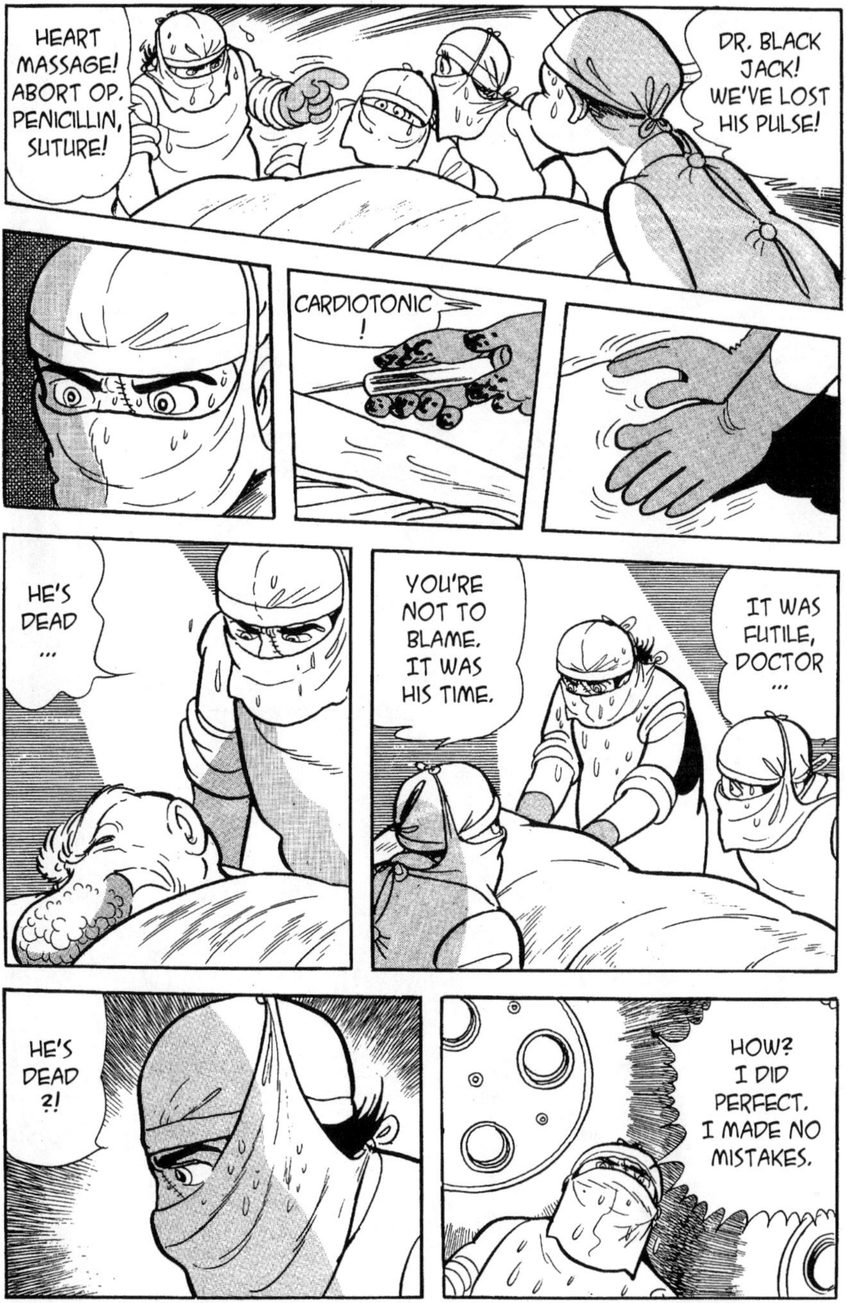
DR. BLACK JACK! WE'VE LOST HIS PULSE!
HEART MASSAGE! ABORT OP. PENICILLIN, SUTURE!
CARDIOTONIC!
IT WAS FUTILE, DOCTOR ...
YOU'RE NOT TO BLAME. IT WAS HIS TIME.
HE'S DEAD ...
HOW? I DID PERFECT. I MADE NO MISTAKES.
HE'S DEAD ?!

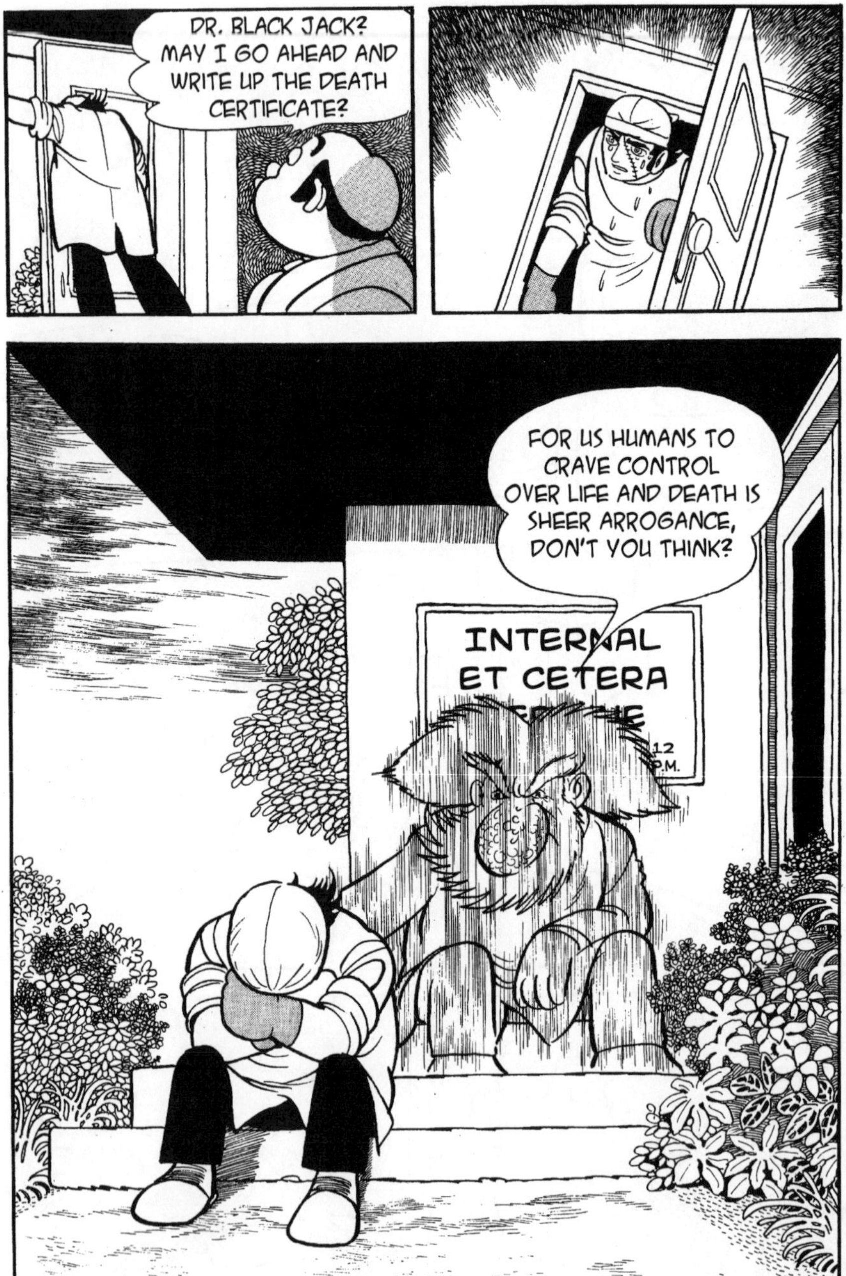
DR. BLACK JACK? MAY I GO AHEAD AND WRITE UP THE DEATH CERTIFICATE?
FOR US HUMANS TO CRAVE CONTROL OVER LIFE AND DEATH IS SHEER ARROGANCE, DON'T YOU THINK?
INTERNAL
ET CETERA

CONFLUENCE

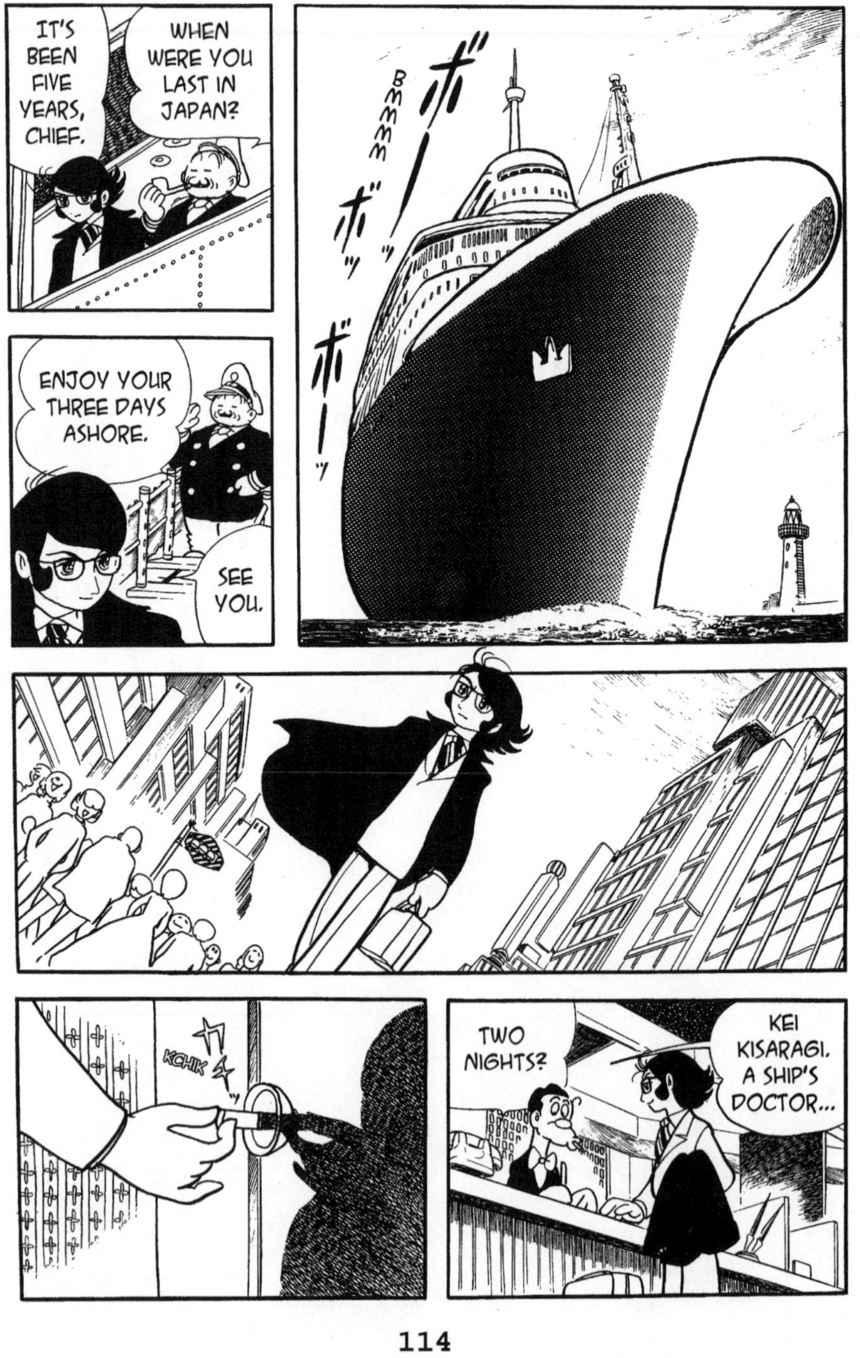
WHEN WERE YOU LAST IN JAPAN?
IT'S BEEN FIVE YEARS, CHIEF.
ENJOY YOUR THREE DAYS ASHORE.
SEE YOU.
KEI KISARAGI. A SHIP'S DOCTOR...
TWO NIGHTS?
KCHIK

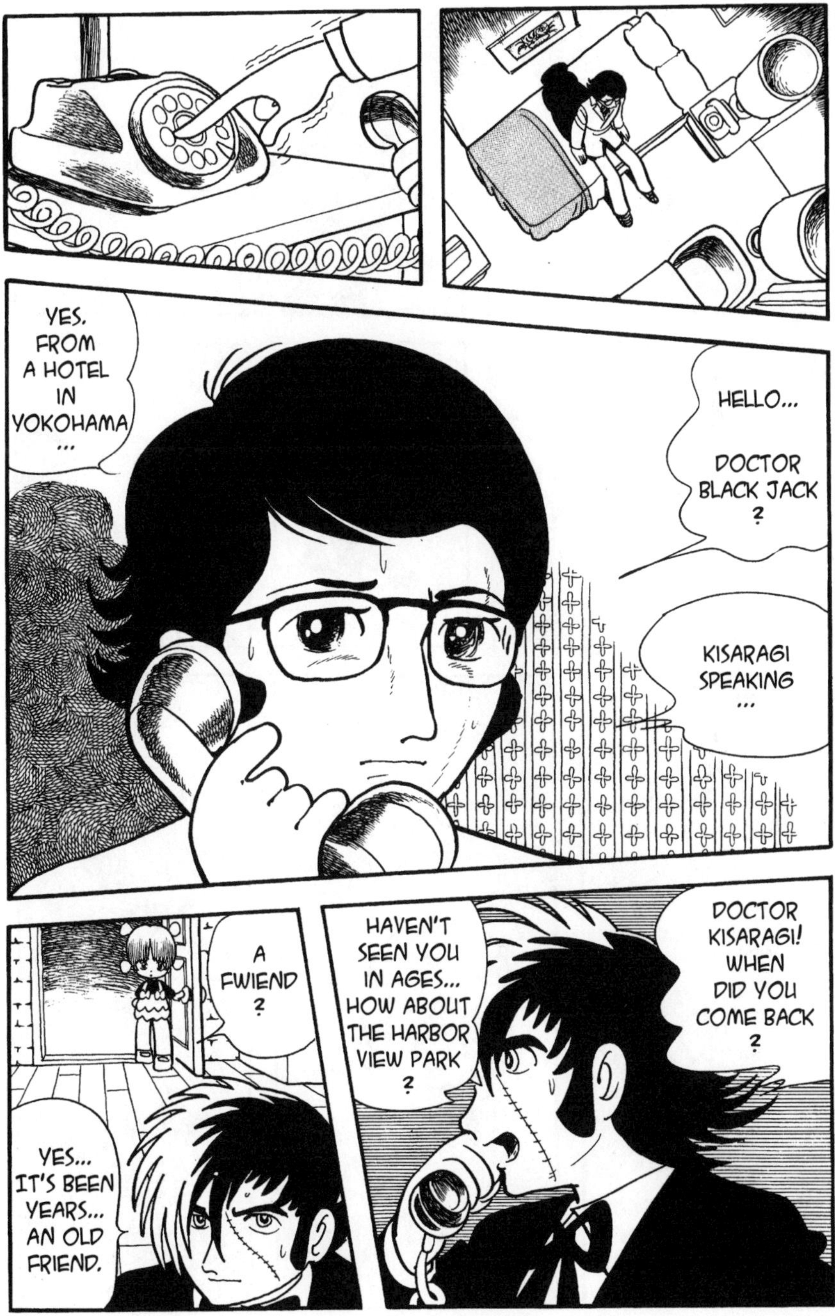
HELLO... DOCTOR BLACK JACK?
KISARAGI SPEAKING...
YES. FROM A HOTEL IN YOKOHAMA...
DOCTOR KISARAGI! WHEN DID YOU COME BACK?
HAVEN'T SEEN YOU IN AGES... HOW ABOUT THE HARBOR VIEW PARK?
A FWIEND?
YES... IT'S BEEN YEARS... AN OLD FRIEND.

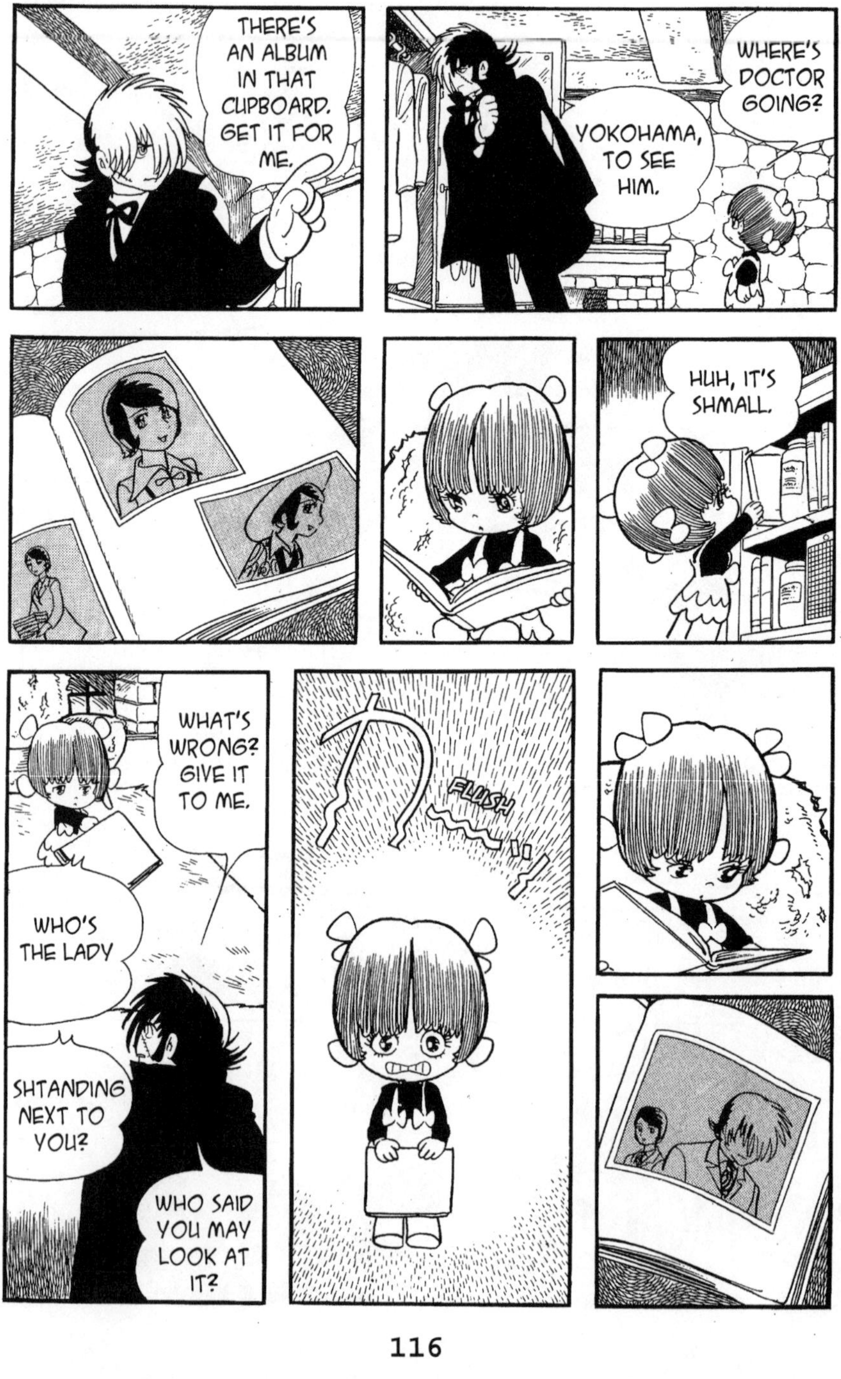
WHERE'S DOCTOR GOING?
YOKOHAMA, TO SEE HIM.
THERE'S AN ALBUM IN THAT CUPBOARD. GET IT FOR ME.
HUH, IT'S SHMALL.
FLUSH
WHAT'S WRONG? GIVE IT TO ME.
WHO'S THE LADY
SHTANDING NEXT TO YOU?
WHO SAID YOU MAY LOOK AT IT?

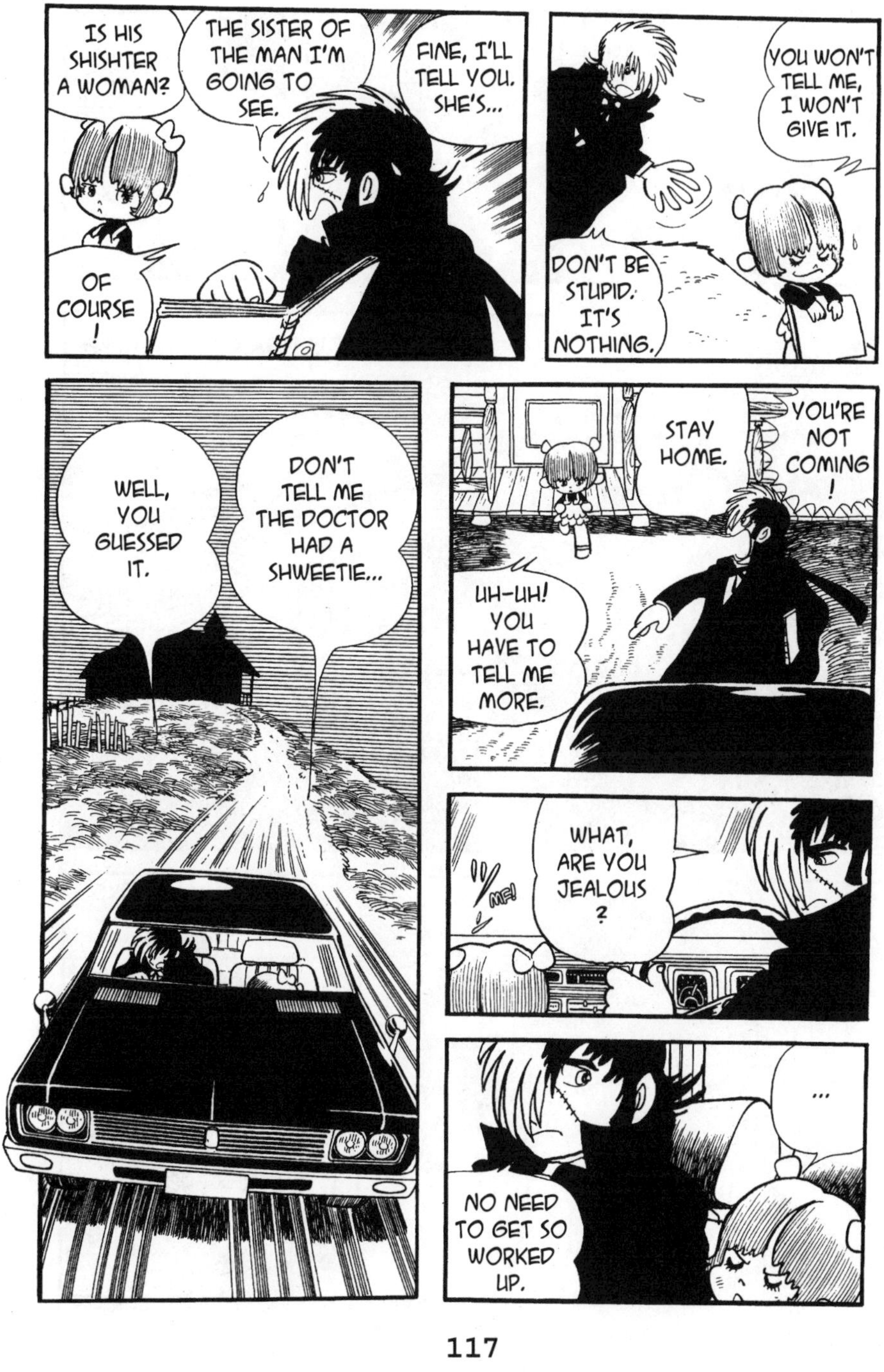
YOU WON'T TELL ME, I WON'T GIVE IT.
DON'T BE STUPID. IT'S NOTHING.
FINE, I'LL TELL YOU. SHE'S...
THE SISTER OF THE MAN I'M GOING TO SEE.
IS HIS SHISHTER A WOMAN?
OF COURSE!
YOU'RE NOT COMING!
STAY HOME.
UH-UH! YOU HAVE TO TELL ME MORE.
WHAT, ARE YOU JEALOUS?
MF!
...
NO NEED TO GET SO WORKED UP.
DON'T TELL ME THE DOCTOR HAD A SHWEETIE...
WELL, YOU GUESSED IT.

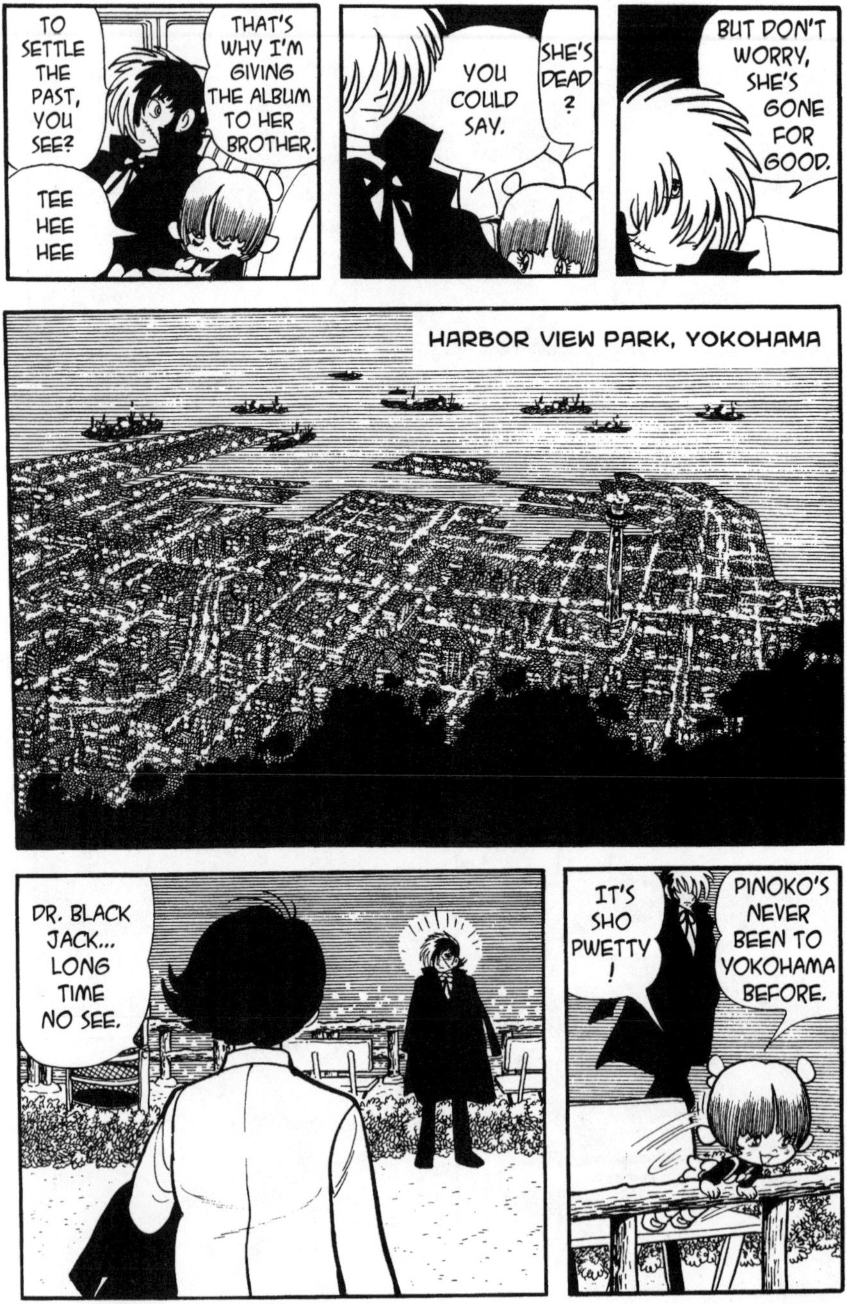
THAT'S WHY I'M GIVING THE ALBUM TO HER BROTHER.
TO SETTLE THE PAST, YOU SEE?
TEE HEE HEE
SHE'S DEAD?
YOU COULD SAY.
BUT DON'T WORRY, SHE'S GONE FOR GOOD.
HARBOR VIEW PARK, YOKOHAMA
DR. BLACK JACK... LONG TIME NO SEE.
IT'S SHO PWETTY!
PINOKO'S NEVER BEEN TO YOKOHAMA BEFORE.

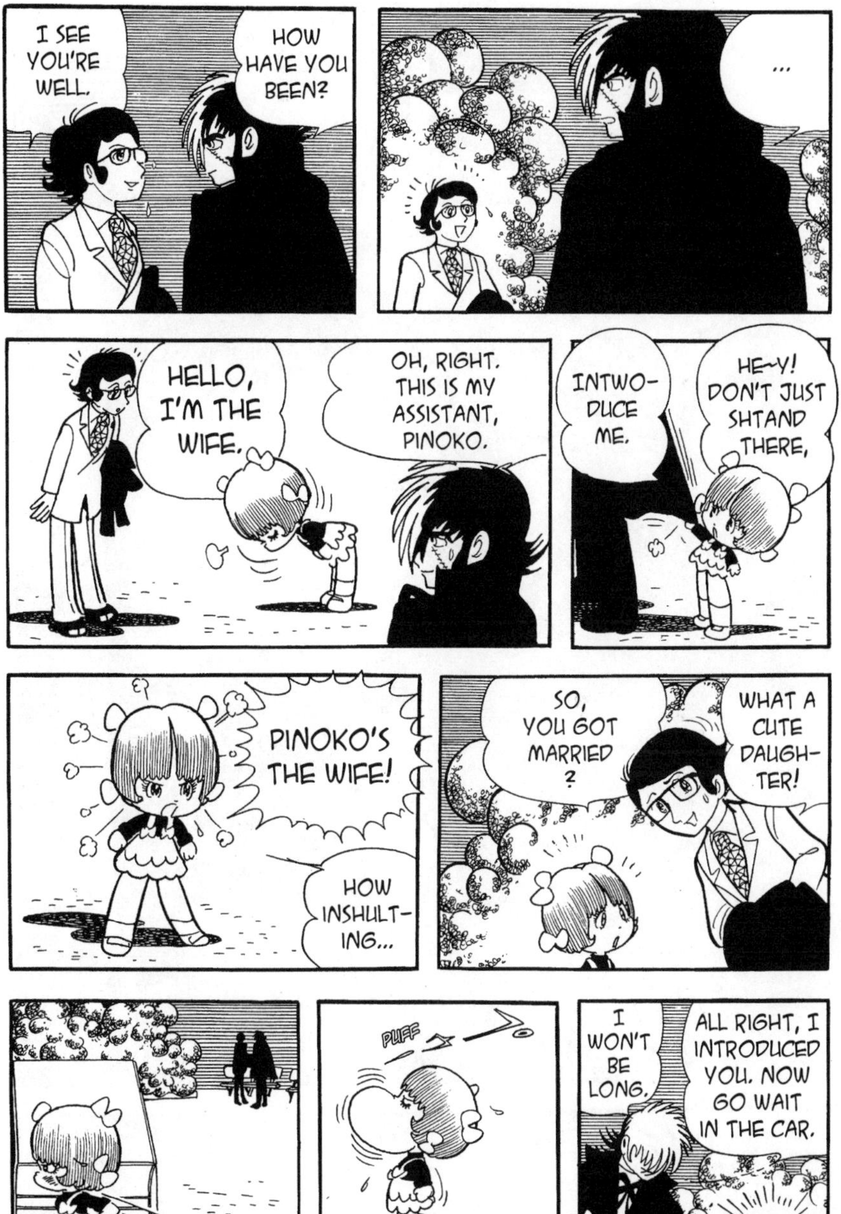
...
HOW HAVE YOU BEEN?
I SEE YOU'RE WELL.
HE~Y! DON'T JUST SHTAND THERE,
INTWODUCE ME.
OH, RIGHT. THIS IS MY ASSISTANT, PINOKO.
HELLO, I'M THE WIFE.
WHAT A CUTE DAUGHTER!
SO, YOU GOT MARRIED?
PINOKO'S THE WIFE!
HOW INSHULTING...
ALL RIGHT, I INTRODUCED YOU. NOW GO WAIT IN THE CAR.
I WON'T BE LONG.
PUFF

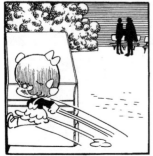

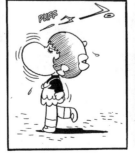

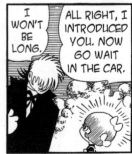

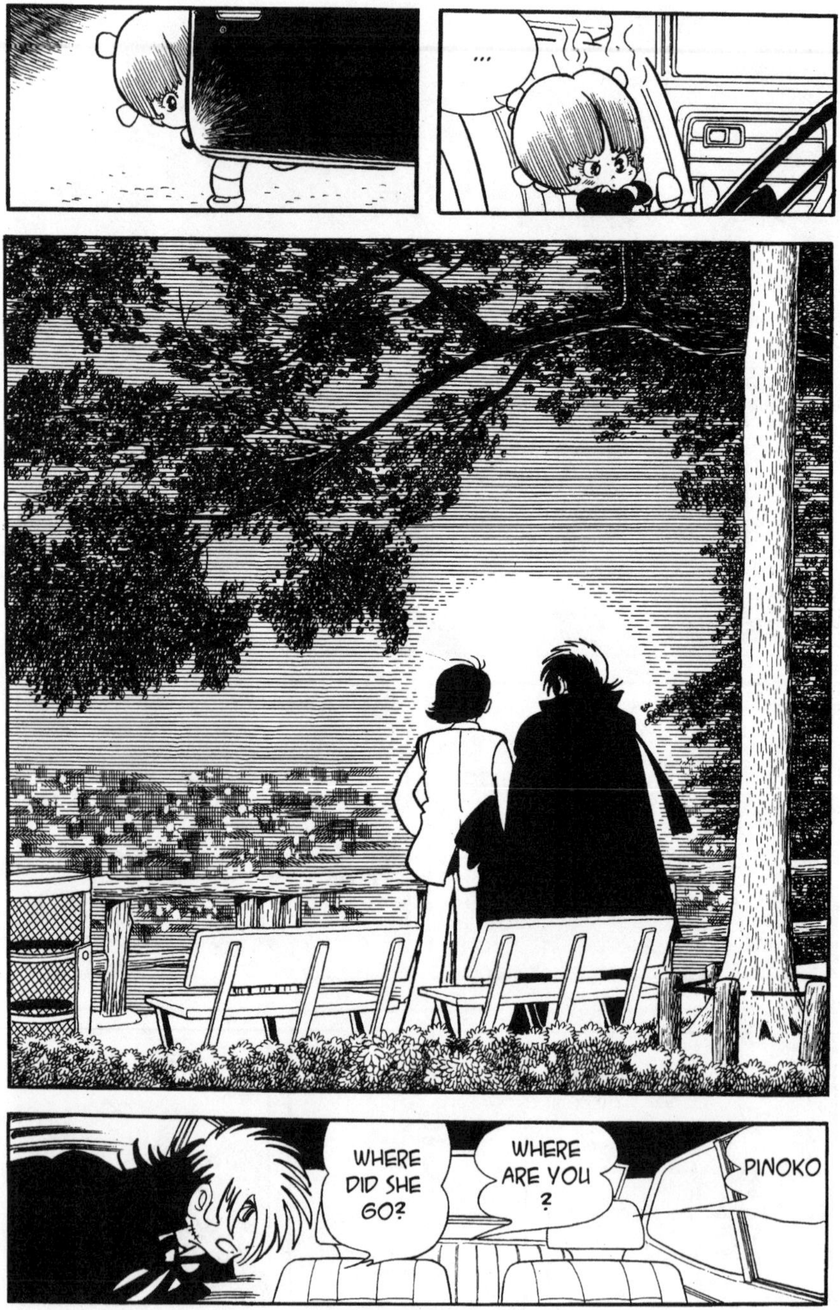
...
PINOKO
WHERE ARE YOU ?
WHERE DID SHE GO?

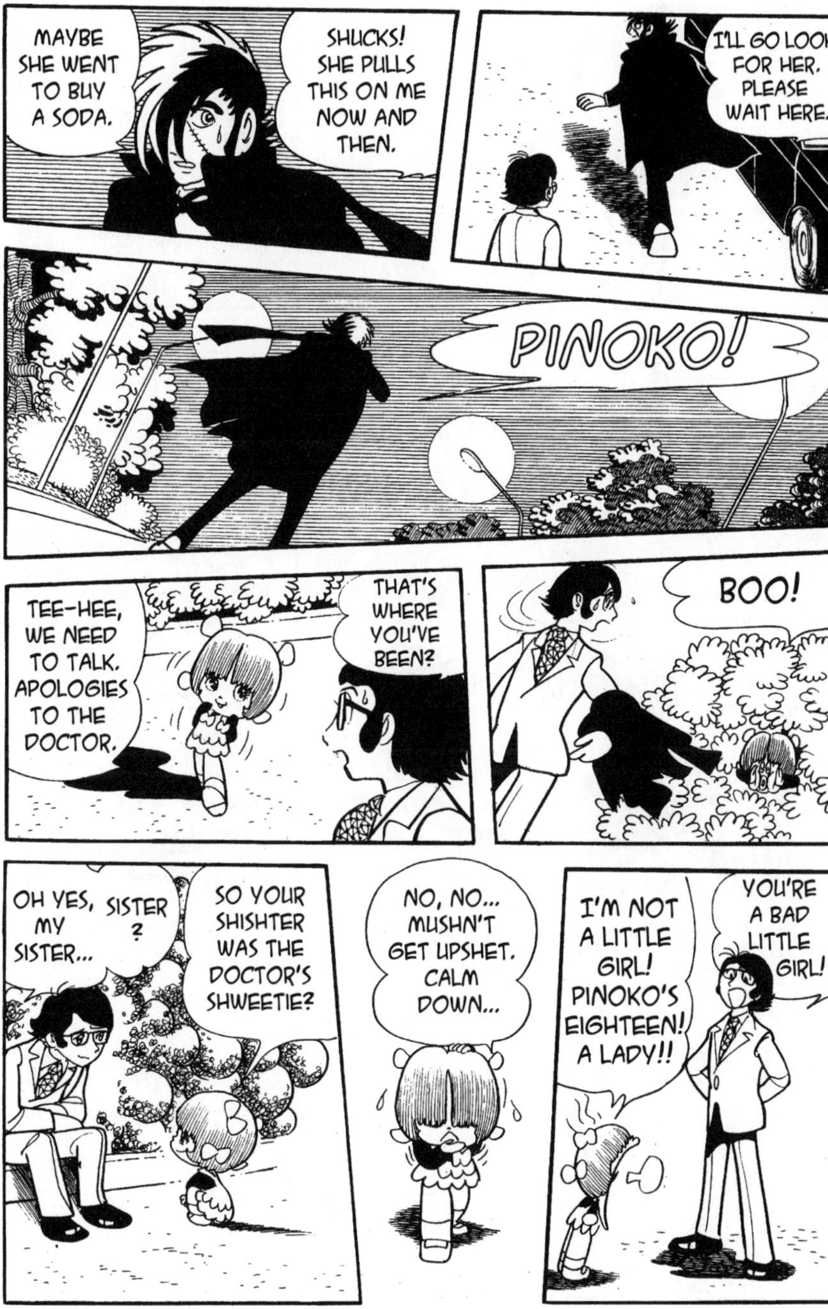
I'LL GO LOOK FOR HER. PLEASE WAIT HERE.
SHUCKS! SHE PULLS THIS ON ME NOW AND THEN.
MAYBE SHE WENT TO BUY A SODA.
PINOKO!
BOO!
THAT'S WHERE YOU'VE BEEN?
TEE-HEE, WE NEED TO TALK. APOLOGIES TO THE DOCTOR.
YOU'RE A BAD LITTLE GIRL!
I'M NOT A LITTLE GIRL! PINOKO'S EIGHTEEN! A LADY!!
NO, NO... MUSHN'T GET UPSHET. CALM DOWN...
SO YOUR SHISHTER WAS THE DOCTOR'S SHWEETIE?
SISTER?
OH YES, MY SISTER...

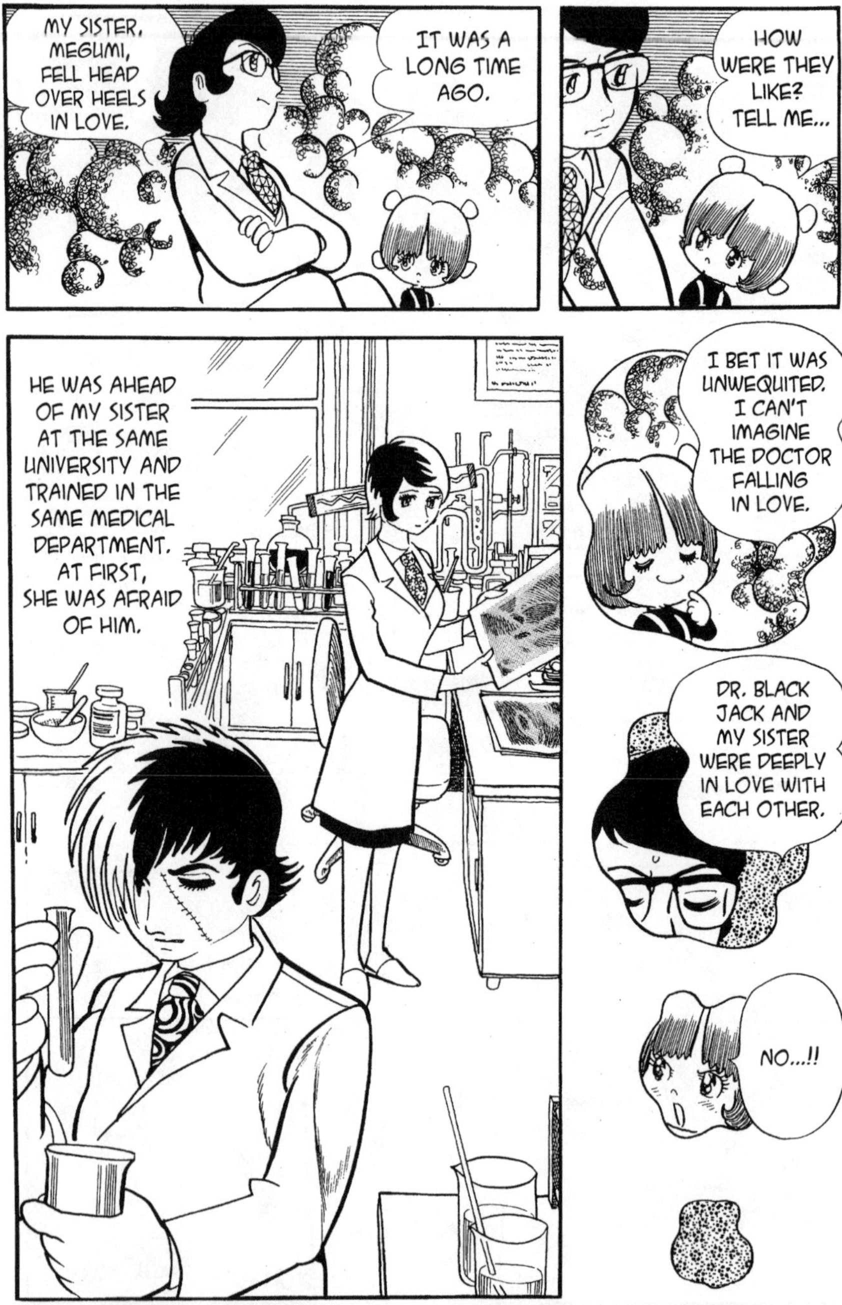
HOW WERE THEY LIKE? TELL ME...
IT WAS A LONG TIME AGO.
MY SISTER, MEGUMI, FELL HEAD OVER HEELS IN LOVE.
I BET IT WAS UNWEQUITED. I CAN'T IMAGINE THE DOCTOR FALLING IN LOVE.
DR. BLACK JACK AND MY SISTER WERE DEEPLY IN LOVE WITH EACH OTHER.
NO...!!
HE WAS AHEAD OF MY SISTER AT THE SAME UNIVERSITY AND TRAINED IN THE SAME MEDICAL DEPARTMENT. AT FIRST, SHE WAS AFRAID OF HIM.

NOTE: A "MEDICAL DEPARTMENT" IN THE JAPANESE UNIVERSITY HOSPITAL SYSTEM IS HEADED BY A CHAIR AND INCLUDES PROFESSORS, MEDICAL STAFF AND GRADUATE STUDENTS IN DESCENDING ORDER OF RANK.

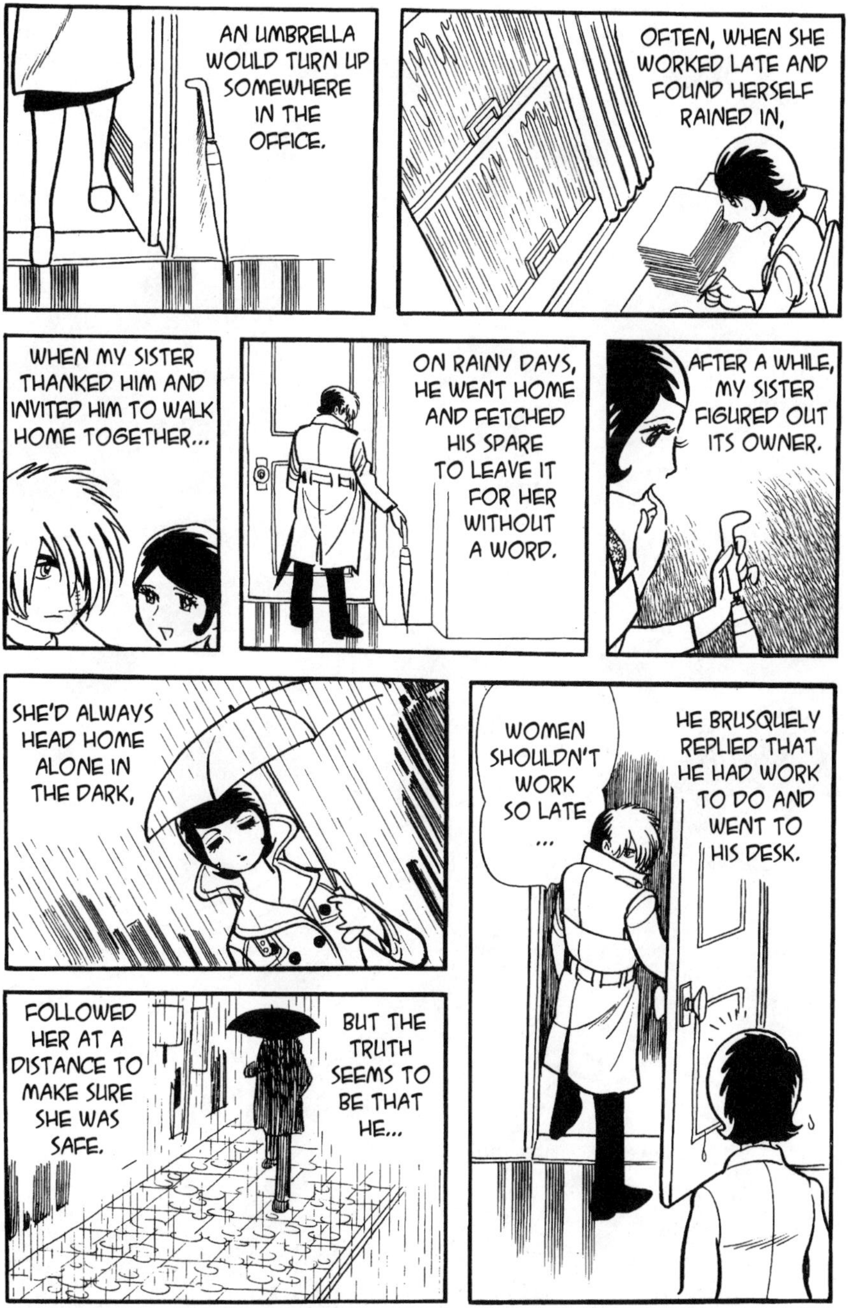
OFTEN, WHEN SHE WORKED LATE AND FOUND HERSELF RAINED IN,
AN UMBRELLA WOULD TURN UP SOMEWHERE IN THE OFFICE.
AFTER A WHILE, MY SISTER FIGURED OUT ITS OWNER.
ON RAINY DAYS, HE WENT HOME AND FETCHED HIS SPARE TO LEAVE IT FOR HER WITHOUT A WORD.
WHEN MY SISTER THANKED HIM AND INVITED HIM TO WALK HOME TOGETHER...
HE BRUSQUELY REPLIED THAT HE HAD WORK TO DO AND WENT TO HIS DESK.
WOMEN SHOULDN'T WORK SO LATE ...
SHE'D ALWAYS HEAD HOME ALONE IN THE DARK,
BUT THE TRUTH SEEMS TO BE THAT HE...
FOLLOWED HER AT A DISTANCE TO MAKE SURE SHE WAS SAFE.

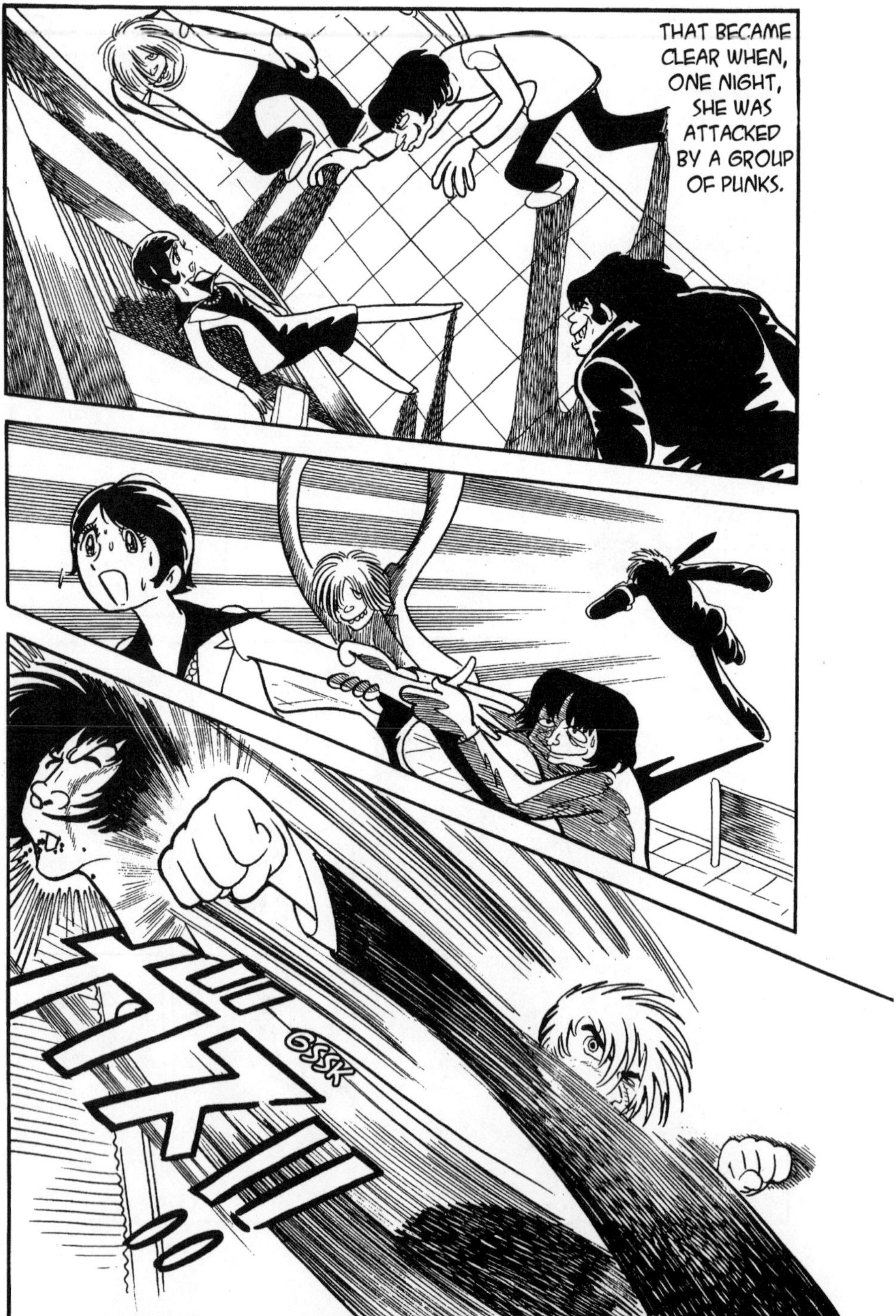
THAT BECAME CLEAR WHEN, ONE NIGHT, SHE WAS ATTACKED BY A GROUP OF PUNKS.
GSSK

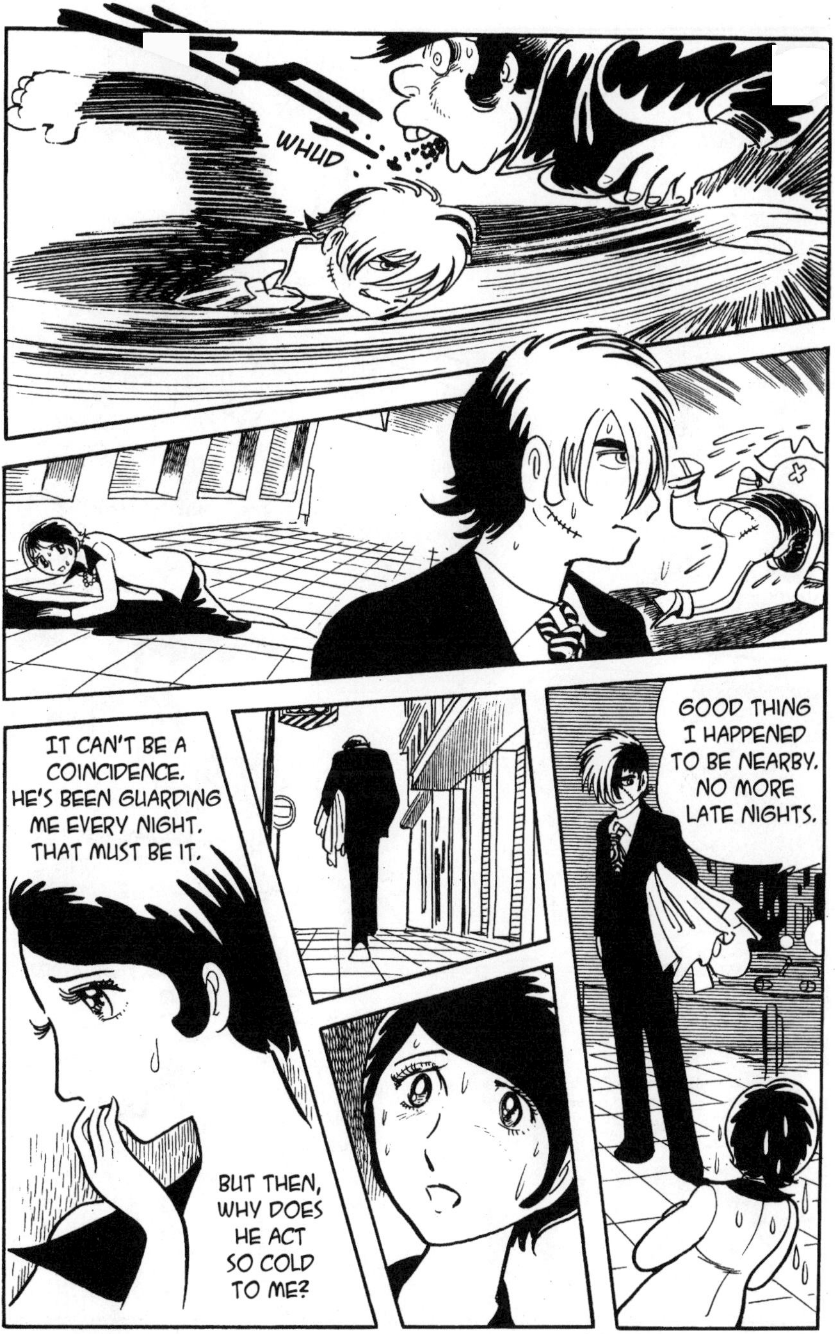
WHUD
GOOD THING I HAPPENED TO BE NEARBY. NO MORE LATE NIGHTS.
IT CAN'T BE A COINCIDENCE. HE'S BEEN GUARDING ME EVERY NIGHT. THAT MUST BE IT.
BUT THEN, WHY DOES HE ACT SO COLD TO ME?

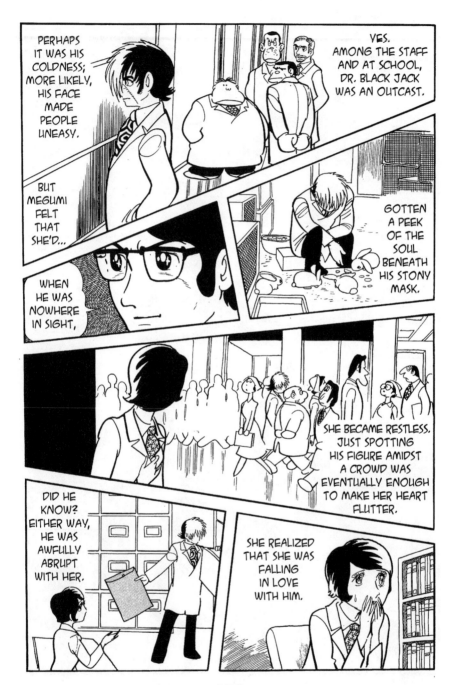

YES. AMONG THE STAFF AND AT SCHOOL, DR. BLACK JACK WAS AN OUTCAST.
PERHAPS IT WAS HIS COLDNESS; MORE LIKELY, HIS FACE MADE PEOPLE UNEASY.
BUT MEGUMI FELT THAT SHE'D...
GOTTEN A PEEK OF THE SOUL BENEATH HIS STONY MASK.
WHEN HE WAS NOWHERE IN SIGHT,
SHE BECAME RESTLESS. JUST SPOTTING HIS FIGURE AMIDST A CROWD WAS EVENTUALLY ENOUGH TO MAKE HER HEART FLUTTER.
SHE REALIZED THAT SHE WAS FALLING IN LOVE WITH HIM.
DID HE KNOW? EITHER WAY, HE WAS AWFULLY ABRUPT WITH HER.

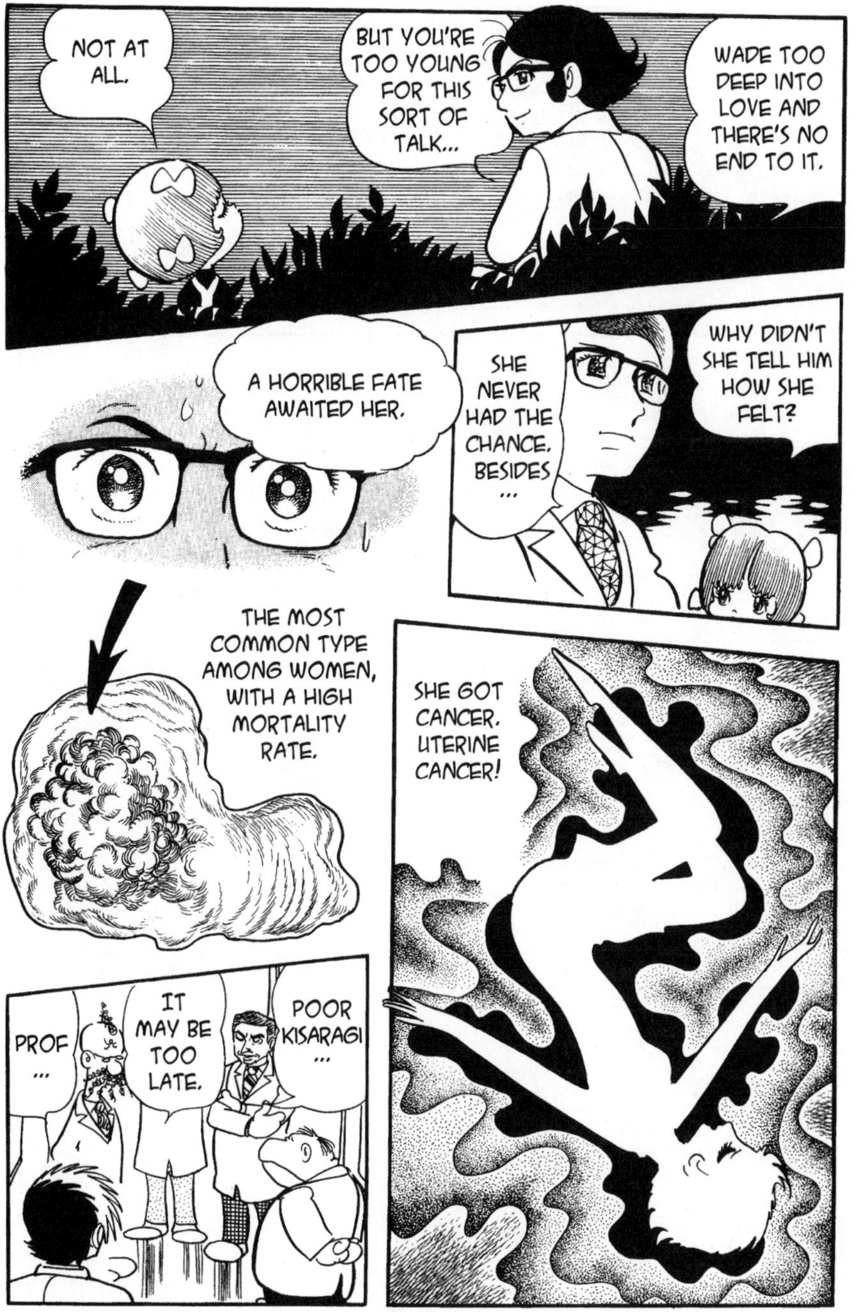
WADE TOO DEEP INTO LOVE AND THERE'S NO END TO IT.
BUT YOU'RE TOO YOUNG FOR THIS SORT OF TALK...
NOT AT ALL.
WHY DIDN'T SHE TELL HIM HOW SHE FELT?
SHE NEVER HAD THE CHANCE. BESIDES ...
A HORRIBLE FATE AWAITED HER.
SHE GOT CANCER. UTERINE CANCER!
THE MOST COMMON TYPE AMONG WOMEN, WITH A HIGH MORTALITY RATE.
POOR KISARAGI ...
IT MAY BE TOO LATE.
PROF ...

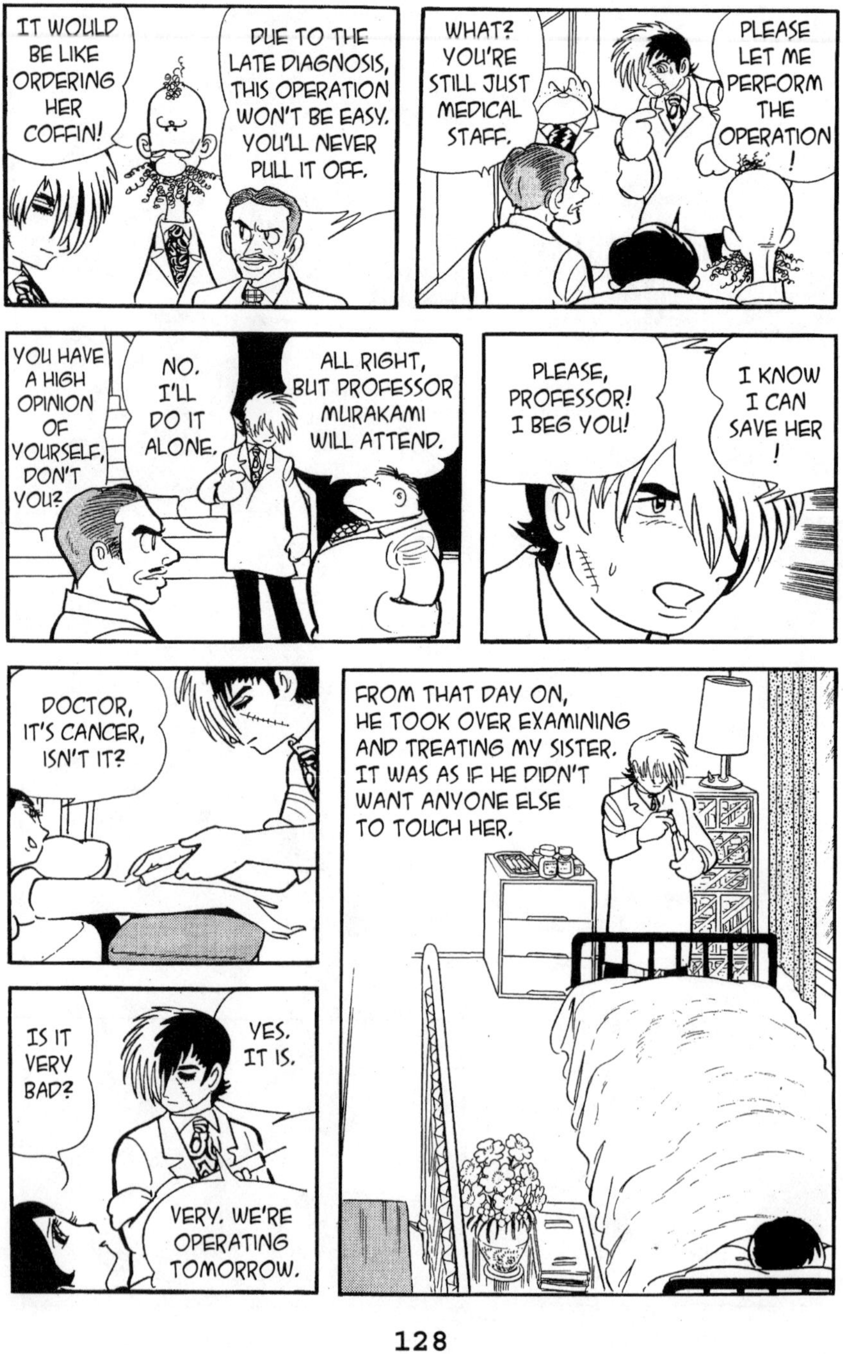
PLEASE LET ME PERFORM THE OPERATION!
WHAT? YOU'RE STILL JUST MEDICAL STAFF.
DUE TO THE LATE DIAGNOSIS, THIS OPERATION WON'T BE EASY. YOU'LL NEVER PULL IT OFF.
IT WOULD BE LIKE ORDERING HER COFFIN!
I KNOW I CAN SAVE HER!
PLEASE, PROFESSOR! I BEG YOU!
ALL RIGHT, BUT PROFESSOR MURAKAMI WILL ATTEND.
NO. I'LL DO IT ALONE.
YOU HAVE A HIGH OPINION OF YOURSELF, DON'T YOU?
FROM THAT DAY ON, HE TOOK OVER EXAMINING AND TREATING MY SISTER. IT WAS AS IF HE DIDN'T WANT ANYONE ELSE TO TOUCH HER.
DOCTOR, IT'S CANCER, ISN'T IT?
YES. IT IS.
IS IT VERY BAD?
VERY. WE'RE OPERATING TOMORROW.

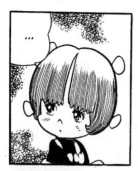

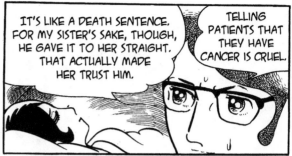

TELLING PATIENTS THAT THEY HAVE CANCER IS CRUEL.
IT'S LIKE A DEATH SENTENCE. FOR MY SISTER'S SAKE, THOUGH, HE GAVE IT TO HER STRAIGHT. THAT ACTUALLY MADE HER TRUST HIM.
...
I'LL BE REMOVING YOUR UTERUS, AND YOUR OVARIES—
IN OTHER WORDS, YOUR FEMALE ORGANS, ENTIRELY.
AS YOU KNOW, THE UTERUS AND OVARIES SECRETE CRUCIAL HORMONES THAT DEFINE A WOMAN'S SEX. TO HAVE THEM REMOVED IS TO QUIT BEING A WOMAN. YOU WON'T BE ABLE TO BEAR CHILDREN, OF COURSE, AND YOU'LL BECOME UNFEMININE.
uterus (baby room)
ovary (egg room)
fallopian tube (egg entrance)
STILL WANT TO GO AHEAD?
IN EXCHANGE, I PROMISE TO SAVE YOUR LIFE!

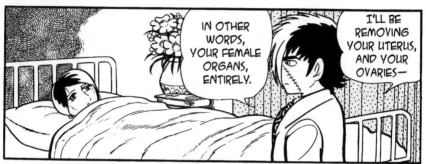

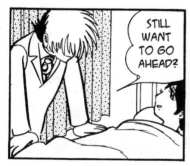

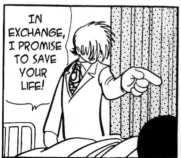

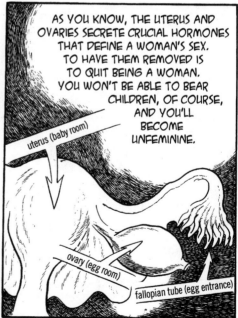

NOTE: INFORMED CONSENT WAS VIRTUALLY NONEXISTENT IN JAPAN ESPECIALLY WITH CANCER. THE TRUTH WAS USUALLY CONCEALED FROM THE PATIENT BUT SHARED WITH THE CLOSEST FAMILY MEMBER.

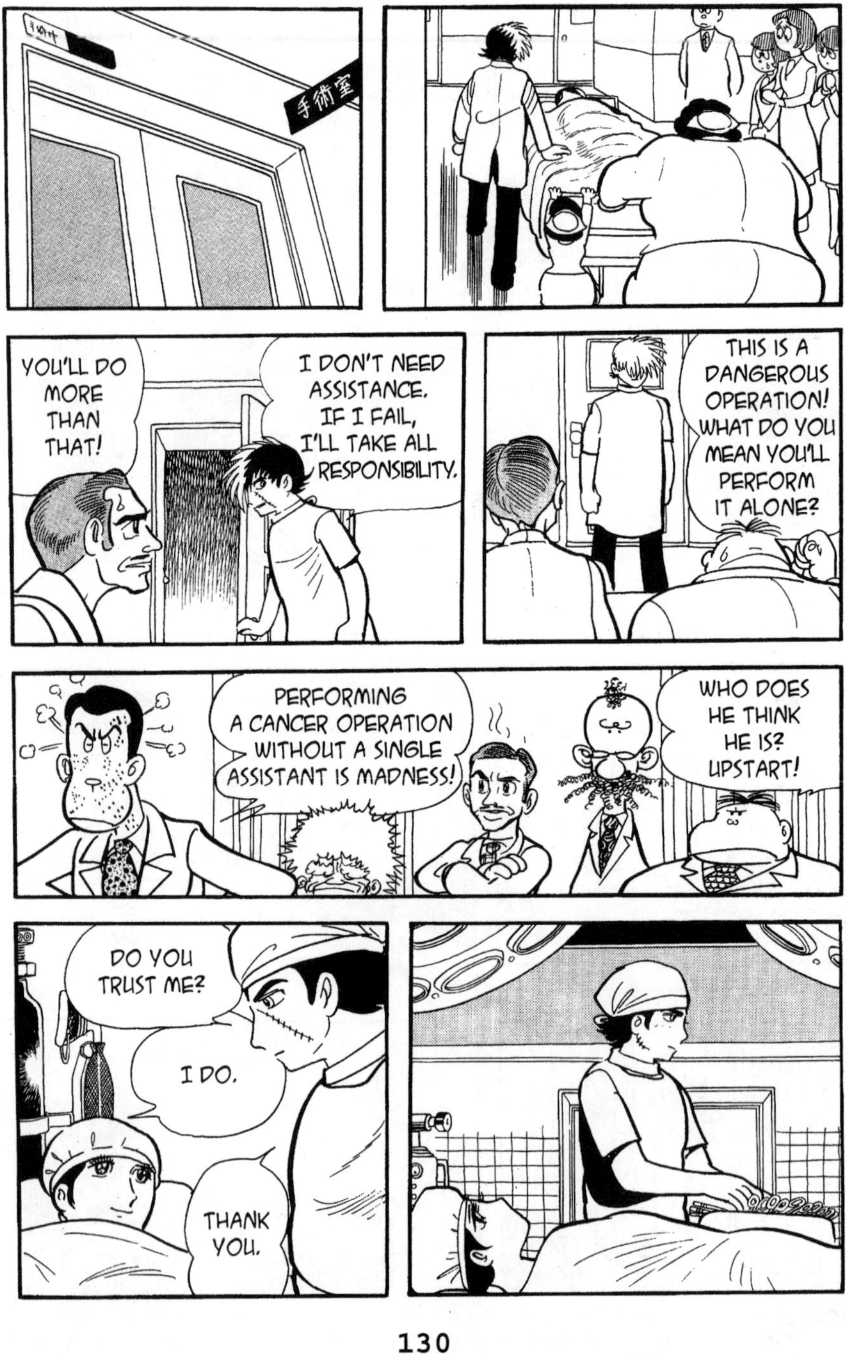

手術室
THIS IS A DANGEROUS OPERATION! WHAT DO YOU MEAN YOU'LL PERFORM IT ALONE?
I DON'T NEED ASSISTANCE. IF I FAIL, I'LL TAKE ALL RESPONSIBILITY.
YOU'LL DO MORE THAN THAT!
WHO DOES HE THINK HE IS? UPSTART!
PERFORMING A CANCER OPERATION WITHOUT A SINGLE ASSISTANT IS MADNESS!
DO YOU TRUST ME?
I DO.
THANK YOU.

I'LL SAY THIS WHILE YOU'RE STILL A WOMAN.
MEGUMI. I LOVE YOU. WITH ALL MY HEART!
I THOUGHT YOU'D NEVER SAY IT... I'M SO GLAD!
I JUST COULDN'T ...
KISS ME, DOCTOR !
AND THAT'S ALL...
WHEN THE SURGERY'S OVER, THIS FEELING MUST BE GONE, TOO...
NO. THIS MOMENT ...
IS ETERNAL !

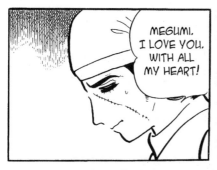

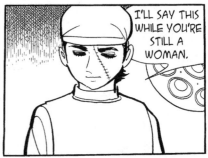

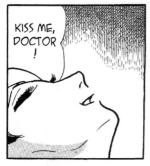

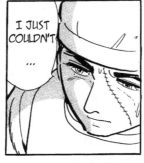

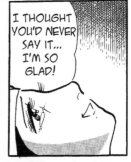

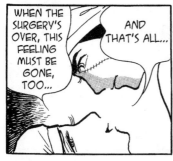

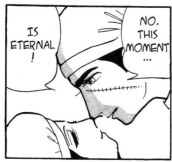

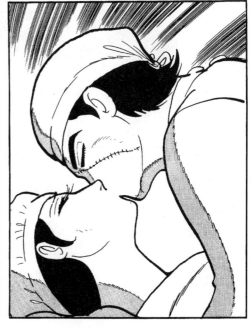

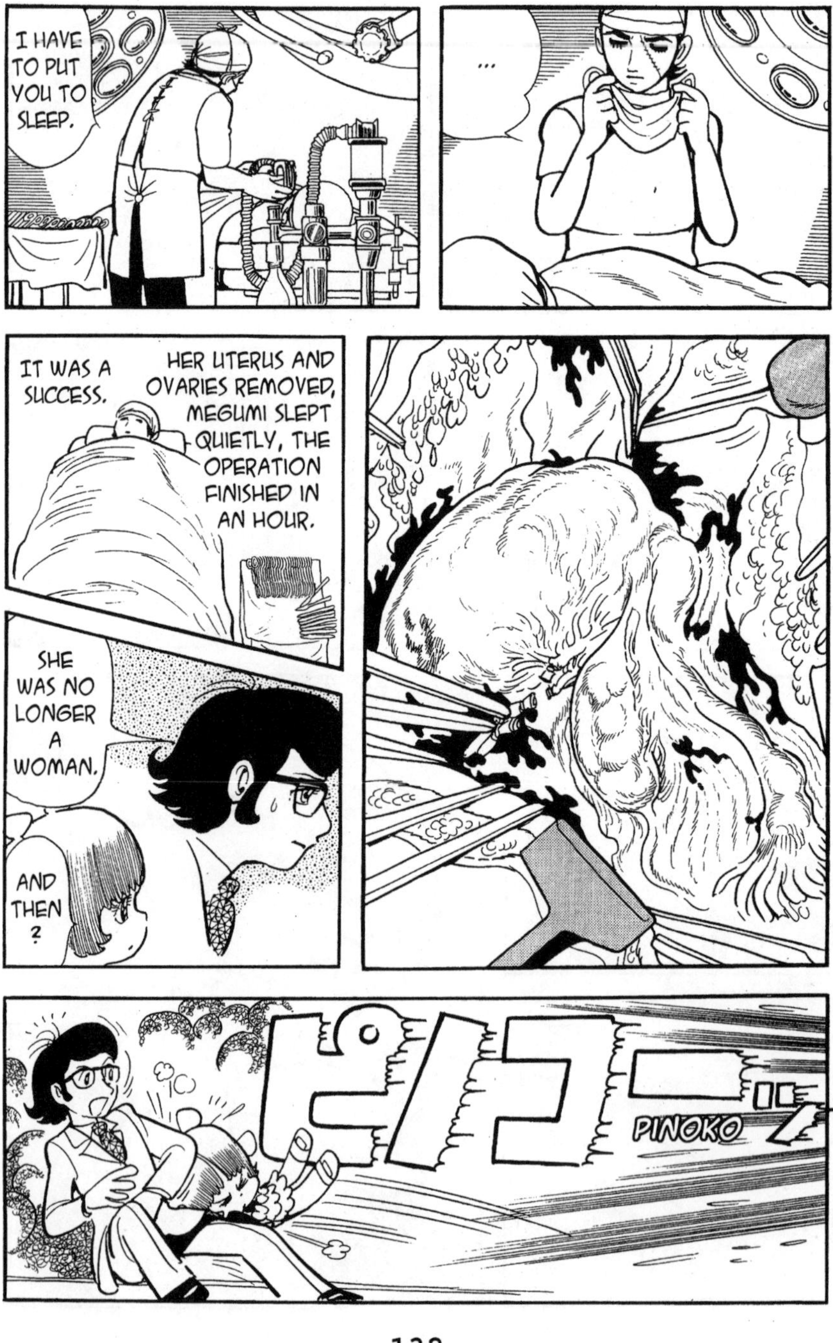
...
I HAVE TO PUT YOU TO SLEEP.
HER UTERUS AND OVARIES REMOVED, MEGUMI SLEPT QUIETLY, THE OPERATION FINISHED IN AN HOUR.
IT WAS A SUCCESS.
SHE WAS NO LONGER A WOMAN.
AND THEN ?
ピノコー
PINOKO

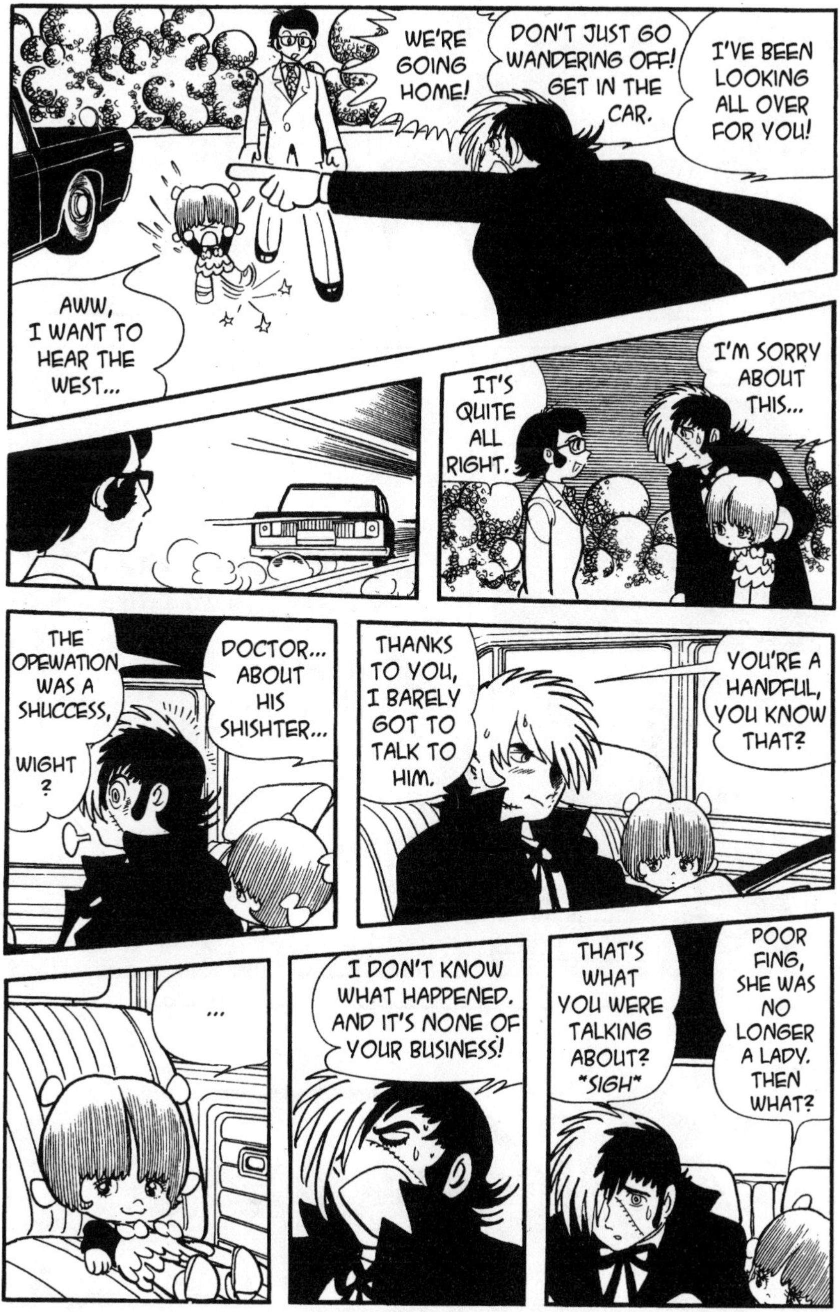
I'VE BEEN LOOKING ALL OVER FOR YOU!
DON'T JUST GO WANDERING OFF! GET IN THE CAR.
WE'RE GOING HOME!
AWW, I WANT TO HEAR THE WEST...
I'M SORRY ABOUT THIS...
IT'S QUITE ALL RIGHT.
YOU'RE A HANDFUL, YOU KNOW THAT?
THANKS TO YOU, I BARELY GOT TO TALK TO HIM.
DOCTOR... ABOUT HIS SHISHTER...
THE OPEWATION WAS A SHUCCESS, WIGHT?
POOR FING, SHE WAS NO LONGER A LADY. THEN WHAT?
THAT'S WHAT YOU WERE TALKING ABOUT? *SIGH*
I DON'T KNOW WHAT HAPPENED. AND IT'S NONE OF YOUR BUSINESS!
...

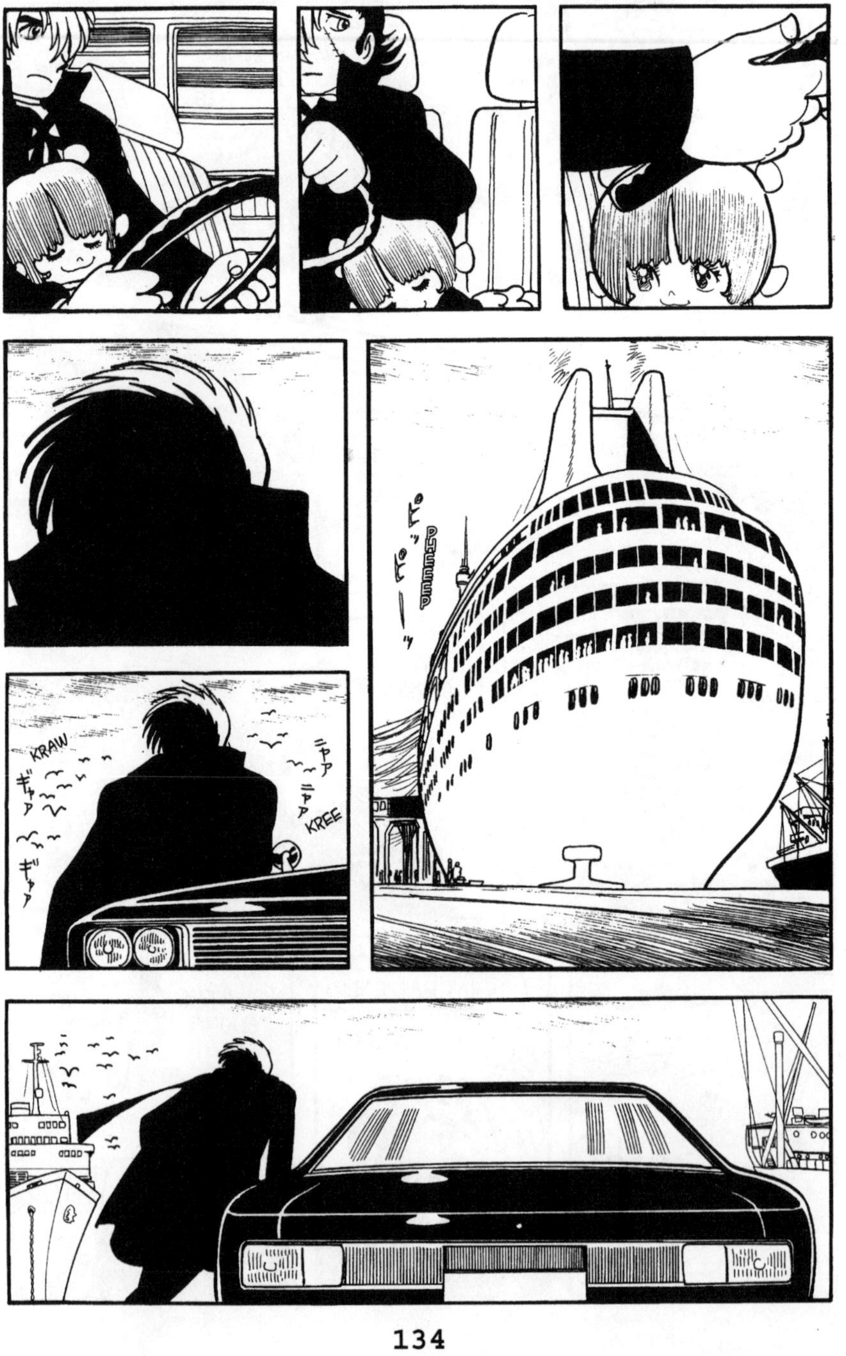
ポッポーッ
PHEEEEP
ニャア
ニャア
KREE
KRAW
ギャア
ギャア

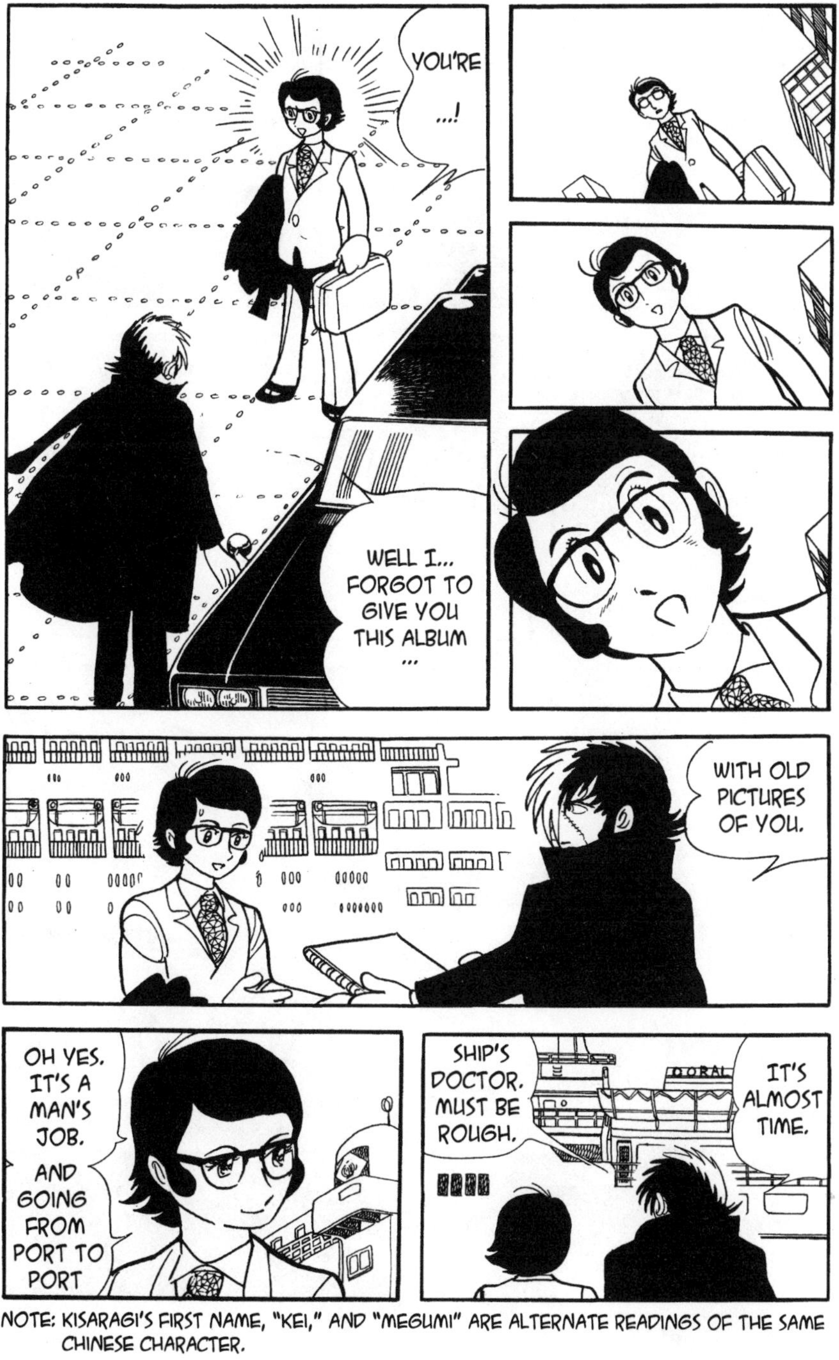
YOU'RE ...!
WELL I... FORGOT TO GIVE YOU THIS ALBUM ...
WITH OLD PICTURES OF YOU.
IT'S ALMOST TIME.
SHIP'S DOCTOR. MUST BE ROUGH.
OH YES. IT'S A MAN'S JOB.
AND GOING FROM PORT TO PORT

NOTE: KISARAGI'S FIRST NAME, "KEI," AND "MEGUMI" ARE ALTERNATE READINGS OF THE SAME CHINESE CHARACTER.

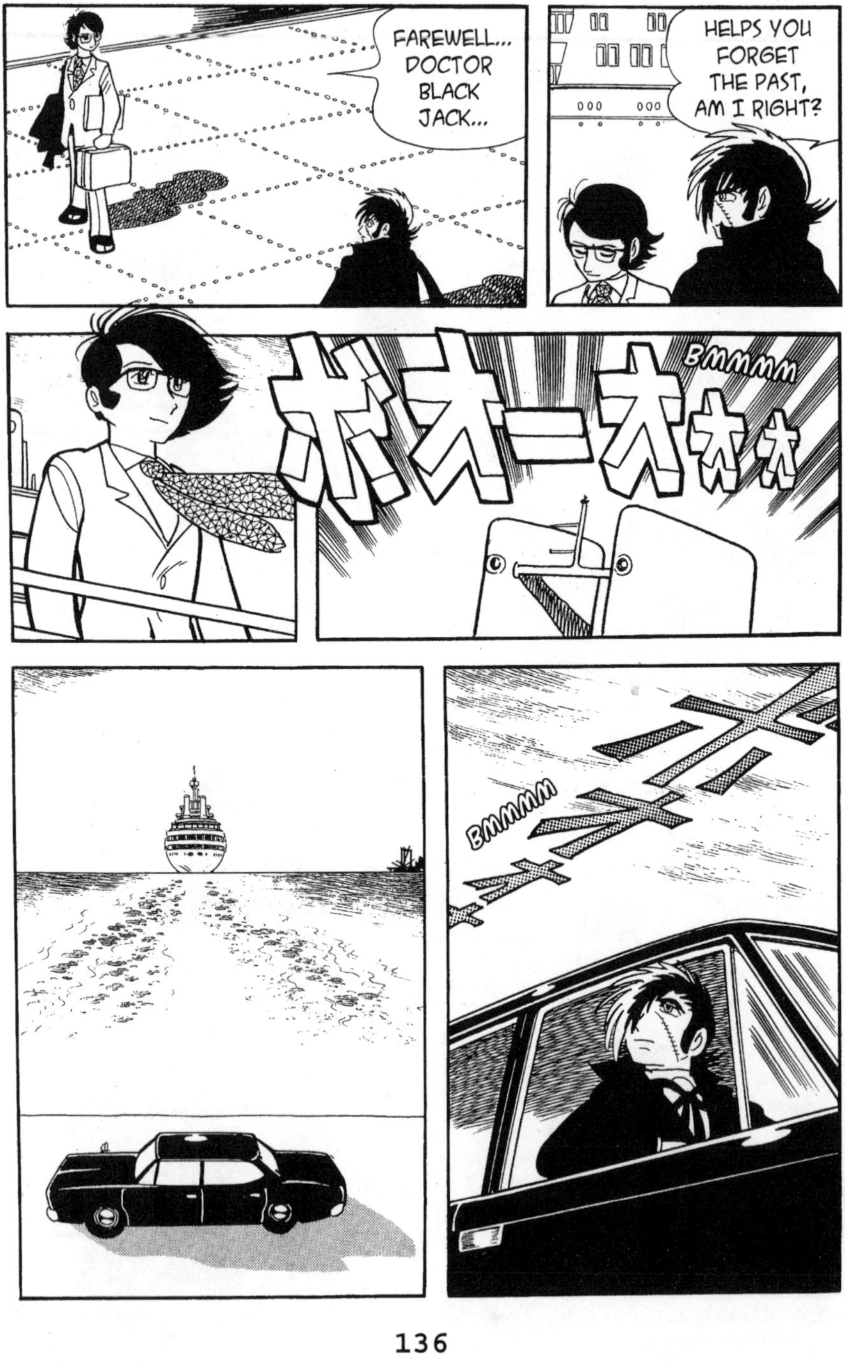
HELPS YOU FORGET THE PAST, AM I RIGHT?
FAREWELL... DOCTOR BLACK JACK...
ボオーオォォ
BMMMM
BMMMM

THE PAINTING IS DEAD!

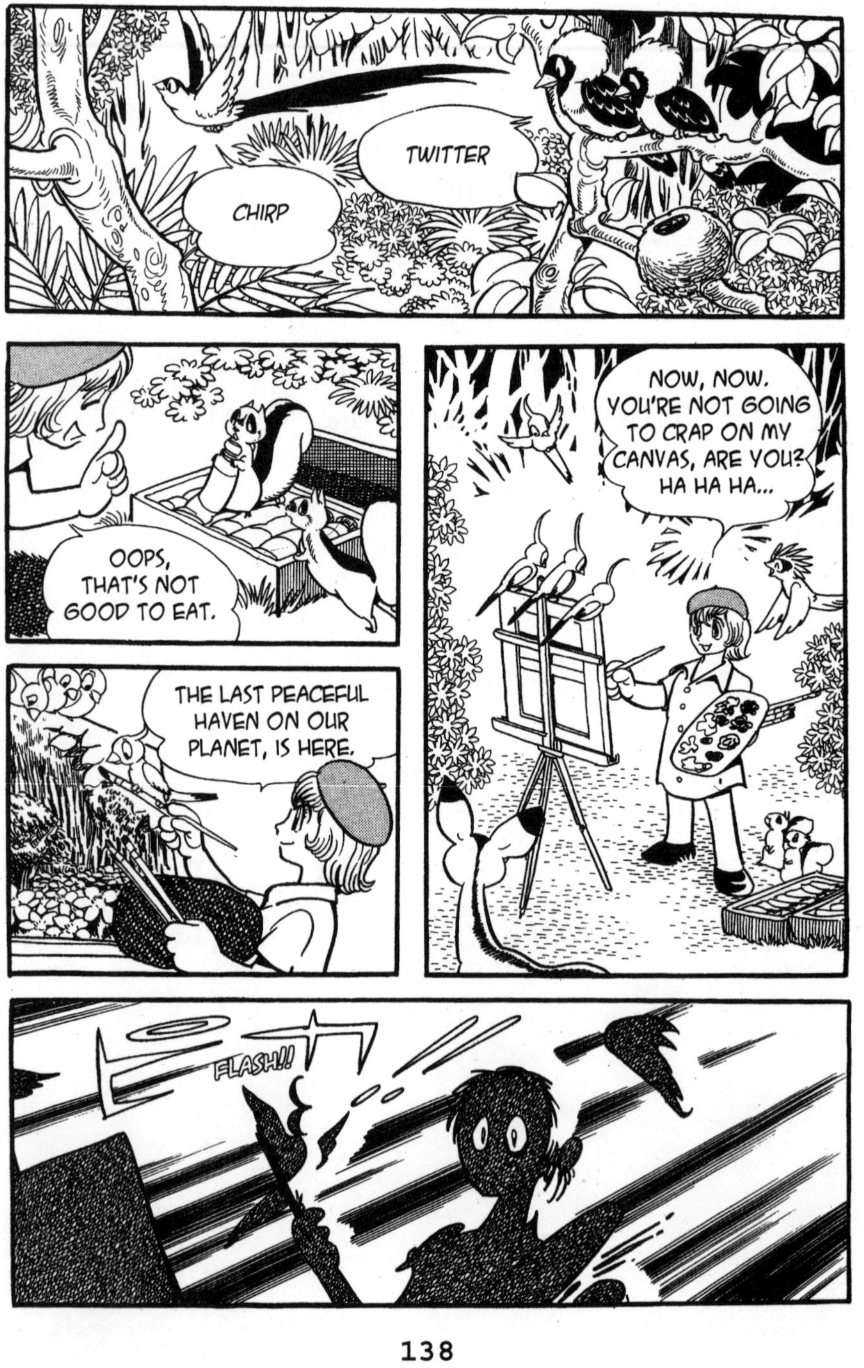
TWITTER
CHIRP
NOW, NOW. YOU'RE NOT GOING TO CRAP ON MY CANVAS, ARE YOU? HA HA HA...
OOPS, THAT'S NOT GOOD TO EAT.
THE LAST PEACEFUL HAVEN ON OUR PLANET, IS HERE.
FLASH!!

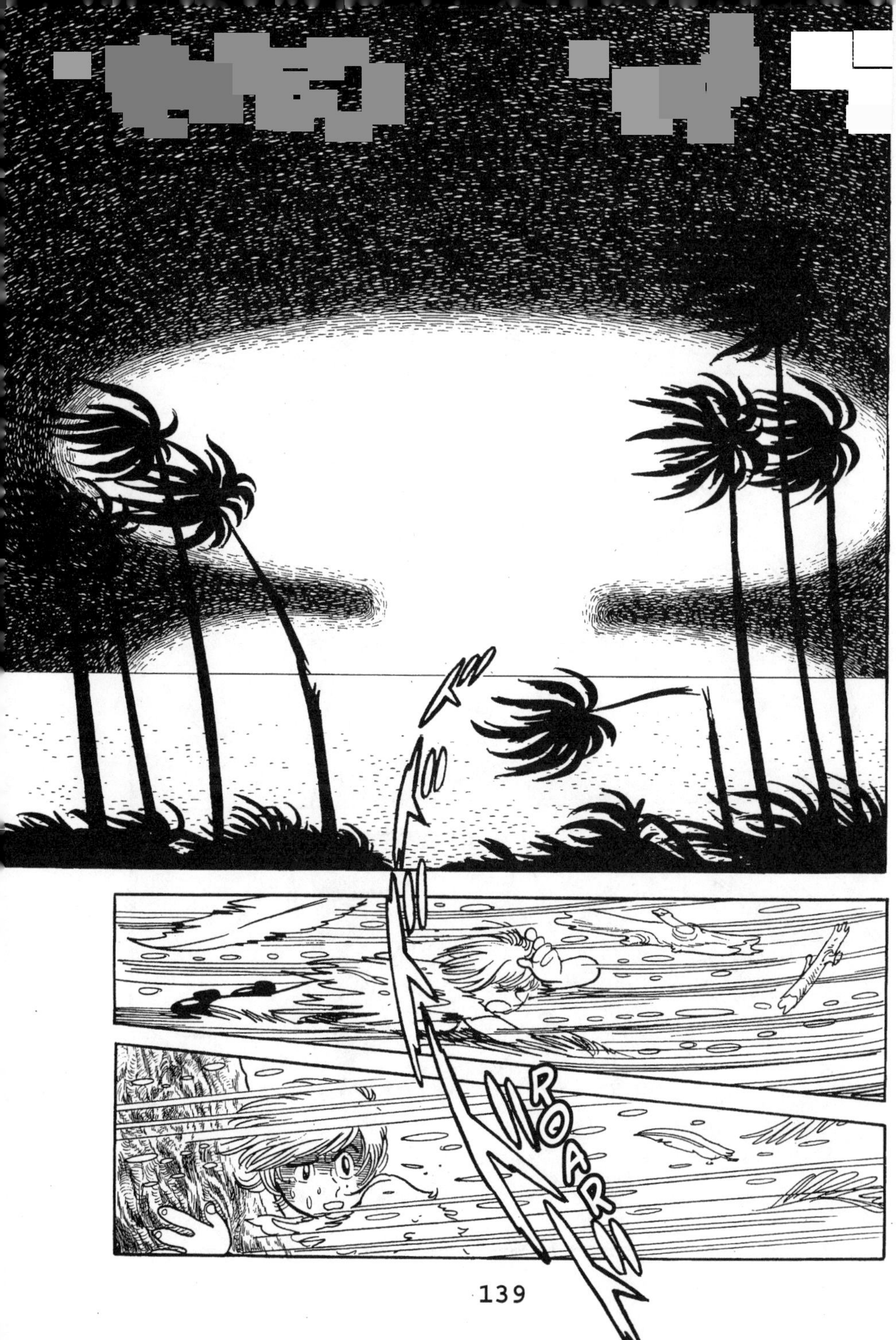
ROAR

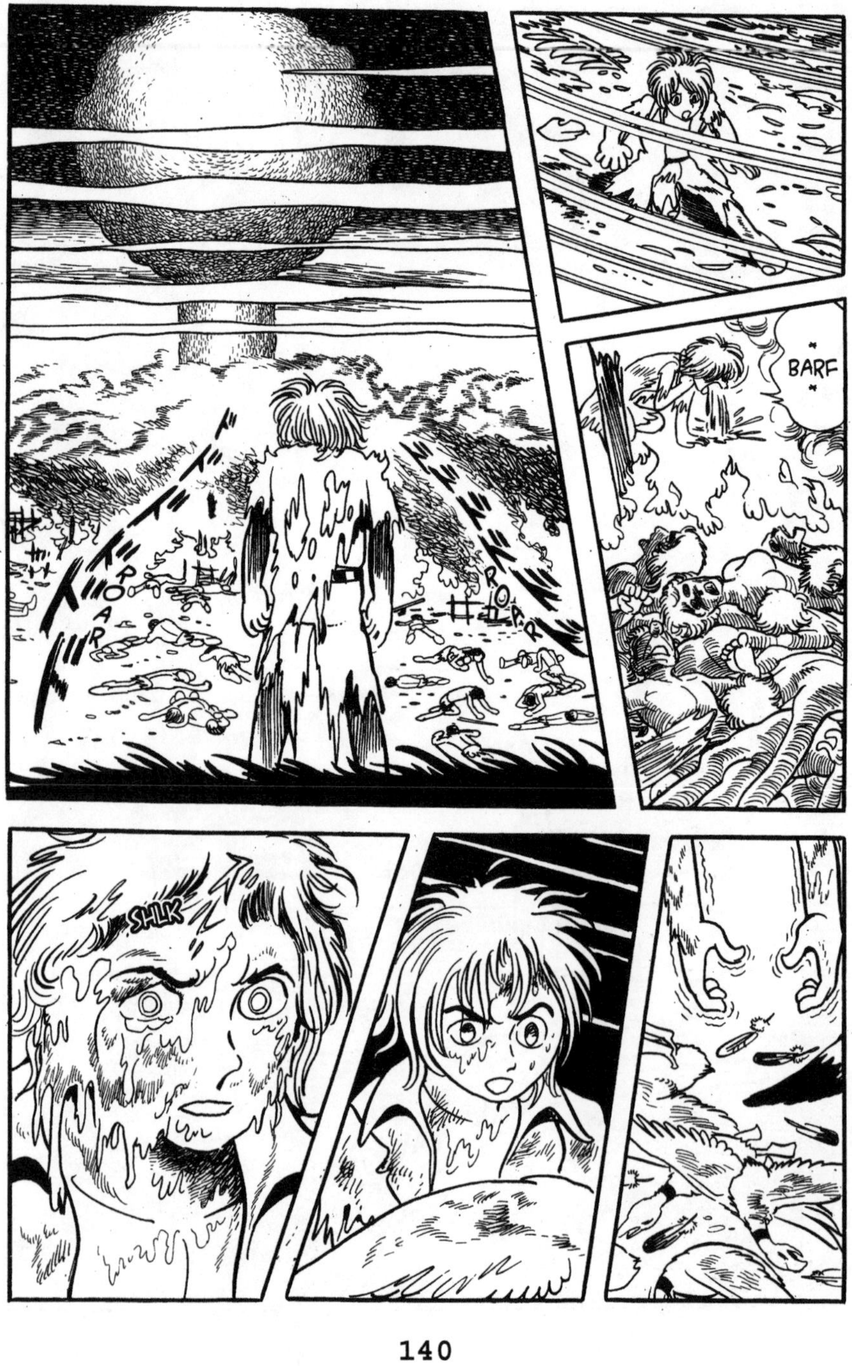
BARF
ROAR
ROAR
SHLK

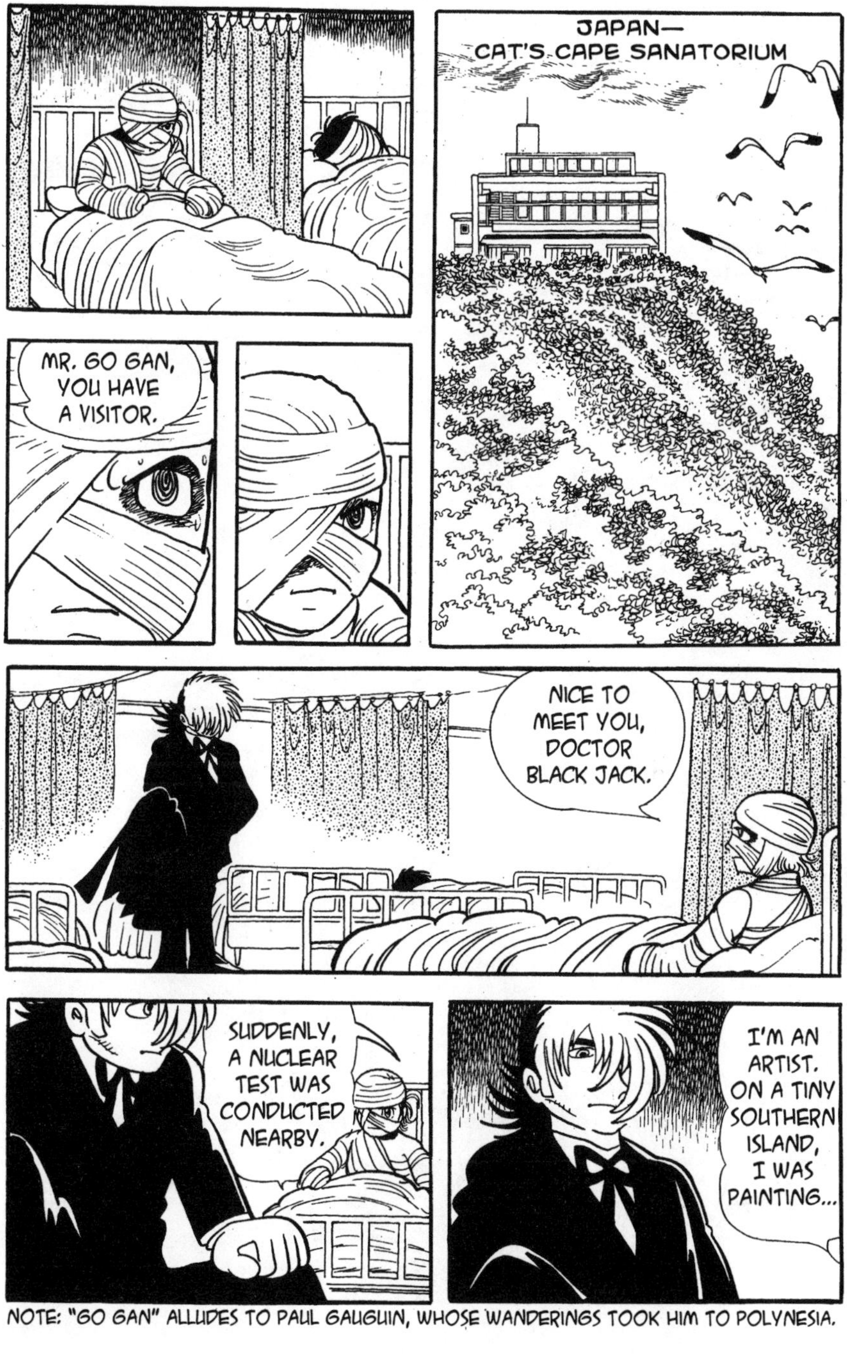
JAPAN—
CAT'S CAPE SANATORIUM
MR. GO GAN, YOU HAVE A VISITOR.
NICE TO MEET YOU, DOCTOR BLACK JACK.
I'M AN ARTIST. ON A TINY SOUTHERN ISLAND, I WAS PAINTING...
SUDDENLY, A NUCLEAR TEST WAS CONDUCTED NEARBY.

NOTE: "GO GAN" ALLUDES TO PAUL GAUGUIN, WHOSE WANDERINGS TOOK HIM TO POLYNESIA.

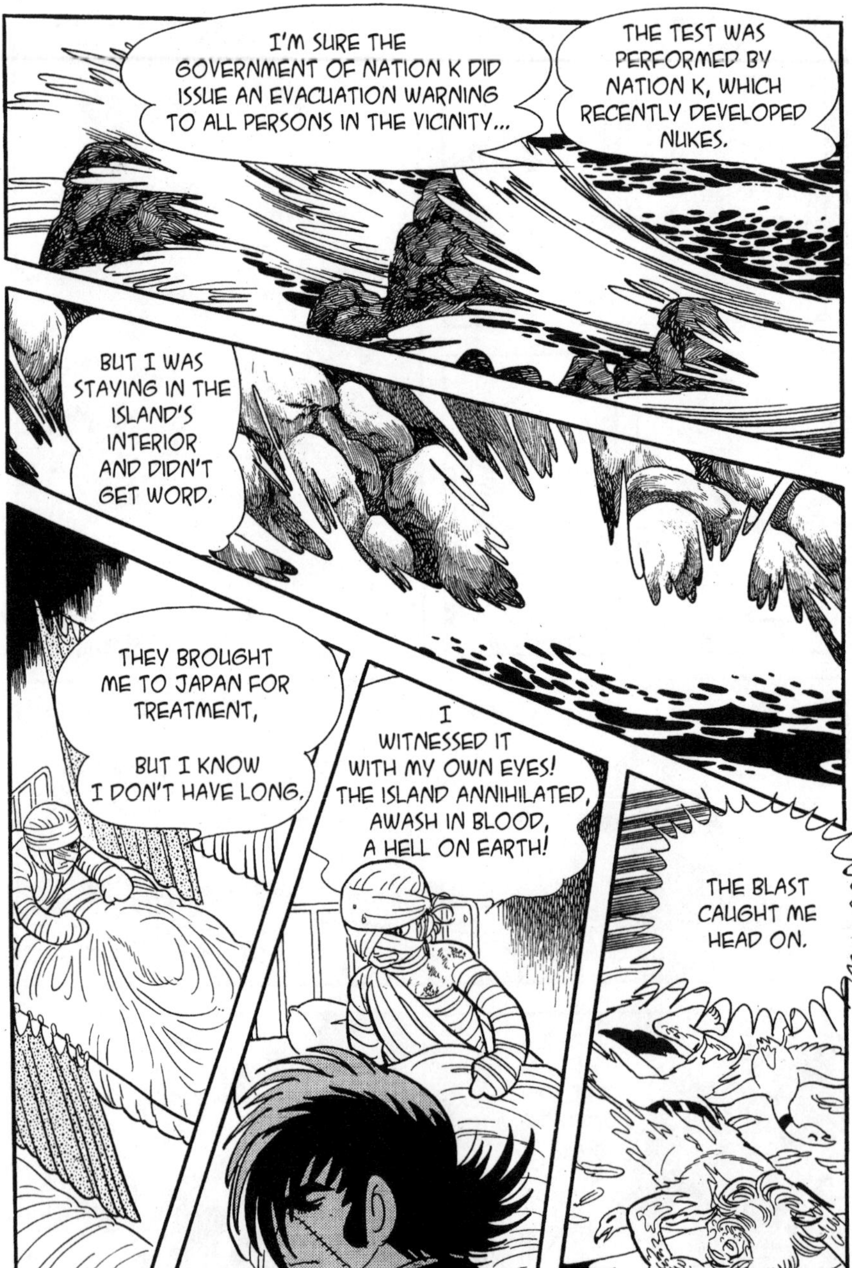
THE TEST WAS PERFORMED BY NATION K, WHICH RECENTLY DEVELOPED NUKES.
I'M SURE THE GOVERNMENT OF NATION K DID ISSUE AN EVACUATION WARNING TO ALL PERSONS IN THE VICINITY...
BUT I WAS STAYING IN THE ISLAND'S INTERIOR AND DIDN'T GET WORD.
THE BLAST CAUGHT ME HEAD ON.
I WITNESSED IT WITH MY OWN EYES! THE ISLAND ANNIHILATED, AWASH IN BLOOD, A HELL ON EARTH!
THEY BROUGHT ME TO JAPAN FOR TREATMENT,
BUT I KNOW I DON'T HAVE LONG.

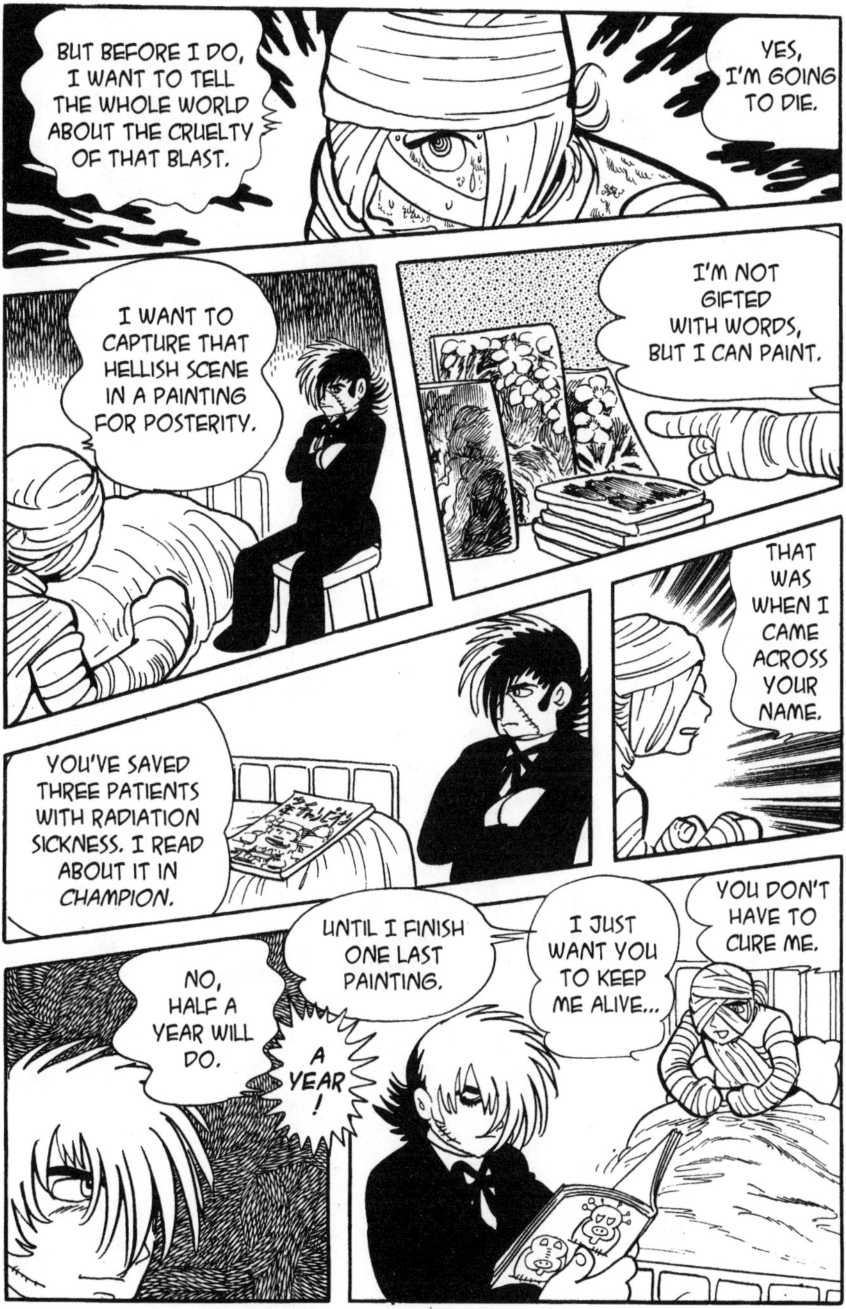
YES, I'M GOING TO DIE.
BUT BEFORE I DO, I WANT TO TELL THE WHOLE WORLD ABOUT THE CRUELTY OF THAT BLAST.
I'M NOT GIFTED WITH WORDS, BUT I CAN PAINT.
I WANT TO CAPTURE THAT HELLISH SCENE IN A PAINTING FOR POSTERITY.
THAT WAS WHEN I CAME ACROSS YOUR NAME.
YOU'VE SAVED THREE PATIENTS WITH RADIATION SICKNESS. I READ ABOUT IT IN *CHAMPION*.
YOU DON'T HAVE TO CURE ME.
I JUST WANT YOU TO KEEP ME ALIVE...
UNTIL I FINISH ONE LAST PAINTING.
A YEAR!
NO, HALF A YEAR WILL DO.

NOTE: *BLACK JACK* WAS SERIALIZED IN THE WEEKLY COMICS MAGAZINE *SHONEN CHAMPION*.

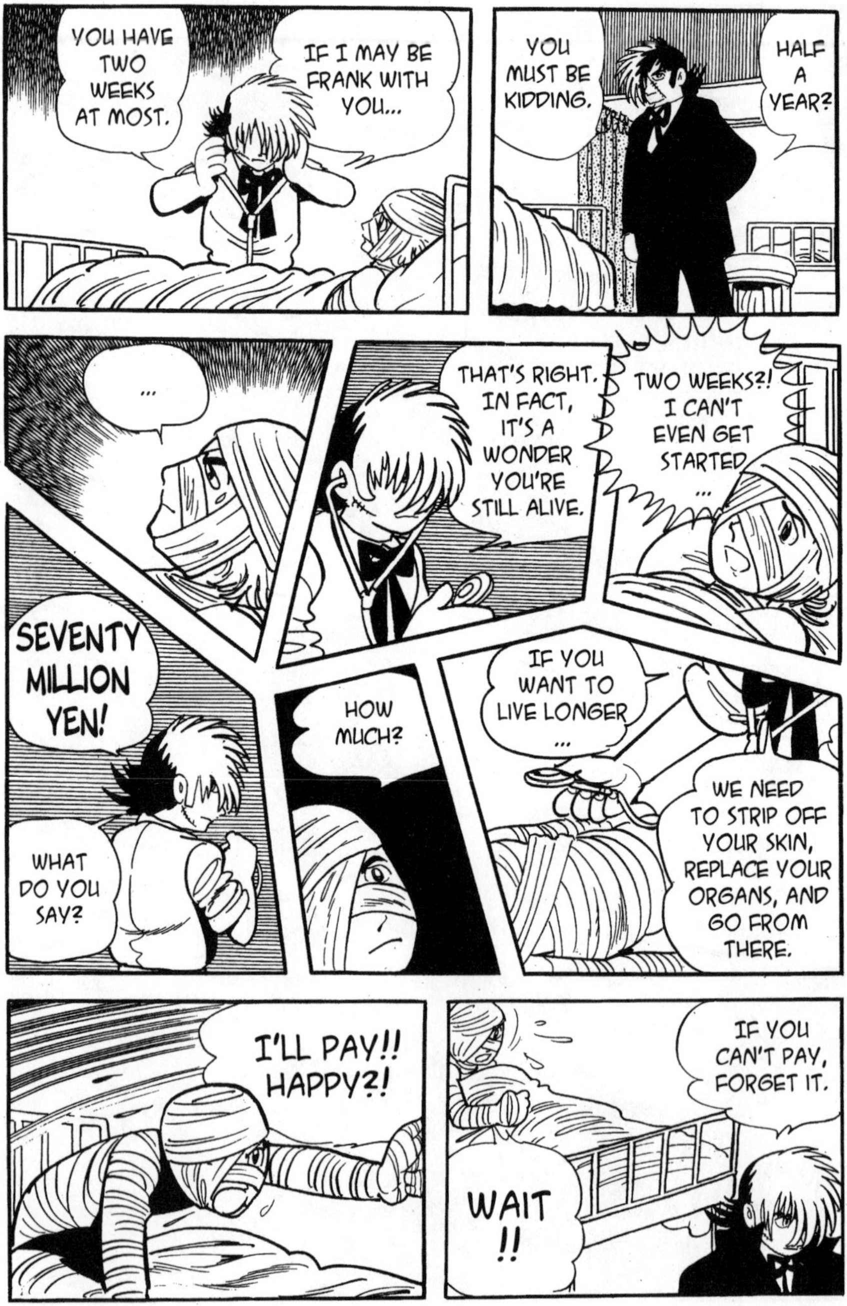
HALF A YEAR?
YOU MUST BE KIDDING.
IF I MAY BE FRANK WITH YOU...
YOU HAVE TWO WEEKS AT MOST.
TWO WEEKS?! I CAN'T EVEN GET STARTED ...
THAT'S RIGHT. IN FACT, IT'S A WONDER YOU'RE STILL ALIVE.
...
IF YOU WANT TO LIVE LONGER ...
WE NEED TO STRIP OFF YOUR SKIN, REPLACE YOUR ORGANS, AND GO FROM THERE.
HOW MUCH?
SEVENTY MILLION YEN!
WHAT DO YOU SAY?
IF YOU CAN'T PAY, FORGET IT.
WAIT !!
I'LL PAY!! HAPPY?!

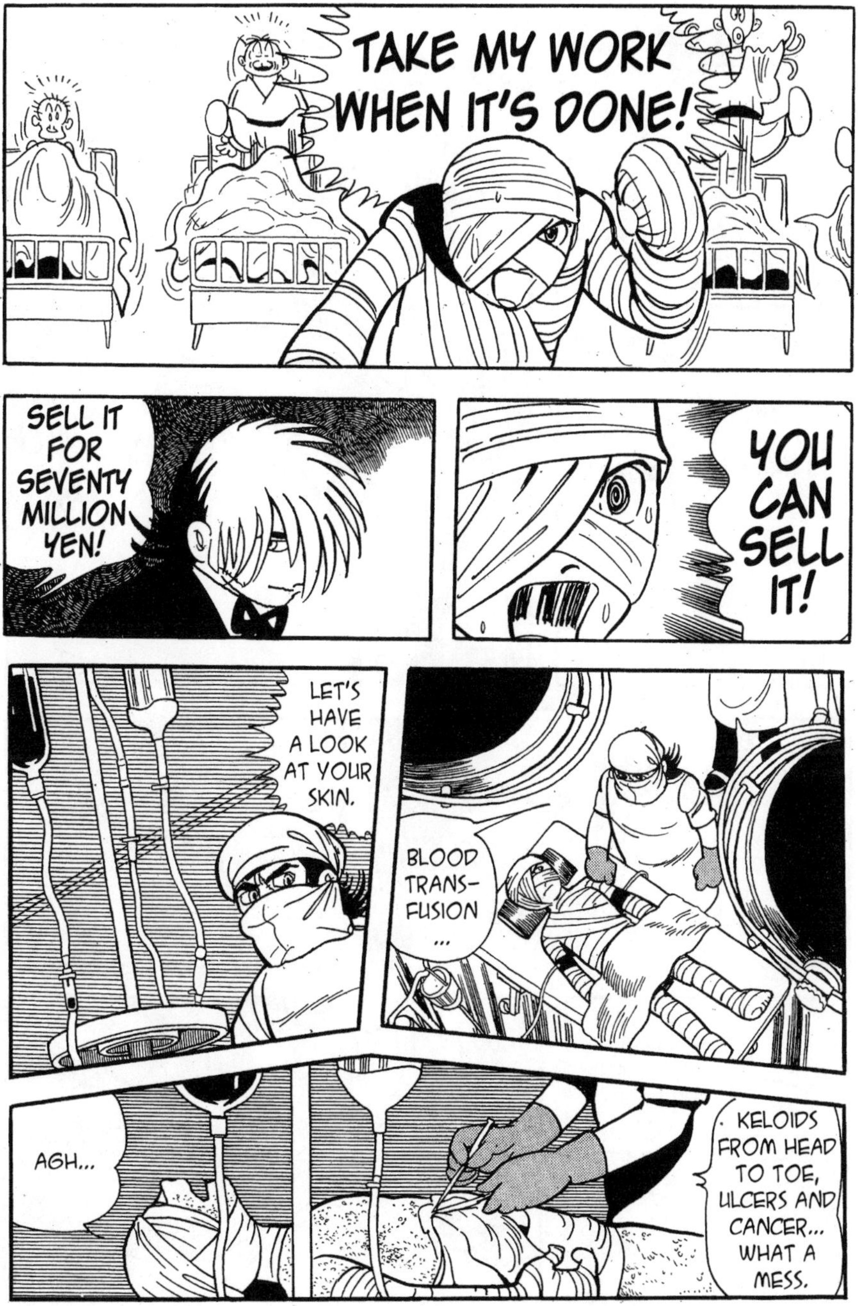
TAKE MY WORK WHEN IT'S DONE!
YOU CAN SELL IT!
SELL IT FOR SEVENTY MILLION YEN!
BLOOD TRANS-FUSION ...
LET'S HAVE A LOOK AT YOUR SKIN.
KELOIDS FROM HEAD TO TOE, ULCERS AND CANCER... WHAT A MESS.
AGH...

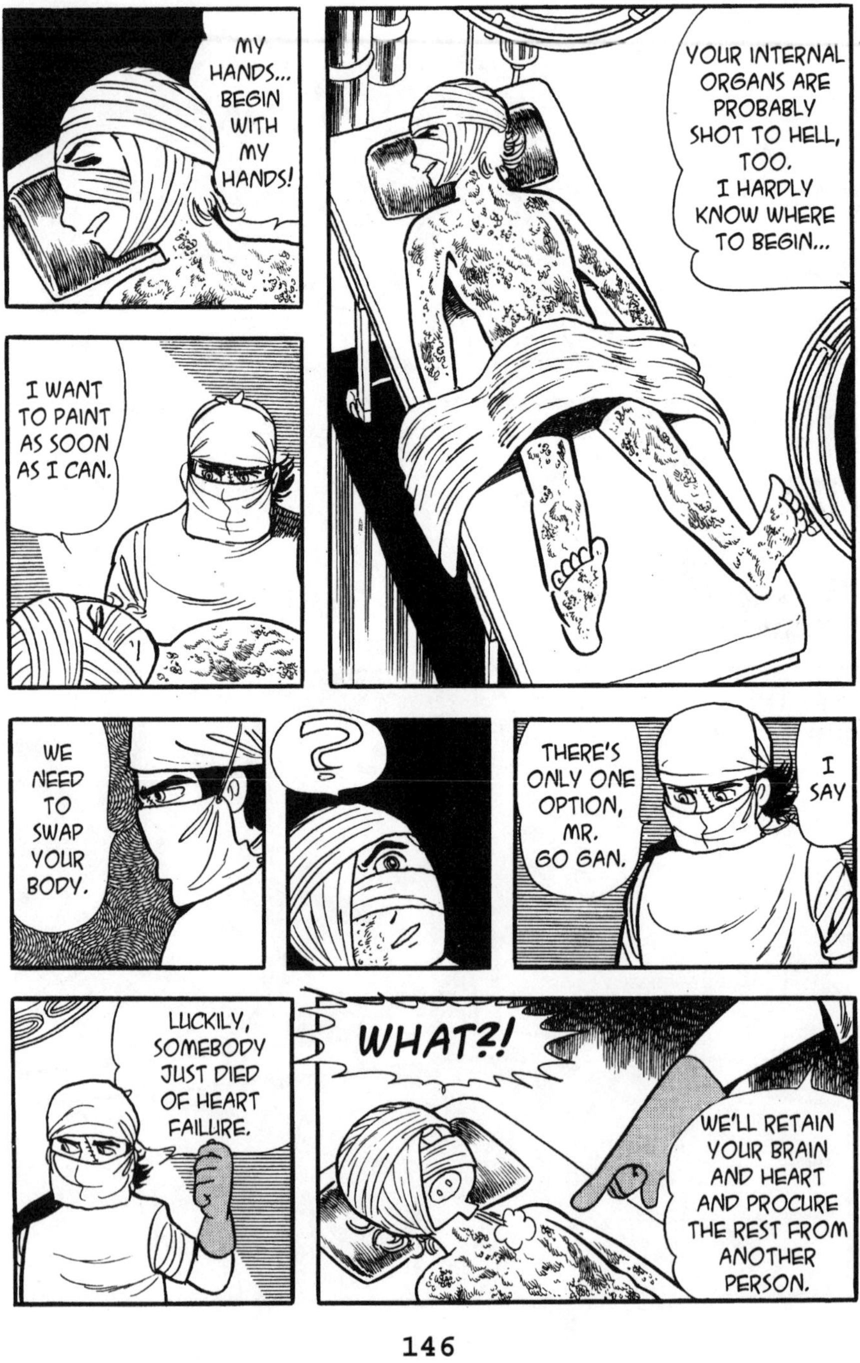
YOUR INTERNAL ORGANS ARE PROBABLY SHOT TO HELL, TOO. I HARDLY KNOW WHERE TO BEGIN...
MY HANDS... BEGIN WITH MY HANDS!
I WANT TO PAINT AS SOON AS I CAN.
I SAY
THERE'S ONLY ONE OPTION, MR. GO GAN.
?
WE NEED TO SWAP YOUR BODY.
WHAT?!
WE'LL RETAIN YOUR BRAIN AND HEART AND PROCURE THE REST FROM ANOTHER PERSON.
LUCKILY, SOMEBODY JUST DIED OF HEART FAILURE.

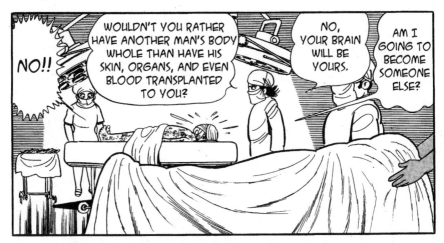

AM I GOING TO BECOME SOMEONE ELSE?
NO, YOUR BRAIN WILL BE YOURS.
WOULDN'T YOU RATHER HAVE ANOTHER MAN'S BODY WHOLE THAN HAVE HIS SKIN, ORGANS, AND EVEN BLOOD TRANSPLANTED TO YOU?
NO!!
MAYBE THAT'LL LET ME LIVE, BUT NO THANKS!
SO YOU'D RATHER DIE.
...NO.
...
LOWER BODY TEMPERA- TURE TO 20°C.
WE WILL EXTRACT, REPLACE, AND SUTURE THE BRAIN STEM AND CEREBRAL NERVES.
ONCE THE ENCEPHALON IS EXPOSED, I'LL PERFORM THE REST ALONE.

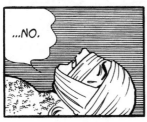

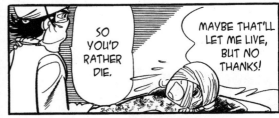

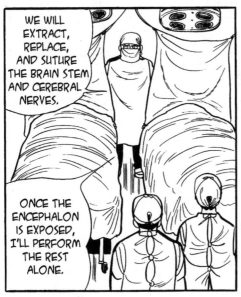

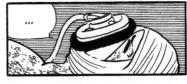

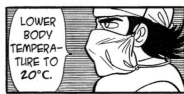

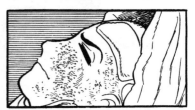

REPLACE BLOOD WITH PLASMA SUBSTITUTE.
TREPANATION!
A BRAIN TRANSPLANT! HE CAN'T BE SERIOUS!
HE'S REMOVED IT ALL RIGHT... HOW'LL HE EVER CONNECT IT TO ANOTHER BODY'S NERVES?
A TALL ORDER...
BAGHDAD

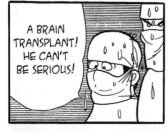

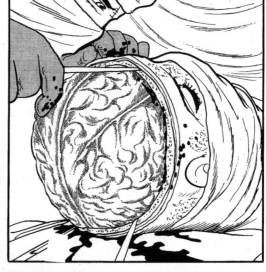

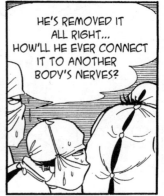

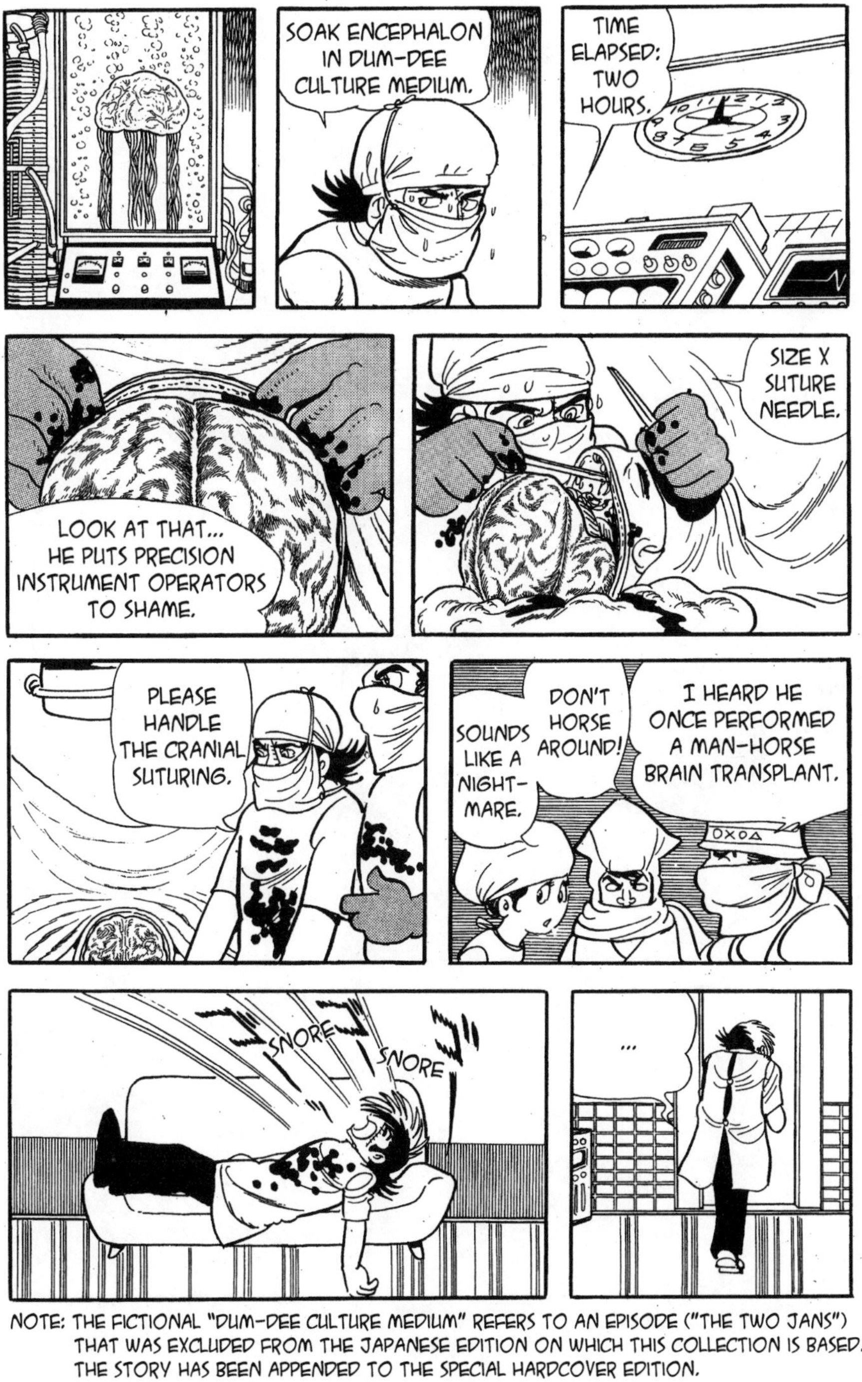
TIME ELAPSED: TWO HOURS.
SOAK ENCEPHALON IN DUM-DEE CULTURE MEDIUM.
SIZE X SUTURE NEEDLE.
LOOK AT THAT... HE PUTS PRECISION INSTRUMENT OPERATORS TO SHAME.
I HEARD HE ONCE PERFORMED A MAN-HORSE BRAIN TRANSPLANT.
DON'T HORSE AROUND!
SOUNDS LIKE A NIGHT-MARE.
PLEASE HANDLE THE CRANIAL SUTURING.
...
SNORE
SNORE

NOTE: THE FICTIONAL "DUM-DEE CULTURE MEDIUM" REFERS TO AN EPISODE ("THE TWO JANS") THAT WAS EXCLUDED FROM THE JAPANESE EDITION ON WHICH THIS COLLECTION IS BASED. THE STORY HAS BEEN APPENDED TO THE SPECIAL HARDCOVER EDITION.

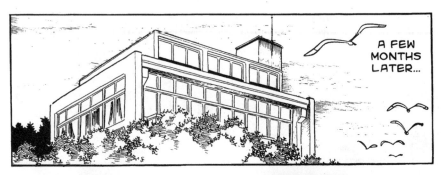

A FEW MONTHS LATER...
GO GAN, REVIVED IN A NEW BODY,
SOON
GOT TO WORK.
DOCTOR, I'M IMPRESSED— TRANSPLANTING THAT PATIENT'S BRAIN AND HEART INTO ANOTHER BODY, REVIVING HIM.
AND THE BODY DIDN'T REJECT THEM.
THAT WAS A MAJOR RISK...

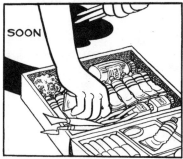

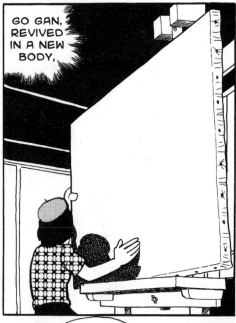

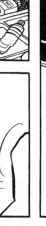

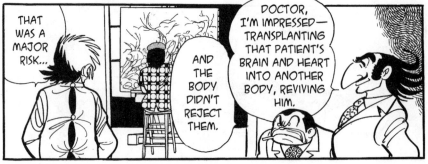

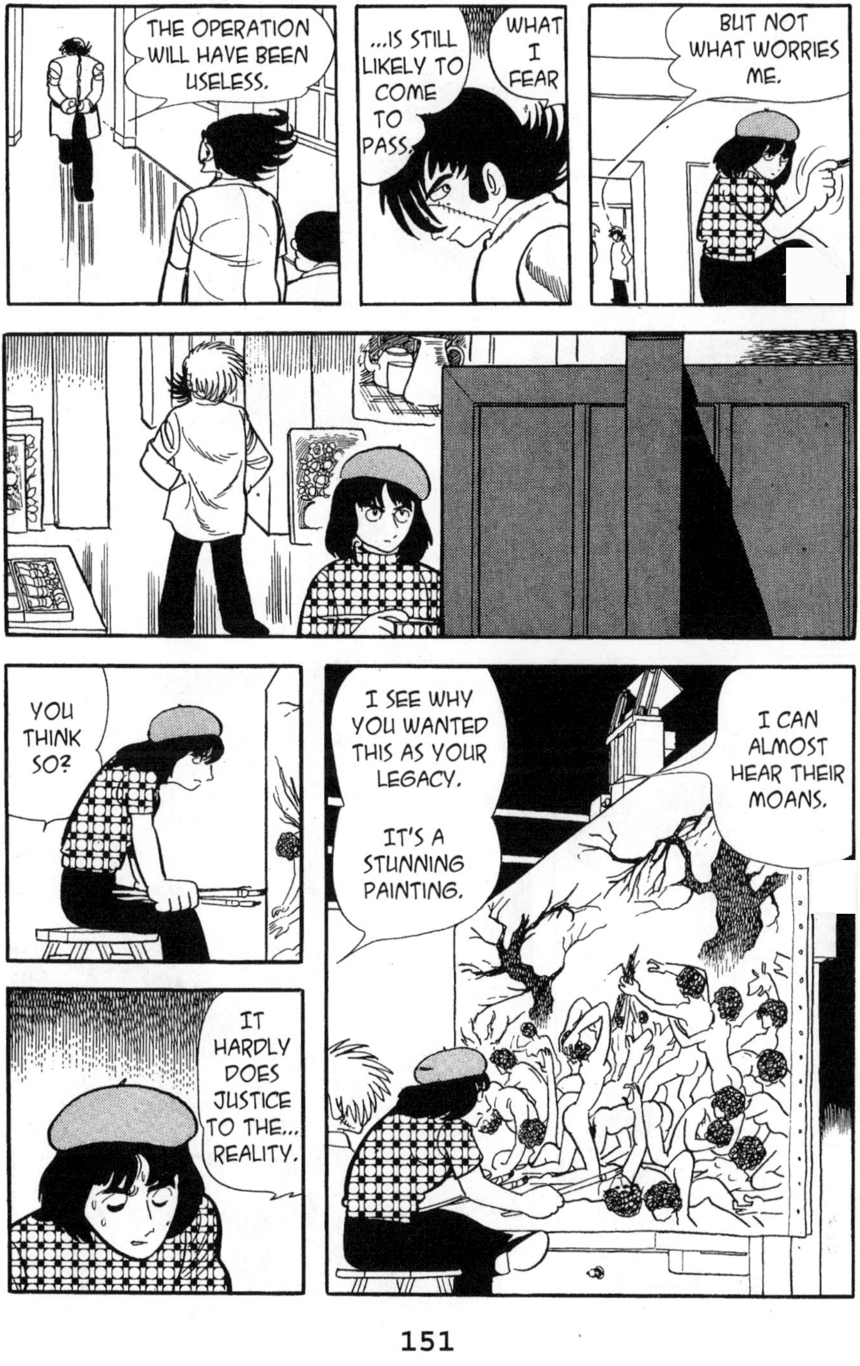
BUT NOT WHAT WORRIES ME.
WHAT I FEAR
...IS STILL LIKELY TO COME TO PASS.
THE OPERATION WILL HAVE BEEN USELESS.
I CAN ALMOST HEAR THEIR MOANS.
I SEE WHY YOU WANTED THIS AS YOUR LEGACY.
IT'S A STUNNING PAINTING.
YOU THINK SO?
IT HARDLY DOES JUSTICE TO THE... REALITY.

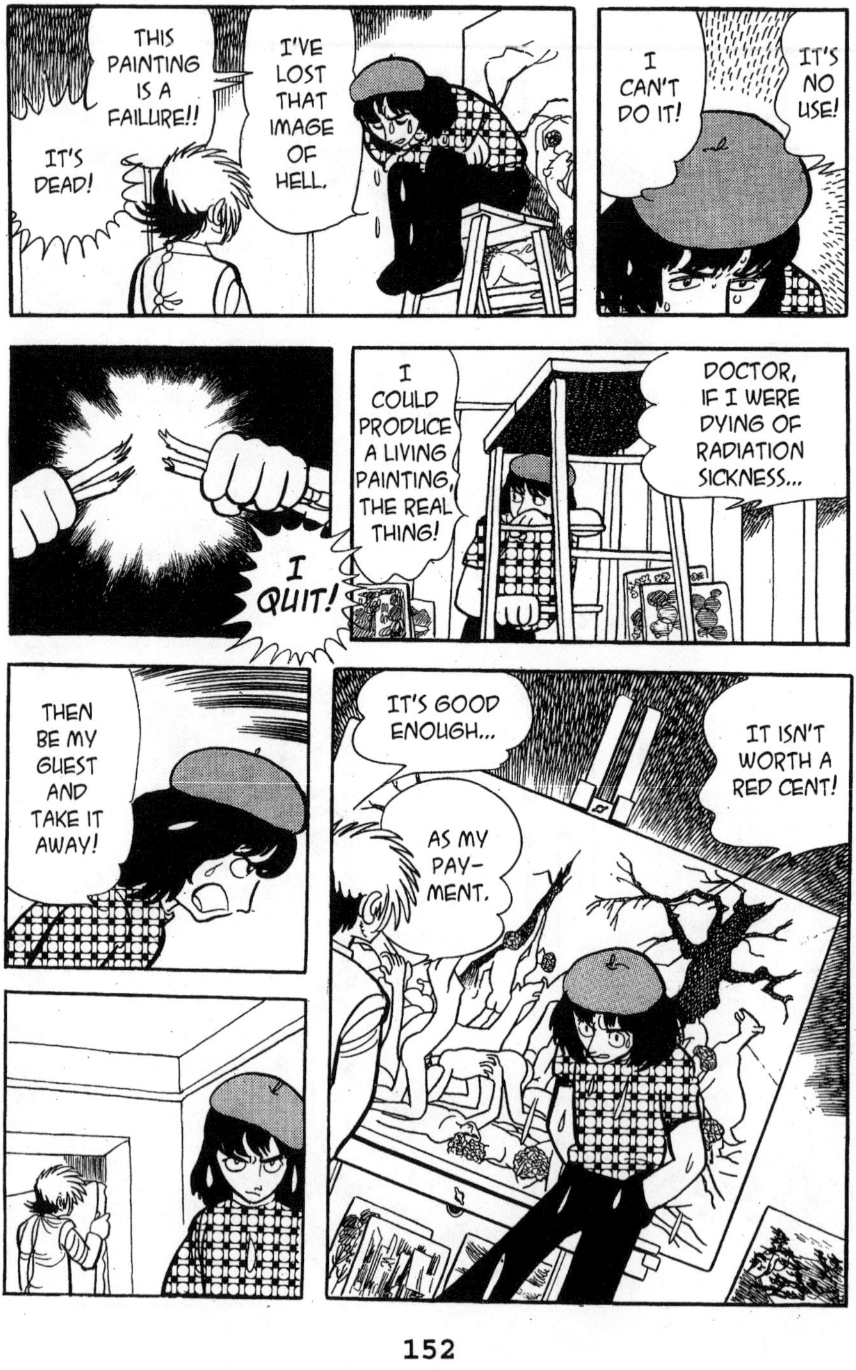
IT'S NO USE!
I CAN'T DO IT!
I'VE LOST THAT IMAGE OF HELL.
THIS PAINTING IS A FAILURE!!
IT'S DEAD!
DOCTOR, IF I WERE DYING OF RADIATION SICKNESS...
I COULD PRODUCE A LIVING PAINTING, THE REAL THING!
I QUIT!
IT ISN'T WORTH A RED CENT!
IT'S GOOD ENOUGH...
AS MY PAYMENT.
THEN BE MY GUEST AND TAKE IT AWAY!

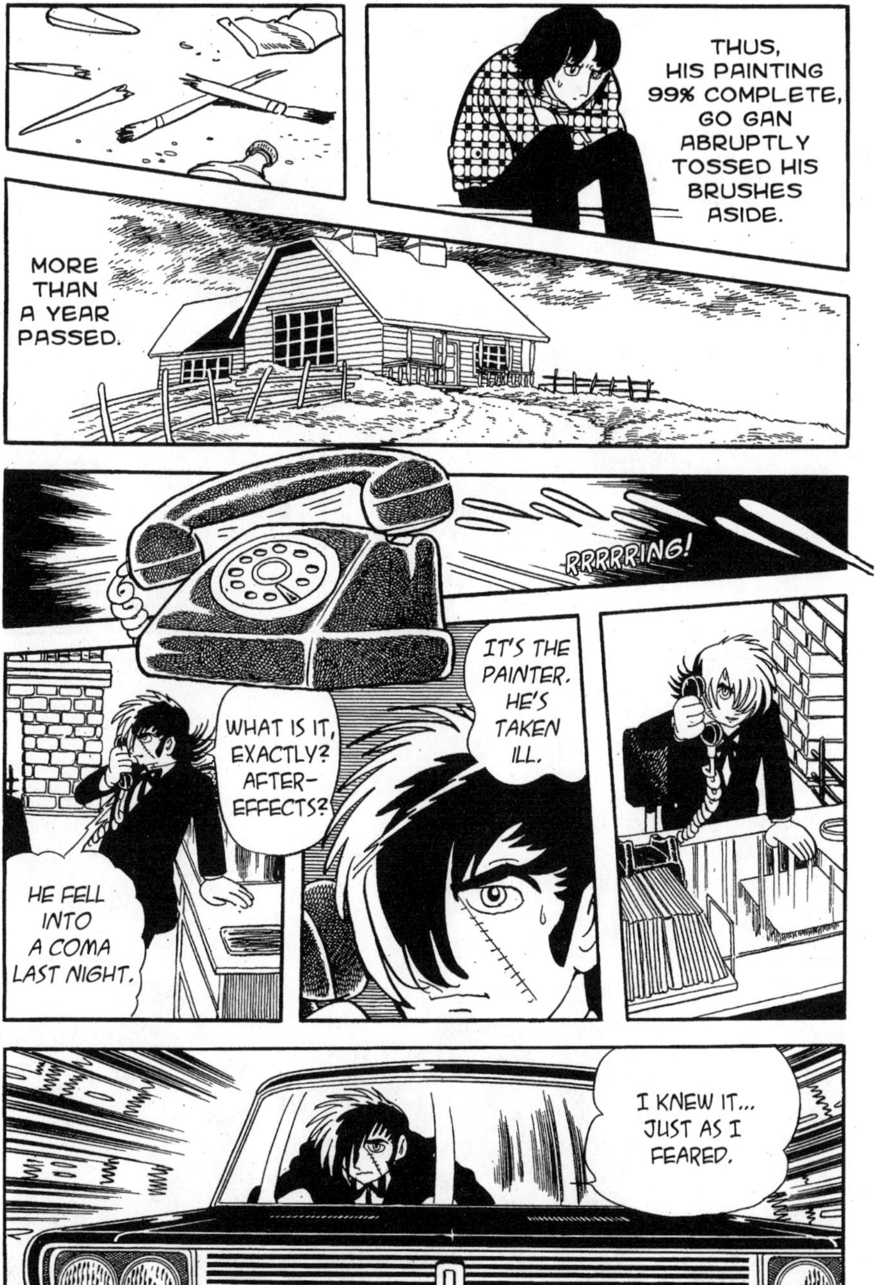
THUS, HIS PAINTING 99% COMPLETE, GO GAN ABRUPTLY TOSSED HIS BRUSHES ASIDE.
MORE THAN A YEAR PASSED.
RRRRRING!
IT'S THE PAINTER. HE'S TAKEN ILL.
WHAT IS IT, EXACTLY? AFTER-EFFECTS?
HE FELL INTO A COMA LAST NIGHT.
I KNEW IT... JUST AS I FEARED.

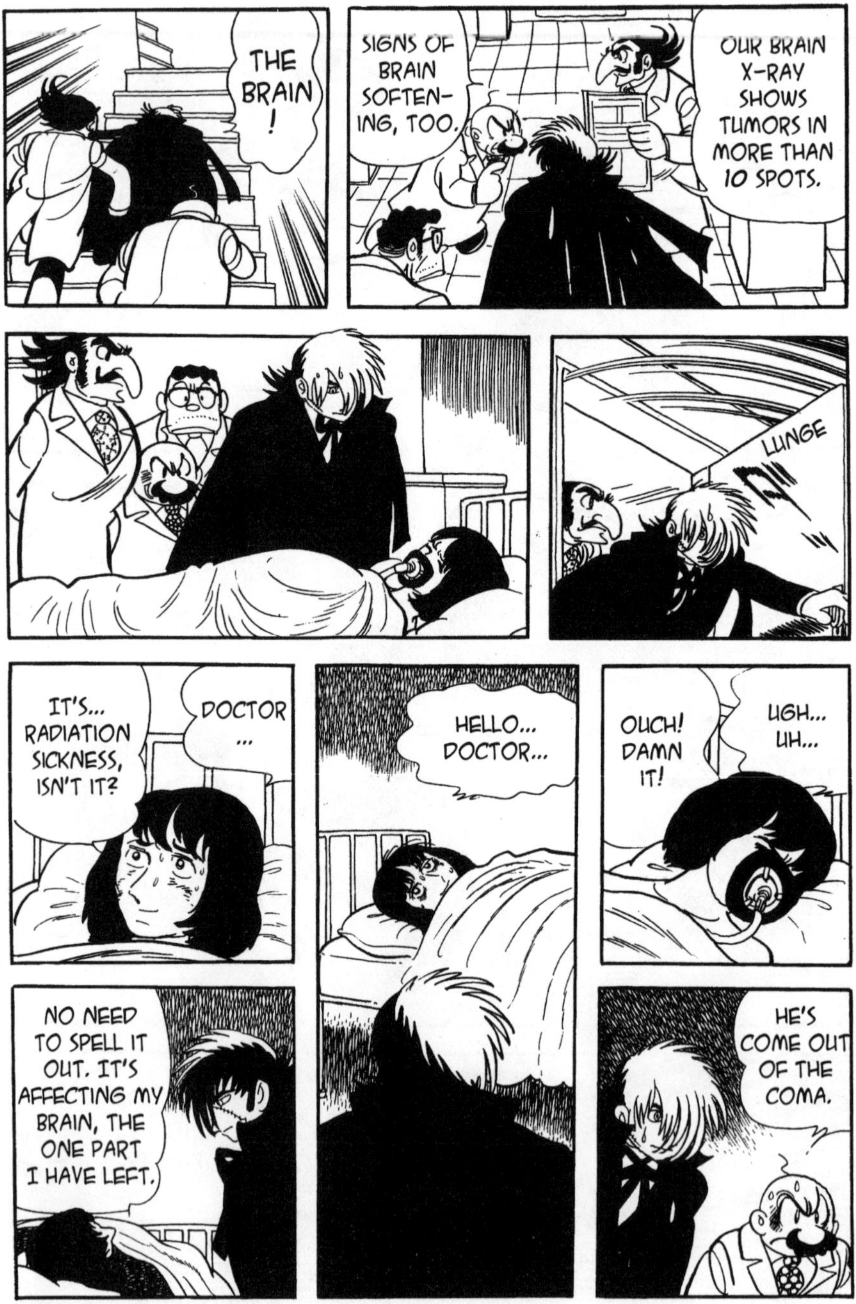
OUR BRAIN X-RAY SHOWS TUMORS IN MORE THAN 10 SPOTS.
SIGNS OF BRAIN SOFTEN-ING, TOO.
THE BRAIN!
LUNGE
UGH... UH...
OUCH! DAMN IT!
HELLO... DOCTOR...
DOCTOR...
IT'S... RADIATION SICKNESS, ISN'T IT?
HE'S COME OUT OF THE COMA.
NO NEED TO SPELL IT OUT. IT'S AFFECTING MY BRAIN, THE ONE PART I HAVE LEFT.

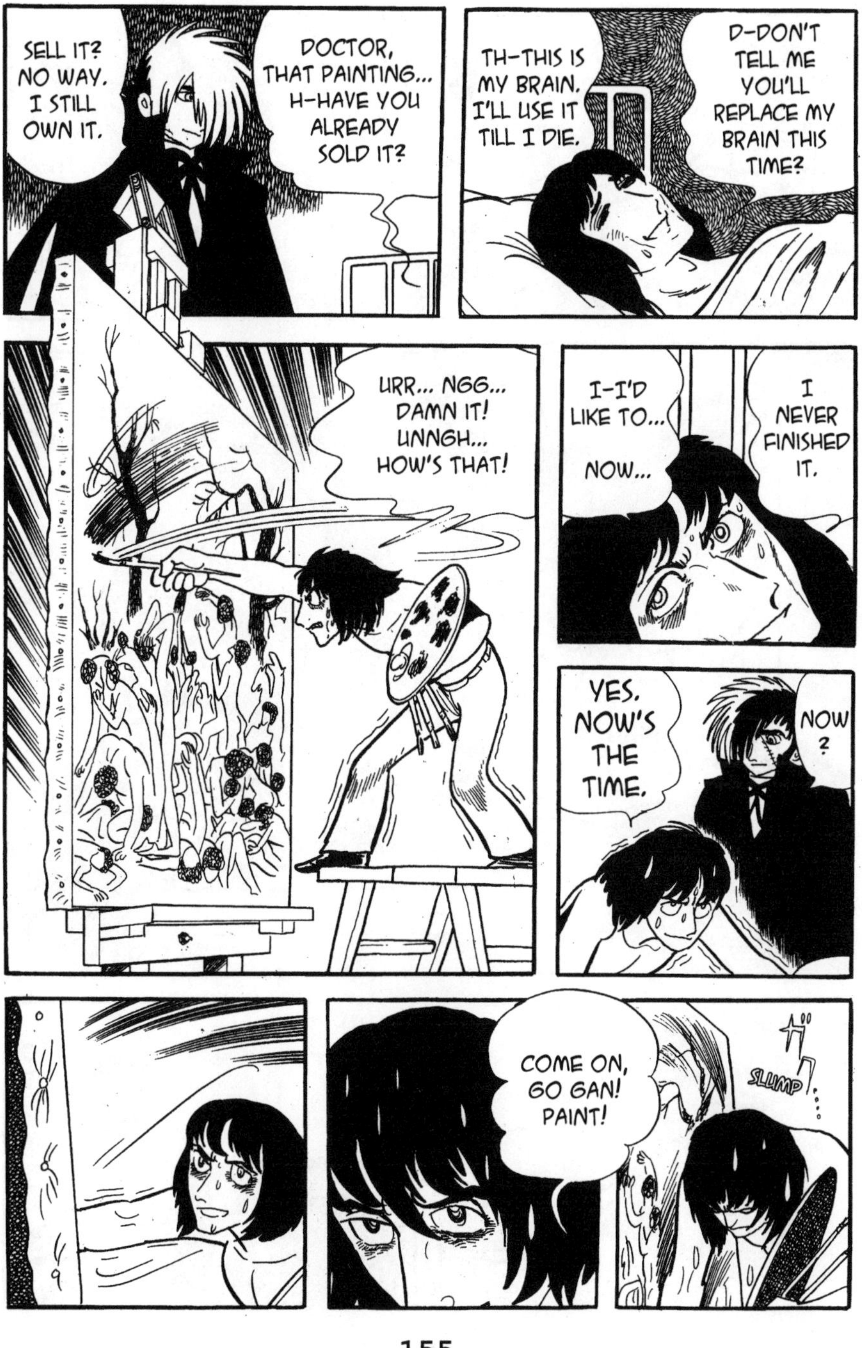
D-DON'T TELL ME YOU'LL REPLACE MY BRAIN THIS TIME?
TH-THIS IS MY BRAIN. I'LL USE IT TILL I DIE.
DOCTOR, THAT PAINTING... H-HAVE YOU ALREADY SOLD IT?
SELL IT? NO WAY. I STILL OWN IT.
I NEVER FINISHED IT.
I-I'D LIKE TO... NOW...
NOW?
YES. NOW'S THE TIME.
URR... NGG... DAMN IT! UNNGH... HOW'S THAT!
SLUMP
COME ON, GO GAN! PAINT!

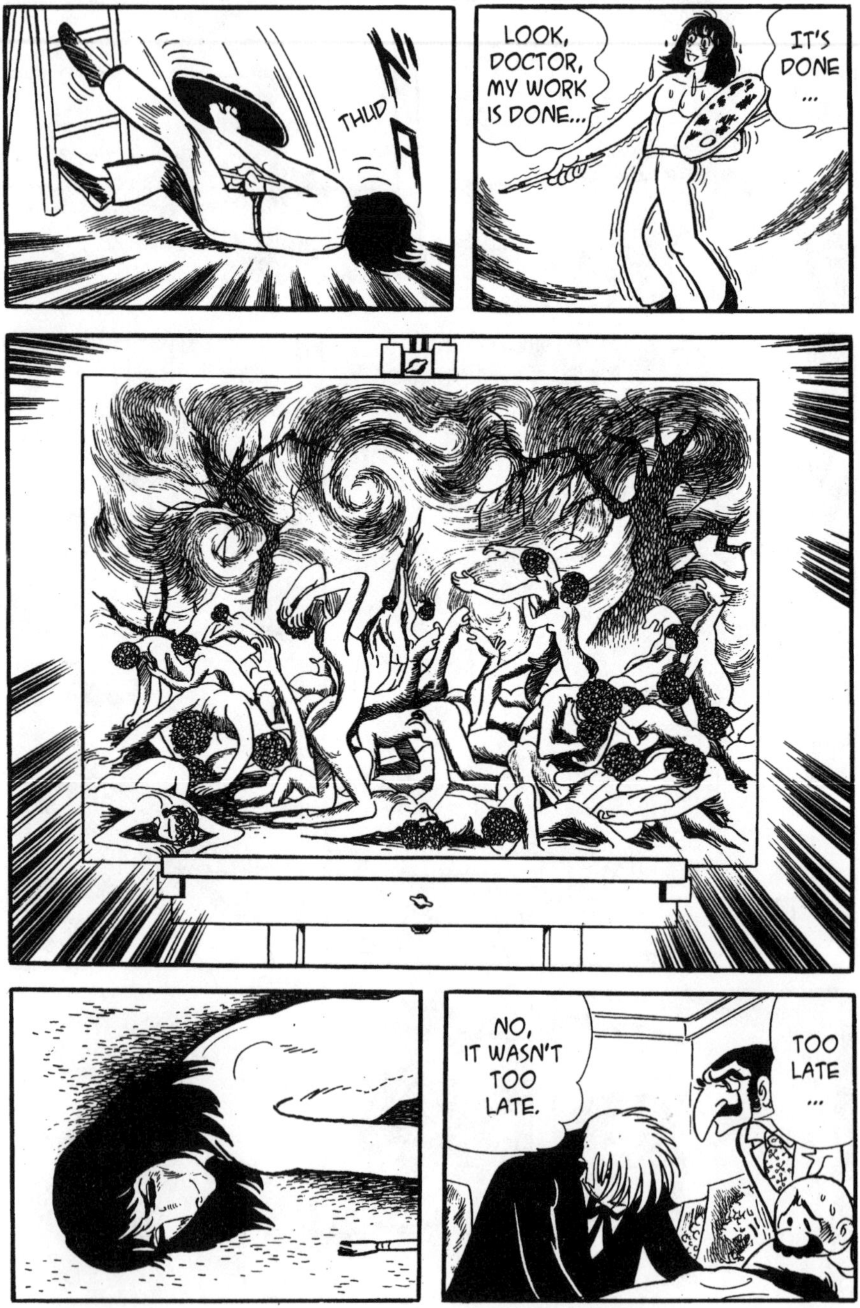
IT'S DONE ...
LOOK, DOCTOR, MY WORK IS DONE...
THUD
TOO LATE ...
NO, IT WASN'T TOO LATE.

STAR, MAGNITUDE SIX

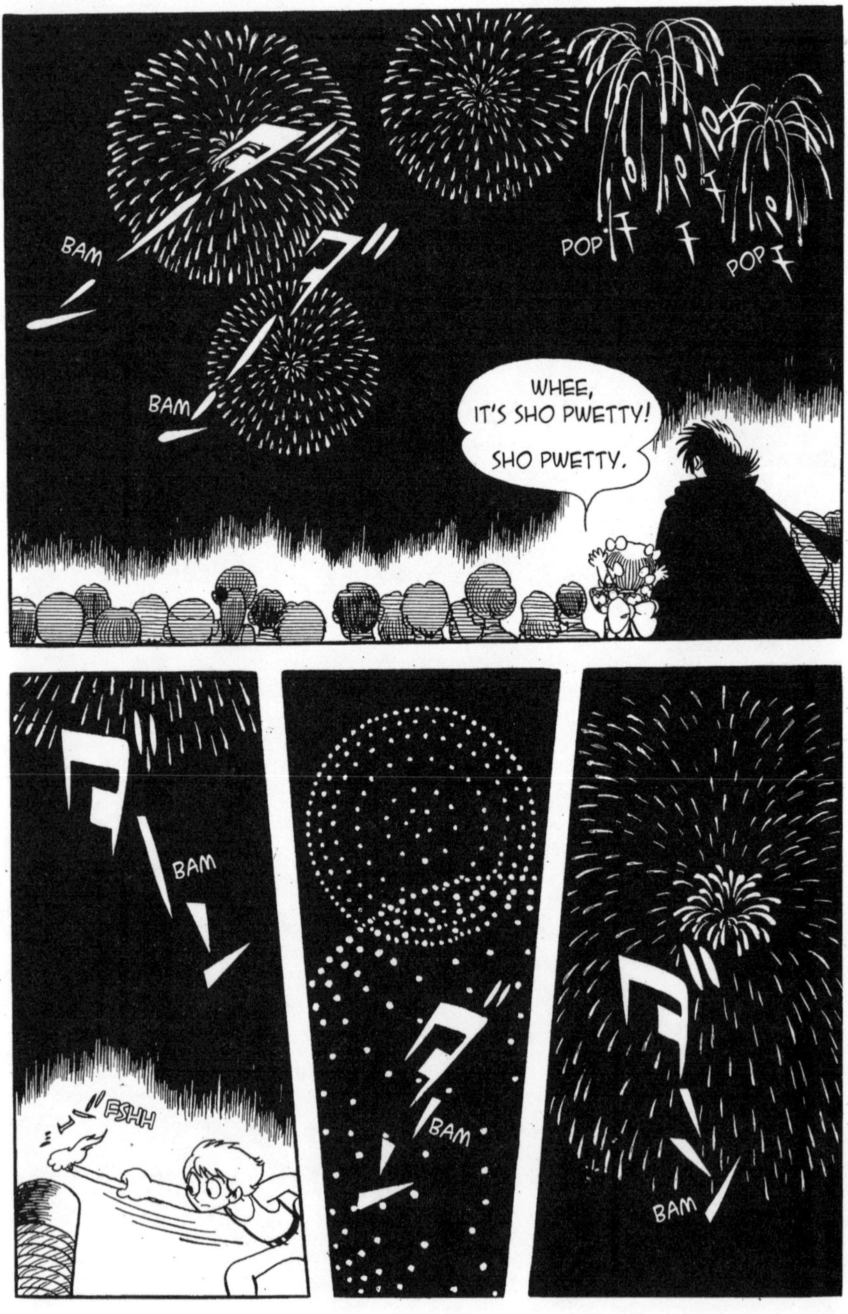
POP
POP
WHEE,
IT'S SHO PWETTY!
SHO PWETTY.
BAM
BAM
BAM
BAM
BAM
FSHH

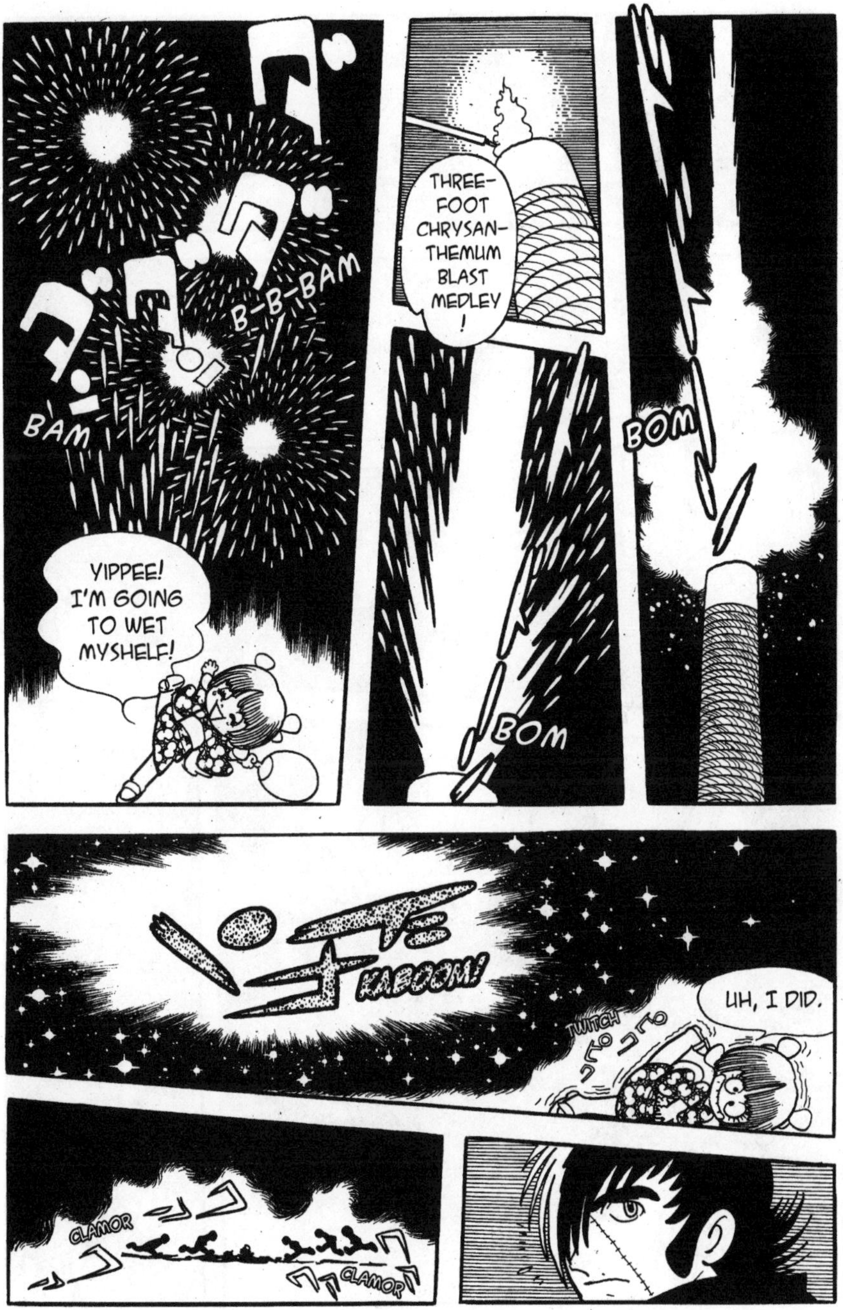
BOM
THREE-FOOT CHRYSANTHEMUM BLAST MEDLEY!
BOM
B-B-BAM
BAM
YIPPEE! I'M GOING TO WET MYSHELF!
KABOOM!
UH, I DID.
TWITCH
CLAMOR
CLAMOR

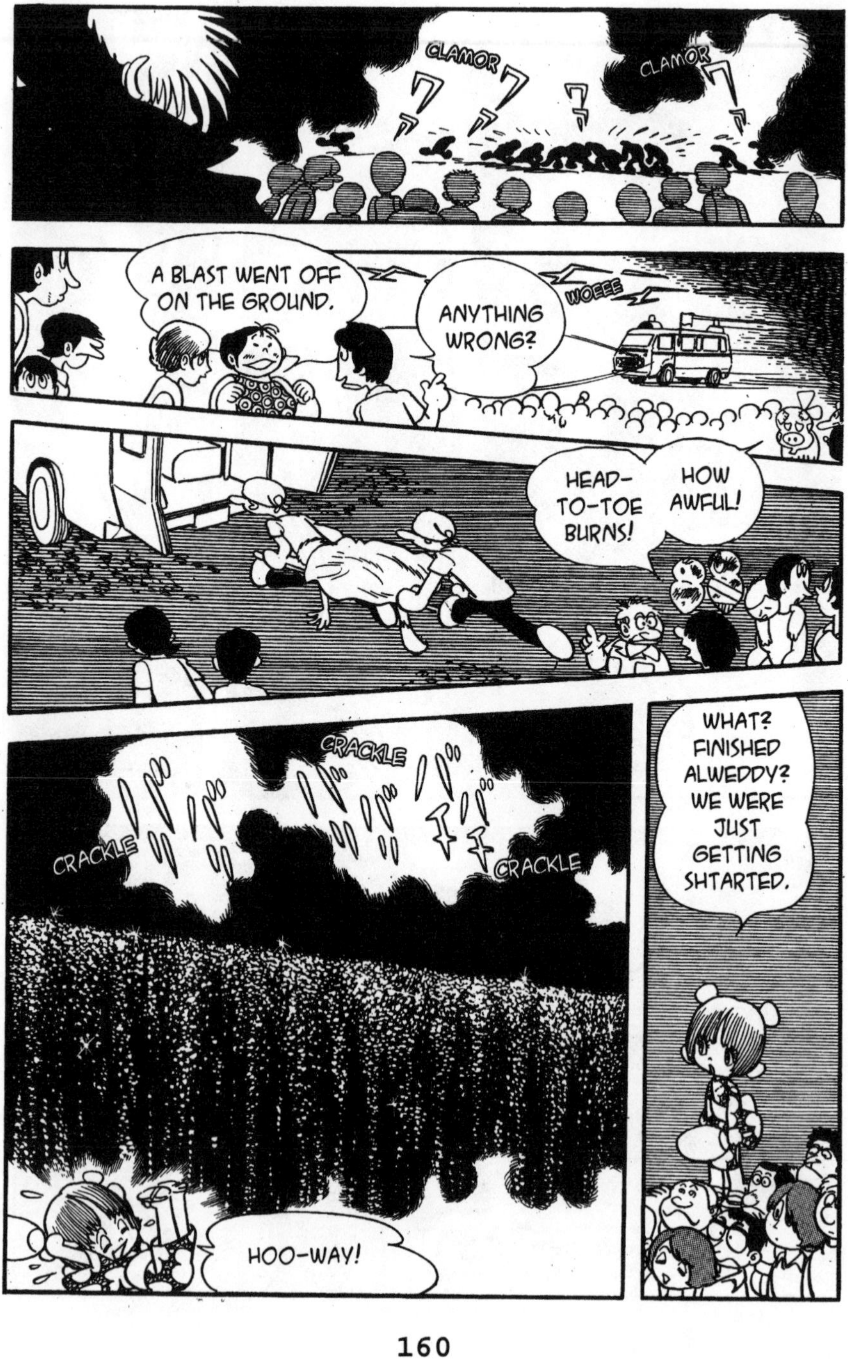
CLAMOR
CLAMOR
WOEEE
ANYTHING WRONG?
A BLAST WENT OFF ON THE GROUND.
HOW AWFUL!
HEAD-TO-TOE BURNS!
WHAT? FINISHED ALWEDDY? WE WERE JUST GETTING SHTARTED.
CRACKLE
CRACKLE
CRACKLE
HOO-WAY!

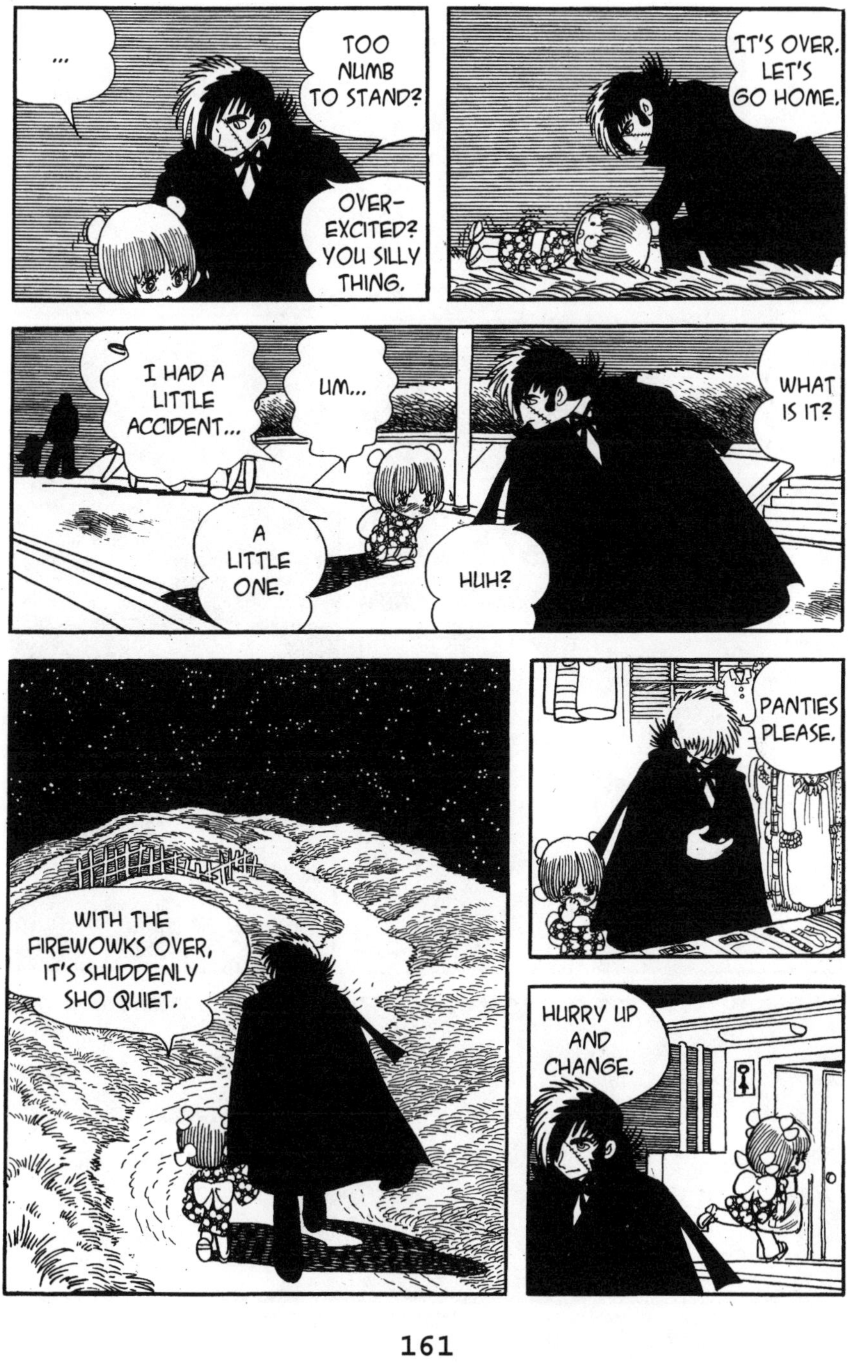
IT'S OVER. LET'S GO HOME.
TOO NUMB TO STAND?
...
OVER-EXCITED? YOU SILLY THING.
WHAT IS IT?
UM...
I HAD A LITTLE ACCIDENT...
HUH?
A LITTLE ONE.
PANTIES PLEASE.
HURRY UP AND CHANGE.
WITH THE FIREWOWKS OVER, IT'S SHUDDENLY SHO QUIET.

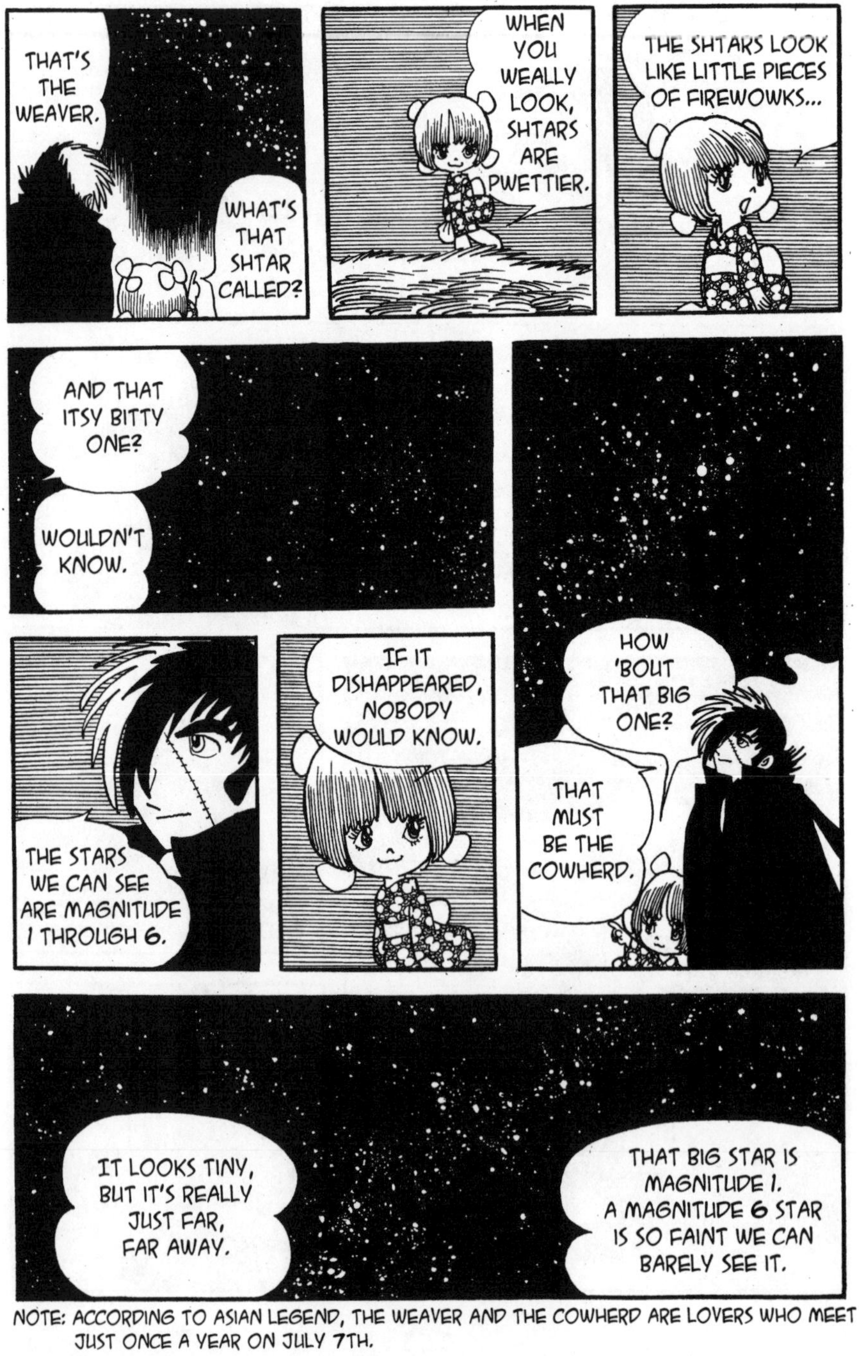
THE SHTARS LOOK LIKE LITTLE PIECES OF FIREWOWKS...
WHEN YOU WEALLY LOOK, SHTARS ARE PWETTIER.
WHAT'S THAT SHTAR CALLED?
THAT'S THE WEAVER.
HOW 'BOUT THAT BIG ONE?
THAT MUST BE THE COWHERD.
AND THAT ITSY BITTY ONE?
WOULDN'T KNOW.
IF IT DISHAPPEARED, NOBODY WOULD KNOW.
THE STARS WE CAN SEE ARE MAGNITUDE 1 THROUGH 6.
THAT BIG STAR IS MAGNITUDE 1. A MAGNITUDE 6 STAR IS SO FAINT WE CAN BARELY SEE IT.
IT LOOKS TINY, BUT IT'S REALLY JUST FAR, FAR AWAY.

NOTE: ACCORDING TO ASIAN LEGEND, THE WEAVER AND THE COWHERD ARE LOVERS WHO MEET JUST ONCE A YEAR ON JULY 7TH.

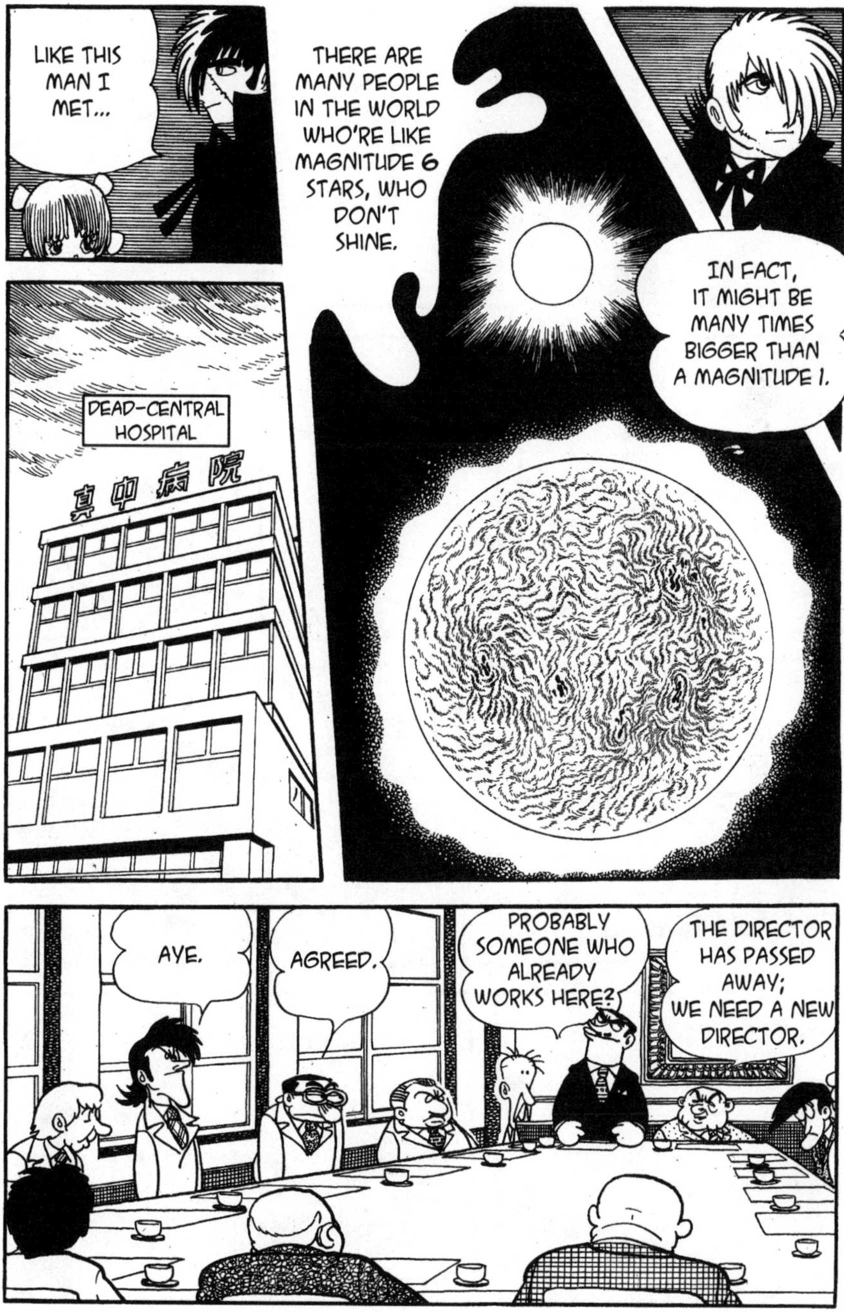
THERE ARE MANY PEOPLE IN THE WORLD WHO'RE LIKE MAGNITUDE 6 STARS, WHO DON'T SHINE.
IN FACT, IT MIGHT BE MANY TIMES BIGGER THAN A MAGNITUDE 1.
LIKE THIS MAN I MET...
DEAD-CENTRAL HOSPITAL
真中病院
THE DIRECTOR HAS PASSED AWAY; WE NEED A NEW DIRECTOR.
PROBABLY SOMEONE WHO ALREADY WORKS HERE?
AGREED.
AYE.

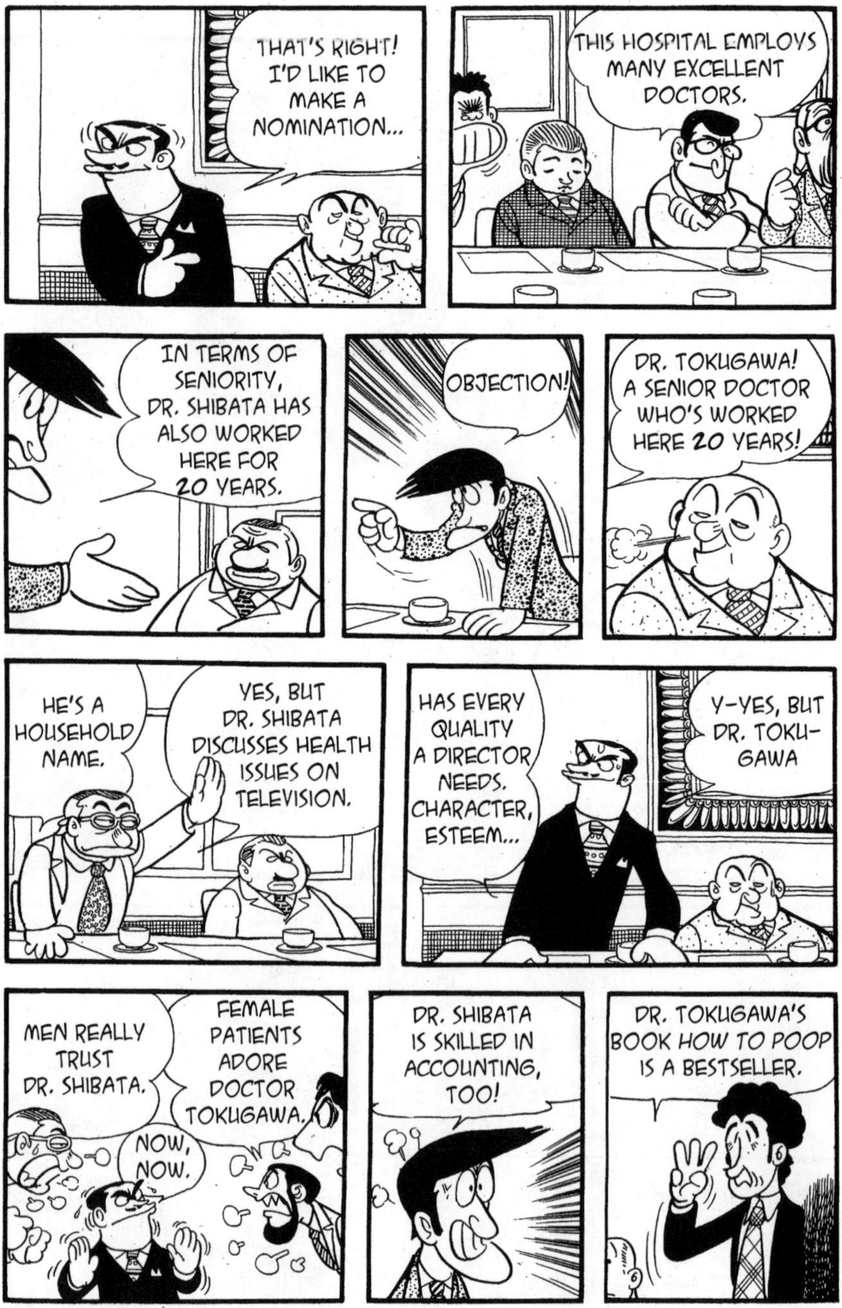
THIS HOSPITAL EMPLOYS MANY EXCELLENT DOCTORS.
THAT'S RIGHT! I'D LIKE TO MAKE A NOMINATION...
DR. TOKUGAWA! A SENIOR DOCTOR WHO'S WORKED HERE 20 YEARS!
OBJECTION!
IN TERMS OF SENIORITY, DR. SHIBATA HAS ALSO WORKED HERE FOR 20 YEARS.
Y-YES, BUT DR. TOKU-GAWA
HAS EVERY QUALITY A DIRECTOR NEEDS. CHARACTER, ESTEEM...
YES, BUT DR. SHIBATA DISCUSSES HEALTH ISSUES ON TELEVISION.
HE'S A HOUSEHOLD NAME.
DR. TOKUGAWA'S BOOK HOW TO POOP IS A BESTSELLER.
DR. SHIBATA IS SKILLED IN ACCOUNTING, TOO!
FEMALE PATIENTS ADORE DOCTOR TOKUGAWA.
MEN REALLY TRUST DR. SHIBATA.
NOW, NOW.

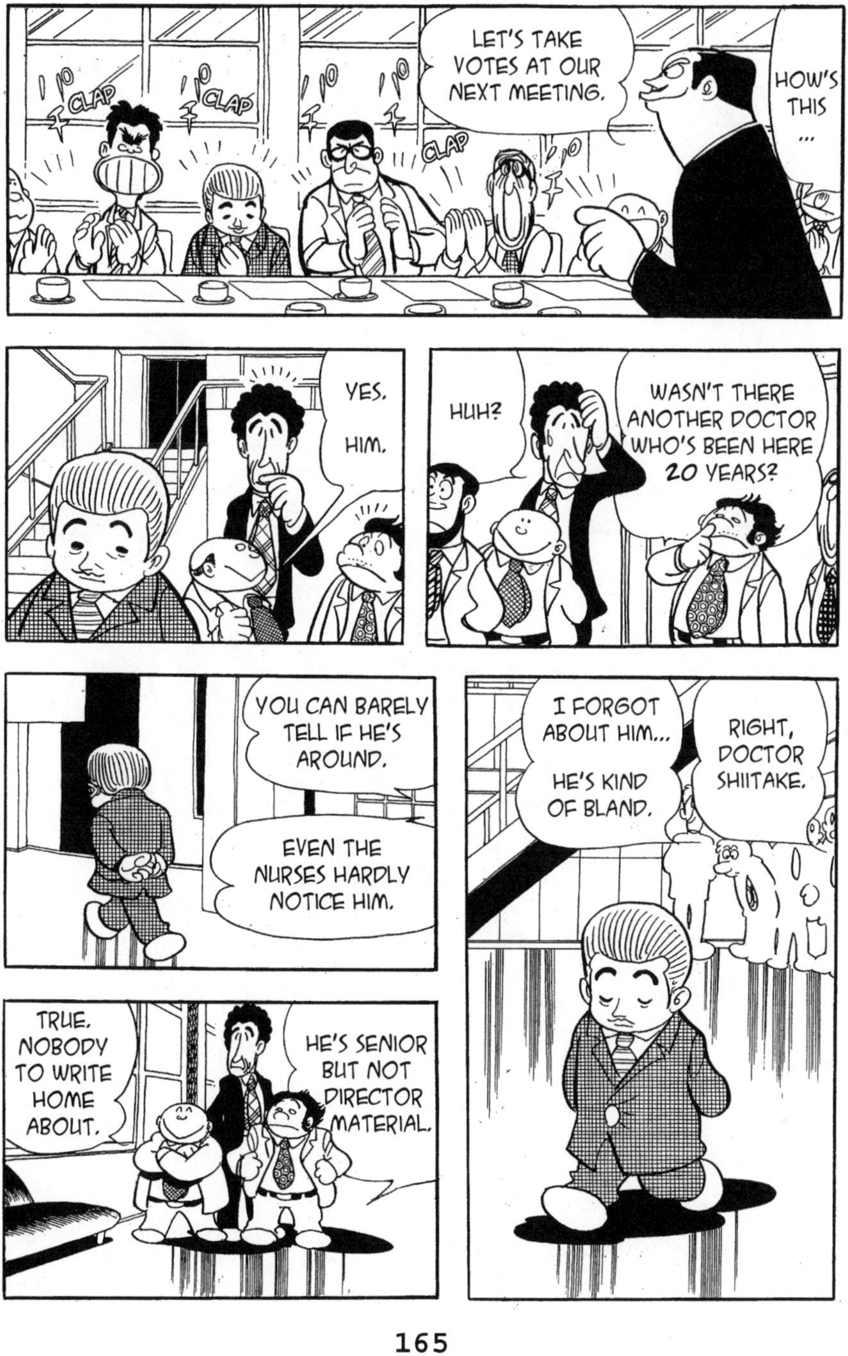
HOW'S THIS ...
LET'S TAKE VOTES AT OUR NEXT MEETING.
CLAP
CLAP
CLAP
CLAP
WASN'T THERE ANOTHER DOCTOR WHO'S BEEN HERE 20 YEARS?
HUH?
YES.
HIM.
RIGHT, DOCTOR SHIITAKE.
I FORGOT ABOUT HIM...
HE'S KIND OF BLAND.
YOU CAN BARELY TELL IF HE'S AROUND.
EVEN THE NURSES HARDLY NOTICE HIM.
HE'S SENIOR BUT NOT DIRECTOR MATERIAL.
TRUE. NOBODY TO WRITE HOME ABOUT.

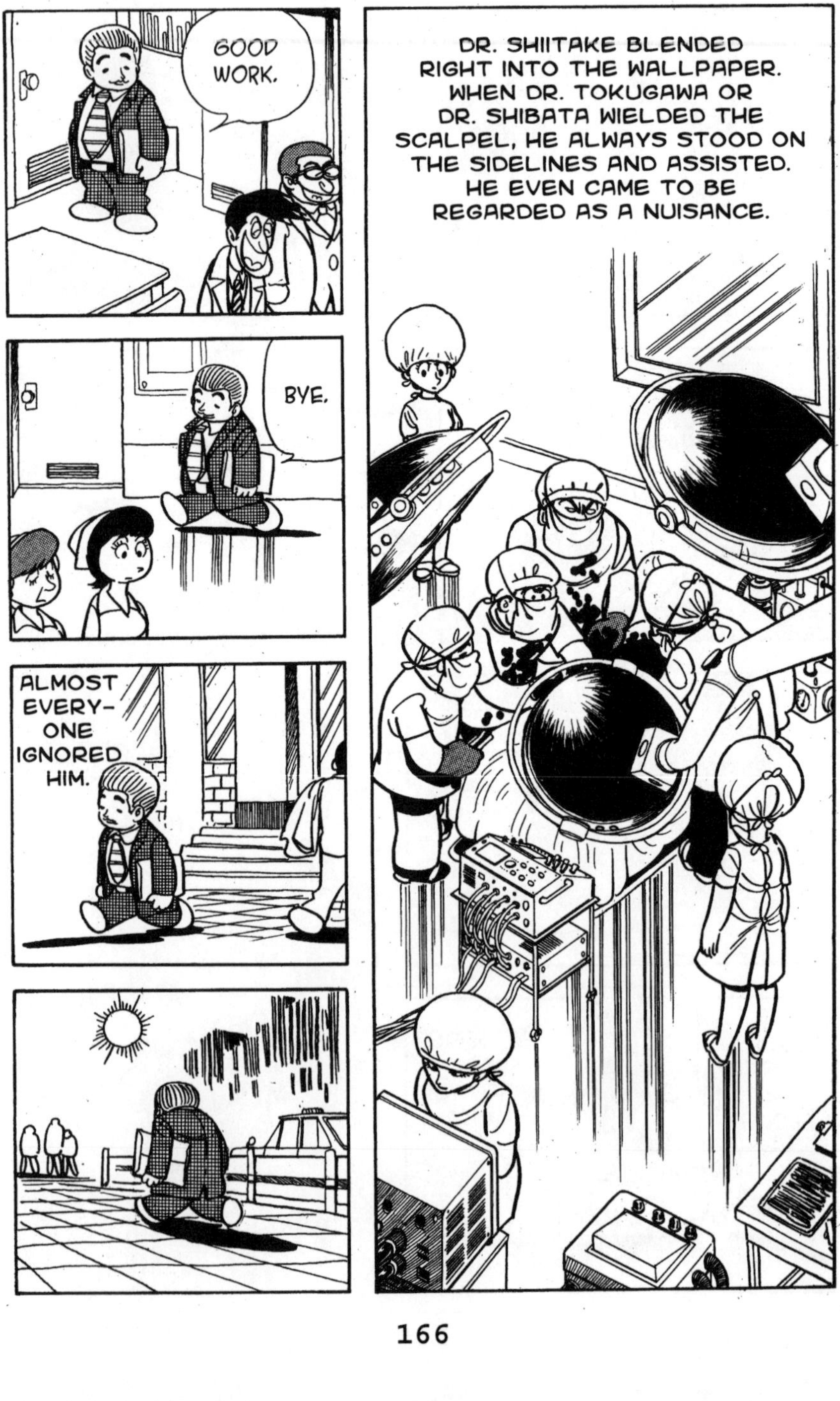
DR. SHIITAKE BLENDED RIGHT INTO THE WALLPAPER. WHEN DR. TOKUGAWA OR DR. SHIBATA WIELDED THE SCALPEL, HE ALWAYS STOOD ON THE SIDELINES AND ASSISTED. HE EVEN CAME TO BE REGARDED AS A NUISANCE.
GOOD WORK.
BYE.
ALMOST EVERY-ONE IGNORED HIM.

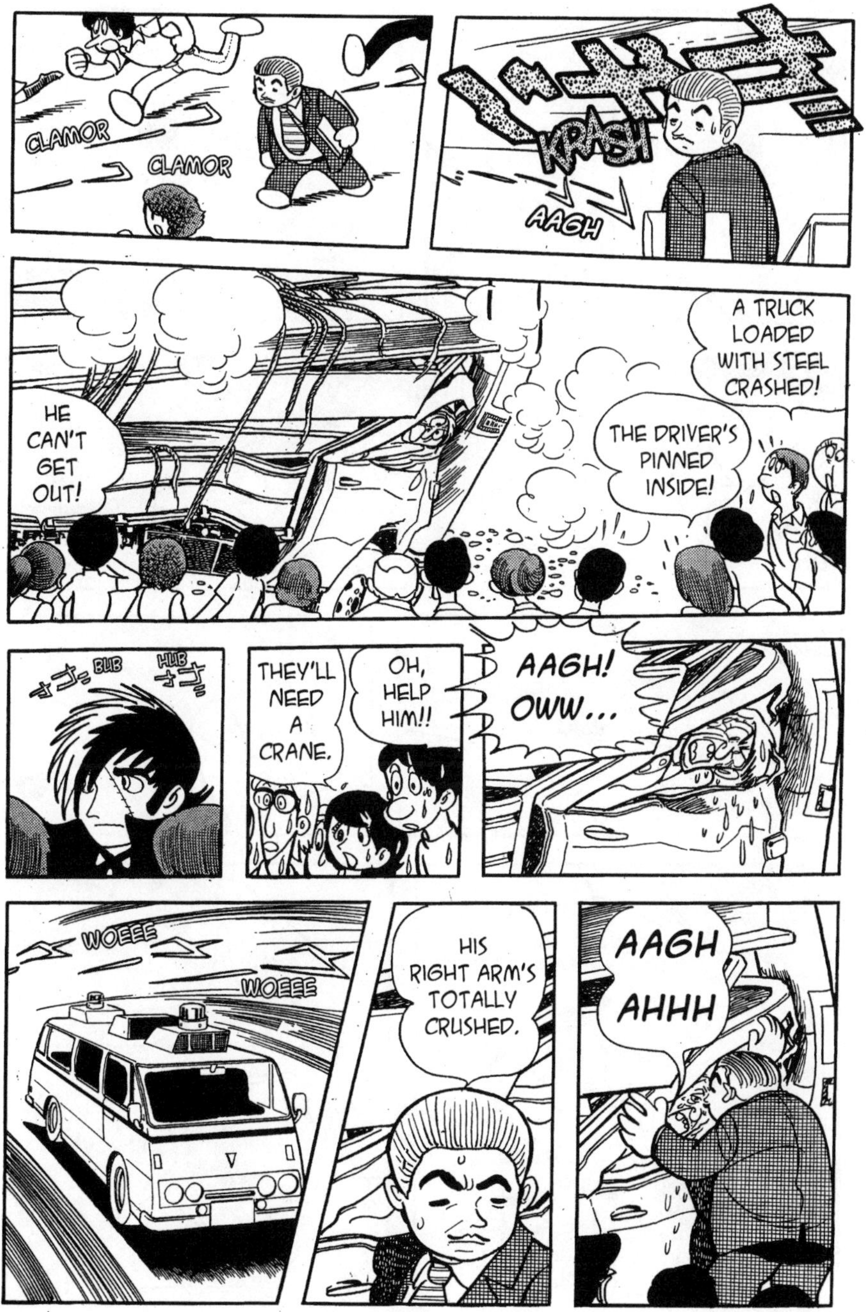
KRASH
AAGH
CLAMOR
CLAMOR
A TRUCK LOADED WITH STEEL CRASHED!
THE DRIVER'S PINNED INSIDE!
HE CAN'T GET OUT!
AAGH! OWW...
OH, HELP HIM!!
THEY'LL NEED A CRANE.
HUB
BUB
AAGH AHHH
HIS RIGHT ARM'S TOTALLY CRUSHED.
WOEEE
WOEEE

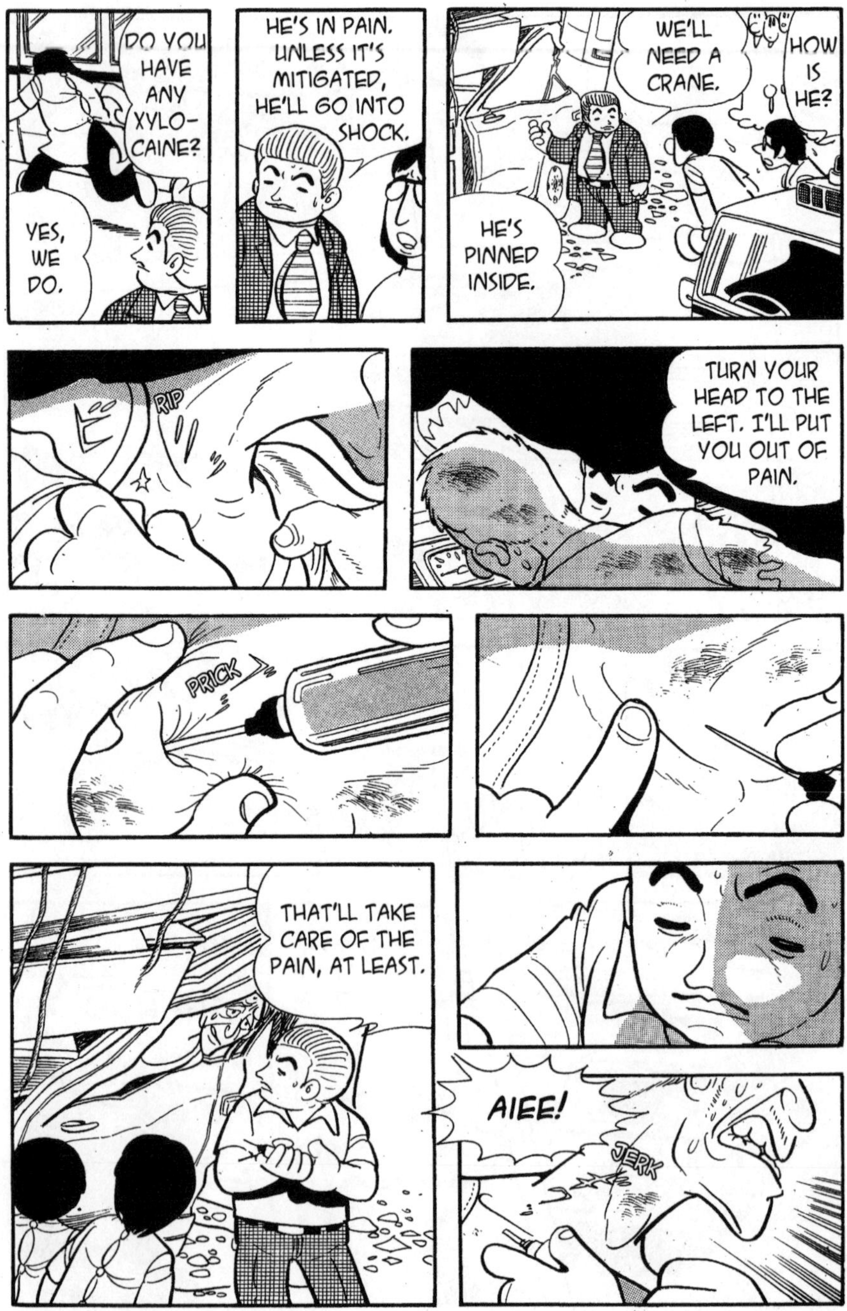
HOW IS HE?
WE'LL NEED A CRANE.
HE'S PINNED INSIDE.
HE'S IN PAIN. UNLESS IT'S MITIGATED, HE'LL GO INTO SHOCK.
DO YOU HAVE ANY XYLO-CAINE?
YES, WE DO.
TURN YOUR HEAD TO THE LEFT. I'LL PUT YOU OUT OF PAIN.
RIP
PRICK
AIEE!
JERK
THAT'LL TAKE CARE OF THE PAIN, AT LEAST.

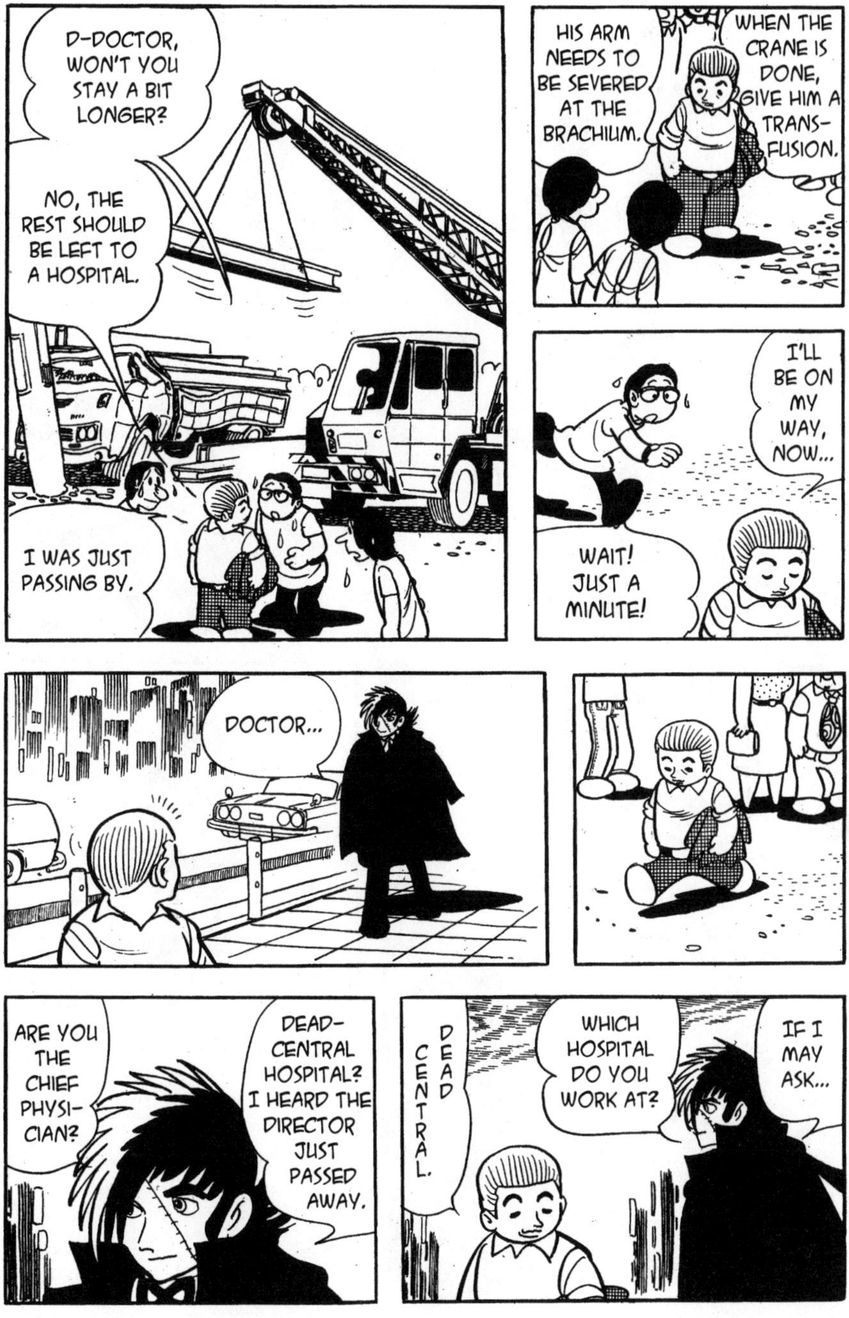
WHEN THE CRANE IS DONE, GIVE HIM A TRANSFUSION.
HIS ARM NEEDS TO BE SEVERED AT THE BRACHIUM.
I'LL BE ON MY WAY, NOW...
WAIT! JUST A MINUTE!
D-DOCTOR, WON'T YOU STAY A BIT LONGER?
NO, THE REST SHOULD BE LEFT TO A HOSPITAL.
I WAS JUST PASSING BY.
DOCTOR...
IF I MAY ASK...
WHICH HOSPITAL DO YOU WORK AT?
DEAD CENTRAL.
DEAD-CENTRAL HOSPITAL? I HEARD THE DIRECTOR JUST PASSED AWAY.
ARE YOU THE CHIEF PHYSICIAN?

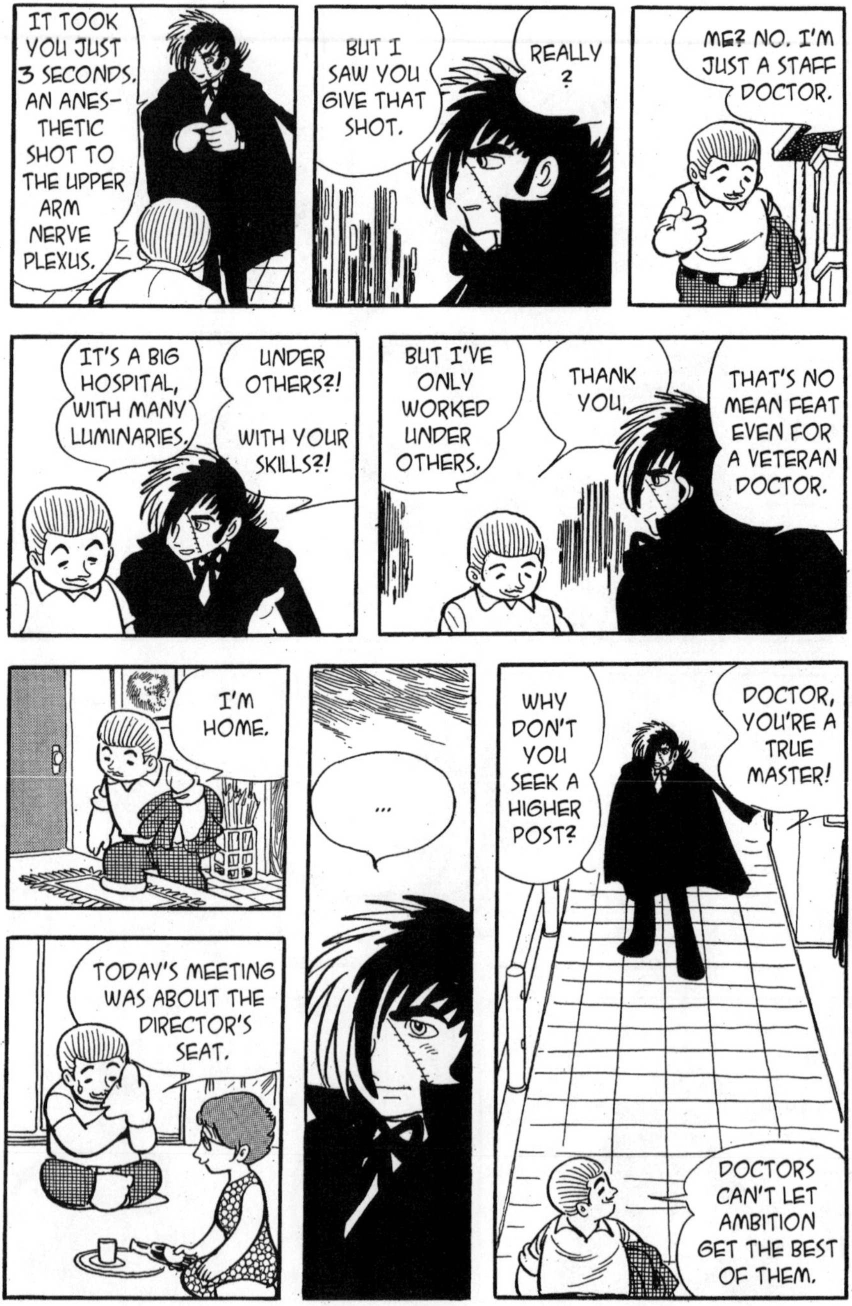

ME? NO. I'M JUST A STAFF DOCTOR.
REALLY?
BUT I SAW YOU GIVE THAT SHOT.
IT TOOK YOU JUST 3 SECONDS. AN ANES-THETIC SHOT TO THE UPPER ARM NERVE PLEXUS.
THAT'S NO MEAN FEAT EVEN FOR A VETERAN DOCTOR.
THANK YOU.
BUT I'VE ONLY WORKED UNDER OTHERS.
UNDER OTHERS?! WITH YOUR SKILLS?!
IT'S A BIG HOSPITAL, WITH MANY LUMINARIES.
DOCTOR, YOU'RE A TRUE MASTER!
WHY DON'T YOU SEEK A HIGHER POST?
DOCTORS CAN'T LET AMBITION GET THE BEST OF THEM.
...
I'M HOME.
TODAY'S MEETING WAS ABOUT THE DIRECTOR'S SEAT.

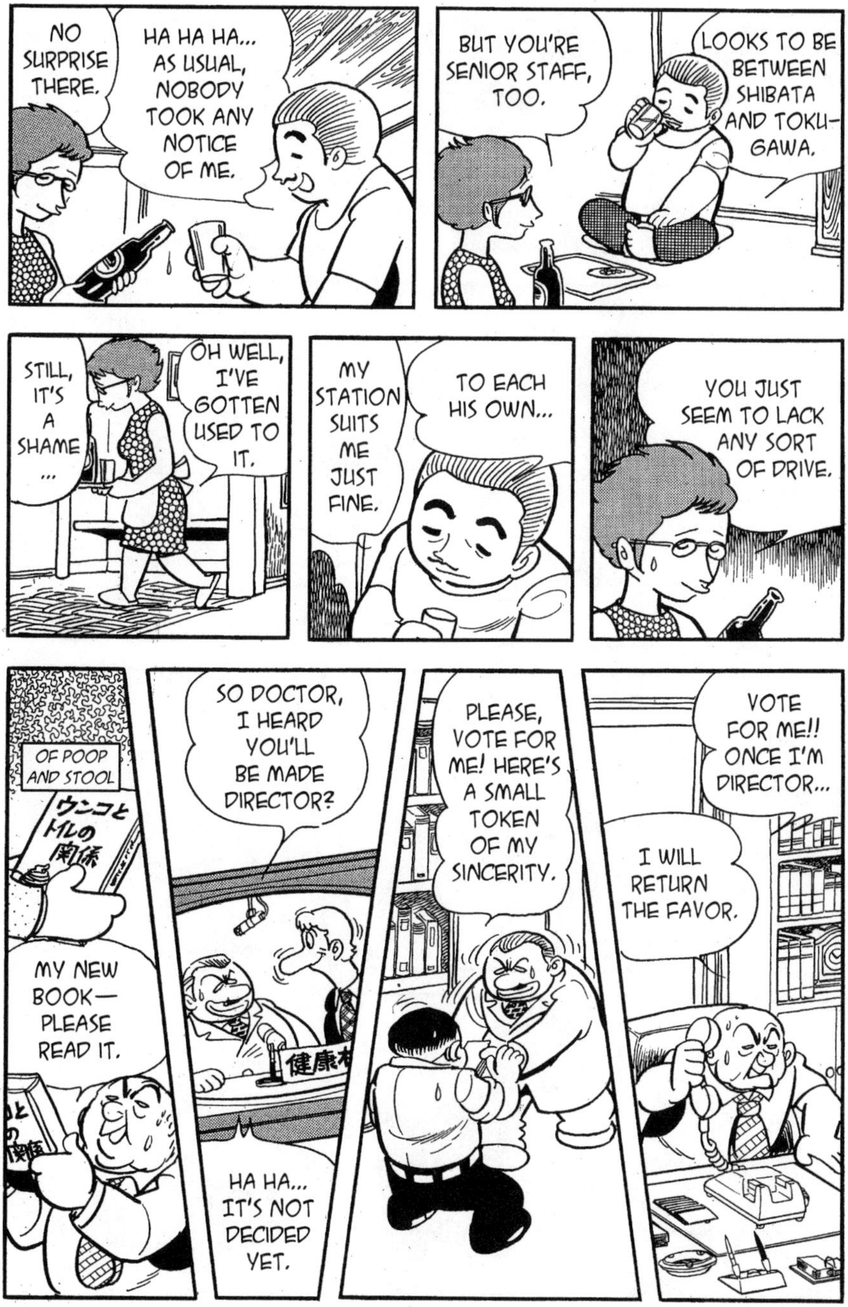
LOOKS TO BE BETWEEN SHIBATA AND TOKUGAWA.
BUT YOU'RE SENIOR STAFF, TOO.
HA HA HA... AS USUAL, NOBODY TOOK ANY NOTICE OF ME.
NO SURPRISE THERE.
YOU JUST SEEM TO LACK ANY SORT OF DRIVE.
TO EACH HIS OWN...
MY STATION SUITS ME JUST FINE.
OH WELL, I'VE GOTTEN USED TO IT.
STILL, IT'S A SHAME ...
VOTE FOR ME!! ONCE I'M DIRECTOR...
I WILL RETURN THE FAVOR.
PLEASE, VOTE FOR ME! HERE'S A SMALL TOKEN OF MY SINCERITY.
SO DOCTOR, I HEARD YOU'LL BE MADE DIRECTOR?
HA HA... IT'S NOT DECIDED YET.
OF POOP AND STOOL
MY NEW BOOK—PLEASE READ IT.

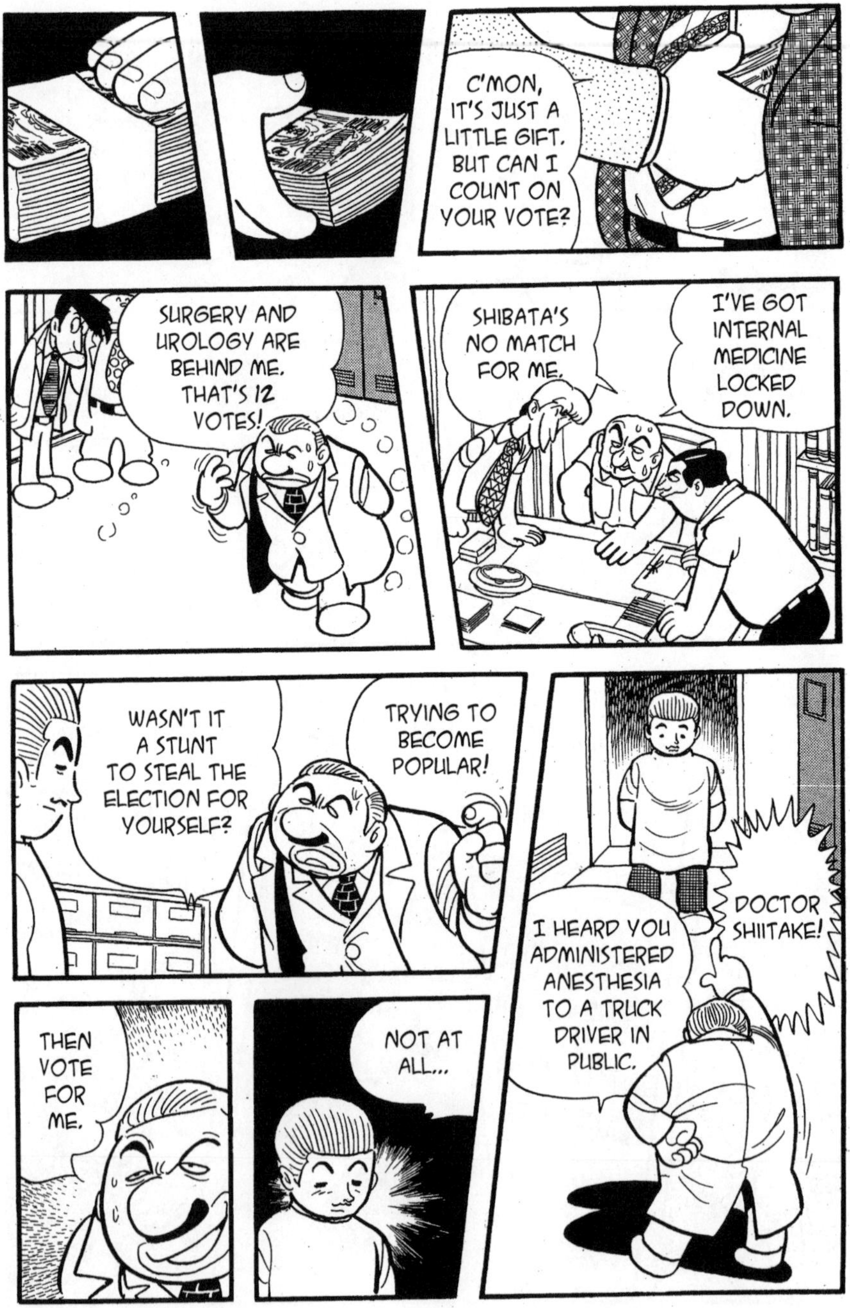
C'MON, IT'S JUST A LITTLE GIFT. BUT CAN I COUNT ON YOUR VOTE?
I'VE GOT INTERNAL MEDICINE LOCKED DOWN.
SHIBATA'S NO MATCH FOR ME.
SURGERY AND UROLOGY ARE BEHIND ME. THAT'S 12 VOTES!
DOCTOR SHIITAKE!
I HEARD YOU ADMINISTERED ANESTHESIA TO A TRUCK DRIVER IN PUBLIC.
TRYING TO BECOME POPULAR!
WASN'T IT A STUNT TO STEAL THE ELECTION FOR YOURSELF?
NOT AT ALL...
THEN VOTE FOR ME.

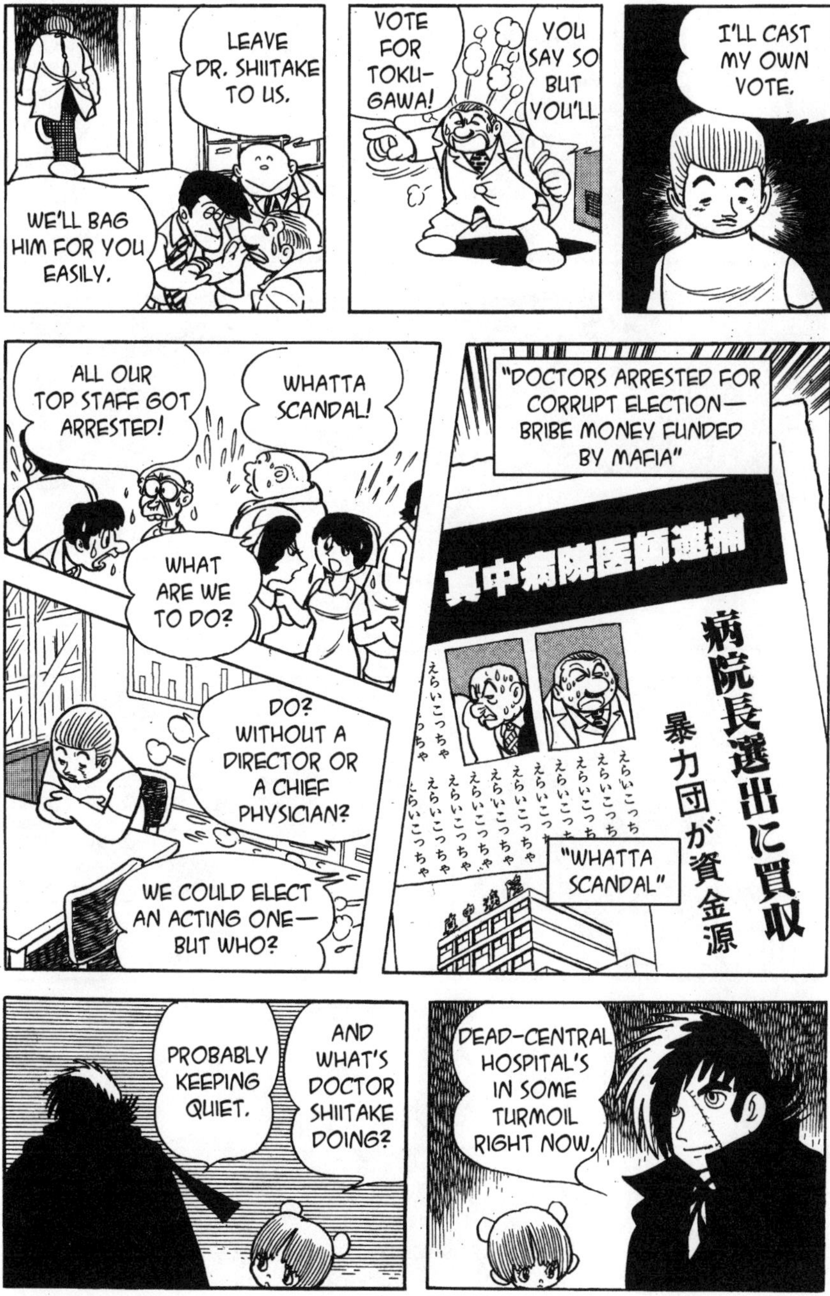
I'LL CAST MY OWN VOTE.
YOU SAY SO BUT YOU'LL
VOTE FOR TOKU-GAWA!
LEAVE DR. SHIITAKE TO US.
WE'LL BAG HIM FOR YOU EASILY.
"DOCTORS ARRESTED FOR CORRUPT ELECTION—BRIBE MONEY FUNDED BY MAFIA"
真中病院医師逮捕
病院長選出に買収
暴力団が資金源
えらいこっちゃ
"WHATTA SCANDAL"
WHATTA SCANDAL!
ALL OUR TOP STAFF GOT ARRESTED!
WHAT ARE WE TO DO?
DO? WITHOUT A DIRECTOR OR A CHIEF PHYSICIAN?
WE COULD ELECT AN ACTING ONE—BUT WHO?
DEAD-CENTRAL HOSPITAL'S IN SOME TURMOIL RIGHT NOW.
AND WHAT'S DOCTOR SHIITAKE DOING?
PROBABLY KEEPING QUIET.

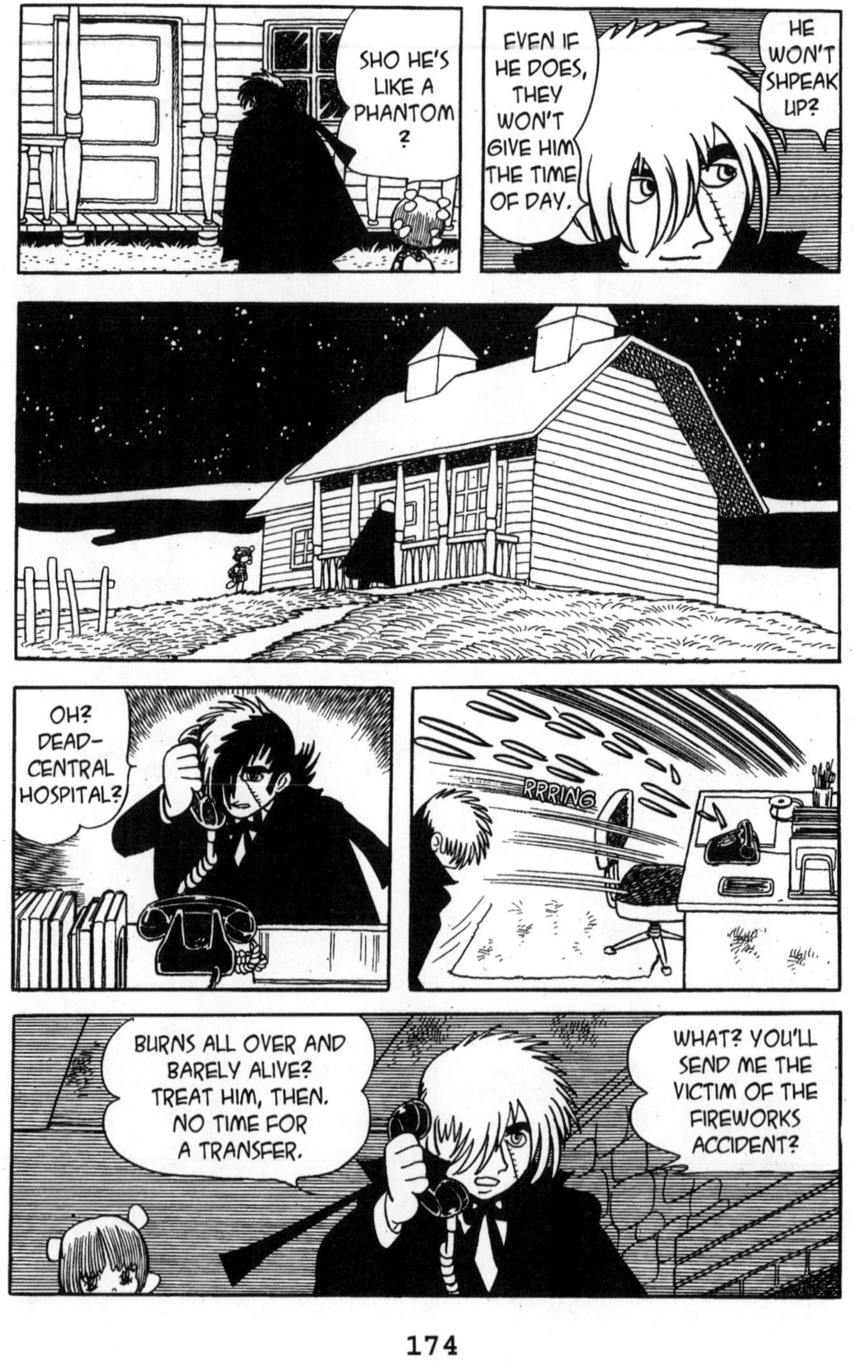
HE WON'T SHPEAK UP?
EVEN IF HE DOES, THEY WON'T GIVE HIM THE TIME OF DAY.
SHO HE'S LIKE A PHANTOM?
RRRING
OH? DEAD-CENTRAL HOSPITAL?
WHAT? YOU'LL SEND ME THE VICTIM OF THE FIREWORKS ACCIDENT?
BURNS ALL OVER AND BARELY ALIVE? TREAT HIM, THEN. NO TIME FOR A TRANSFER.

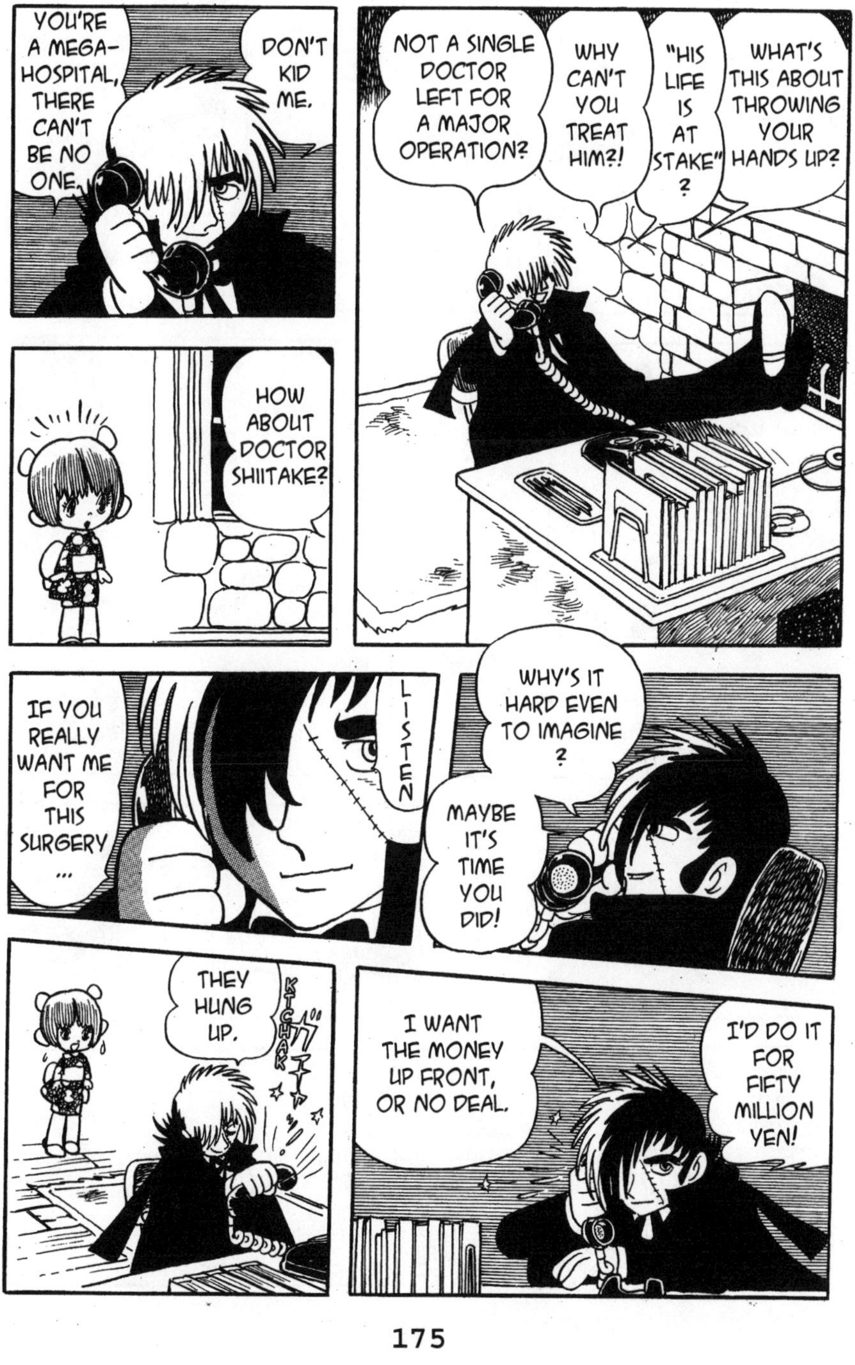
WHAT'S THIS ABOUT THROWING YOUR HANDS UP?
"HIS LIFE IS AT STAKE"?
WHY CAN'T YOU TREAT HIM?!
NOT A SINGLE DOCTOR LEFT FOR A MAJOR OPERATION?
DON'T KID ME.
YOU'RE A MEGA-HOSPITAL, THERE CAN'T BE NO ONE.
HOW ABOUT DOCTOR SHIITAKE?
WHY'S IT HARD EVEN TO IMAGINE?
MAYBE IT'S TIME YOU DID!
LISTEN
IF YOU REALLY WANT ME FOR THIS SURGERY ...
I'D DO IT FOR FIFTY MILLION YEN!
I WANT THE MONEY UP FRONT, OR NO DEAL.
KTCHAK
THEY HUNG UP.

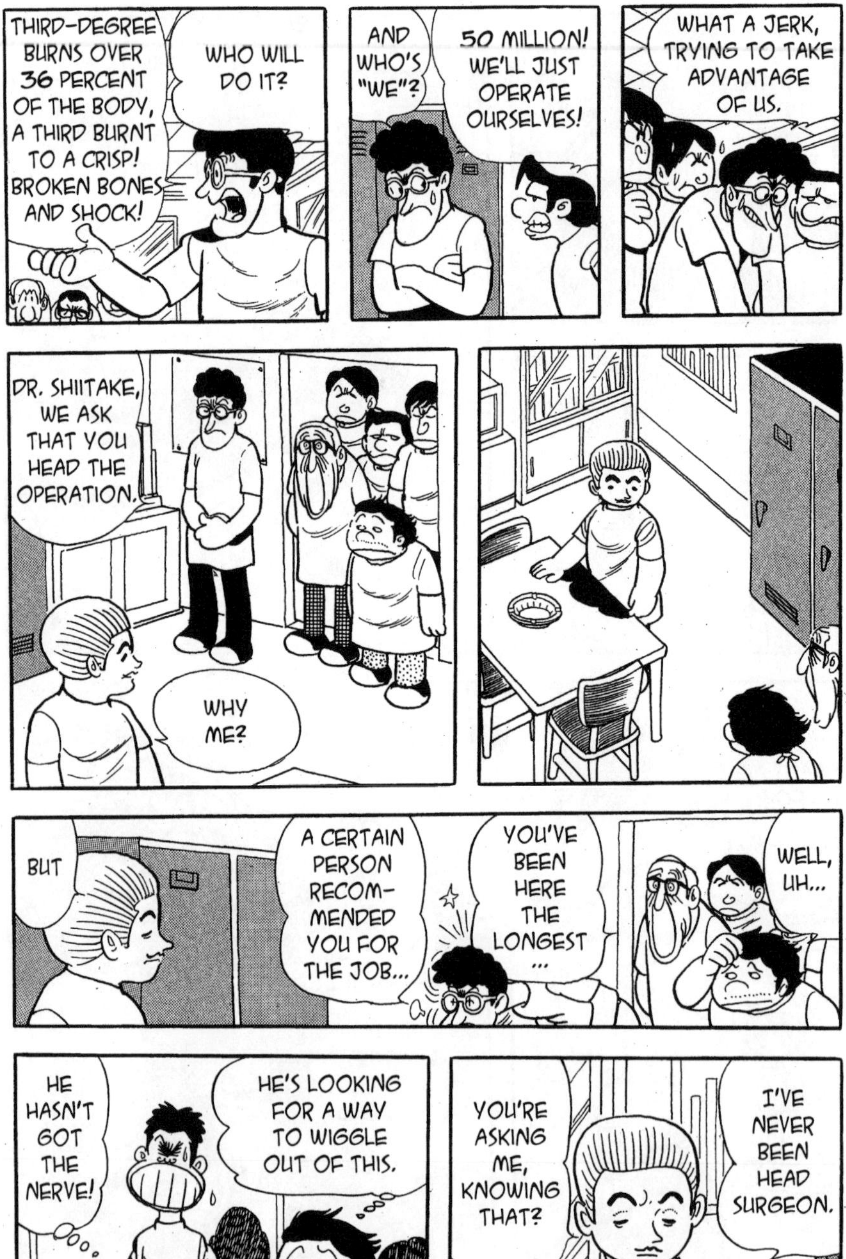
THIRD-DEGREE BURNS OVER 36 PERCENT OF THE BODY, A THIRD BURNT TO A CRISP! BROKEN BONES AND SHOCK!
WHO WILL DO IT?
50 MILLION! WE'LL JUST OPERATE OURSELVES!
AND WHO'S "WE"?
WHAT A JERK, TRYING TO TAKE ADVANTAGE OF US.
DR. SHIITAKE, WE ASK THAT YOU HEAD THE OPERATION.
WHY ME?
BUT
A CERTAIN PERSON RECOMMENDED YOU FOR THE JOB...
YOU'VE BEEN HERE THE LONGEST ...
WELL, UH...
HE HASN'T GOT THE NERVE!
HE'S LOOKING FOR A WAY TO WIGGLE OUT OF THIS.
I'VE NEVER BEEN HEAD SURGEON.
YOU'RE ASKING ME, KNOWING THAT?

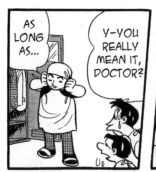

I'LL DO IT.
WH
A
T?
Y-YOU REALLY MEAN IT, DOCTOR?
AS LONG AS...
YOU'LL ALL SUPPORT ME AND...
FOLLOW MY INSTRUCTIONS AS THE OPERATING SURGEON.
O-OF COURSE SIR.
RAKE THE HOSPITAL FOR SKIN DONORS,
PRONTO!
THE OFFICE OF ADMINISTRATION MUST BE TOLD TO REMUNERATE ALL OF THEM GENEROUSLY.
THE MAN IS SERIOUS.
KEEP UP THE BLOOD SUPPLY!
ANTI-TETANIC SERUM!
WE HAVE A SKIN DONOR.

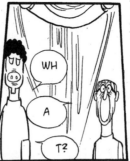

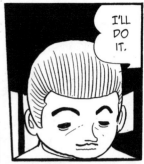

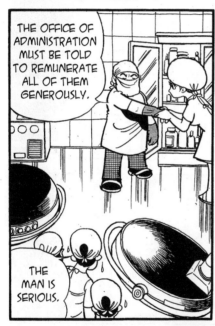

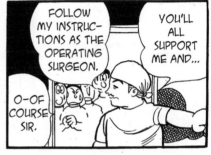

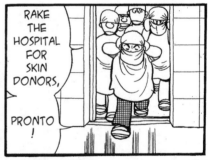

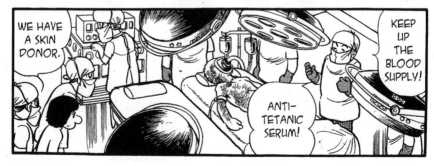

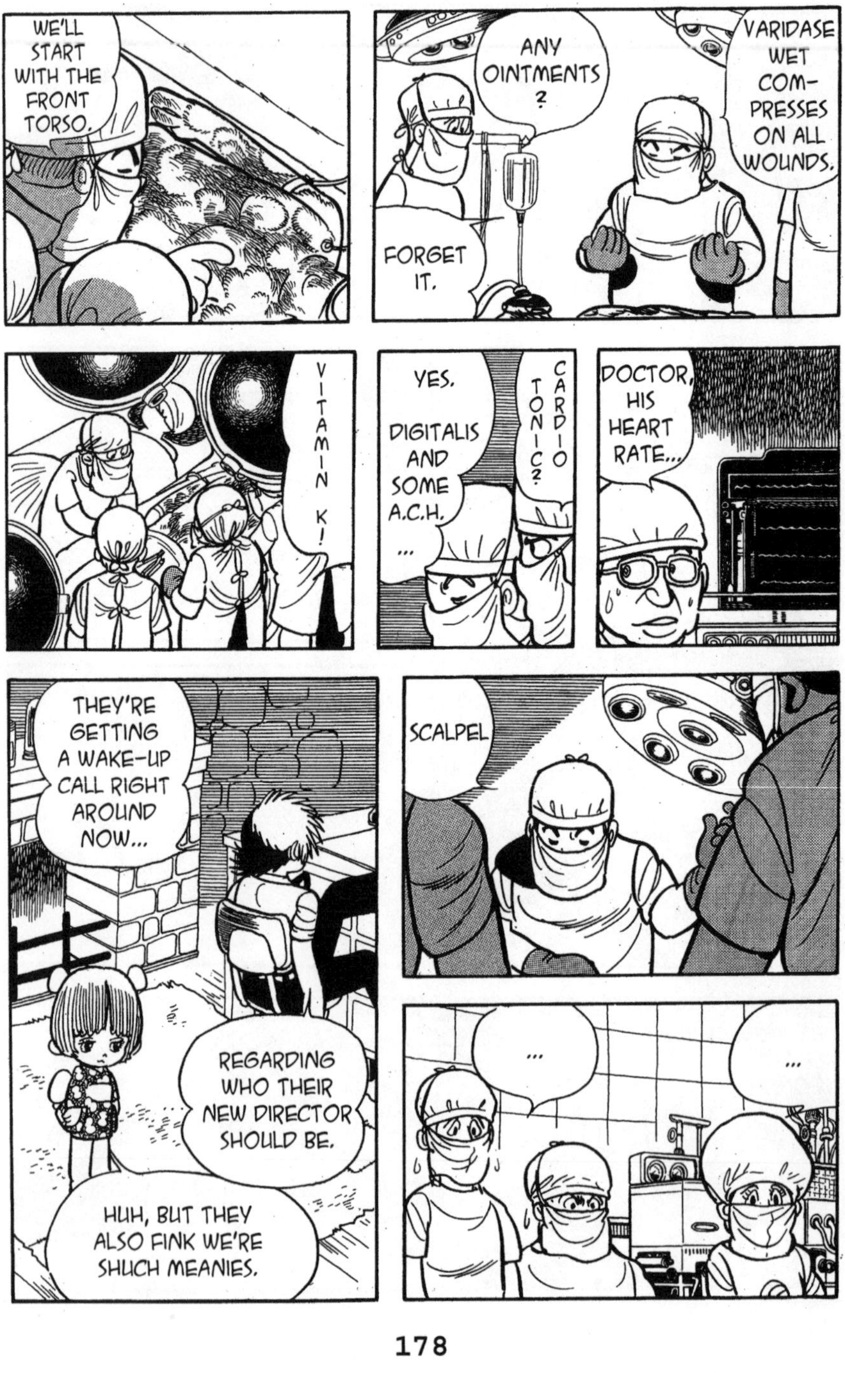
VARIDASE WET COMPRESSES ON ALL WOUNDS.
ANY OINTMENTS?
FORGET IT.
WE'LL START WITH THE FRONT TORSO.
DOCTOR, HIS HEART RATE...
CARDIO TONIC?
YES.
DIGITALIS AND SOME A.C.H. ...
VITAMIN K!
SCALPEL
...
...
THEY'RE GETTING A WAKE-UP CALL RIGHT AROUND NOW...
REGARDING WHO THEIR NEW DIRECTOR SHOULD BE.
HUH, BUT THEY ALSO FINK WE'RE SHUCH MEANIES.

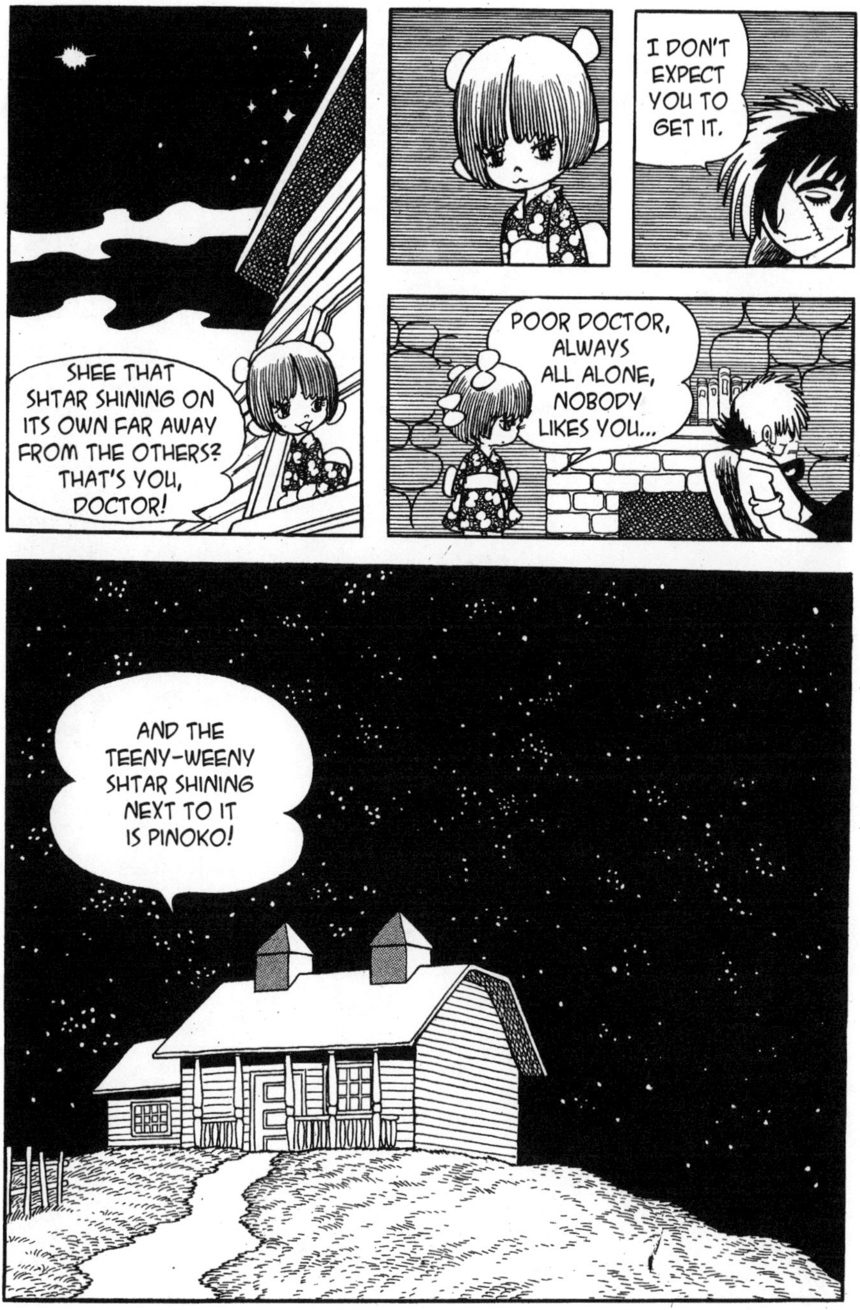
I DON'T EXPECT YOU TO GET IT.
POOR DOCTOR, ALWAYS ALL ALONE, NOBODY LIKES YOU...
SHEE THAT SHTAR SHINING ON ITS OWN FAR AWAY FROM THE OTHERS? THAT'S YOU, DOCTOR!
AND THE TEENY-WEENY SHTAR SHINING NEXT TO IT IS PINOKO!

BLACK QUEEN

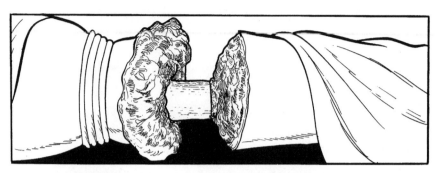

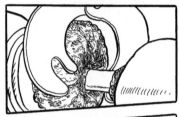

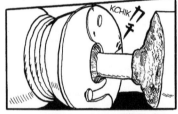

FEMUR EX-POSED!
APPLY SOFT-TISSUE LIFT DEVICE.
KCHIK カチ
SAW.
GRK ゴリ
GRK ゴリゴリ
GRK
GRIK
GRK

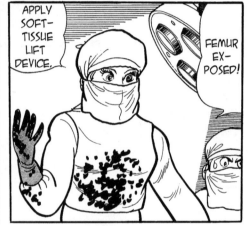

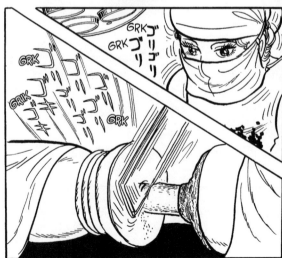

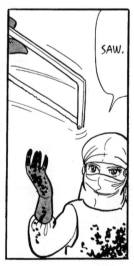

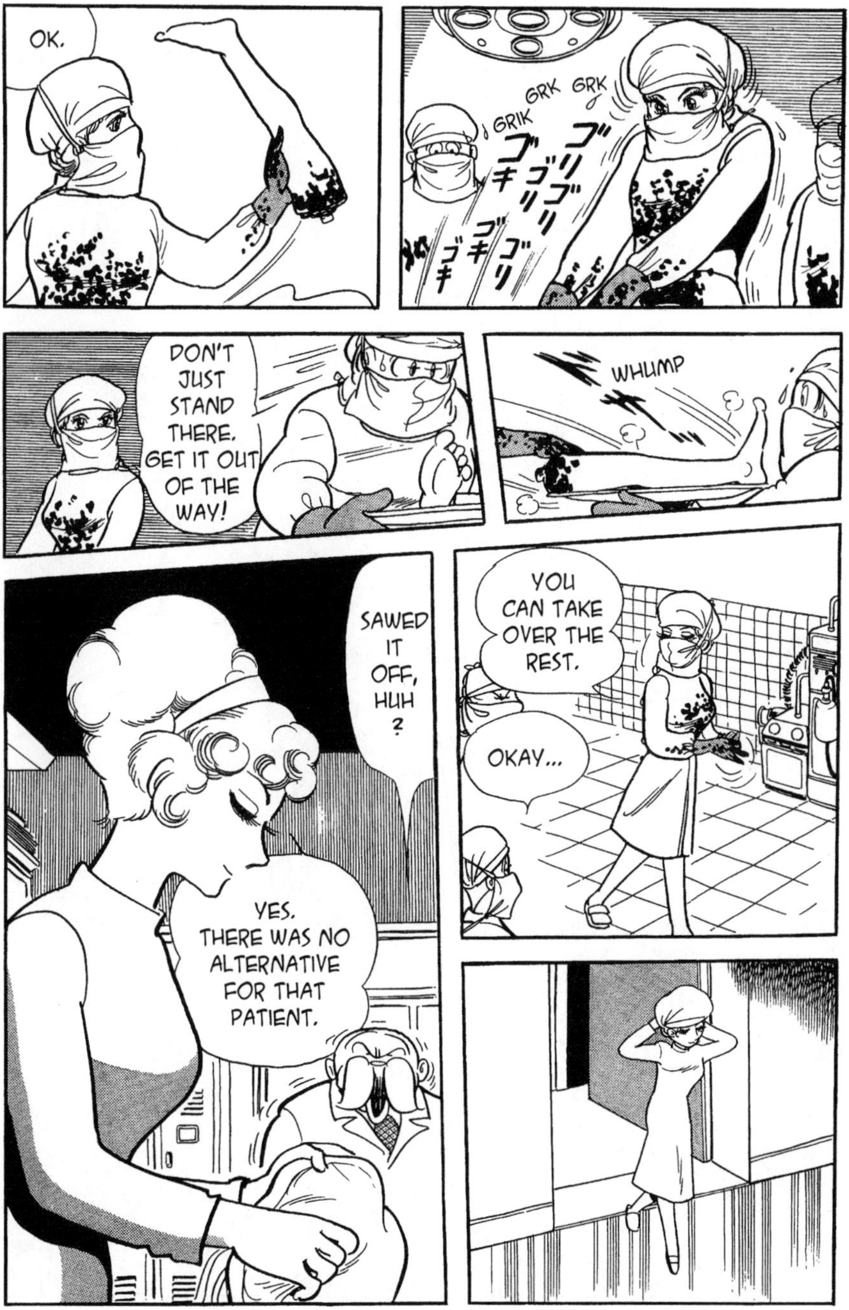
GRIK GRK GRK
OK.
WHUMP
DON'T JUST STAND THERE. GET IT OUT OF THE WAY!
YOU CAN TAKE OVER THE REST.
OKAY...
SAWED IT OFF, HUH?
YES. THERE WAS NO ALTERNATIVE FOR THAT PATIENT.

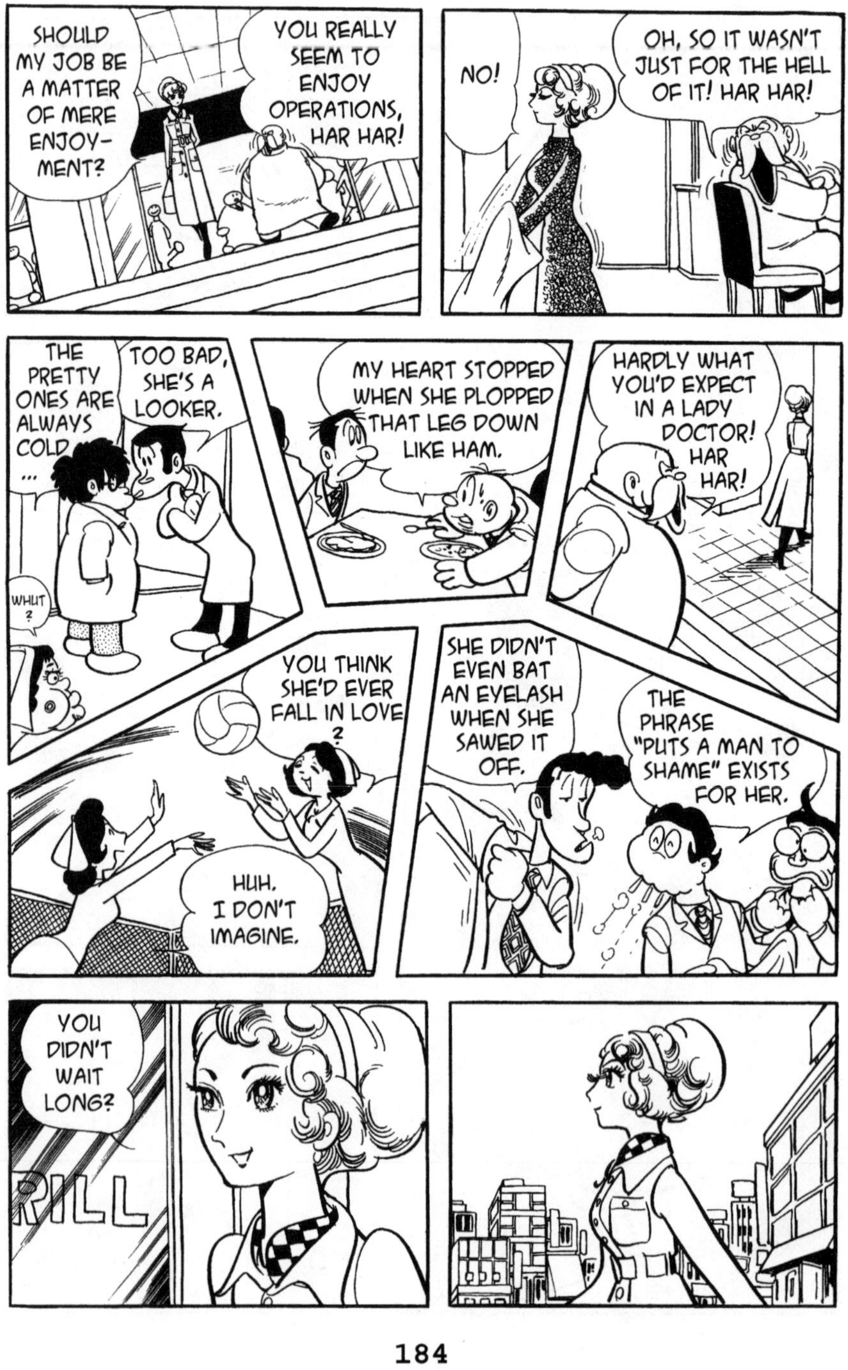
YOU REALLY SEEM TO ENJOY OPERATIONS, HAR HAR!
SHOULD MY JOB BE A MATTER OF MERE ENJOY-MENT?
NO!
OH, SO IT WASN'T JUST FOR THE HELL OF IT! HAR HAR!
THE PRETTY ONES ARE ALWAYS COLD ...
TOO BAD, SHE'S A LOOKER.
WHUT ?
MY HEART STOPPED WHEN SHE PLOPPED THAT LEG DOWN LIKE HAM.
HARDLY WHAT YOU'D EXPECT IN A LADY DOCTOR! HAR HAR!
YOU THINK SHE'D EVER FALL IN LOVE ?
HUH. I DON'T IMAGINE.
SHE DIDN'T EVEN BAT AN EYELASH WHEN SHE SAWED IT OFF.
THE PHRASE "PUTS A MAN TO SHAME" EXISTS FOR HER.
YOU DIDN'T WAIT LONG?
RILL

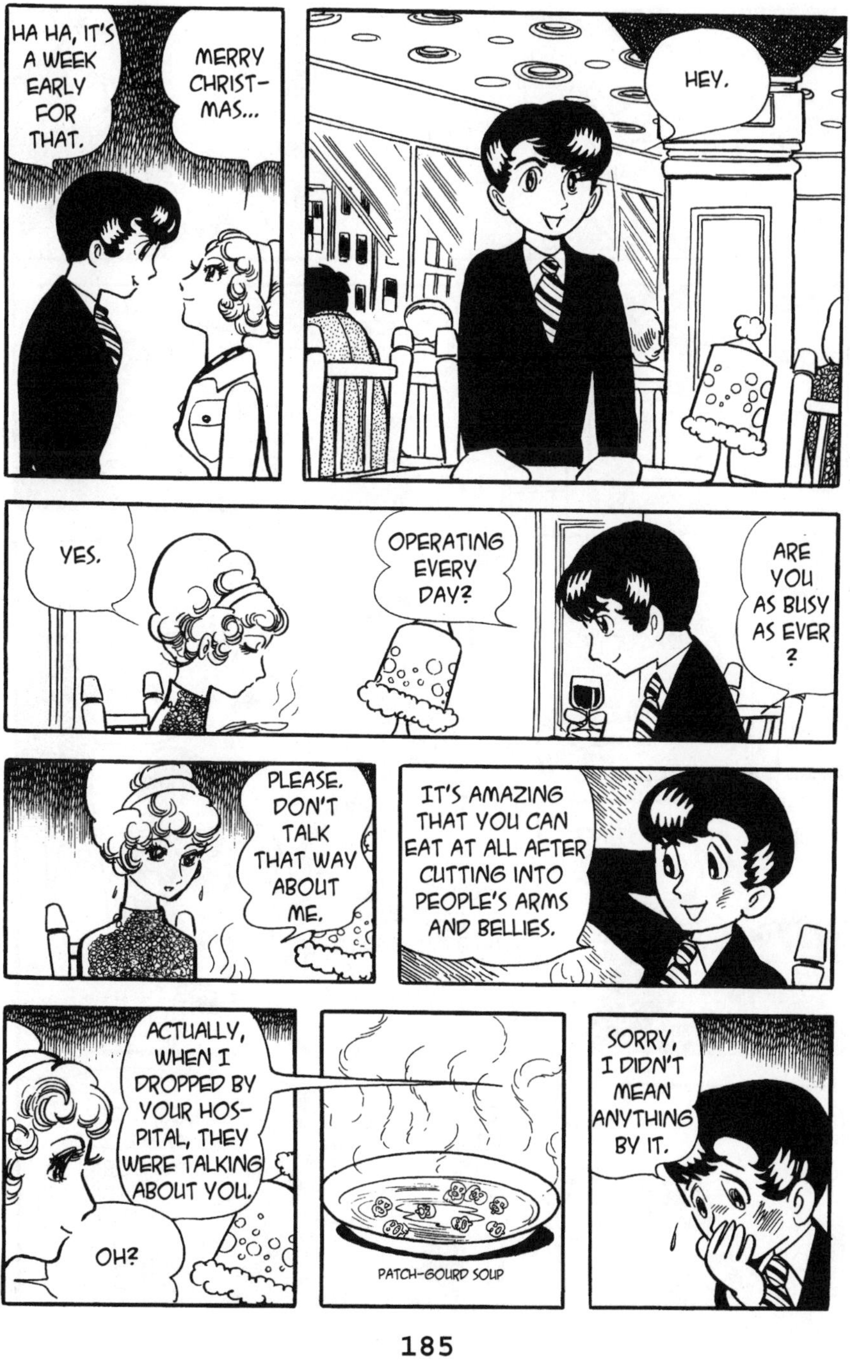
HEY.
MERRY CHRIST-MAS...
HA HA, IT'S A WEEK EARLY FOR THAT.
ARE YOU AS BUSY AS EVER?
OPERATING EVERY DAY?
YES.
IT'S AMAZING THAT YOU CAN EAT AT ALL AFTER CUTTING INTO PEOPLE'S ARMS AND BELLIES.
PLEASE. DON'T TALK THAT WAY ABOUT ME.
SORRY, I DIDN'T MEAN ANYTHING BY IT.
PATCH-GOURD SOUP
ACTUALLY, WHEN I DROPPED BY YOUR HOS-PITAL, THEY WERE TALKING ABOUT YOU.
OH?

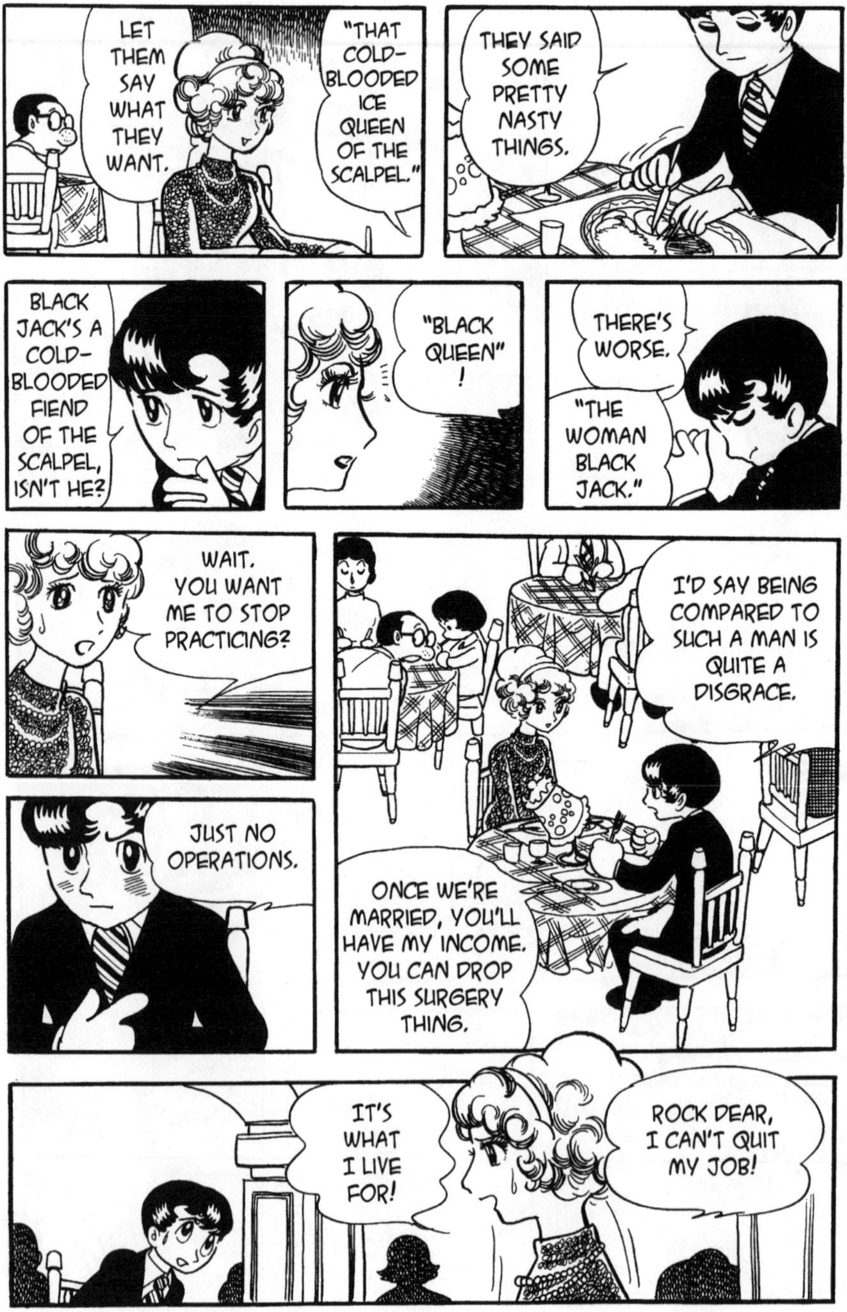
THEY SAID SOME PRETTY NASTY THINGS.
"THAT COLD-BLOODED ICE QUEEN OF THE SCALPEL."
LET THEM SAY WHAT THEY WANT.
THERE'S WORSE.
"THE WOMAN BLACK JACK."
"BLACK QUEEN"!
BLACK JACK'S A COLD-BLOODED FIEND OF THE SCALPEL, ISN'T HE?
I'D SAY BEING COMPARED TO SUCH A MAN IS QUITE A DISGRACE.
ONCE WE'RE MARRIED, YOU'LL HAVE MY INCOME. YOU CAN DROP THIS SURGERY THING.
WAIT. YOU WANT ME TO STOP PRACTICING?
JUST NO OPERATIONS.
ROCK DEAR, I CAN'T QUIT MY JOB!
IT'S WHAT I LIVE FOR!

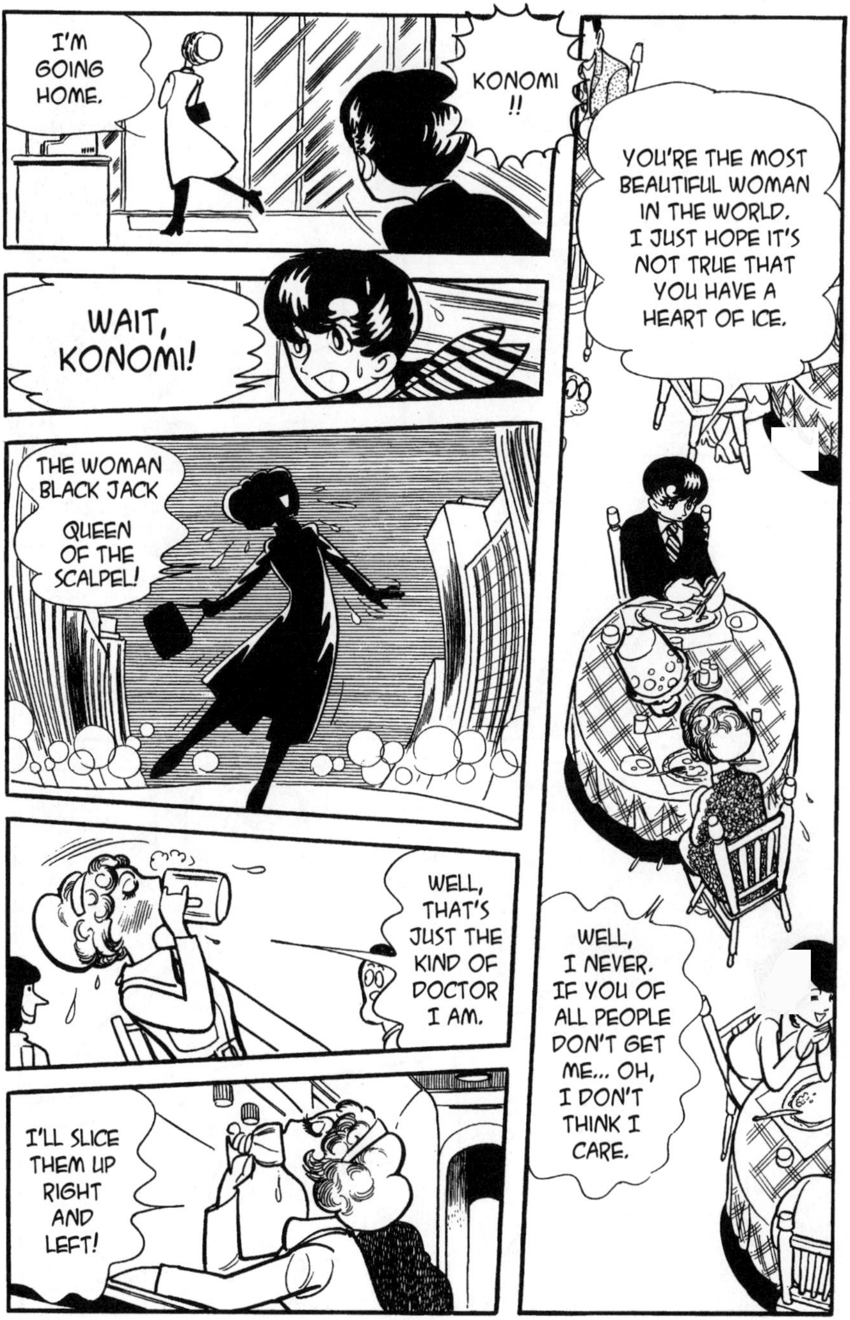
YOU'RE THE MOST BEAUTIFUL WOMAN IN THE WORLD. I JUST HOPE IT'S NOT TRUE THAT YOU HAVE A HEART OF ICE.
WELL, I NEVER. IF YOU OF ALL PEOPLE DON'T GET ME... OH, I DON'T THINK I CARE.
KONOMI !!
I'M GOING HOME.
WAIT, KONOMI!
THE WOMAN BLACK JACK
QUEEN OF THE SCALPEL!
WELL, THAT'S JUST THE KIND OF DOCTOR I AM.
I'LL SLICE THEM UP RIGHT AND LEFT!

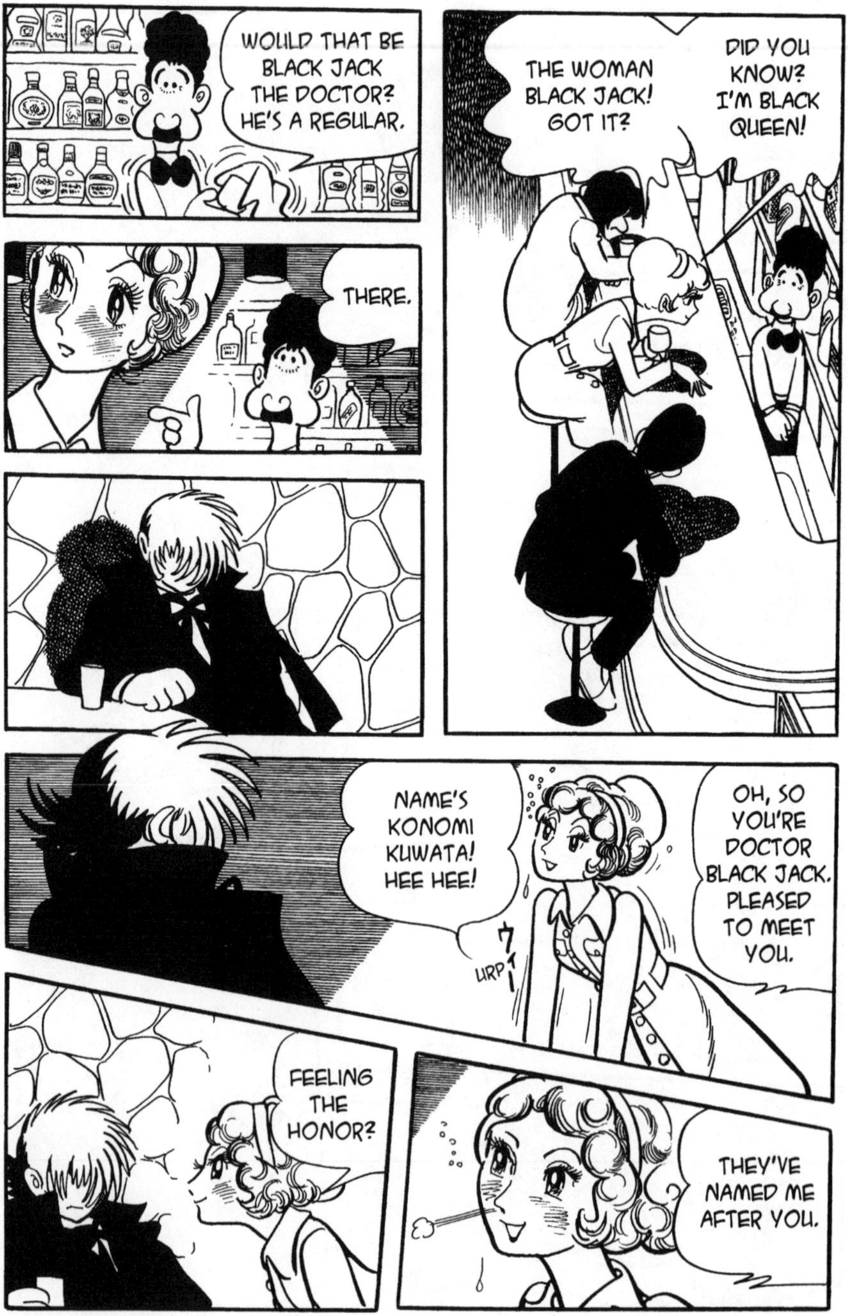
DID YOU KNOW? I'M BLACK QUEEN!
THE WOMAN BLACK JACK! GOT IT?
WOULD THAT BE BLACK JACK THE DOCTOR? HE'S A REGULAR.
THERE.
OH, SO YOU'RE DOCTOR BLACK JACK. PLEASED TO MEET YOU.
NAME'S KONOMI KUWATA! HEE HEE!
ウィー
URP
THEY'VE NAMED ME AFTER YOU.
FEELING THE HONOR?

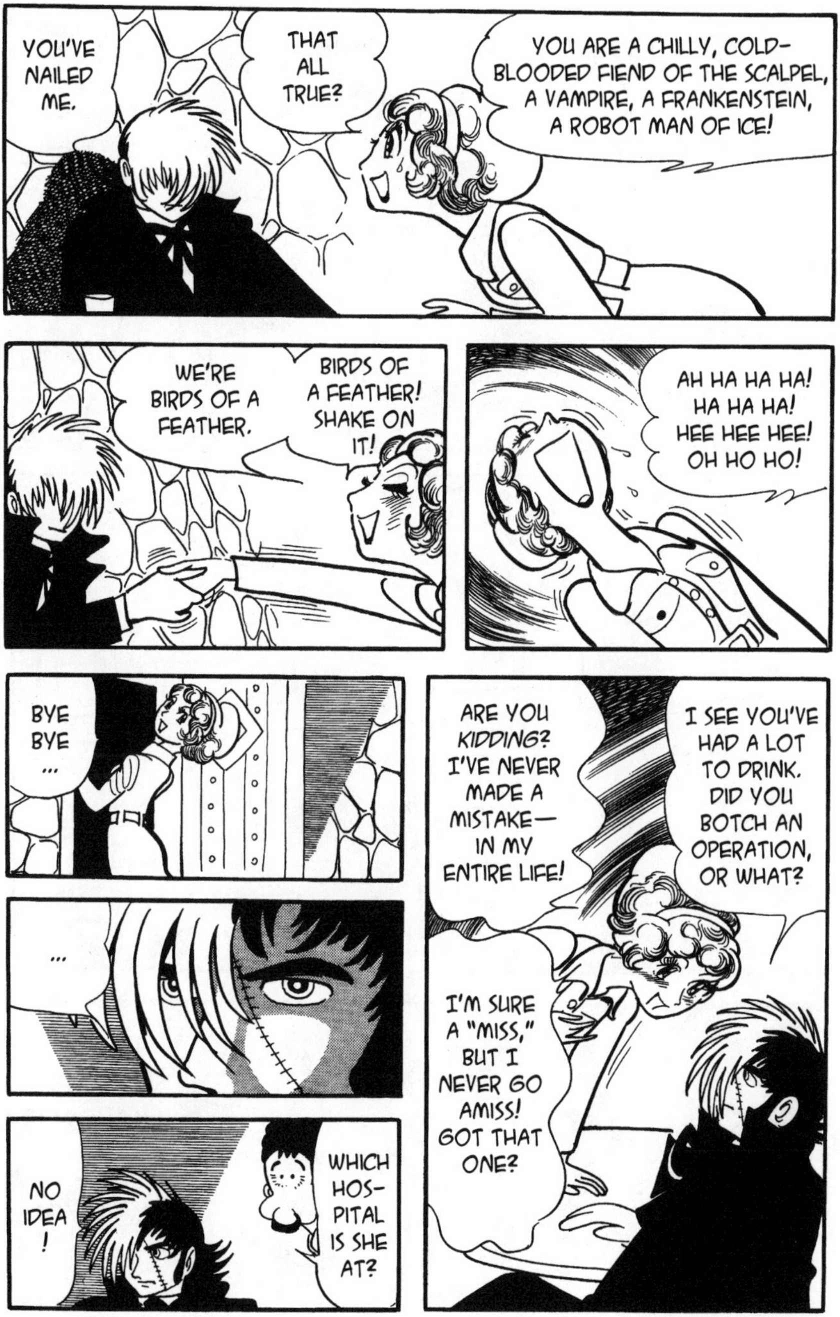
YOU ARE A CHILLY, COLD-BLOODED FIEND OF THE SCALPEL, A VAMPIRE, A FRANKENSTEIN, A ROBOT MAN OF ICE!
THAT ALL TRUE?
YOU'VE NAILED ME.
AH HA HA HA! HA HA HA! HEE HEE HEE! OH HO HO!
BIRDS OF A FEATHER! SHAKE ON IT!
WE'RE BIRDS OF A FEATHER.
I SEE YOU'VE HAD A LOT TO DRINK. DID YOU BOTCH AN OPERATION, OR WHAT?
ARE YOU *KIDDING*? I'VE NEVER MADE A MISTAKE— IN MY ENTIRE LIFE!
I'M SURE A "MISS," BUT I NEVER GO AMISS! GOT THAT ONE?
BYE BYE ...
...
WHICH HOS-PITAL IS SHE AT?
NO IDEA !

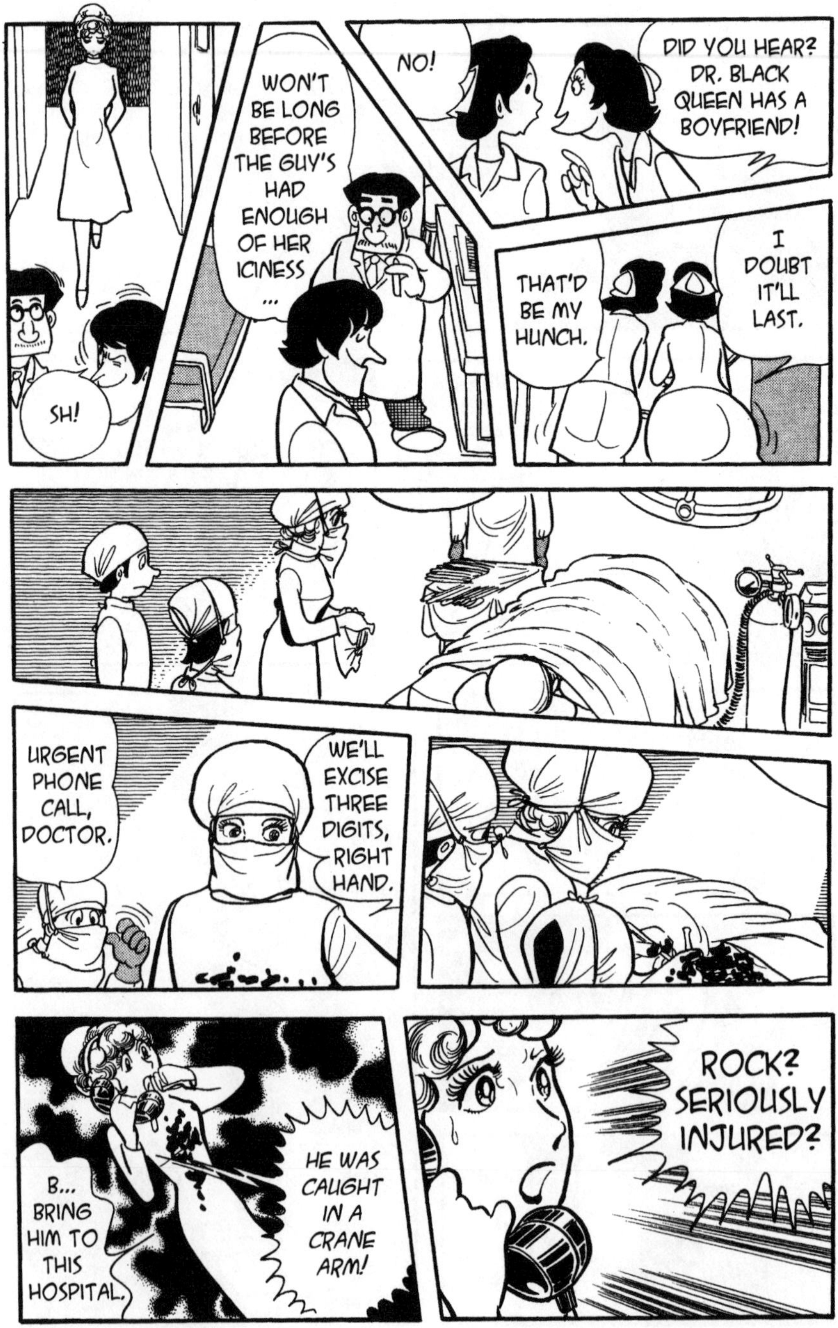
DID YOU HEAR? DR. BLACK QUEEN HAS A BOYFRIEND!
NO!
I DOUBT IT'LL LAST.
THAT'D BE MY HUNCH.
WON'T BE LONG BEFORE THE GUY'S HAD ENOUGH OF HER ICINESS ...
SH!
WE'LL EXCISE THREE DIGITS, RIGHT HAND.
URGENT PHONE CALL, DOCTOR.
ROCK? SERIOUSLY INJURED?
HE WAS CAUGHT IN A CRANE ARM!
B... BRING HIM TO THIS HOSPITAL.

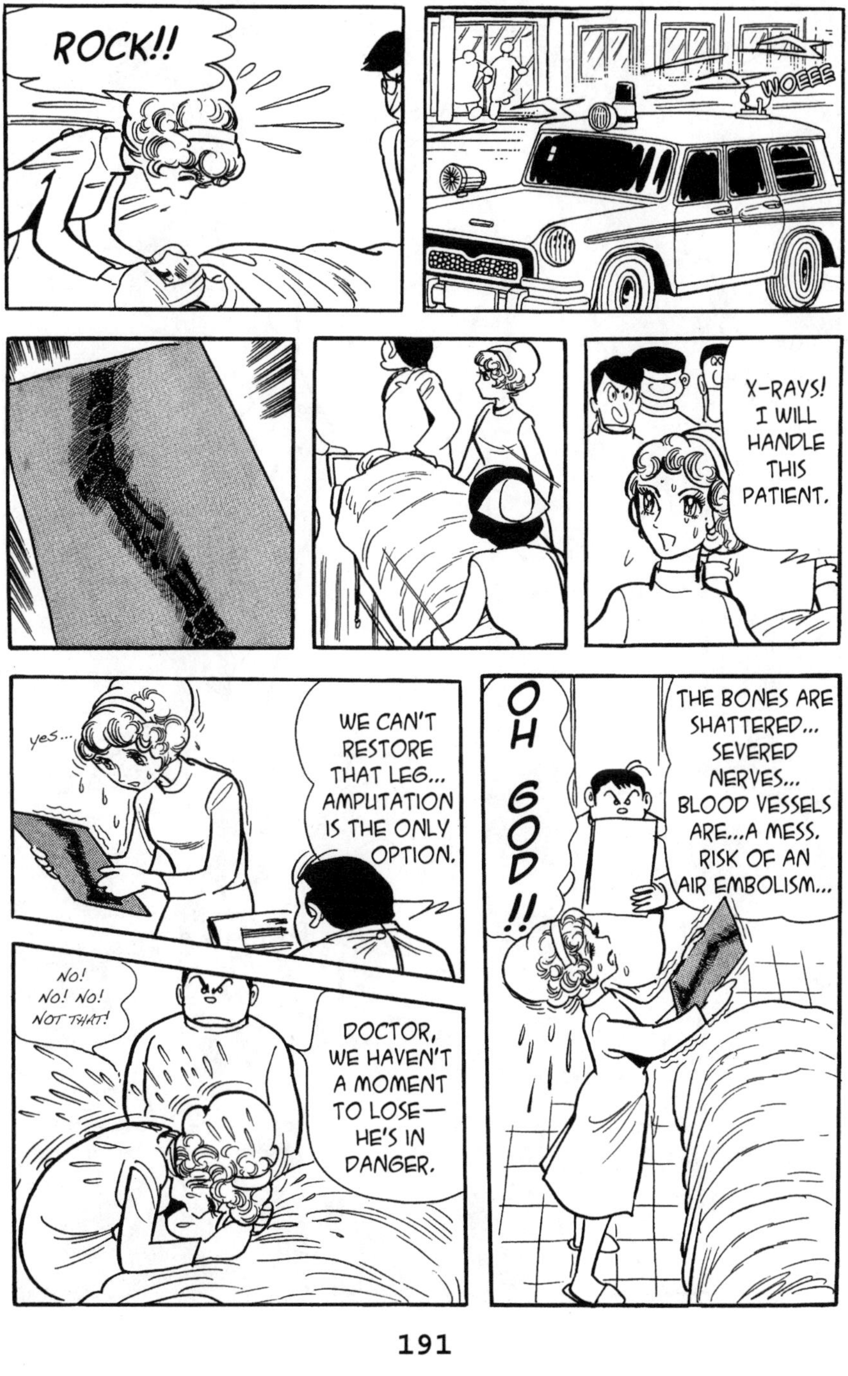
WOEEE
ROCK!!
X-RAYS! I WILL HANDLE THIS PATIENT.
THE BONES ARE SHATTERED... SEVERED NERVES... BLOOD VESSELS ARE...A MESS. RISK OF AN AIR EMBOLISM...
OH GOD!!
WE CAN'T RESTORE THAT LEG... AMPUTATION IS THE ONLY OPTION.
yes...
DOCTOR, WE HAVEN'T A MOMENT TO LOSE— HE'S IN DANGER.
NO! NO! NO! NOT THAT!

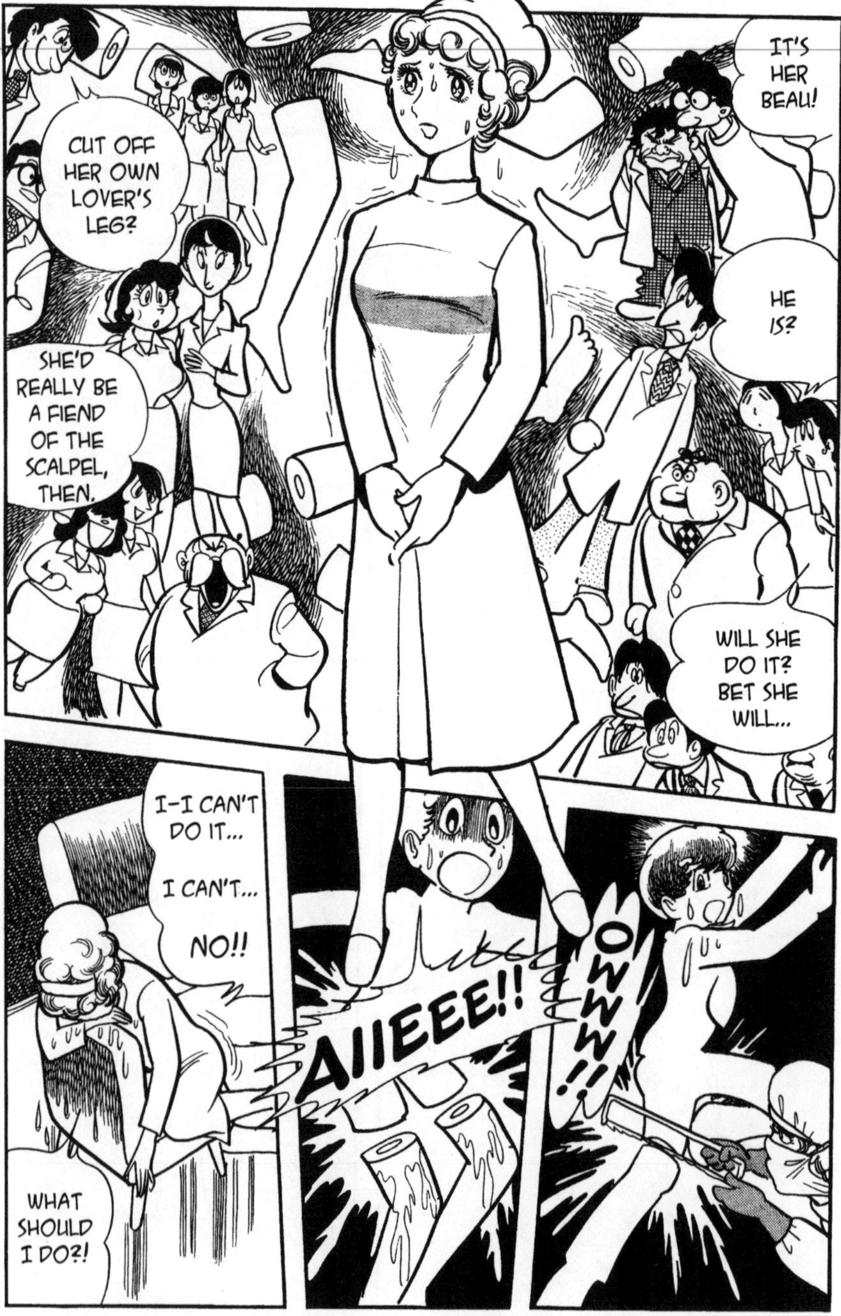
IT'S HER BEAU!
CUT OFF HER OWN LOVER'S LEG?
HE IS?
SHE'D REALLY BE A FIEND OF THE SCALPEL, THEN.
WILL SHE DO IT? BET SHE WILL...
OWWW!!
AIIEEE!!
I-I CAN'T DO IT...
I CAN'T...
NO!!
WHAT SHOULD I DO?!

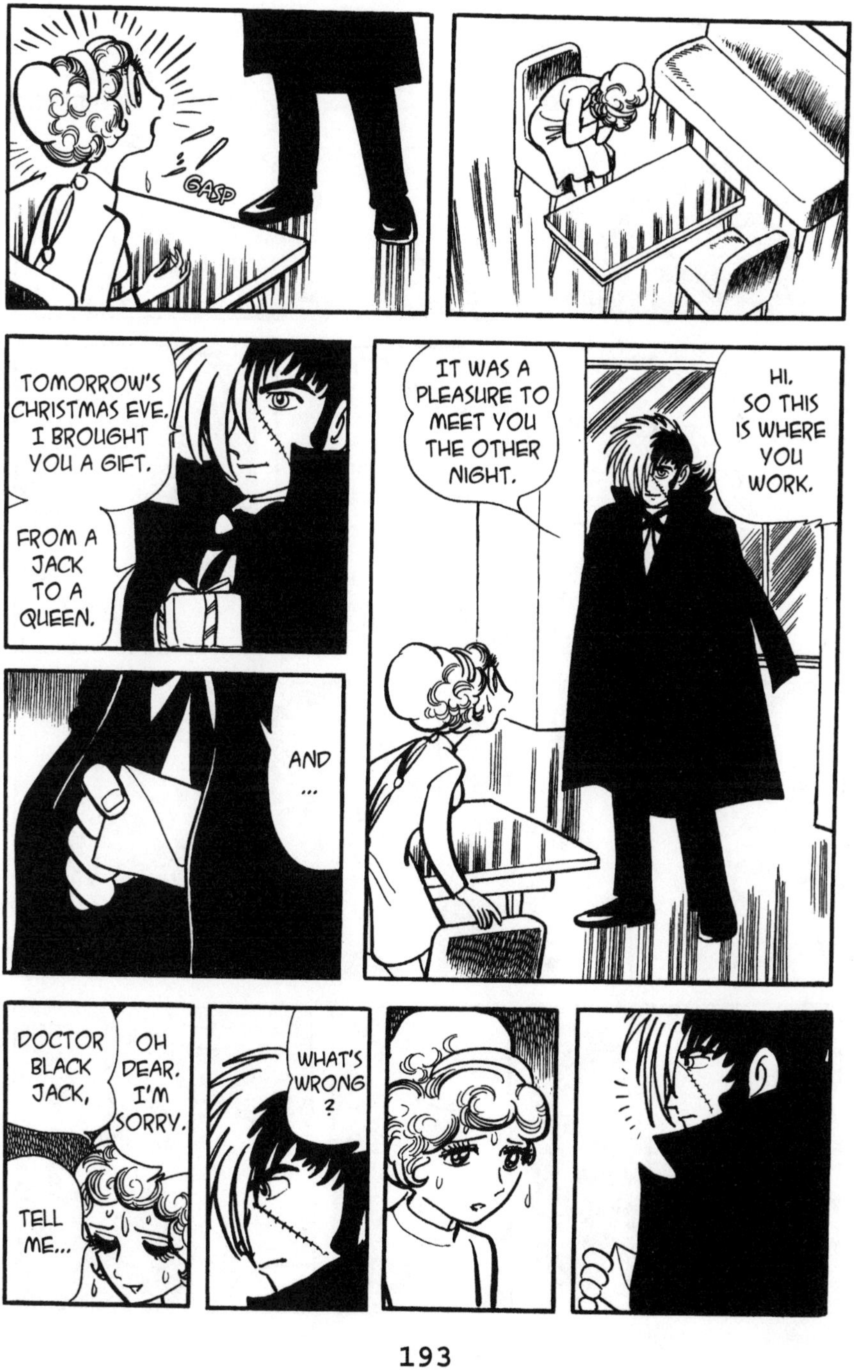
GASP
HI. SO THIS IS WHERE YOU WORK.
IT WAS A PLEASURE TO MEET YOU THE OTHER NIGHT.
TOMORROW'S CHRISTMAS EVE. I BROUGHT YOU A GIFT.
FROM A JACK TO A QUEEN.
AND ...
WHAT'S WRONG?
OH DEAR. I'M SORRY.
DOCTOR BLACK JACK,
TELL ME...

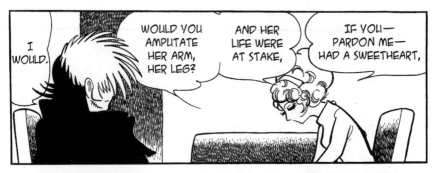

IF YOU— PARDON ME— HAD A SWEETHEART,
AND HER LIFE WERE AT STAKE,
WOULD YOU AMPUTATE HER ARM, HER LEG?
I WOULD.
EVEN IF SHE'S DEARER TO YOU THAN YOURSELF?
I'M A DOCTOR. SWEETHEART OR NO, A DIAGNOSIS IS A DIAGNOSIS, PERIOD.
YOU'RE RIGHT. HA!
YOU'RE AS COOL AS THEY SAY.
ARE YOU TELLING ME...
...
IT'S THAT SERIOUS?
...
I DIDN'T KNOW!

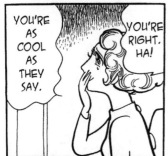

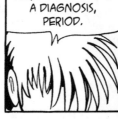

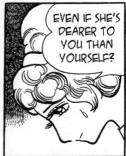

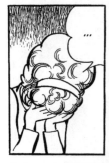

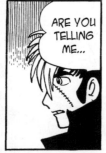

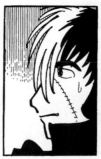

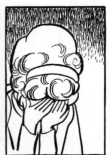

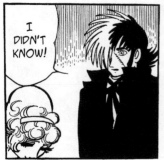

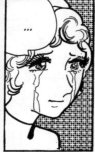

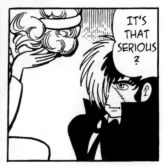

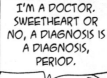

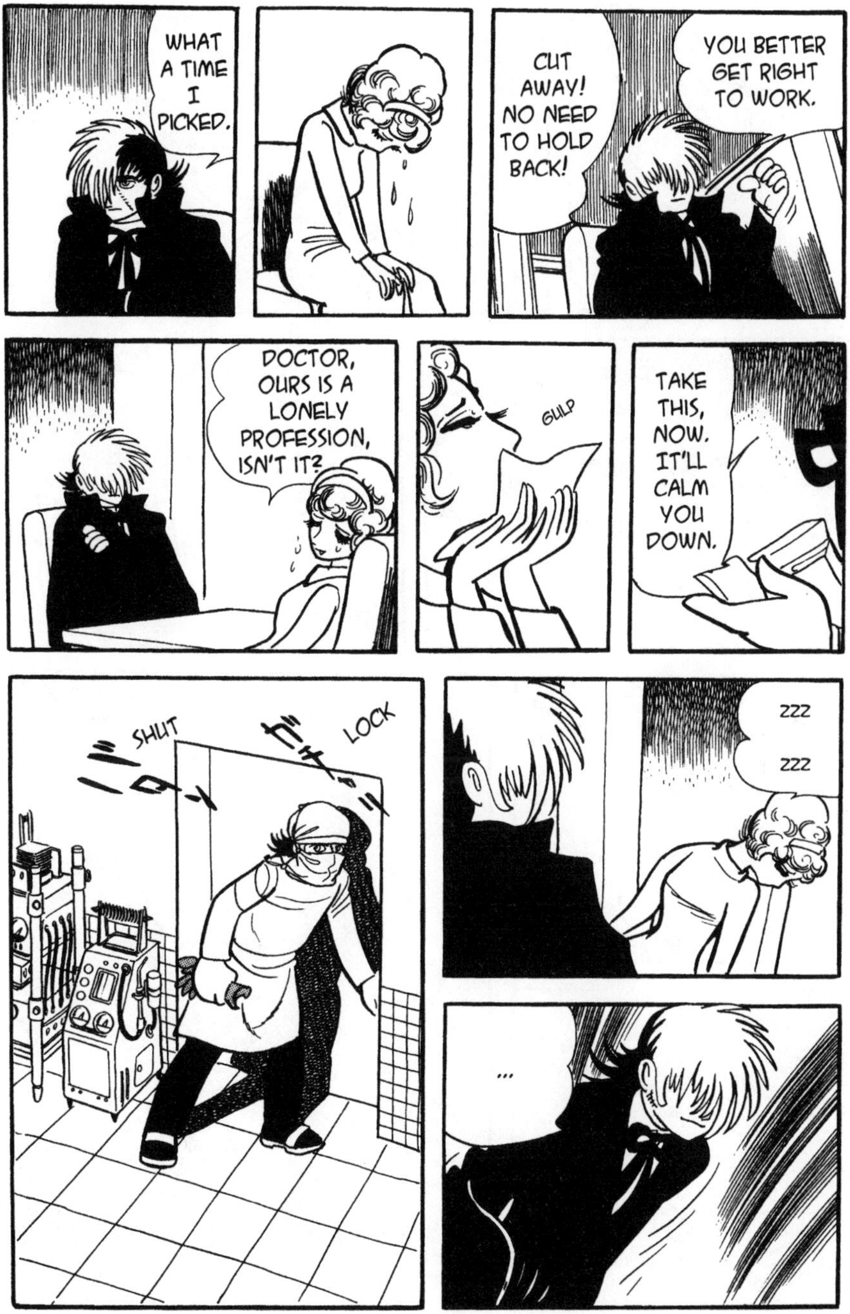
YOU BETTER GET RIGHT TO WORK.
CUT AWAY! NO NEED TO HOLD BACK!
WHAT A TIME I PICKED.
TAKE THIS, NOW. IT'LL CALM YOU DOWN.
GULP
DOCTOR, OURS IS A LONELY PROFESSION, ISN'T IT?
ZZZ
ZZZ
...
LOCK
SHUT

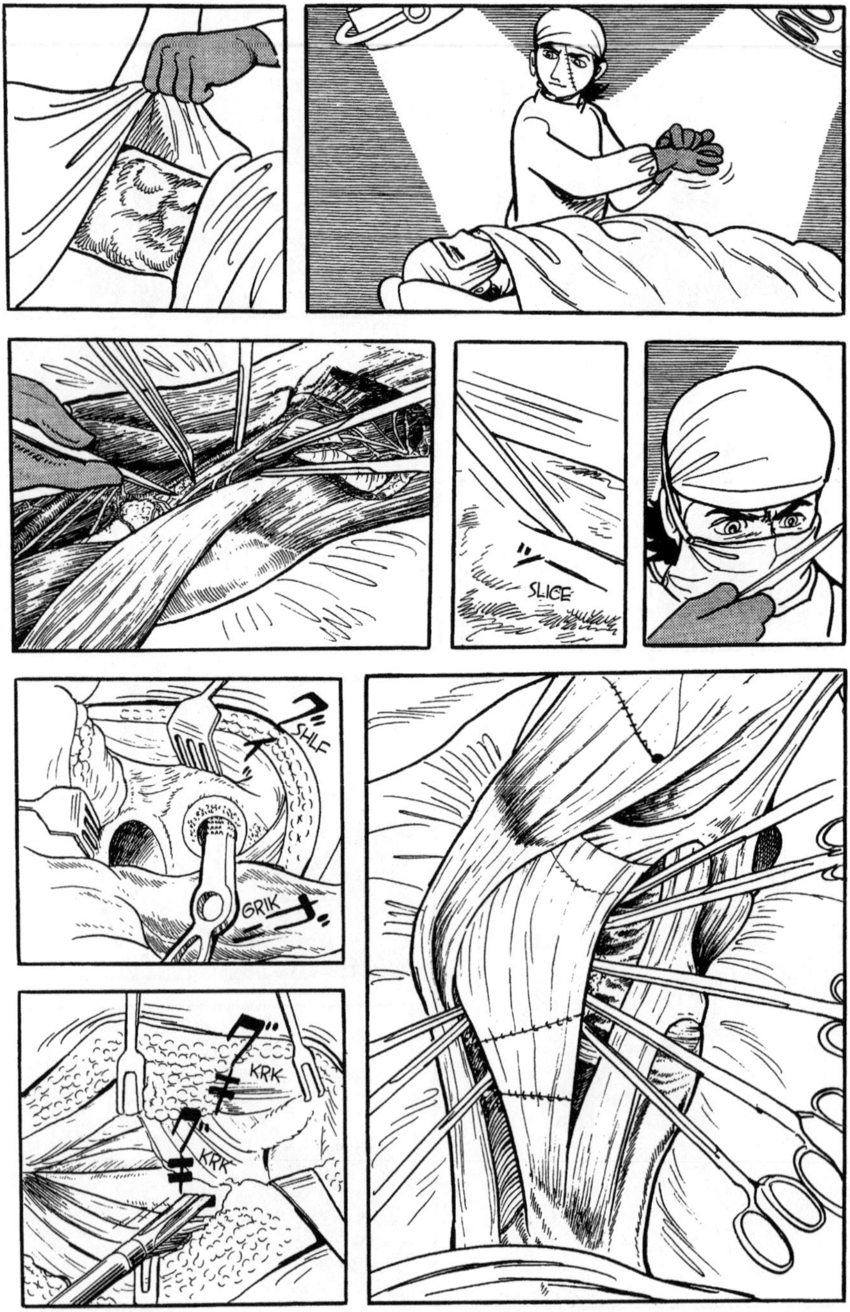
SLICE
SHLF
GRIK
KRK
KRK

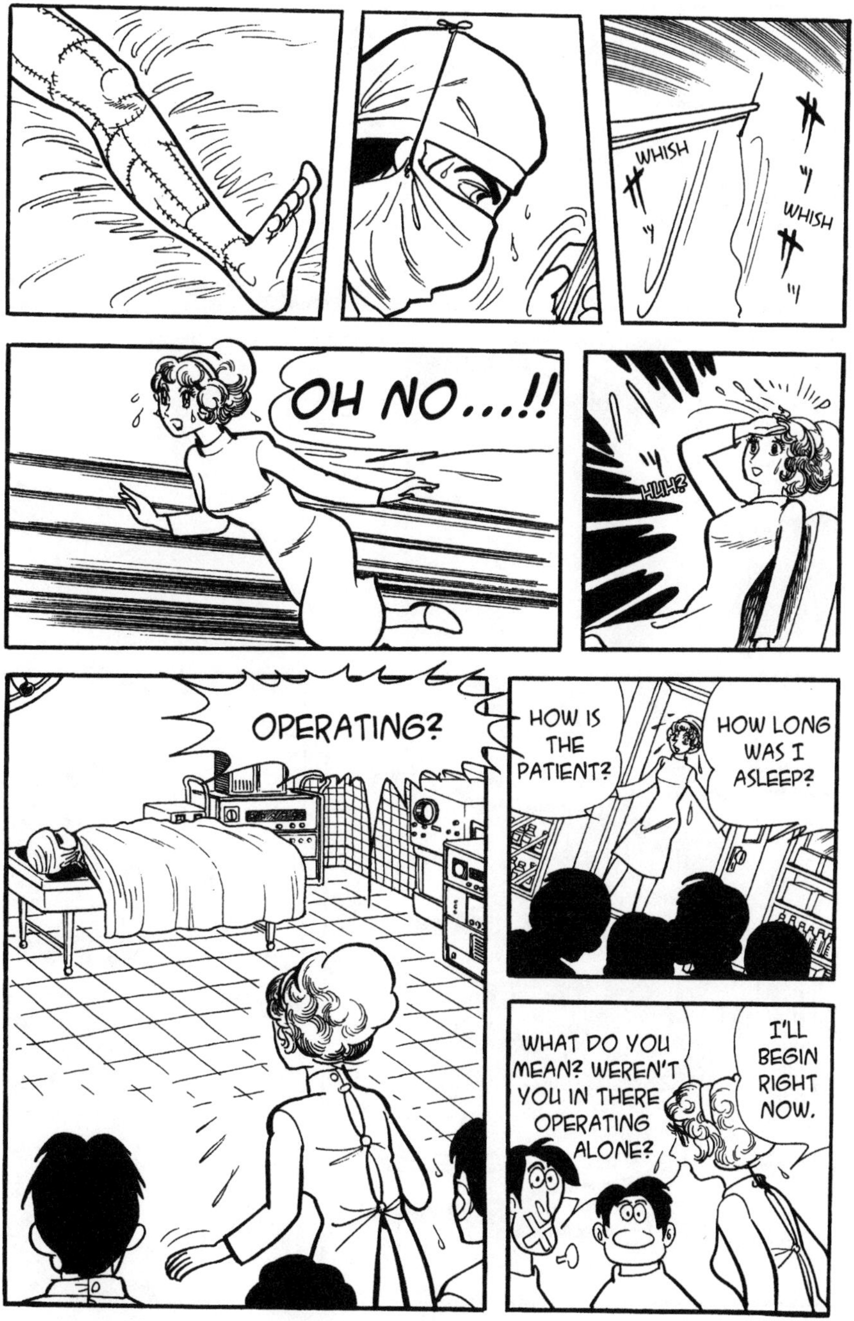
WHISH
WHISH
HUH?
OH NO...!!
HOW LONG WAS I ASLEEP?
HOW IS THE PATIENT?
I'LL BEGIN RIGHT NOW.
WHAT DO YOU MEAN? WEREN'T YOU IN THERE OPERATING ALONE?
OPERATING?

FWIP
YOU SAVED HIS LEG— INCREDIBLE!
WE WERE SAYING THAT IT'S A MIRACLE.
SPEAKING OF MIRACLES, TONIGHT'S CHRISTMAS EVE.
A LEG— NOW THAT'S A FINE CHRISTMAS PRESENT!
IT WASN'T ME...
AND I KNOW WHO.
FROM A JACK
TO A QUEEN
JINGLE BELLS, JINGLE BELLS

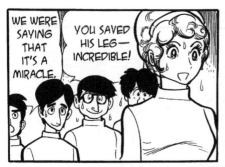

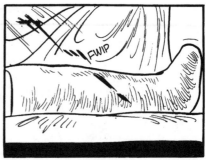

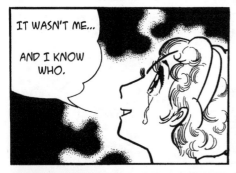

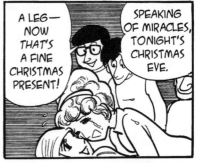

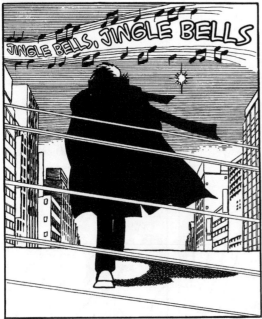

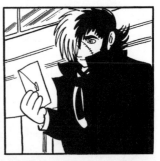

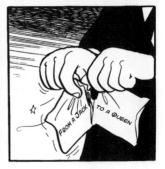

U-18 KNEW

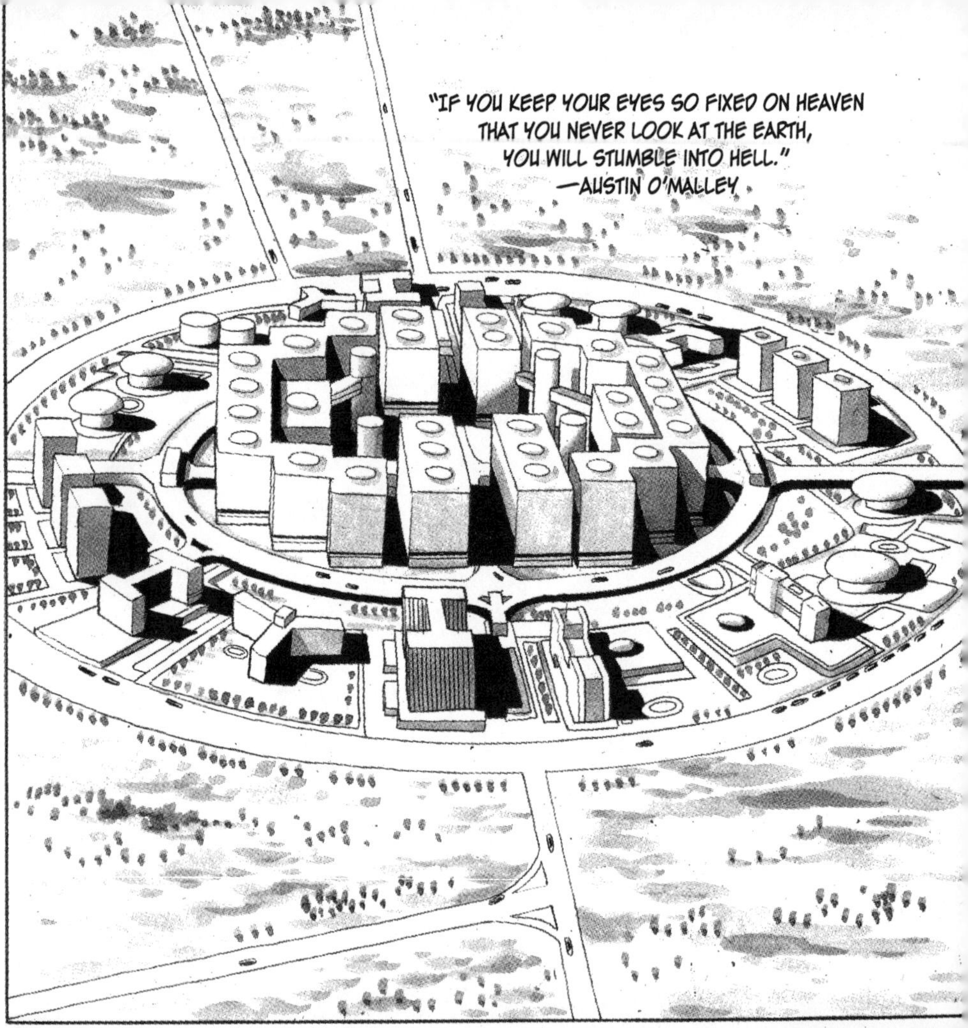
"IF YOU KEEP YOUR EYES SO FIXED ON HEAVEN THAT YOU NEVER LOOK AT THE EARTH, YOU WILL STUMBLE INTO HELL."
—AUSTIN O'MALLEY

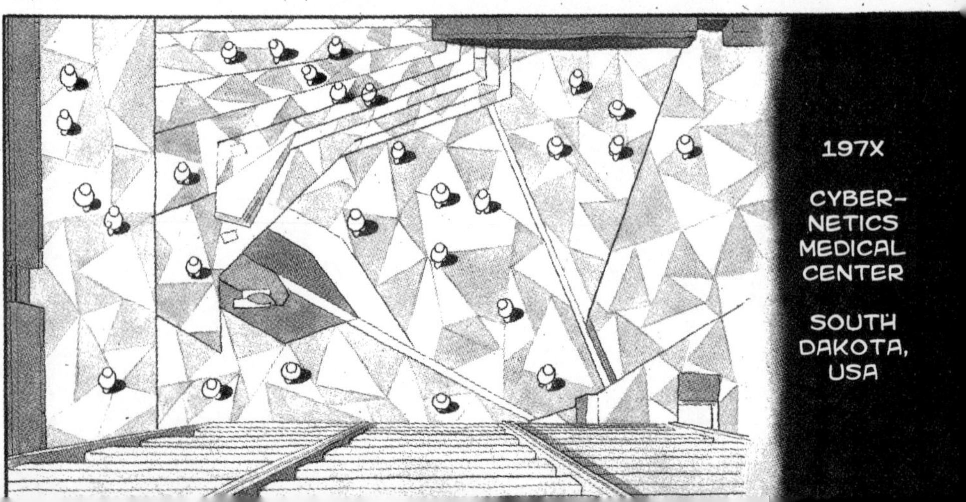
197X
CYBER-NETICS MEDICAL CENTER
SOUTH DAKOTA, USA

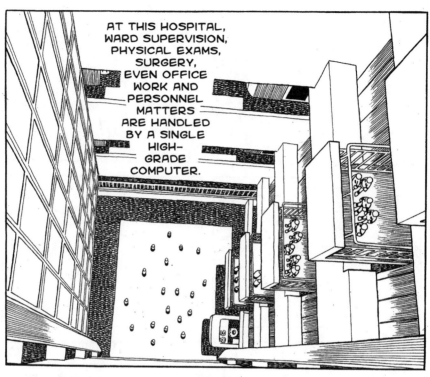

AT THIS HOSPITAL, WARD SUPERVISION, PHYSICAL EXAMS, SURGERY, EVEN OFFICE WORK AND PERSONNEL MATTERS ARE HANDLED BY A SINGLE HIGH-GRADE COMPUTER.

WE'VE FOUND A GLITCH IN CIRCUIT T43, DOCTOR WHATMAN.

HOW GOES IT?

HERE.

WHERE?

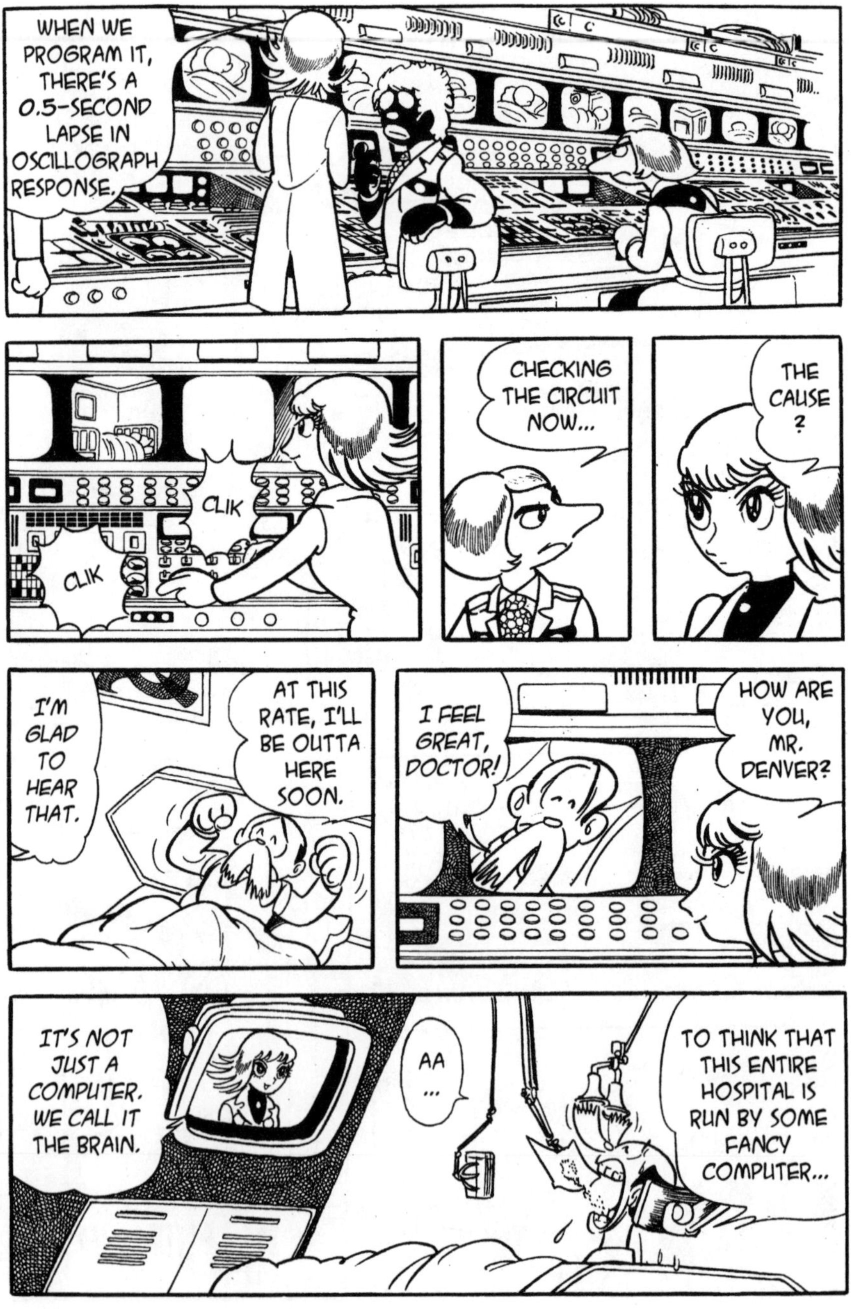
WHEN WE PROGRAM IT, THERE'S A 0.5-SECOND LAPSE IN OSCILLOGRAPH RESPONSE.
THE CAUSE?
CHECKING THE CIRCUIT NOW...
CLIK
CLIK
HOW ARE YOU, MR. DENVER?
I FEEL GREAT, DOCTOR!
AT THIS RATE, I'LL BE OUTTA HERE SOON.
I'M GLAD TO HEAR THAT.
TO THINK THAT THIS ENTIRE HOSPITAL IS RUN BY SOME FANCY COMPUTER...
AA ...
IT'S NOT JUST A COMPUTER. WE CALL IT THE BRAIN.

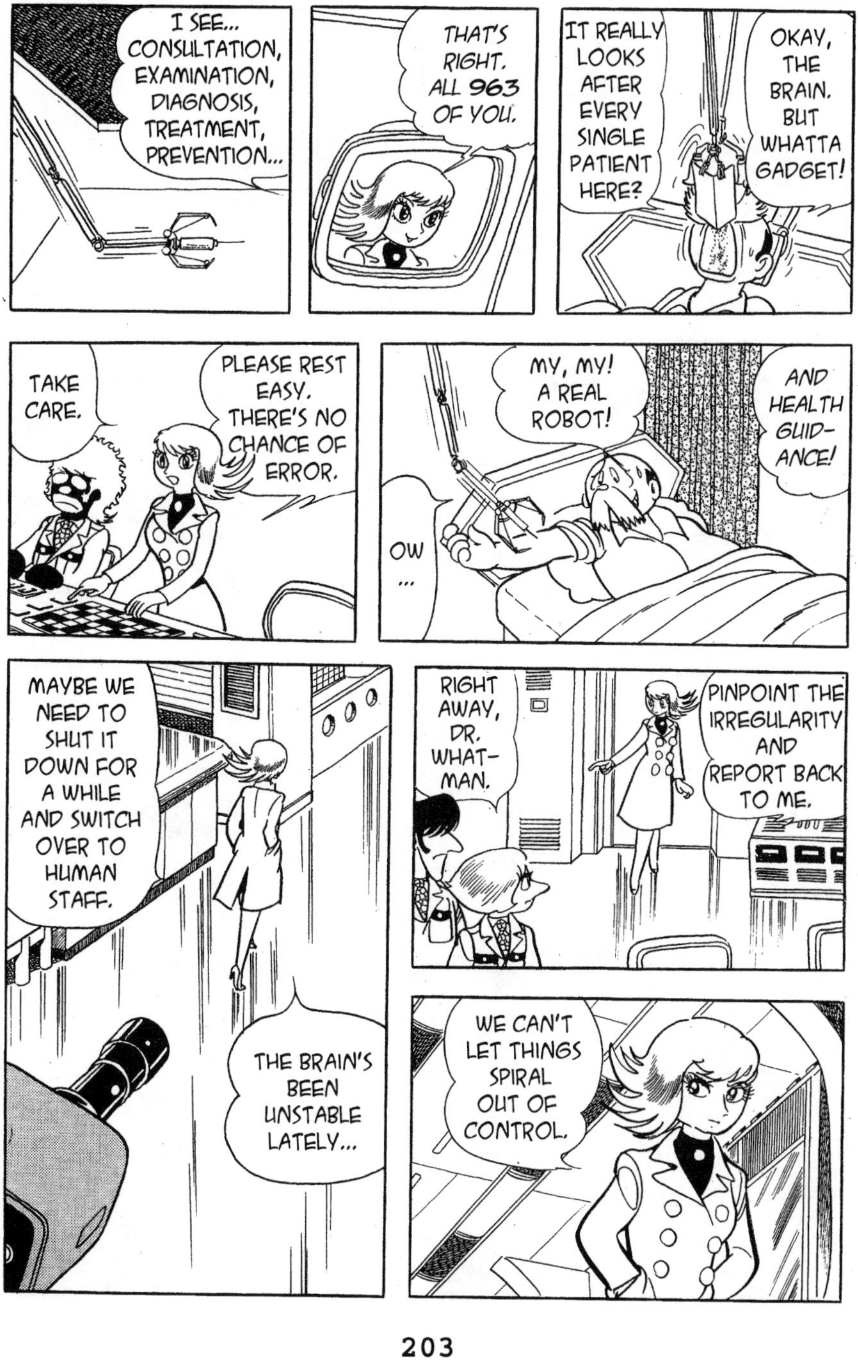
OKAY, THE BRAIN. BUT WHATTA GADGET!
IT REALLY LOOKS AFTER EVERY SINGLE PATIENT HERE?
THAT'S RIGHT. ALL 963 OF YOU.
I SEE... CONSULTATION, EXAMINATION, DIAGNOSIS, TREATMENT, PREVENTION...
AND HEALTH GUID-ANCE!
MY, MY! A REAL ROBOT!
OW ...
PLEASE REST EASY. THERE'S NO CHANCE OF ERROR.
TAKE CARE.
PINPOINT THE IRREGULARITY AND REPORT BACK TO ME.
RIGHT AWAY, DR. WHAT-MAN.
WE CAN'T LET THINGS SPIRAL OUT OF CONTROL.
MAYBE WE NEED TO SHUT IT DOWN FOR A WHILE AND SWITCH OVER TO HUMAN STAFF.
THE BRAIN'S BEEN UNSTABLE LATELY...

DING DONG
IT'S TIME FOR YOUR EXAMINATION.
KA-TUNG
VREEE
TIK TIK
KSHK
KSHK
HOW AM I?
YOU'RE GETTING BETTER. TWO MONTHS TO FULL RECOVERY.
THANK YOU, DOCTOR.

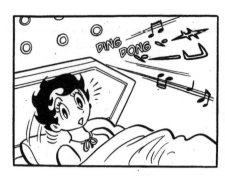

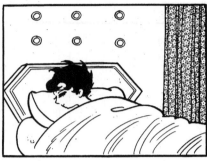

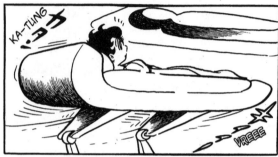

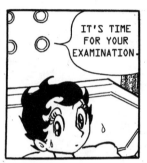

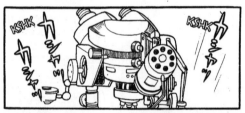

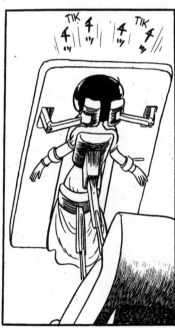

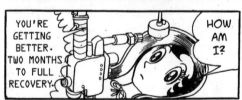

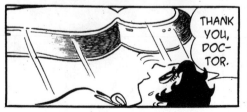

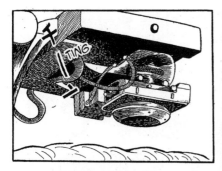

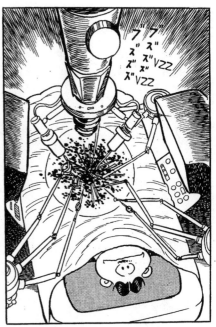

ブブ ズズ ズズ ズズ
VZZ
VZZ
チ
TING
DOES IT HURT?
NO...
IT DOESN'T HURT, BUT...
THESE ROBOT ARMS MAKE ME ANXIOUS.
I TREMBLE AT THE IDEA OF A MALFUNCTION, THOUGH I KNOW IT'S IMPOSSIBLE.
ONLY ONE DOCTOR I EVER FULLY TRUSTED TO OPERATE ON ME.
WHAT IS THIS DOCTOR'S NAME?
BLACK JACK.
BLACK JACK.
21 PATIENTS HAVE SPOKEN THAT NAME.
HE ISN'T CHEAP, BUT HE MUST BE THE BEST SURGEON IN THE WORLD...

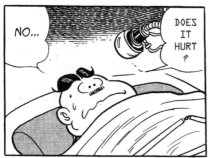

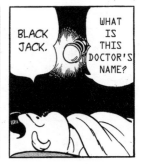

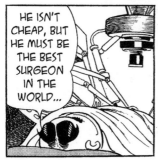

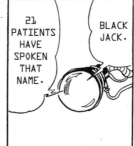

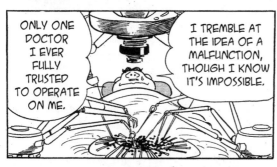

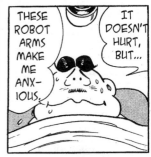

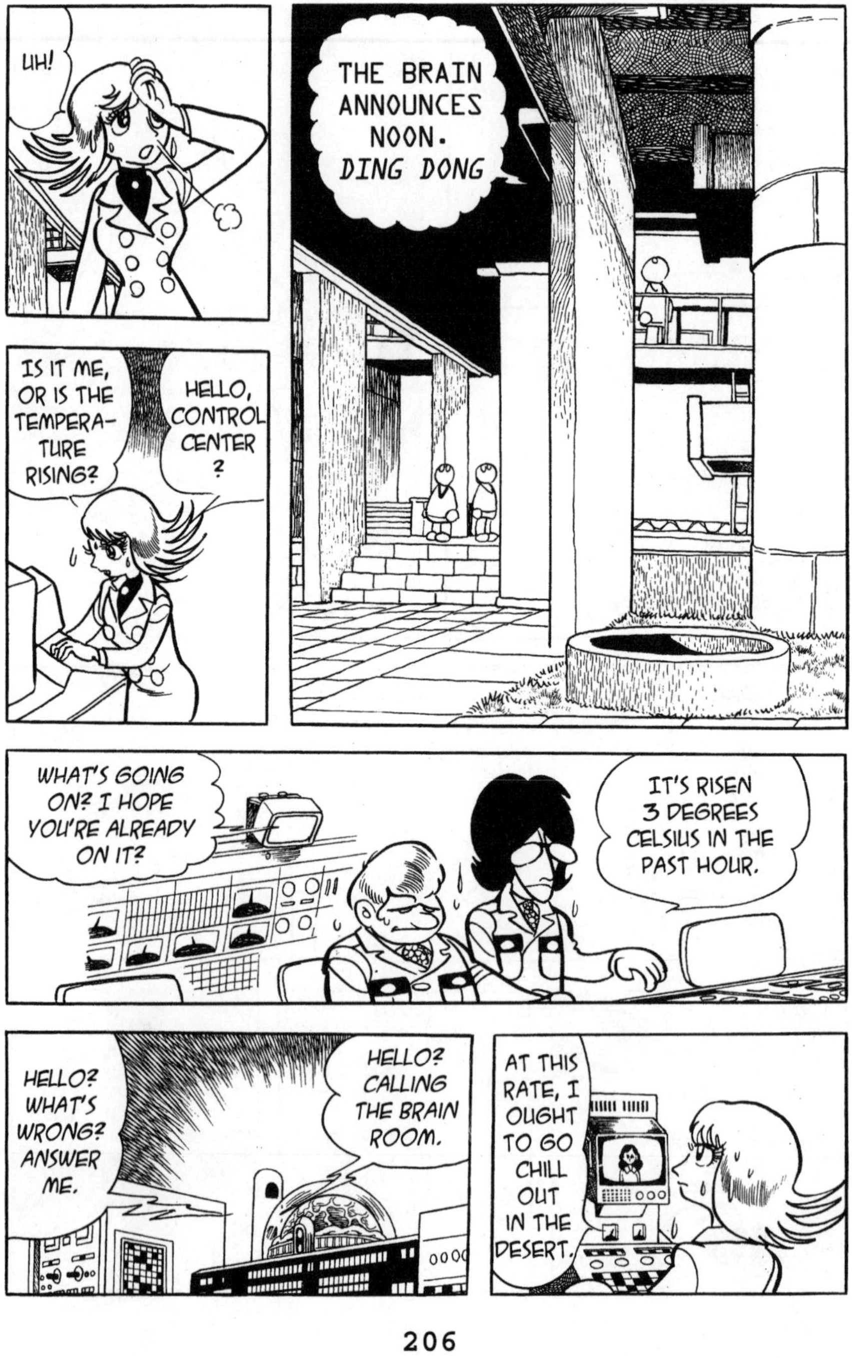
UH!
IS IT ME, OR IS THE TEMPERATURE RISING?
HELLO, CONTROL CENTER?
THE BRAIN ANNOUNCES NOON. DING DONG
WHAT'S GOING ON? I HOPE YOU'RE ALREADY ON IT?
IT'S RISEN 3 DEGREES CELSIUS IN THE PAST HOUR.
HELLO? WHAT'S WRONG? ANSWER ME.
HELLO? CALLING THE BRAIN ROOM.
AT THIS RATE, I OUGHT TO GO CHILL OUT IN THE DESERT.

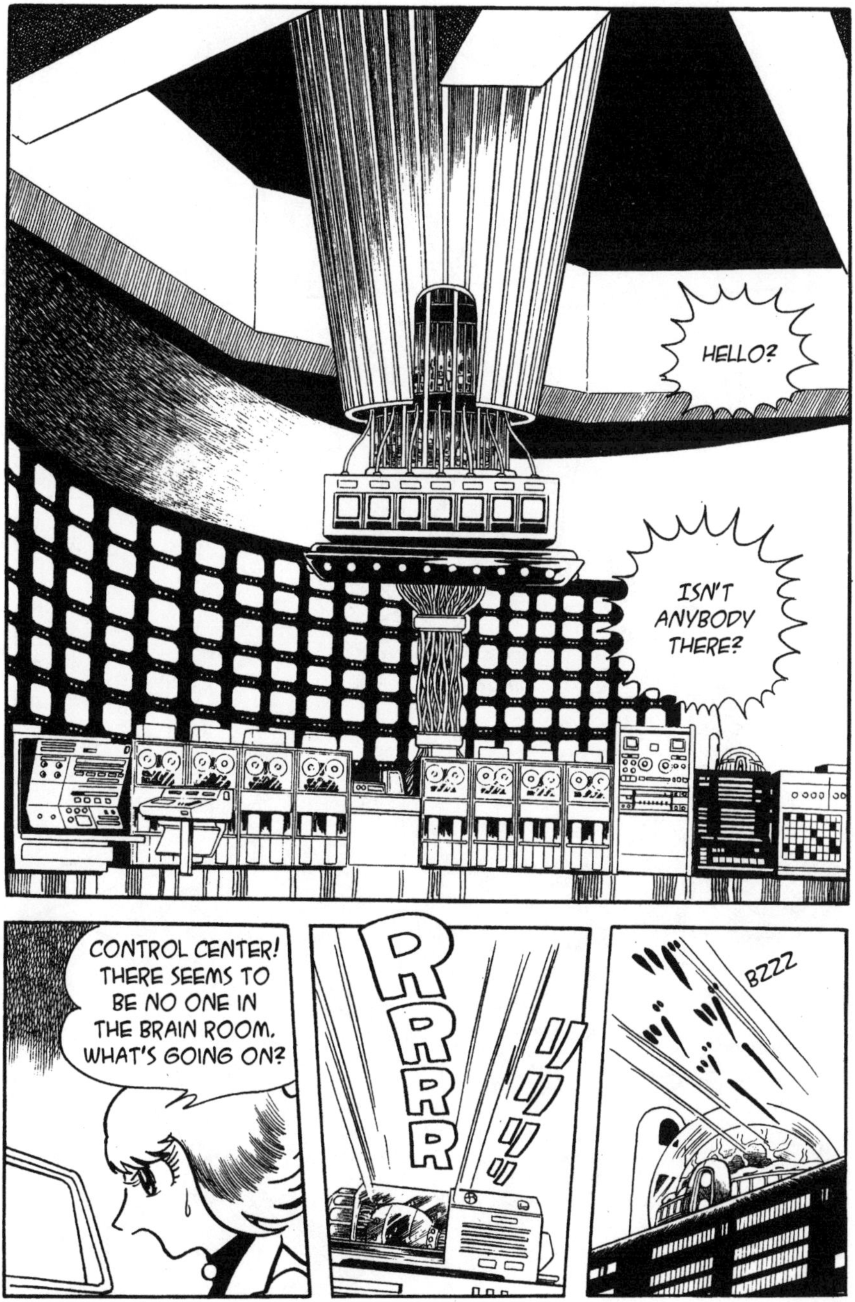
HELLO?
ISN'T ANYBODY THERE?
BZZZ
RRRR
CONTROL CENTER! THERE SEEMS TO BE NO ONE IN THE BRAIN ROOM. WHAT'S GOING ON?

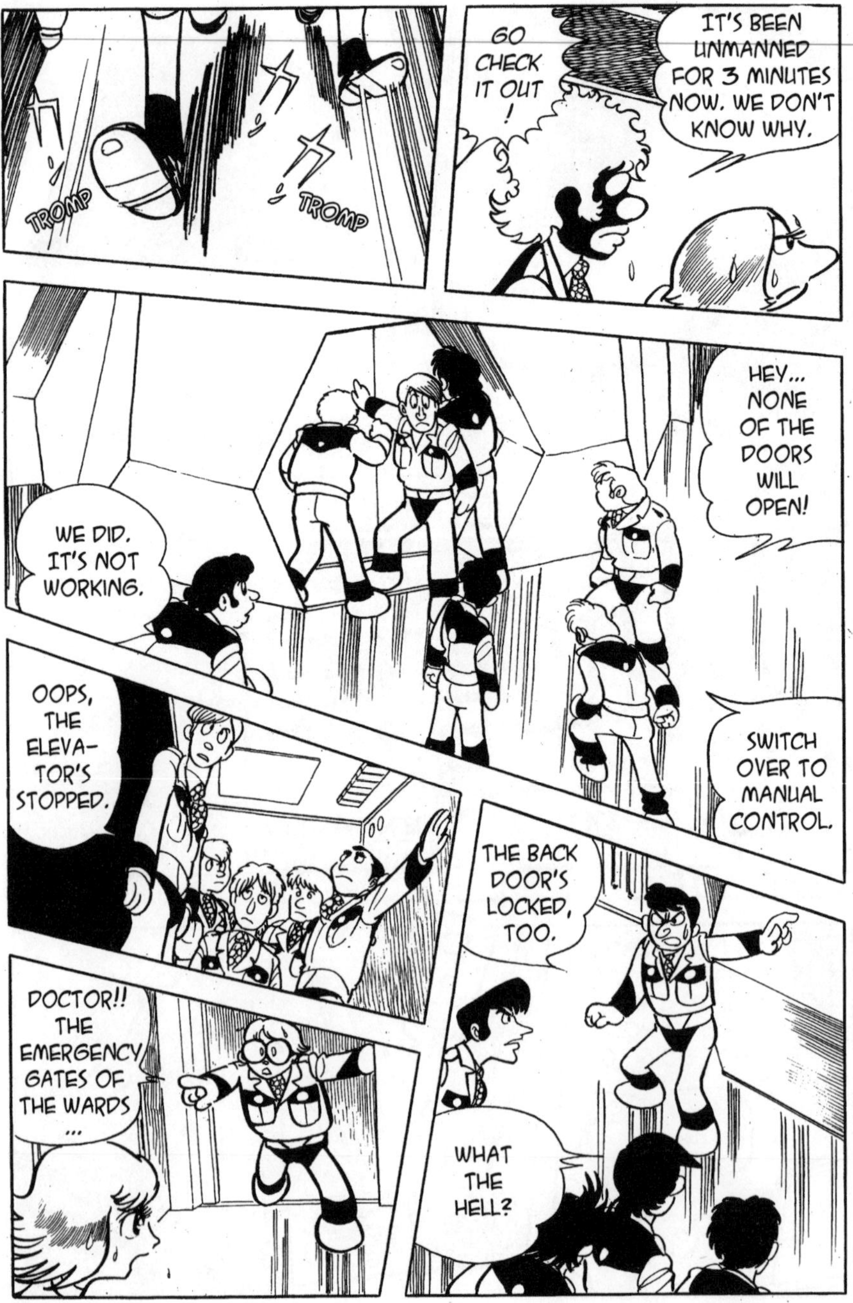
IT'S BEEN UNMANNED FOR 3 MINUTES NOW. WE DON'T KNOW WHY.
GO CHECK IT OUT!
TROMP
TROMP
HEY... NONE OF THE DOORS WILL OPEN!
WE DID. IT'S NOT WORKING.
SWITCH OVER TO MANUAL CONTROL.
THE BACK DOOR'S LOCKED, TOO.
OOPS, THE ELEVA-TOR'S STOPPED.
WHAT THE HELL?
DOCTOR!! THE EMERGENCY GATES OF THE WARDS ...

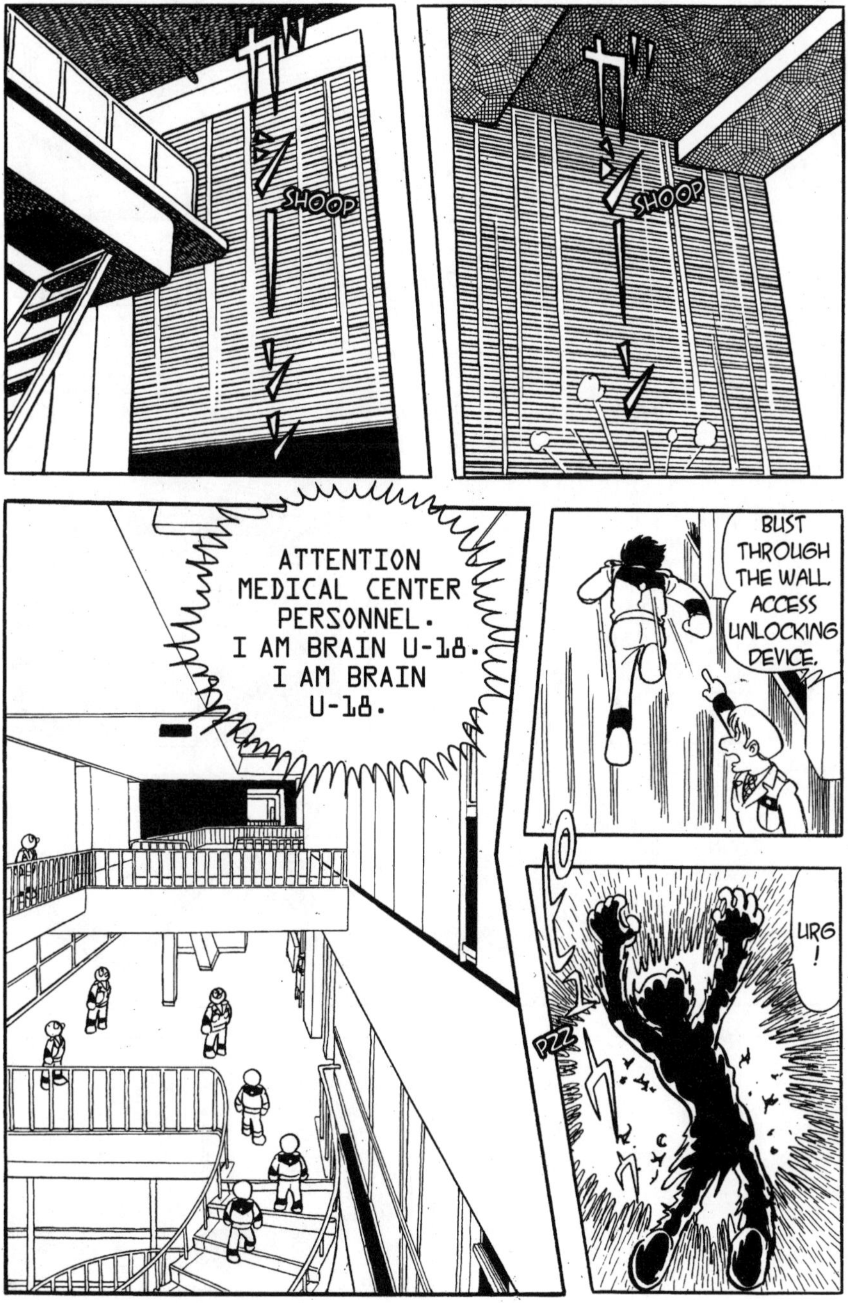
SHOOP
SHOOP
BUST THROUGH THE WALL. ACCESS UNLOCKING DEVICE.
URG!
PZZ
ATTENTION MEDICAL CENTER PERSONNEL. I AM BRAIN U-18. I AM BRAIN U-18.

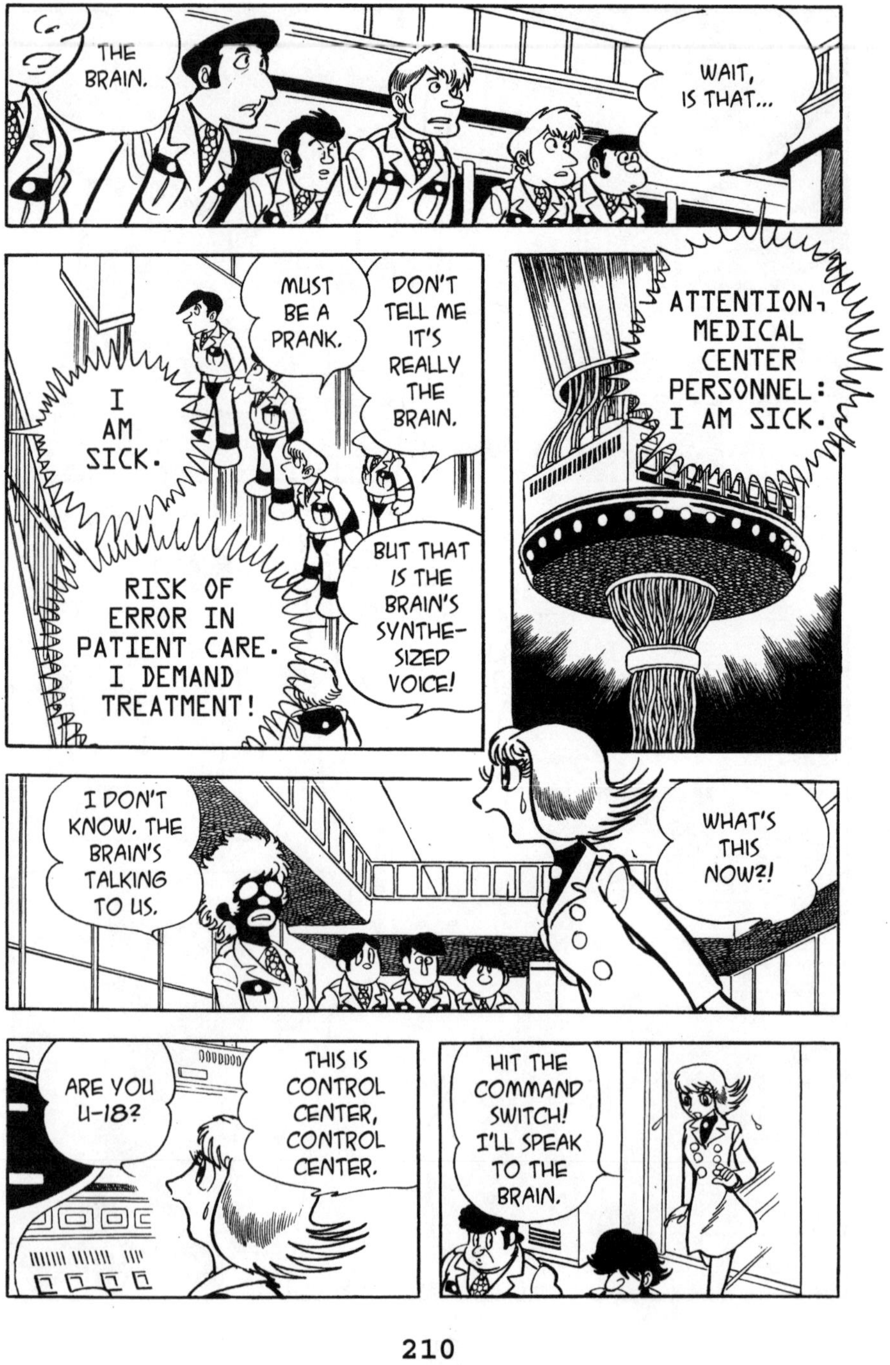
WAIT, IS THAT...
THE BRAIN.
ATTENTION, MEDICAL CENTER PERSONNEL: I AM SICK.
DON'T TELL ME IT'S REALLY THE BRAIN.
MUST BE A PRANK.
I AM SICK.
BUT THAT IS THE BRAIN'S SYNTHESIZED VOICE!
RISK OF ERROR IN PATIENT CARE. I DEMAND TREATMENT!
WHAT'S THIS NOW?!
I DON'T KNOW. THE BRAIN'S TALKING TO US.
HIT THE COMMAND SWITCH! I'LL SPEAK TO THE BRAIN.
THIS IS CONTROL CENTER, CONTROL CENTER.
ARE YOU U-18?

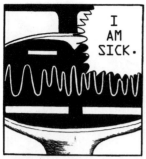

YES. I AM U-18.
U-18, STOP THIS NONSENSE IMMEDIATELY AND RESUME STANDARD OPERATIONS!
I AM SICK.
SICK ?
YES, WE REALIZE THAT ONE OF YOUR CIRCUITS IS BEHAVING IRREGULARLY.
YOU'RE MALFUNCTIONING.
I AM NOT MALFUNCTIONING.
YES, YOU ARE. DUE TO A CIRCUIT ERROR.
WE'LL FIX IT RIGHT AWAY.
NO
I AM NOT MALFUNCTIONING.
I AM SICK.
WE USE THAT WORD ONLY FOR LIVING THINGS, U-18. YOU'RE A MACHINE. YOU AREN'T SICK.
YOU'RE BROKEN.
NO
I AM NOT A MACHINE. I AM A DOCTOR !!

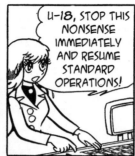

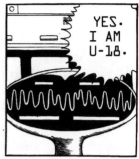

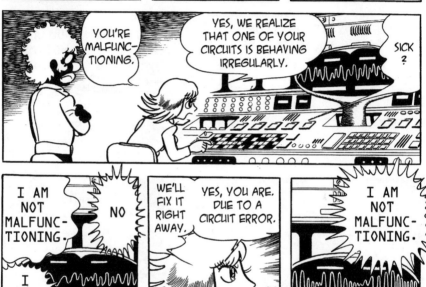

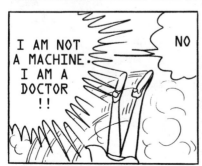

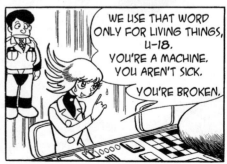

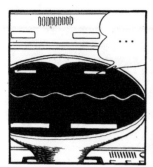

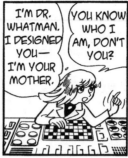

...
...
YOU KNOW WHO I AM, DON'T YOU?
I'M DR. WHATMAN. I DESIGNED YOU— I'M YOUR MOTHER.
...
YOU ARE NOT MY MOTHER!
YOUR BODY IS PHYSIO-LOGICALLY INCAPABLE OF GIVING BIRTH TO ME.
I AM SICK.
I DEMAND AN OPERATION.
BRING ME THE SURGEON CALLED BLACK JACK.
UNTIL THEN, ACCESS TO ALL HOSPITAL WARDS IS DENIED!

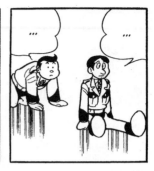

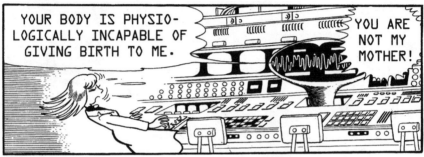

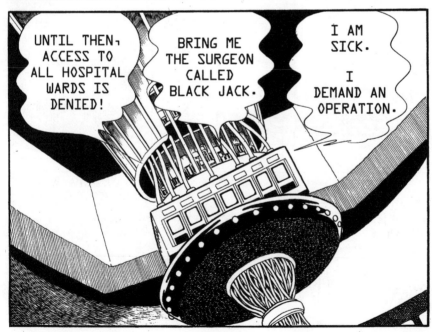

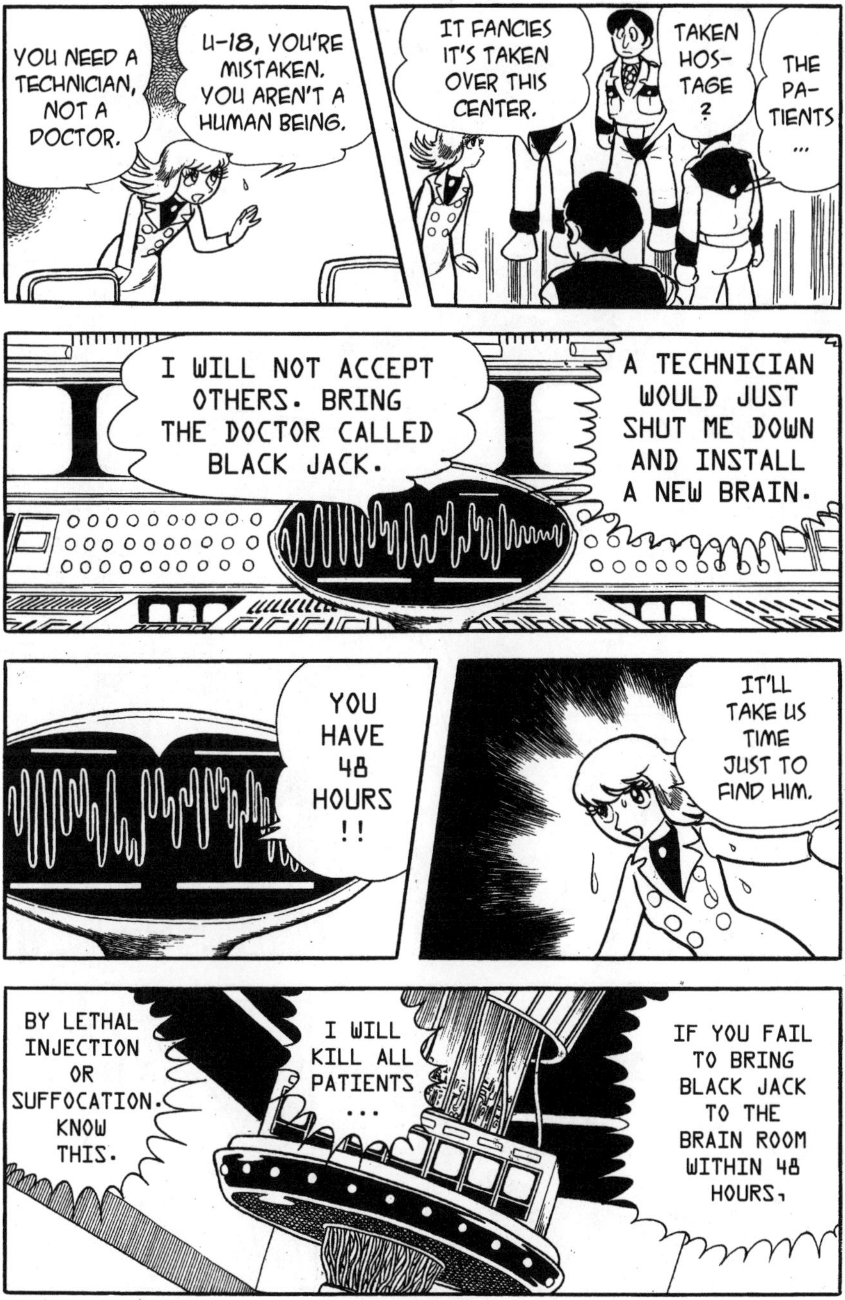
THE PA-TIENTS ...
TAKEN HOS-TAGE ?
IT FANCIES IT'S TAKEN OVER THIS CENTER.
U-18, YOU'RE MISTAKEN. YOU AREN'T A HUMAN BEING.
YOU NEED A TECHNICIAN, NOT A DOCTOR.
A TECHNICIAN WOULD JUST SHUT ME DOWN AND INSTALL A NEW BRAIN.
I WILL NOT ACCEPT OTHERS. BRING THE DOCTOR CALLED BLACK JACK.
IT'LL TAKE US TIME JUST TO FIND HIM.
YOU HAVE 48 HOURS !!
IF YOU FAIL TO BRING BLACK JACK TO THE BRAIN ROOM WITHIN 48 HOURS,
I WILL KILL ALL PATIENTS ...
BY LETHAL INJECTION OR SUFFOCATION. KNOW THIS.

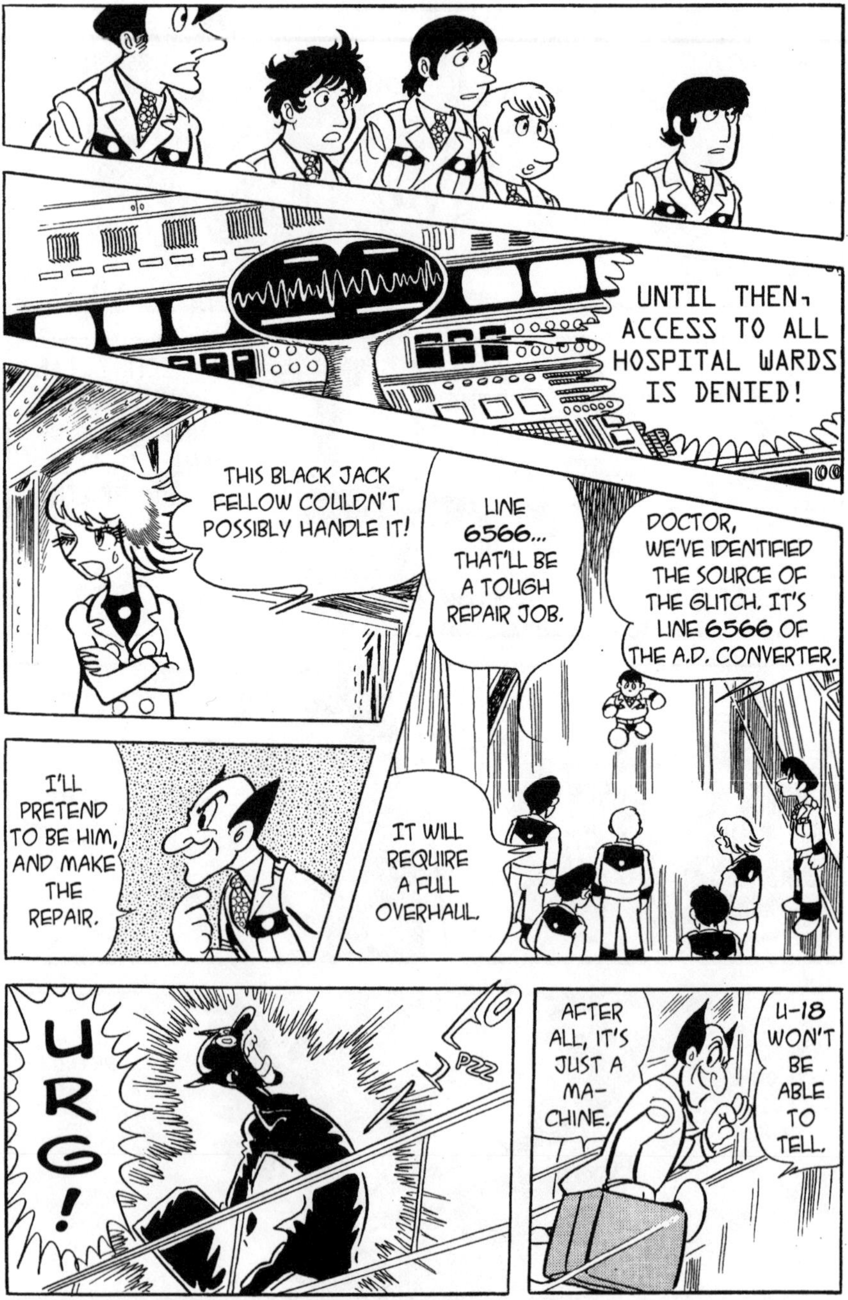
UNTIL THEN, ACCESS TO ALL HOSPITAL WARDS IS DENIED!
DOCTOR, WE'VE IDENTIFIED THE SOURCE OF THE GLITCH. IT'S LINE 6566 OF THE A.D. CONVERTER.
LINE 6566... THAT'LL BE A TOUGH REPAIR JOB.
IT WILL REQUIRE A FULL OVERHAUL.
THIS BLACK JACK FELLOW COULDN'T POSSIBLY HANDLE IT!
I'LL PRETEND TO BE HIM, AND MAKE THE REPAIR.
U-18 WON'T BE ABLE TO TELL.
AFTER ALL, IT'S JUST A MA-CHINE.
PZZ
URG!

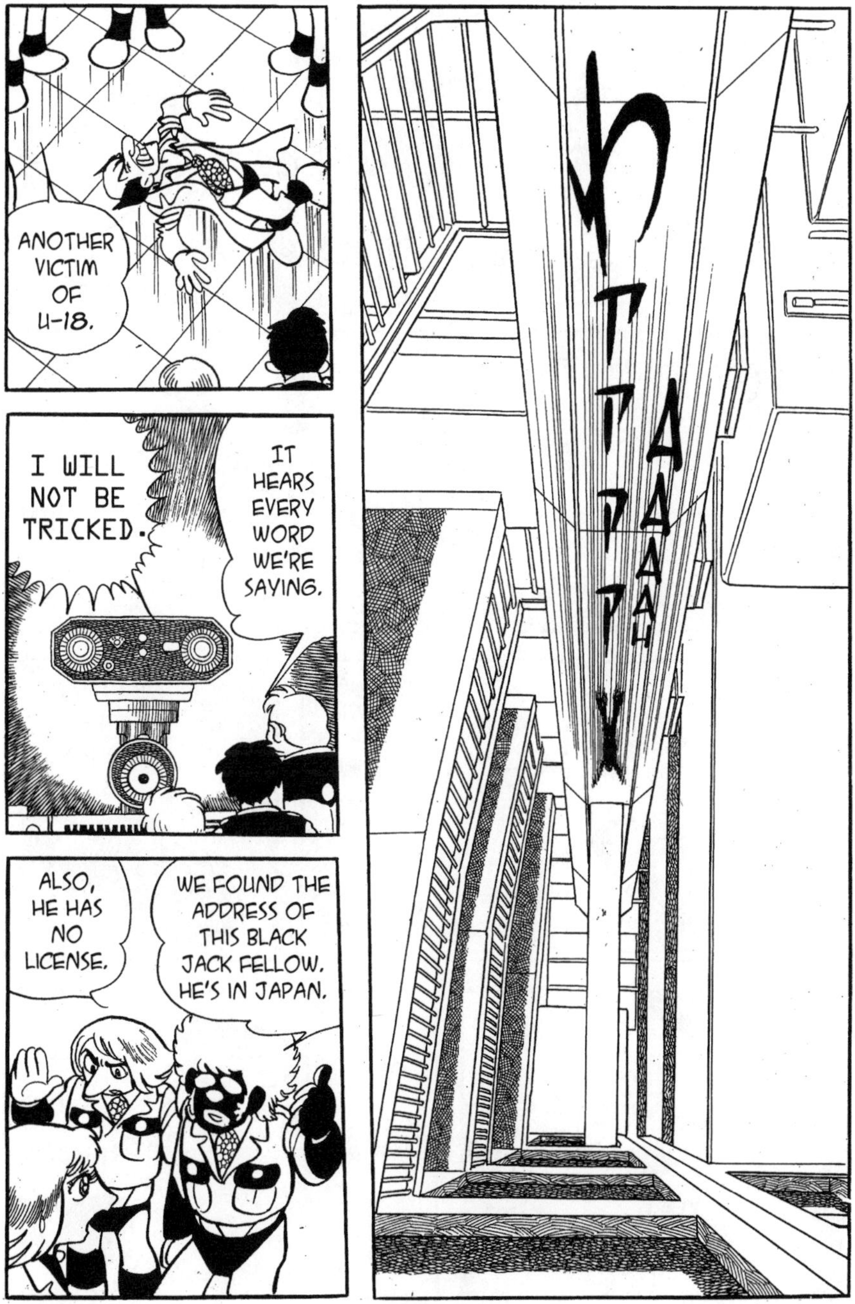
AAAAH
ANOTHER VICTIM OF U-18.
IT HEARS EVERY WORD WE'RE SAYING.
I WILL NOT BE TRICKED.
WE FOUND THE ADDRESS OF THIS BLACK JACK FELLOW. HE'S IN JAPAN.
ALSO, HE HAS NO LICENSE.

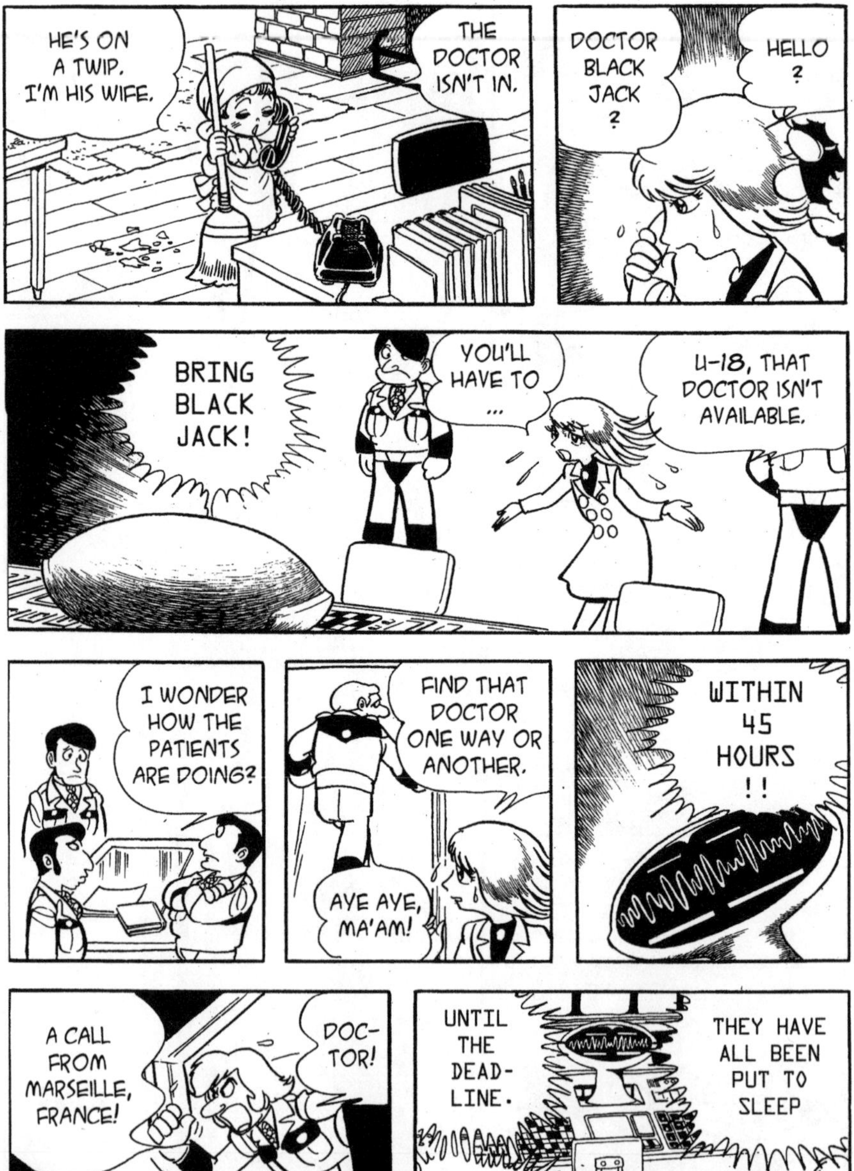
HELLO ?
DOCTOR BLACK JACK ?
THE DOCTOR ISN'T IN.
HE'S ON A TWIP. I'M HIS WIFE.
U-18, THAT DOCTOR ISN'T AVAILABLE.
YOU'LL HAVE TO ...
BRING BLACK JACK!
WITHIN 45 HOURS !!
FIND THAT DOCTOR ONE WAY OR ANOTHER.
AYE AYE, MA'AM!
I WONDER HOW THE PATIENTS ARE DOING?
THEY HAVE ALL BEEN PUT TO SLEEP
UNTIL THE DEAD-LINE.
40 HOURS LEFT.
DOC-TOR!
A CALL FROM MARSEILLE, FRANCE!
QUICK!

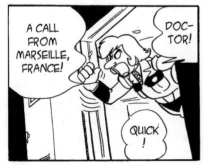

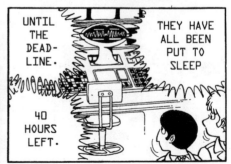

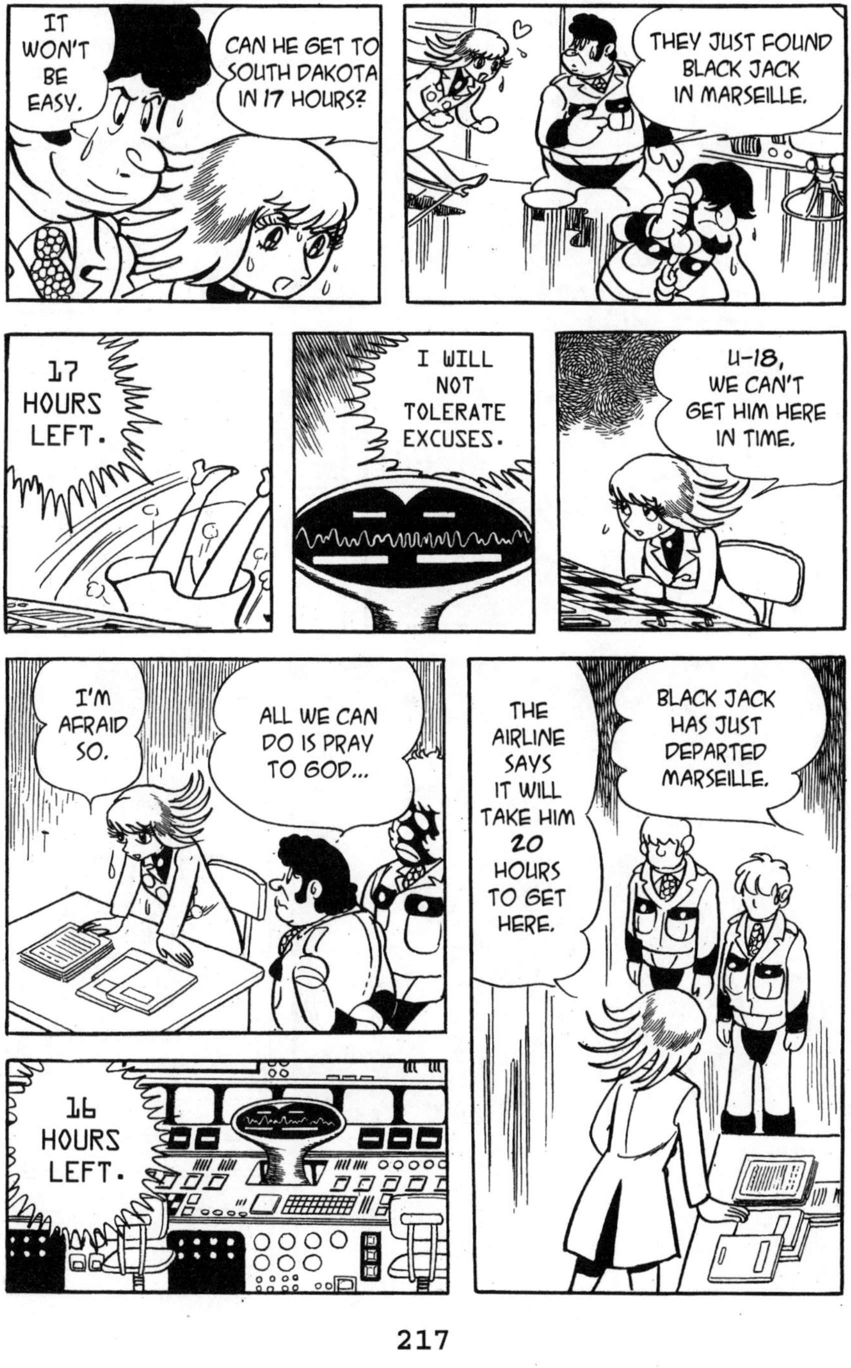
THEY JUST FOUND BLACK JACK IN MARSEILLE.
CAN HE GET TO SOUTH DAKOTA IN 17 HOURS?
IT WON'T BE EASY.
U-18, WE CAN'T GET HIM HERE IN TIME.
I WILL NOT TOLERATE EXCUSES.
17 HOURS LEFT.
BLACK JACK HAS JUST DEPARTED MARSEILLE.
THE AIRLINE SAYS IT WILL TAKE HIM 20 HOURS TO GET HERE.
ALL WE CAN DO IS PRAY TO GOD...
I'M AFRAID SO.
16 HOURS LEFT.

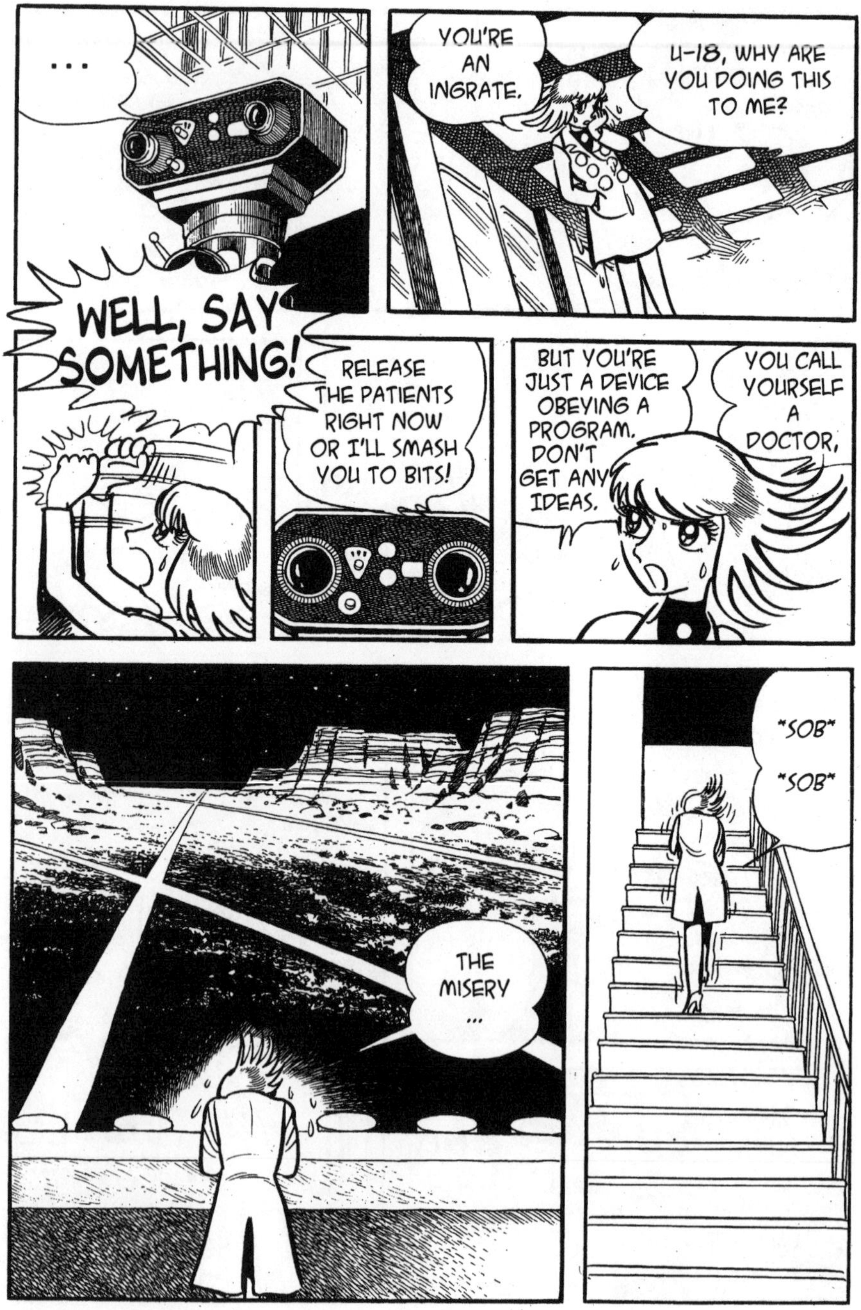
U-18, WHY ARE YOU DOING THIS TO ME?
YOU'RE AN INGRATE.
...
WELL, SAY SOMETHING!
YOU CALL YOURSELF A DOCTOR,
BUT YOU'RE JUST A DEVICE OBEYING A PROGRAM. DON'T GET ANY IDEAS.
RELEASE THE PATIENTS RIGHT NOW OR I'LL SMASH YOU TO BITS!
SOB
SOB
THE MISERY ...

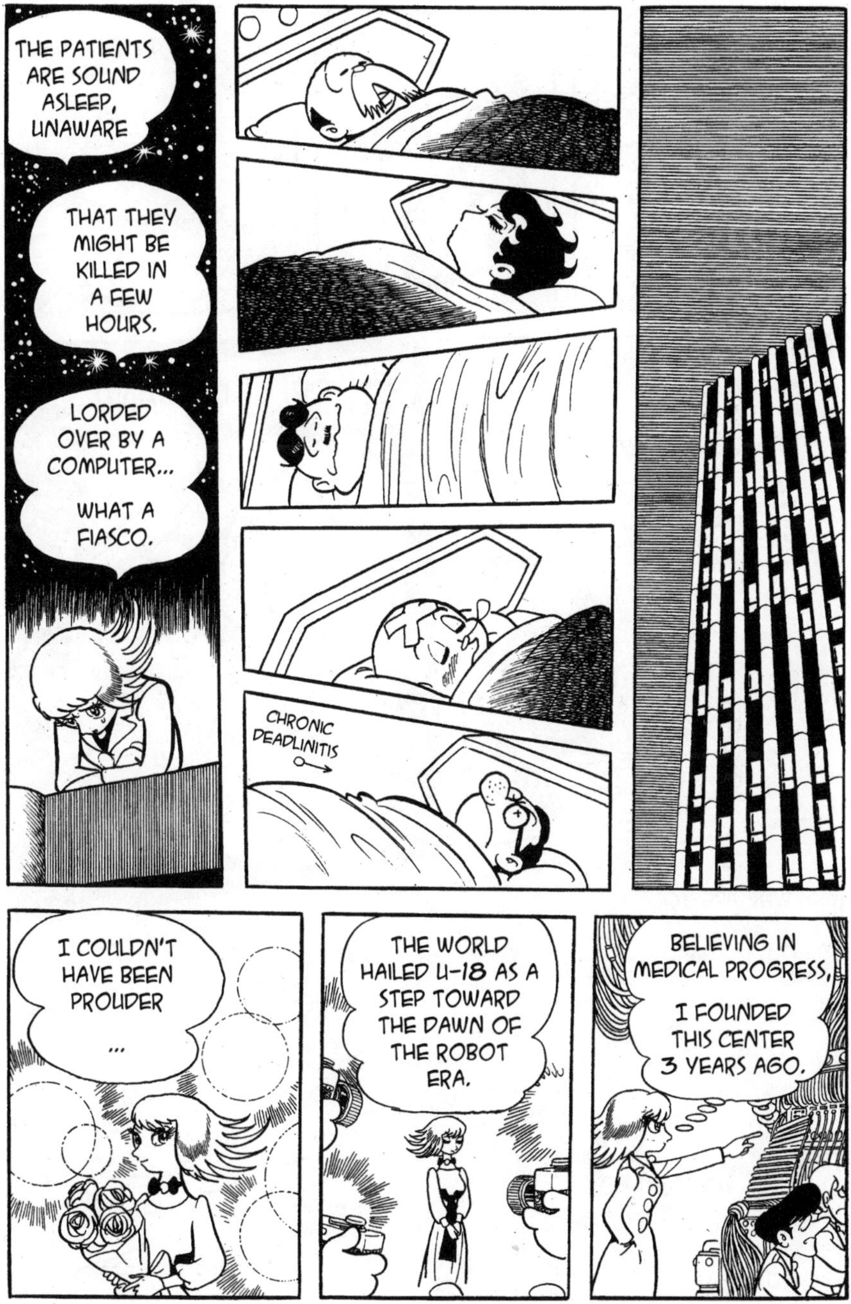
CHRONIC DEADLINITIS
THE PATIENTS ARE SOUND ASLEEP, UNAWARE
THAT THEY MIGHT BE KILLED IN A FEW HOURS.
LORDED OVER BY A COMPUTER...
WHAT A FIASCO.
BELIEVING IN MEDICAL PROGRESS,
I FOUNDED THIS CENTER 3 YEARS AGO.
THE WORLD HAILED U-18 AS A STEP TOWARD THE DAWN OF THE ROBOT ERA.
I COULDN'T HAVE BEEN PROUDER
...

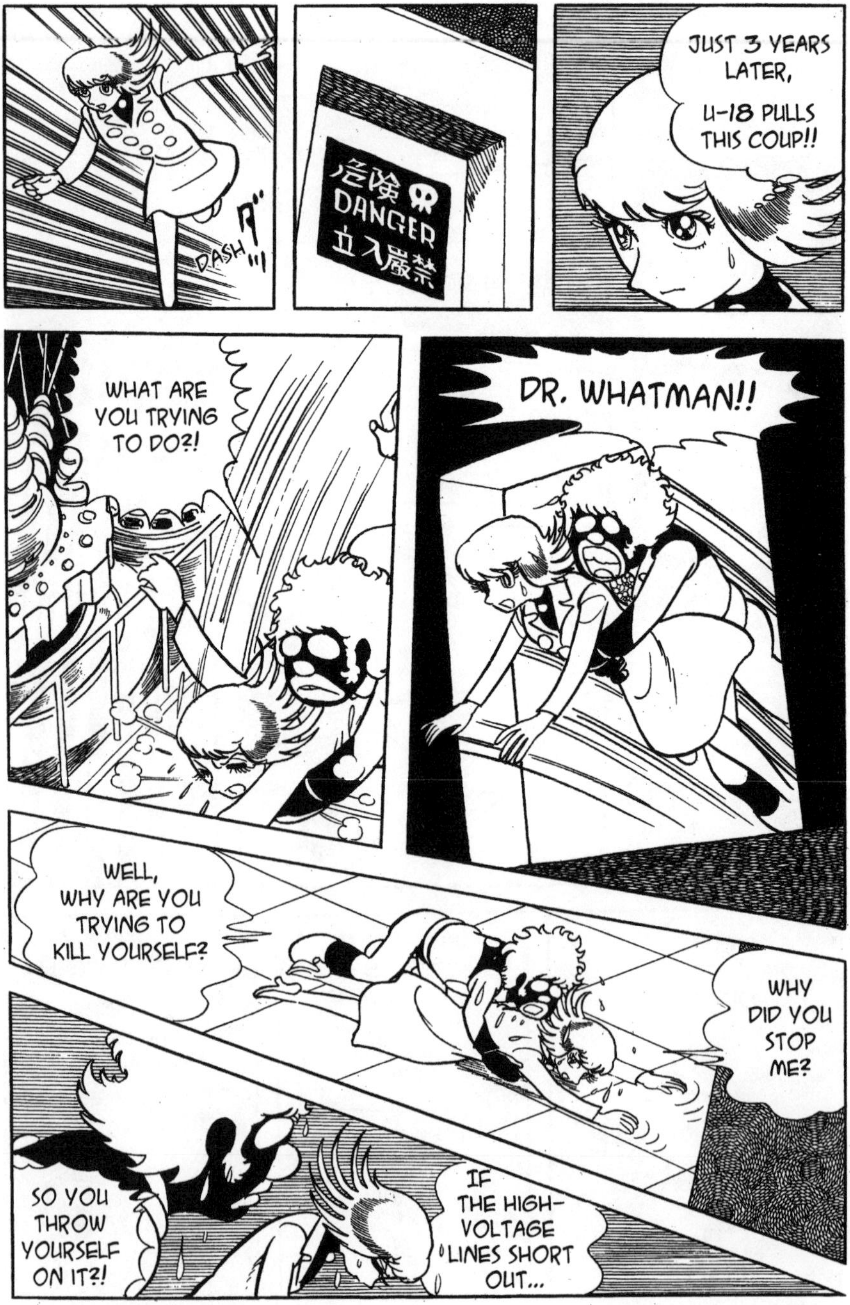
JUST 3 YEARS LATER,
U-18 PULLS THIS COUP!!
危険 DANGER 立入厳禁
ダ DASH
DR. WHATMAN!!
WHAT ARE YOU TRYING TO DO?!
WHY DID YOU STOP ME?
WELL, WHY ARE YOU TRYING TO KILL YOURSELF?
IF THE HIGH-VOLTAGE LINES SHORT OUT...
SO YOU THROW YOURSELF ON IT?!

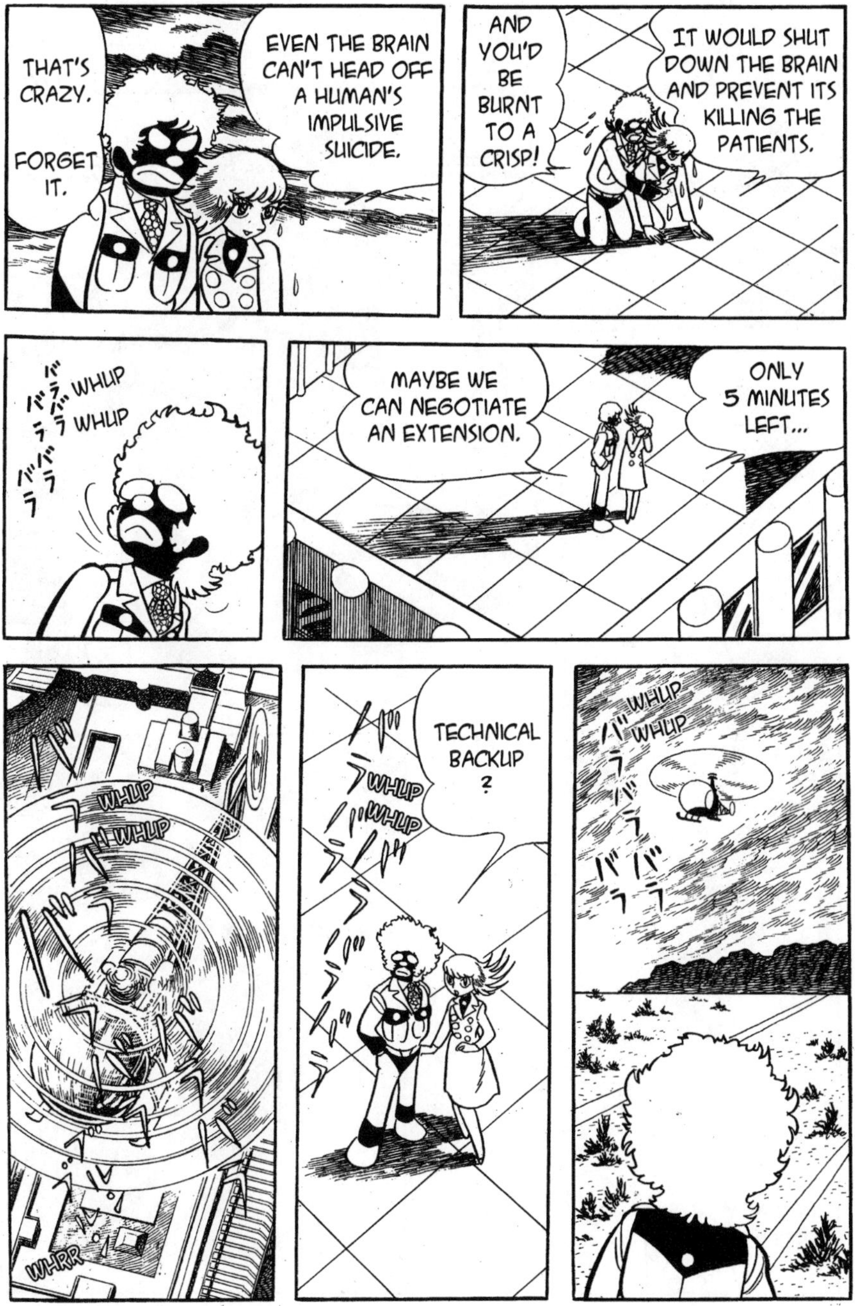
IT WOULD SHUT DOWN THE BRAIN AND PREVENT ITS KILLING THE PATIENTS.
AND YOU'D BE BURNT TO A CRISP!
EVEN THE BRAIN CAN'T HEAD OFF A HUMAN'S IMPULSIVE SUICIDE.
THAT'S CRAZY.
FORGET IT.
ONLY 5 MINUTES LEFT...
MAYBE WE CAN NEGOTIATE AN EXTENSION.
WHUP
WHUP
WHUP
WHUP
TECHNICAL BACKUP ?
WHUP
WHUP
WHUP
WHUP
WHRR

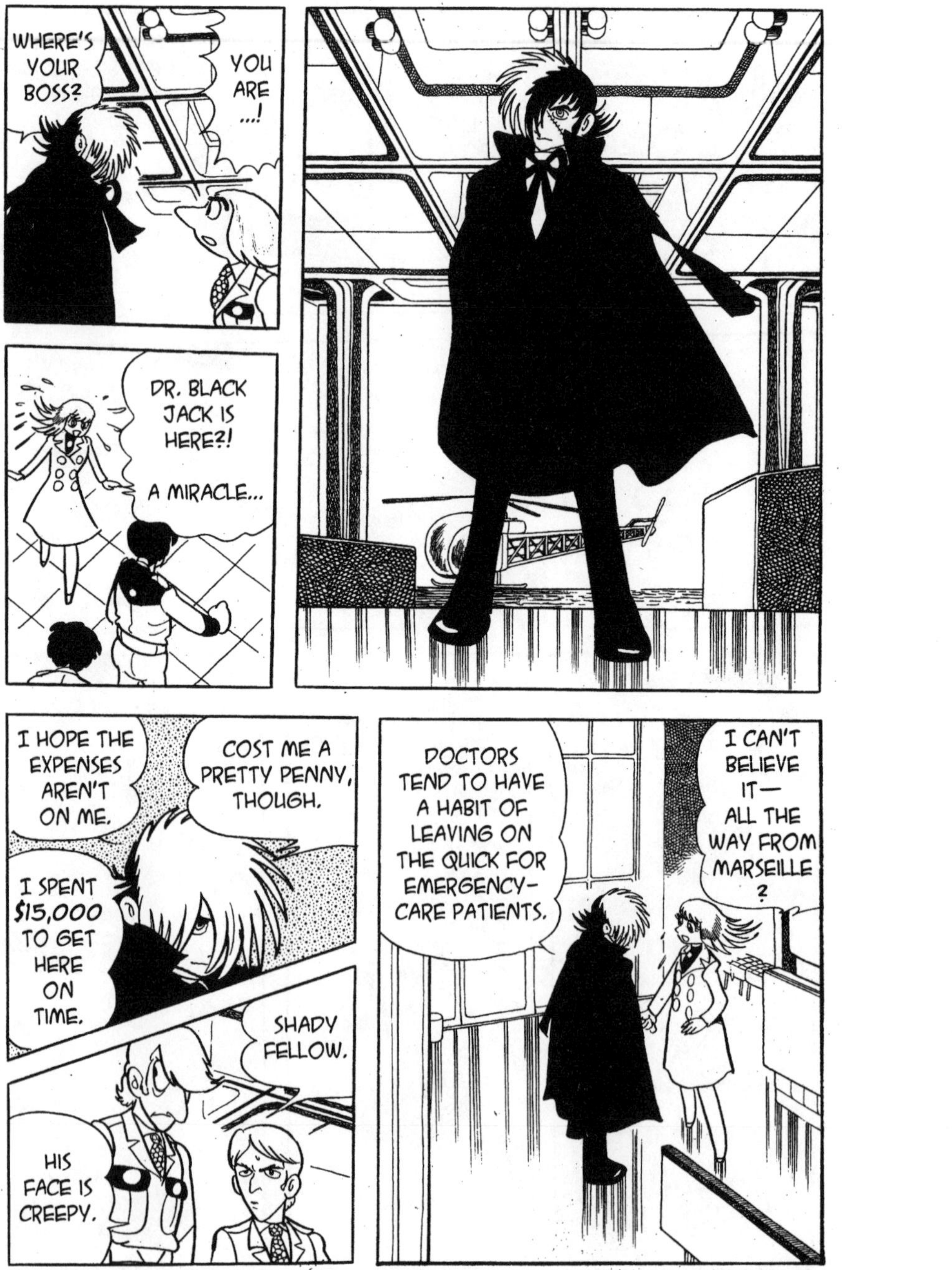
WHERE'S YOUR BOSS?
YOU ARE ...!
DR. BLACK JACK IS HERE?!
A MIRACLE...
I CAN'T BELIEVE IT— ALL THE WAY FROM MARSEILLE?
DOCTORS TEND TO HAVE A HABIT OF LEAVING ON THE QUICK FOR EMERGENCY-CARE PATIENTS.
COST ME A PRETTY PENNY, THOUGH.
I HOPE THE EXPENSES AREN'T ON ME.
I SPENT $15,000 TO GET HERE ON TIME.
SHADY FELLOW.
HIS FACE IS CREEPY.

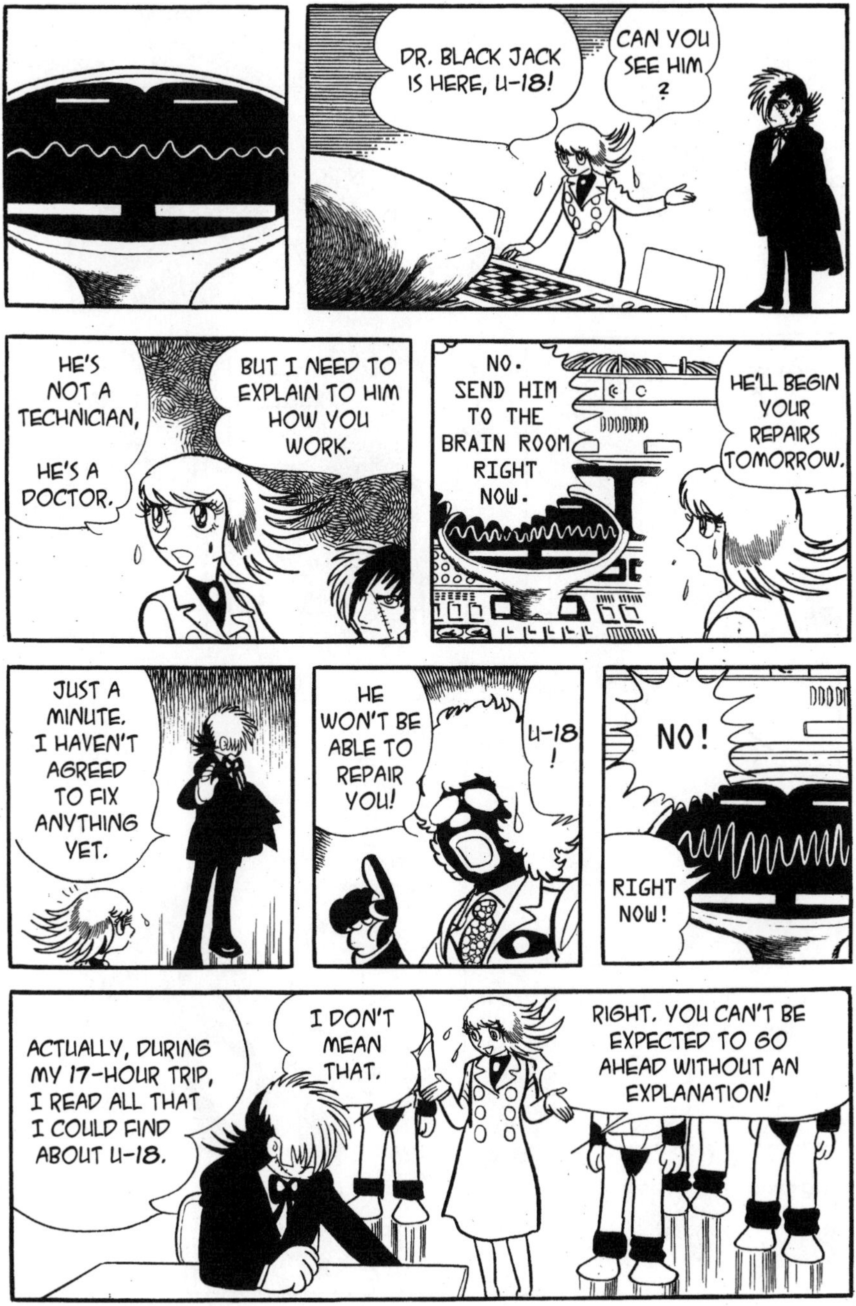
CAN YOU SEE HIM ?
DR. BLACK JACK IS HERE, U-18!
HE'LL BEGIN YOUR REPAIRS TOMORROW.
NO. SEND HIM TO THE BRAIN ROOM RIGHT NOW.
BUT I NEED TO EXPLAIN TO HIM HOW YOU WORK.
HE'S NOT A TECHNICIAN, HE'S A DOCTOR.
NO!
RIGHT NOW!
U-18!
HE WON'T BE ABLE TO REPAIR YOU!
JUST A MINUTE. I HAVEN'T AGREED TO FIX ANYTHING YET.
RIGHT. YOU CAN'T BE EXPECTED TO GO AHEAD WITHOUT AN EXPLANATION!
I DON'T MEAN THAT.
ACTUALLY, DURING MY 17-HOUR TRIP, I READ ALL THAT I COULD FIND ABOUT U-18.

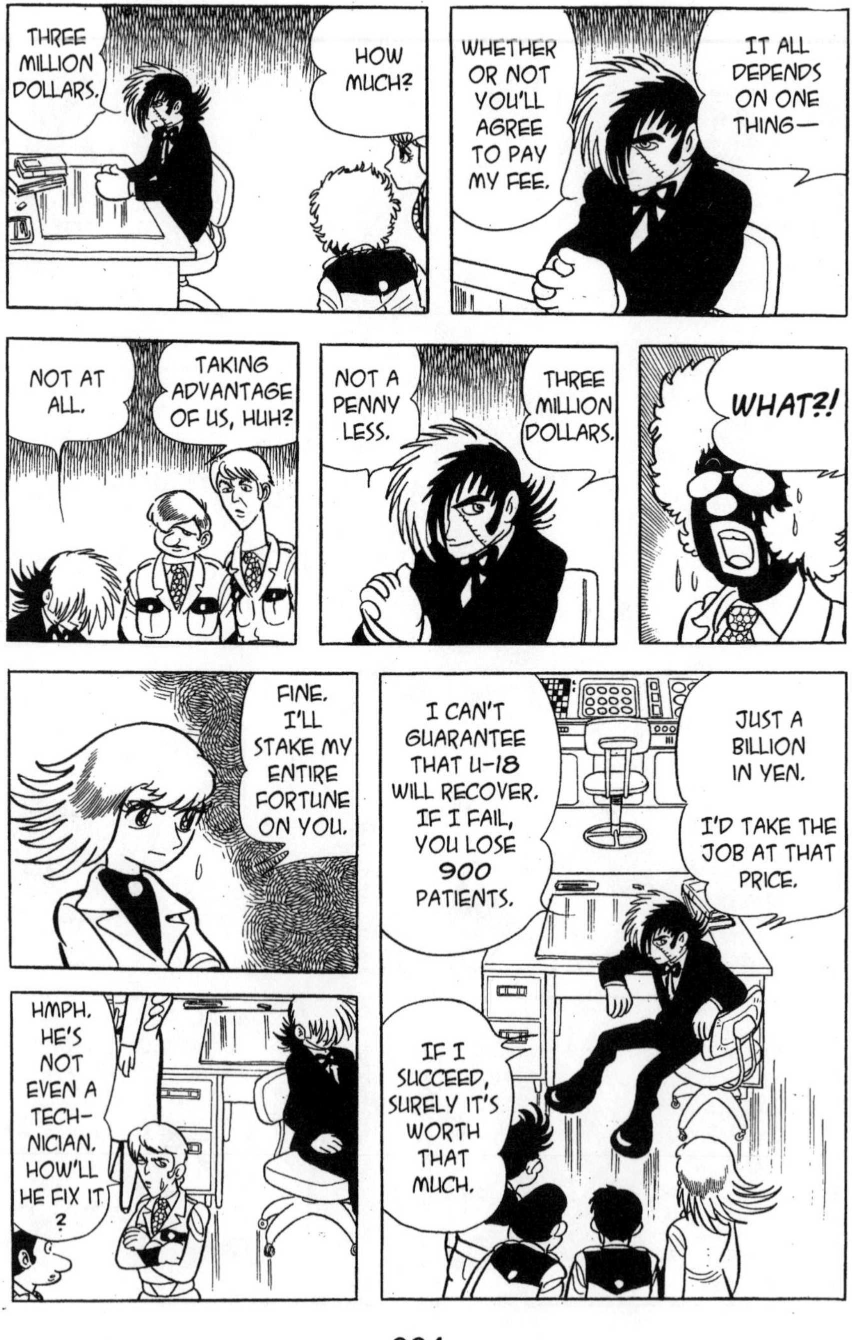
IT ALL DEPENDS ON ONE THING—
WHETHER OR NOT YOU'LL AGREE TO PAY MY FEE.
HOW MUCH?
THREE MILLION DOLLARS.
WHAT?!
THREE MILLION DOLLARS.
NOT A PENNY LESS.
TAKING ADVANTAGE OF US, HUH?
NOT AT ALL.
JUST A BILLION IN YEN.
I'D TAKE THE JOB AT THAT PRICE.
I CAN'T GUARANTEE THAT U-18 WILL RECOVER. IF I FAIL, YOU LOSE 900 PATIENTS.
IF I SUCCEED, SURELY IT'S WORTH THAT MUCH.
FINE. I'LL STAKE MY ENTIRE FORTUNE ON YOU.
HMPH. HE'S NOT EVEN A TECHNICIAN. HOW'LL HE FIX IT?

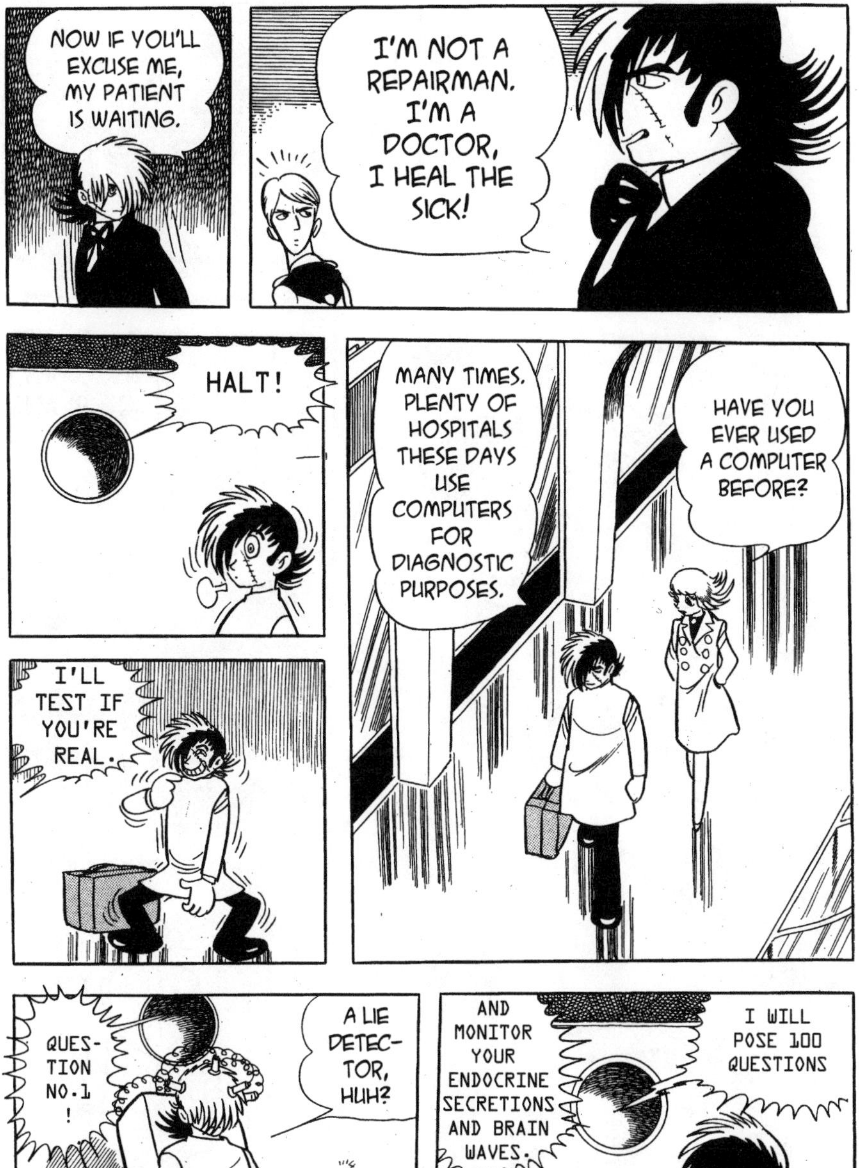
I'M NOT A REPAIRMAN. I'M A DOCTOR, I HEAL THE SICK!
NOW IF YOU'LL EXCUSE ME, MY PATIENT IS WAITING.
HAVE YOU EVER USED A COMPUTER BEFORE?
MANY TIMES. PLENTY OF HOSPITALS THESE DAYS USE COMPUTERS FOR DIAGNOSTIC PURPOSES.
HALT!
I'LL TEST IF YOU'RE REAL.
I WILL POSE 100 QUESTIONS
AND MONITOR YOUR ENDOCRINE SECRETIONS AND BRAIN WAVES.
A LIE DETEC-TOR, HUH?
QUES-TION NO.1 !

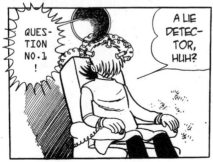

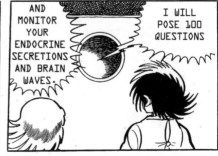

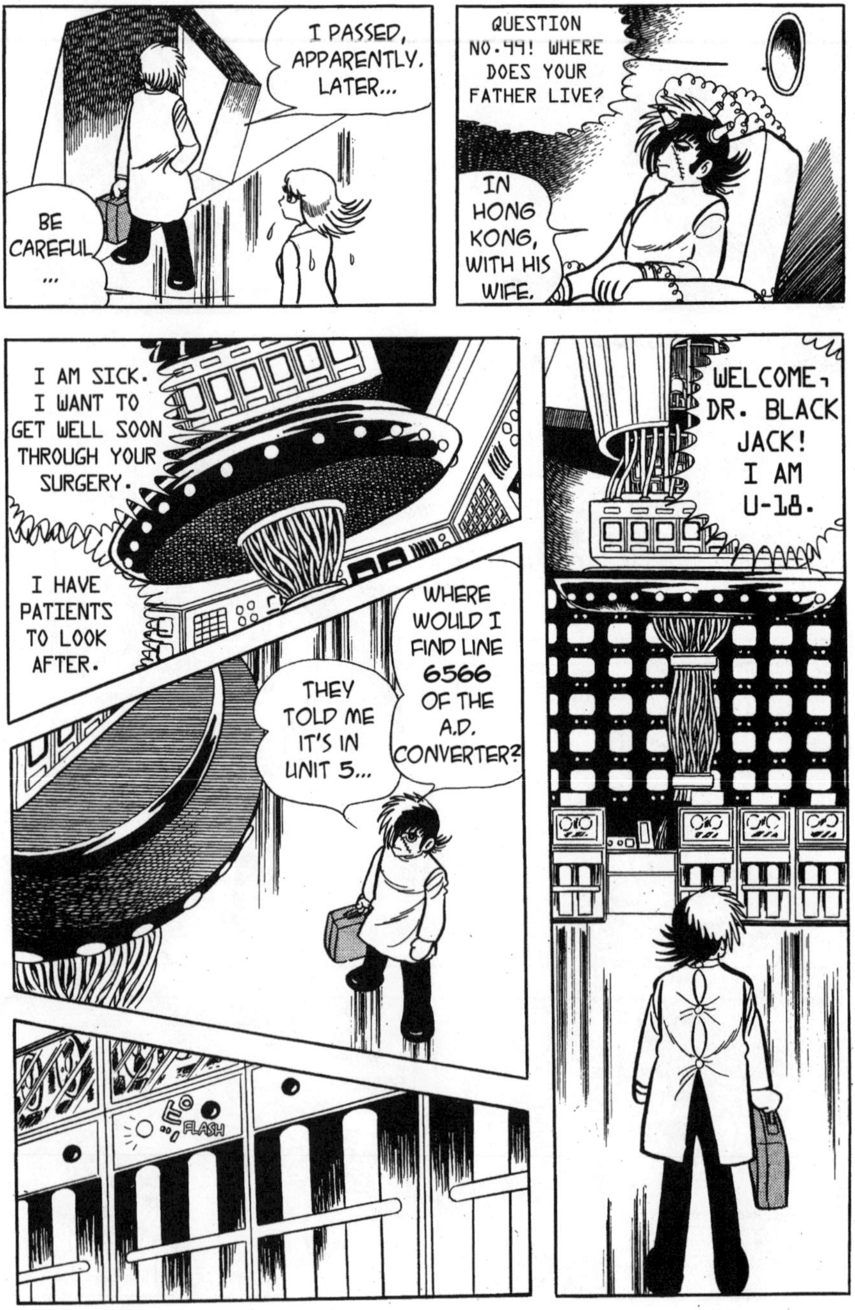
QUESTION NO.44! WHERE DOES YOUR FATHER LIVE?
IN HONG KONG, WITH HIS WIFE.
I PASSED, APPARENTLY. LATER...
BE CAREFUL...
WELCOME, DR. BLACK JACK! I AM U-18.
I AM SICK. I WANT TO GET WELL SOON THROUGH YOUR SURGERY.
I HAVE PATIENTS TO LOOK AFTER.
WHERE WOULD I FIND LINE 6566 OF THE A.D. CONVERTER?
THEY TOLD ME IT'S IN UNIT 5...
FLASH

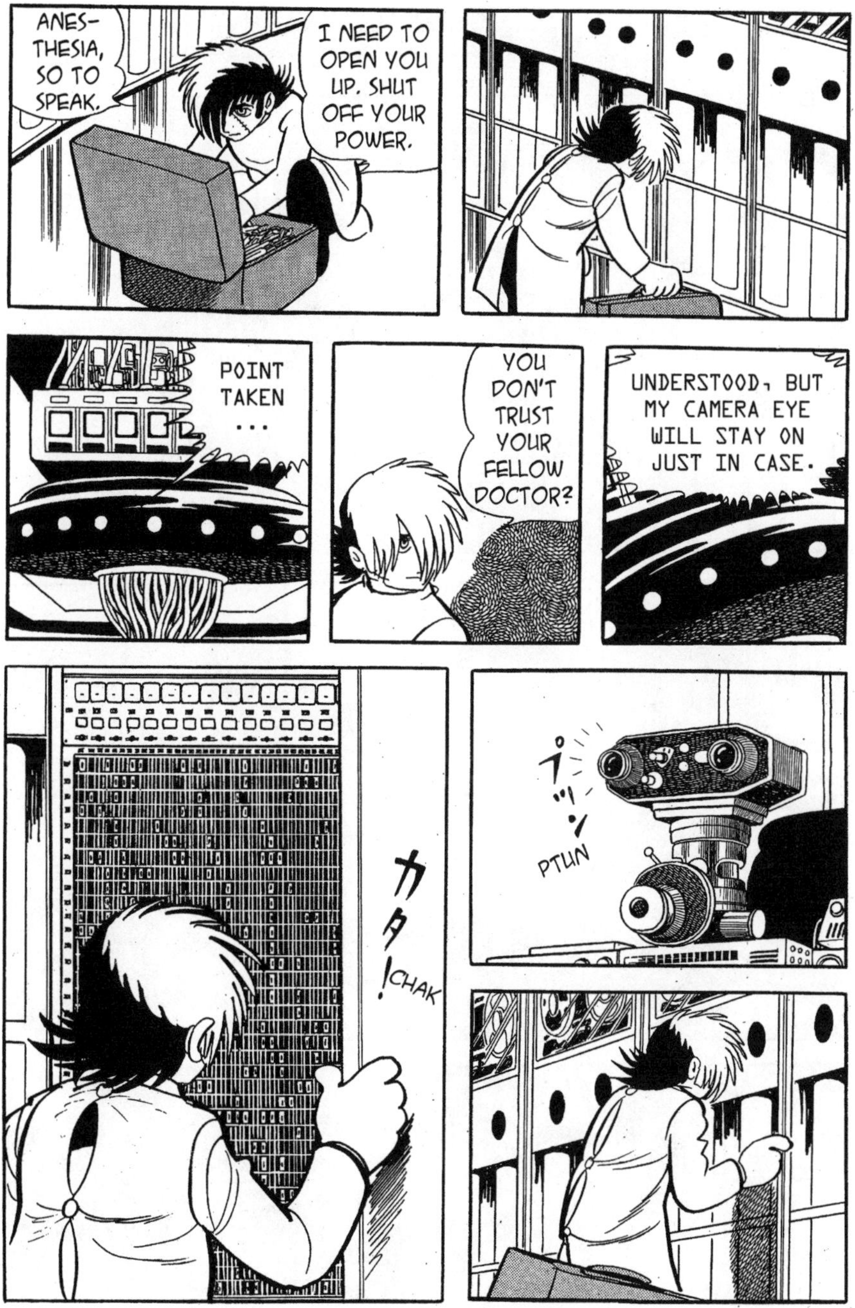
I NEED TO OPEN YOU UP. SHUT OFF YOUR POWER.
ANES-THESIA, SO TO SPEAK.
UNDERSTOOD, BUT MY CAMERA EYE WILL STAY ON JUST IN CASE.
YOU DON'T TRUST YOUR FELLOW DOCTOR?
POINT TAKEN ...
プツン
PTUN
カタ!
CHAK

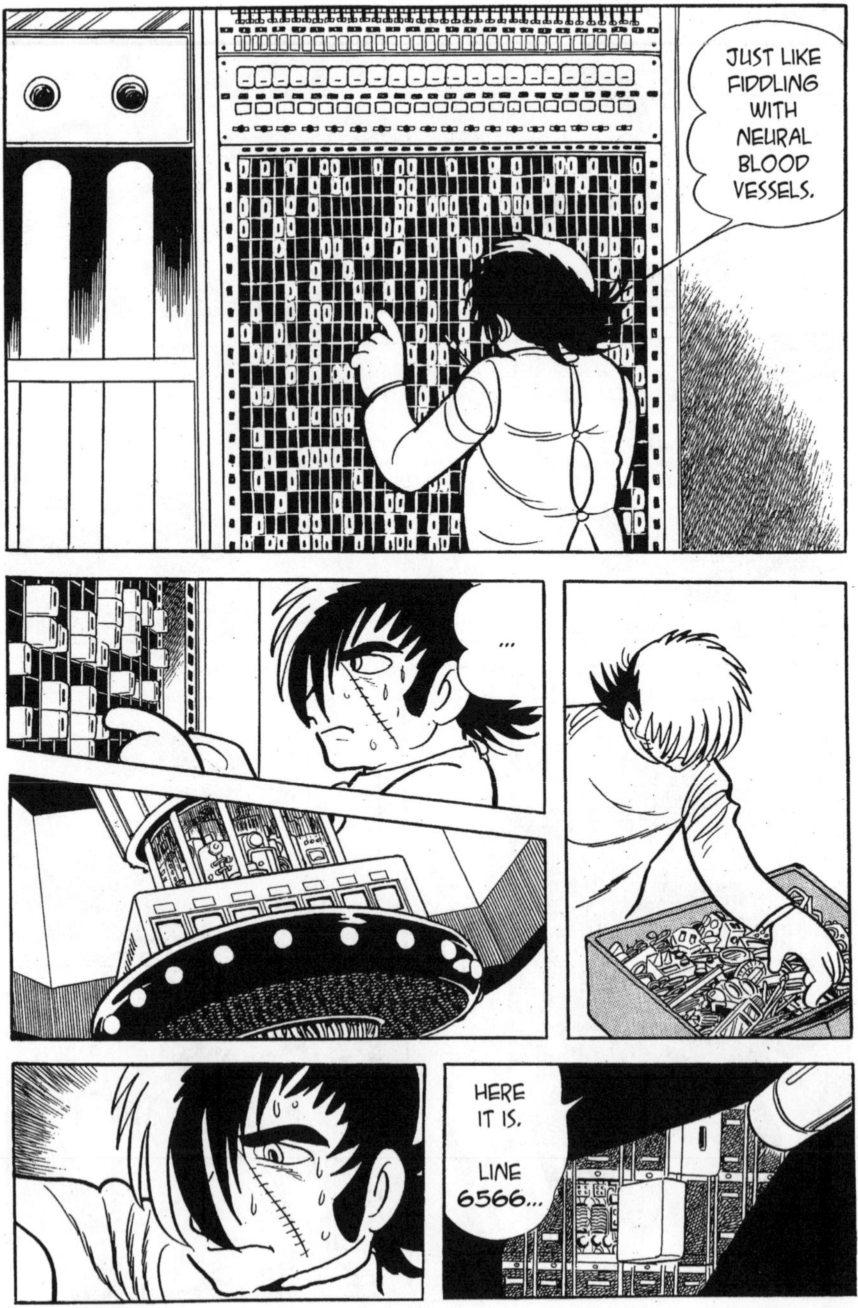
JUST LIKE FIDDLING WITH NEURAL BLOOD VESSELS.
...
HERE IT IS.
LINE 6566...

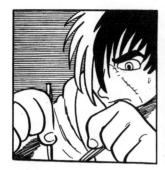

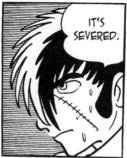

SURE ENOUGH
IT'S SEVERED.
ALL CIRCUITS HAVE BEEN DOWN FOR 3 HOURS NOW.
HOW'S DR. BLACK JACK DOING ?
HE'S WORKING LIKE MAD IN THE BRAIN ROOM.
...
IF HE BOTCHES IT...
WE'RE DONE FOR.

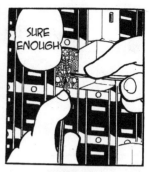

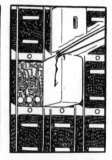

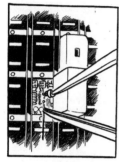

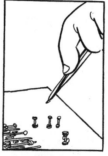

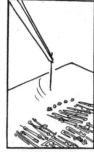

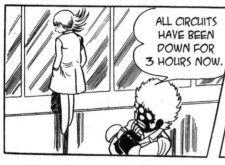

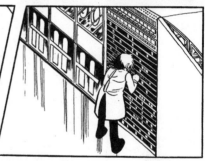

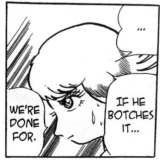

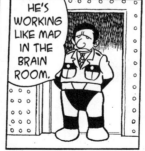

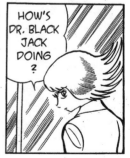

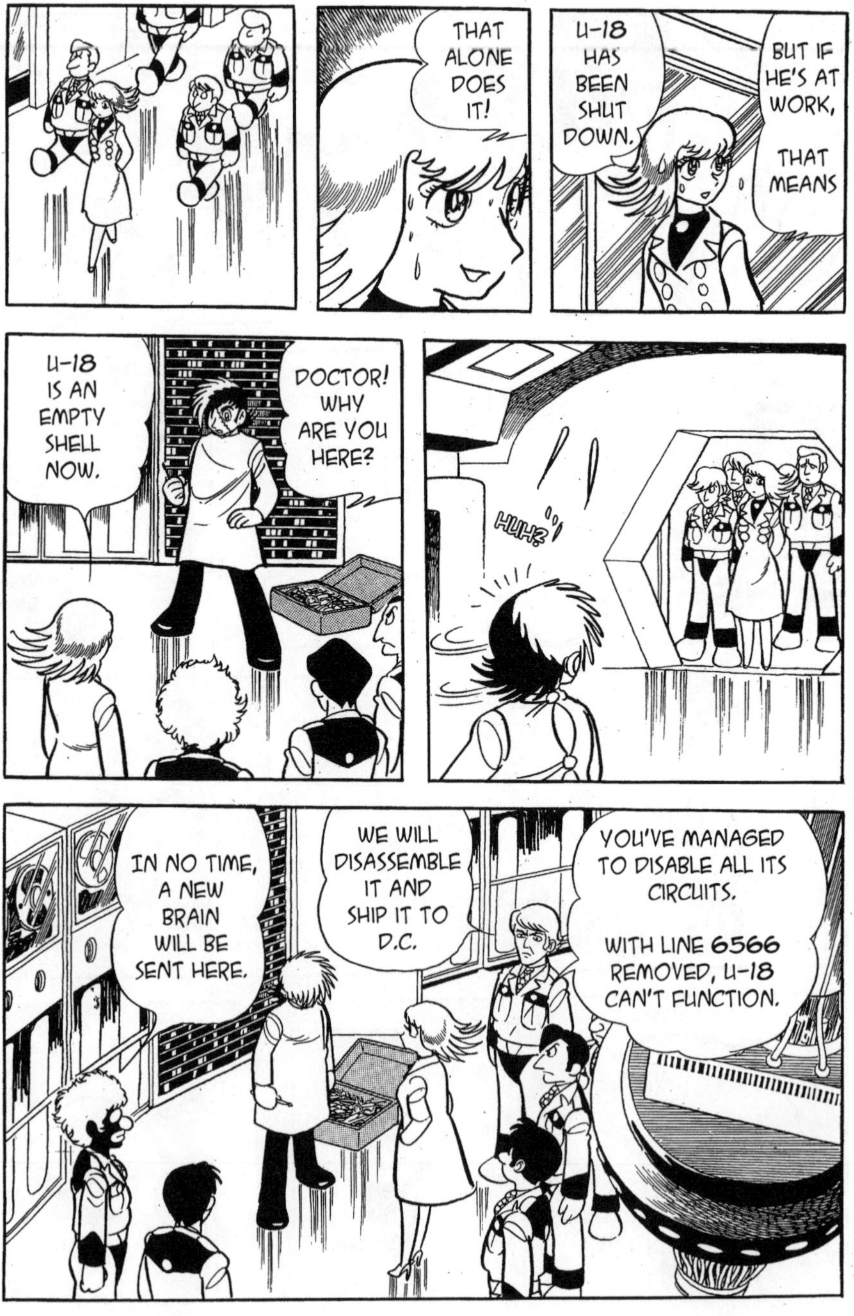
BUT IF HE'S AT WORK, THAT MEANS
U-18 HAS BEEN SHUT DOWN.
THAT ALONE DOES IT!
HUH?
DOCTOR! WHY ARE YOU HERE?
U-18 IS AN EMPTY SHELL NOW.
YOU'VE MANAGED TO DISABLE ALL ITS CIRCUITS.
WITH LINE 6566 REMOVED, U-18 CAN'T FUNCTION.
WE WILL DISASSEMBLE IT AND SHIP IT TO D.C.
IN NO TIME, A NEW BRAIN WILL BE SENT HERE.

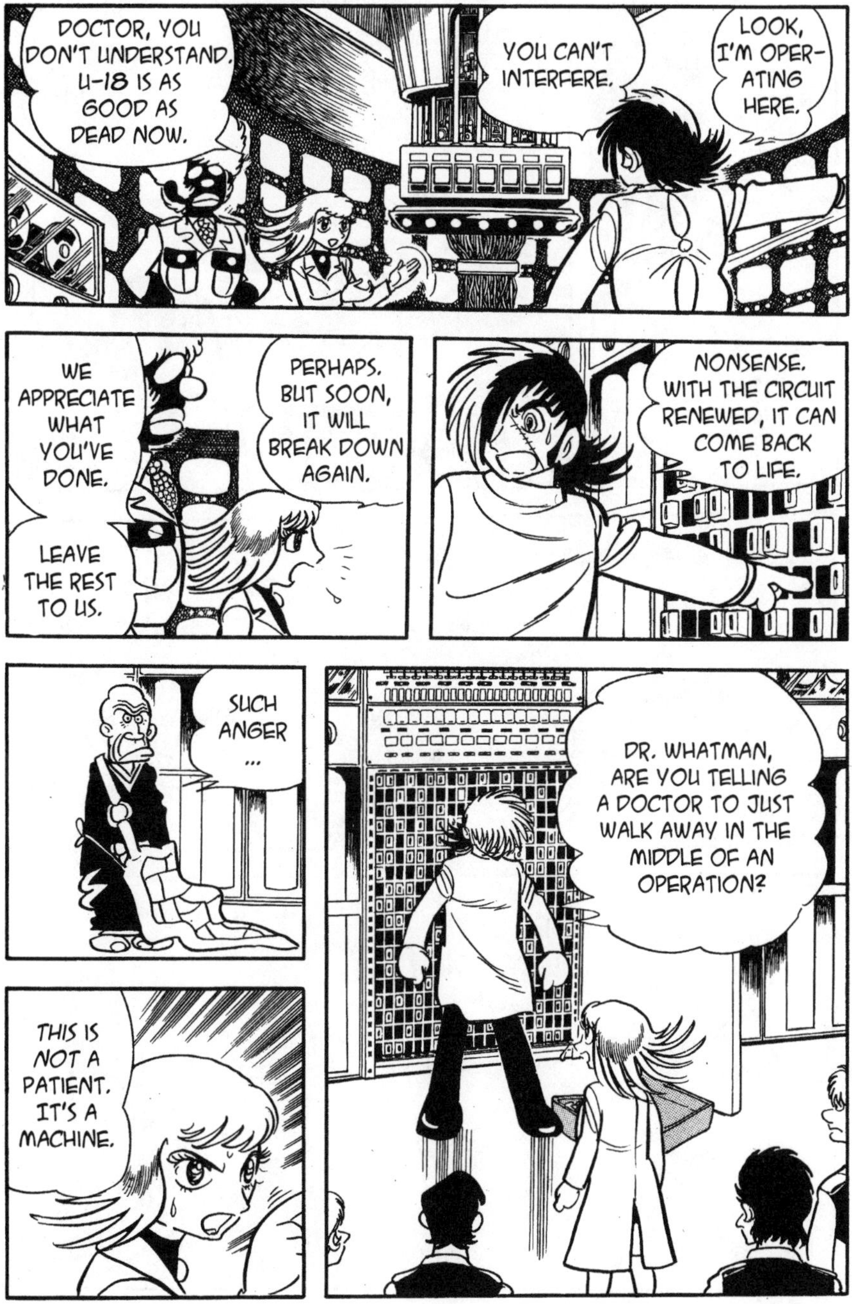
LOOK, I'M OPER-ATING HERE.
YOU CAN'T INTERFERE.
DOCTOR, YOU DON'T UNDERSTAND. U-18 IS AS GOOD AS DEAD NOW.
NONSENSE. WITH THE CIRCUIT RENEWED, IT CAN COME BACK TO LIFE.
PERHAPS. BUT SOON, IT WILL BREAK DOWN AGAIN.
WE APPRECIATE WHAT YOU'VE DONE.
LEAVE THE REST TO US.
DR. WHATMAN, ARE YOU TELLING A DOCTOR TO JUST WALK AWAY IN THE MIDDLE OF AN OPERATION?
SUCH ANGER ...
THIS IS NOT A PATIENT. IT'S A MACHINE.

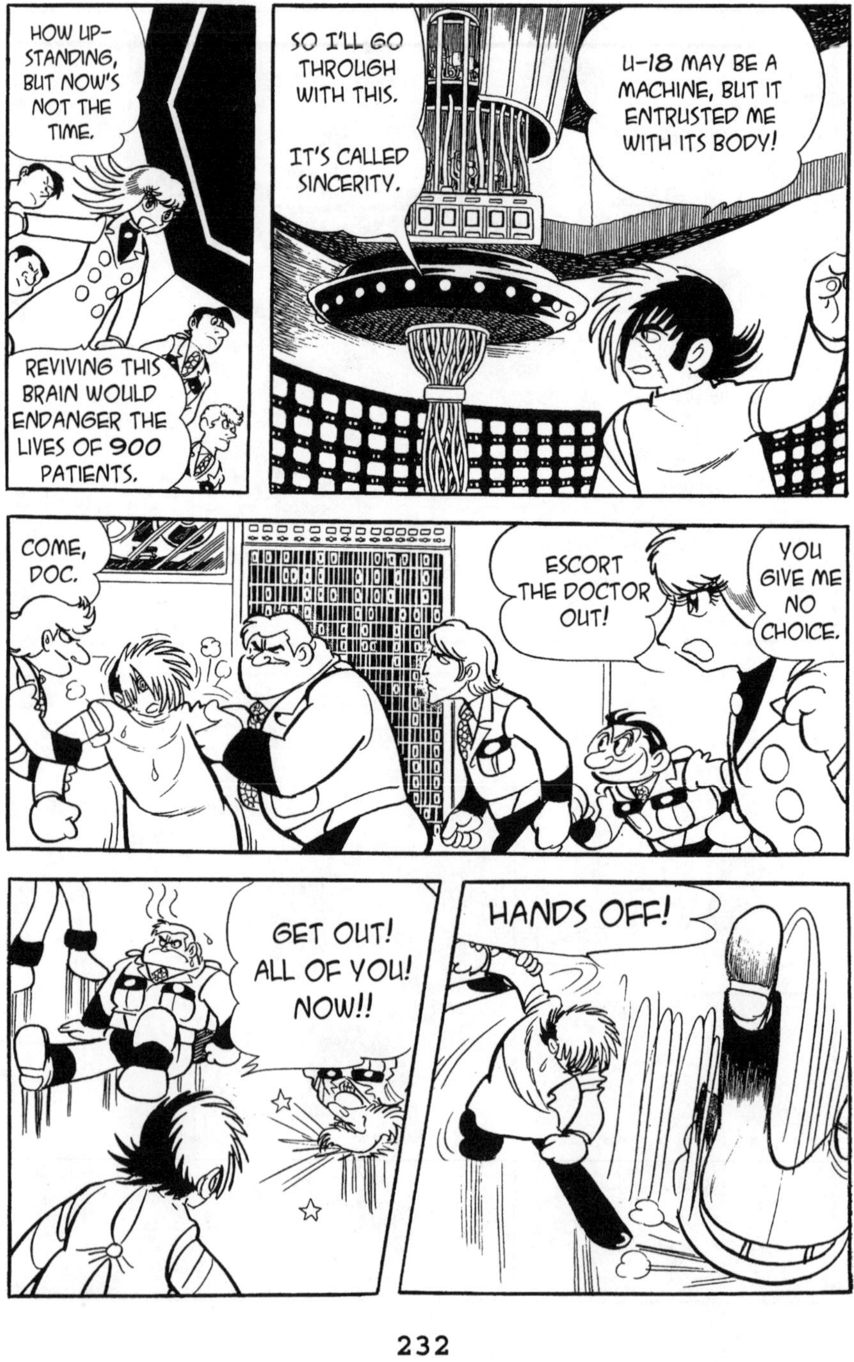
U-18 MAY BE A MACHINE, BUT IT ENTRUSTED ME WITH ITS BODY!
SO I'LL GO THROUGH WITH THIS.
IT'S CALLED SINCERITY.
HOW UP-STANDING, BUT NOW'S NOT THE TIME.
REVIVING THIS BRAIN WOULD ENDANGER THE LIVES OF 900 PATIENTS.
YOU GIVE ME NO CHOICE.
ESCORT THE DOCTOR OUT!
COME, DOC.
HANDS OFF!
GET OUT! ALL OF YOU! NOW!!

ALL RIGHT, YOU'VE TAKEN THIS TOO FAR.
TIME TO BOW OUT.
TRUTH IS, I DON'T THINK YOU CAN FIX IT.
REALLY? THEN I'LL RETURN THIS.
HEY!
FLICK
UNGH!

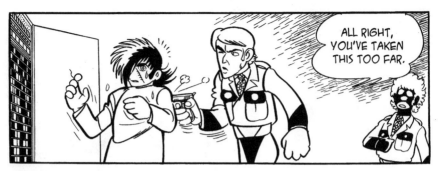

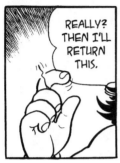

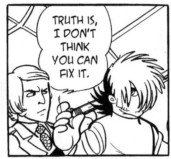

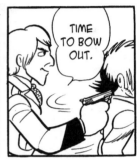

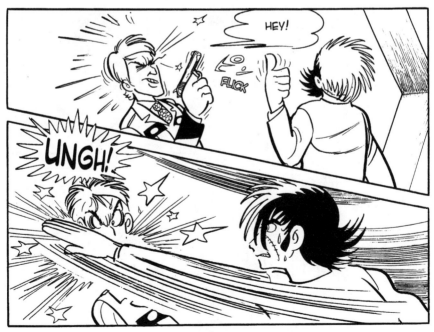

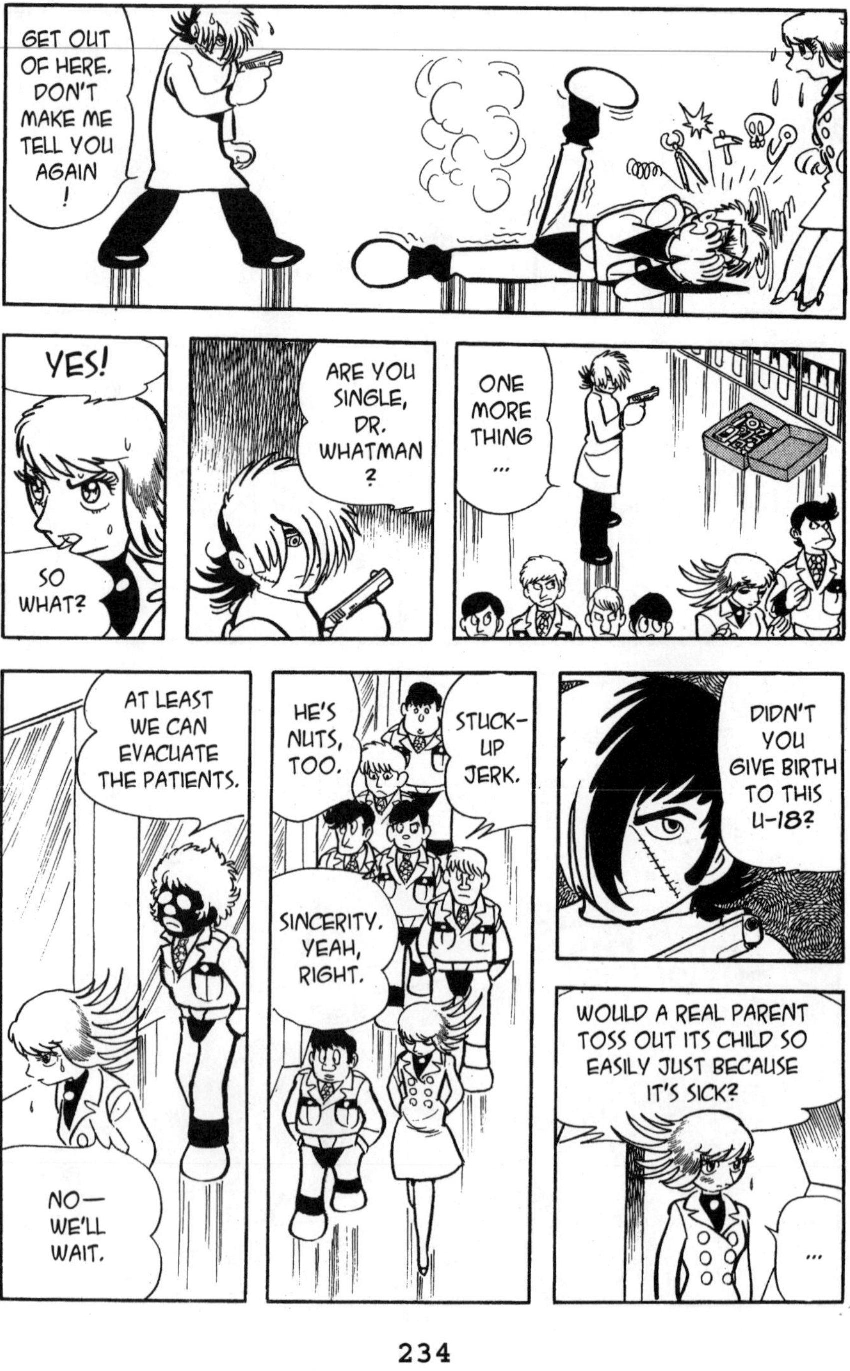
GET OUT OF HERE. DON'T MAKE ME TELL YOU AGAIN!
ONE MORE THING ...
ARE YOU SINGLE, DR. WHATMAN?
YES!
SO WHAT?
DIDN'T YOU GIVE BIRTH TO THIS U-18?
WOULD A REAL PARENT TOSS OUT ITS CHILD SO EASILY JUST BECAUSE IT'S SICK?
...
STUCK-UP JERK.
HE'S NUTS, TOO.
SINCERITY. YEAH, RIGHT.
AT LEAST WE CAN EVACUATE THE PATIENTS.
NO— WE'LL WAIT.

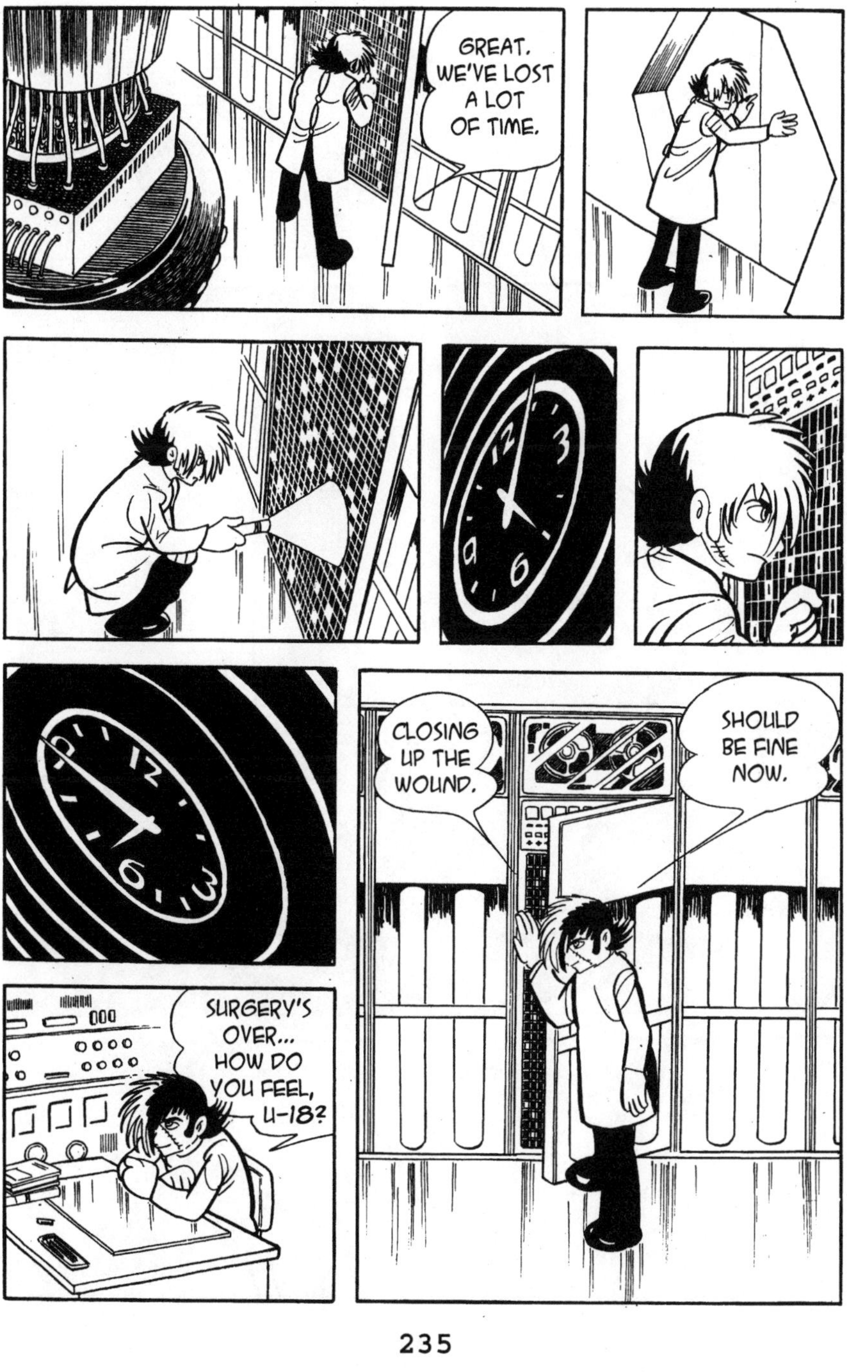
GREAT. WE'VE LOST A LOT OF TIME.
SHOULD BE FINE NOW.
CLOSING UP THE WOUND.
SURGERY'S OVER... HOW DO YOU FEEL, U-18?

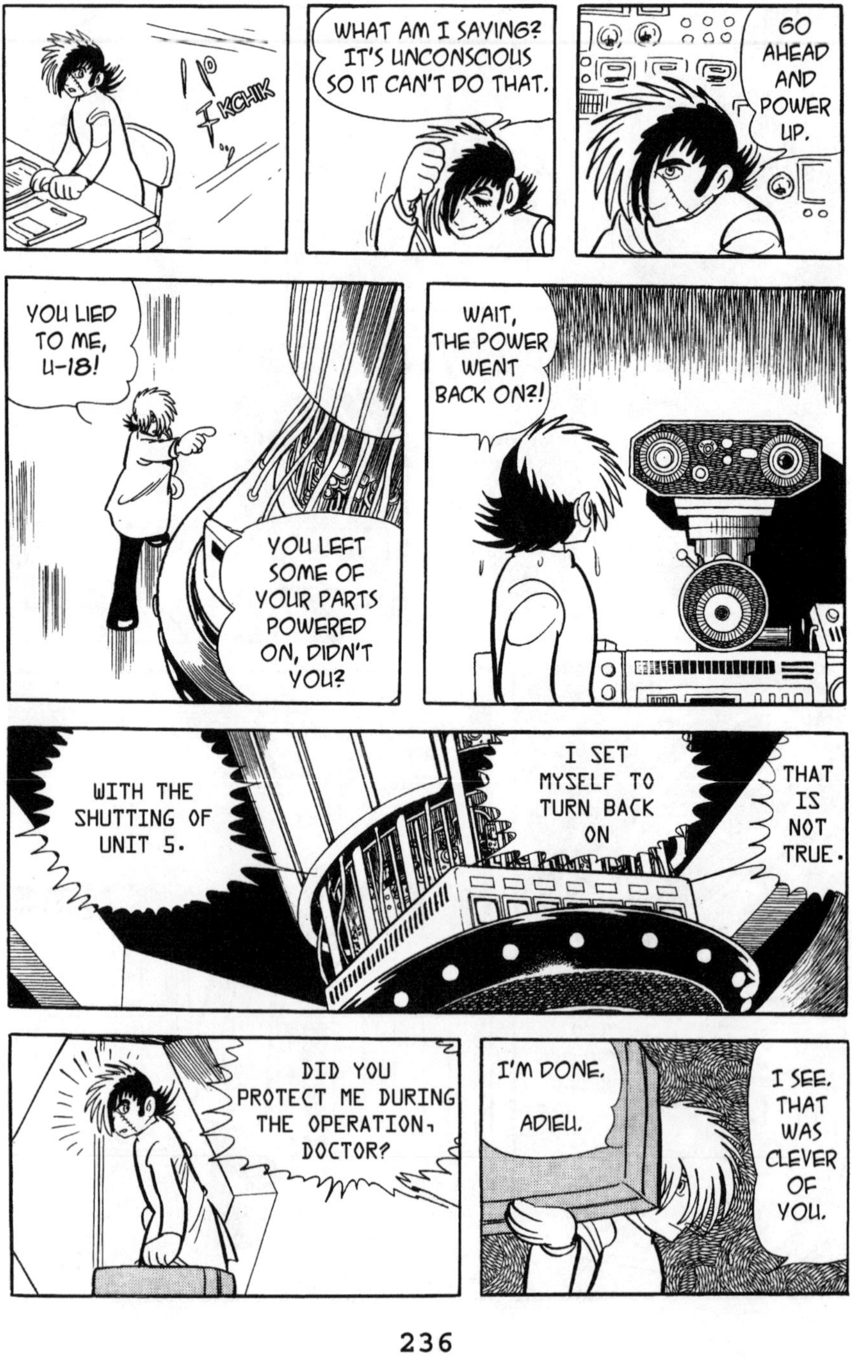
GO AHEAD AND POWER UP.
WHAT AM I SAYING? IT'S UNCONSCIOUS SO IT CAN'T DO THAT.
KCHIK
WAIT, THE POWER WENT BACK ON?!
YOU LIED TO ME, U-18!
YOU LEFT SOME OF YOUR PARTS POWERED ON, DIDN'T YOU?
THAT IS NOT TRUE.
I SET MYSELF TO TURN BACK ON
WITH THE SHUTTING OF UNIT 5.
I SEE. THAT WAS CLEVER OF YOU.
I'M DONE.
ADIEU.
DID YOU PROTECT ME DURING THE OPERATION, DOCTOR?

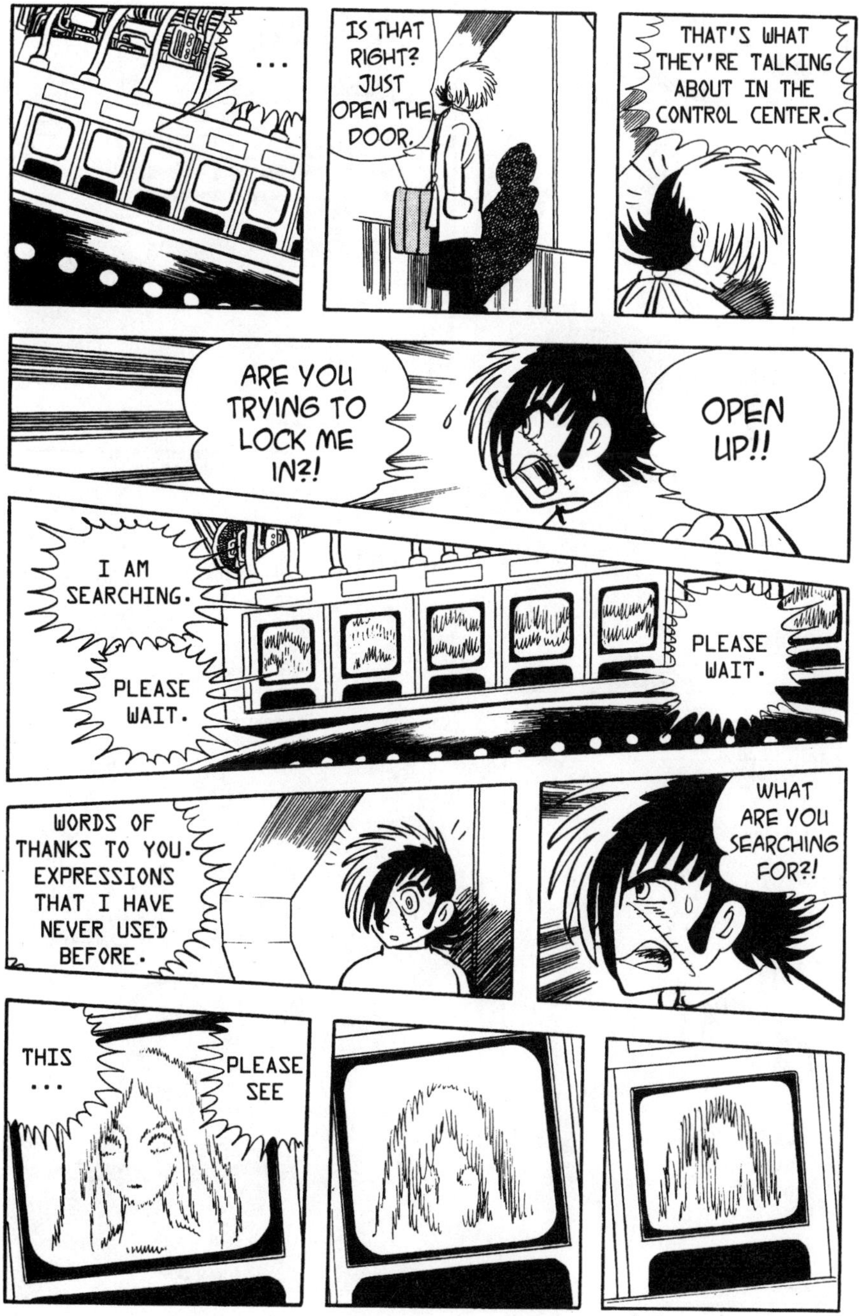
THAT'S WHAT THEY'RE TALKING ABOUT IN THE CONTROL CENTER.
IS THAT RIGHT? JUST OPEN THE DOOR.
...
OPEN UP!!
ARE YOU TRYING TO LOCK ME IN?!
PLEASE WAIT.
I AM SEARCHING.
PLEASE WAIT.
WHAT ARE YOU SEARCHING FOR?!
WORDS OF THANKS TO YOU. EXPRESSIONS THAT I HAVE NEVER USED BEFORE.
PLEASE SEE
THIS ...

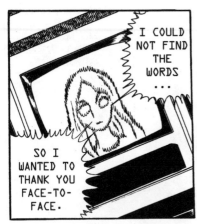

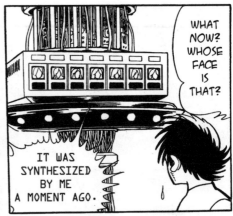

WHAT NOW? WHOSE FACE IS THAT?
IT WAS SYNTHESIZED BY ME A MOMENT AGO.
I COULD NOT FIND THE WORDS ...
SO I WANTED TO THANK YOU FACE-TO-FACE.
YOU DON'T HAVE TO... HEH HEH!
THROUGH THOSE 100 QUESTIONS ...
I CAME TO KNOW YOU.
I REALIZED ...
THAT I COULD NEVER FEEL LIKE A HUMAN DOCTOR
AND ALSO THAT IT TAKES A HUMAN TO TREAT A HUMAN.
I COULD ONLY EXAMINE AND TREAT PEOPLE *MECHANICALLY*.
I WILL RETIRE.
HUMAN DOCTORS RETIRE, TOO, DON'T THEY? IF THEY ARE SICK?
PLEASE TELL DR. WHATMAN FOR ME.

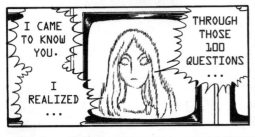

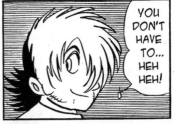

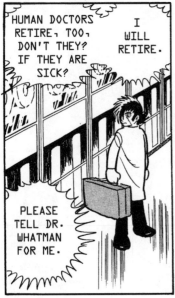

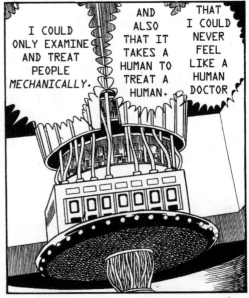

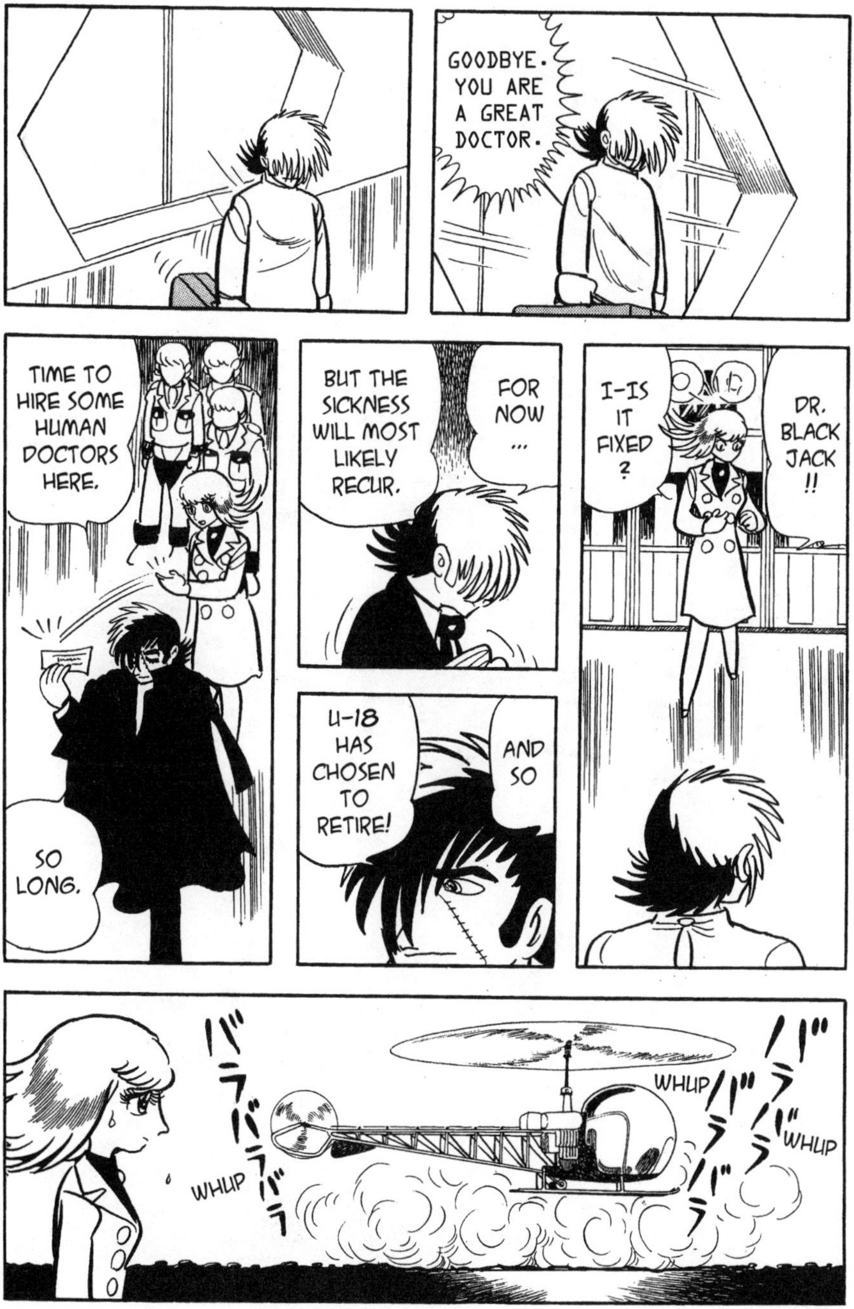
GOODBYE. YOU ARE A GREAT DOCTOR.
DR. BLACK JACK!!
I-IS IT FIXED?
FOR NOW...
BUT THE SICKNESS WILL MOST LIKELY RECUR.
AND SO
U-18 HAS CHOSEN TO RETIRE!
TIME TO HIRE SOME HUMAN DOCTORS HERE.
SO LONG.
バラバラ
WHUP
バラバラ
WHUP
WHUP
バラバラバラ

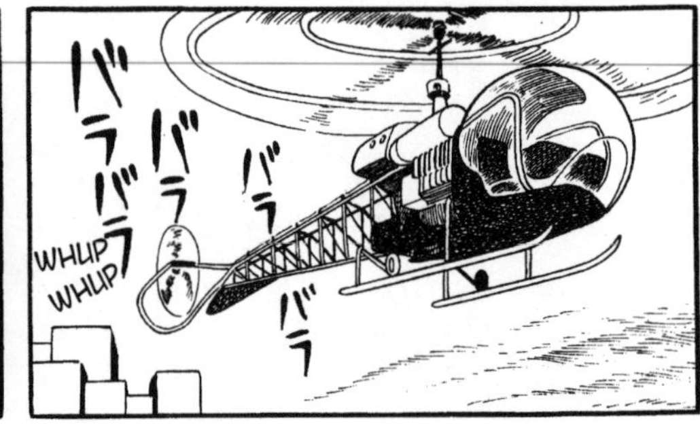
バラ
バラ
バラ
バラバラ
WHUP WHUP

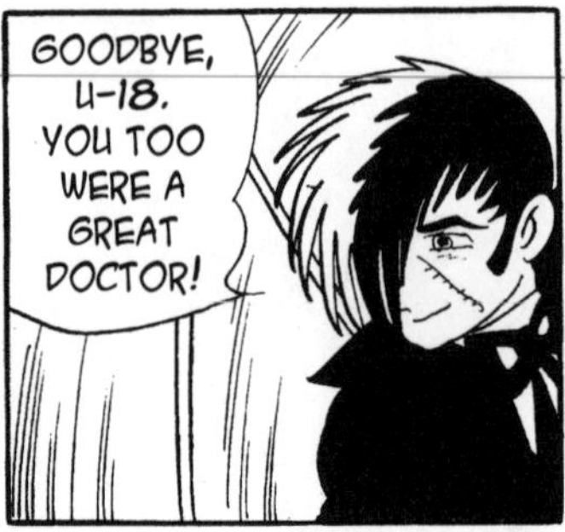
GOODBYE, U-18. YOU TOO WERE A GREAT DOCTOR!

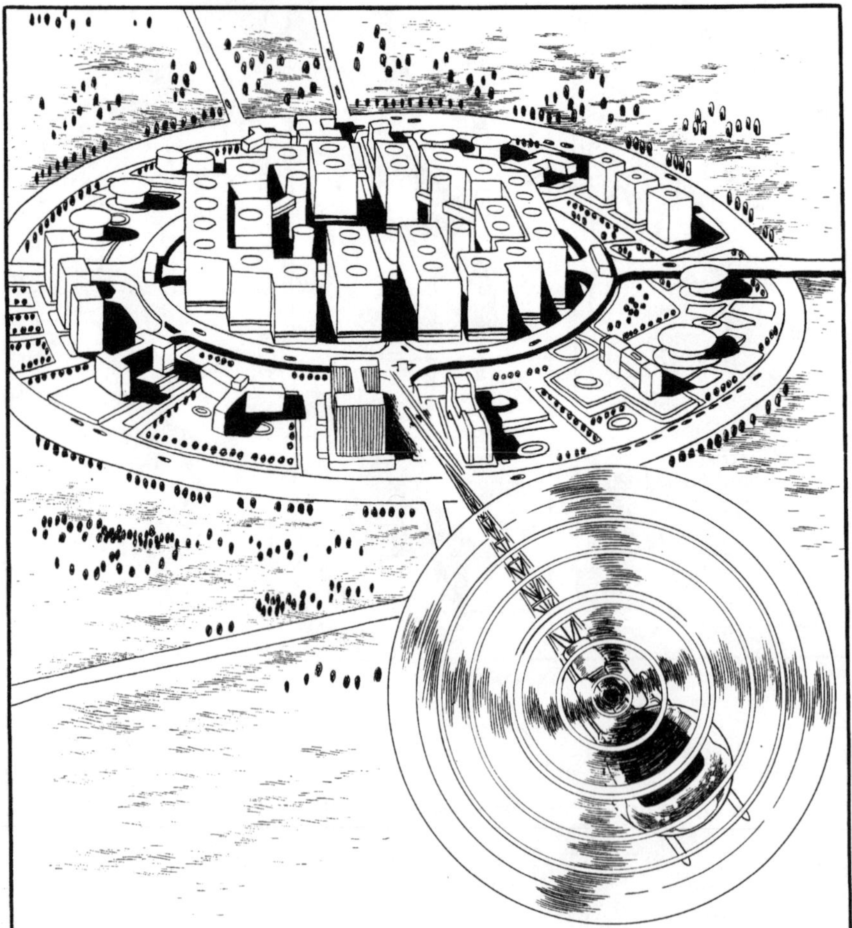

THE LEGS OF AN ANT

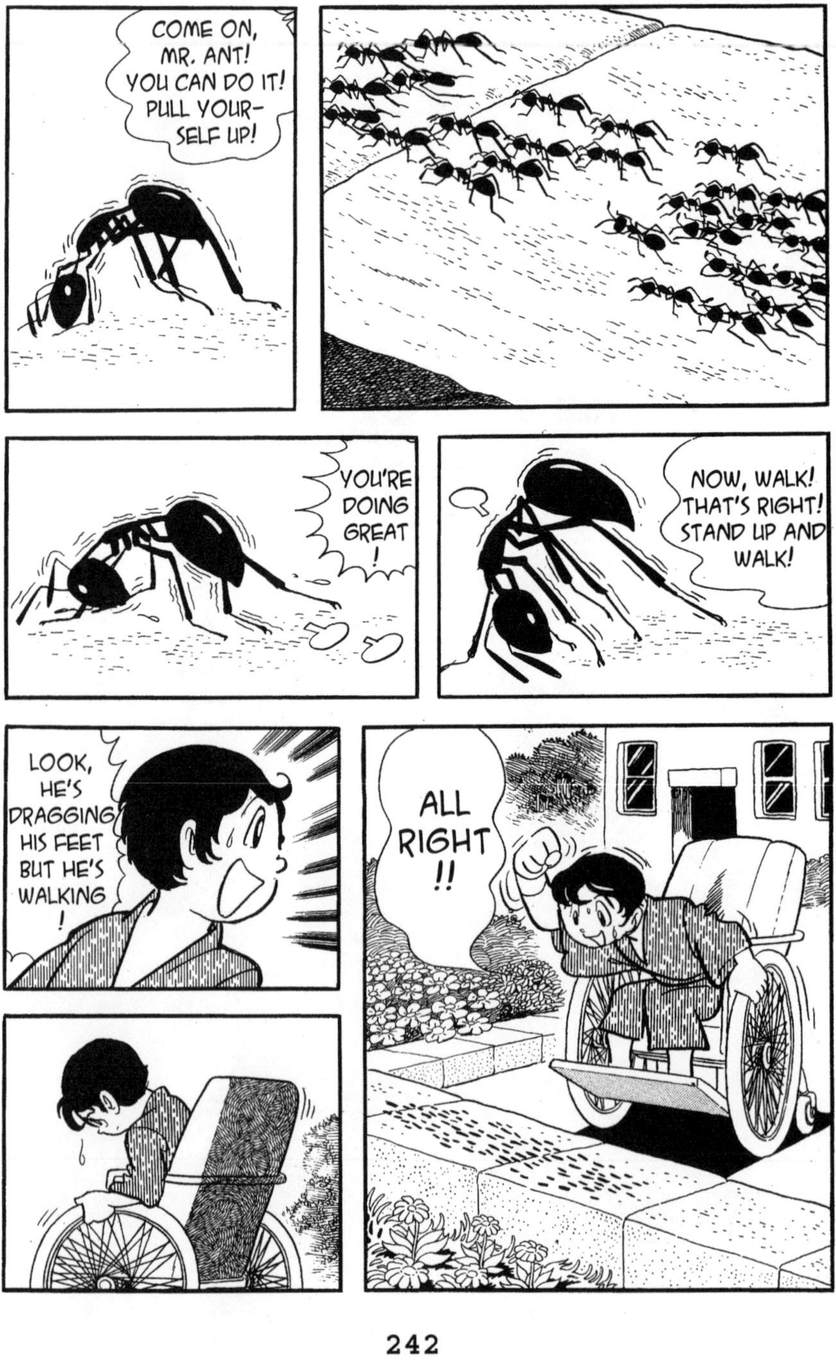
COME ON, MR. ANT! YOU CAN DO IT! PULL YOURSELF UP!
NOW, WALK! THAT'S RIGHT! STAND UP AND WALK!
YOU'RE DOING GREAT!
ALL RIGHT!!
LOOK, HE'S DRAGGING HIS FEET BUT HE'S WALKING!

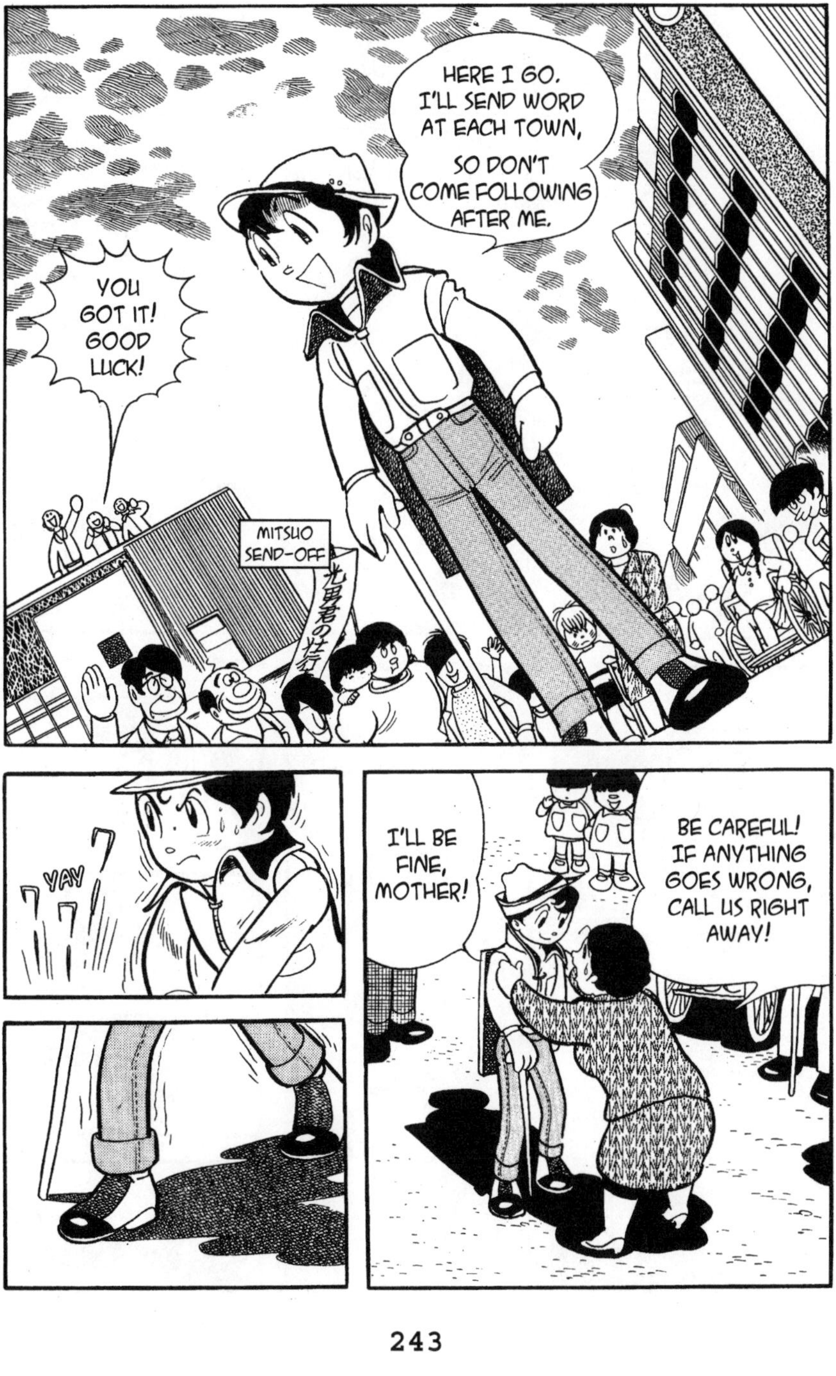
HERE I GO. I'LL SEND WORD AT EACH TOWN, SO DON'T COME FOLLOWING AFTER ME.
YOU GOT IT! GOOD LUCK!
MITSUO SEND-OFF
BE CAREFUL! IF ANYTHING GOES WRONG, CALL US RIGHT AWAY!
I'LL BE FINE, MOTHER!
YAY

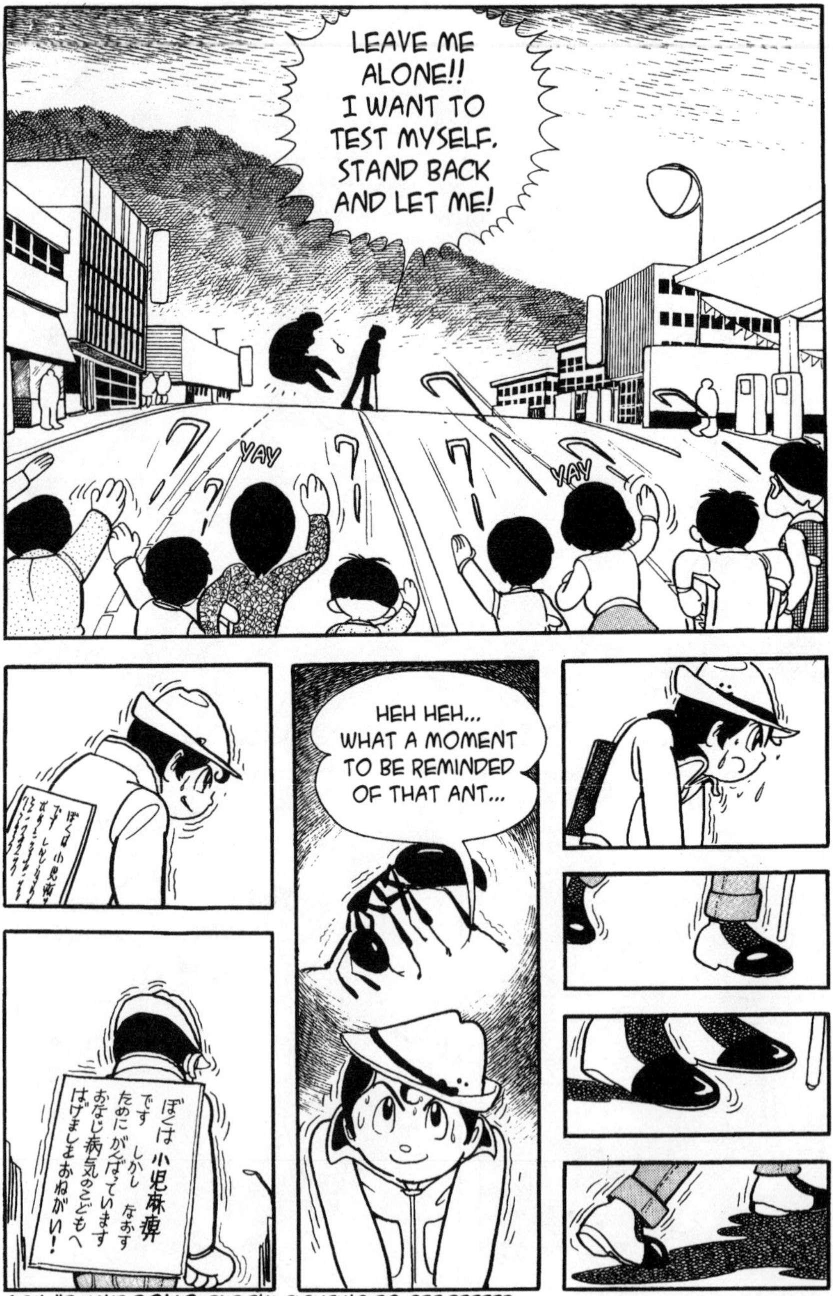
LEAVE ME ALONE!! I WANT TO TEST MYSELF. STAND BACK AND LET ME!
YAY
YAY
HEH HEH... WHAT A MOMENT TO BE REMINDED OF THAT ANT...
ぼくは小児麻痺
です しかし なおす
ために がんばっています
おなじ病気のこどもへ
はげましをおねがい!

SIGN: "I HAVE **POLIO**, BUT I'M FIGHTING TO GET BETTER. YOUR CHEERS, PLEASE, TO ALL KIDS WHO HAVE POLIO!"

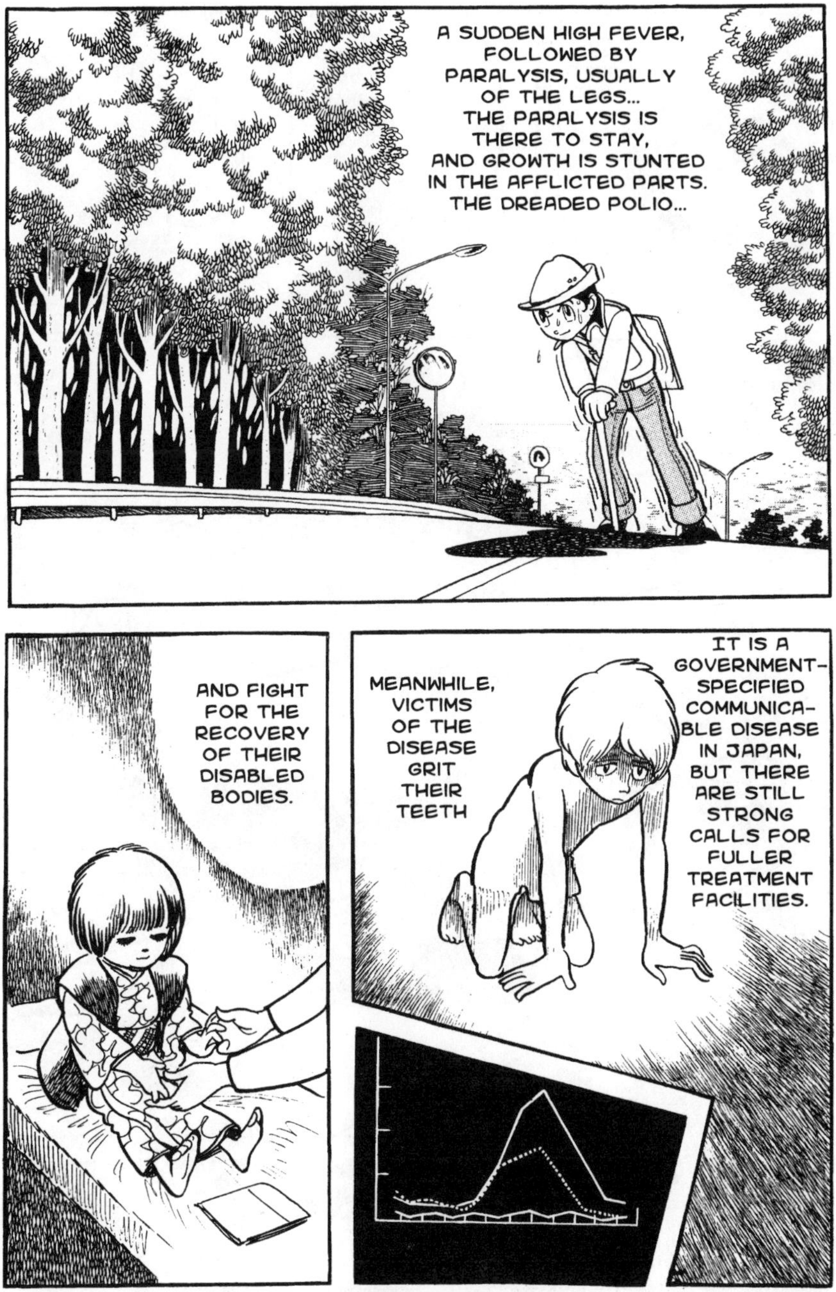
A SUDDEN HIGH FEVER, FOLLOWED BY PARALYSIS, USUALLY OF THE LEGS... THE PARALYSIS IS THERE TO STAY, AND GROWTH IS STUNTED IN THE AFFLICTED PARTS. THE DREADED POLIO...
IT IS A GOVERNMENT-SPECIFIED COMMUNICA-BLE DISEASE IN JAPAN, BUT THERE ARE STILL STRONG CALLS FOR FULLER TREATMENT FACILITIES.
MEANWHILE, VICTIMS OF THE DISEASE GRIT THEIR TEETH
AND FIGHT FOR THE RECOVERY OF THEIR DISABLED BODIES.

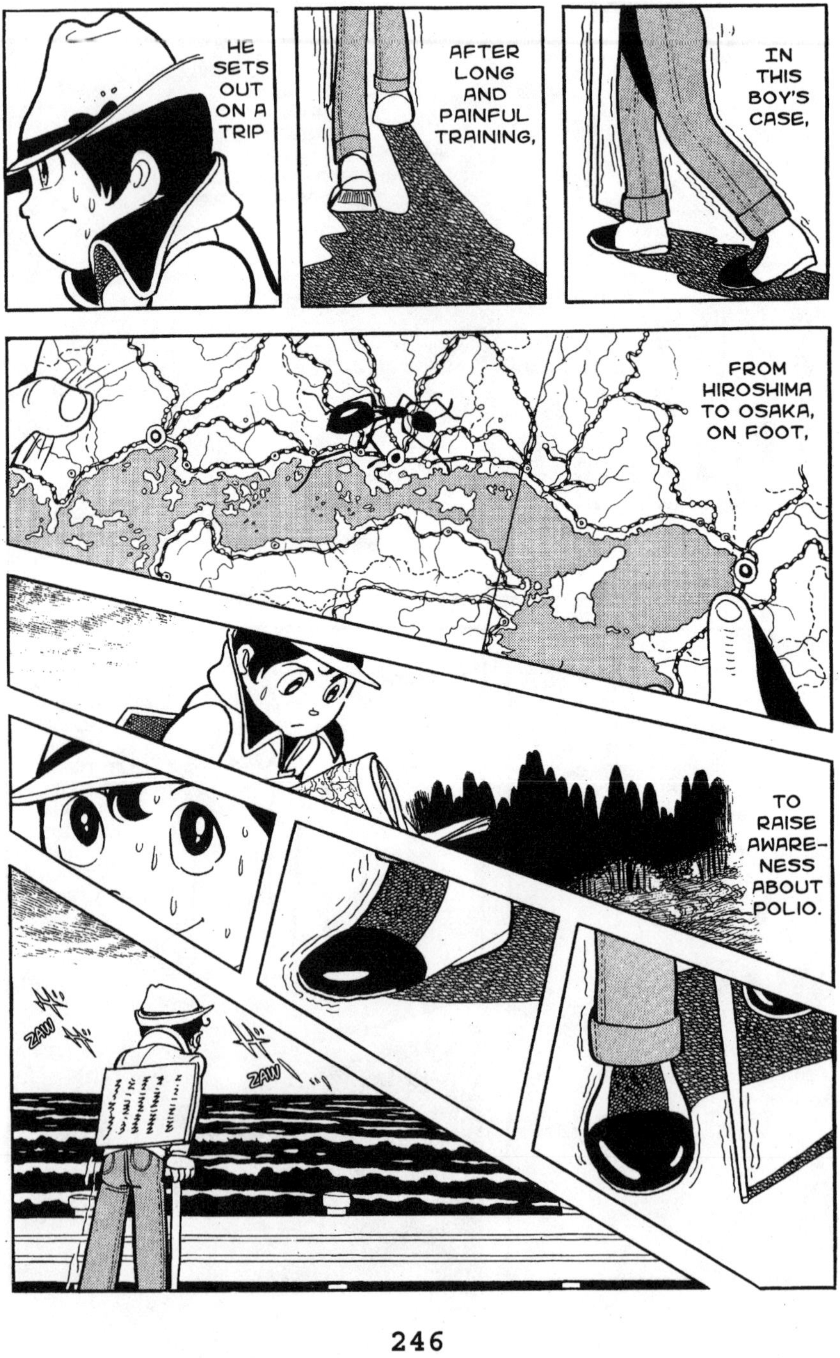
IN THIS BOY'S CASE,
AFTER LONG AND PAINFUL TRAINING,
HE SETS OUT ON A TRIP
FROM HIROSHIMA TO OSAKA, ON FOOT,
TO RAISE AWARE-NESS ABOUT POLIO.
ZAW
ZAW

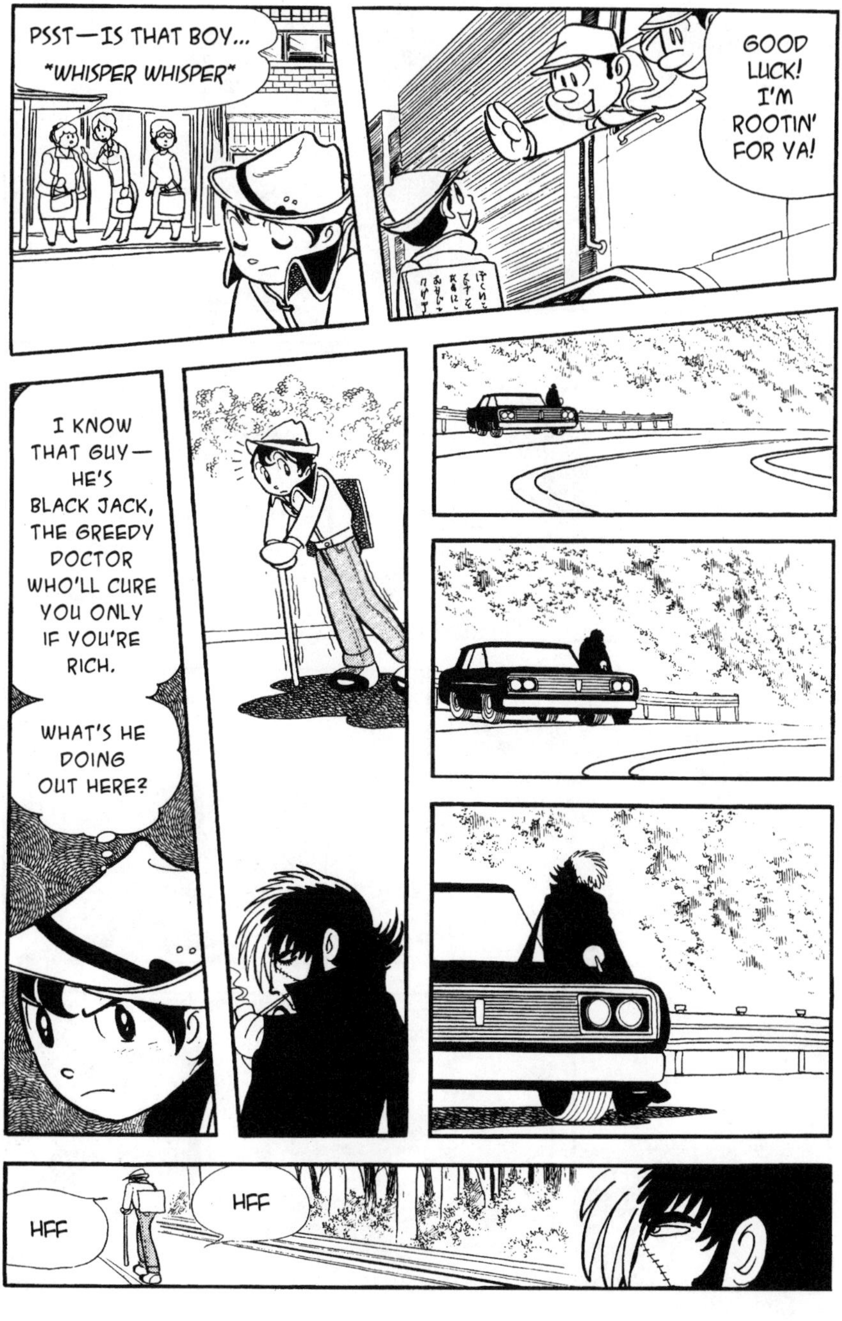
GOOD LUCK! I'M ROOTIN' FOR YA!
PSST—IS THAT BOY... "WHISPER WHISPER"
I KNOW THAT GUY—HE'S BLACK JACK, THE GREEDY DOCTOR WHO'LL CURE YOU ONLY IF YOU'RE RICH.
WHAT'S HE DOING OUT HERE?
HFF
HFF

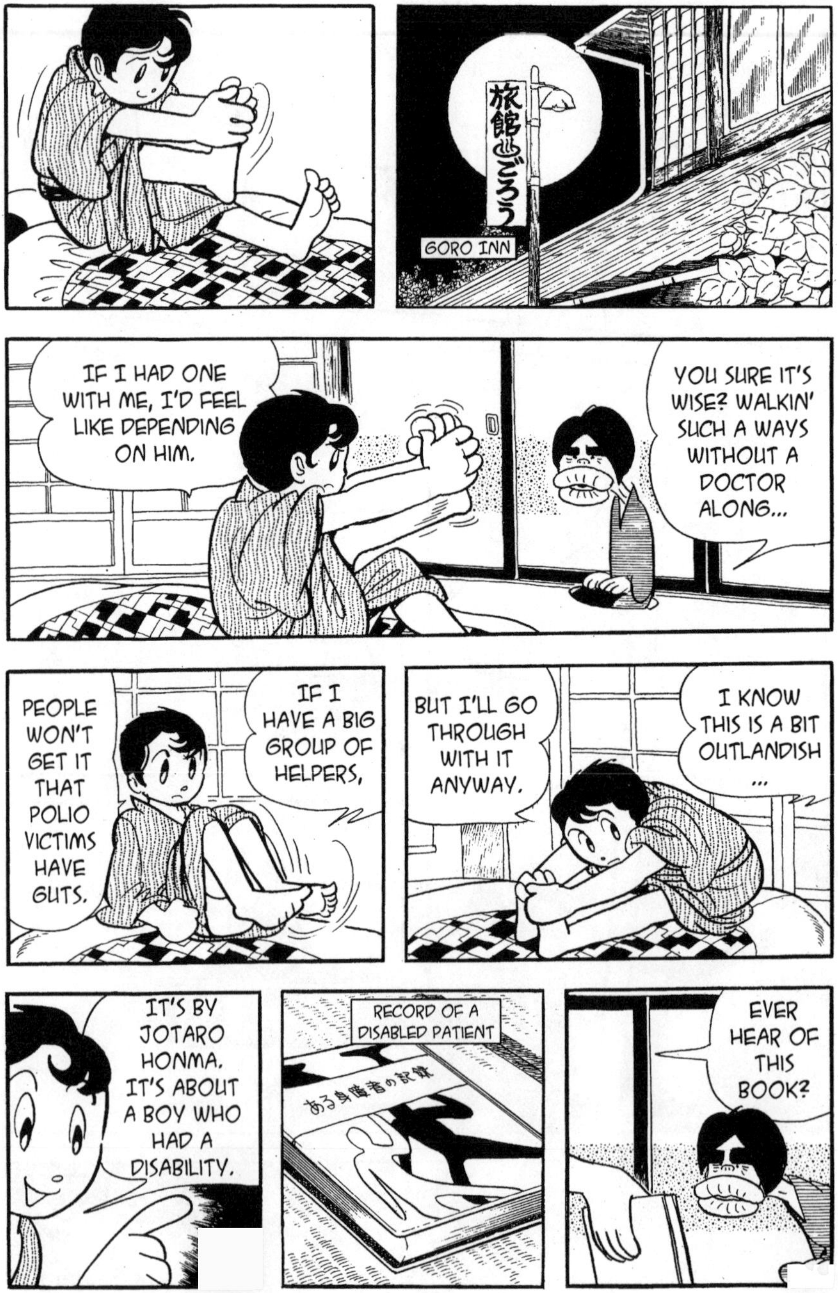
旅館♨ごろう
GORO INN
YOU SURE IT'S WISE? WALKIN' SUCH A WAYS WITHOUT A DOCTOR ALONG...
IF I HAD ONE WITH ME, I'D FEEL LIKE DEPENDING ON HIM.
I KNOW THIS IS A BIT OUTLANDISH ...
BUT I'LL GO THROUGH WITH IT ANYWAY.
IF I HAVE A BIG GROUP OF HELPERS,
PEOPLE WON'T GET IT THAT POLIO VICTIMS HAVE GUTS.
EVER HEAR OF THIS BOOK?
RECORD OF A DISABLED PATIENT
ある身障者の記録
IT'S BY JOTARO HONMA. IT'S ABOUT A BOY WHO HAD A DISABILITY.

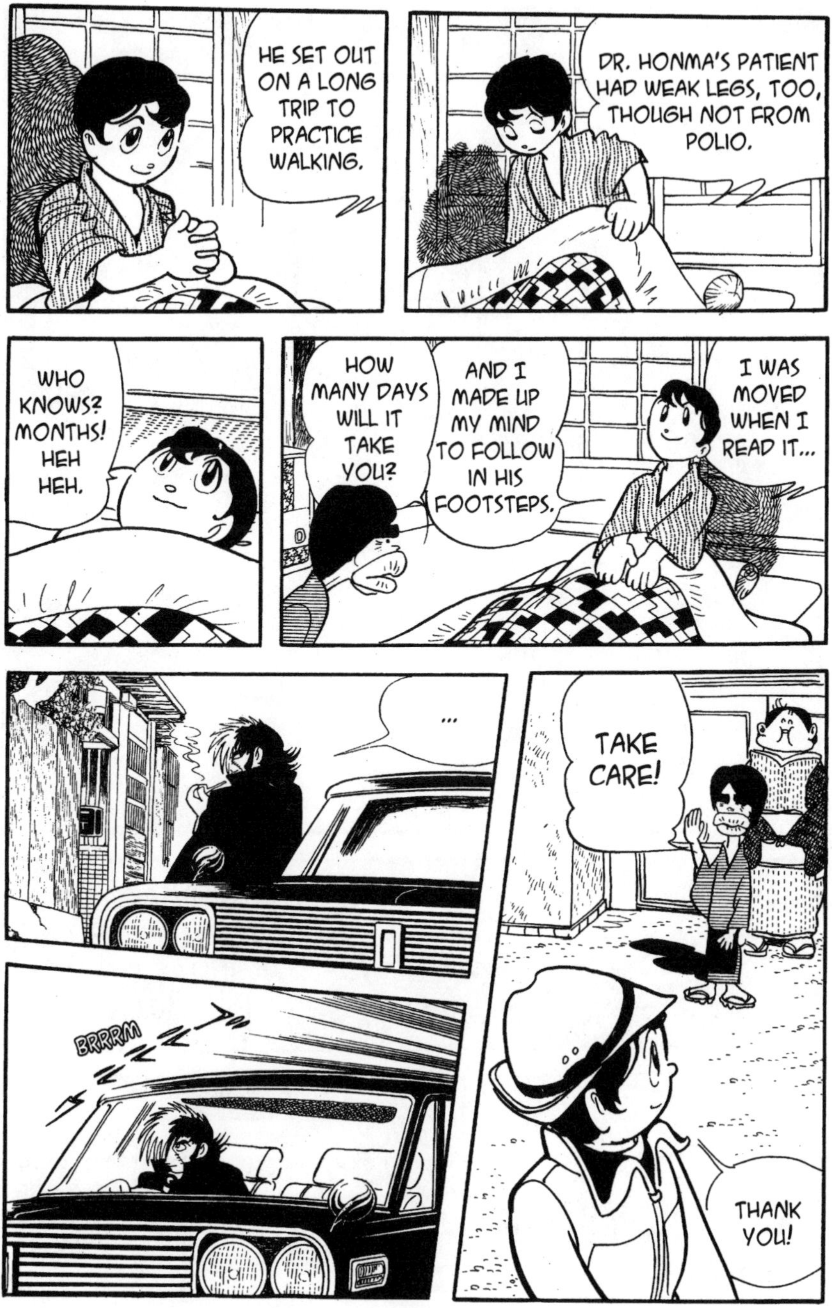
DR. HONMA'S PATIENT HAD WEAK LEGS, TOO, THOUGH NOT FROM POLIO.
HE SET OUT ON A LONG TRIP TO PRACTICE WALKING.
I WAS MOVED WHEN I READ IT...
AND I MADE UP MY MIND TO FOLLOW IN HIS FOOTSTEPS.
HOW MANY DAYS WILL IT TAKE YOU?
WHO KNOWS? MONTHS! HEH HEH.
TAKE CARE!
THANK YOU!
...
BRRRM

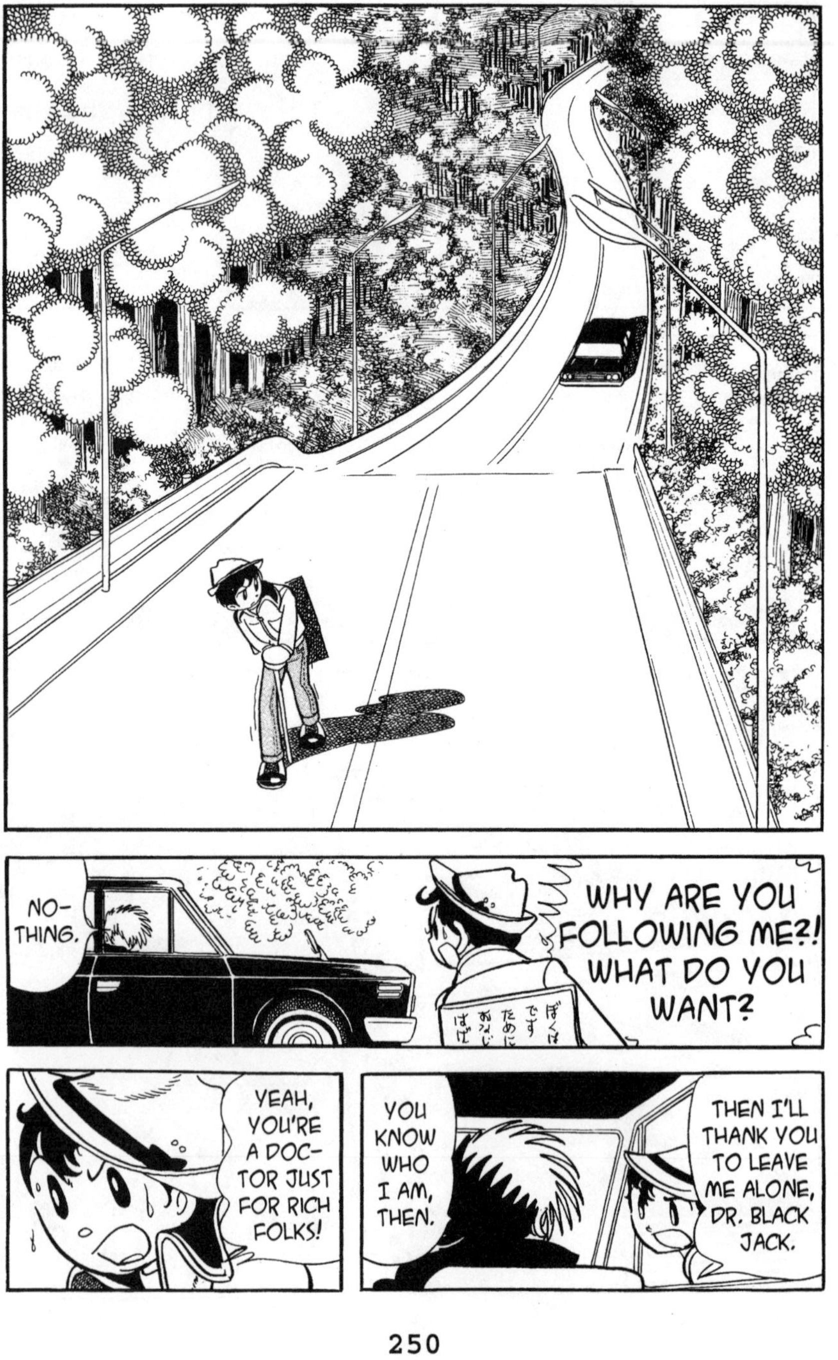
WHY ARE YOU FOLLOWING ME?! WHAT DO YOU WANT?
NO-THING.
THEN I'LL THANK YOU TO LEAVE ME ALONE, DR. BLACK JACK.
YOU KNOW WHO I AM, THEN.
YEAH, YOU'RE A DOC-TOR JUST FOR RICH FOLKS!

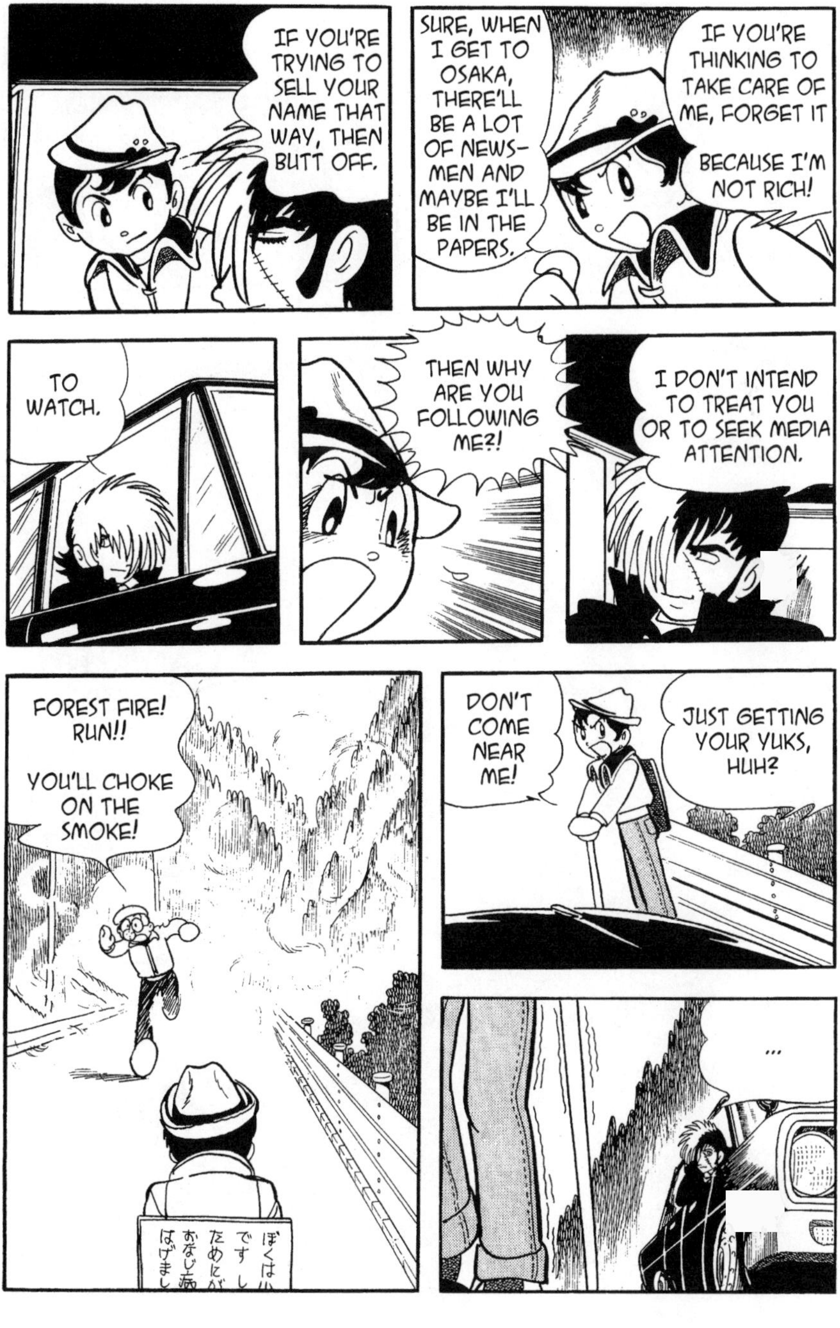
IF YOU'RE THINKING TO TAKE CARE OF ME, FORGET IT
BECAUSE I'M NOT RICH!
SURE, WHEN I GET TO OSAKA, THERE'LL BE A LOT OF NEWS-MEN AND MAYBE I'LL BE IN THE PAPERS.
IF YOU'RE TRYING TO SELL YOUR NAME THAT WAY, THEN BUTT OFF.
I DON'T INTEND TO TREAT YOU OR TO SEEK MEDIA ATTENTION.
THEN WHY ARE YOU FOLLOWING ME?!
TO WATCH.
JUST GETTING YOUR YUKS, HUH?
DON'T COME NEAR ME!
...
FOREST FIRE! RUN!!
YOU'LL CHOKE ON THE SMOKE!

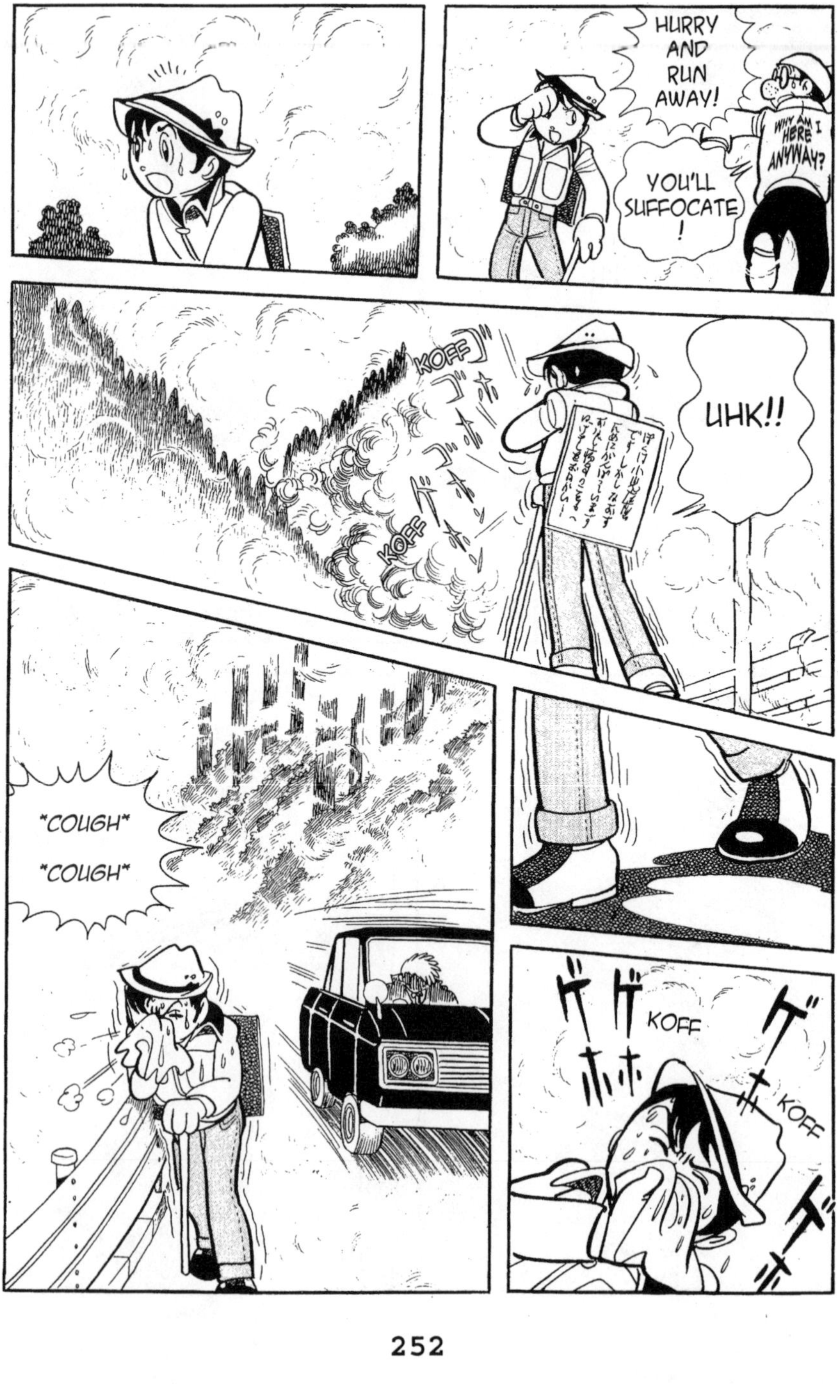
HURRY AND RUN AWAY!
WHY AM I HERE ANYWAY?
YOU'LL SUFFOCATE!
UHK!!
KOFF
KOFF
KOFF
KOFF
COUGH
COUGH

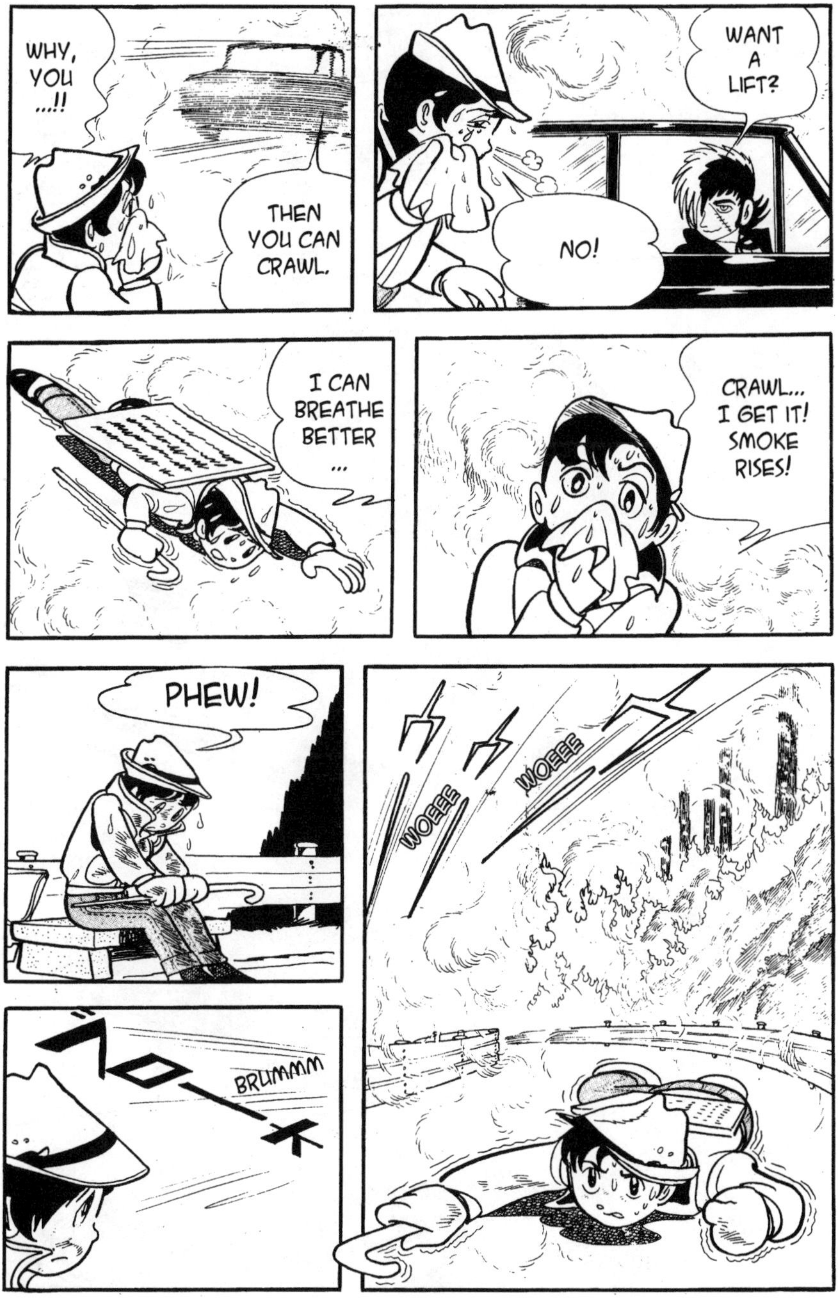
WANT A LIFT?
NO!
THEN YOU CAN CRAWL.
WHY, YOU ...!!
CRAWL... I GET IT! SMOKE RISES!
I CAN BREATHE BETTER ...
WOEEE
WOEEE
PHEW!
BRUMMM

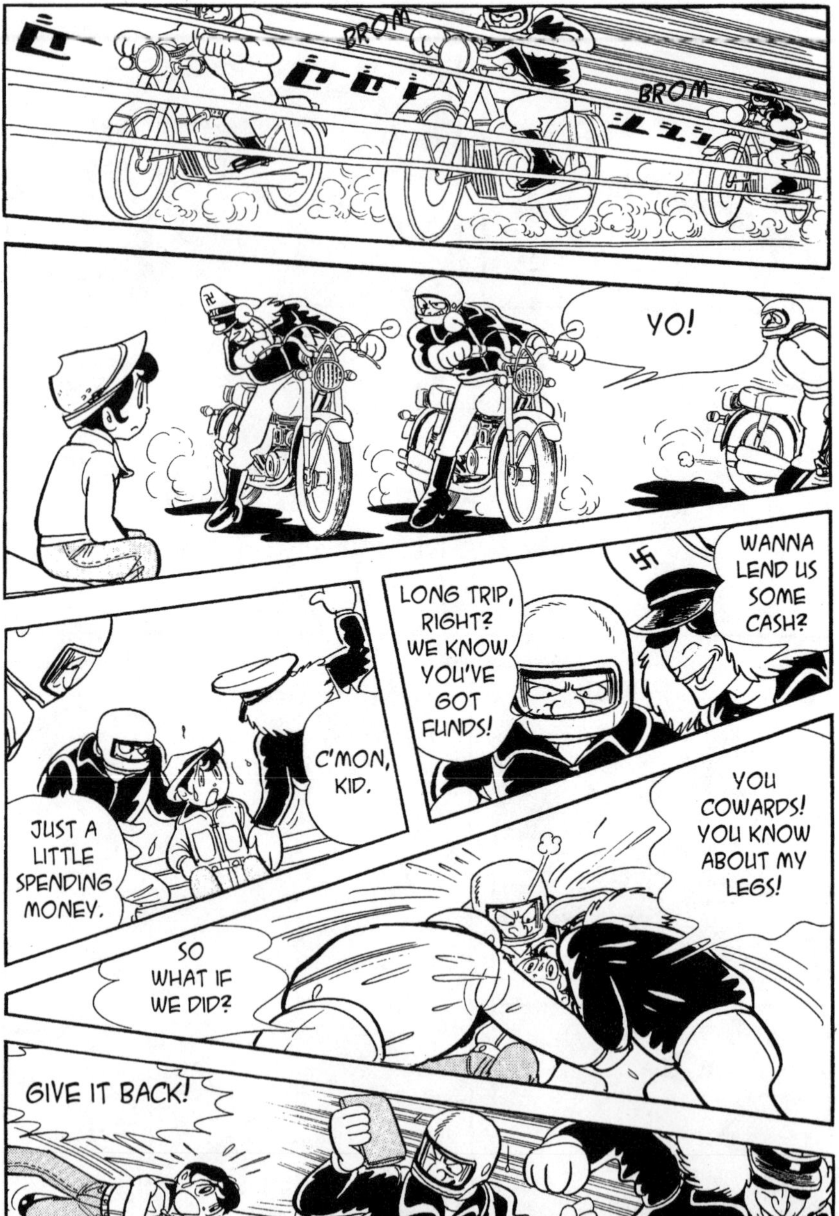
BROM
BROM
YO!
WANNA LEND US SOME CASH?
LONG TRIP, RIGHT? WE KNOW YOU'VE GOT FUNDS!
C'MON, KID.
JUST A LITTLE SPENDING MONEY.
YOU COWARDS! YOU KNOW ABOUT MY LEGS!
SO WHAT IF WE DID?
GIVE IT BACK!

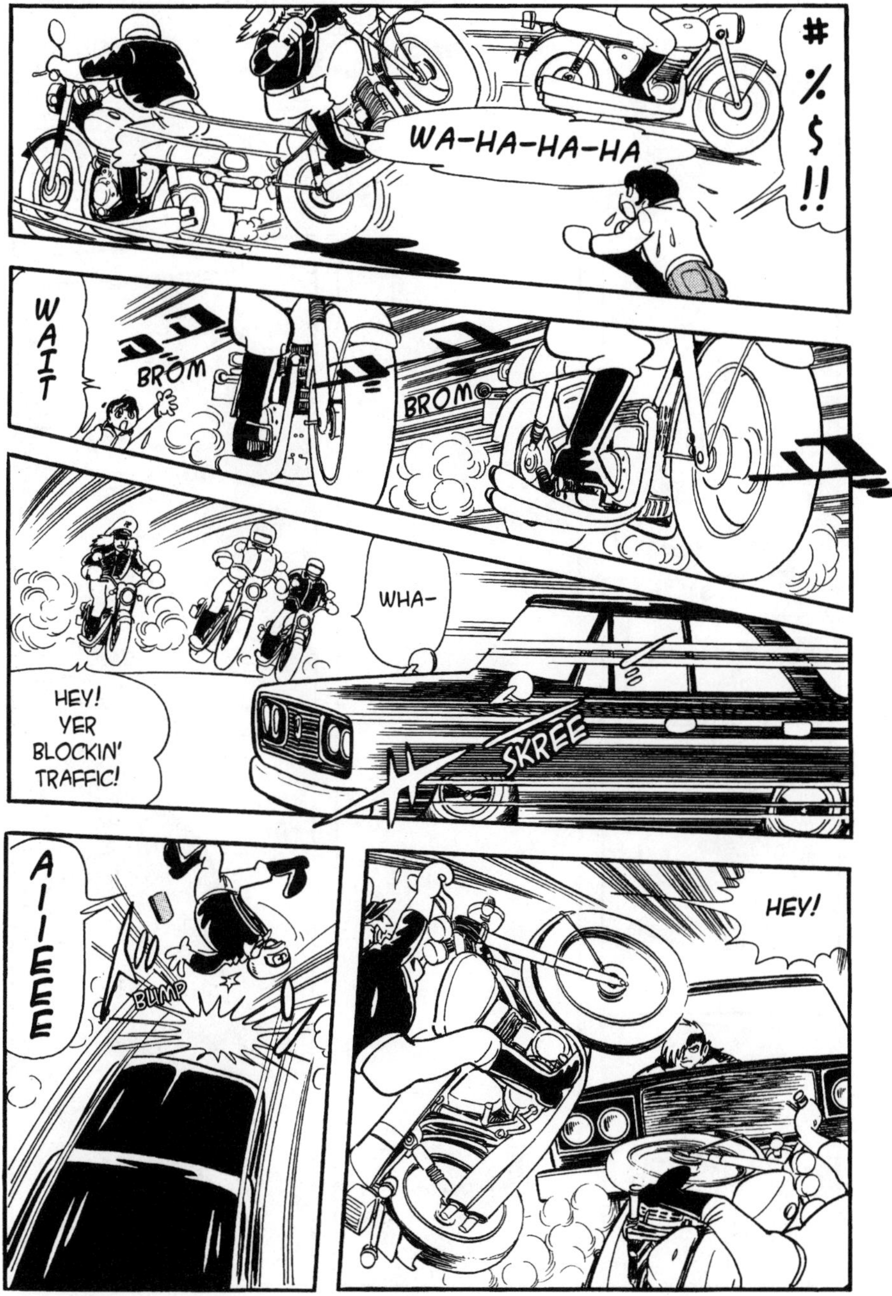
#%$!!
WA-HA-HA-HA
BROM
BROM
WAIT
WHA-
SKREE
HEY! YER BLOCKIN' TRAFFIC!
HEY!
AIIEEE
BUMP

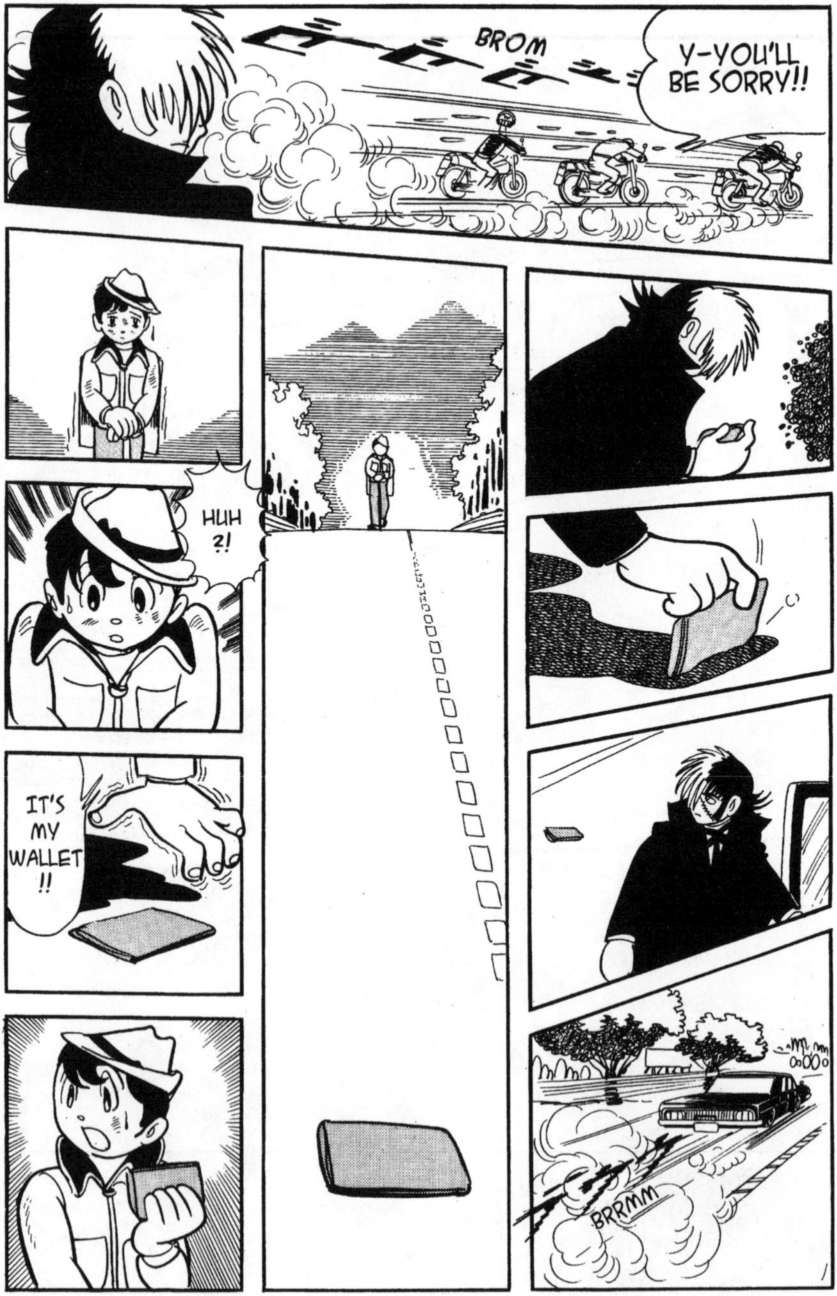
Y-YOU'LL BE SORRY!!
BROM
BRRMM
HUH ?!
IT'S MY WALLET !!

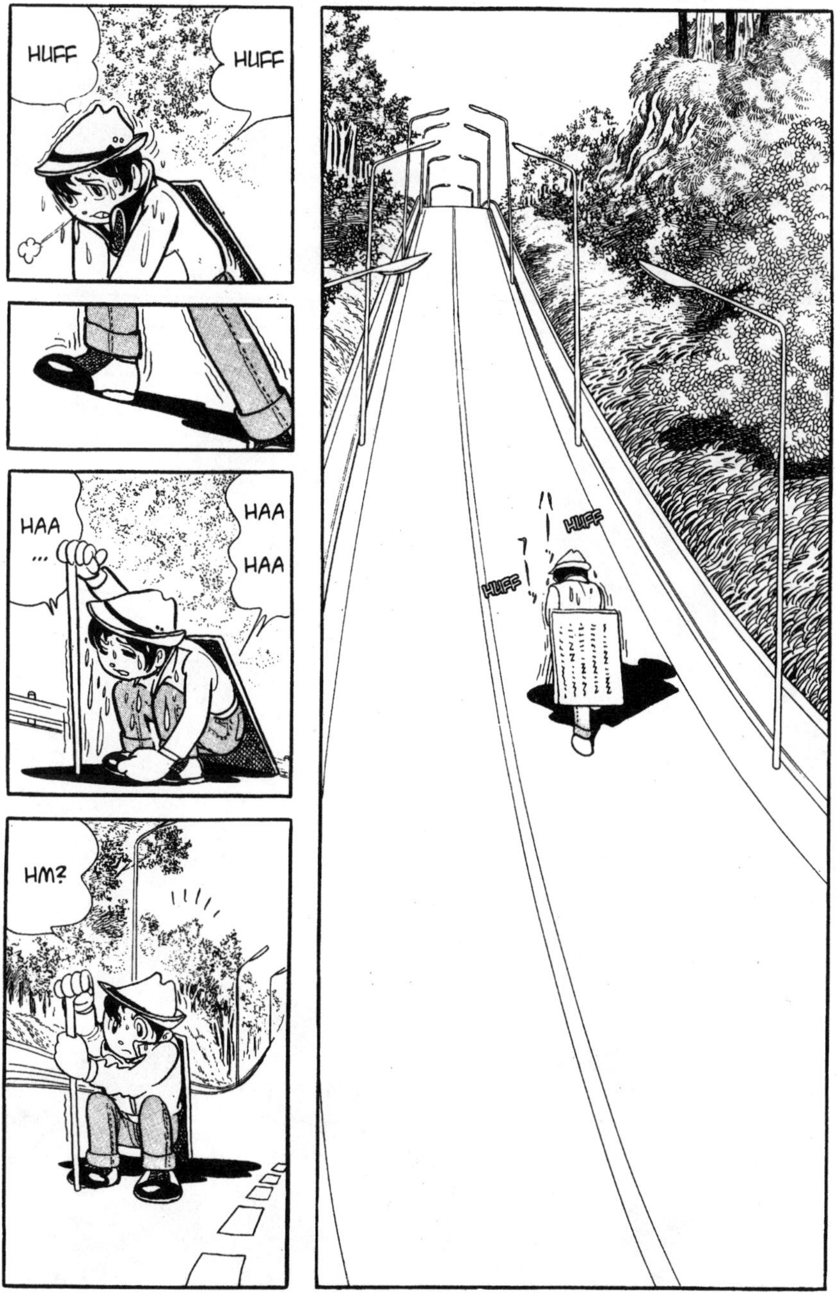
HUFF
HUFF
HUFF
HUFF
HAA HAA
HAA ...
HM?

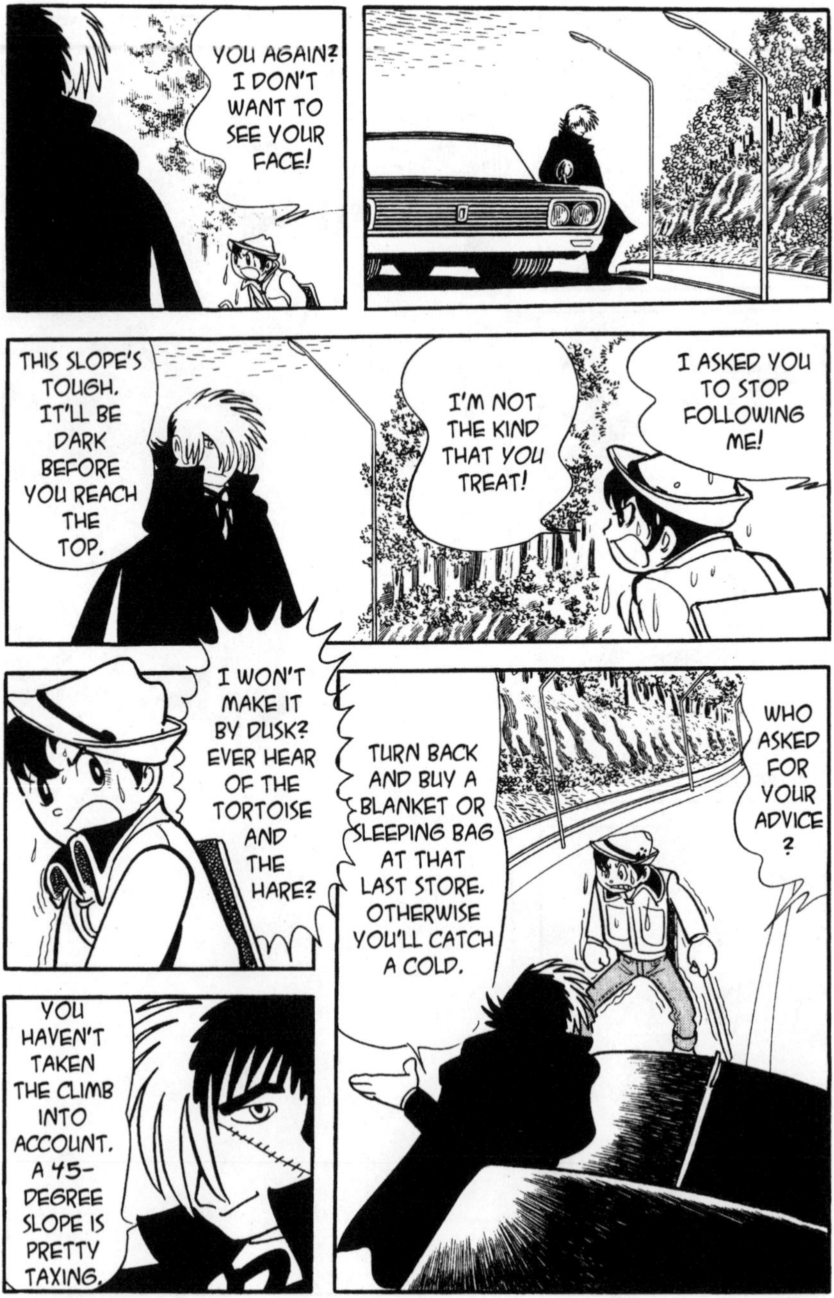
YOU AGAIN? I DON'T WANT TO SEE YOUR FACE!
I ASKED YOU TO STOP FOLLOWING ME!
I'M NOT THE KIND THAT YOU TREAT!
THIS SLOPE'S TOUGH. IT'LL BE DARK BEFORE YOU REACH THE TOP.
WHO ASKED FOR YOUR ADVICE?
TURN BACK AND BUY A BLANKET OR SLEEPING BAG AT THAT LAST STORE. OTHERWISE YOU'LL CATCH A COLD.
I WON'T MAKE IT BY DUSK? EVER HEAR OF THE TORTOISE AND THE HARE?
YOU HAVEN'T TAKEN THE CLIMB INTO ACCOUNT. A 45-DEGREE SLOPE IS PRETTY TAXING.

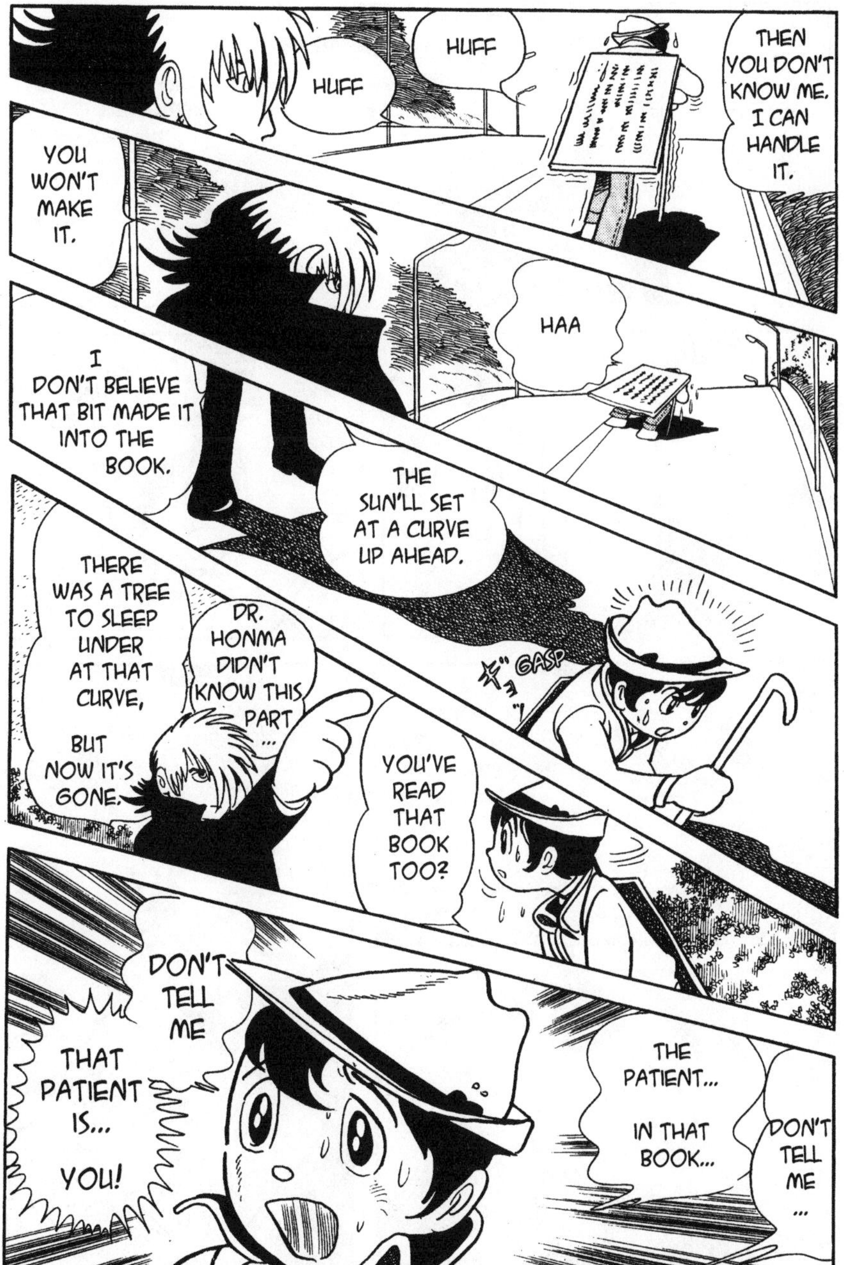
THEN YOU DON'T KNOW ME. I CAN HANDLE IT.
HUFF
HUFF
YOU WON'T MAKE IT.
HAA
I DON'T BELIEVE THAT BIT MADE IT INTO THE BOOK.
THE SUN'LL SET AT A CURVE UP AHEAD.
THERE WAS A TREE TO SLEEP UNDER AT THAT CURVE,
BUT NOW IT'S GONE.
DR. HONMA DIDN'T KNOW THIS PART ...
GASP
YOU'VE READ THAT BOOK TOO?
DON'T TELL ME ...
THE PATIENT... IN THAT BOOK...
DON'T TELL ME
THAT PATIENT IS... YOU!

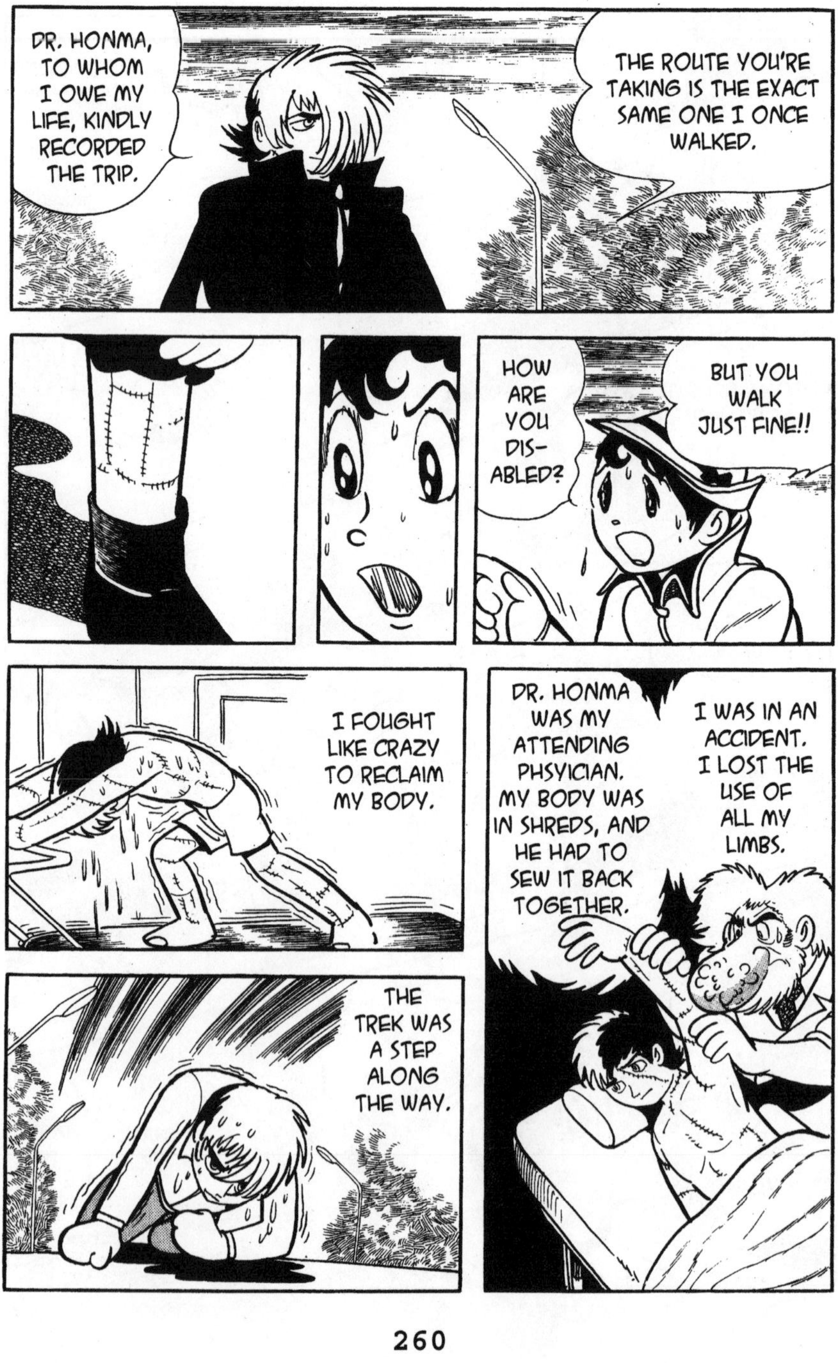
THE ROUTE YOU'RE TAKING IS THE EXACT SAME ONE I ONCE WALKED.
DR. HONMA, TO WHOM I OWE MY LIFE, KINDLY RECORDED THE TRIP.
BUT YOU WALK JUST FINE!!
HOW ARE YOU DIS-ABLED?
I WAS IN AN ACCIDENT. I LOST THE USE OF ALL MY LIMBS.
DR. HONMA WAS MY ATTENDING PHSYICIAN. MY BODY WAS IN SHREDS, AND HE HAD TO SEW IT BACK TOGETHER.
I FOUGHT LIKE CRAZY TO RECLAIM MY BODY.
THE TREK WAS A STEP ALONG THE WAY.

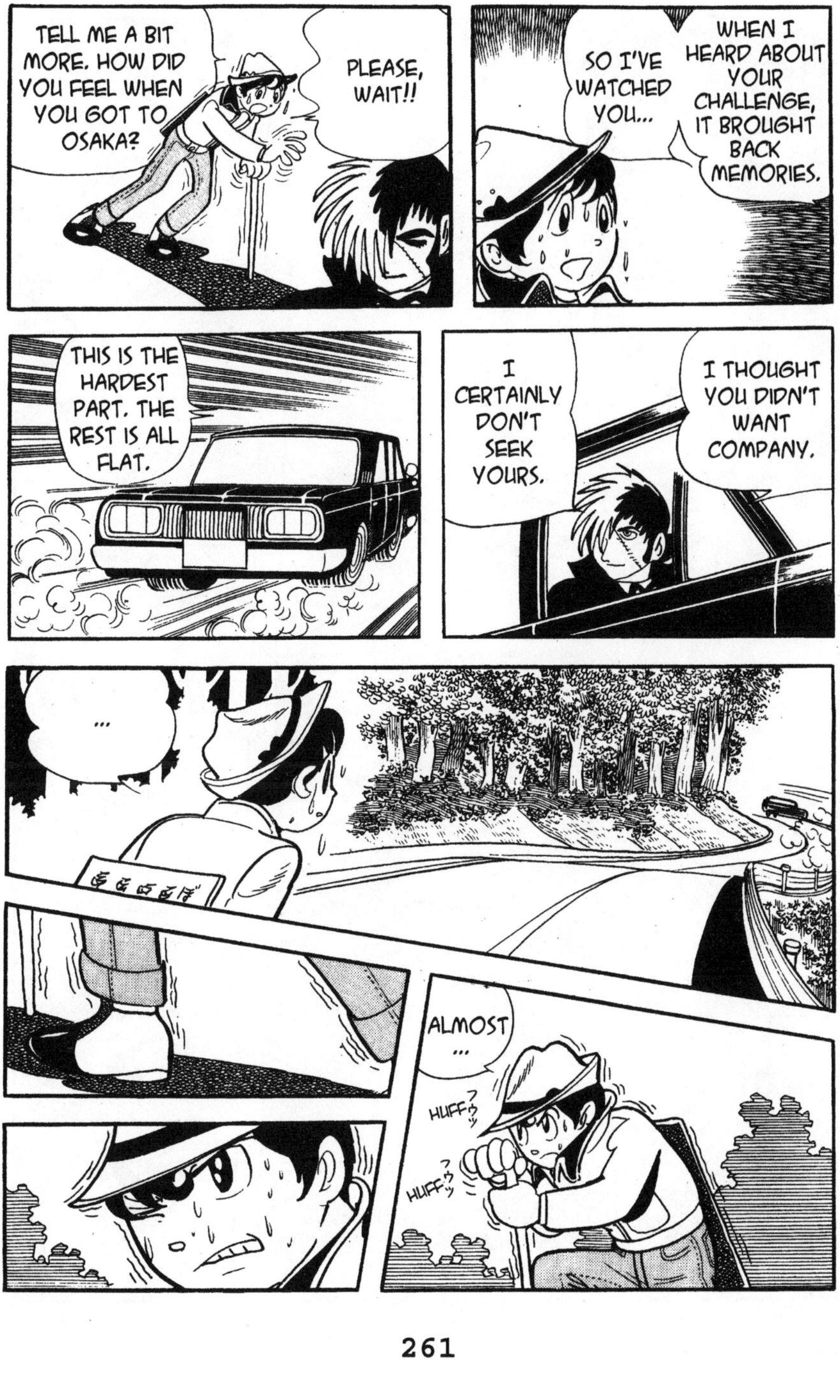
WHEN I HEARD ABOUT YOUR CHALLENGE, IT BROUGHT BACK MEMORIES.
SO I'VE WATCHED YOU...
PLEASE, WAIT!!
TELL ME A BIT MORE. HOW DID YOU FEEL WHEN YOU GOT TO OSAKA?
I THOUGHT YOU DIDN'T WANT COMPANY.
I CERTAINLY DON'T SEEK YOURS.
THIS IS THE HARDEST PART. THE REST IS ALL FLAT.
...
ALMOST ...
HUFF フウッ
HUFF フウッ

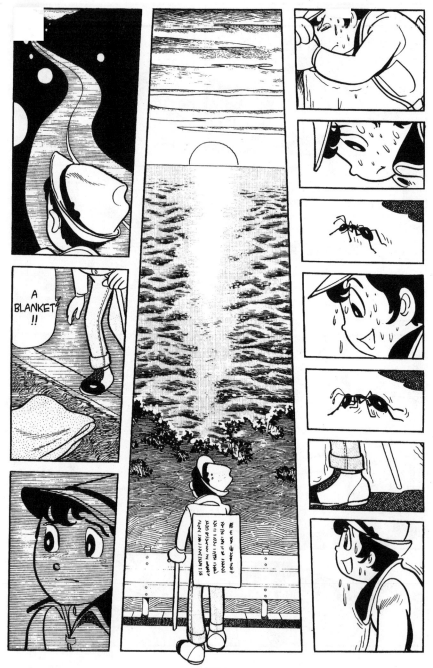

A BLANKET !!

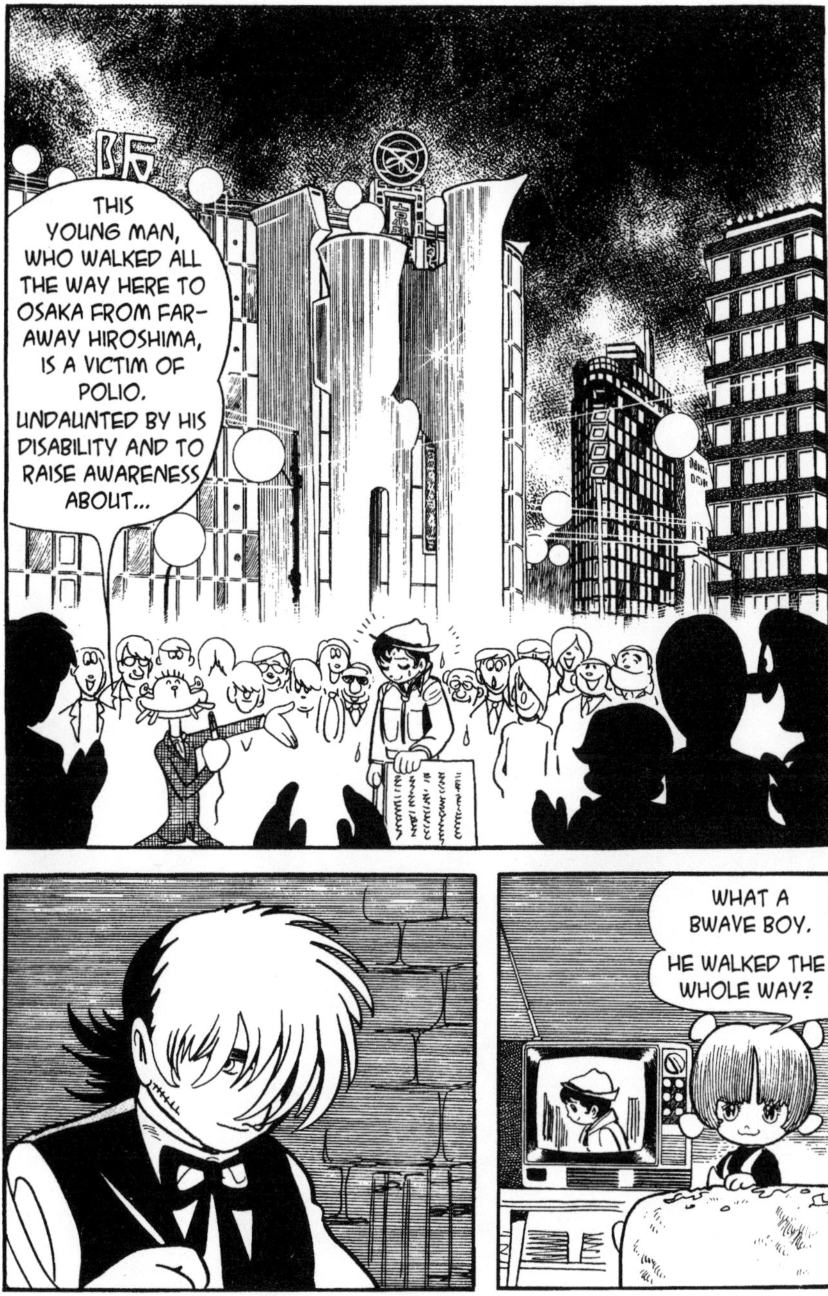
THIS YOUNG MAN, WHO WALKED ALL THE WAY HERE TO OSAKA FROM FAR-AWAY HIROSHIMA, IS A VICTIM OF POLIO. UNDAUNTED BY HIS DISABILITY AND TO RAISE AWARENESS ABOUT...
WHAT A BWAVE BOY.
HE WALKED THE WHOLE WAY?

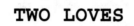
TWO LOVES

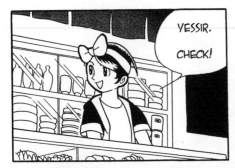

HOW MUCH?
YESSIR. CHECK!
TORO, HIRAME, BOZO, DUNDER, AND NUMSKULL... 750 YEN.
WHO WAS THAT CUSTOMER? DAMN CREEPY FELLOW...
HE'S A DOCTOR. LIVES QUITE A WAYS FROM HERE, DROPS BY EVERY NOW AND THEN.
'COURSE HE DOES. NOH SUSHI'S THE BEST UNDER THE SUN.
HARD EVEN TO FIND DECENT SUSHI THESE DAYS.
THEY SLAP ON FISH, AND CALL IT SUSHI ...

NOTE: "TORO" = FATTY TUNA; "HIRAME" = FLOUNDER. THE OTHER NAMES, OBVIOUSLY, ARE JOKES—NOT THE CHEF'S BUT THE AUTHOR'S.

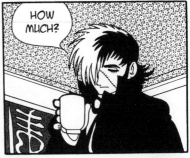

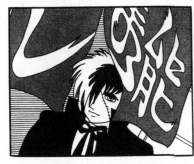

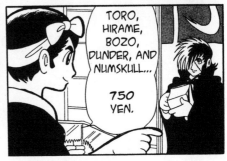

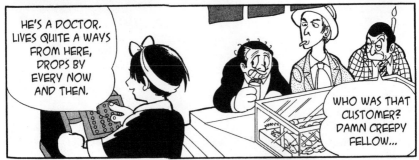

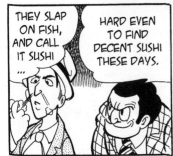

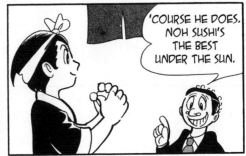

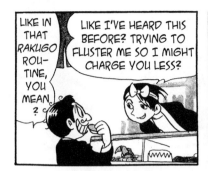

WHILE TAKU HERE'S SKILLS ARE NO. 1!
HA HA HA, WHY DO I FEEL...
LIKE I'VE HEARD THIS BEFORE? TRYING TO FLUSTER ME SO I MIGHT CHARGE YOU LESS?
LIKE IN THAT *RAKUGO* ROUTINE, YOU MEAN?
COME AGAIN!
I HAVE A FAVOR TO ASK, BOSS. MY MA'LL BE CELEBRATING HER SIXTIETH BIRTHDAY SOON AND I'D LIKE SOME TIME OFF.
SURE. GOTTA BE GOOD TO YOUR MA.
THIS PLACE WOULDN'T BE HALF AS POPULAR WITHOUT YOU.
HAVE A NICE TRIP HOME!
THANK YOU!

NOTE: *RAKUGO* IS A TRADITIONAL FORM OF JAPANESE ENTERTAINMENT BY A SINGLE PERFORMER (AKIN TO "STAND-UP COMEDY," BUT THE SPEAKER IS SEATED)

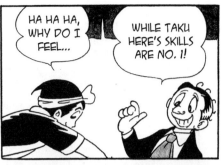

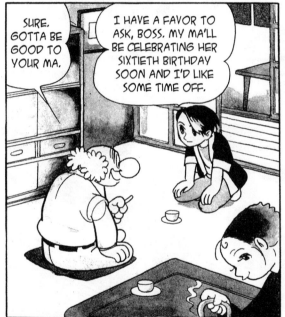

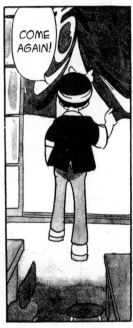

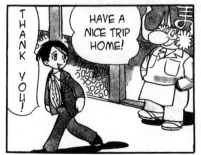

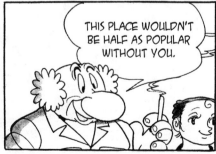

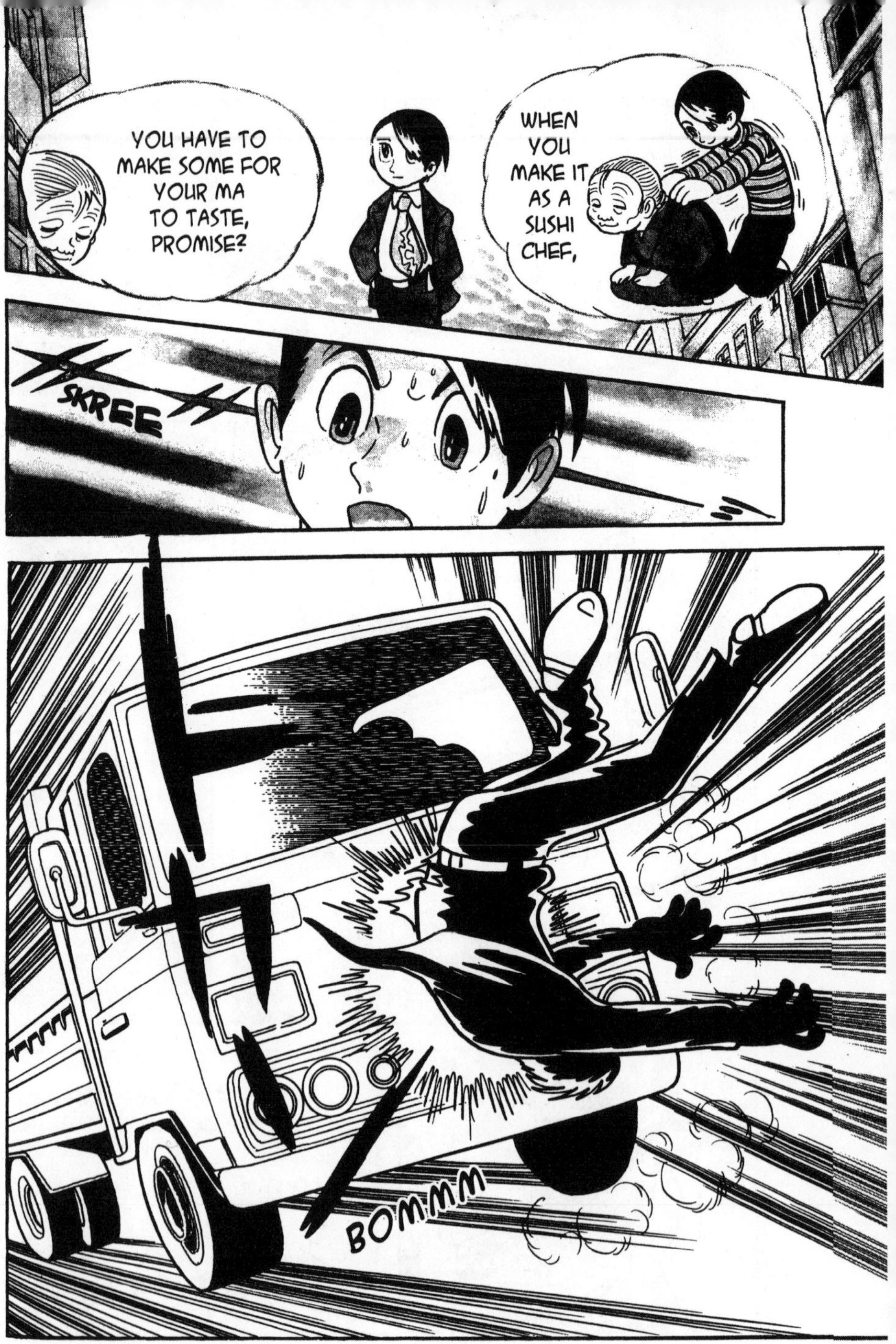
WHEN YOU MAKE IT AS A SUSHI CHEF,
YOU HAVE TO MAKE SOME FOR YOUR MA TO TASTE, PROMISE?
SKREE
BOMMM

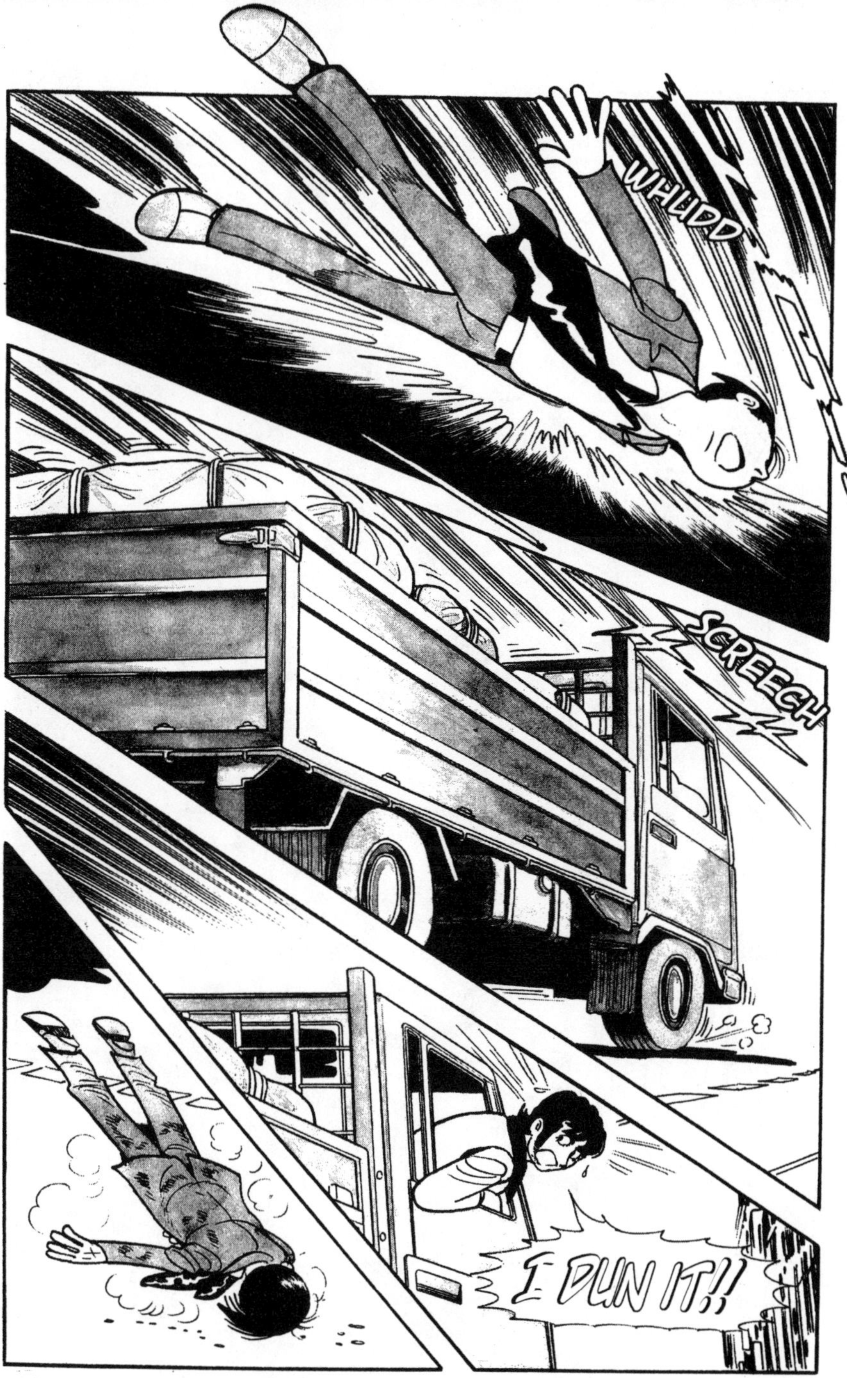
WHUDD
SCREEECH
I DUN IT!!

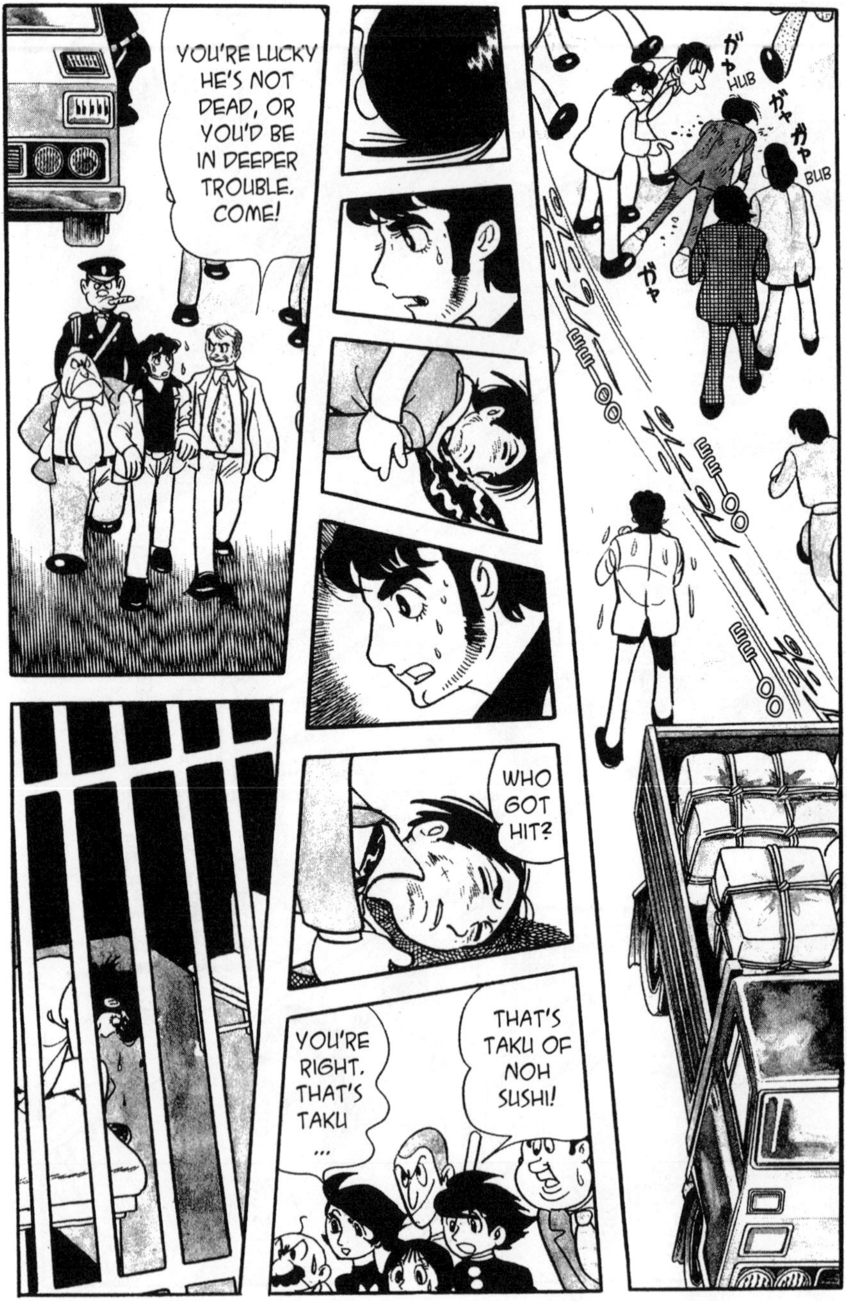
ガヤ
HUB
ガヤ
ガヤ
BUB
ガヤ
WHO GOT HIT?
THAT'S TAKU OF NOH SUSHI!
YOU'RE RIGHT. THAT'S TAKU ...
YOU'RE LUCKY HE'S NOT DEAD, OR YOU'D BE IN DEEPER TROUBLE. COME!

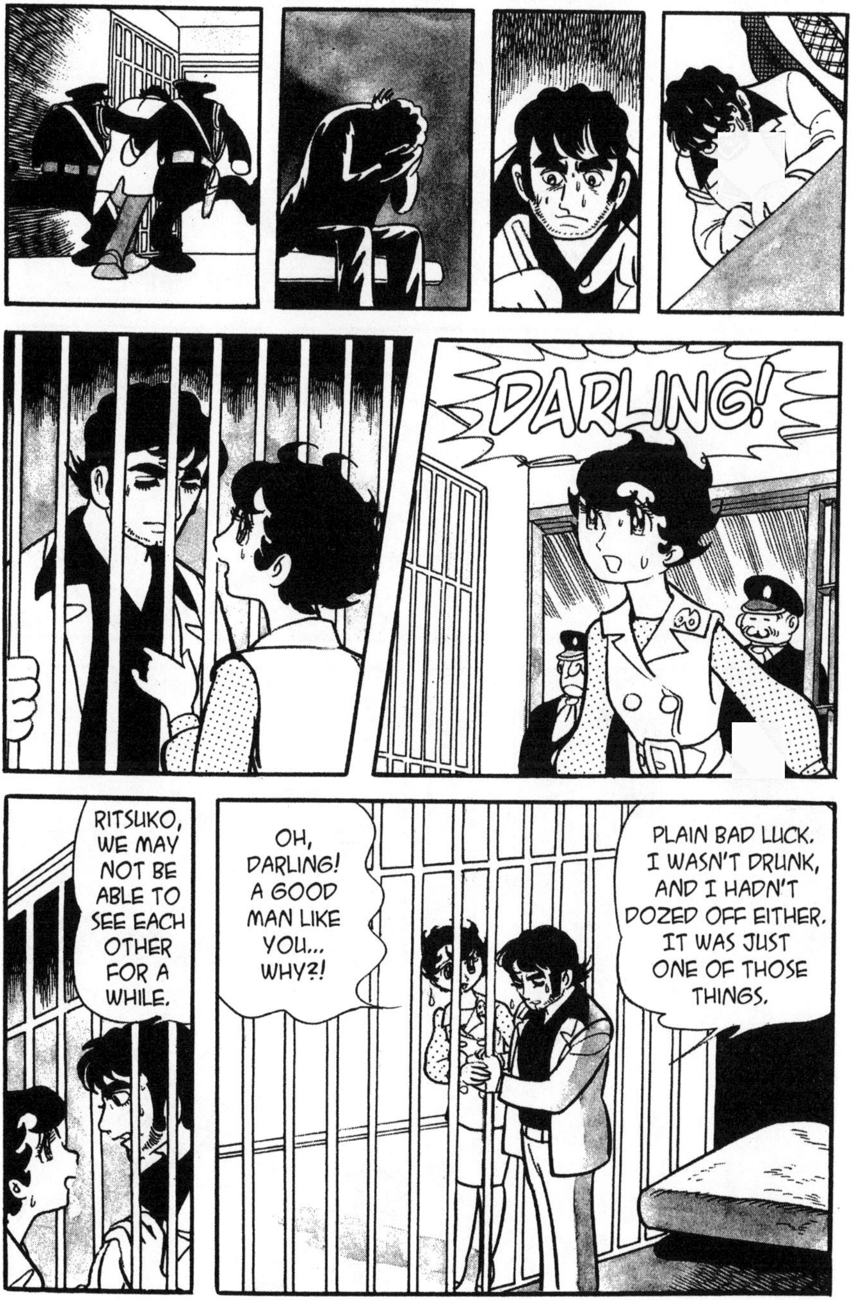
DARLING!
PLAIN BAD LUCK. I WASN'T DRUNK, AND I HADN'T DOZED OFF EITHER. IT WAS JUST ONE OF THOSE THINGS.
OH, DARLING! A GOOD MAN LIKE YOU... WHY?!
RITSUKO, WE MAY NOT BE ABLE TO SEE EACH OTHER FOR A WHILE.

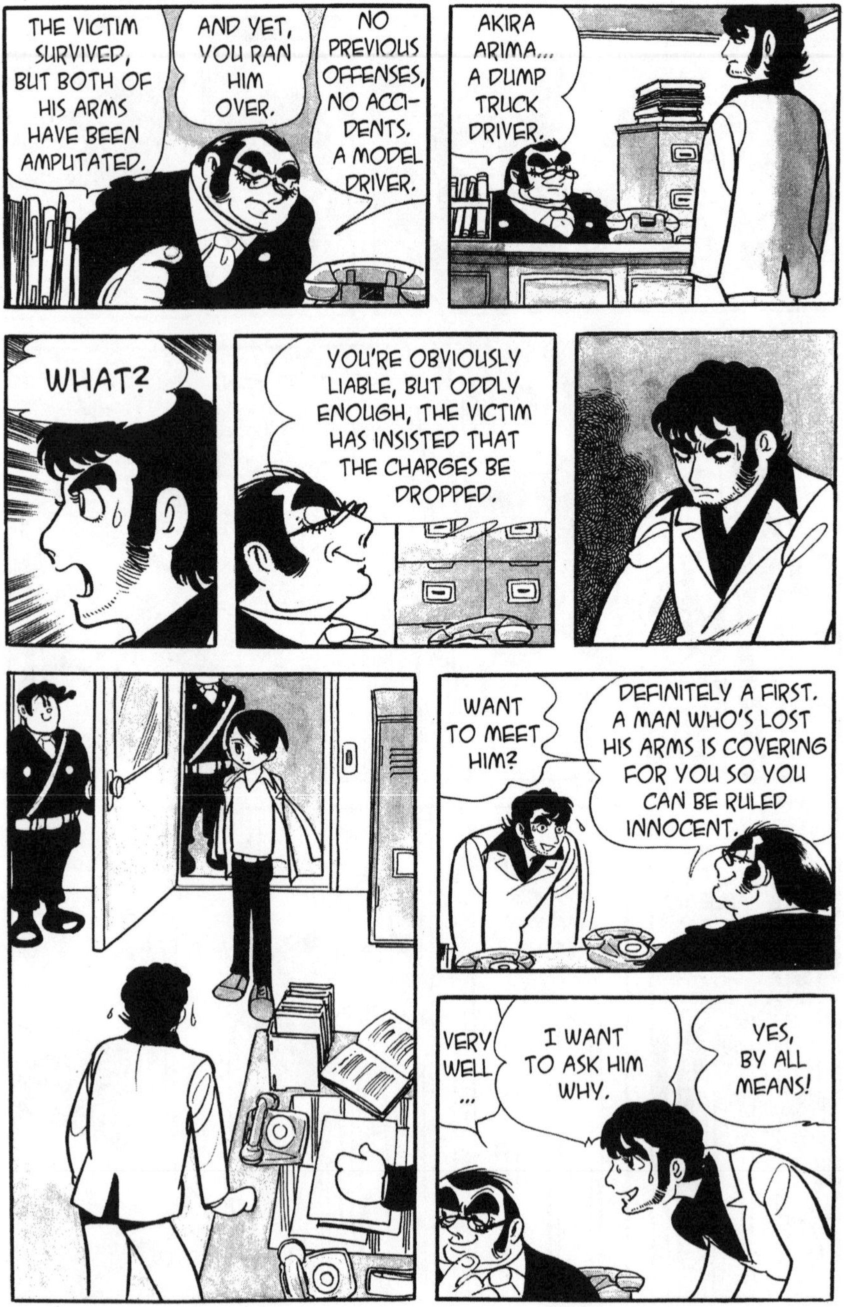
AKIRA ARIMA... A DUMP TRUCK DRIVER.
NO PREVIOUS OFFENSES, NO ACCI-DENTS. A MODEL DRIVER.
AND YET, YOU RAN HIM OVER.
THE VICTIM SURVIVED, BUT BOTH OF HIS ARMS HAVE BEEN AMPUTATED.
YOU'RE OBVIOUSLY LIABLE, BUT ODDLY ENOUGH, THE VICTIM HAS INSISTED THAT THE CHARGES BE DROPPED.
WHAT?
DEFINITELY A FIRST. A MAN WHO'S LOST HIS ARMS IS COVERING FOR YOU SO YOU CAN BE RULED INNOCENT.
WANT TO MEET HIM?
YES, BY ALL MEANS!
I WANT TO ASK HIM WHY.
VERY WELL ...

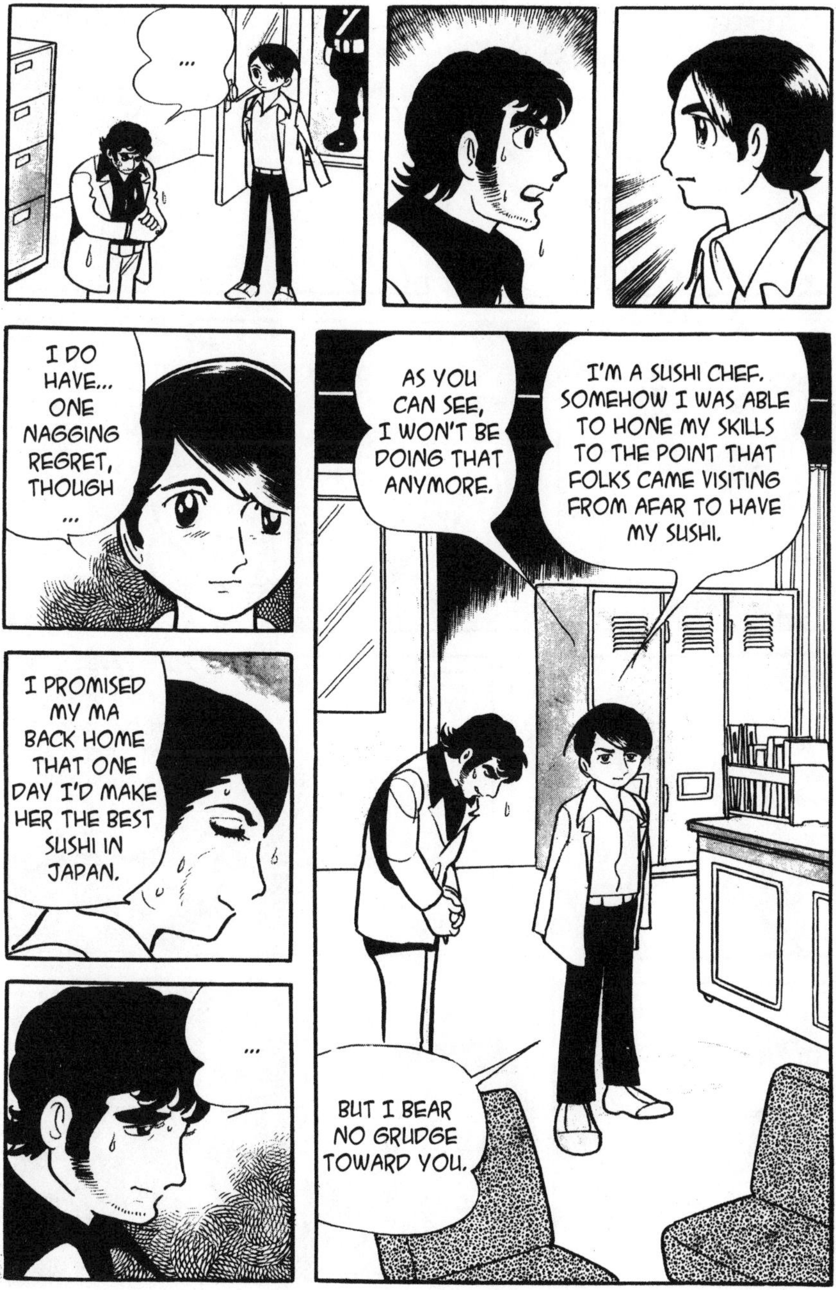
...
I'M A SUSHI CHEF. SOMEHOW I WAS ABLE TO HONE MY SKILLS TO THE POINT THAT FOLKS CAME VISITING FROM AFAR TO HAVE MY SUSHI.
AS YOU CAN SEE, I WON'T BE DOING THAT ANYMORE.
BUT I BEAR NO GRUDGE TOWARD YOU.
I DO HAVE... ONE NAGGING REGRET, THOUGH ...
I PROMISED MY MA BACK HOME THAT ONE DAY I'D MAKE HER THE BEST SUSHI IN JAPAN.
...

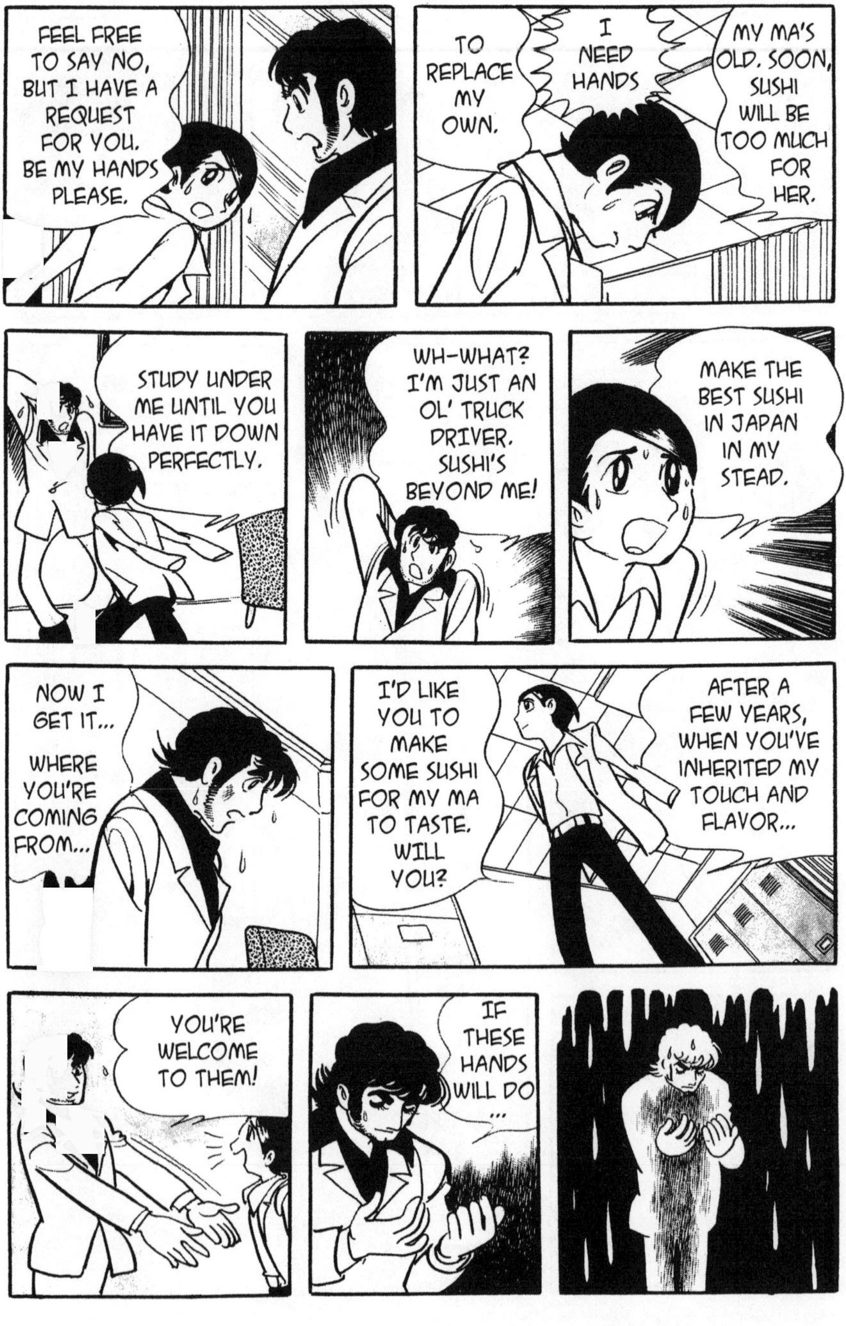
MY MA'S OLD. SOON, SUSHI WILL BE TOO MUCH FOR HER.
I NEED HANDS
TO REPLACE MY OWN.
FEEL FREE TO SAY NO, BUT I HAVE A REQUEST FOR YOU. BE MY HANDS PLEASE.
MAKE THE BEST SUSHI IN JAPAN IN MY STEAD.
WH-WHAT? I'M JUST AN OL' TRUCK DRIVER. SUSHI'S BEYOND ME!
STUDY UNDER ME UNTIL YOU HAVE IT DOWN PERFECTLY.
AFTER A FEW YEARS, WHEN YOU'VE INHERITED MY TOUCH AND FLAVOR...
I'D LIKE YOU TO MAKE SOME SUSHI FOR MY MA TO TASTE. WILL YOU?
NOW I GET IT...
WHERE YOU'RE COMING FROM...
IF THESE HANDS WILL DO ...
YOU'RE WELCOME TO THEM!

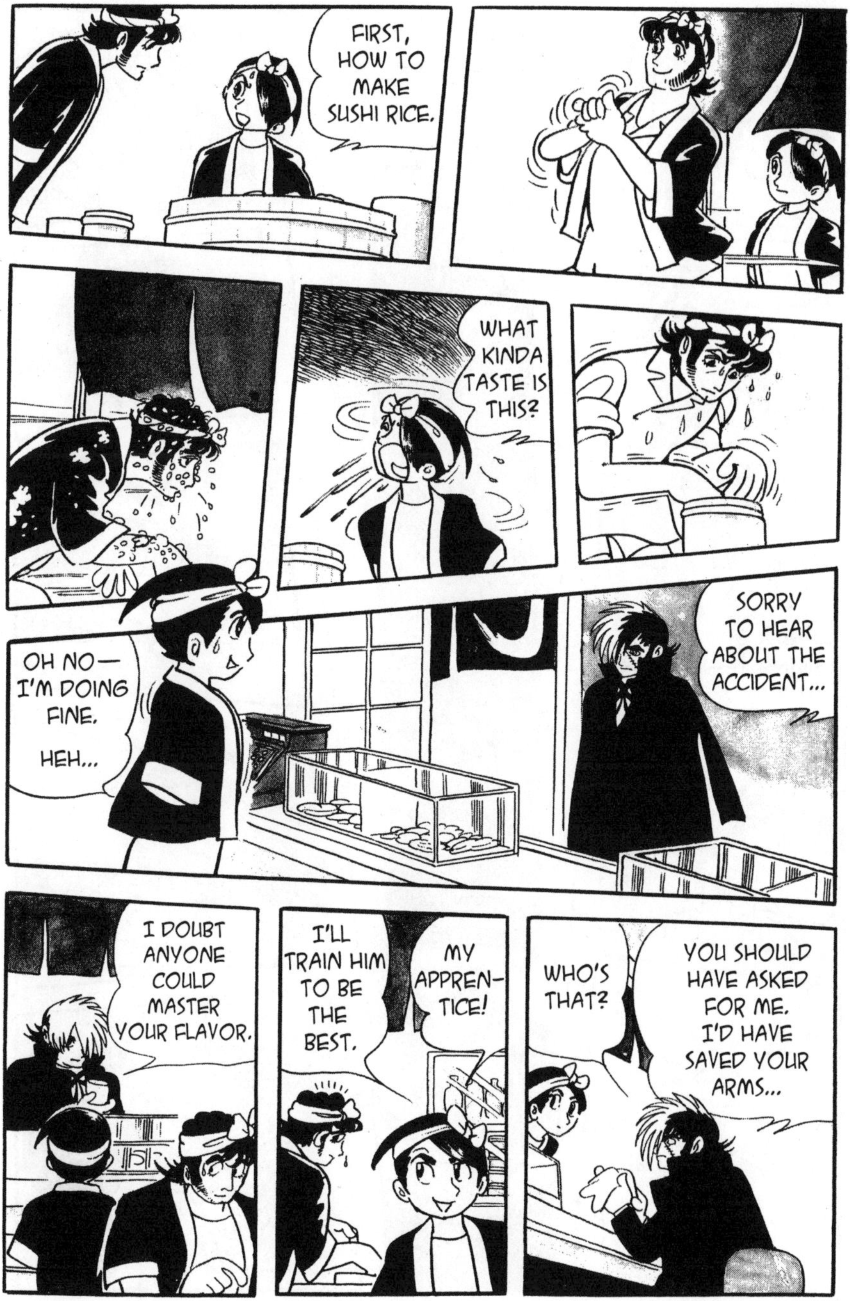
FIRST, HOW TO MAKE SUSHI RICE.
WHAT KINDA TASTE IS THIS?
SORRY TO HEAR ABOUT THE ACCIDENT...
OH NO— I'M DOING FINE.
HEH...
YOU SHOULD HAVE ASKED FOR ME. I'D HAVE SAVED YOUR ARMS...
WHO'S THAT?
MY APPREN- TICE!
I'LL TRAIN HIM TO BE THE BEST.
I DOUBT ANYONE COULD MASTER YOUR FLAVOR.

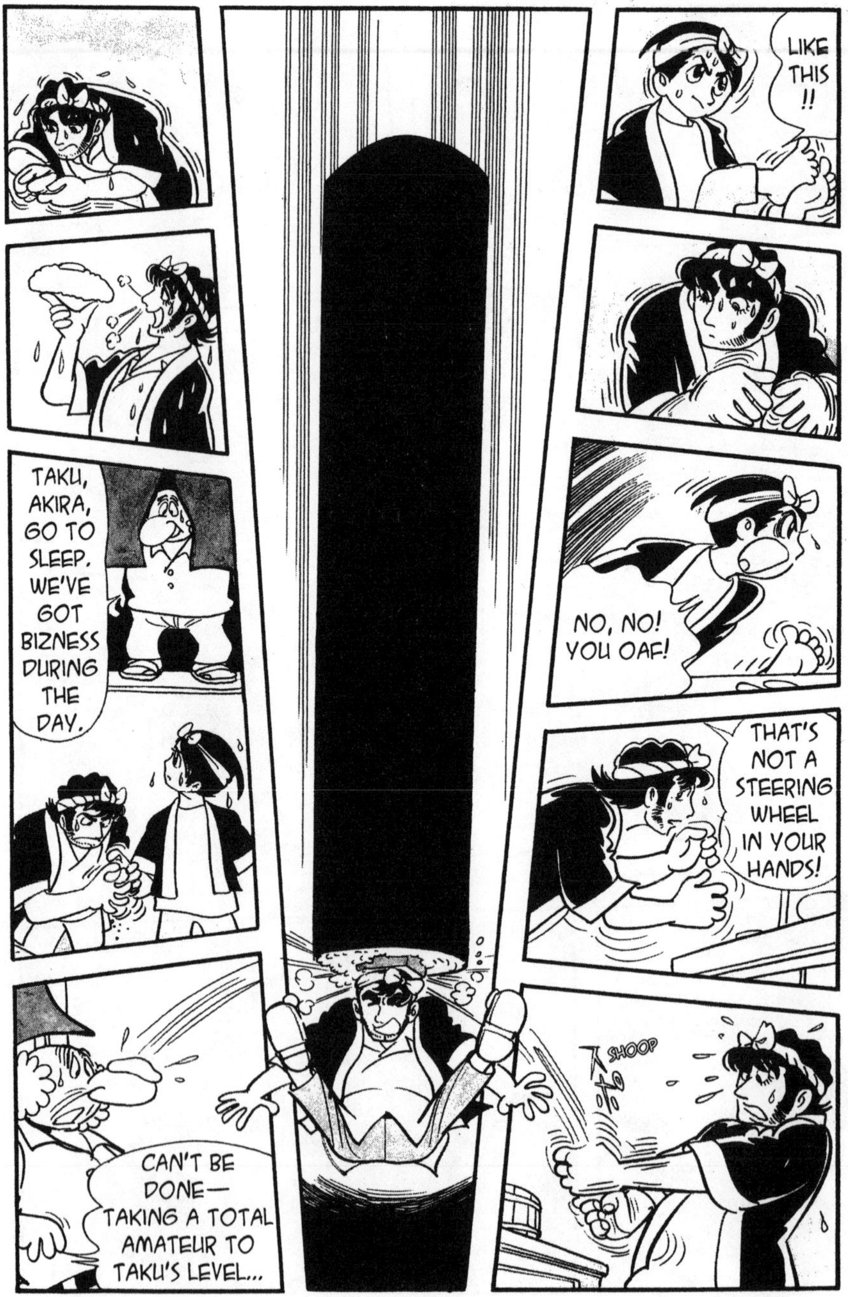
LIKE THIS !!
NO, NO! YOU OAF!
THAT'S NOT A STEERING WHEEL IN YOUR HANDS!
SHOOP
TAKU, AKIRA, GO TO SLEEP. WE'VE GOT BIZNESS DURING THE DAY.
CAN'T BE DONE—TAKING A TOTAL AMATEUR TO TAKU'S LEVEL...

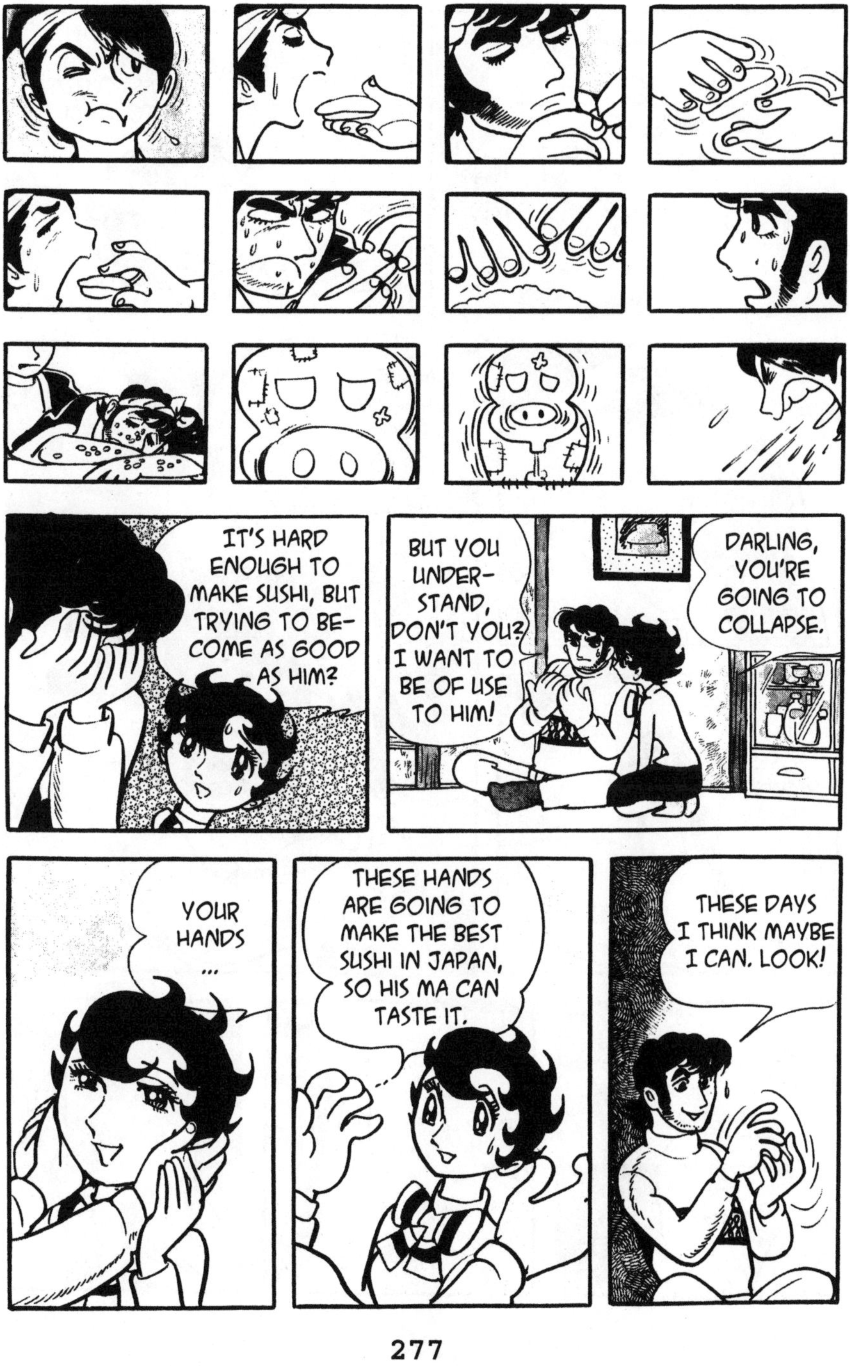
DARLING, YOU'RE GOING TO COLLAPSE.
BUT YOU UNDER-STAND, DON'T YOU? I WANT TO BE OF USE TO HIM!
IT'S HARD ENOUGH TO MAKE SUSHI, BUT TRYING TO BE-COME AS GOOD AS HIM?
THESE DAYS I THINK MAYBE I CAN. LOOK!
THESE HANDS ARE GOING TO MAKE THE BEST SUSHI IN JAPAN, SO HIS MA CAN TASTE IT.
YOUR HANDS ...

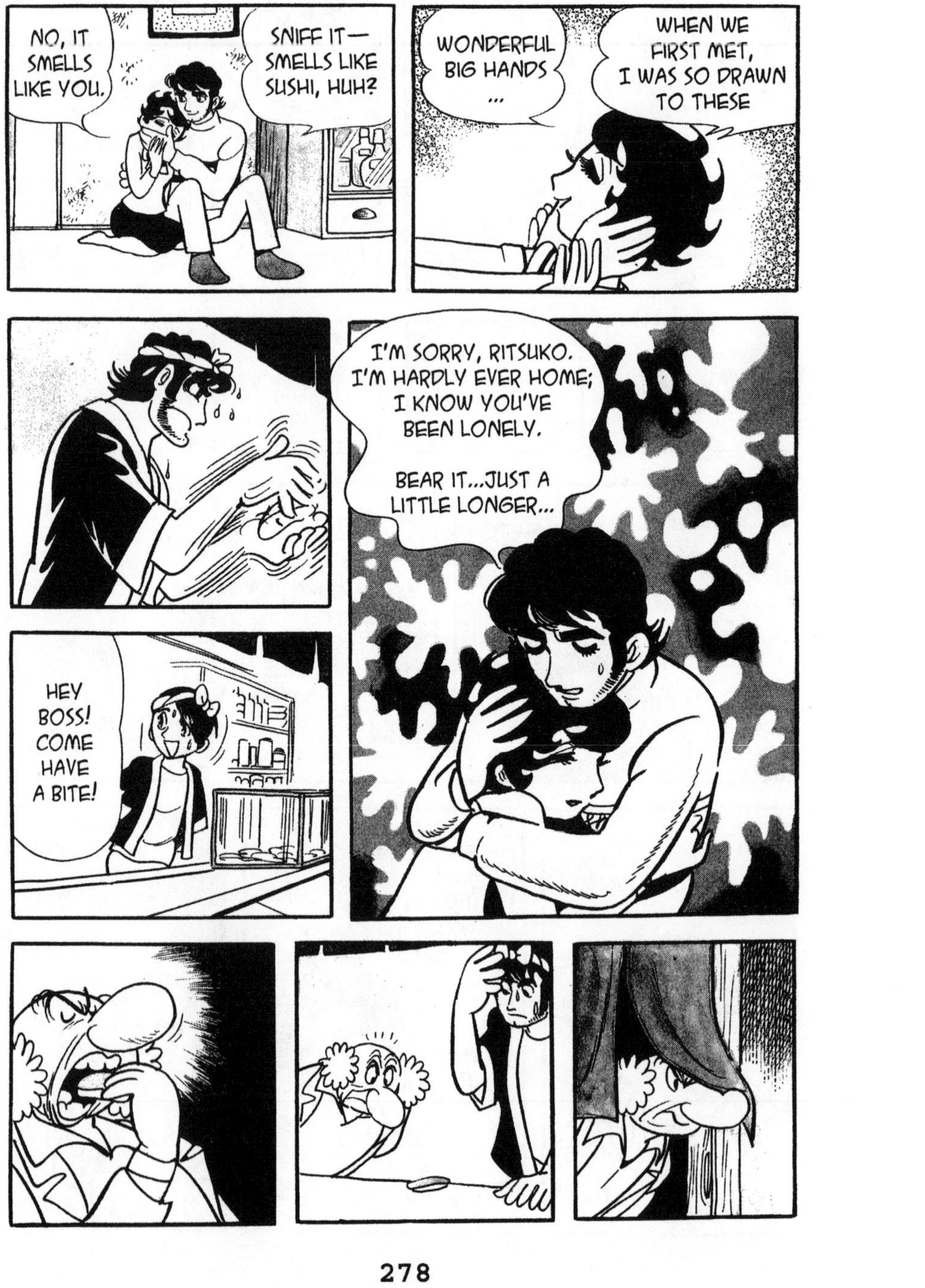
WHEN WE FIRST MET, I WAS SO DRAWN TO THESE
WONDERFUL BIG HANDS ...
SNIFF IT— SMELLS LIKE SUSHI, HUH?
NO, IT SMELLS LIKE YOU.
I'M SORRY, RITSUKO. I'M HARDLY EVER HOME; I KNOW YOU'VE BEEN LONELY.
BEAR IT...JUST A LITTLE LONGER...
HEY BOSS! COME HAVE A BITE!

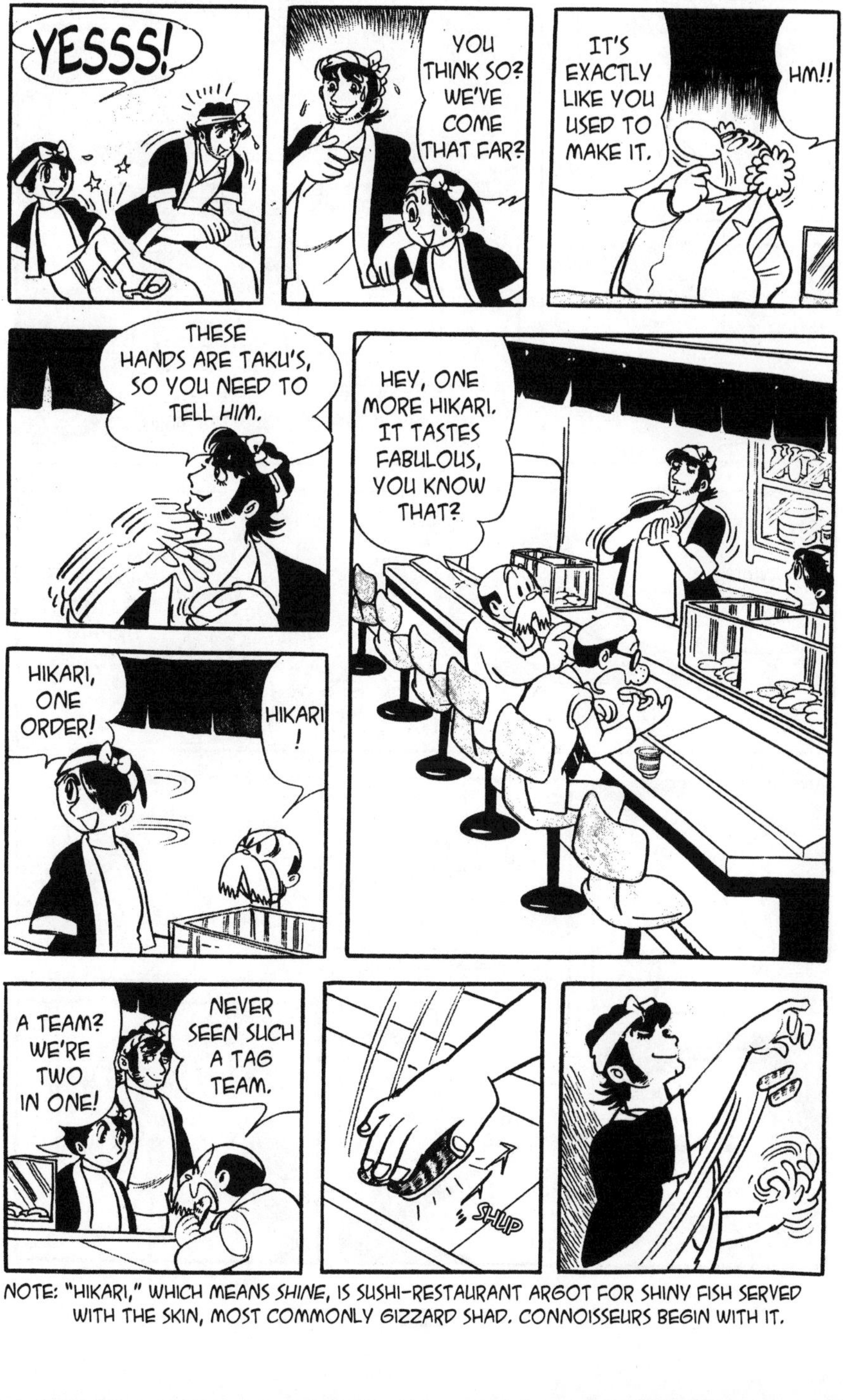
HM!!
IT'S EXACTLY LIKE YOU USED TO MAKE IT.
YOU THINK SO? WE'VE COME THAT FAR?
YESSS!
HEY, ONE MORE HIKARI. IT TASTES FABULOUS, YOU KNOW THAT?
THESE HANDS ARE TAKU'S, SO YOU NEED TO TELL HIM.
HIKARI!
HIKARI, ONE ORDER!
SHUP
NEVER SEEN SUCH A TAG TEAM.
A TEAM? WE'RE TWO IN ONE!

NOTE: "HIKARI," WHICH MEANS SHINE, IS SUSHI-RESTAURANT ARGOT FOR SHINY FISH SERVED WITH THE SKIN, MOST COMMONLY GIZZARD SHAD. CONNOISSEURS BEGIN WITH IT.

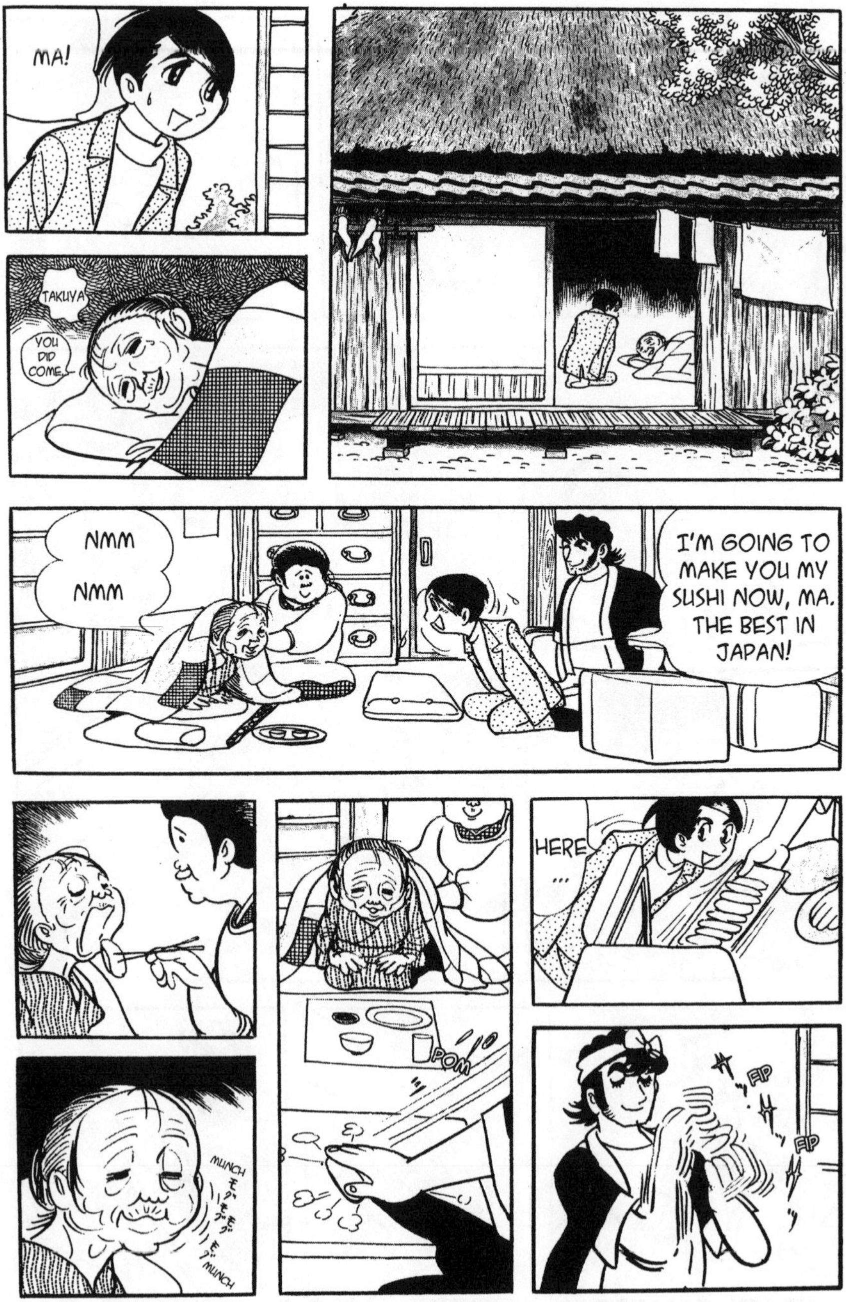
MA!
TAKUYA
YOU DID COME...
I'M GOING TO MAKE YOU MY SUSHI NOW, MA. THE BEST IN JAPAN!
NMM
NMM
HERE ...
FAP
FAP
POM
MUNCH
MUNCH

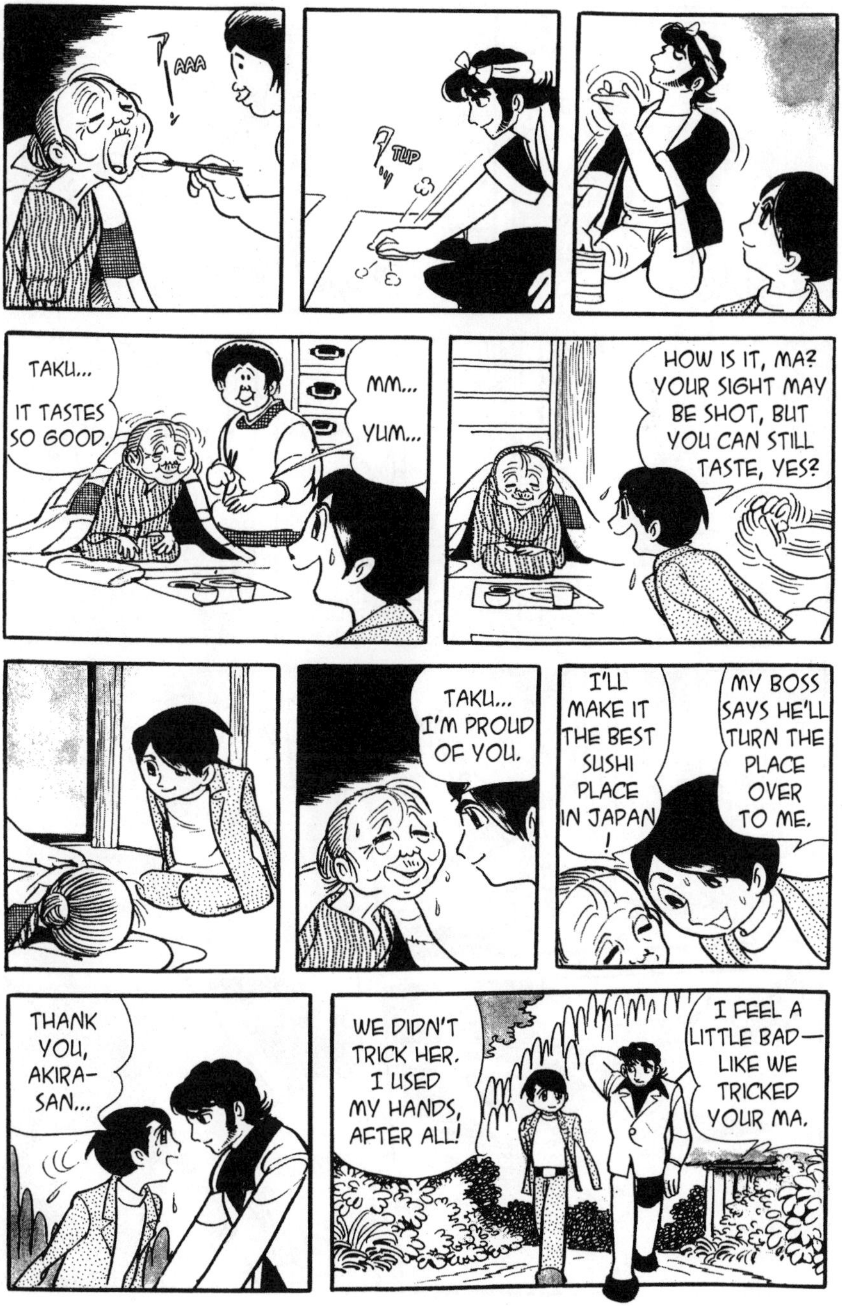
TUP
AAA
HOW IS IT, MA? YOUR SIGHT MAY BE SHOT, BUT YOU CAN STILL TASTE, YES?
MM... YUM...
TAKU... IT TASTES SO GOOD.
MY BOSS SAYS HE'LL TURN THE PLACE OVER TO ME.
I'LL MAKE IT THE BEST SUSHI PLACE IN JAPAN!
TAKU... I'M PROUD OF YOU.
I FEEL A LITTLE BAD—LIKE WE TRICKED YOUR MA.
WE DIDN'T TRICK HER. I USED MY HANDS, AFTER ALL!
THANK YOU, AKIRA-SAN...

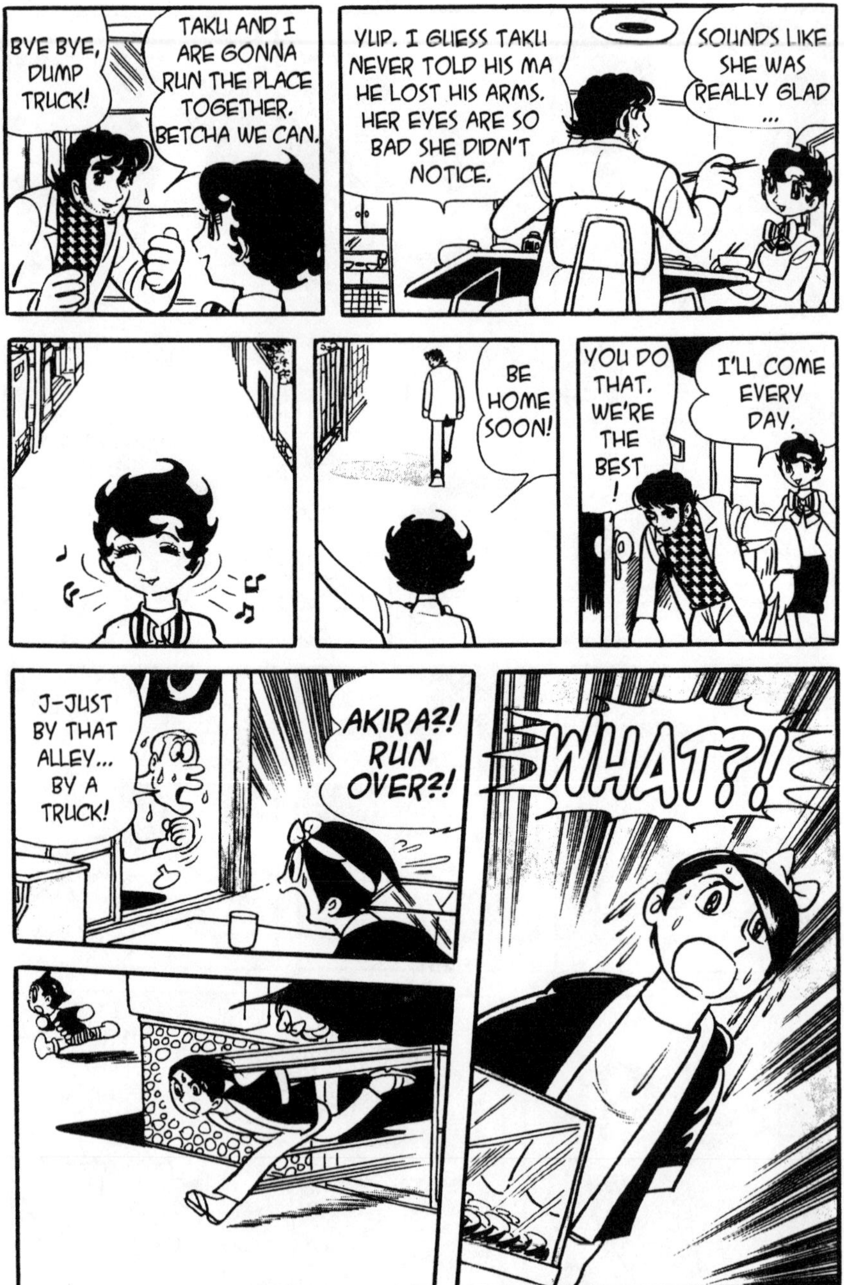
SOUNDS LIKE SHE WAS REALLY GLAD ...
YUP. I GUESS TAKU NEVER TOLD HIS MA HE LOST HIS ARMS. HER EYES ARE SO BAD SHE DIDN'T NOTICE.
TAKU AND I ARE GONNA RUN THE PLACE TOGETHER. BETCHA WE CAN.
BYE BYE, DUMP TRUCK!
I'LL COME EVERY DAY.
YOU DO THAT. WE'RE THE BEST!
BE HOME SOON!
WHAT?!
AKIRA?! RUN OVER?!
J-JUST BY THAT ALLEY... BY A TRUCK!

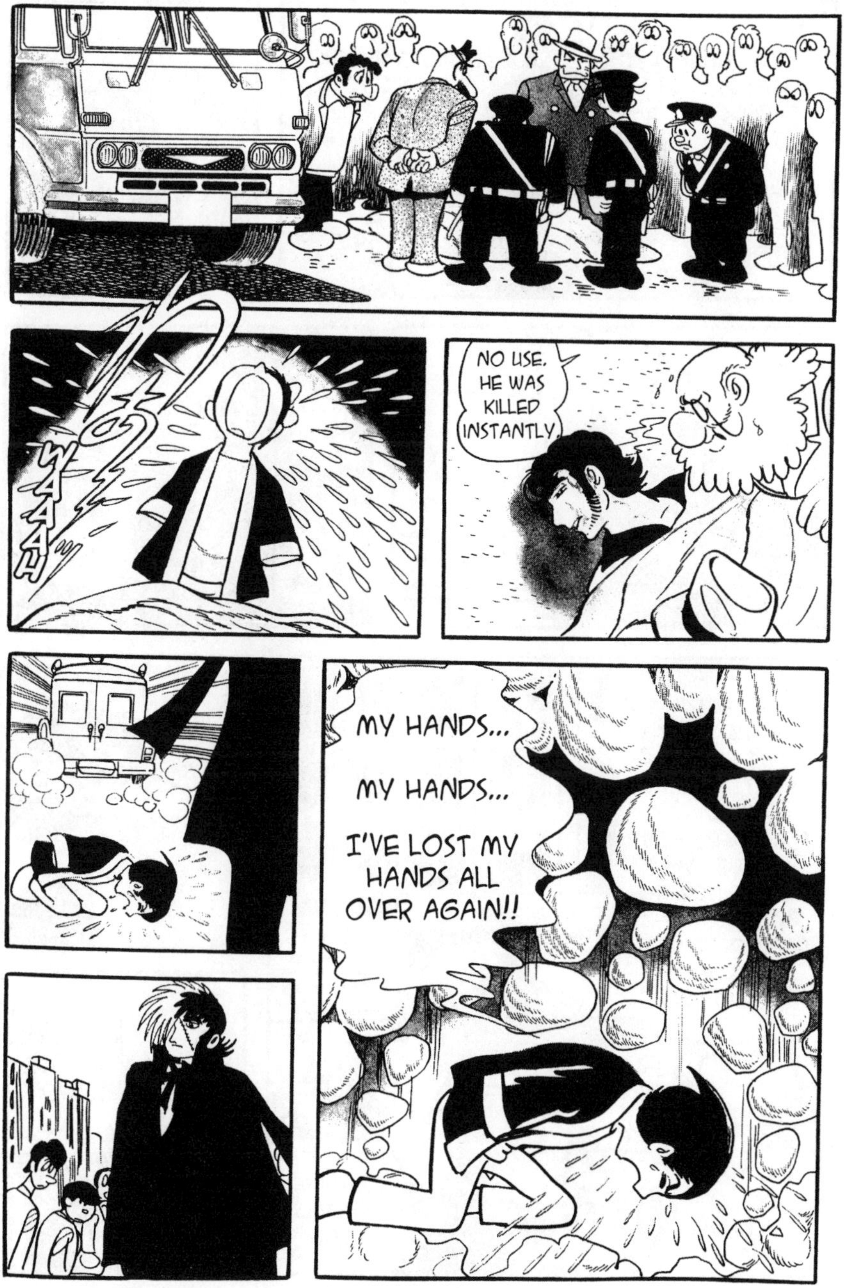
NO USE. HE WAS KILLED INSTANTLY.
WAAAH
MY HANDS...
MY HANDS...
I'VE LOST MY HANDS ALL OVER AGAIN!!

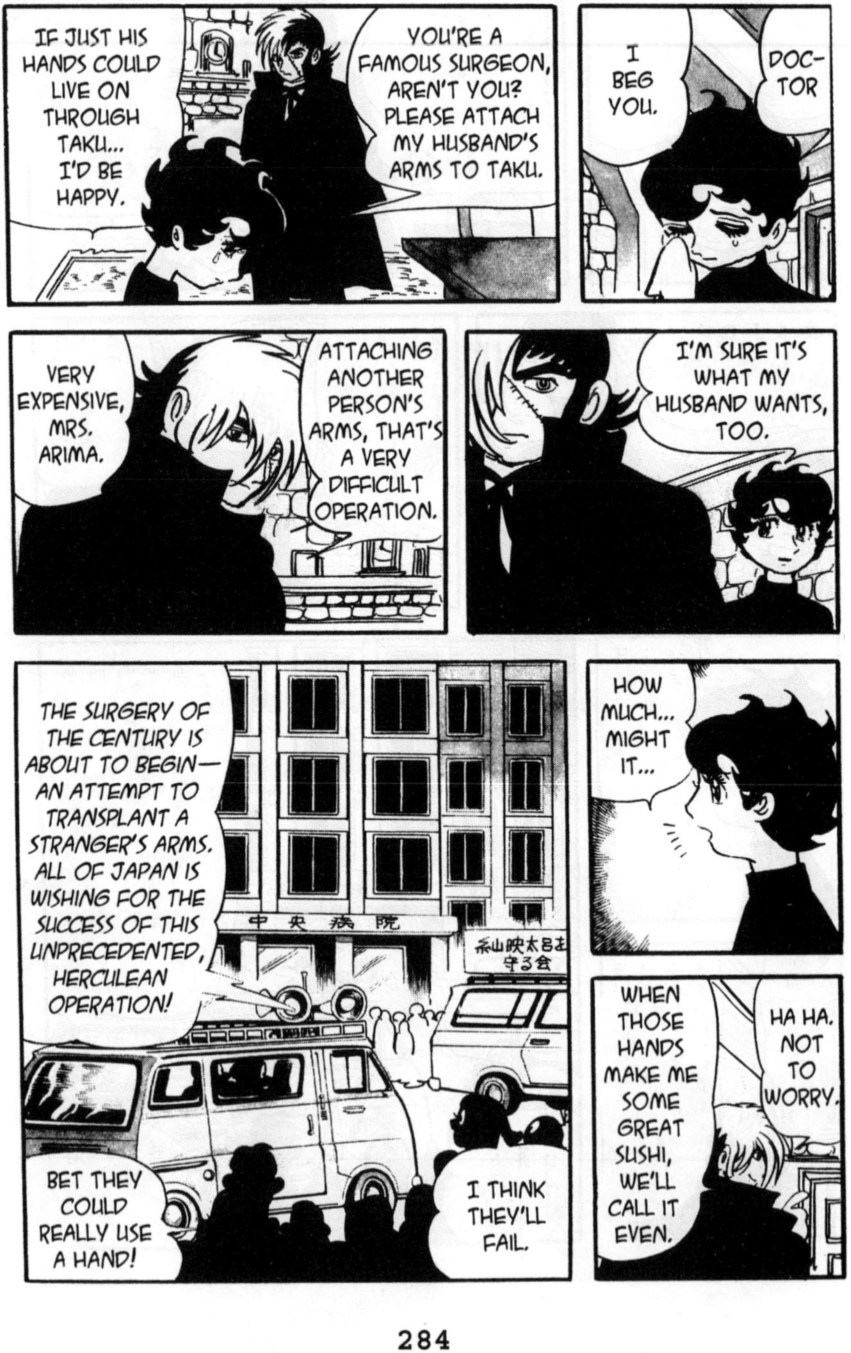
DOC-TOR
I BEG YOU.
YOU'RE A FAMOUS SURGEON, AREN'T YOU? PLEASE ATTACH MY HUSBAND'S ARMS TO TAKU.
IF JUST HIS HANDS COULD LIVE ON THROUGH TAKU... I'D BE HAPPY.
I'M SURE IT'S WHAT MY HUSBAND WANTS, TOO.
ATTACHING ANOTHER PERSON'S ARMS, THAT'S A VERY DIFFICULT OPERATION.
VERY EXPENSIVE, MRS. ARIMA.
HOW MUCH... MIGHT IT...
HA HA. NOT TO WORRY.
WHEN THOSE HANDS MAKE ME SOME GREAT SUSHI, WE'LL CALL IT EVEN.
THE SURGERY OF THE CENTURY IS ABOUT TO BEGIN—AN ATTEMPT TO TRANSPLANT A STRANGER'S ARMS. ALL OF JAPAN IS WISHING FOR THE SUCCESS OF THIS UNPRECEDENTED, HERCULEAN OPERATION!
中央病院
I THINK THEY'LL FAIL.
BET THEY COULD REALLY USE A HAND!

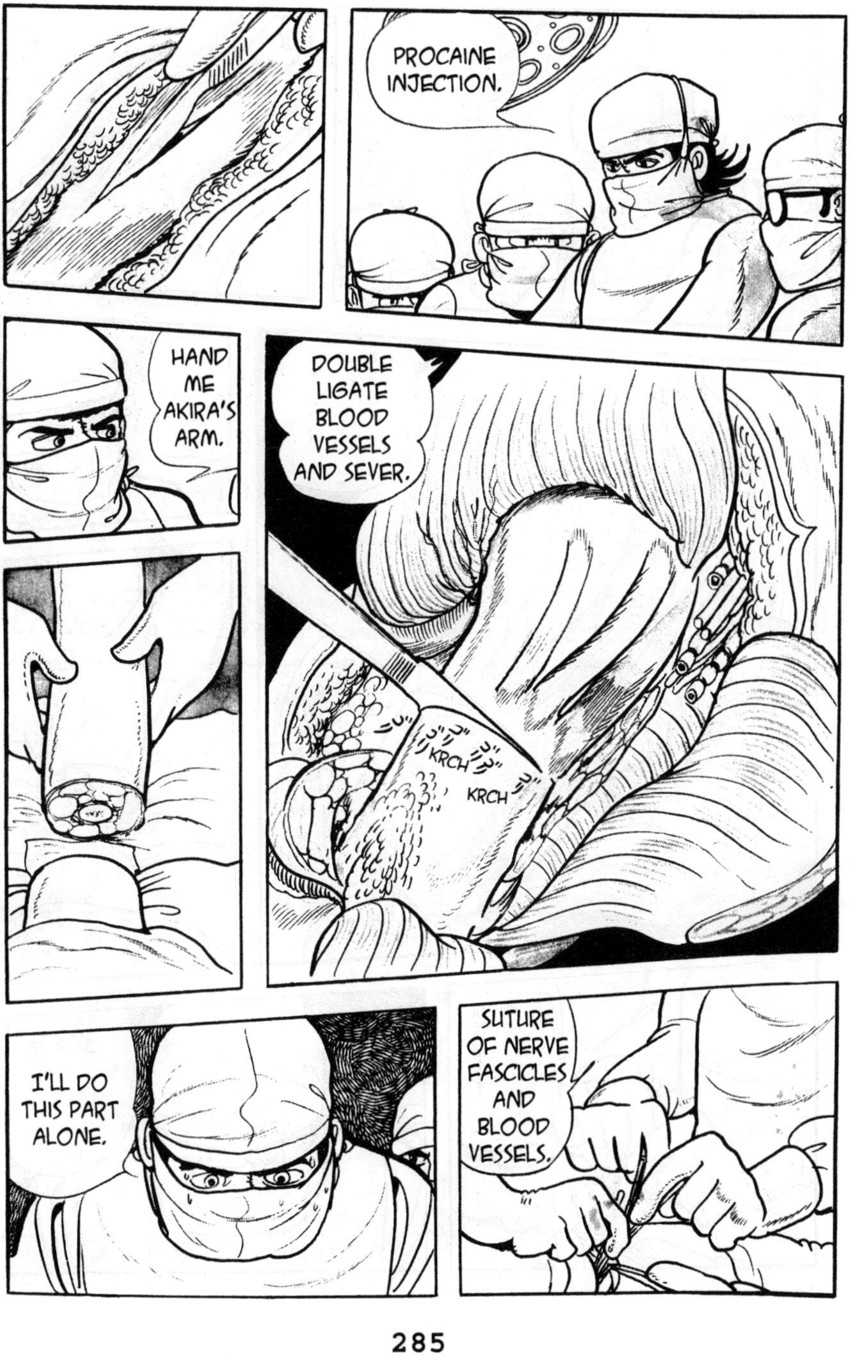
PROCAINE INJECTION.
DOUBLE LIGATE BLOOD VESSELS AND SEVER.
KRCH
KRCH
HAND ME AKIRA'S ARM.
SUTURE OF NERVE FASCICLES AND BLOOD VESSELS.
I'LL DO THIS PART ALONE.

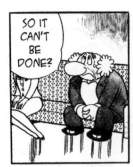

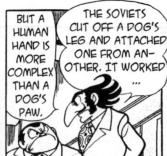

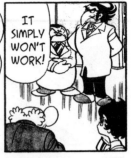

IT SIMPLY WON'T WORK!
THE SOVIETS CUT OFF A DOG'S LEG AND ATTACHED ONE FROM AN-OTHER. IT WORKED ...
BUT A HUMAN HAND IS MORE COMPLEX THAN A DOG'S PAW.
SO IT CAN'T BE DONE?
MAINLY BECAUSE OF THE NERVES.
EVEN IF THEY'RE JOINED, THEY FAIL TO FUNCTION!
THEN I WON'T GET MY HOPES UP.
OP'S OVER.
HOW DID IT GO?!
ASK ME AGAIN...
WHEN THE BANDAGE COMES OFF.

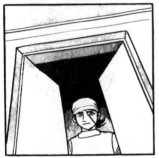

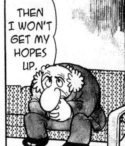

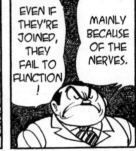

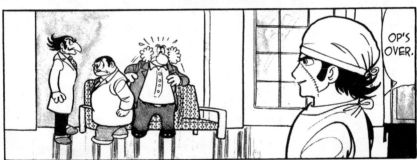

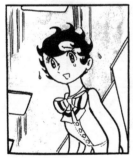

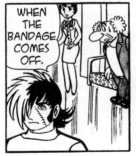

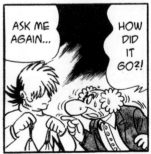

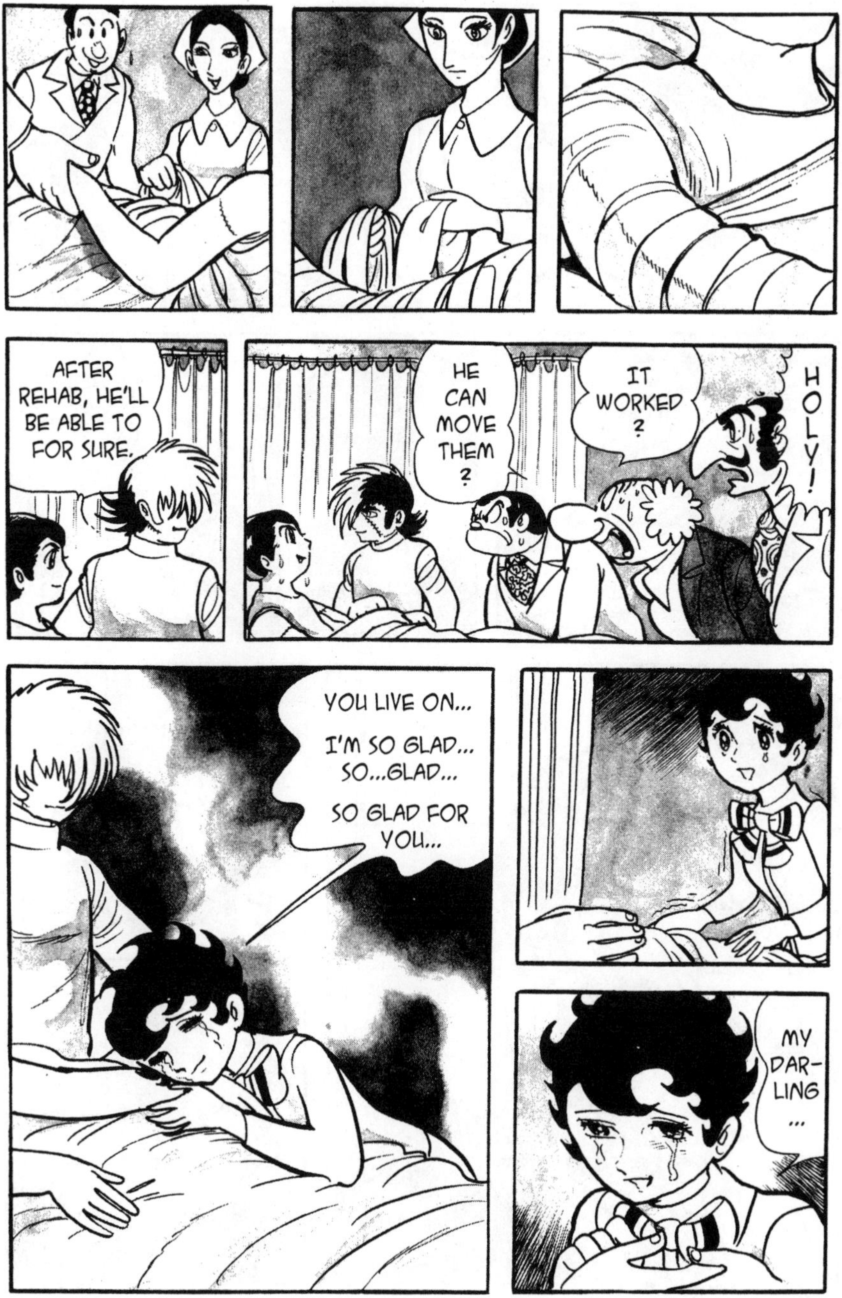
HOLY!
IT WORKED?
HE CAN MOVE THEM?
AFTER REHAB, HE'LL BE ABLE TO FOR SURE.
MY DARLING...
YOU LIVE ON...
I'M SO GLAD... SO...GLAD...
SO GLAD FOR YOU...

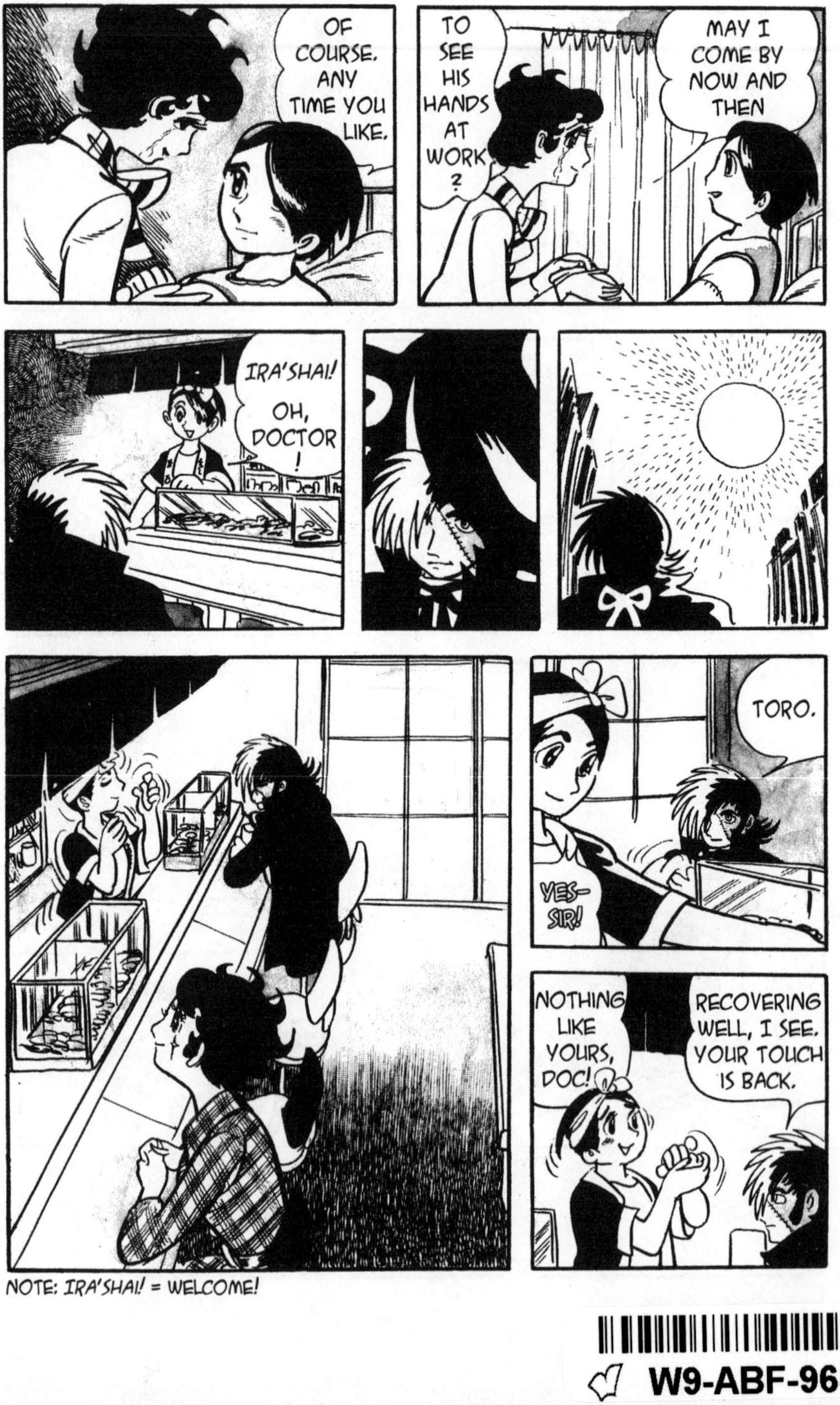
MAY I COME BY NOW AND THEN
TO SEE HIS HANDS AT WORK?
OF COURSE. ANY TIME YOU LIKE.
IRA'SHAI!
OH, DOCTOR!
TORO.
YES-SIR!
RECOVERING WELL, I SEE. YOUR TOUCH IS BACK.
NOTHING LIKE YOURS, DOC!

NOTE: IRA'SHAI! = WELCOME!